SILK
AND
SONG

DANA STABENOW, born in Alaska and raised on a 75-foot fish tender, is the author of the award-winning, bestselling Kate Shugak series. The first book in the series, *A Cold Day for Murder*, received an Edgar Award from the Mystery Writers of America. Contact Dana via her website: www.stabenow.com.

outside of Bengal, and we saw one village that we were told was destroyed by them, but we never saw any ourselves." He smiled. "Carrying the Khan's paiza must be a guarantor of safe passage through the very bowels of hell itself, I think."

"How could it be otherwise?" Bayan said simply.

The eyes of the two men met. There was a long silence which Marco was determined not to break.

Bayan sighed. "I have spoken with our heavenly master, the Khan. He has said you may escort the Princess Kokachin to the court of King Arghun." A tart note entered into his voice. "He says it is to be hoped that you will succeed where those three nitwits of Arghun's failed."

Marco tried to conceal the leaping of his heart beneath a judicious expression. "To be fair, they couldn't know their chosen route home would lead through a civil war. It was simply bad luck."

"You make your own luck," Bayan said, who had certainly made enough of his own to be an authority. "At any rate, you, your father and your uncle will together be named the guardians of the Princess Kokachin. Your job is to deliver her safely to her bridegroom in the Levant."

"As always it is our very great joy to obey the wishes of the Son of Heaven," Marco said.

The promptness of this reply earned him a raised eyebrow. "As you say," Bayan said. "Your expedition will also be accompanied by delegations to the Pope in Rome, and to the kings of France, Spain, and England. You will be entrusted with messages to other leaders of Christendom as well."

"Expedition?" Marco said. "How large is this caravan going to be?"

"You will not be going overland, you will be going by sea," Bayan said, "in fourteen ships. The expedition is even now being assembled in Kinsai." He smiled to see Marco for once at such a loss for words. It didn't happen often.

"I am—humbled, as will be my father and my uncle, by the Great Khan's trust in us to lead such a grand mission." Marco knew a flood of happiness that at long last he would be going home, equalled only by the surge of satisfaction that it would be in such style. "When do we leave?"

"The court astrologers have decreed the last of the spring tides will be the most propitious day for your departure."

Marco cast an involuntary glance through the open door, where the garden was in full bloom.

"Yes, I know, my friend, we have left your departure a little late." Bayan leaned forward, a grave expression on his face, and dropped his voice to that barely above a whisper. "Within these four walls," he said, "I will tell you, my friend, that I do not know how much longer the Khan will live. His illness has progressed to where he rarely leaves his chambers. Very few are admitted into his presence." Bayan grimaced. "You'll know how bad it must be when I tell you that Chi Yuan sent for me, of all people, to visit our master the Great Khan in hopes I would ease his depression. A bit ironic, when we both know that Chi Yuan will be first in line with a dagger aimed at my heart when our master the Great Khan breathes his last."

Marco was silent. The struggle for power between the Mandarins and the Muslims at the court of Cambaluc was legendary. If Chi Yuan, a Mandarin and a jealous guard of the Great Khan's private life, had sent for Bayan of the Hundred Eyes, a Muslim, to relieve the Great Khan's spirits, they must be low indeed.

"He is leaving this life," Bayan said, his expression somber, "and he knows it. While he lives, you are safe here in Everything Under the Heavens. When he dies…"

The two men sat together in silence.

It was nothing Marco had not known before he had requested this audience. Many times over the past several years, ever since the Khan's health had begun to fail, the Polos had petitioned to leave the court and return home to Venice. Each time they had been refused, partly because the Great Khan feared what the loss of such effective tools would do to his own power and prestige, and partly because he was truly fond of them.

There was that much more urgency for his departure now that the Khan lay dying. The twelve barons of the Shieng were jealous of his influence over their leader. While the Khan lived, their spite would be kept in check. When the Khan died…

"If we leave so soon, then I must return home at once," Marco said at last. "There is much to be done." His smile was rueful. "Shu Lin will be furious to be given so little time to pack."

Bayan did not smile back. "Alas…"

Marco stiffened. "There is a problem?"

Bayan placed his cup on the low table with exact precision, and delivered his next statement in a manner that showed that he knew just how unwelcome the words would be. "Our master the Great Khan has said that the beautiful Shu Lin and your equally lovely daughter, Shu Ming, must await your return here in Cambaluc."

"What!" Marco found himself on his feet without remembering how he got there.

Bayan smoothed the air with both palms. "Gently, my friend, gently. Sit. Sit."

After a tense moment Marco subsided to his pillows, his mind in turmoil. "But he gave her to me. She was a gift from the Great Khan, to me personally, Marco Polo, his most valued emissary. Or so he said." He could not quite keep the bitterness from his voice.

"Our master the Great Khan does not go back on his given word," Bayan said.

"But he holds my wife and my daughter hostage against my return!"

Again, Bayan smoothed the air. Again he said, "Gently, my friend, and lower your voice, I beg you. The eyes and ears of our master the Great Khan are everywhere, even here." He settled his hands on his knees and leaned forward again. "Commend Shu Lin and Shu Ming into the care of someone you trust. Escort the Princess Kokachin to her betrothed. When enough time has passed that our master the Great Khan's attention has turned elsewhere, I will send her to you."

"And if he dies in the meantime?"

"Gently, my friend, I beg you, gently. She is only a woman, and with you gone will have no status, and therefore offer no threat to anyone at court."

"She is safer with me gone, you mean."

"Yes." The soft syllable was implacable.

Marco sat in a leaden silence filled with despair.

Bayan leaned forward to put a hand on Marco's shoulder. "Think," he said, giving the other man a hard shake. "You must leave – you, your father and your uncle – for your own safety, for the sake of your very lives. Our master the Great Khan knows this as surely as do we ourselves, and he has found this way to make use of you for the last time. But you have been his friends for twenty years, and our master the Great Khan's heart aches at your parting. This is his way of ensuring himself that you come back to him."

Their eyes met. This was Marco's last departure from the court of the Great Khan, and both men knew it.

"How will I tell her?" Marco said heavily.

Bayan sat back. "Her father was one of the twelve barons of Shieng. She will understand."

She had. There were tears, but tears only of sorrow at their parting, and none of anger or remonstration. She did not blame him for his decision to leave his wife and daughter behind. Indeed, she said, as Bayan had, "If the Great Khan is as ill as Bayan says, it will be safer for us if you are gone when he dies." She had smiled up at him with wet but resolute eyes. "If Bayan says he will send us to you, then he will send us to you. We will be parted for only a short time. Have courage, my love."

That night in their bed he gathered her into his arms and buried his face in her dark, fragrant hair. Here was wealth beyond measure, the highest status, unlimited privilege. Here was work he could do, and do well. Here was Shu Lin, beautiful and loving and loyal beyond words, and Shu Ming, three years old, as intelligent and healthy a child as any father could wish.

But here also was a once-strong and visionary ruler rendered timid and withdrawn by age, weary of spirit, limbs swollen with the gout that came from a diet of meat and sweets washed down with koumiss. He must leave, and he must leave soon. His father and his uncle were impatient to be away, and both of them had remonstrated with him over his reluctance to leave Shu Lin behind. The thought flashed through his mind that they would be glad not to have to explain her presence at Marco's side to their family in Venice.

"You have all the courage for both of us, it seems," he said.

Three-year-old Shu Ming was harder to convince, and his last sight of her was sobbing in her mother's arms. Wu Hai, Marco's partner in business and in many journeys over the years, stood at Wei Lin's side: square, solemn, solid. Wu Hai, one of the most successful businessmen from Cambaluc to Kinsai, was a man of worth and respectability. He had the added advantage of being well known to Shu Lin and Shu Ming.

"I give you my word," Wu Hai had said with a gravity befitting one undertaking a sacred oath, "your wife and your daughter will be no less in my house than members of my own blood."

Marco looked long upon the faces of his wife and child, and did not turn away until the firm hand of his uncle Maffeo pressed hard upon his shoulder.

The three Polos went out beneath the wooden arch that was the entrance of the only home Marco had known for the last twenty years. The sound of his daughter softly weeping followed him into the street.

He never saw wife, nor daughter, nor home again.

2

1294, Cambaluc

K UBLAI KHAN DIED before Marco reached Venice, even before the Polos managed at last to deliver Princess Kokachin safely to her bridegroom. As the lady's consistently bad fortune would have it, he was also dead, murdered before ever she reached the kingdom of the Levant.

In Cambaluc, Kublai Khan's grandson, Temur, took the throne after months of uncertainty, followed by a struggle for power that did little to reinforce the stability of the Mongol realm. Trade went forward, of course, because nothing stopped trade, and Wu Hai returned from a trip to Kinsai shortly after Temur came to power.

Full of plans to open a new route to the pearl merchants of Cipangu, it was, shamefully, a full day before he noticed that Shu Lin and Shu Ming were missing. It took another day and making good on a threat to have his majordomo stripped to the waist and whipped before the assembled members of the family before he could discover where they were. He went straight to Bayan, the new emperor's chief minister.

By then, Shu Lin was dead.

Bayan did Wu Hai the courtesy of summoning him to his house to deliver the news in person. "Almost before the Great Khan breathed his last, the Mandarins and the Mongols were at each other's throats. Both factions were determined to remove any obstacles to their acquisition of power, as indeed was Temur Khan. Any favorites of the old Khan were suspect, and subject to immediate... removal."

"I understand," Wu Hai said, rigid with suppressed fury and guilt. "Marco, his father and his uncle were beyond their reach. His wife and child were not."

Bayan cleared his throat and dropped his eyes. "It may be that there was an informer who directed attention their way."

Wu Hai stood motionless, absorbing this. What Bayan was too tactful to say was that very probably someone in Wu Hai's own household had sold Shu Lin and Shu Ming in exchange for favor at the new court. His first wife had never liked Wu Hai's association with the foreign traders who brought him the goods he sold, that had made his fortune, that had provided the substantial roof over her head, the silks on her back and the dainties on her table.

"They were thrown into the cells below the palace," Bayan said. "From what I can discover, Shu Lin sold herself to the guards in exchange for Shu Ming's safety."

There was a brief, charged silence as both men remembered the delicate features and graceful form of the dead woman, and both flinched away from images of what she must have endured before her death.

There was shame in Bayan's face at his failure to protect his friend's wife and child. He had gravely underestimated the lengths to which desperate courtiers would go to curry favor with the new khan, and he admitted it now before a man who had also failed in his duty to a friend.

In a subdued voice, Wu Hai said, "And Shu Ming?"

Bayan's face lightened. "Alive. The doctors say she has suffered no harm. No physical harm." Bayan nodded at the open door of his study, and Wu Hai went through into the garden, where once again the plum trees were in bloom. Shu Ming sat with her back to one of the trees, surrounded by fallen petals, a tiny figure in white silk embroidered with more plum blossoms. Of course, he thought, Bayan's people would have dressed her in mourning. He stopped some distance away, so that she would not be frightened.

It was unfortunate that she looked more like her father than her mother: long-limbed, hair an odd color somewhere between gold plate and turned earth, eyes an even odder color somewhere between gray and blue, and, most condemning, round in shape, untilted, foldless. Her foreignness hit one like a blow, he thought ruefully. It would be all too easy to pick her out of any household in Everything Under the Heavens, and given the provincial and xenophobic nature of the native population, she would always be a target simply by virtue of breathing in and breathing out.

And now, her mother dead, her father gone beyond the horizon, she had no status in the community, no rights, no power. Her father had left them both well provided for, and Wu Hai had secured those funds—had, he thought bitterly, taken better care of their funds than he had of their persons. But money would not be enough to buy her acceptance in Cambaluc.

The tiny figure had not moved, sitting cross-legged, her hands laying loosely in her lap, her eyes fixed on the middle distance. Her hair had been ruthlessly shorn, no doubt to rid her of the lice that infested every prison, and the cropped head made the slender stem of her neck look even more fragile rising up from the folds of her white tunic. There was almost no flesh remaining on her body. Her skin was translucent, her cheekbones prominent beneath it. Her tiny hands looked like paper over sticks.

He cleared his throat gently.

She turned her head to look at him, and he saw with a pang that she seemed somehow much older.

He bowed. "You see before you one Wu Hai, your father's most unworthy friend. Do you remember me?"

12

She inclined her head, her expression grave. "Of course I do, uncle," she said, giving him the correct honorific with the precisely correct emphasis and intonation. Again like her father, he thought, she had a facility for any language, her tongue adapting readily from Mongol to Mandarin.

"I am sorry I was away from home for so long," he said.

"My mother is dead, uncle," she said.

"To our loss and great sorrow," he said.

"And my father is gone."

"This, too, I know," he said.

"What will you do with her?" Bayan said before they left.

Wu Hai looked down at Shu Ming's tearstained face, asleep on his shoulder. "I have a son," he said.

"Ah," Bayan said, a thoughtful hand stroking his mustaches. "Have you given any thought to what your family will say?"

"I have no other family," Wu Hai said.

Bayan said no more.

Wu Hai returned to his home and turned everyone in the house into the street with what they had on their backs, wife and servants all, with the sole exception of his son.

His wife sobbed and groveled at his feet. "Where will I go, husband? What will I do?"

Before them all he deliberately put the sole of his foot against her shoulder and shoved her through the gate. She rolled and rose to her feet, the lacquer on her face running in great rowels down her cheeks. "You had a wife!" Her voice rose to a scream. "What need had you of another!"

"She had a husband," Wu Hai said. He surveyed the throng of people gathered around her. Not one of them could meet his eyes.

He remembered the delicate features and the gentle disposition of his friend's wife, brutalized and despoiled and then destroyed, from nothing more than petty jealousy.

"I have no wife," he said, raising his own voice so that it would be heard over the sobs and wails of the people who had once formed his household. So they would understand fully the price of betrayal, he himself closed the heavy wooden doors in their faces. The bar dropped inexorably into its brackets with a loud and final thud.

He turned to face his son.

Wu Li was a sturdy and handsome fellow, standing with his legs braced and his thumbs in his belt in imitation of his father. He met Wu Hai's eyes squarely, although his face was a little pale.

"Do you understand what happened here, my son?" Wu Hai said.

The boy hesitated, and then nodded once, firmly. "I do, father."

"What, then?"

Unflinching, the boy said steadily, "There is no excuse for betraying a guest in one's home."

Wu Hai's wife had been an unaffectionate and inattentive mother. He nodded. "It is well," he said.

He sold the house for an extortionate price to one of Temur's new-minted nobles and built a new home on property he owned outside of the city. It sat on the banks of the Yalu, and he built a dock and warehouses there as well, which, once Temur's policies allowed the realm to recover from the economic instability caused by the ruinous wars of his grandfather, proved to be a profitable move.

The first ceremony conducted beneath the roof of the new house was the marriage of his son, Wu Li, 9, to Shu Ming, 5. The marriage was in name only until both children had come of age, but in the interim it gave Shu Ming rank and citizenship, entitled to all the rights and at least the outward respect of the citizens of Everything Under the Heavens.

Temur was an enlightened ruler who appointed people to positions of responsibility regardless of their ethnicity or religion. At court Mongols worked beside Han Chinese, Muslims, Confucians and even a few Latins, usually priests who were missionaries for their faiths, but some merchants as well. In this he was truly the grandson of Kublai Khan. But Wu Hai, who until the end of his life held himself responsible for the betrayal and death of Shu Lin, wasn't taking any chances with the life of her daughter. He ignored the whispers in the Chinese community, the covert looks his family received when abroad, even the mutterings of his own parents.

He was every bit as honorable a man as Marco had believed him to be when he committed his wife and daughter into Wu Hai's care.

3

1312, Five days from Kashgar

JOHANNA HAD GRADUATED to her own camel.

Her father, Wu Li, had told her that if she managed to keep her seat from the beginning of Kuche to the city of Kashgar that he would let her off the leading string for the journey home. Shu Ming's protest had died on her lips when she met Wu Li's indulgent glance.

Johanna's camel was young and small, but what she lacked in size and maturity she made up for in energy and a fierce determination to be out in front. At Johanna's nudge she lengthened her stride to something approaching a canter.

"Johanna," Wu Li said in a warning voice.

"I'm sorry, father," Johanna said, with an impish glance over her shoulder. "She wants to run."

"Wu Li," Shu Ming said, and he looked at her with an expression warring between guilt and pride.

He shrugged, a twinkle in his eye. "She wants to run."

Shu Ming looked at the receding figure of their daughter. "They both want to run," she said.

By now three lengths ahead of Deshi the Scout, Johanna was concentrating so hard on keeping her balance while at the same time keeping her back straight that she didn't see the body until her camel stumbled over it. Her only consolation was that

Deshi had not seen it either, although to be fair the rest of the remnants of the other caravan were well buried in the shifting desert sand. Johanna was almost thrown—almost, but luckily not quite.

Nevertheless, Wu Li had seen. He kicked his camel into a trot and arrived at her side at the same time as Deshi the Scout. "All right, daughter?"

All three of them stared at the desiccated limb that her mount's hoof had exposed.

Johanna swallowed. "All right, father."

"Good. Stay in your saddle."

Her back straightened and her chin rose. "Of course, father."

Shu Ming had seen, too, and came up fast, and when she yanked on the reins her camel stopped so abruptly that its hindquarters slid out from beneath it and rider and camel both skated past on the sand. On any other day the sight would have provoked laughter and teasing. Today Johanna managed only a shaken smile.

Deshi the Scout already had his bow out and an arrow nocked, his face stern as he scanned the horizon. Wu Li pulled his mount around and raised a hand. The line of camels halted, some expressing their displeasure by groaning and spitting. One kicked out with his right hind leg, narrowly missing Mangu the Cook, who let loose with a string of cheerful curses that died on his lips when he looked ahead to see what the problem was.

Wu Li kicked his camel into a kneeling position and slid down, loosening his knife as he went, but the bodies were days dead and the only sound on this lonely expanse of undulating dunes was the rasp of wind on sand. He looked at Deshi the Scout, who withdrew to the nearest rise, there to keep a watch in every direction at once.

By the time they had uncovered the bodies of three camels, a horse, and thirteen people, it was almost sunset. Wu Li sent a rider ahead to Kashgar to alert the authorities and to let Shu Shao know they would be late in arriving. Mangu located a small oasis with an even smaller spring and two frail date palms half

17

a league from the road and supervised the setting up of a camp while Wu Li gathered what evidence he could to reconstruct what had happened.

Deshi the Scout found a scrap of sheer red fabric. The edge was hemmed with gilt spangles. "Gujarat weave," he said.

"There are no women or children among the bodies," Wu Li said. "Muslim bandits, then. Every year they move further east. Remember the Buddhist shrine we found last year?"

"What was left of it I do." Deshi the Scout hawked and spat. "This kind of thing didn't happen when the old Khan was alive."

Wu Li agreed, but silently: even here, a thousand leagues from the capitol, one could never be sure who was listening. Kublai Khan's heirs had been competent but they were not visionaries, and they had allowed the politics of court and the luxuries of the throne to distract their attention from the disintegrating infrastructure of their empire. Over the years the Road had become slowly but steadily more perilous.

They ate without appetite and mostly in silence that evening, and turned in early. Wu Li took the first watch, knife at his side, bow at his knee.

They had not pitched the yurts in case they had to move suddenly and quickly. For a long time into that very long night Johanna watched the figure of her father, back to the coals of the fire, the fronds of the two palms hanging limp and listless over his head, a black sky glittering with stars above.

Johanna woke to meet the alert eyes of Deshi the Scout. The rising sun set fire to the endless eastern horizon and illuminated his grave smile. She crept from beneath the blankets she shared with Wu Li and Shu Ming and retired behind a convenient dune to attend to the call of nature.

She squatted, holding her trousers out of the way. The stream of urine steamed in the cold morning air, the acrid smell striking her nostrils. She was almost finished when the sand directly beneath her feet heaved up. She screamed and tumbled backwards, head over heels. She scrambled to her feet, hauling at her trousers.

Her scream had a particularly piercing and far-reaching quality, and behind her she heard startled voices and loud oaths. "Johanna! Where is Johanna?" her mother cried.

Before her astonished gaze the sand rose up and assumed a human shape. For a wild moment she thought a demon was materializing before her eyes, an apparition out of one of Deshi's tales that would pull her back beneath the sand with him, there to devour her whole. She screamed again, backing away, tripping over her own feet and falling once more.

The sand cascaded in sheets from the apparition. As Wu Li and Shu Ming hurtled around the dune on one side and Deshi the Scout came around it from the other, weapons drawn and ready for action, the figure was revealed to be a boy hardly older than Johanna herself.

He was thin to the point of emaciation, his blue eyes red-rimmed, his hair stiff with sand, his skin peeling from sunburn. He wore only a filthy kilt that might once have been white in color, and leather sandals.

His only possession was a sword as tall as he was. A luminous steel blade rising from a heavy hilt encrusted with stones. As Wu Li and Deshi approached he raised the blade high, or tried to, the muscles of his scrawny arms bunched with effort. He actually got it up over his head, staggering a little, before the weight of all that metal got the better of him and his arms trembled and gave way. The sword dropped behind him, point down in the sand, his hands still grasping the hilt.

Tears made runnels in the dirt caked on his cheeks, but he didn't seem afraid. On the contrary, he was swearing like Mangu the Cook when the millet burned to the bottom of the pot. "I'll kill you!" he said. He was trying to shout but his voice came out in a hoarse croak. "Don't you touch me, or I'll kill you all!"

Wu Li and Deshi the Scout, who had halted, exchanged a glance. The boy had spoken in Aramaic.

Wu Li turned back to the boy and spoke in the same language. "Gently," he said. "We mean you no harm."

The boy wiped his face on his shoulder, leaving both smeared with dirt and tears and snot, a fearful sight. "I'll kill you all," he said, but the fierceness had drained out of him. His head drooped as if it was suddenly too heavy for his neck.

Johanna, yanking the drawstring of her pants tight, was red-faced and furious, embarrassed at being frightened by a boy no older or bigger than she was. She opened her mouth to call him every name she could think of, and after a life spent on the road with her father, her supply was endless. She encountered her father's eye, and shut her mouth again.

"My name is Wu Li," said her father. "I am a merchant of Cambaluc, traveling to Kashgar." He gestured. "We have food. Grant us the honor of sharing it with you."

Perhaps it was the formality of his speech, or perhaps it was the manner in which he made it, man to man. The boy's shoulders straightened, and when Wu Li turned and walked back to their camp he followed, the tip of the sword leaving a thin line in the sand behind him.

Mangu brought him a meal of dried dates and fresh baked naan and the boy tore into it with ferocious greed and looked around for more. "Gently, my friend," Wu Li said, "gently. You have been hungry too long to eat too much all at once." He handed the boy a skin full of water. "Drink now, small swallows. Let your stomach remember how to digest its food."

The rest of the company served themselves. The warm bread and the hot black tea took the edge off their hunger and the rising sun burned the chill from the morning air.

"What is your name?" Wu Li said.

The boy blinked. "Jaufre," he said at last, as if only just remembering it himself.

"And how do you come to be here, Jaufre?"

The boy looked at the steam rising from the thick earthenware cup. "My father was a guard on a caravan traveling from Baghdad to Karakorum."

Wu Li looked at the sword laying at the boy's side. "That is his sword?"

A grubby hand touched the hilt for reassurance. "Yes."

"I see."

As did they all. Even beneath all the grime, it was obvious the sword was made of the finest steel – probably Damascus steel, Wu Li thought – and he suspected that the stones in the hilt might be genuine gemstones. A valuable asset, indicating either the wealth of its owner or great favor on the part of the patron who had bestowed it. It was doubtful that a caravan guard could ever afford to buy one such for himself.

That Jaufre had it now meant that his father was dead, because such a weapon would not have left his possession any other way. Wu Li only wondered how the boy had taken it without the raiders noticing.

He said, "And you traveled with your father?"

"Yes." The boy's face twisted. "And my mother."

Behind her Johanna heard Shu Ming draw in a breath.

"You were attacked," Wu Li said. It wasn't a question.

"Yes."

"By whom?"

"Many men. On horses."

"Horses? Not steppe ponies?"

"No. Horses."

Not Mongols then, Wu Li thought. "How were the men dressed?"

The boy looked confused but answered readily. "Mintans and trousers."

"On their heads?"

"Sariks."

"With their faces covered?"

The boy nodded.

"Beda," Deshi the Scout said.

"Or Turgesh," Wu Li said. "Although I've never heard of either of them this far east before." He turned back to the boy and spoke again, keeping his voice matter of fact. "Your father?"

The boy's chin trembled and then firmed. "I buried him."

"How did they not see you?" Wu Li indicated the sword with his chin. "Or the sword?"

"He fell on me, to hide me from them." The boy drew in a shaky breath, and Wu Li could only imagine how the moments had passed for the boy, held motionless beneath the dying weight of his father. "And then before they could search him the wind came and blew the sand. I let it cover me." He swallowed and looked away. "Us. I think I must have fallen asleep."

Lost consciousness, more like, Wu Li thought.

"When the storm stopped, I woke up and they were gone. So," the boy said drearily, "I buried him, and I took his sword, and I walked until I found water."

Shu Ming made a soft sound of distress, and Wu Li knew she was picturing in her mind the small, desolate figure alone on the trackless yellow sands, beneath the scorch of an unforgiving sun. "How did you find water?"

"There were birds," the boy said. "I followed them."

"Lucky," Deshi said in Mandarin.

Smart, Wu Li thought. "And your mother?" he said.

The boy's face contorted with the effort not to cry. "They took her. They took all the women. And the camels and the horses that weren't killed in the fighting." His head drooped. "I looked for tracks, but the wind blew them all away."

Wu Li raised his head and met Shu Ming's eyes. "How long ago was that?"

The boy squinted at the rising sun. "Eight days? Nine?" He shook his head, exhaustion showing plainly on his face. "I buried myself in the sand every night to keep warm, and again every day when the sun got too hot to bear."

"You did well," Wu Li said.

The boy's head jerked up. "I hid," he said with bitter emphasis.

"And you're alive," Wu Li said.

The boy stared at him. "I didn't even try to fight them."

"You're alive," Wu Li said again. "What made you show yourself this morning?"

The boy reddened and he glared at Johanna. "She peed on me!"

Johanna, who had been rapt with interest at the tale thus far, went red again in her own turn. "I didn't know you were there!"

Everyone burst into laughter, except for the two combatants. Wu Li recovered first, and said mildly, "Well, Jaufre, we will be glad to offer you safe passage to Kashgar, if that is your wish." Again he gave the illusion of Jaufre having a choice, and Jaufre, who was old enough to know better, was grateful for this sparing of his dignity, even if he was too young to put a name to it.

Wu Li looked up at the circle of faces. "Finish your breakfasts, water the camels and fill the water skins. We move on as soon as we strike camp."

He didn't say what he was thinking, what they were all thinking. With Persian bandits marauding this far east, the sooner they were behind caravansary walls, the better.

They were away in half an hour, the boy Jaufre in the saddle behind Johanna, the sword strapped to the saddlebag behind him. It was difficult to remain aloof in such close proximity. He smelled, but it wouldn't have been polite to say so and besides, it wasn't his fault. After a while she said in a stiff little voice, "My name is Johanna."

She'd given up hope of a response to her overture when he said, "Johanna. Johanna? There was a queen named Johanna once. Or so my father told me."

"Really?"

"She was the sister of a great warrior king named Richard the Lionheart," Jaufre said. His voice was dull, but he seemed determined to pay his passage on the back of her camel with the full story. "They were from my father's country, an island far to the west. She was sent to marry the king of another island. And then he died, and she was held hostage, and her brother had to rescue her."

"And then what happened?"

"I don't remember all of it. She was shipwrecked on the way home and her brother had to rescue her again, and then she almost married two other kings, and then she did marry a count of the Franks, and led his army while he was away."

"And then what?"

"I think she became a nun."

"What's a nun?"

Jaufre seemed to wake up a little at this question. "You don't know what a nun is?"

"No. What is it?"

"Well, it's—she is like a monk, only she's a woman."

"Oh." All the monks Johanna had met were Buddhists, and male. It was hard to imagine a woman dressed in a skimpy orange robe and bare feet whose only possession was a wooden bowl used for both eating and begging. She wondered if the other Johanna had had to shave her head, like the monks did, and if so, what kept her crown on afterward.

They rode in silence after that. From time to time during that first long day, as the road passed swiftly beneath, she would seek out the familiar, reassuring figures of her mother and her father.

To have lost one was unthinkable. To lose both? Unendurable.

"You will stay with us," she said to the horizon of undulating sand, to the bleached blue of the sky overhead, to the rump of Deshi's camel. She was staking a claim.

Jaufre, drained from his ordeal and hypnotized by the rhythm of the camel's swaying gait, had fallen asleep with his head on her shoulder, drooling a little from the corner of his mouth.

"You will stay with us," she said again, more softly this time, but with even more conviction.

He snored, too.

4

THERE WERE NO stories or singing around the fire that night or any other between there and Kashgar. They reached the city in three days instead of five, pushing their mounts hard, making dry camps with everyone taking turns on watch during the night, arms to hand, even Johanna and her small bow, no one getting much sleep. Johanna saw the relief on her father's face when the high walls of the city came into view.

They halted in the yard of the large caravansary that sat just outside the city walls. Dusty camels knelt, bawling out their hunger, and ostlers moved in a continual dance to remain just out of reach of their snapping yellow teeth.

A young woman approached, neat in clean robes correctly tied, and bowed. "It is good to see you safely arrived, Master Wu." She bowed to Shu Ming. "Sister."

"It is good to have arrived safely, Shasha," Wu Li said with a certain grimness. "Your own journey?"

"Without incident, master. Niu Gang and I made excellent time." Her tone and expression were bland but her eyes were sharp as they scanned the rest of the party, noting the addition of Jaufre perched behind Johanna with interest but no surprise. "I have secured rooms for our party and hired staff for our stay. Niu Gang is arranging feed for the camels with the stable master.

Six merchants, including the venerable Wen Yan, have requested first looks at our goods, and the magistrate requests an appointment at your earliest convenience."

Wu's expression eased and he gave her a formal bow. "As always, Shu Shao, you reward my trust tenfold."

She bent her head without embarrassment and without arrogance, accepting the compliment as no more or less her due. Jaufre, looking on, thought that she wore the assurance of a woman many years her senior. Johanna, too, seemed to him much older than her six.

But then Jaufre, though he did not realize it then, felt like an old man himself. A life lived on the Road encouraged the early acquisition of skills of all kinds. You either survived it or you did not. If you did, you matured fast.

Wu Li busied himself with supervising the unloading of the bolts of silk and bales of tea and crates of porcelain. Shu Shao led Shu Ming and Johanna to their rooms. They were on the second floor, in a corner. Shu Ming opened the shutters of two windows that looked out over a garden with a blue-tiled fountain tinkling in the middle of it.

"Very nice," Shu Ming said. "How much are we paying?"

"No more than we can afford."

The two women smiled at each other.

Their hair was drawn severely back into identical thick braids, but there any similarity ended. Shu Ming was taller, her hair a tawny mass with gold glints, her eyes a golden brown. Shu Shao's hair was smooth and black, her face a round-cheeked oval of olive skin, with tilted eyes as dark as her hair. Shu Ming moved with unconscious grace, her eyelashes casting long shadows on her cheeks. Shu Shao moved with economy and purpose, and her gaze was direct, alert and missed nothing. Shu Ming smelled of peonies in full bloom. Shu Shao smelled of peonies, too, and of ginger and ginseng and licorice and cinnamon. Shu Shao was nearer in age to Johanna but her assurance and self-possession made her seem older than both of them.

"Mother?"

Shu Ming turned to smooth back a curl that had escaped from Johanna's fat bronze braid. "What is it, my love?"

Johanna raised serious eyes to her mother's. "I think Jaufre should stay with us."

The hand stilled.

"Jaufre is the boy?" Shu Shao said.

Shu Ming nodded. "And why is that exactly?" she said to Johanna.

Johanna was only six, and the complexities of human emotion were as yet beyond her articulation. "Because we found him," she said. "Because he belongs to us."

"He belongs to himself, Johanna," Shu Ming said, but her voice was gentle.

"He doesn't have anyone else, mother." Eyes a shade darker than her own were openly pleading. "There is no one he knows here in Kashgar, and no family or home waiting for him in Baghdad. There is only us."

Shu Ming was silent for a moment.

It was a great grief to her that thus far Johanna had been the only child she had been able to carry to term, and her only child to have survived birth. Married to Wu Li almost before she could remember as a matter of survival, it was her very great fortune to have been joined to someone who loved her and cared for her enough to take her with him on his journeys, to have not taken, at least not yet, another wife or concubine. He had never betrayed by word or deed his wish for more children, for a son to inherit his father's business, to carry his father's line forward into immortality, to honor his father's and his father's bones. She looked into Johanna's eyes, and she feared what the future had in store for her daughter. A woman alone, without family, was in peril by her very existence on the earth.

She thought of Jaufre, that fierce young boy who had been ready to take on Wu Li and Deshi the Scout and their entire caravan in defense of himself and his father's sword.

Young as she had been, Shu Ming never forgot the days and weeks she had spent in the cells below the palace in Cambaluc, of the things she had seen, of the things her mother had done for a drop of water or a grain of rice. She alone in Wu Li's entourage truly understood the repressed horror that dulled Jaufre's eyes.

Given his ordeal, there would have been no reproaches if all he had done was eat and sleep and ride over the past three days, but instead he had contributed to the daily work of the caravan with ability and determination. He knew as well as Johanna the knots required to secure a pack on a camel's back and he didn't balk at joining her in collecting dried dung from the Road for that night's campfire. Shu Ming had spared a bit of water to clean off the worst of the dirt and had cobbled together a change of clothing, so his appearance was much improved. She liked both the erectness of his spine and the directness of his gaze, and found him well-spoken when addressed.

He also looked a lot more like her daughter than almost anyone else they knew back in Cambaluc, with the exception of those foreign merchants and priests who always clustered about the royal court, seeking attention and favor.

She reminded herself that he was scarcely older than her daughter, and smiled at Johanna. "Let us see what your father says."

Johanna smiled. She knew what that meant, and she danced away to tell Jaufre he was coming home with them.

His brow knotted. "I can't come with you, Johanna," he said.

"Why not?" she said, dismayed.

"I have to find my mother," he said.

When called before Wu Li that evening after dinner, he repeated himself. "I have to find my mother."

Wu Li looked at the small, militant figure planted in front of him, and knew respect, even an odd sense of pride in this foundling. Still, he could not allow the boy to go haring off into the blue. Chances were he would only end up in a slave market, too. But it would be much better if the boy came to that realization on his own. "Do you know where she has been taken?"

The boy hesitated, and then gave his head a reluctant shake.

"Do you have a plan as to where to begin to look?"

A longer pause. Another shake of the head.

Wu Li sat back, scratching his chin in a thoughtful manner. "I see. Well, I can put some inquiries to people I know here in Kashgar. We will need a description. Did you look like her?"

"No. She had dark hair and eyes. I look like my father." The firm chin gave just a suspicion of a quiver before his face resumed its determined cast.

"Was she Persian?"

"Greek," the boy said. "My father was from Britannia."

"A Crusader?" Wu Li said. Or the son of one, perhaps, as the last Christian outpost in the Levant had fallen to the Mamluks over twenty years before.

"A Templar."

"Ah." A lapsed one, then, as Templars were supposed to be celibate. It happened. Wu Li's agent in Antioch was a former Templar who had renounced Christianity for Islam and embraced the notion of multiple wives and unlimited concubines with tireless enthusiasm. "About your mother," he said. "The slave market in Kashgar is the largest between here and Kabul. It is possible she and the others captured from your caravan will be brought here to be sold." He reflected briefly on how much such a sale might bring. Generally speaking, a woman who had had a child would not fetch the highest price, which was reserved for virgins. But Jaufre was a handsome lad and had probably had equally handsome parents. Wu Li could only hope that if his mother was found, the price would not be beyond the reach of his purse, as he well knew that he would be expected to meet it by wife and daughter both. "What is your mother's name?"

"Agalia," the boy said. "It means joy in Greek."

"Pretty," Wu Li said, keeping his inevitable reflections to himself.

The boy left, step light with hope.

"Do you really think it is possible we may find her here?" Shu Ming said later.

Wu Li shrugged. "It is possible. But not likely. And we must be very careful. Slavery is not illegal in Kashgar."

She was combing her damp hair with the intricately carved sandalwood comb he had brought her from Mysore the year Johanna was born, the only year she had not traveled with him. Yet again he was conscious of the gratitude due his father, who had chosen so well for his son's bride. The condemning looks that her obvious foreign blood drew in Cambaluc, the shunning by the Chinese community there, it was all worth it for a life spent with a woman like this at his side. Beautiful, intelligent, adventurous. What more could one want in a mate?

And they weren't in Cambaluc now. He stretched out on the bed and put his hands behind his back to watch her as she bent over, her hair hanging almost to the floor, and began with short, patient strokes to disentangle first the very ends of the thick mane, working slowly up to her scalp. When she was finished she stood up straight and tossed her hair back, where it fell in a flyaway cloud of shining brown curls, with the most intriguing streaks of gold and bronze and cinnamon. She was flushed and smiling, having felt his eyes on her all the while, knowing how much he enjoyed watching her at this particular task.

The first night at their destination was always a special night, no matter how tired or travelworn they were. The first night was a celebration of the return of privacy after weeks and sometimes months spent sleeping in tents in the open or in caravansary rooms shared with ten others. The ritual included bathing, clean clothes, a meal of local delicacies they could eat sitting on clean mats, a long, delicious night in a clean, comfortable bed, and no need to set a guard or to rise too early the following morning.

She was wrapped in the Robe of a Thousand Larks, a garment of gold silk elaborately embroidered in silk thread with the brilliant colors of many larks in many attitudes, yellow throats arched, plump orange chests puffed out, black and yellow banded wings spread in flight, green heads cocked to one side, red beaks open in song. Bordered with brilliant flowers and green leaves and black branches, bound closely to the waist with a matching sash, it seemed to Wu Li that the robe made all the light in the world gather in this one room solely to illuminate Shu Ming's slender, elegant figure.

And it made his hands itch to loosen the knot of that sash.

She set the comb carefully to one side and walked to him, and the whereabouts of Jaufre's mother and indeed everything else were forgotten for the rest of the evening.

The next morning he presented himself at the magistrate's office as requested and saw with pleasure and not a little relief that the magistrate was not alone. "Ogodei!"

He stepped forward and the two men exchanged a hearty embrace. From a corner of his eye he took note of the magistrate's visible relaxation, and he hid a smile. Having a captain of a Mongol ten thousand in one's backyard was never a cause for joy unconfined.

"Wu Li, my good friend." A man of ability, vigor and stamina, the Mongol chief was dressed in soldier's robes, his long black mustaches rivaling Bayan's own. He looked fit and bronzed from long days spent in the saddle, patrolling the western borders of the Khan's vast empire. "I find you, as always, far from home."

Wu Li laughed. "The last time was, when? Khuree, at the summer court, at the ceremony of the gifts?"

"Worse!" Ogodei covered his eyes and gave a dramatic shudder. "In Kinsai last fall. You had just returned from Cipangu, that far and obstinate country, laden with fine pearls and full of plans as to where and to whom to sell them." He laughed, throwing back his head. "As I recall, you sold some to me."

"But then," Wu Li said, a glint in his eye and a manifestly false tone of apology in his voice, "there are so many likely recipients for them."

This time Ogodei's crack of laughter was so loud it made the magistrate jump, although for the sake of his dignity he did his best to conceal it. "True enough, Wu Li, my old friend. I am rich in wives and in concubines." He cocked an eyebrow. "And the beautiful Shu Ming?"

"Flourishing."

"And your daughter?"

"Healthy, shooting up like a weed in springtime." Wu Li exchanged a bow with the magistrate. "What brings you to the edge of the world, O great captain of the Khan?"

The three men settled into chairs and leaned forward to discuss the state of their mutual world.

Later, Wu Li gave Shu Ming the gist of it. "Jaufre's caravan was not the only one attacked this season. Reports have been coming in from as far as Kabul, and even beyond. The Persian tribes are becoming ever more bold in their incursions. The Khan has placed several of his ten thousands to patrol the Road this season and deal with any trouble."

"He's missed some," Shu Ming said.

He shot her a warning glance. It took only one informer to turn criticism to treason.

"You will still look for Jaufre's mother?" Shu Ming said.

"I gave the boy my word," Wu Li said, and Shu Ming said no more.

Wu Li was as good as his word. He had been closely questioned by Ogodei and the magistrate on the remains of Jaufre's caravan, and had used the interview to pose cautious questions of his own. He omitted any mention of Jaufre, and he had laid the most strict prohibition on all his people from making any public reference as to how the boy had come to be among them. Since

Kashgar was the nearest available market for stolen goods, it stood to reason someone affiliated with the thieves would be in the city, very much alive to the news of an eyewitness and bound to pass it on. Ogodei was a vigorous and capable captain and Wu Li had no doubt his progress up the ranks would be steady and possibly even legendary, but even he could not guarantee the safety of one small boy in a city the size and duplicity of Kashgar. Anonymity was a much more sensible solution.

Wu Li bought a cap for the boy to cover hair that, when washed, proved to be the color of gold – a distinctive, memorable and in these parts unusual shade – and told him to wear it every moment he was outside their rooms in the caravansary.

Over the next week as Wu Li met with his agent in Kashgar, his fellow merchants and prospective buyers, he let fall a judicious word here and there that he was looking for a Greek woman answering to the name of Agalia. A free woman, recently widowed, who might through a series of unfortunate circumstances have had the additional misfortune of falling prey to slavers. He wasn't asking for himself, but family in Antioch had contacted Basil the Frank, his agent in Baghdad, and as a favor to Basil… Yes, yes, of course, the utmost discretion…

The Honorable Wu Li of Cambaluc, following in the footsteps of his father, the Honorable Wu Hai, had taken great care over many visits to maintain good relations with the city of Kashgar, paying into the city's treasury with every appearance of good will his tithe of monies earned through sales of his goods. He had even taken on a local orphanage as a personal concern, in donations of cash, food and goods. Neither was he a stranger to the local mosque, Buddhist monastery, or Nestorian church. He had no intention of embarrassing any good citizen of Kashgar for legally acquiring property in the form of a slave. But if such a slave had been purchased, it was just possible that she could be sold again, immediately, and at a modest profit. The Honorable Wu Li would be very grateful, and as every citizen of Kashgar knew, such gratitude had a way of manifesting itself in very real terms, if not immediately then at some time in the future. The citizens of Kashgar, traders to the bone, took always the long view.

In the meantime, Jaufre and Johanna, shadowed at a discreet distance by Deshi the Scout, sallied forth into the great bazaar, where a surgeon pulled a rotten molar from the mouth of a groaning patient with his wailing wife at his side. Next to the surgeon's shop a blacksmith replaced a cast shoe on a braying donkey. Another stall featured an endless array of brilliant silks, presided over by a black-veiled woman who, when the imam issued the call to prayer, excused herself from her customers, produced a small rug, and knelt to prostrate herself toward the east.

There were tents filled with nothing but soaps, powders to clean one's hair, picks to clean one's fingernails, pumice to smooth one's callouses, creams and lotions to soften one's skin, perfumes to make one irresistible to the opposite sex. There was cotton by the bale and by the ell, and tailors to make it up into any garment one wished. Carpenters made chair legs and rolling pins and carts. Herbalists made up mixtures of spices to season lamb, ease a head cold, hasten a birth. A tinsmith cut rolled sheets of tin into pieces for buckets, tubs, pots and pans. An ironworker fashioned chisels and hammers. Potters sat behind rows of bowls, pitchers and urns glazed in golden brown and cool green.

One huge tent was filled with coarse sacks with the tops open and the sides partly rolled down to display a vast selection of dried fruits and nuts, apricots from Armenia, olives from Iberia, almonds and dates from Jordan, pistachios from Balkh. There were carts piled high with sheep's lungs dyed pink and green and yellow and stuffed with spiced meats and cooked grains. One sweating man rendered a pile of pomegranates as tall as he was into cups of cool, tart, ruby-red juice, unperturbed by the dozens of wasps and flies buzzing around him. "Hah, daughter of the honorable Wu Li! You have returned to Kashgar!"

34

Johanna beamed at him. "Well met, Ahmed! Yes, we have returned, and we are here to trade."

He refilled their cups without charge, trading Kashgar gossip for the gossip of the Road, and Jaufre was impressed by Johanna's knowledge and confidence, and the ease with which she slipped between Mandarin, the language spoken among members of the caravan, and Persian, the lingua franca of Kashgar. He was even more impressed by the respect Ahmed accorded Johanna, and the gravity with which he listened to her replies to his questions. Fifty years Ahmed's junior, she barely came up to his waist, and yet he attended her conversation with a serious frown that didn't look as if he were indulging a child.

Next to Ahmed's stall green-glazed earthenware jars of olive oil, big enough to hold both Johanna and Jaufre with room to spare, were stacked against bales of hay. The vendor had set up a crude wooden table with a bowl of the oil available for tasting. Placed conveniently next door was a naan stall. A woman in a colorful scarf tied low on her forehead, her sleeves turned back to her elbows, was kneading a mass of dough in a large open bowl. Her husband presided over the oven, a tall earthenware pot larger than the oil urns buried in glowing coals. He tore off chunks of dough to pat them into rounds and slap them against the inside surface of the pot. When that side had browned he peeled them off and slapped them down again on the other, uncooked side. The smell of baking bread made Johanna's stomach growl and the baker's wife smile. She gave them two rounds each, saying with a twinkle, "Still the finest bread in all of Kashgar, yes, young miss?"

"Oh, yes, thank you, Malala! Is Fatima here?"

"She is, young miss," Malala said. "She is on an errand for me at present, but doubtless you will see her while you are here. Inshalla." She waved them off so she could serve a growing line of hungry customers. Half of them called out greetings to Johanna and inquiries after the goods her father would be selling.

"Who's Fatima?" Jaufre said.

"Malala and Ahmed's daughter," Johanna said. "I've known her forever."

They stood next to the olive oil stall, tearing off chunks of warm naan to dip into the sample bowl and wolf it down. The olive oil man topped off the bowl and continued his pitch to the crowd. "The very finest olive oil to be had within a thousand leagues! The first pressing of the season, from the vineyards of Messenia! A delicate flavor and a sturdy body, perfect for both cooking and dressing!" He smiled benignly down at the two urchins with his product dripping off their chins. "And, ladies and gentlemen, the best prices this side of the Levant!" He leaned forward and said to Johanna, "Young miss, you will tell your father, the honorable Wu Li, that Yusuf the Levantine says this is the best press of oil in a generation, yes? The cooks of Cambaluc will pay any price for it."

Johanna nodded, her solemnity belied somewhat by the smearing of the best press of oil in a generation across her face with the back of her hand. "Be sure I will tell him so this evening, Yusuf."

He bowed, his hand on his heart. "Then I am content. Approach, good sirs, approach! Oil of Messenia, the first pressing! The taste, ah, the taste!" He kissed his fingers to the sky. "The taste will make you swoon!"

He winked at Johanna and she fainted dead away into the arms of a startled Jaufre, to the chuckles of the surrounding crowd.

After that they went to wool sheds to watch the sheep being shorn, where the shearer gave Johanna samples of this year's wool clip with an adjuration that she hand them over to Wu Li as soon as possible because everyone knew how fine was the wool harvested from the flocks of Ibrahim the Berber and his supply was already dangerously low. They proceeded to the cow barns to watch the auction, and then to the horse yard, where they spent the rest of the afternoon watching a group of men comprising three generations of the same family buy a small Arabian stallion with a hide as black as ebony, from another

36

family of four generations. A representative of each generation from each family got to ride him the length of the yard and back again. He was a lovely sight, his graceful neck arched, his nose stretched out to drink the wind, his tail flying behind him as he seemed to float above the ground that passed so swiftly beneath his hooves. "See the tall man?" Johanna said. "The tallest man is always the broker."

"And if he isn't tall?" Jaufre said.

"Then he wears a tall hat," Johanna said.

They watched the tall man conduct the lengthy negotiations between the two parties, and as the sun slanted low over the white bulk of the Pamir Mountains a boy not much more than their own age was allowed to lead the stallion away, his face lit with joy and pride.

They returned to the caravansary at dusk, lips stained with pomegranate juice, oil on their chins and bread crumbs caught in the folds of their clothes. Jaufre, who had spent the day in a very good imitation of a carefree child, saw Wu Li and was recalled immediately to the fact of his recent history. The anxiety that made him seem so much older than his years settled over his features again.

Before he had to force himself to ask, Wu Li answered. "I'm sorry, Jaufre. There is still no word."

That evening, as the sun was just a memory in the western sky and the full moon only a pearly promise in the east, everyone staying in the caravansary gathered in the courtyard, around a large fire that had burned down to a circle of glowing coals. The members of the individual caravans grouped together to recline on blankets and lean against saddles. Everyone brought food and shared it: dumplings from Cambaluc, skewers of barbecued goat's liver from Yarkent, pickled eggs from Kuche, chicken tagines spiced with salty lemon from Maroc, black olives from

Greece, the wonderful naan of Kashgar, all of it washed down with delicious sips of wine from Cyprus, decanted with pride from a wooden barrel by a trader who had brought it all the way from Antioch.

Jaufre, sitting miserable and silent behind Johanna, couldn't remember when the music began, or how, but at some point he became aware of words being sung, accompanied by an instrument of some kind. He looked up and saw four members of the caravan from Antioch, the one that had brought the wine from Cyprus, sitting together on a blanket placed near the fire so that its light could fall on their faces, eyes half closed. One voice was very deep, the other three much higher. They were accompanied by a fifth man on a wooden wind instrument with a flared lip, whose notes were sweet and plaintive.

It was a dialect of Persian with which he was unfamiliar, but after the first verse he began to catch the words. It was a marching song, sung by a caravaner always on the Road, the dust of the desert sticking in his throat, the thin air of the mountains leaving him gasping for breath, the pickpockets of Samarkand relieving him of what little money the girls of Trebizond had left behind. The Road was mother, went the chorus, the Road was father, the Road was sister, the Road was brother, the Road was home for such as they. The triumphant finish was greeted by enthusiastic applause, and one by one each of the companies stepped forward to sing their own songs, of first love, of lost love, of lost virginity, of ancient legends and not too modern wars, of the monsters that lurked in the dark around every corner of the Road. The Antioch caravan sang a forlorn song about a lost Jerusalem and the Tashkent caravan retaliated with a song about a pillaging group of ruthless Crusaders annihilated to the last man by righteous warriors of the Crescent. At the ending of each song both groups shouted good-natured insults that no one took seriously.

The moon was directly overhead by now and bright enough to cast long shadows in the courtyard. A group of Tuaregs assembled before the fire, their cheches wonderfully twisted and knotted about their heads, their hands and faces blue from the indigo dye that stained their clothes. They sat in a semicircle, each with his legs wrapped around skin drums of various sizes and graduated notes. One began a simple rhythm of single beats. After a moment or two a second drum joined in, countering the first's rhythm. A third rhythm wove joyfully above and below first and second. A fourth used his drum to back up a song in which he was instantly joined by his brethren. A fifth man shook heavy metal rattles in rhythm with the drums and began to dance around the circle and then into the seated audience, shaking his rattles and enticing them to join in. It wasn't hard, as even Jaufre couldn't keep his feet still.

Johanna noticed, and put her lips to his ear. "Do you know the song?"

He shook his head.

"They sing of Tin Hinan, the Tamenokalt from Tafilalt. A long time ago she united all the Tuaregs into one tribe. They call her 'the mother of us all.'" Her eyes sparkled in the firelight. "The song says that she is buried in a desert even larger than the Taklamakan, where the sand is red, not yellow, and the dunes are as high as mountains."

"You would like to see it," he said.

She looked surprised. "Of course. I want to see everything. Don't you?"

Before he could answer a cry went up. "Wu Li! Shu Ming! Young miss! Young miss! Young miss!"

Jaufre, surprised out of his misery, looked at his companions.

Wu Li rose to his feet and bowed, his face grave but his eyes twinkling. He raised Shu Ming to her feet with a courtly hand and led his family of three to the blanket by the fire. They settled down, Shu Ming plucking at the strings of a delicate lap harp, Wu Li with a small skin drum that produced a soft beat beneath the heels of his hands. Johanna sat before them, Shu Shao and Deshi the Scout arrayed themselves behind them, and the five voices blended as one. Wu Li's was low and mellow, Shu Ming's warm and feminine, Johanna's high and pure, Shu Shao and Deshi the Scout underpinning the rhythm in time with Wu Li's drum.

White petals, soft scent
Friend of winter, summoner of spring
You leave us too soon.

The camel drivers of Wu Li's caravan hummed the base note, giving it a rich, full presence in the still courtyard. The firelight flickered on the blue-tiled walls of the caravansary, looming up out of the dark all around them. The fountain tinkled, and the stars shone overhead in defiance of the radiant light of the moon.

Jaufre, listening, understood dimly that the song was not about a plum tree at all. Somehow, scarcely aware, the hard knot of agony and loss beneath his breastbone began to ease, just a little.

The next day Wu Li, having emptied the last pack of every item either brought with them from Cambaluc or acquired along the way, and having crossed and crossed again every street and alley of Kashgar where there was something for sale, began to entertain offers to buy or trade. Jaufre ushered the sellers into Wu Li's presence, and announced their names and their goods. He was alive to the importance of first impressions and took care with his bows and his manners.

Johanna stood at Wu Li's elbow, guardian of Wu Li's bao. This was a small jade cylinder with Chinese characters carved in bas relief on one end. When a deal was struck, Johanna would remove the lid from a tiny, shallow jade pot, revealing it to be filled with a red paste, which Jaufre later learned was a mixture of ground cinnabar, oil and threads of silk. Wu Li would press the end of the bao into the paste and stamp a small square of paper, upon which had been written the details of the deal just concluded with the merchant then before him.

The bao was Wu Li's seal, the three carved characters representing his family name and the words "trader" and "honest." The seal had been conferred on his father by the khan and was known from one end of the Road to the other and on all its various routes. It represented Wu Li's word and bond to deal fairly with all who did business with him. All sellers left Wu Li's tent clutching a square of paper with the agreed-upon figures scribbled on it and the stamp of the House of Wu in one corner, a guarantee of good faith payment immediately upon presentation. Most of them exchanged it for coin when Wu Li's men appeared to load the purchased goods onto a camel, but a seller could choose not to accept coin for his goods immediately. Instead, they might redeem the piece of paper a month or even a year from the day it was stamped, for coin or for goods of equal value, from Cipangu to Venice.

Yusuf the Levantine, self-confessed dealer in the very finest olive oil to be had within a thousand leagues, bewailed the price Wu Li refused to go above, but he winked at Jaufre on his way out, tucking his precious piece of paper securely into his sash.

Jaufre looked at Johanna. She smiled and stood even more proudly behind her father.

Three weeks after the caravan had arrived in Kashgar, they were making preparations to leave. Wu Li, Shu Ming, Shu Shao, and Deshi the Scout gathered in a group to debate the best, as in most profitable, route home.

Wu Li had acquired a new map from a local Kashgar dealer, an Arabic map drawn more than 170 years before according to the faded date in one corner. A name was barely legible in another. "Al-Idrisi," Johanna said haltingly, spelling it out. Wu Li had been teaching her Arabic writing, and she looked at him to see how well she had done.

"Al-Idrisi," her father said. "All. E. Dree. Si."

"Al-Idrisi," Johanna said with more confidence.

The map was impressive in its clean lines and sharp geographical features and even more so in its startling lack of religious icons and exhortations. What Wu Li knew of it was accurate, something that could not often be said of any map not drawn by himself or his agents. It was a reproduction, of course, and the parchment crackled with age, but he and Johanna could easily adapt it into his route book.

The book was a collection of maps of all the routes Wu Li had ever traveled, some with his father and his father's great friend Marco Polo, but mostly they were from later travels of his own, bound in a small volume between supple calfskin stamped with his seal. One page led to another so that to follow—or retrace—a certain route all one had to do was turn the page forward or back. Each page was annotated in Wu Li's neat characters, the names of his agents in each location, the best vendors in oil and carpets and spices, the names of the more reasonable government officials along the way. Or the more reasonably priced ones.

The route book was every bit as valuable a possession as Wu Li's bao, compiled over twenty years of almost constant travel. They consulted it now in a body: himself, Shu Ming, Shu Shao, Deshi the Scout, and Johanna, with Jaufre sitting behind her, a fascinated if slightly unwilling auditor. After all, he thought, it wasn't as if he was going with them.

"We should take the southern route home," Shu Shao said.

"You never want to miss the spice market, Shasha," Johanna said.

Shasha smiled but did not deny it.

"It is true," Deshi the Scout said. "Spices are small and light and very valuable for their weight."

Deshi the Scout was always in favor of any commodity that

was easy to pack and that would not weigh down the camels on the Road, especially not on the Road home.

"Nutmeg," Shu Ming murmured. It was the most precious of spices in the East, revered by any cook worthy of the name, and was held by healers to have medicinal properties as well.

"There is all the nutmeg one could want in Kinsai," Wu Li said.

Shu Shao smiled. "We are not in Kinsai," she said.

Wu Li looked around the circle and laughed. "Is it a conspiracy, then?" Without waiting for an answer he gave a decisive nod. "The southern route, then, through Yarkent." He shook his head. "Other than the oil, we have picked up very little in bulk here in Kashgar." He looked at Deshi the Scout. "We should make good time."

Deshi the Scout nodded.

"I have some news good enough to make us all sleep easier on the Road," Wu Li said. "Ogodei and his ten thousand accompany us at least as far as Yarkent."

Wu Li saw Shu Ming's shoulders relax. The memories of Jaufre's caravan must have been preying on her mind. Well, and they had preyed upon his own.

She looked up and saw him watching her, and knew her thoughts to be his own. She smiled at him.

"And after Yarkent?" Wu Li said. "Straight home to Cambaluc?"

There seemed to be no objection. Wu Li dismissed them to their various chores, and he and Johanna settled in to transferring the information from the new map into Wu Li's route book. There were no roads on it, of course, and much of the distance involved had to be guessed at, but Johanna yearned for what lay at the edges of the pages. Wu Li gave an indulgent laugh. "We will travel them all one day," he told her.

"To the ends of the pages?" she said, her eyes drawn to the islands floating off the western edge of the map.

He tousled her hair. "To the ends of the earth itself," he said.

She beamed up at him, and Jaufre knew a moment's envy, not

only for Johanna's possession of a father still living, but for the prospect of a shore not yet seen.

Wu Li was supervising the padding and packing of the two dozen amphorae of oil the next day when he felt a plucking at his elbow. He turned and saw a city clerk, an older man bent and shortsighted from years of stooping over his accounts. "Tabari," he said, inclining his head courteously. "Forgive me, I did not see you standing there. How may I help you?"

He listened to Tabari's hurried speech with a bent head. Shu Ming, on the other side of the courtyard, saw the gathering frown beneath his polite expression.

Tabari brought news of a beautiful woman who had fetched the highest price that year on the Kashgar slave block. He knew the names of several people who had attended the auction, and after suitable reward shared them with Wu Li.

After an afternoon and a following morning spent knocking on Kashgar doors, bribes in hand, the one man Wu Li could find who would admit to having been present and who was willing to describe what had happened rolled his eyes and patted his heart. "Ah, you should have seen her, my friend! Not young, no, but ripe enough that the juice would run down your chin when you took a bite. Eyes so dark and liquid you could imagine diving into them, hair like black silk, and a figure—" his hands sketched an improbable shape in the air "—Oh, my friend. A proud one, too, head high, unashamed, though they stripped her for the bidding. It was fierce, I will tell you." He sighed reminiscently.

If only Barid the Balasagan's purse had measured up to his appreciation for a beautiful woman, it was clear that Wu Li's search would have ended there. Barid winked at Wu Li and gave him a nudge with his elbow. "But I know you for a stolid married man these many years, my friend. What is this, that you ask after another woman? If she knew, Shu Ming would carve out your liver and eat it while you bled to death in front of her, eh? What? A name?" He scratched his head. "Was she the one they called the Rose of Jordan? No, no, that was that skinny girl with the missing teeth. I think they called this one the Lycian Lotus. Eh? Who won? Some sheik from the west, I heard. Bedu, Turgesh." He gave a vague wave of his hand, indicating everything west of Kashgar. "Berber, maybe. No, I didn't catch his name. What? Who sold her?" He scratched his chin. "Anwar the Egyptian. At least he was the one looking the most satisfied at the end of the day. It's wonderful how he manages to offer the primest of prime goods every time, eh?"

Not so wonderful, if Anwar the Egyptian worked as a receiver of stolen goods for Persian raiders, Wu Li thought.

Anwar the Egyptian was brusque. "She was only one of a group I bought two days before. Her buyer?" He eyed Wu Li. "Honorable Wu Li, of course I wish to be of help, but—thank you." A jingle of coin. "Yes, I remember now. A sheik from the west. I don't remember his name."

Wu Li doubted that. "Where in the west?" he said.

The slaver shrugged. "It is a vast area, the west. Many places, many people." His smile did not reach his eyes. "Many sheiks."

Wu Li suppressed a sigh and reached again into his purse.

Anwar the Egyptian eyed the coin, gold this time, that Wu Li was fingering. "He said something about one more stop on his way home, to pick up a new sword."

"Do you think it was her?" Shu Ming said that evening.

"She matches Jaufre's description, but then so does every other woman between here and Antioch."

"Lycia is a place in Greece," Shu Ming said. "I think. Or near it."

"Yes," Wu Li said. "And he says his mother was Greek."

"And a new sword for someone rich enough to pay that much

45

for a slave means Damascus," Shu Ming said. "How far away is Damascus?"

"Two thousand leagues and more," Wu Li said. "Too far."

They sat in heavy silence for a moment.

"You'll have to tell him."

"Yes." But he didn't stir.

"What troubles you, my husband?"

"You remember why I wanted her to have a western name?"

She was startled by what seemed to be an abrupt change of subject, because Wu Li always spoke to the purpose. "Johanna?"

He nodded. "Johanna," he said. He smiled a little. "Wu Johanna."

She smiled, too, at the incongruity, at the odd conjoining of east and west in a single name. "Of course I remember," she said. "She looks western." *As I do,* she could have said. "Her grandfather is seen in her face for any who look upon her." She laid a hand on his arm. "I agreed with you, Li. Her face already sets her apart. It would have been silly, even cruel, to put a Chinese name to that face."

He nodded, his hand coming up to clasp hers. "But it is more than that, Ming. You have seen as well as I the change. In spite of the Khan's efforts, fear and hatred of foreigners grows in Cambaluc, more every year. I have even heard talk of expelling them all, of closing the ports to foreign ships."

She knew what he said was true, and said nothing.

"I fear Johanna will never find a home in Cambaluc," he said. "I feared it when she was born. I wanted her to have a name she could wear easily if…"

"If she lived somewhere other than Cambaluc."

He let out a long, slow sigh. "Yes."

She was silent for a moment. "She wants him to stay with us."

"I know," Wu Li said. "I like what I see of the boy."

"As do I."

"And I was thinking that it would be good for her to have someone, a companion who looks like her—"

A brother, Shu Ming thought. The brother I could not give her. The son I could not give you.

"—a friend who will walk with her through the years. She will have all I own, but I fear it will not be enough. She is too foreign. She could be married for my fortune, and disposed of when we are gone."

They sat in silence for a few moments, and then Wu Li rose to his feet. "But you are right, my wife. I must tell him. The decision must be his."

Jaufre listened in solemn silence, Johanna sitting close by his side. In the past weeks, the two had grown inseparable. "I am sorry, Jaufre," Wu Li said. "There is no more to be done."

The boy's face was white and strained. Johanna, looking at him anxiously, understood. Both of his parents had been alive and whole and present a month before. She looked at her mother and her father sitting across from them, the tea tray between them forgotten by them all.

Into the silence, Wu Li said, "I understand your need to find her, Jaufre, and it does you credit. But she could be anywhere now, and there is no place even for you to begin to look. 'A sheik in the west' is not helpful. There are hundreds of sheiks. Thousands. And your own father owned a blade of Damascus steel."

Wu Li glanced at Johanna, whose eyes were raised trustfully to his face. Just so had Jaufre no doubt once looked at his father, with absolute faith, certain that he could make all well. "This is my thought," he said. "My daughter and my wife, I myself have come to value you highly. Shu Shao and Deshi the Scout both speak well of you, and I value their counsel. There is a place for you in our family. Return with us to Cambaluc, and let yourself grow into a man." Wu Li sighed. "And when that day comes, set out in search of your mother, if it is what you still wish to do."

The cry was wrenched from him. "She could be dead by then, Wu Li!"

"She could be dead now." Wu Li felt Shu Ming's eyes upon him. This was unlikely, they both knew. Anyone who had paid the price quoted by an awed Barid the Balasagan would have taken very great care of so valuable a property, but if Jaufre set out in pursuit he would be dead shortly thereafter of any one of a number of causes, or a slave himself, in which case his mother would be dead to him and he to her for all time. The world was vast and travel across it slow. Chances were weighted heavily against mother and son ever meeting again, but any small hope Jaufre had of it lay in joining the Wu household.

And this, Jaufre, displaying what would become a lifelong ability to recognize the truth, however unpalatable it was and however much it cost him, came to understand for himself. When they left Kashgar three days later, he rode behind Johanna, swaying over the sand on the back of the young camel.

If he looked over his shoulder too often, surely no one was so cruel as to mention it.

5

1320, Cambaluc

The route to Cipangu to trade silk for pearls, initiated by Wu Hai and carried forward with efficiency and dispatch by Wu Li, had become an annual event in the trading house of Wu. This had been a most profitable year, partially due, Wu Li had to admit, if only to himself, to Johanna's ability to make friends wherever she went. In this case she had ingratiated herself into the society of the women pearl divers of Ama, who had taught her the art of holding her breath underwater for a long enough time as to strike terror into the hearts of her parents waiting anxiously on shore. But what could they do?

"She's too old to scold and too tall to beat," Wu Li said ruefully.

His wife gave him a fond look. "As if you have ever done either."

By the time they reached the Edo docks, Wu Li was concerned enough over the value of their cargo that he hired another half dozen guards from the always steady supply found on any port. One, a youngish thickset man whose black quilted armor and well-kept naginata argued a fall from samurai grace, was so anxious to board ship that he accepted the first salary offer Wu Li made. By the time they reached Kinsai, having proved his value in two encounters with pirates, he was outspoken in his belief that he was deserving of a bonus amounting to twenty-five percent of the value of the trade goods he had helped to protect. He said so, loudly, and this sounded like a fine idea to the other Nippon guards Wu Li had hired in Edo. They stood in front of him in a half-circle, hands resting on their weapons in a manner completely lacking in subtlety.

"The value of your contribution to the success of our voyage is not in dispute, Gokudo," Wu Li said, answering threat with courtesy. "Indeed, it was my intention to pay you a bonus of ten percent of the worth of the goods you have helped us shepherd safely to port. However."

His eyes hardened and he made a motion with one hand. Deshi the Scout and a dozen other retainers materialized behind the Nippon guards, armed with swords, pry bars and belaying pins.

"Because of your greed," Wu Li said, courtesy giving way to contempt, "and your inability to make your case for reimbursement without threat, you will receive the salary we agreed on in Edo, and not one tael more."

There was the promise of an incipient riot, but Wu Li's men were in sufficient number to quell it before the Mongol authorities were alerted and all his profit went in fines for failure to keep the peace. "My thanks, Deshi," Wu Li said, and for the first time noticed that the scout was pale and shivering. "My friend, you are ill! Return home at once and seek out Shu Shao. She will know what to do."

Unfortunately, in this instance, Shu Shao, already a healer of some repute, did not.

The next morning, Shu Ming fell ill. She complained of loose stool in the morning, and three hours later she, too, was pale and shivering, her skin clammy to the touch, her heart hammering beneath her skin at a frantic, irregular pace. She complained of thirst, when her mind wasn't wandering, which it did more and more as the day wore on. They tried giving her clear soup and tea but she couldn't keep anything down, and by the afternoon her sodden bedclothes had to be changed every hour.

Before nightfall, she was dead.

So was the maid who laundered her sheets, the stable boy, Deshi the Scout, and 3,526 other citizens of Cambaluc.

In the horrible weeks that followed, Wu Li went about looking like a ghost. Johanna attended him white-lipped and withdrawn. Jaufre suffered the loss of his second mother with outward calm and inward agony, taking over the mews and the stables while Shu Shao took charge of the kitchen, and all went on tiptoe for fear that the master of the house would shatter like glass at one wrong word.

One day a month later Jaufre went out to the stables and found Johanna seated on a bale of hay next to Edyk the Portuguese, deep in earnest conversation. She looked more animated than she had since the day her mother died. Edyk was holding one of Johanna's hands in both of his own, and as Jaufre came around the corner he raised it to his lips.

Johanna looked up and saw Jaufre. She pulled her hand free and jumped to her feet. "Edyk has come."

"So I see." The two men exchanged a cool glance.

"I am sorry for the trouble that has visited the house of the Honorable Wu Li," Edyk said with a formal bow.

Jaufre inclined his head a fraction. He could not rue the lightening of sorrow on Johanna's face, even if he suspected that their recent troubles were not what had brought Edyk the Portuguese to the house of Wu Li.

Edyk the Portuguese was in his early twenties and, like Johanna and Jaufre, the child of expatriate Westerners, with eyes too round for Cambaluc comfort. A brawny young man, thickly-muscled, again like Johanna and Jaufre he moved with the assurance of someone accustomed to an active life. He had his father's brown eyes and his mother's black hair and a charming smile all his own. He was a trader, as the honorable Wu Li had been a trader, and traveling the trade routes with him Johanna had watched that smile melt feminine hearts from Kinsai to Kashgar.

He was shorter than Jaufre by a head, which was some comfort to the crusader's son, but he made up for his lack of height with a dynamic personality and a great deal of personal charm and energy. He was an up-and-coming merchant in Cambaluc, one of the group of foreign traders resident there by permission of the Khan who accounted for the bulk of foreign goods imported into the city. Since the death of the Great Khan, raiders on the Silk Road had moved from a rarity to a steadily increasing threat. In response, the Cambaluc merchants had banded together in a cooperative association, exchanging information on road conditions and organizing communal caravans at set times during the year. Pooling their resources, they could hire more guards, which increased their chances of a safe arrival at their destination, alive and with their goods intact, and, when they had finished their trading, a safe return home. Their profit would be less from the increased competition at their destinations, but at least they were sure of living to travel and trade another day.

The Honorable Wu Li had been among the proponents of this cooperative, and Edyk the Portuguese had been among the first to join. Young, only five years older than Jaufre and Johanna, intelligent, talented and ambitious, he was quick to see the benefits of Wu Li's proposal, and a caravan traveling under Wu Li's direction hadn't left Cathay in the last three years in which Edyk the Portuguese had not been a full partner, carrying silk west and driving a carefully selected group of purebred horses east. He favored Arabians, but when available he did not turn up his nose at draft horses like the Ardennais, mules, and the occasional zebra, which could be bred with horses to make a hardy pony good for narrow trails at high elevations, a breed championed by a certain faction of Mongol nobles who were willing to pay any amount to acquire better transportation for their troops.

He'd met Johanna during the Cambaluc merchants' first communal caravan, early one morning when he'd come down to inspect his father's picket line and had found her galloping up on his most obstreperous stallion. "His front right shoe is a little loose, I think," she had said without introduction, and slid from the stallion's back to pick up his right front foot, beckoning Edyk closer for an inspection of the offending shoe. She had been right.

Edyk's father had been a rogue Cistercian monk, born in Portugal, who had abandoned a life of contemplation and cloister for one of travel and adventure. Like Johanna's grandfather, upon reaching the East he had offered his services to the court of the Great Khan. Those services had been able enough to achieve recognition and reward, again like Johanna's grandfather, in the form of Edyk the Portuguese's mother, the daughter of a Chinese concubine. Again, like Johanna and Jaufre, by virtue of his foreign blood he was shunned by Cambaluc society, and not much more welcomed by the ruling class.

Foreign traders, the proximate cause of so much Mongol wealth, were regarded as somewhere in between, and their children, especially the children of favorite foreigners and ex-Mongol concubines, were even then regarded as a breed apart, not quite other but not quite equal, either. Like Johanna and Jaufre and lacking an alternative, Edyk was drawn to others of his kind.

Where Johanna went Jaufre followed and the three of them had become nearly inseparable over the years, but recently Jaufre had noticed a change in Edyk's manner toward Johanna; less brotherly and more, well, affectionate, was the only word for it. It set Jaufre's teeth on edge.

"North Star's foal was born last night," Edyk said.

In spite of himself, Jaufre brightened. "All well?"

Edyk grinned. "He was running before he could walk. A winner, I'll wager."

And he would, Jaufre thought, and Edyk the Portuguese would win, too. Upon succeeding to his father's business three years before, Edyk had shifted emphasis from general goods to livestock, in particular racing stock, and had made a name for himself in buying and backing winners.

"And North Star?" Johanna said.

"Well, though I think this is the last time I will breed her. She has done enough for my stables."

"What are you calling him?"

Edyk smiled at her. She was taller than he was but it didn't seem to bother him. "What would you like me to call her, Golden Flower?"

Jaufre didn't like the caressing tone in his voice, and still less did he like Edyk's employment of Johanna's Cambaluc name. "What color is his coat?"

Edyk's smile lessened. "He is pure white, nose to tail."

A short silence fell. They all knew that white was the color of death. Johanna and Jaufre were still wearing white in honor of Shu Ming's death, although they would be putting it off when the month of official mourning had passed. "Will Chinese gamblers bet on a white horse?" Jaufre said.

"They will on this one," Edyk said with more assurance. "And Mongol gamblers certainly will. We're just lucky it's a colt and not a filly."

Johanna and even Jaufre in spite of himself nodded emphatic agreement. A vast herd of white mares was maintained by the Mongol emperor for the production and fermenting of their milk. If North Star had born a female, Edyk would have been expected to gift it to the Mongol court, no matter how fast a foal out of North Star might be expected to run. Koumiss was more of a staple in the Mongolian diet than bread or meat.

"Then call him North Wind," Johanna said. "Let him be named for how fast he will run."

A slow smile spread across Edyk's face. "Perfect," he said, and swung Johanna up into his arms and whirled her around.

Jaufre, watching, schooled his expression to something that felt a little less like murder.

54

On the other side of Cambaluc, where families who could trace their ancestries back to the Shang dynasty lived closely together in a section renowned for its insularity, xenophobia and self-regard, another meeting was taking place, with consequences reaching much farther than the selection of a lucky name for a winning horse.

The house was every bit as large as its neighbors, but its appearance had declined with the fortunes of its owners. Luck had not followed the Dai family for three generations. Once one of the richest trading concerns in Everything Under the Heavens, the hopes of everyone under the Dai roof were now vested in the person of Dai Fang, an exquisite beauty of twenty years. Like Johanna, she was the only child of her house. Her mother was an invalid, her father inconstant, and when one day at the age of fifteen Dai Fang discovered that the only food in the house was two eggs laid by a stringy hen who had then immediately died, she had shut her father in a room with the cheapest bottle of rice wine she could find and had stepped forward to take the reins of the family business into her own hands.

Over the past five years, those hands had proved to be capable. Intelligent and ruthless, with an invaluable talent for identifying well in advance of demand that one luxury item that the wives and concubines of Cambaluc simply could not do without that year. Allied with a charm of manner that had seduced many an older trader with more experience and a much harder head, Dai Fang made agreements and partnerships profitable enough to draw the Dai fortunes back up over the edge of disaster. When she had balanced the books at the end of the previous year, for the first time in four years the knot in her belly eased a little. They would not starve. The house would not have to be sold to pay their debts. Her mother could have the services of a decent nurse, who could also provide herbal remedies for Dai Yu's own needs. If disaster in the form of sandstorm or flood or raiders did not descend upon next year's caravan, the house of Dai might even see a profit. A modest one, to be sure, but encouraging after so many years of loss.

It was at this inopportune moment that her father sobered up enough to notice that his daughter had reached the venerable age of twenty without being married. Unable to bear the shame, he entered into an arrangement with a matchmaker and began interviewing prospective sons-in-law. This was not to Dai Fang's taste at all, not least because of Gokudo, her father's Nippon sergeant of the guard, hired for a pittance a year before.

"He will never allow you to marry me," Gokudo said. Twenty-six, a hard-muscled man of middle height, his hands were rough and calloused from work with the spear with the curved blade he called the naginata, the weapon he only put down when he joined Dai Fang in her bed. Even now, it leaned against the wall within easy reach.

"No," she said. "The honorable Dai Fu would be horrified at the very thought of joining the revered house of Dai with a man not born in Everything Under the Heavens."

He looked down at her, his amusement showing in his face.

"What?"

He shook his head. Far be it from him to draw her attention to the fact that the honorable Dai Fu's daughter shared her bed, enthusiastically and without inhibition, with a man not himself born in Everything Under the Heavens. A warrior nobleman exiled from his own country, he was still a foreigner here, forced to sell his services as a lowly bodyguard to a failed merchant, a man whom he would never even have met, let alone associated with were he still heir to those rights, privileges and duties conferred by five hundred generations of birth, influence and favor.

But then taking a lover was of much less importance than taking a husband.

He took a deep, steadying breath, calming yet again the shame and the fury that burned always in his breast. His father had picked the losing side in a struggle for power and their family was no more. It was futile to dwell on the past, although the day would come when… Again he forced away thoughts of vengeance and retribution. They were a waste of energy best spent elsewhere.

And there were compensations to his present occupation, to be sure. Slowly he drew back the coverlet and let himself enjoy the sight of her smooth, unblemished skin, the small, ruby-crowned breasts, the mystery between her lissome legs concealed by a tight weave of black hair. He had trimmed that cap of hair himself, with a sharp knife and infinite care. As he watched, she stretched, opening her legs, legs that ended in tiny, folded-back feet that had been bound since birth, a grotesquerie that had charmed him at first sight.

A delicate film of moisture made her skin glow in the moonlight. He felt his body respond, and he smiled. After all, what need had Dai Fang of sure feet? It was off them that he liked her best. And if she married judiciously...

He looked up to meet her eyes as his hand traveled up the inside of her thigh. "Then we must select the proper husband for you."

She sighed, arching her back. "And you have some suggestions along those lines, I suspect."

He was on her and in her, ferocious, sudden, his hand clapping brutally over her mouth as she cried out in surprise. "As it happens."

Servicing his mistress required only the attention of his body, and left his mind free to plot the various ways he could bring Dai Fang's attention to the newly bereaved state of that most prosperous Cambaluc merchant, the honorable Wu Li.

In the end the choice was obvious, and Dai Fu required very little persuading to open negotiations. The honorable Wu Li was of impeccable lineage with extensive holdings who had recently lost his wife and who had no son. There was of course the matter of having looked outside his race for his first wife, but that could be excused on the grounds of his father's misplaced loyalty to an absent associate, an honorable if foolish act. Dai Fang was a young woman of excellent family and considerable beauty. It took very little encouragement for Dai Fang to arrange a meeting between her father and the honorable Wu Li, a meeting at which she contrived to be present. He wasn't interested until she allowed herself to display some knowledge of trade. Further questions, delicately put beneath Dai Fu's benevolent if slightly drunken eye, revealed a shrewd mind, wrapped in a traditional and delightfully feminine package.

In appearance she was as unlike Shu Ming as she could be, and so Wu Li overlooked her bound feet, and the calculating look in her eyes.

The matter was arranged in a week. The sensation this caused in Wu Li's household lasted longer than that, but by not so much as the lift on an eyebrow did Dai Fang reveal any knowledge of the information the spies in the honorable Wu Li's house reported daily to Gokudo. Her plans were laid and Wu Li so completely in her thrall that she felt confident that she would be able to see them through.

The marriage took place a month later. Dai Fang's mother's nurse, an invaluable consultant, was able to supply her with an effective means of convincing Wu Li of her innocence. He was entirely beguiled, displaying a tenderness for her that first night that was as touching as it was tedious.

She left the nurse with her mother, but she took Gokudo with her as her personal bodyguard when she moved into Wu Li's house.

And so infatuated with his new wife was Wu Li that he did not recognize Gokudo as the guard he had hired in Edo at the end of his last voyage to Cipangu.

6

1322, Cambaluc

"MY HUSBAND IS dead," the widow said.

Not "Your father." Not the more formal "The head of the house of Wu." Just the exclusive, proprietary "My husband." The widow was selfish even in her alleged grief.

There was also a hard glitter of triumph in her dark eyes, for those with the wit to see it.

"I know," the girl said. The words were calm, devoid of grief or sorrow, devoid, indeed, of any expression at all.

The widow's mouth tightened into a lacquered red line. "How?" She had forbidden any communication between the mongrel's servants and her own, on pain of severe punishment.

The girl shrugged without answering. Her eyes met the widow's without expression, without humility and, most inexcusably, without fear.

The widow felt the familiar rage well up in her breast. Her hands trembled with it, curling into claws, the resemblance enhanced by the long, enameled fingernails. She saw the little mongrel looking at them, still with no expression on her alien face, and inhaled slowly, straightening her fingers from claws into hands once more.

Behind her Gokudo stirred, a brief movement, a rustle of clothing, but it was enough to remind her of what was at stake.

The little mongrel still had friends at court, associates of Wu Li who remembered him with respect and fondness and who might be persuaded to listen to any grievances Wu Li's daughter might have with her father's second wife.

Gokudo was of course quite correct. The Khan's attention must be avoided, and it required only her own self-control. The widow caused her rage to abate by sheer willpower, until she was able to look on her husband's daughter and only child with at least the appearance of indifference. Soon the little mongrel would be out of the house and out of her life.

The mongrel wasn't little, being indecently tall, towering over everyone in the house and over most of the citizens of Cambaluc for that matter, but the widow never thought of her any other way. The little mongrel was nothing but a blight on the honored ancestors of the house of Wu, upon the sacred ancestors of Everything Under the Heavens itself, and what was worse, the little mongrel cost more than any two other members of the household to feed and clothe. Since the widow had cajoled her honorable husband Wu Li into letting her take over his accounts after his accident, she knew just how much extra silk it took to keep the length of the little mongrel's legs and arms decently covered, and how many bowls of noodles it took to fill her apparently bottomless belly.

If the little mongrel's size had not damned her beyond redemption, her features surely would have. Her eyes were not a decent, modest brown or culturally acceptable black but instead a blue so light the irises were almost gray, with no hint of fold in the eyelid. The little mongrel lacked even the common courtesy to drop her gaze out of respect in the presence of her elders, and especially her betters.

And as tightly confined as fashion and tradition decreed in a single braid that reached her waist, the little mongrel's hair was still as unruly and unmanageable as the little mongrel herself, escaping a wisp at a time to curl round the pale face with its odd cheekbones, enormous nose and grossly oversized mouth.

The hair had not even the saving grace of color, that thick rich black fall of hair one might expect of the honorable Wu Li's daughter, but instead a brown streaked with bronze, acquired during the improperly hatless and shockingly astride daily rides with her father and that foreign stableboy the honorable Wu Li had so carelessly chosen first as his daughter's playmate and later as her personal guard. Perhaps Wu Li had felt that the essential outlandishness in each made them fit only for their own company. Certainly they were inseparable.

Wu Li's widow was pleased enough with this reasoning to ignore the presence of Gokudo at her shoulder. He was the noble warrior of an honorable race strong enough to defeat two invasions by Kublai Khan himself, not to be compared to the descendant of a race of men who could not hold a land they had conquered for even fifty years.

The little mongrel's stepmother averted her eyes before her inventory could take in the abomination of close-cut fingernails and unbound feet, but she was shocked to her very soul at such an unfeminine disregard for the proprieties. That the little mongrel herself was without sense or shame was expected but that Wu Li would have allowed either was unbelievable. Foreign, the widow thought with an inward shudder, the most insulting epithet in her language.

Yes: in birth, appearance and demeanor, altogether an unsatisfactory little mongrel to dispose of, but disposed of she must be if the widow wished to gather the reins of her husband's importing business into her own supremely competent hands, and that she most certainly wished to do.

All that remained was the safe disposition of the sole heir of Wu Li's body.

Fortunately a solution to the problem was ready to hand. The widow smiled to herself, and said, "Ceremonies for your father will take place three days from now." She paused, and added with a bow that was as patronizing as it was slight, "You may attend."

The little mongrel displayed no proper gratitude for the

61

magnanimity thus offered. There was no bow of acknowledgement, no polite murmur of appreciation. Her blue-gray eyes remained steady on the widow's face. Truth be told, that unflinching gaze was a little unnerving.

Again, Gokudo shifted behind the widow. Her eyes moved to the marble-topped table reposing in isolated splendor against one wall. On its carved and polished top rested two items, carefully centered. One was the jade box that held Wu Li's bao. The other was the fat leather-bound journal that held the names of all of Wu Li's agents in cities far and near, and his annotated maps of trading routes as far as the Middle Sea. The power these two items represented was enough to soothe her irritation.

She turned her head to see the little mongrel watching her. She dropped her eyes and smoothed the heavy blue silk of her dress. "There is another matter we must discuss. Sit down." She beckoned a servant forward with one graceful sweep of a hand heavy with rings. "Will you have tea?"

The girl folded her long frame down onto a pillow, crossing her legs and resting a hand on each knee instead of kneeling with bent head and clasped hands in an attitude of proper attentiveness. She refused tea. Impolite and graceless as well as ugly, the widow noted, not without pleasure.

They waited as the tea was poured and the servant retired. The widow sipped delicately at the fragrant liquid in the paper-thin porcelain cup. After a moment of appreciative contemplation of the delicate design traced on its rim, she said, her tone casual, "I have received an offer of marriage for you."

"Have you?" The strange light eyes met hers. "From whom?"

The widow allowed herself a small, playful smile. "It is from the son of Maffeo the Portuguese."

The blue eyes widened so slightly that if the widow had not been watching so closely for any change of expression she would have missed it. "Is it?" was all the little mongrel said.

"It is, and a very generous offer, too," her father's widow said. "He offers silk, spices, an interest in future trading ventures."

"Generous indeed," the little mongrel said, after a moment.

"And of course you have known each other since you were children."

"Of course."

Her stepmother looked up suspiciously but could perceive no sarcasm in that clear, alien gaze. She folded her tiny hands in her lap and regarded their long polished nails, longer than the fingers themselves, with thoughtful attention. "Altogether a most suitable match."

"Isn't it, though," the little mongrel said, her tone almost amiable.

Her father's widow smiled again, broadly this time. "Then, if you have no objection, I will put the matter in hand at once."

"As you wish, my father's second wife," the girl said.

Again her stepmother looked sharply for guile in those strange eyes. She found none. It was not that she had expected outright opposition, but she had been spiteful enough to hope that some aspect of the little mongrel's planned future would be displeasing to her. Instead, the girl seemed acquiescent, amenable even, to be disposed of so quickly and so efficiently.

It was with a faint feeling of disappointment that she terminated the interview, and turned with relief to the affairs of her husband's trading empire.

Hers now.

7

P RIDE KEPT JOHANNA'S departing step to a stroll much slower than her usual ground-eating stride. The widow's creature scowled and closed the door so swiftly and so firmly behind her that her robe nearly caught in the crack. She paused for a moment to consider it, the heavy mahogany panels carved with the symbols for health and prosperity, the massive bronze ring pulls.

The heavy bronze lock.

The door had been closed against her, to keep her out, to separate her from her father and, more importantly, any claim on his estate. She understood that quite well.

She smiled. It would never occur to the widow or her Nipponese creature that the barrier of the door worked both ways.

She turned and made straight for her own suite, the two small rooms in the back of the house to which she had been relegated upon the occasion of her father's remarriage. If asked, Johanna would have replied truthfully that she preferred her new location, as it was closer to the stables, the mews and the kitchen, and horses, falcons and food ranked very high in importance in her life. Her lyra she kept next to her bed, so that music was never out of her reach.

Once in her room she threw off the heavy silk robe, the wonderfully embroidered Robe of a Thousand Larks that had once belonged to her mother which she had donned for the visit of state to her father's second wife, and pulled on trousers and tunic made of heavier raw silk. It was dyed a rich black and trimmed with dull black sateen. Black for travel, not white for mourning. She had been adamant in the face of Shasha's remonstrations. She would not at this late date bow to the traditions of a place that had treated her like an outsider all her life.

She smoothed one hand over the nubbled texture. She had bargained for the fabric herself, on their last trip to Suchow. The blue-gray eyes went blank for a moment and she stood still, unmoving, staring at nothing.

She shook herself out of her reverie and raised her voice. "Shasha? Where are you?"

"In the kitchen."

Shu Shao, now a kitchen drudge, was stirring a steaming pot over the stove. She looked up, ran her eyes over the girl's tall form, and said, "I remember the trip to Shandong with your father to buy that silk. It was the first time he permitted you to conduct the bargaining."

"I remember," Johanna said. Unable yet to bring herself to speak casually of her father, she gestured at the empty kitchen. "Where is everyone?"

Shasha snorted. "Over in her quarters."

"You can't blame them, Shasha," Johanna said. "They have to eat." She smiled. "And it will be easier for us to talk."

Shasha's brown eyes were as keen and clever as ever between their narrow lids. She examined the girl before her. "So?"

"So, we go."

Shasha felt a loosening of the apprehension that had been slowly accumulating since Wu Li had brought home his second wife. "When?"

"Three days. After the cremation."

"So soon?"

"It must be." Johanna grimaced. "She has arranged a marriage for me."

"Who?"

"Edyk."

Shasha's lids drooped until she looked half asleep. She resumed her stirring. "Hmmm."

"What is that supposed to mean?"

"What?"

"That 'hmmm.' You 'hmmm' and you nod to yourself. I hate it when you do that."

Shasha lifted the spoon out of the pot and set it to one side. "He does love you."

"I know that," Johanna said. "I love him. It doesn't matter. It wouldn't work."

"You think not?"

There was as much pain as there was certainty in Johanna's reply. "I know not."

Shasha nodded again. She moved the pot to the back of the stove and reached for two bowls. "Bird's nest."

"My favorite."

The woman and the girl ate in companionable silence. Johanna asked for more and Shasha took great pleasure in filling the bowl to its rim for the second time.

"What?" Johanna said, catching sight of her expression.

Shasha shook her head. Wu Li's widow's complaints that Johanna ate twice as much as the hungriest horse in the stables lent spice to every bite of food the girl took. Shasha was willing to admit it lent a certain zest to ladling it out, too.

Johanna finished her third helping, set her bowl aside and stretched. She met the older woman's eyes with a gravity that sat heavily on her young features. "I must show you something, Shasha," she said.

She led the way to her bedroom, going straight to the silken tapestry hanging above her bed, caught up one corner and without hesitation ripped out the lining. Six small packages fell to the bed, each was wrapped in translucent rice paper and tied with string. With a certain solemn ceremoniousness in her manner she untied the string and unfolded the paper. She tilted the package and a gleaming stream of stones fell out, so deeply red they seemed as if they might set the coverlet on fire. Indeed, Shasha picked up one of the stones and where the gem rested her skin felt near to scorching. "From Mien," she said, and it wasn't a question. She let the stone slip from her hand back to the patched and faded coverlet.

"Yes," the girl said. She stirred the little heap of gems with a pensive forefinger. "We were coming home on the Grand Canal from Kinsai. The night before we started, this funny little man in a dhow tied up next to us." She smiled at the memory. "All those junks, and his was the only dhow. We had never seen one so far from Calicut before. Father invited him on board for dinner and when he realized I was a girl he dropped his jib and tied it round him with one of the jib sheets." At Shasha's puzzled look she smiled. "All he wore for traveling was a turban, you see."

Shasha laughed.

"His name was Lundi. He had a hooded snake he kept in a basket that lapped milk out of a saucer like a cat. He drank too much wine after dinner and started telling the story about Princess Padmini of Rajputana and the Moslem invader Ala-ud-din, only the way he told it Ala-ud-din got to Rajputana before Padmini killed herself. I could tell Father was about to send me to bed when Lundi's turban fell off and all these rubies fell out. It was like the story of From-Below-the-Steps and the night it rained emeralds. They were so beautiful. Father bought all of them on the spot."

Johanna smiled again. "Edyk said the last time he was in Kinsai that Lundi had bought a house by the river and filled the garden with hooded snakes and the house with pretty concubines, all named Padmini."

They stood in silence, staring down as the fiery swath of color glittered up at them. Johanna put her arm around the older woman's shoulders. "Some in the hems of my clothes, some in yours, some in Jaufre's. We leave in three days."

"Does she—"

"She knows nothing of them. Father gave them to me and told me to hide them." Her expression was bleak. "He said he thought I might need them one day."

"Well," Shasha said, voice very dry, "at least the man wasn't a complete fool."

There was a brief, taut silence. "Never speak of my father in that way again, Shasha," Johanna said. "Do you understand me?"

Oh, I understand perfectly, Shu Shao thought. "He was only a man, Johanna, and he was so lonely and so lost after Shu Ming died. And Dai Fang is very beautiful."

Johanna turned abruptly. "I'll tell Jaufre," she said over her shoulder, "and then I'm going to Edyk's."

Shasha thought before speaking this time, and then said, very carefully, "Is that wise?"

"Perhaps not," Johanna said, pausing in the doorway. "But it is only fair."

With a lithe, confident stride she was gone, leaving Shasha to reflect ruefully on the wisdom of tying her future to someone as proud and as stubborn and as reckless as Johanna.

But then what could one expect of a child born beneath the broom star? The signs had been there the night of Johanna's birth for all to read. Did the appearance of that cloud banner, that peacock feather in the skies over Everything Under the Heavens not signify the wiping out of the old and the establishment of the new? Certainly the description fit Johanna who, raised by a liberal and loving father, never bothered with the traditional limitations placed on the behavior of females, or children for that matter.

Shasha chuckled. Wu's widow would—and had—taken the legend of the broom star even further, to anticipate drought, famine and disease as a natural consequence of Johanna's birth and continued presence in Wu Li's house. Wu Li had put up with much from his second wife but he had stopped that nastiness in its tracks, so firmly that the second wife had never referred to

Johanna again in his presence. If she could not speak ill of the girl, she would not speak of her at all.

Shasha swept up the rubies in her hands and smiled to herself. At least life on the road with Johanna would never be dull.

She thought of Jaufre, and her smile faded. No, not dull at all.

Jaufre had been moved from the house to the stables at the same time Shasha had been moved from the family quarters to the kitchen. He was seated now on a leather folding stool outside his room, coaxing another year's use out of a worn bridle.

"I've just come from a royal audience," she said. "Wu Li's widow has finally seen fit to inform me of my father's death."

"Twenty-four hours after the fact," Jaufre said. His hands stilled and his eyes lifted to hers. "It was better this way, Johanna," he said. "After the accident, it was only a matter of time. Wu Li was not the man to live without his legs."

She turned her face into an errant ray of sunshine and closed her eyes against the glare. "I know. It's just…"

His hand, hard and warm and slightly sweaty, raised to her cheek. "I know."

She pressed her face into his palm. He allowed it for a moment, and then pulled away to resume work on the bridle.

She pulled out a wisp of hay and chewed it, watching him work. He was as unnaturally tall as she, with smooth, tanned skin and startlingly light hair, the first and still the only golden hair she had ever seen, even on the Road. It was thick and clipped short and in the sun gleamed like a polished helmet. His eyes were blue, too, but much darker, like the sky after sunset. He was muscular and agile from work with the bow and the staff and with the horses and hawks and the soft boxing he practiced daily in the garden, taught him by Deshi the Scout since Jaufre had first joined the Wu household. When Johanna had expressed an interest Deshi the Scout had begun teaching her, too.

After Deshi's death they continued to practice, rising at dawn every morning. After Shu Ming's death, they had both found comfort in the ritual. After Wu Li's remarriage, they had done so under the occasional eye of the second wife's personal guard. He seemed amused. Once Jaufre had said beneath his breath, "I wonder, does he know what happens when we speed this up?"

"Let's not show him," Johanna said with her voice barely above a whisper. "Let's... keep it in reserve."

She made no mention of the way Gokudo sometimes looked at her, of how uncomfortable his presence made her feel. Even on the Road, before the eyes of hundreds of strangers, never had she felt so threatened. She was determined that the widow's bodyguard would have no prior knowledge of just how well the widow's husband's daughter could protect herself at need.

Jaufre looked up to see her eyes fixed on some distant thought, and allowed himself the rare pleasure of a long, unguarded look. A late ray of sun kissed her cheek to gold, and threw her profile into proud relief: the straight nose, the high, shadowed cheekbones, the full lips that curled upwards at their corners, the chin that was somehow delicate and determined at the same time. His eyes strayed to the rich bronze braid of hair, the curls that slipped from their braid to cup her cheeks, coil over her shoulders and around the promising swell of her breasts. Her waist was narrow, her hips slim but rounded, flowing into the long, smooth length of her legs sprawling negligently beside his in the hay.

She was a woman now, not the child she had been when she had convinced him to join his fortunes with the honorable house of Wu. He closed his eyes, took a deep and he hoped unobtrusive breath, and focused once more on the bridle.

Her voice disturbed his thoughts. "Jaufre?"

"What?"

"Your father was a Frankish Crusader," she said.

He shrugged. "So he said. He left his crusade to ride as a caravan guard. Not a very good one, obviously, or our caravan wouldn't have been slaughtered to the last man by Persian bandits."

He spoke without bitterness, but she remembered the lonely, unmarked mound they had left behind, sand heaped by hand as high as he could make it, grains already shifting with the wind. "And your mother was Greek?"

His hands stilled on the bridle. "Yes. Why?"

"All the Greeks I've met are dark," she said. "Was your father fair-haired, as you are?"

He nodded, still working on the bridle. "He said that where he came from, some island to the west, many people have fair hair."

"It is very beautiful."

He grinned, and two deep dimples creased his cheeks. "So all the ladies tell me." She threw a handful of straw at him and he ducked, laughing. "Why so many questions today? You know all you need to know about me."

The full lips curved slightly. "Perhaps."

He resumed work on the bridle. "So. When do we go?"

"Three days from now."

"After the ceremonies for Wu Li."

"Yes."

"Where?"

"We could go first to Khuree," she said tentatively, as if she already knew it was a bad idea.

Jaufre shook his head. "That's the last place we want to go. You are the granddaughter of Marco Polo, Johanna. If the Khan learns that we are traveling west he will turn us into official envoys."

"But he might give us a paiza, as he did my grandfather and his father and uncle. We would have safe conduct anywhere in the world."

"Yes, he might; in fact he probably would, and then we would be bound to his service. He would load us down with missives to the Christian Pope and to all the kings in the West. There would be no time for our own business in the middle of all that

71

tedious diplomacy." He made a disgusted sound. "You've seen them at court, all twittering out of the sides of their mouths, no one meaning a word they say. No, I thank you."

She hid a smile.

"And then we would have to return." He looked at her. "We're not coming back, are we?"

"No," Johanna said. "No, we are not."

"So. Does the widow know we are leaving?"

"No," Johanna said.

He looked at her. "You can hate her if you want to, Johanna. She deserves your hatred."

"There is something else," she said, missing the grim certainty of his last words.

Before she could tell him what, there was movement at the stable door, and they looked up to see Gokudo watching them, one hand tucked into the wide sash he wore around his waist. It was as black as his topknot of hair, as black as the padded armor he wore at all times, as black as the ebony shaft of the tall spear he invariably carried. The curved point of the steel blade set into the top of the spear reflected the sunlight in a blaze that could hurt the eyes, were one to look at it too closely.

Johanna found herself on her feet, Jaufre at her side. A distant part of her mind noticed that they had all three assumed the same stance, shoulders braced, body weight over spread feet, knees slightly bent. Jaufre's hand settled on the hilt of the dagger at his waist. Her own hands hung loosely at her sides, ready for the knives strapped to her forearms to drop into her hands.

Tension sang in the air, until a horse whinnied loudly and thumped his stall.

Gokudo laughed suddenly: a deep, rolling belly laugh that filled the room. "Ha, my young friends," he said in his heavily accented Mandarin. "You are alert. That speaks well for the security of the honorable House of Wu."

Jaufre gave a curt nod. "Did you wish for a horse, Gokudo?"

"I did not, young Jaufre, not at present." The guard gave an

72

airy wave. "Just out for a stroll about the premises." He smiled. He had very white, very even teeth. "All must be in order for the festivities."

Jaufre felt Johanna tense next to him and said smoothly, "Surely you meant the ceremonies, Gokudo."

Gokudo's smile faded. "Surely, I did," he said gently. "Anything else would have been an insult to the memory of the Honorable Wu Li, and an affront to his descendants."

His gaze lingered on Johanna's artificially still face, before it slid slowly and deliberately down the length of her body. He held his gaze for just long enough to offend but not quite long enough to incite, before stepping past them to enter Jaufre's room without invitation. It was small and spare; a cot, a table, an oil lamp, a small chest for clothes. The only decoration was a large sword hanging from the wall, its encrusted hilt older than the leather scabbard it was encased in.

Again without invitation, Gokudo took down the sword and pulled it free. "Eh, Damascus steel." He looked down the blade, first one side and then the other. He pulled back a sleeve, licked his arm and ran the edge of the sword down his skin. "A fine edge, too," he said, inspecting the fine black hairs on the blade and the smooth, unblemished patch of skin it had left behind. "However did you come by such a thing, young Jaufre?"

Ignoring the implied insult, Jaufre said evenly, "It was my father's."

"Ah." Gokudo contemplated the blade, and its scabbard. "You don't use it."

"No."

"A pity." He walked past them into the yard, there to toss the sword into the air and catch it by the hilt as it fell again. "What balance," he said, admiring. "Obviously created by the hand of a master smith." He tossed it into the air again.

Jaufre stepped in front of it to catch it this time. The smack of hilt into hand shouted "Mine!" to anyone within earshot.

When he turned Gokudo was watching him with an assessing

eye. "I, too, own a sword, young Jaufre. Perhaps they should meet." He smiled again. He smiled a lot. "In practice, of course."

"Of course," Jaufre said.

Gokudo saluted him, tucked his hands back into his sash, and walked to the house with his usual jaunty step.

Jaufre watched him go, his eyes narrowed. "I wonder how much he heard."

"Nothing," Johanna said. "We were almost whispering."

He looked at her. "He was marking territory, Johanna."

"I noticed," Johanna said with mild sarcasm. "You can't fight him, Jaufre."

He doesn't want to fight me, Jaufre thought. He wants to kill me. "I know," he said. And he thought he knew why.

"Buy time," she said. "It's only three days."

"How?"

"Ask him for lessons with the sword," she said.

"Not from him," Jaufre said. "Never from him. He wears the black armor."

She shrugged. "All Cipangu mercenaries wear black armor."

He looked down at her, a faint smile lightening his expression. "And all Cipangu mercenaries are samurai. Which means they are very, very good at their craft."

"You're afraid of him," she said, not quite a question.

He gave her an incredulous look. "You aren't?" She raised an eyebrow. "Johanna, they say he can take two heads at once with that spear of his."

"They don't say it, he does," she said. "A tale told to frighten children."

"And I'm one of the children?"

She almost apologized before she saw the raised eyebrow, and laughed. "Stop trying to pick a fight."

His own smile faded. "Don't ever turn your back on Gokudo. He could kill us both without a thought and go in to enjoy his breakfast afterward. And he is the widow's creature, through and through."

"Her lover, too," she said, her voice flat.

He turned, surprised. "I didn't know you knew."

"The only person in this house who didn't know was my father," she said.

"If you kill her, we won't live to leave Everything Under the Heavens."

"It is the only reason she is still living," Johanna said, her expression bleak.

He was relieved to hear it, but there was no harm in driving the lesson home. "Well—that, and the fact that her personal guard is an ex-samurai."

She shrugged. "A thug, merely."

"For someone who has spent so much time in Cipangu, you are remarkably ignorant of its culture," Jaufre said with a deadly calm that finally pierced her insouciance. "Samurai are highly trained warriors, educated not just in personal arms but in strategy and tactics as well. This is a man who could not only take off our heads with one swipe of that pig-sticker of his, he could also organize the invasion of Kinsai."

"If he's so great, what is he doing a thousand leagues from home?"

"I don't know," Jaufre said. "He could have offended one of the shogun. He could have been on the losing side of a war." He shrugged. "He could be a spy, sent to Cambaluc to send home information on the stability of the Khan's court. Although I don't think so."

"Why not?"

"Spies, good spies, fade into the background. Gokudo? Likes to put on a show."

She watched Gokudo as he moved across the courtyard. Gokudo, who strutted rather than walked everywhere he went. He held his naginata, sharp, polished, as a badge of office. As a deadly threat.

She looked at the sword Jaufre held. "Maybe you should get in a few lessons with that thing. We should be ready to fight."

"Only if we can't run," he said. "And you know I prefer the bow."

Gokudo reached the front door of the house and went inside, the shadowed interior seeming to swallow his black figure whole.

"Jaufre?"

"What?" he said, going back inside to resheathe and rehang his father's sword on the wall of his room.

"Edyk has offered for me, something my father's widow undoubtedly refers to as a miracle sent from the Son of Heaven himself, as she is now busily planning my marriage."

His hands stilled on the sword but he didn't look around. "He loves you."

"He thinks he does."

"He loves you," Jaufre repeated.

"It doesn't matter," she said. "It wouldn't work. He wouldn't be happy." She paused. "I wouldn't be happy, to stay here in Cambaluc."

"You're sure?"

"I'm sure," she said firmly, and the hard, painful knot in his gut that had been twisting steadily tighter relaxed a little; not much, but enough to let him turn and face her, mask in place. "Besides," she added, with her sudden smile, "we have places to go, you and I and Shasha."

"Money?"

"We have enough. More than enough. Father made sure of that. Shasha will show you. And we can always earn our way. You're a soldier and a caravan master. Shasha's a cook and a healer. And you said yourself I'm as good a horseman and falconer as any you've ever seen, and if worst comes to worst, we can always sing for our suppers." She grinned. "And I know I'm a better diver, even if you won't admit it."

"Cipangu again," he said, a reminiscent smile pulling up one corner of his mouth.

"I brought back more of the rose pearls than you did," she said, with an impish, sidelong glance.

"Only because the fish charmer failed to keep a shark from the diving ground and the rest of us had brains enough to get out of the water," he replied promptly.

"Until you dived in to pull me out. I think you were more afraid of my bringing back more pearls than you had, than you were afraid that I might be eaten by the shark."

He remembered that Gokudo was from Cipangu, and good memories were swamped by a returning flood of recent events. He stooped to pick up the bridle he had been working on before Gokudo had come in on them. "And Edyk?"

Her smile vanished as quickly as it had come. "I'm going to see him now. To say goodbye."

He heard the thud of his blood in his ears. The knot in his gut was back, tied more tightly than it had ever been before. His eyes cleared and he saw that the bridle had snapped in two in his hands.

"Jaufre?" she said. "Is something wrong?"

He stood up abruptly and tossed the pieces of bridle into the scrap barrel. When he turned to where she could see his face again it had resumed its usual genial mask. "I'll saddle the Shrimp."

And he did, and he tossed her into the saddle, and he waved her off with a smile, although it was more of a rictus. Shu Shao came out to stand beside him as Johanna kicked the sedate Shrimp into a jolting trot and passed through the wooden gates. "She's off to see Edyk, then?"

He nodded, not trusting his voice to speech.

She nodded. "I'm to show you something."

He followed her into the house, where she produced the rubies of Mien from her sewing basket. "We are to sew these into the hems of our clothes."

"As Shu Ming said her father did," he said.

She nodded. They were both speaking in whispers, and Shasha had left the door wide open so that they might hear if anyone approached. He leaned in and said, "Shasha, do you know?"

She looked wary. "Know what?"

He took a deep breath. "How Wu Li truly died?"

She cast a quick glance through the door. "Which time?" she said.

He was startled into normal speech, quickly shushed by a gesture. "He didn't fall from his horse, Shasha," he said, his voice low again. "His cinch was cut nearly through."

She was silent for a long moment. "A pity the fall didn't kill him," she said at last.

"Shasha!"

She looked at him, her expression heavy with the burden of knowledge. "A pity the fall didn't kill him," she repeated.

"Why?" But he was afraid he already knew.

"Because," she said, "then the widow would not have dispatched Gokudo to finish the job with Wu Li's own pillow."

He went white. "Shasha. Are you sure?"

"He fought," she said distantly. "I saw blood beneath his fingernails. Before she had me removed from his room, of course."

Following his accident Wu Li had been left without the use of his legs, and there were other, internal injuries at which the learned doctors summoned from the city could only speculate. Now he wondered just how learned those doctors were, and how much the widow Wu had paid them to say what she wanted Wu's household to hear. "Is there no one we can tell? No one to whom we can appeal for justice?"

"Who?" Shasha said simply.

Jaufre cast around for a name. "Ogodei?" he said. "He's a baron of a hundred thousand now. He was a friend to Wu Li."

"And with his promotion he was posted to the west," she said. "He was the first person I thought of. No, Jaufre. There is no one else that I can think of. Wu Li spent just enough time and money at court to keep his business free of their interference. He did not cultivate the kind of friendships we would need to make an accusation against the widow."

They stood in miserable silence before sounds came from the kitchen of the beginnings of dinner.

Shasha gave him a little push toward the door.

"Johanna can't know, Shasha," he heard himself say.

"No," Shasha said grimly. "She most certainly can't."

8

JOHANNA SLID DOWN from the Shrimp's back, patting her heaving sides. Patiently she lifted the mare's right front hoof and dug out an offending piece of rock that had become wedged in her hoof. The Shrimp rewarded her efforts by leaning her entire weight on her back.

"You," Johanna said, "are an ungrateful wretch and you should have been turned into fertilizer years ago." She jabbed the horse's belly with an elbow and the Shrimp huffed out an indignant breath and shifted her weight enough for Johanna to finish the task.

Johanna let the Shrimp's hoof fall, and straightened, stretching.

Beneath her Cambaluc stretched on forever, its many rooftops glittering in the afternoon sun, the palace of the Great Khan bulking large to overshadow its neighbors. Johanna stood still, looking her fill. In her expression was appreciation for the beauty of the great city, and respect for the industry and achievement of its citizens, but there was no affection, no pride of place, and none of the sorrow one might expect from one anticipating a permanent exile.

Chiang, Edyk's manservant, answered her knock and bowed her into the house at once. Hearing her voice Edyk jumped up with a glad smile and held out both hands. "Johanna!"

Johanna waited for Chiang, loitering next to the door with a carefully disinterested look on his face, to leave the room. When at last he did, with a reluctant, backwards glance, she said without preamble, "My father's widow tells me you have offered to marry me."

Edyk's welcoming smile changed to a frown and his hands dropped. He looked at her searchingly. "The offer was made to your father last year. He told me it was for you to decide, but that in any case I must wait until you were older. He didn't tell you?"

The breath went out of her on a long sigh and she shook her head. "No. No, he wouldn't. He wouldn't want to pressure me, and he knew his second wife and I were not… close."

He touched her shoulder; a gentle, comforting touch. "I know."

She reached up to caress his hand lightly. His arms went out but before he could embrace her she stepped away. "I have come here to explain why I must refuse, Edyk."

He stood very still, his breath caught in his throat; even his heart seemed to cease beating. Jaufre could have told him that Johanna always had that effect on the men in her life, but it had been a long time since Edyk had been willing to listen to anything Jaufre might have to say about Johanna. "What?" someone said, and Edyk realized the stranger's voice was his own. "Johanna, what did you say?" He started forward.

She held up one hand, palm towards him. "Don't! Don't touch me, not yet. Listen. Listen to me, please, Edyk." She stretched out a hand to slide a rice paper door to one side. The plum trees in the garden beyond were flowering and the aroma of their blossoms slipped into the room, curling into every corner, pervasive and bittersweet. Edyk would never be able to smell a plum blossom again without remembering this moment.

Her back to him, Johanna said in a steady voice, "I can't marry you, Edyk. It would be impossible. For both of us."

Now his voice was hard and angry, with an undercurrent of fear. "That's nonsense and you know it. We've grown up side by side, we were friends before we ever—well, you know. Before."

She almost smiled at his stutter over how their relationship had changed. "I know."

"And," he added, "we're both foreigners, in a land that is determined to keep us that way."

"My father was as Chinese as the Son of Heaven himself," she said, an edge to her voice.

"But your mother was half Chinese and half Venetian," he said flatly, "the same as mine is Chinese and Portuguese. Look in your mirror. The Venetian won out. It doesn't matter that we were born here. We are strangers in a strange land, as Bishop John taught us from the book of the Christian god. And we always will be."

"No," she said carefully, back in control. "I won't be. At least I won't be a stranger in this land."

"What do you mean?"

"I mean that I'm leaving, Edyk."

"What?"

She closed her eyes and inhaled the scent of the blossoms. "I'm leaving Cambaluc, Edyk, and Everything Under the Heavens."

"What!" He was really frightened now. He jerked her around to face him. "You're leaving? You're leaving me?"

"Yes."

"To go where? And why?"

"Perhaps," she said, considering, "perhaps I will look for my grandfather."

He snorted. "He's been gone, how long now, thirty years? You never met him, you don't know him. He may be dead, he most likely is, and then where will you be? And even if he is alive, what makes you think he'd want anything to do with you, when he never bothered to stay in contact with his own daughter, your mother?"

"Edyk," she said, her expression relaxing a little. "Have you never wanted to get up of a morning and start walking west?"

He looked at her, a veteran of trading trips north, south, east and, yes, west, and raised an eyebrow.

"All right," she said. "But have you never wished to keep going, to follow the sun to where it sets? To see the fountains of fire in Georgiana? To visit the enchanters of Tebet? To fight the dragons at the edge of the ocean?" The sadness in her eyes faded, to be replaced by excitement and anticipation. It was a look Edyk had seen before, and did not rejoice in now.

She waited, part of her hoping he would agree with her, part of her hoping he would offer to dower his wives and children, sell his business and come with them on the road. When he didn't, she sighed, although it didn't hurt as much as she had imagined it would. "It doesn't matter if my grandfather is alive or dead, Edyk. He is merely an excuse to start me on my way. You know me." She smiled. "You know me better than almost anyone else. Would you expect anything less?"

He took a hasty step away from her, and then back. "And who will take care of you?"

"I can take care of myself," she said.

Edyk could not honestly quarrel with her superb if arrogant self-confidence. Neither was he ready to acknowledge defeat. "You know what the roads are becoming, now that the Great Khan is dead."

"Shasha and Jaufre will be with me."

"Jaufre!" he exclaimed. "Jaufre is going with you?"

"Yes."

"I might have known," he said bitterly.

Johanna looked surprised. "Certainly you might have known," she agreed. "We grew up here together, children of foreigners. We have suffered the shunning of the people of the Son of Heaven all our lives. He wants to leave as badly as I do, and unlike you he is free to do so. And he is my best and oldest friend."

"Johanna." He took both her hands in his and held them tightly. "I know I've never said the words, but I thought you knew. I love you, Johanna. I want to marry you. I want to spend the rest of my life with you. Don't leave me here all alone."

The sadness in her eyes was displaced again, this time by

laughter. "And what would Blossom and Jade have to say to that?"

"But they love you!" he protested. "They always have."

"As your friend, yes," she said. "As a third wife?" She shook her head, and the corners of her mouth quirked upwards.

Watching the generous curve of her lips he felt again that sharp, fierce tug of desire, and this time he let it show in his eyes. "Is it the bride price?" he said roughly. "I'll double it. Triple it, even."

She shook her head. "I don't want to be bought," she said gently. "And Edyk, you know you don't want to buy me."

"Then come to me freely," he said. "Come to me naked, I don't care. I want you for my wife, Johanna."

She shook her head again; a final, negating movement.

He recognized the signs. Johanna had a kind of determined, implacable ruthlessness Edyk had never before encountered in a woman. In Johanna's world, there were the people she cared for, and then there was everyone else: worthy of curiosity, certainly, perhaps even of courtesy... perhaps. The people she cared for—he totted them up mentally and even before one was dead could fit them all on the fingers of one hand—were worthy of any sacrifice, mental, emotional, physical.

There has never been such a woman, he thought, looking at the gallant chin, the squared shoulders, the bronzed hair escaping its braid to curl riotously around her face, the eyes the color of the sky over Kesmur just before dawn. He let his eyes drift down her body, over the swell of her breasts, the indentation of her waist, the long legs. "But I want you," he said at last, hazarding his all in a voice gone thick with need. "Johanna, I want you."

"Then take me," she said huskily. His eyes met hers and he felt a shock of recognition at the desire he saw reflected there. "I want you, too. I need you. And I want something for myself. Something for my very own, to take away with me, to keep me warm on the long dark nights away from you." He was frozen with disbelief and she took a step forward and caught at his hand. "Edyk, please," she said, and raised his hand to her breast. "Please love me."

He felt the rich weight of her breast, the nipple already hard beneath the palm of his hand, and pulled her into his arms, bringing his mouth down on hers so roughly her lip split. He tasted blood and lifted his head to see her eyes half-closed, her skin flushed, her lips parted. Her tongue came out to touch the cut, and with a groan he was unable to suppress cradled himself between her thighs, sliding his hands over her bottom to lift and rub her against him. She responded, eagerly if inexpertly, and such was his instantaneous need that he would have taken her then and there, on the floor, if she had not called to him in a voice soft and shaken with desire. "Edyk, Edyk, not here. Not here," she repeated when he raised his head again, dazed, almost uncomprehending. She smoothed his hair back with one trembling hand. "Anyone could come in."

He pulled away from her. "Where, then?" he demanded, unsmiling, the planes of his face hard and strained.

"The lake. The summerhouse. We will be alone there."

He looked at her, his eyes burning, his mouth compressed. "The summerhouse is two hours from here, Johanna."

She smiled at him, a rich, bewitching smile of shared desire that promised him everything she had to give and more. "Then we'd better get started, hadn't we?"

At her smile his body responded promptly and he cursed her. She laughed. He flung open the door and bellowed for Chiang, who appeared almost immediately, still with that carefully nurtured expression of disinterest. "Saddle North Wind," Edyk snapped, and turned back to Johanna.

She was still laughing. "North Wind?" she said. "You actually ride North Wind?"

"He's the fastest horse in my stables and he doesn't race again until next week," he said grimly.

Her smile was provocative. "And he lets you ride him?"

"He will if you're with me." And indeed when Chiang brought

the horse around from the stables he caught Johanna's scent and whinnied eagerly, almost trotting with Chiang dangling at the end of his reins. He almost danced to a stop and nosed eagerly at the front of her tunic. She laughed and fed him a piece of carrot and rubbed his ears.

"I should never have let you near him as a colt," Edyk said grimly. He threw Johanna up into the saddle without ceremony, yanked the reins from Chiang and vaulted up after her.

"The Shrimp!" Johanna said protestingly.

"The Shrimp! Great Khan! You rode the Shrimp up here? I'm surprised either of you finished the trip alive." He pulled her back against him, and heard her gasp. "Yes," he said with satisfaction. "You want to go to the summerhouse, fine, but we'll ride the Wind there together, Johanna." He kicked the white stallion into a canter. North Wind, a horse with a mind of his own, thought it should be a gallop and Edyk was only too willing to oblige.

All the same, it was the longest, most torturous journey Edyk the Portuguese, veteran of many crossings of the Taklamakan Desert, was ever to make. Once out of the city the road narrowed to a rough trail and became steep and rocky. North Wind of necessity slowed to a walk. Johanna leaned back in the cradle of Edyk's arms, her body rubbing against his with the Wind's every step. By the time they reached the lake, hidden at the head of a small valley south of Cambaluc, Edyk was frantic with the need to get at her, to lay her skin bare to his eyes and his touch.

Johanna was no less frantic to let him. All the long way up to the lake, Edyk's hands and lips were never still, and his voice, husky with desire, had whispered in between kisses and bites exactly what he was going to do to her, and how. When his feet hit the ground she hurled herself forward into his arms, almost knocking him over. She could feel him press into her belly and she rubbed up against him, moaning.

He slid his hands over her hips and held her still. He let his head fall back and drew a great rush of air into his lungs, holding it, and then letting it expel from his chest in an explosive rush.

"Johanna, wait," he said. Loving had always been enjoyable for him, sweet, a mutually-pleasing frolic. With Johanna the pleasure was so intense it was almost pain, a demon that had him by the scruff of the neck who wouldn't let go until he had satisfied it, and he knew he must slow himself down or he would hurt her. He clenched his teeth and made an effort to speak intelligibly. "This is your first time, isn't it?"

"You know it is," she muttered, licking at the drop of sweat that had collected in the hollow of his throat, sliding her hands down his back to pull him tightly against her. He caught her hands and she made a frustrated sound and tried to pull free. "I want to touch you, Edyk. Let me."

He raised her chin with one hand and looked into the clear eyes that were now dark with thwarted desire. "I want to let you," he said softly. "But I'm all sweaty from the ride, and so are you. Let's swim first."

"I don't want to swim," she said crossly, urging him forward again.

He gave a laugh that turned into a shaken groan. Again he caught her hands and said with difficulty, "Stop that. I don't want to swim either, but we have to slow this down a little." He looked into her eyes and whispered, "Trust me to do this right, Johanna."

She closed her eyes tightly for a moment. When she opened them again the desire was still there but on a leash. "All right," she said. "What do you want me to do?"

He pulled her towards the lake. "We have to take off our clothes to swim, don't we?"

She brightened, marched down to the water's edge and without further ado pulled her tunic over her head. The setting sun played over her flushed skin, gilding her nipples. Her trousers followed her tunic and the sun turned the soft curls between her long legs to gold. The sight nearly drove him to his knees. "Johanna," he said, his throat thick. "You're as beautiful as I thought you would be. No. More beautiful than I ever dreamed."

She reached for him with impatient hands, pulling his tunic over his head, finding the ties of his trousers and slipping them down. She stood back to look at him, from dark eyes to wide shoulders to strong arms to narrow hips to sturdy legs and back up to rampant, strutting desire. "So are you."

She stretched out a hand to touch him. He grabbed it and used it to lead her into the lake. The water was lukewarm, but to their overheated skins still a shock. They cupped it in trembling hands and smoothed it over their bodies. Johanna leaned forward to follow her hands with her lips, sipping the water from his skin from mouth to chest to thigh, to touch her tongue to the length of flesh upright and hot and hard against his belly.

He pulled her out of the lake and into his arms. Her skin, cool from the water, shivered delightfully against his and he bent his head and placed his lips to her breast. One hand knotted in her hair, the other slipped between her legs to find her wet and hot, and with a groan he kissed his way down her body to bury his mouth in her. She cried out her pleasure, back arching like a bow, and would have fallen but for his arms steadying her.

"Johanna, Johanna," he muttered against the soft skin of her belly. "I'm sorry, I can't wait any longer."

"Finally." He almost laughed at the breathless exasperation in her voice, and forgot to when she slid to her knees, her mouth seeking out his, her hands exploring. "Please, Edyk," she sobbed, clutching at his shoulders. "Please."

"All right," he said through gritted teeth, and pulled her down on him, so that for the first time she felt all that heat and pride pressed up inside her. If there was pain she never felt it. She came to climax at once, crying out in sheer delight, opening her eyes afterwards to see him staring at her, his eyes burning, his body still hard within her, and then she felt the cool grass against her spine as he laid her down.

He brushed the hair back from her face, kissed her – tiny, teasing kisses – holding himself inside her as the sweet shuddering of her body slackened. Then he began to move, long, deep strokes, pushing slowly all the way up, then pulling as slowly out, loitering both within her heated flesh and without, teasing her, taunting her, urging her on to renewed desire. She gasped at the return of feeling, staring up at him with wide astonished eyes and parted lips. He smiled. Her hips began to lift to his and he threw back his head. "Yes." When he drew almost all the way out she dug her nails into his back in protest and her inner muscles closed around him. He groaned and began thrusting faster and harder and deeper. She wrapped her legs around him and met him thrust for thrust. When he plunged inside her for the last time she convulsed and cried out, a low, disbelieving sound joined to his own growled pleasure.

They lay speechless in the light of the rising moon for a long time afterward. When he had recovered he shifted his weight. Wordlessly she clutched him to her, silently protesting, and he subsided, content to remain where he most longed to be.

Presently she stirred, and he raised his head to see her eyes sparkling in her flushed face, tendrils of hair clinging to her skin, her braid damp and tangled against her neck. In a voice lazy with pleasure she observed, "Now I know what Jade and Blossom have been giggling about for the last three years."

"What!"

She said reasonably, "Well, we had to talk about something, and they can't ride and I don't embroider, and all we had in common was you."

He stared at her for a long, long moment. She grinned, and he threw back his head and shouted with laughter. She laughed with him, and the sound of it pealed across the still water of the lake and lingered beneath the boughs of the drooping willow trees.

Thinking of it afterwards, he supposed they must have eaten and slept, but all he could remember was the laughter and the loving, on the floor, in the grass, in the lake, sometimes they even made it as far as the bed. She gave him everything her smile had promised and more. His thoughts, his hands, the strands of his hair, the pores of his skin, his nostrils were filled with the taste and texture and smell of her. He memorized the straight, arrogant bridge of her nose, the sultry curve of her mouth, the vulnerable hollow of her throat, the sweet slope of her breast, the silken texture of her skin, the seductive smell of her femininity. She responded completely, openly, wholeheartedly, without reservation or shyness, her astonished pleasure at each new sensual delight a reward in itself. He taught her the difference between loving and rutting, he seduced her sweetly and showed her how to return in kind; every skill he had learned from every woman he had ever loved he exerted to show her how much he cared, how much he needed, how much he wanted this one woman in his arms, in his life.

He could not bear to think of life without her, and so he didn't think of it. "We will build a home in Kinsai," he murmured into her hair late into their second night at the summerhouse. "We will have many sons, and we will teach them to bargain and to trade, and take them with us when we travel. I love you, Johanna."

"I love you, Edyk," she whispered.

His last thought before he fell into a deep, dreamless sleep with her locked securely in his arms was, she'll never leave me now.

But when he woke the next morning, she was gone.

So was North Wind.

9

Nᴏʀᴛʜ ᴡɪɴᴅ ᴡᴀs not the only priceless possession to have gone missing in Cambaluc that morning.

The house of the late, honorable Wu Li was in an uproar as his widow stormed through every room, leaving chaos in her wake. Drawers were yanked out, their contents dumped on the floor, the drawers tossed aside. Shiny lacquered boxes were wrenched open, found wanting, and hurled against the wall. Tall porcelain vases were turned upside down and shaken in vain for anything that might have been secreted there, and when they proved empty were shattered into a hundred pieces on every hearthstone.

"Where are they?" the widow said. Her voice rose to a shriek. "Where are they!"

The kitchen was a scene of bedlam by the time she finished there. The undercook bled from four parallel scratches on his cheek from the widow's nails. Every pot was taken from its hook, every pan from its shelf, the spit pulled from the wall and used as a club to strike the drab assigned to turn it. The drab lay unconscious in a corner, breathing stertorously through bubbles of blood that extended and retracted through her nostrils. One of the maids was blinded, possibly permanently, having caught the brunt of the widow's rings across her eyes. The rest of the servants had fled, or were cowering beneath tables and chairs and behind doors and bureaus, hoping against hope to escape her notice.

Gokudo was made of sterner stuff. "My lady," he said.

She snarled and whirled, both hands curled into bejeweled claws. "Where are they?" she shouted, advancing on him.

"I do not know, my lady," he said.

She raised a hand, long, now-broken fingernails already stained with blood. "Tell me where they are! The stables!" She stepped forward. "Get out of my way!"

Gokudo stood his ground. "Wu Li's daughter is gone," he said.

She didn't appear to hear him, at first, the mad light in her eyes undiminished, the claw of a hand still upraised to strike. He repeated himself, raising his voice, enunciating each word in a slow, clear voice. "The daughter of the honorable Wu Li is gone from this house. As is Shu Shao the kitchen drudge and Jaufre the stable boy."

This time she heard him.

They stood there, facing each other, motionless, no sound in the kitchen except for the heavy breathing of the widow, the whimpers of the undercook, and the crackle of a cinder, raked out from the hearth in the struggle over the spit and now doing its best to set fire to the floor.

Her hand dropped. "Show me," she said.

It was the first time she had been in the little mongrel's room. The smallness of the room, the shabbiness of its furnishings did not register with her.

What did register was the narrow bed, neatly made, and the box resting in the middle of the plumped pillow with the carefully mitered corners. Clad in layers of black lacquer, scarlet leaves twining around the join between lid and base, the box was in itself a work of art a handspan square. It had been made for its purpose, and it looked well used, and well loved.

Wu Li's widow had no thought for the craftsmanship of the thing. She snatched it up and tugged. The lid was so well made that the seal created a vacuum that resisted her efforts. She tugged in vain. She even broke another nail. Tears of rage began to course down the widow's painted cheeks, and she flung the box at Gokudo. "Open it!"

Gokudo got his hands up just in time to stop the box from hitting him in the face. He found the catch on the lid, and it opened with a huff of sound, the lid standing up on its intricately hand-crafted brass hinges. He held the box out at arm's length so she could see inside. He could already tell what it contained by its weight.

She remained bent over the box, staring inside it with burning eyes.

There was a commotion at the front of the house. The widow didn't move, and Gokudo swore and went to see what it was.

Edyk the Portuguese was struggling with the door man. "Where is she? Where is North Wind? Where are they? Tell this fool to let me go!"

"Release him, Bo He," Gokudo said.

Bo He, an elderly gentleman in a ruffled state, stepped back and smoothed his coat. "As my mistress wishes," he said.

Gokudo raised his hand to strike him for his insolence, but Edyk the Portuguese stepped forward. "Where is she? Where is Johanna? Is North Wind in your stables? Take me to them at once!"

"We shelter neither your whore nor your nag in this house, Edyk the Portuguese," Gokudo said, not bothering to hide his sneer.

Edyk stopped and stared at him. "Johanna isn't here? Where is she? When do you expect her back?"

Gokudo laughed, and Edyk raised his hand to strike him. Gokudo slapped it to one side and followed up with a sharp blow to Edyk's sternum with the flat of his other hand. Edyk flew backward, tumbling to the ground in the center of the courtyard. He made as if to scramble to his feet and froze with the point of Gokudo's naginata at his throat.

"Get up," Gokudo said contemptuously. "Please, do get up."

Edyk dropped and rolled out out of reach and got back on his feet. He snatched up a hoe someone had let fall in a bed of narcissus during the widow's rampage and dropped into a guard stance, only to have the blade of the naginata slice off the head. Instead of retreating as Gokudo had every right to expect, Edyk thrust with the end of the stick, striking Gokudo hard in the chest. By the time the samurai caught his breath Edyk was gone and the bodyguard could hear the sound of hoofbeats from the other side of the gate, departing rapidly.

He cursed when he got his breath back, loudly and fluently in his native tongue, and spun around to see Bo He watching. He didn't like the expression on the majordomo's face so he cut it off. He stepped over the gurgling remains of the old man's body and went back into the house to find Dai Fang.

She had returned to her own quarters and was in the restored orderliness of her sitting room with a pot of tea steaming in front of her. The madness of her fury was gone, vanished as if it had never been, to be replaced by a cold and deadly intensity that caused a ripple of unease to break out down the back of even his warrior spine.

She poured tea for both of them, and presented his cup with both hands. "Find her," she said.

"My lady—"

She raised her eyes to his. "Find her, and bring her to me."

He did the only thing she would permit. He bowed his head, accepted the tea, and said, "As my lady wishes."

Her voice stopped him at the door. "And Gokudo?"

"My lady?"

Her glittering eyes raised to his. "In what condition she is returned to the home of her father is of no concern to me."

He bowed again, and thought, not for the first time, of the bronze braid wrapped around his fist, and of forcing wide the long, lissome legs of the daughter of the house. "As my lady wishes."

10

Spring, 1322

THE YAMBS THE Great Khan commanded to be built half a century before that greeted those traveling the road west at every eighth league had yet to fall into disrepair, and the great trees he planted to show the way were just beginning to leaf out as Johanna's tiny group passed between them. Occasionally they met an imperial mailman, hurrying to complete his sixty daily leagues, but for most of the way the road was as bare of company as her companions were bare of conversation.

Jaufre had been curt and uncommunicative since Johanna's return from the summerhouse, riding North Wind. Johanna, rebuffed in her efforts to share her wonderful new feelings of freedom and independence, was bewildered and resentful and surly in turn. Shasha, glancing surreptitiously from one to the other as if to gauge the amount of unvented spleen gathering in each youth, kept her own counsel.

And the glittering roofs of Cambaluc faded in the distance. They followed the road west, stopping at Shensi only to feed and water the horses and find a quick meal for themselves. They traveled well into the night, made a cold camp and were up again before the sun the following morning.

"What's the rush?" Jaufre said finally, and irritably.

Johanna settled the saddle in place, looking over North

Wind's back at the road they had come down the day before. "My father's second wife doesn't like being crossed," she said. As if aware that this was a meager explanation for driving them down the road like a slave trader late for an auction, she added, "She will be very angry that she will now not receive the commission on Edyk's marriage settlement." She checked again to see that the clasp on the leather pouch she wore at her waist was secure.

"Wu Li's widow will be delighted to be rid of us," Jaufre said, yanking at a cheek strap so hard that his horse whinnied and danced in reproof. "Three less bellies to fill, three less servants to pay. The heir to Wu Li's estate conveniently missing. I doubt she'll make any effort to come after you."

"Nonetheless, I, too, will rest more easily when we are out of her reach," Shasha said, watching Johanna with a speculative gaze.

Johanna saw Shasha watching her. She flushed and dropped her hand.

"Well then, perhaps you could just tell us where it is we're going in such a hurry," Jaufre said with awful sarcasm.

Johanna froze up. "I would have thought you would recognize the road," she said, as haughty as a mandarin's mistress.

Shasha beat a strategic retreat and waited for the explosion from a safe distance. She hoped it would be a loud one. With blows, even. Anything to clear the air.

A bright ray of morning sun flooded their campsite with light. Johanna was here, Jaufre thought in sudden realization: here, with him. She had not stayed behind with Edyk. She had turned her back on the security of marriage, a life of ease and comfort, and the affection of a man sure to love her and indulge her all her life long.

She had not chosen that life. Instead, she was traveling

the Road west with him, Jaufre. The Road was no refuge, no sanctuary, no safe haven. At every league there was a new and almost invariably fatal disease waiting to infect them, thieves and bandits eager to rob them, rival merchants hoping to cheat them, bears and wolves with their next meal on their minds. There were poisonous snakes and insects and wells poisoned by nature or by man. They could be struck by lightning on the plains, smothered in sand in the desert, buried in snow in the mountains. They could lose their way. They could be deliberately misdirected, and attacked.

But here she was, with him, on that Road. Edyk the Portuguese was a memory back in Cambaluc, and Cambaluc was falling farther behind them every day.

North Wind shied at a dragonfly and pulled at his picket, his white coat gleaming in the dawn light. North Wind, the preeminent race horse of his day and Edyk's pride and joy, now Johanna's saddle horse.

Jaufre burst out laughing. Johanna looked around, startled. Still laughing, he reached out to pull her braid in not quite his old, brotherly manner, but close enough to lay her hackles. Johanna melted instantly, grinning at him, every constraint falling away, not thinking to question why there had been any constraint to begin with.

Shasha muttered to herself. They looked at her. "So we go to Chang'an," she said. "And who do we meet in Chang'an?"

"Guess," Johanna said.

Shasha stared at her with rising suspicion. "Johanna, you wouldn't!"

"I would, too," Johanna said.

Shasha groaned. "Not old No-Nuts!"

"The very same," Johanna said proudly. She moved to tie her bedroll to the back of North Wind's saddle, and added in a reproving voice, "And I don't think that's a very respectful way to refer to my honorable uncle, either."

Jaufre turned his face so that Shasha wouldn't see his grin.

Shasha took a deep breath and swore with a surprising range and fluency.

Johanna widened her eyes and said in a shocked voice, "But, Shasha! I thought you liked Uncle Cheng!" Shasha wasn't finished swearing and Johanna said reproachfully, "Such is gratitude. And after Uncle Cheng rescued your teeth from that prince in Zeilan, too."

"If that idiot hadn't tried to buy off the local priest with pork instead of beef, my teeth wouldn't have been in any danger in the first place," Shasha said tartly.

"Well," Johanna said, vaulting astride North Wind and glancing at the increasing light on the eastern horizon, "the sooner we start the sooner you can abuse him all you like to his face. We've got to hurry. He wrote me that he wants to start no later than the night of the new moon."

"Isn't that tonight?" Jaufre said.

The sound of North Wind's hoofbeats racing away was her reply.

And indeed Wu Cheng was seen to be pacing impatiently up and down in front of the East Gate of Chang'an, alternately kicking and cursing any camel unfortunate enough to get in his way.

Johanna waved. "Uncle Cheng! Uncle Cheng!"

He halted, staring at the three horses galloping in his direction, and then waved back vigorously before turning to shout at the packers. There was a great flurry of movement and the sounds of disgruntled camels spitting and snapping and groaning as they levered themselves up, one half at a time.

"Nice horse," Wu Cheng said when Johanna reined in. If North Wind looked familiar to him, Wu Cheng, an inveterate gambler, possessed the discretion not to say so. He scowled at Shasha. "You had to bring her?"

She grinned. "Of course, Uncle. It wouldn't do for you to be bored on the journey."

The scowl deepened. Unintimidated, Johanna said, "How big is the caravan this year, Uncle? It looks enormous."

The scowl faded. One sure way to divert Wu Cheng was to praise his caravan. "A thousand camels."

Johanna knew her duty and was properly impressed. "Imagine!"

Wu Cheng grinned. "Well, maybe nine hundred, and of course not all my own."

"How many other traders travel with us?"

The scowl came back. "A dozen, so far, and a more useless pack of ninnies I never saw—"

"—in all my days on the Road, and they are many—" Jaufre said.

"—no more idea of the dangers than a newborn babe, and of less use—" Johanna said.

"—and all I'm doing by agreeing to take them into my caravan," said Shasha, unable to resist, "—is inviting disaster down upon all our heads."

Wu Cheng stared, and then threw back his head and laughed: a big, booming noise that turned the heads of everyone in line at the Gate. "Well, well," he said, "it may be that I have guided this caravan before." He cuffed Johanna lightly across the ears. She ducked out of the way, grinning. "Put your horses with the others, then, and find your camels. The girls of Dunhuang, Turpan, and Kashgar are waiting for us!" he bellowed, and there was a ragged cheer from his men. He mounted his camel and it came gruntingly up on all four ungainly legs. Wu Cheng adjusted his seat and squinted at the horizon, alert to a telltale wisp of cloud or column of dust.

Shasha and Jaufre both noticed that while Wu Cheng watched the western horizon, Johanna watched the east. Jaufre thought it was because of Edyk. Shasha did not.

They would both have been surprised. The sun was sinking in a magnificent red-orange blaze, casting a golden shadow over the land. Everything Under the Heavens had never seemed as beautiful to Johanna as it did now, and she discovered to her surprise that there were tears in her eyes.

Goodbye, my father, she thought. Thank you for giving me life. Thank you for giving me my freedom. I love you. I will always love you. And I will live my life to make you proud.

She bowed her head, and Jaufre, riding behind, saw the last ray of the setting sun strike her bronzed hair, and knew he would forgive her anything. He urged his camel to come alongside hers and reached for her hand. She looked up, smiling through her tears, and her hand clasped his in return.

He told himself that it was enough.

For now.

They traveled through the night, eating in the saddle, and did not stop until the sun broke free of the horizon the next morning and the temperature began to rise. They made a dry camp, spreading bedrolls beneath yurts and awnings of light cloth fixed between the camels' saddles and tent poles stuck in the sand. The guards dug latrines. The cooks busied themselves with what would be their main and only hot meal each day. Smoke from the fires curled lazily into a clear, colorless sky slowly darkening to a brassy blue.

The encampment was the size of a small city and indeed resembled one from the top of a dune a short distance away. Clustered at the top of the dune were Uncle Cheng and Johanna's party, mounted again on their horses. North Wind was fidgety and finicky, wanting to stretch his neck into a run. Jaufre's bay gelding was composed and businesslike and disinclined to put up with any of North Wind's nonsense. Shasha rode a flirtatious little gray mare who in movement seemed to dance rather than canter.

"My nephew has joined his ancestors, then," Cheng said.

Johanna let her eyes trace the tops of the tents of their wayfaring village, outlined against the yellow dunes. It was a familiar sight, lacking only the energetic, capable figure of her father. "He has, uncle."

Cheng rested a hand on her knee. "It is better so." His eyes met Jaufre's, and he frowned slightly at the hard expression he saw there.

"I know, uncle," Johanna said. "But—"

"But," he said, nodding, and gave her knee a final pat before sitting erect in the saddle again. He himself was riding a venerable donkey who carried himself and Wu Cheng with something of an air, as if he knew he provided transportation for the leader of their expedition and was determined to lend them both dignity.

Cheng himself bore little resemblance to his nephew, being taller and much heavier. The mandarins and the eunuchs were warring factions at court, with the old khan favoring the eunuchs, and castration was seen as a way into power by ambitious parents. Cheng had been offered up for the procedure at the age of ten, and was rewarded with an immediate entrance into the Royal Academy. This was followed by a post at court, where a combination of ability and relative honesty saw his star rise fast and far.

He was among the inner circle of the previous khan, which contributed to his subsequent banishment when the new khan took power and brought in his own eunuchs. He went to Wu Hai, in whose business he had invested most of his own earnings, and Wu Hai put him on the first caravan heading west, which very probably saved his life from the same purge that had taken the life of Johanna's grandmother. He made his home in Chang'an and once it was safe to return to Cambaluc became an infrequent but familiar guest in Wu Li's house. One of Johanna's earliest memories was of sitting on Uncle Cheng's knees during one of his many visits, learning a complicated game of changing patterns played with a knotted round of string.

"Where do you go, then?" Cheng said. He had met Wu Li's second wife. He knew without being told at least one reason why they were leaving Everything Under the Heavens.

"West," Jaufre said.

"Ah," Cheng said. "And how far?"

"Until the ocean drops off the edge of the world, uncle," Johanna said, tears banished now, "and the dragons who live there burn us up with their fiery breath."

Wu Cheng laughed. "As far as that? A very long journey, indeed." He paused. "It is a new and very different world to which you travel, Johanna."

"Yes, and won't it be exciting!" she said. "You know father never traveled beyond Kashgar on our western journeys. I've always wondered what the Pamirs look like from the other side. What an adventure, uncle!"

Her uncle could have said many things in response to this blithe comment, but held his fire, for the moment. "I will be sad to see you go," he said instead. "It is not likely we will meet again on this earth."

"Who is to say?" Johanna said, not wanting to agree but knowing this was most likely true. "We might meet on the Road again one day, honorable uncle."

Wu Cheng smiled. "We might at that, honorable niece."

She felt for the pouch at her waist. Had her father's widow missed them yet? Very likely, and how furious she would be, and how much more so with no abomination of a child to take it out on, and how much more furious than that when she sent out riders and discovered that Johanna was now out of her reach. Johanna contemplated her father's widow's reaction with a great deal of satisfaction.

On her left, Shasha noticed the gesture, and wondered at the unease that whispered up her spine.

Jaufre noticed only the smile pulling at the corners of Johanna's lips. "You look happy," he said.

She breathed in, deeply. "Do you smell that, Jaufre?"

"What?" He sniffed. "You mean the salt air?"

She shook her head, still smiling. "Freedom," she said.

He thought about it, even as she nudged North Wind into motion. The stifling tension that had infused the house of the honorable Wu Li from the moment he had brought his second wife home. The inchoate threat everyone had felt the day Dai Fang introduced Gokudo. The year full of encroaching snubs and slights as Dai Fang moved Jaufre out of the house and into the stables, Johanna from her suite near the garden to her room off the scullery, Shasha from her position as one of the family to that of a kitchen maid.

The only time they had been able to breathe was on the road with Wu Li. Jaufre had a very clear memory of his own father, but he was long dead and so would Jaufre had been, were it not for Wu Li and Shu Ming and Shasha, and always and ever, Johanna. He knew who his family was.

He nudged his bay into a stride to match North Wind's, at least temporarily. Johanna turned her head to meet his eyes. "Freedom," he said.

"Freedom!" they shouted together, and their horses, in that inexplicable way that horses do, divined the high spirits of their riders and moved smoothly into a gallop, kicking up a cloud of dust that hung in the air, obscuring their passing, leaving only an echo of laughter behind.

Until the dust settled again, and left their tracks plain for anyone with the eyes to see.

Heading west. Always and ever, west.

11

WHEN THEY ROSE again at dusk, the last trader to join their caravan had arrived and there was a flurry of packing and loading. When it was done Uncle Cheng called the leader of each merchant group traveling with them into a conference. "I am Wu Cheng. Most of us have traveled together before but for those who are new to me, this is how it goes. We sleep days and travel nights. You are expected to be packed and ready to travel at dusk each day. You care for your own livestock. You buy and cook your own food, and I don't want to be arbitrating any arguments over how you like your rice boiled. If someone gets sick, they will be quarantined until we arrive at the first available town or caravansary. If someone gets hurt to the point that it affects their ability to travel, they will be left at the first available town or caravansary. This caravan is not a traveling hospital."

He let that sink in before going on. "If there is a fire, everyone turns out to fight it, and each morning everyone is responsible for locating the camels carrying the water sacks, which will every morning always be picketed next to the guards' tents, which every morning will always be next to my yurt." He pointed. "The one marked by the red and yellow pennon. Can everyone see it?"

Everyone nodded, very solemn, even those who had heard it many times before. They had to camp closely together for security, which also put everyone and their goods at risk if a fire broke out.

"Fighting for whatever reason, inclination, drunkenness, gambling or sheer bad temper," Uncle Cheng said. "Not in camp, and see my previous remarks about anyone getting hurt; I don't care whether you started it or not. My plan is to get this caravan to Kashgar in seventy days, before the worst of the summer heat, and anyone who delays us in any way or for any reason will be left behind, willing or unwilling." He tucked his hands in his belt and stared around the circle.

He looked perfectly calm and even relaxed, but Johanna and Jaufre exchanged a knowing glance. Jovial Uncle Cheng could appear quite intimidating at will.

"There are women and children traveling with us. None of them are to be interfered with in any way. If any such interference does occur and the report is credible, the offender will be taken under guard to the nearest city or caravansary and remanded to the custody of the local magistrate, with a recommendation of extreme prejudice." He jerked a thumb at the man standing next to him. "And that's only if my havildar doesn't see fit to deal with the offender first. In which action, whatever it is, he will always have my full authority and support."

Johanna couldn't quite make out the man standing in Uncle Cheng's shadow, who seemed to bow slightly and then efface himself.

"Please don't test us in this. It will not end well for you." Uncle Cheng's smile was thin. "Although it may well end you entirely."

Another uncomfortable silence, broken by a Persian sheik in flowing robes and grizzled beard. "Worthy Wu Cheng, are there reliable reports on the road ahead?"

"Sheik Mohammed," Wu Cheng said with a respectful bow in return. "Are we at risk of attack by bandits, do you mean?"

The sheik inclined his head.

Uncle Cheng stroked his long, thin mustaches. "Well, we are at less risk traveling together simply because there are so many

105

of us. Bandit gangs don't generally tend to attack large numbers. But we've all heard the stories. We must be alert and vigilant, and I beg of you all, urge your people to be discreet. It is well known that the larger bands have agents of their own in some of the larger towns, and they will be looking for easy targets."

"And if we are attacked?" another voice said, this one belonging to the man standing next to the sheik. He was younger and like enough to the sheik to claim him as father.

"We will defend ourselves," Uncle Cheng said. "You all carry arms and know how to use them or I wouldn't have allowed you to join this caravan. Keep your weapons in good working order and within reach. My havildar will instruct you further, one at a time, on this evening's march, but what it boils down to is if we come under attack we bunch up in a group. They will always pick off stragglers. Any pack camel here would be worthy of the effort, especially if they manage to capture any people, who I'm sure I don't have to tell you can be sold as slaves at the greatest possible profit."

He let the words linger on the air for a moment, and then brought his two ham hands together in a loud smack. "We will be traveling fast but there will be time to buy and sell along the way. If a majority of you think we ought to stay an extra day at the market in, say, Kuche, or Yarkent, I will certainly acquiesce to the will of the majority. However, I will expect us to make up the extra day on the road."

He smiled again, more widely, and such was his personal charisma that Johanna felt an immediate lessening of tension around the circle. "I have planned an extra full day's stop at every oasis town we travel through, so if we stay on schedule there will be regular opportunities for rest, refit, and to buy supplies. And for wine, women and song."

There was a ripple of laughter and a relaxation of tension.

"All right," Wu Cheng said briskly. "Mount up."

106

The first few days of travel were all confusion and vexation. Various groups wishing to travel together jockeyed for position in line and generally succeeded only in embroiling themselves, their animals and surrounding travelers in a hopeless tangle of reins, stirrups and leading strings. They were straightened out again by sweating, swearing handlers and guards, and provided Uncle Cheng with multiple opportunities to demonstrate in six different languages his comprehensive and inspiring command of invective. During one of these instructional episodes Shasha saw Johanna sitting to one side, repeating certain phrases silently. Johanna looked up to see Shasha watching and had the audacity to grin.

On the second day a trader from Balkh managed to mislay ten camels. The rest of the caravan carried on while Uncle Cheng's havildar and a squad of guards were sent out to retrieve them. They returned in the middle of the night, missed in the dark by most of the caravaners, who were treated the following morning to the unpleasant spectacle of a thief and his three co-conspirators stripped to their waists and beaten until their backs were bloody. The missing camels were produced and returned to their grateful owner, who became a shade less grateful when Uncle Cheng assessed two of the camels as payment in full for the retrieval.

The lesson was well taken by everyone watching, but both were unsettling sights for the rest of them to take to their beds that morning. That evening, before the caravan set off again, by Uncle Cheng's express command the four thieves were left to make their way back to Chang'an as best they could, stripped of their shoes and with no water or food to ease their way.

Johanna lingered at the tail end of the caravan, watching the four pitiful figures staggering eastwards.

Unnoticed, Uncle Cheng had ridden up beside her. "Well, niece? Do you judge me to be too harsh?"

She turned to meet his eyes and said without flinching, "No, uncle. I'm just surprised you didn't kill them outright."

The corner of his mouth quirked.

"But then," she said demurely, "there would be no one left alive to attest to the swift and certain justice of that greatest of all caravan masters, the mighty and terrible Wu Cheng."

He burst out laughing. Hearing it, the four felons broke into a staggering run. "Hah! What a caravan master you would have made yourself, honorable niece!"

"And," she said, jerking a thumb over her shoulder at the receding caravan, "none of them will forget it, either. Not the punishment, and certainly not the finder's fee."

He pulled his camel's nose around. "Not from here to Kashgar," he agreed cheerfully. "Serves them right for being so careless of their stock. And it is good to teach a strong lesson early in the trip. It saves much trouble later on."

"Really, uncle," Johanna said drily, "you owe them a debt of gratitude."

"Indeed I do, honorable niece," he said, "and I have paid it. They yet live."

The four would-be thieves toiled up over a dune and dropped out of sight.

There were the usual difficulties between incompatible personalities, tribes and religions, but Uncle Cheng dealt firmly with anything that upset his peace and the peace of the traders traveling under his protection. One hapless Turgesh tripped over a tent pole and fell headlong into a tent full of Muslim women, and only quick footwork prevented a full-blown riot on the part of the women's male relatives. There were the usual rivalries between traders as well, but again Uncle Cheng was quick to take notice and nip anything incendiary in the bud before it had a chance to flower into a fruit that would poison the entire enterprise.

By the time they reached Lanchow, the Golden City, the caravan had settled into the formation it would take for the rest of the journey. People were creatures of habit. If Hamid the Persian, dealer in silks, wools and other fine fabrics, took his place in line between Meesang the Sayam, buyer and seller of precious and semi-precious gemstones, and Wasim the Pashtun, purveyor of copper goods, one morning, chances were he could be found traveling between these two worthies for the duration of the trip.

Johanna reveled in the freedom of the Road with every league gained in distance from Cambaluc. On the Road it didn't matter that her eyes were too round or that she was too tall or that her hair was the wrong color. There was no enforced separation of races on the Road; on the Road she didn't have to be careful not to speak the Mongol tongue within the hearing of Mongol ears. Persian, Jew, Turgesh, Sogdian, Persian, Frank, Chinese, it did not matter. They were all one to Uncle Cheng, and for the duration of the trip his was the only authority to which they bowed. It was all the stronger because they had surrendered to it voluntarily, for the safety of one meant the safety of all.

In the meantime, she, Jaufre and Shasha were meeting old friends. One such they encountered at their first camp. "Johanna! Johanna!"

Johanna looked toward the sound of her voice. "Fatima!" she said.

The slim, dark girl ran up to her and embraced her with enthusiasm, laughing with pleasure. Fatima, daughter of Ahmed the baker and Malala his wife, was in fact a child of laughter, a pretty girl of Johanna's age, wearing a short jacket over a tunic and an ankle-length skirt, all heavy with colorful embroidery, with unbound hair confined beneath a spangled blue veil. "But what is this! What are you doing on the Road this early? Usually I don't see you until Kashgar." She looked around. "But where is Wu Li?"

She was put in possession of recent events and her laughter faded, but only momentarily, and indeed Johanna could not wish otherwise. "And Shasha," Fatima said, leaving Johanna to embrace the other woman. "And Jaufre," she said, turning to him. Fatima was also something of a flirt. She ran an appraising eye over his long length. "Much… taller," she said. "Than when I last saw you."

She hugged him, too, for what seemed like a much longer time than she had Johanna or Shasha.

Jaufre grinned down at her. "Why, thank you, Fatima. And how is Azar these days?"

Fatima released him, laughing. "Azar is just fine, Jaufre the Frank, and thank you for asking."

"Are you married yet?"

Fatima looked at Jaufre with a speculative eye. "Not yet. I'm waiting to see if I get a better offer."

Jaufre laughed at this. Johanna frowned. Shasha noticed.

"We are joining your caravan, did you know?" Fatima said. "We let our last leave without us because Father said the caravan master didn't know where he was going."

There was general rejoicing, and plans were made immediately to pitch their camps together. Shasha didn't think that either Johanna or Jaufre noticed how ably Johanna was able to keep herself between Jaufre and Fatima at all times.

They made new friends, too, as the journey continued. One of the most interesting was Félicien the Frank, a thin young man with curious eyes in a sun-burned face and dark, untidy curls confined by a floppy cap. His bare cheek proclaimed his youth and his worn but sturdy clothes a purse only irregularly full. His only possessions were a lute and an aged donkey whose complaints in transit could be heard from one end of the caravan to the other. Félicien was not a trader, but a traveler, he told them one evening around the communal campfire. "A goliard, they call us sometimes where I come from," he said.

"Where do you come from?" Johanna said.

"What's a goliard?" Jaufre said.

"A goliard is a student," Félicien said.

"A student," Jaufre said. "Of what?"

Félicien waved an airy hand. "Oh, of the world, my dear Jaufre. Of the world and all its manifest glories."

"How long have you been, ah, studying the world?"

"This will be my third summer on the Road."

"So long," Johanna said, who had noticed that Félicien had not answered her question about where he was from. "How do you pay your way? If you don't trade…" The goliard was lean but not thin, so he wasn't starving.

Félicien quirked an eyebrow, but it appeared he recognized the genuine curiosity behind a question posed by a life made possible and prosperous by trade. "I tell stories," he said. "I sing. I write cansos, and, if I'm paid well enough to hire a fast horse afterward, I write sirventes."

"You sing?" Johanna said.

"What's a canso?" Jaufre said.

"What stories?" Shasha said.

Félicien laughed, displaying a set of very fine teeth, even and white and well cared-for, an unusual sight in a Frank. "Yes, I sing. A canso is a love song. What stories—oh, all stories, any story that will find a few coins in my pocket afterward. But King Arthur and the Round Table is a speciality." He gave a slight bow.

"What's a sirvente?" Jaufre said, stumbling a little over the word.

Félicien grimaced. "A hate song," he said, and would be drawn no farther into the subject. Instead he sang them a lilting ditty in the Frankish tongue that he translated into Persian on the fly, about an unlovely swineherd and a passing poet that had everyone around the fire rocking with laughter. Johanna understood much more than she would have before Edyk and the three days at the summerhouse, and laughed along with the rest.

Félicien's voice was high and clear and pure and he could put a soulful quaver into the most mundane verse, causing gentlemen to clear their throats and ladies to wipe surreptitiously at the corners of their eyes. He ended his impromptu concert with a short song called "A Monk's View."

111

O wandering clerks
You go to Chartres
To learn the arts
O wandering clerks
By the Tyrrhenian
You study Aesclepion
O wandering clerks
Toledo teaches
Alchemy and sleight-of-hand

O wandering clerks
You learn the arts
Medicine and magic
O wandering clerks
Nowhere learn
Manners or morals
O wandering clerks

It scanned and rhymed in French, and by then everyone
was shouting along whenever the line "O wandering clerks!"
made an appearance. At the finish Félicien leapt to his feet and
flourished his cap in an elaborate bow. Quite a few coins were
tossed into it. Laughter in this case was demonstrably more than
its own reward. Johanna took thoughtful note.

From that evening forward Félicien found himself at their
campfire more often than not. His stories were in high demand
and his voice a welcome addition to their own. He was also
a font of information on places beyond the Middle Sea, and
Jaufre drank all these in thirstily, especially any scrap concerning
Britannia.

Their course took them not directly west; rather, they moved
from city to city as trading opportunities and market values

112

offered opportunity. The topography was initially mostly flat, dry plain, sandy dunes interspersed with expanses of loose black pebbles and hard-packed dirt. The Tian Shan Mountains, snow-capped peaks keeping august distance from the riffraff, were succeeded by the Flaming Mountains, which formed a bare rock wall against the northwestern horizon. "They aren't flaming," Johanna said, disappointed that they didn't live up to their name.

"They aren't really of a height to deserve the term 'mountains,' either," Jaufre said critically.

The barely undulating plain was interrupted just often enough for comfortable travel by oasis towns, built on rivers that snaked back and forth for a few leagues before vanishing into the ground, only to reappear again leagues away. The ruins of ancient villages perched on yellow sandstone wedges, marooned high in the air by the erosion of the water's flow. Tiny farms were tucked in along the riverbanks, fields of cotton beginning to bud between straight rows of slender poplars radiant in silvery green. Grape vines sent investigatory tendrils across wooden frames and fruit trees were small white clouds of blooms. Everywhere the bees were happily drunk on nectar, buzzing dizzyingly from blossom to blossom.

In Lanchow they traded not at all, the city being too near Chang'an and Cambaluc for profit such as Wu Li had taught them to expect. If they did not trade, however, they could look to see what luxuries were going for the highest prices that year, and store that information away for future profit. Midway between the spice market and a row of apothecaries shops Johanna, Jaufre and Félicien were offered a full saddlebag of grayish grainy matter that the seller, hand on his heart, earnestly swore upon the bones of his ancestors was dried ground testicle of Jacob's sheep, a proven aphrodisiac—"Guaranteed to warm the coldest woman on the darkest winter night, sahib!" The seller, a wizened little man in a filthy jellaba and an even filthier turban fastened with a chipped red brooch that couldn't even pretend to be a ruby, clutched at Jaufre's sleeve. "Yes, yes, and a known curative for shingles, croup, headache, stomach ache and toothache besides!" When Jaufre smiled and shook his head the old man said, "Where else will you find such rare and wonderful goods, young sir? Where?"

"Where, indeed," Johanna said, but Jaufre was made of kinder stuff and pressed a small coin into the old man's hand. It disappeared, but they left the old man pulling his wispy beard and calling out after them, "Is it Wuwei that you journey to next? No, no, not Wuwei, young sir, young miss, as your life depends upon it! Those fellows on the other side of the river are robbers and murderers, they are deviants and pederasts, they rape their mothers, they slay their fathers! Stay safe here where you deal always with honest men! I spit, I spit—" suiting his word to the deed so that Jaufre had to step quickly out of range "—all good people spit on the monsters there!"

"Well, we can't say we haven't been warned," Félicien said, and Johanna could tell by the faraway look in his eyes that he was already composing his next song, something scurrilous to do with the perverse occupations of the dread Wuwei-ers, no doubt.

They met Shasha coming out of the spice market. "Anything worth buying?" Jaufre said.

"I will wait for Yarkent," Shasha said, and Jaufre and Johanna laughed. Félicien looked between them, quizzical, and Johanna said, "Just wait. When we get to Yarkent, you'll see."

In Wuwei, the Lanchow marketplace prophet's dire prophecies notwithstanding, Johanna found a Khuree merchant with two bales of sable pelts, so expertly cured they rivaled silk for suppleness and sheen. The Khuree knew what he had and the bargaining was fierce, but in the end Johanna bore the sables off in triumph, secure in the knowledge that the return on investment to be had farther down the Road would be well worth her while.

Jaufre found a smith who made belt knives of simple yet elegant design, with edges honed to a sharpness that, the smith said with pride, "cut your eye just to look at it." Jaufre tested a few of the edges and the smith wasn't far wrong. They were beautiful and useful and small in bulk and weight, a hundred of them tucked easily into a single pack.

Shasha visited the spice bazaar and said, "I will wait for Yarkent."

"What's in Yarkent?" Félicien said again, and again Jaufre and Johanna would only shake their heads.

In Kuche the donkey carts were tethered in the dry riverbed as the muezzin's call to prayer summoned their drivers to the mosque. On Saturday the sun rose on a bustling market. Jaufre found a vendor with two camel load's worth of fragrant sandalwood that he knew would do well in Kashgar. Johanna sought out a wool merchant with whom Wu Li had a long and profitable relationship, who could be relied upon not to leave his bales open in transit so as to gather desert sand on the road and so increase their weight, although she kneaded a handful before making an offer because it was expected of her father's daughter. The wool merchant offered her hot, sweet mint tea and commiseration upon the loss of such a noble father, and she bought ten bales of his finest wool for a weaver in Kashgar who would know how to value it.

Shasha, upon inquiry, said with a certain self-conscious dignity that she had seen nothing of interest beyond an inferior frankincense priced so high as to be amusing to any experienced trader.

"And you'll wait for Yarkent," Jaufre said.

Johanna laughed, and Shasha glared, and the three of them returned to camp in high spirits.

"Honorable niece," Uncle Cheng said, intercepting them before their yurt.

"Honorable uncle," Johanna said, wondering at the twinkle in his eye. "Have you prospered in Kuche?"

"I have," he said, the twinkle more pronounced. "I believe I may prosper even more tomorrow."

"We remain another night then, uncle?" Jaufre said.

"We do," Uncle Cheng said with a slight bow and a beaming smile that made all three of them instantly suspicious. "We do indeed."

"Is the market extended for another day?"

"It is not," Uncle Cheng said. "But there are to be races."

Jaufre and Shasha both watched with foreboding as Johanna's expression changed to resemble Uncle Cheng's in a way no two persons who looked so infinitely dissimilar should do.

Race day dawned in Kuche clear and cool, the aromas of baking bread and animal manure jostling for place. Jaufre woke to find Johanna already gone, and looked across the yurt to see Shasha staring back at him. "This is not wise," she said. "It will draw attention."

"What," he said, grumbling his way into his clothes; "you think Edyk the Portuguese hasn't noticed yet that his horse is missing?"

The dry riverbed had been transformed, all the donkey carts moved to the sides and tethered to roots beneath the overhang. The center of the riverbed was taken up with a group of child acrobats who tumbled down gracefully from quickly-formed human pyramids to somersault between running camels. A strongman, an ex-soldier by the contemptuous curl of his lip, bent a sword in half, then straightened it out again. A magician made a little girl's doll disappear, made it reappear when the little girl opened her mouth to cry, and then produced a silver drachma from her brother's ear. Lines formed before letter writers, spare quills tucked behind their ears, their assistants scraping industriously at previous letters written on already venerable pieces of vellum. An astrologer was doing a rousing business in horoscopes, musicians piped their pipes and strummed their sitars and beat their drums with greater and lesser skill, and the inevitable Kuchean dancing girls entranced wide-eyed country boys with hips that seemed to move independently of the rest of their bodies. Or they did before the boys' mothers came up to smack their ears and chase them back to their families, there to fall victim to the prostitutes beckoning seductively from the trees growing along the top of the riverbank.

There were at last five men taking bets, by Jaufre's count. The first race was a donkey race, their riders children waving colorful banners. At least half the children fell off at the start, one let his banner become tangled in his donkey's hooves and the donkey fell and his rider with him, and the winner crossed the finish line going backwards. Most of the bettors were parents, and two over-excited fathers fell into an argument that deteriorated into fisticuffs and had to be separated before the next race, to the vociferous dismay of the bystanders who had been placing bets on the outcome.

The second race was between camels: long, lean racing beasts with light racing saddles and professional riders – small, wiry men who listened to their owners' last-minute advice with impassive expressions before throwing a leg over their mounts and kicking them groaning and spitting to their feet. Ten of them lined up for the start and all ten disappeared around the first bend in the river, their progress reported on by shouting, red-faced men stationed above. Betting would continue until the halfway mark, when one of the men waved a black flag violently back and forth and the touts stepped down from their rocks. A few minutes later a roar began far off and increased as the racers drew nearer.

The camels burst round the last bend in the river, brown blurs with their noses stretched out in front of them and ungainly legs kicking sand up all the way back to Cambaluc. They had been slow off the mark but they more than made up for it now, and Jaufre found himself yelling along with everyone else as the two leading camels flashed across the finish line.

There was some considerable conversation between the racers, the owners and the spectators as to who had won. In the end it came down to an older gentleman of dignified mien and snow-white turban, who tucked his hands in his cuffs and delivered his verdict.

Half the crowd groaned and the other half cheered and lined up for their winnings. The touts looked relieved, so the favorite must have won. Jaufre couldn't tell one camel from another and he hadn't placed any bets so the matter was less pressing to him.

The sun was overhead and the scene devolved into a talking, laughing, jostling crowd reliving the camel race second by second. The acrobats came back out, and the Kuche dance troupe, and men and women appeared bearing trays of pomegranate juice and rounds of bread and dried apricots and almonds roasted with salt. A puppet show told the story of a Mongol soldier who eloped with the sultan's daughter, who then died of the smell of her affianced on the first night, eliciting gales of laughter and a respectable handful of coins. A tightrope walker stretched a rope between two trees and held a crowd of people breathless as he jumped, skipped, leaped and did handsprings twenty feet above the river bed. A very talented contortionist made everyone uncomfortable and three jugglers tossed flaming torches back and forth as if they were apples. The torches disappeared and were replaced by knives, which disappeared in their turn to be replaced by duck eggs. Each of the jugglers caught an egg in each hand and one in their mouths without breaking any, and bowed to much applause.

This seemed to be the signal to clear the course for the next race, and there was no mistaking the air of excitement that rippled over the crowd.

"A great event in these parts, evidently."

Jaufre turned to see Sheik Mohammed standing next to him. Immaculate as ever in white robes, his jeweled knife tucked into his belt, his son Farhad standing next to him and the two omnipresent guards alert behind. He surveyed the crowd along the river bed with an aloof expression. He didn't quite draw his skirts in so as not to be polluted by contact with common folk, but nevertheless managed to give the distinct impression that he was entitled to reascend to his own social level at any given moment, and would do so upon the least provocation.

"There is almost always a race in Kuche," Jaufre said.

"So it seems. Do you have a horse in the race?"

"I don't," Jaufre said, and if the sheik noticed the emphasis Jaufre placed on the first word he took no notice. "Do you?"

"I do," the sheik said. He grinned, and it was a surprisingly friendly grin, albeit with an edge to it. "And you would be advised to bet on it, Jaufre of Cambaluc."

Jaufre felt a smile spread across his face. "Would I?" he said.

Soon afterward the contestants lined up, and Jaufre felt the sheik stiffen next to him. He turned his face away so that the sheik couldn't see his grin.

North Wind was the only all-white horse among the racers, and Johanna the only female rider. There was some murmuring about this in the crowd, but Kuche was a caravan town and had seen many more odd things in its day. Then someone recognized her. "Wu Li's daughter! Wu Li's daughter! Wu Li's daughter!" Her name was shouted in Persian and Mandarin, in Uigur and Mongol, in Armenian and what Jaufre thought might have been Hebrew, but it was a long time since he'd heard it. No matter. They remembered Johanna, and Wu Li, in Kuche.

Johanna laughed out loud and waved first to one side of the crowd and then the other. It was only the most curmudgeonly of watchers who did not recognize the joy and pride she took in her horse.

Not that he was hers, Jaufre thought, and scanned the crowd for an officer of the court, merely out of habit.

"A bet on the Honorable Wu Li's daughter and her fine steed, young sir?"

Jaufre looked down to meet the bland eyes of Shasha, stick of charcoal poised over a rough wood tablet, her leather purse heavy at her waist, Félicien guarding her back, and stifled a laugh. Shasha gave an imperceptible shrug, as if to say, What else was I supposed to do?

"No?" she said. "And you, fine sir? A late entrant, to be sure, and untested this far west, but surely worthy of the wager?"

The sheik gave Shasha a sharp glance. "If I bet, I bet on my own horse, madam."

Shasha bent her head. "My apologies, fine sir," she said, and vanished discreetly into the crowd, Félicien a step behind her. A few moments later Jaufre heard her voice. "A bet on the white horse? Of course, my fine sirs, of course! The odds? Come, come, you have only to look at him! The sheik's horse is known never to have a lost a race? Then it is time he did, and I say the white stallion is the one to do it! Ten to one? Eight to one? Very well, five to one, and welcome, fine sir!"

Jaufre very carefully did not look at the man next to him, but on the sheik's other side his son choked and turned it quickly into a cough when his father glared at him.

The sheik's horse was easy to spot, an Arab stallion with a gleaming mahogany coat clothing a fine collection of muscle and bone. He danced impatiently on small, neat hooves, ready to be off. His rider kept glancing at Johanna as if he couldn't believe his eyes. Jaufre felt the sheik shift and still himself again with a palpable effort. Looking that impervious all the time must come with a price.

"How can you bear it?" the sheik's son said to Jaufre in an undertone.

"Bear what?" Jaufre said, his eyes like the sheik's son's trained on the woman on the white stallion.

"Your woman's face uncovered before so many men's eyes," Farhad, the sheik's son, said.

"She's not my woman," Jaufre said. Not yet, he thought.

He didn't notice the sheik's son coming to attention next to him at his words.

The race official cried out and the crowd fell silent, all eyes on the starting line and the seven horses standing there in relative degrees of serenity. The sheik's stallion looked ready to explode out of its skin, North Wind looked carved from marble, and the other five horses simply faded out of existence by comparison. Voices went up as last frantic bids were made. Jaufre didn't see

Uncle Cheng but he was sure he was in the crowd somewhere with silver coin running through his fingers like water.

The official, perched above the fray on the edge of the river's bank, counted to three. At two the sheik's mahogany stallion quivered all over and strained at the bit. North Wind looked bored. The official cried out "Go!" His arm dropped sharply.

And North Wind went from a period of calm repose, probably speculating on the content of his next meal, to a full-length extended gallop in one stride.

Jaufre had seen it before, many times, and it never failed to amaze him. Johanna lay flat on North Wind's back, her face pressed against his neck, her hands buried in his mane. She rode him bareback—"North Wind would never allow me to fall"— with her knees drawn up and her heels pressed tightly against his sides. Her braid was blown free in three strides, on the fourth they were passing Jaufre's position and on the seventh they had reached the first bend.

"Allah forfend!" the sheik said. "What a horse!"

But Jaufre had eyes only for Johanna. So did the sheik's son, although Jaufre didn't notice.

The ground shook beneath the thud of hooves striking sand and North Wind was a full length ahead of the sheik's stallion as they went out of sight, and five lengths ahead of him when they thundered back across the finish line ten minutes later. Here, North Wind deigned to prance and preen, just a bit. The stallion snapped at him and North Wind moved neatly out of reach and nipped the stallion's rider on the thigh, startling something very like a squeal out of him.

And quite right, too, Jaufre thought, shoving his way through the crowd. "Congratulations," he said to Johanna, who brought her leg over North Wind's neck and slid neatly to the ground.

She shook her head, hands busily reassembling her braid. "It wasn't fair, really. No other horse here had a chance against North Wind."

The rider of the mahogany stallion overheard her and reddened.

"No," another voice said. "They didn't."

The stallion's rider paled, and Jaufre turned to see that Sheik Mohammed had followed him through the crowd. The sheik's son was next to him and this time Jaufre saw him look at Johanna, his admiration evident.

"Surely he is a descendant of Bucephalus himself," the sheik said to Jaufre. "I will buy him from you."

"He's not mine," Jaufre said shortly.

The sheik gave him an incredulous look, and turned to Johanna.

He's not hers, either, Jaufre thought.

"I will buy your horse, then," the sheik said to Johanna, reluctantly and somewhat uncomfortably, as if he was unaccustomed to speaking directly to women.

"Certainly," Johanna said with a glittering smile.

"Name your price," the sheik said.

North Wind poked his nose over Johanna's shoulder and blew in her ear. "All the gold in Byzantium, all the pearls in Cipangu, and all the rubies in Mien," she said, with a grin at Jaufre, and at Shasha and Félicien as they arrived, out of breath. Shasha was carrying a noticeably heavier purse. "There is no price too high for North Wind. Besides, I can't sell him."

The sheik reached out a hand and North Wind's teeth snapped again, short of their target only because Johanna said in firm voice, "No." She patted his neck. "I would be cheating you, sheik. He wouldn't go with you if I did sell him. There is no rope strong enough to tie him to you while I am still in the world. He would savage every other horse and trample every guard and break down every door in your stables, to make his way back to me. He's done it before. And he would certainly never allow your man on his back."

"That," Jaufre said reluctantly, "is really true." He reflected on Edyk's troubles with riders, or more specifically on North Wind's troubles with riders. Any races he had run were won in spite of them, and Edyk had forfeited more than one race because North

Wind had dumped his rider before the finish line. No rider had ever volunteered for a second race on North Wind's broad back.

Jaufre looked at Johanna in sudden realization. She met his eyes, a smile in her own.

"He followed you down from the summerhouse," Jaufre said later.

She nodded. "I tried to leave him in his stall at Edyk's, but he kicked it down and came after me. I think, somehow, he knew, and he would not be left behind."

She was grooming North Wind, who had been fed and watered and who was now picketed and drowsing with his weight on three legs. He was almost purring beneath the rhythmic stroke of the bristles.

"And I didn't want to miss the ceremony for Father," Johanna said, "and by then it was too late."

"Why didn't you tell us?"

"If you could have seen your expressions when I rode up! I couldn't resist, Jaufre."

Her grin was impish, her eyes twinkling, her voice on the edge of laughter. He knew no other woman who would be so unconcerned that he had thought her guilty of such an enormous theft. His hand went out but she had turned back to North Wind and didn't see it.

She smoothed out a nonexistent tangle and stepped back, North Wind gleaming in the evening light. They were staying another night in Kuche on the strength of Wu Cheng's winnings. Uncle Cheng even now was hosting an uproarious party for the city's dignitaries behind city walls, catered by every food vendor and wine merchant within a day's ride. It would very likely continue until they were ready to depart the following evening.

"Sheik Mohammed is serious about buying him," Jaufre said.

"North Wind is just as serious about not being bought," Johanna said, and took her leave of her equine familiar with a last, loving stroke. "There are new baths in the city," she said. "Shasha went ahead. Shall we?"

I 2

Kuche

T HE WATER WAS hot and the attendants scrubbed hard. As they
emerged again into the street an hour later, not far away
they could hear the sounds of people still enjoying their wine at
Uncle Cheng's expense. "Should we join them?" Jaufre said.

Johanna yawned hugely. "I'm for bed." She smiled at him, her
face still flushed from her bath.

Without knowing he did it, Jaufre raised a hand and brushed
back a wayward bronze curl that had escaped from her damp
braid to tangle in her eyelashes.

Johanna's smile faded and they stood staring at each other.

Shasha cleared her throat. "Bed, yes, indeed," she said. "It's
been a long day."

They both jumped. Jaufre shook his head as if trying to clear
it and without a word turned on his heel.

Johanna stood where she was, her mouth half open, watching
Jaufre's receding back.

She had not thought of love beyond Edyk. If things had been
different she might have married him and lived with him and
borne his children and traveled and traded with him. Leaving
him had been the most difficult thing she had ever done.

The Road had taught her that no one, man or woman,
was ever quite done with love, but she had never applied that

knowledge to her own life. Perhaps it was simply because she hadn't had time, she thought now. After all, they were not even five hundred leagues from Cambaluc. It was only a little over a month since the idyll in the lake house. She could still feel Edyk's lips against hers, her body rising to his, the joy they had taken in each other's response. It wasn't as if she didn't ache for him, as if the hunger she had felt then had stopped the instant she passed beneath the Great West Gate of Cambaluc. She had dreamed of his hands on her, only to wake, heart pounding, restless, wanting, reaching for him.

She had no doubt that she could find physical relief with any one of the men she saw looking at her in that way. But if the Road had taught her much truth about the relations between men and women, her parents had showed her that such relations could be very good and very lasting. She was well aware that most marriages were transactional, trading a child for a stake in a business, or a foothold in an influential family, or simply a dowry big enough to provide for both children and their children for life.

Or as a convenient way to dispose of an unwanted stepdaughter.

Jaufre had always been there beside her, her fellow trader, her brother in arms, her co-conspirator in whatever devilry their fertile minds could devise. She had felt Jaufre's hands on her a thousand, a thousand thousand times over the years, throwing her up into the saddle, steadying her hands on a new bow, nudging her elbow to the proper position in Fair Lady Works at Shuttles before Deshi the Scout saw that she was wildly out of form. There was no one with whom she felt more comfortable than Jaufre.

This, though. The way his eyes seemed to darken as he watched his hand slide the lock of hair back behind her ear. The touch of his fingers on the skin of her cheek, a touch that seemed to sear straight down through her body, igniting feelings that she had only ever felt for Edyk. She looked down, bewildered, to see her nipples hard against the silk of her tunic, and the dark hollow between her legs felt as if it were about to open, hot, slippery, welcoming.

"Coming?" Shasha said blandly, and like Jaufre, bereft of words, Johanna followed her.

The caravansary in Kuche was undergoing restoration ("The Kuche caravansary has been under construction since before I was born," Johanna had said upon hearing the news) and Uncle Cheng had set up camp outside the walls, arranging their goods and sleeping tents at the heart of a circle of livestock in turn inside a circle of constantly patrolling guards. Their yurt was next to Uncle Cheng's, and the pickets for their mounts on the other side of the guards' tents. It was the safest possible place in the caravan. Even the most accomplished thief would not have dreamed of trying his luck there.

Which was why, perhaps among other reasons, they were taken completely by surprise. Johanna saw Jaufre duck under the flap and heard him stumble and swear.

"What's wrong, Jaufre?" Shasha said, following him inside. Johanna caught the flap before it closed. It dropped behind her and the light from the torches that lit the camp only dimly in the first place was cut off.

The yurt seemed to explode. Something hit her in the chest and she staggered back into the wall of the canvas, which sagged precariously beneath her weight. "What—" Some disturbance of the air warned her at the last minute and she let herself slip to the ground as something large passed over her head. There was a loud metallic clang and an oath from Jaufre, followed by the sound of flesh striking flesh. They were under attack, she thought, incredulous.

The fight was all the more eerie because it was so quiet. Johanna heard Jaufre grunt with effort, she heard Shasha panting, although she could barely hear either over the heart trying to jump out of her chest. She decided to change that and scrambled to her feet, shouting at the top of her voice. "Help! Help! Thieves! Help! Help! Thieves in the camp, help, help, help!"

Outside the tent she heard a distant whinny. Inside the tent there was a guttural curse in a voice that sounded familiar but to which she could not put a name, and then a thud. Another smack of flesh on flesh, and Shasha cried out.

"Shasha!" Johanna said. "Help, thieves, help, thieves!" She fumbled in the dark for the tent flap but it was too dark and she was all turned around.

There was a sound of swiftly approaching thunder, which confused her. It was a cloudless night with a sky full of stars. There could be no approaching storm, and then there was one, in the shape of eleven hundredweight of furious horse, who charged into the yurt at full speed and laid about him indiscriminately with hoof and teeth.

"North Wind!"

"Ouch!"

"Johanna, get outside and calm that beast down!"

Two slashing hooves brought the yurt down around them, tent poles cracking, ropes loosening into an inextricable tangle, and Johanna caught a sliver of light and dove through the opening seconds before she would have been caught in the mess. Above her, North Wind, magnificent in his rage, bugled a war cry through his nose and prepared to renew his assault. She darted in to grasp his halter and before he could rear again let all of her weight dangle from it.

He threw up his head and whinnied, still lunging and rearing and dropping his hooves with a fine lack of discrimination for private property, in his fury bringing down the yurt next to theirs. Fatima and Malala and Ahmed were going to be very annoyed. Fortunately no cries of distress were heard from inside. Like everyone else they must still be in the city and in the very short space of time granted her for coherent thought she was deeply grateful.

She released the halter to throw her arms around his neck and wiggled her way onto his back, laying flat, arms and legs tight around him. "It's all right, boy, it's all right, now, calm down, calm down, it's me, I'm all right." She kept talking, nonsense words mostly, hoping the sound of her voice would calm him. Even then he nearly had her off twice, and when he finally recognized that it was indeed Johanna on his back he reached back with his head, snatched a mouthful of tunic and hauled her down to the ground, where he proceeded to examine her stem to stern with his nose.

"Stop it! North Wind! Stop it! Let me up! I'm fine! By all the Mongol gods, I'm fine!"

From the corner of her eye she saw a figure struggle free of the collapsed yurt and race off, but it was too dark to see who it was. A second figure followed the first and this time North Wind helped him on his way with a judicious kick from his right hind leg. It caught the fleeing man squarely in the seat of the pants and raised him a good two ells in the air. Confounding all expectation he landed on his feet, staggered a few steps and was unfortunately at speed by the time Jaufre had fought himself free of the wreck, vanishing into the thicket of yurts surrounding them.

Jaufre rooted around in the debris to extricate Shasha. North Wind grudgingly allowed Johanna back on her feet. By this time many people had responded to Johanna's shouts and North Wind's battle cry, including Félicien, who stared wide-eyed at the wreckage of the yurt and at the scrapes and bruises sustained by his friends, none of whom by great good fortune were worse hurt. Many of the others had only just returned home from drinking a great deal at Uncle Cheng's expense and were much more jolly than the occasion warranted. They weren't much help getting the yurt back up, either.

"I knew racing North Wind was a bad idea," Shasha said.

She was sporting a spectacular pair of black eyes. Jaufre had a cut on his cheek extending from his right temple almost to the corner of his mouth. It was very thin, as if made by an extraordinarily sharp blade. All three of them were bruised and stiff.

Johanna held up her mother's Robe of a Thousand Larks. It had been slashed nearly in two, the collar alone holding the garment together. The embroidered birds on the cut edge were already beginning to unravel. "Why didn't they just steal it?" she said, fighting tears.

Shasha, tight-lipped, looked up. "They didn't even bother to unbuckle my pack, they just cut it open."

Jaufre held up his own pack, now in two pieces, in reply.

The smells of cumin and cinnamon and coriander permeated the yurt and Jaufre tied back the flap to air it out. He felt the comforting weight of his father's sword resting along his spine and was grateful that his most prized possession was never out of his sight. He found himself leaning over to finger the reassuring lumps in the hem of his coat, and looked up to see Shasha doing the same.

"They took nothing," he said, frowning at the pile he had made of his belongings.

"Or they didn't find what they were looking for," Shasha said.

Johanna said nothing.

Uncle Cheng, red of eye and short of temper, summoned his havildar. This was Firas, a wiry man of middle height with a sparse beard and a scimitar with a grip bound in leather so frequently in use it looked as if it had been molded to fit his and only his hand. He was new to them and indeed to Uncle Cheng, having held the post of head of guard for less than two years. He followed them back to the yurt once it was light enough to see, and surveyed the scene with dark, remote eyes. "Did you see anyone?"

He spoke to Jaufre in Farsi and Johanna answered in kind. "We were at the baths. When we came back, they were inside the yurt, and attacked us as we entered."

"Nothing at all?" he said, again to Jaufre. "No strangers loitering around?"

"You heard her," Shasha said. "Do you think we would have left the tent unguarded, that we wouldn't have sounded the alarm if we had suspected something like this might happen?"

He looked at her for a long moment, and then bent his head in a gesture somewhere between a nod and a bow. "As you say. Do you have any idea yet what is missing?"

"That's just it," Jaufre said. "Nothing seems to be missing. Cut open, ripped apart, but not missing."

Firas meditated for a moment, his eyes dwelling for a moment on Jaufre's sword. "A fortunate circumstance. Or happy forethought."

"Perhaps both," Shasha said. "Old No—the honorable Wu Cheng's hospitality was offered to all in the camp and in the city. The camp was nearly deserted when we came back from the baths. What self-respecting thief would pass up such an opportunity?"

"There were guards," Firas said mildly.

"Not that anyone would notice," Shasha said with acid precision.

His eyes returned to her and she thought he almost smiled. "As you say," he said again. "Still, one must consider all the possibilities. Have you recently turned off any servants who might be nursing a grudge? Dealt with a merchant who might think you had cheated him? Offended an ex-lover?"

"None of those things," Johanna said, and then looked at Jaufre.

"What?" he said.

"That fat redheaded dancer in Dunhuang," she said.

He reddened. "That short Portuguese trader in Cambaluc," he said.

In the subsequent smoldering silence, Shasha cleared her throat delicately. "No," she said, "nothing like that, havildar. At least not recently."

Their eyes met in understanding. "I will inquire," he said, and this time it was a genuine bow, denoting respect and admiration for one newly met.

Shasha waited until he was gone. "All right, Johanna."

Johanna looked at her, surprised at the sharp edge to the other woman's voice. "What?" she said.

"What's in your purse?" Shasha said.

"What?" Jaufre said.

Johanna blushed a fiery red to the roots of her hair. "I don't know what you're talking about."

"Oh yes, you do," Shasha said. "You've been riding with your chin on your shoulder since we left Cambaluc. He—" she jerked her head at Jaufre "—thinks it's because you're pining for Edyk. I think it's because you think we might be pursued." She gestured at the mess in the yurt. "And now I think that we have been, and that they've caught up to us."

"I don't know what you're talking about," Johanna said, but her hand went to the leather purse at her waist.

"What?" Jaufre said again.

"Whatever you took, it put us in danger." Shasha snatched the Robe of a Thousand Larks from Johanna's hands. "You could have been wearing this when it was sliced into pieces."

Johanna flinched and Shasha tossed the robe aside. "I love you, Johanna, I'd lay down my life for yours and so would Jaufre, but we have a right to know why."

Jaufre didn't say "What?" a third time because it might sound like it was the only word he knew.

They waited.

"Oh, all right," Johanna said, sighing. She fumbled at her waist and opened the purse, holding it out to display what was inside.

Jaufre blinked and opened his mouth, but was able to produce only a splutter.

Shasha put her hand over her eyes and shook her head. "Johanna. Johanna. What were you thinking, girl?"

"Pursued?" Jaufre said, finding his vocabulary and gaining in volume. "There is at minimum a band of hired mercenaries on our trail, if not an entire imperial cohort!"

Nestled inside the leather purse was the jade box containing the Wu bao.

Tucked in cozily next to it was Wu Li's worn, leather-bound journal.

Baos were hereditary, increasing in value as they aged from

generation to generation. New ones were awarded only rarely and usually only after a lifetime spent proving one's worth as a trader, or after an especially hefty bribe. Penalties for forgeries were harsh, which only began with stripping the offender of the right to trade in Everything Under the Heavens, and usually ending in prison. In short, the widow Wu would be unable to conduct the business of the Wu Li trading consortium without the Wu Li bao, and certainly, Jaufre thought bitterly, a mercenary troop's fee would be less expensive than the extortionate bribery necessary to moving a petition for a new bao through the bureaucracy at court.

As for the journal…In a faint voice Shasha said, "The journal? You took Wu Li's journal, too?"

"They were my father's," Johanna said. "And now they are mine."

"You do realize that the Honorable Wu Li's second wife may disagree?" Jaufre said with awful sarcasm.

"Of course she does," Shasha said. The strength in her legs gave out, as much from Johanna's revelation as from the lumps she had taken in the recent fracas, and she sat down with a thump on the nearest tangle of belongings. "She knows perfectly well that Wu Li's widow is sure to be nothing short of enraged. That's why she stole them." She raised her head. "Isn't it, Johanna?"

"Well, she certainly didn't see fit to give them to me as part of my dowry," Johanna said. "As she most certainly should have done."

Shasha cast her eyes heavenward for guidance.

"Johanna," Jaufre said in a controlled voice, "you understand, don't you, that without the bao, Dai Fang will be unable to trade commercially? At least until she's able to get a new one?"

"And that that could take years?" Shasha said.

"And that even if she does manage to acquire her own bao that her tithe will increase? Which will cut significantly into her profits?"

"And that even if she can get a new one quicker than that, that you hold the keys to the entire Li network in Wu Li's journal?" Shasha said. "That she won't know the names of debtors or agents in Kashgar or Antioch or Alexandria, or the names of Wu trading partners anywhere along the Road?"

Johanna grinned. "No, she won't, will she?" The other two were rendered momentarily speechless, and Johanna seized her advantage. "You're not worried that she'll follow us, are you? The Dishonorable Dai Fang wouldn't dream of subjecting herself to the barbarian practices of any race so unfortunate as to find itself living outside the borders of Everything Under the Heavens."

"Oh, agreed," Jaufre said.

"Of course she wouldn't," Shasha said.

"But Gokudo would," Jaufre said.

A thoughtful silence fell.

"If she ordered him to, Johanna," Jaufre said, "he would carve all three of us into bite-size pieces with that pig-sticker of his." And he would enjoy it, he thought. He raised his hand to the wound on his cheek. Gokudo had displayed the sharpness of the blade on his naginata many times. If indeed one of last night's visitors was Gokudo, then they were all very lucky that the samurai had not chosen to attack them in the open.

All three of them looked at the Robe of a Thousand Larks, mutilated with a single, sharp slash, and all three imagined what would have happened if Johanna had been wearing it when the blade struck.

Johanna was the first to recover. "Nonsense," she said robustly, as if volume and confidence alone could rout what were now, surely, only the ghosts of their past. "If the Dishonorable Dai Fang sent Gokudo after us, she would have sent him at once, the instant she noticed what was missing."

"So?"

"So why did he wait until Kuche to try to get them back?" Johanna said.

"Kuche is the first place we have spent outside caravansary walls," Shasha said.

"Nonsense," Johanna said again, albeit with less certainty. "We made camp in the desert dozens of times."

"Johanna," Jaufre said, with awful patience, "it would be much easier and much safer for Gokudo to hide his presence among the many strangers housed each night in a city, especially a city along the Silk Road. It would be much more difficult to approach an armed, isolated camp the size of ours."

"He's been following us," Shasha said.

"Since Cambaluc," Jaufre said, "waiting his chance."

"And," Johanna said slowly, "Uncle Cheng travels only as far as Kashgar on this trip." She looked at Jaufre, and at Shasha. "After that, we're on our own."

There followed an awkward silence. "I'm not sorry I did it," Johanna said at last. "They were Father's. By right they are now mine." She tucked the bao and book back into her purse and tied it shut. She looked defiant, and righteous, and unrepentant, and a hundred other things that would get them all killed well before Kashgar. "Besides," she said, "we won. They didn't get what they came for, and we ran them off."

Jaufre exchanged a long, expressionless look with Shasha. "As you say," he said at last, echoing the havildar. It was a useful phrase.

"Let's get this mess cleaned up," Shasha said.

Firas, listening on the other side of the canvas wall of the yurt, now slipped silently away.

Later, with Johanna safely out of earshot, Shasha said, "The bao. And the book."

"One or the other I might be able to defend," Jaufre said, trying to work back up to the righteous wrath he had experienced that morning and not quite managing it. "The book, certainly. But both?"

"Not to mention the horse," Shasha said.

He stopped and looked at her. "I completely forgot about the horse." His voice shook. "Do you think Edyk went to the house looking for North Wind?"

Shasha's lips trembled. "Can you imagine what the widow's reaction would have been when she found the bao and the book missing? And then Edyk arriving, demanding the return of North Wind?"

Jaufre started to grin. "I wonder if the Honorable Wu Li's house is still standing."

"Perhaps," she said unsteadily. "Pieces of it." She strove for control. "Still, this is serious, Jaufre."

"Of course you're right," he said. "At the very least we should begin standing watches."

They looked at each other and broke down completely, laughing so immoderately that they had to cling to each other for support. Outside, passersby wondered what was going on in the big yurt that was so funny.

Uncle Cheng delayed their departure for another day while Firas investigated. Meantime, Shasha was summoned to the caravan master's presence and requested to provide something to ease his wine-induced aches and pains. She snorted and brewed him a strong dish of steeped betony, which he gagged over but didn't dare dump out, not under that stern eye. And it did help, he had to admit, later and most reluctantly. At least he stopped feeling as if he were bleeding from his ears.

There were almost two thousand people in their caravan, over five thousand in Kuche and hundreds more in caravans large and small in constant arrival and departure. Everyone within and without the city walls was intent upon the engrossing subjects of their own commerce and trade and profit. There was little interest to be spared for suspicious strangers bent on burglary and mayhem, unless it was burglary and mayhem directed at themselves. Firas' inquiries thus bore little fruit, as he duly reported to Uncle Cheng, to which meeting Uncle Cheng had summoned Jaufre.

"As was to be expected, Uncle Cheng," Jaufre said. "We will keep a stricter guard in future."

He and Firas left together, and Jaufre was about to go his own way when Firas said, "A moment of your time, young sir."

"Havildar?"

"I wonder if I might see your weapon?"

Jaufre hesitated, and then with some reluctance drew his father's sword from its sheath.

Firas examined it with the eye of an expert, holding it up to judge the straightness of the blade, testing the edge, flipping it into the air and catching it again to assess its balance. All of the things, in fact, that Gokudo had done, although Gokudo had done it without permission. The havildar was a weapons master determining the effectiveness of a tool, expert, impartial, interested in an academic way but with no acquisitiveness. Jaufre, watching him, felt himself relax.

"A noble blade, young sir," Firas said, returning it hilt first. "I would see it in practice."

Jaufre felt the blood run up into his face. "It was my father's sword, havildar. He died before he could instruct me."

"Ah." Firas nodded, his eyes resting on something over Jaufre's shoulder. "I myself practice with such of my men who are so inclined at dawn each day before we march. Your blade and ours are of different models, but I would guess that much of the basic moves would be the same."

Jaufre weighed his father's sword. It had always felt somehow right and proper in his hand, a deadly extension of his own muscle and bone. At any time these past five years Jaufre could have asked one of the imperial guards for instruction. He wasn't sure why he had not.

Today, he thought of the items in Johanna's purse, of the fight in the yurt, of Shasha's black eyes and the cut on his cheek. He was good with knife and bow and almost as good as Johanna with the staff. Sword skill he had none. He thought again of the long slash up the back of Shu Ming's Robe of a Thousand Larks, and thought of how Johanna's face looked lit from within whenever she donned it to sing around an evening campfire.

"I am grateful for the invitation, havildar," Jaufre said, sliding the sword back into its sheath. "And pleased to accept."

Firas noted how easily the movement was completed. Jaufre's sword was not light in weight. There might be more to this slim young man than met the eye. "Just before dawn then, young sir, beyond the cook tents."

Jaufre was there well before dawn, Johanna at his side, as they worked through the thirty-two movements of soft boxing. They went through them three times, seamless, synchronized, one movement flowing naturally into the next. As the horizon brightened they sank down into horse stance, palms loosely cupped and parallel in front of them, held position for a slow count of ten, and rose smoothly again to a standing position.

"I see, young sir," said a voice behind them, "that while you may not have had lessons in the wielding of your father's sword, you are not entirely deficient in lessons of self defense."

"We were taught the art from a very young age," Johanna said, "by my father's man, Deshi the Scout."

He bowed slightly. "Honor is due such a fine teacher. Is it that I am to instruct the young lady in swordsmanship as well?"

Johanna inclined her head, matching dignity with dignity. "No, havildar, I have no such weapon. Though I would like to observe, if you please." Her voice was mild. Her eyes were not.

Firas almost smiled, or so it seemed to Jaufre.

He remembered that first practice for the rest of his life, although there was little of the thrust and parry he would learn later. Light increased in the east, flowing over the horizon onto the broad plain beneath. The hundreds of donkey carts tethered to scrub brush growing from the sandy sides of the river, the churned sand of the river bed the only evidence of yesterday's races. The call of the muezzin. The low curses of men waking, the crackle of cook fires, the smell of bread baking.

"I'm not a warrior, Firas," Jaufre said by way of explanation for the ignorance and ineptitude he was about to display. "I'm a trader."

"You carry a sword," the havildar said, unsurprised at this unsolicited confidence. "Sooner or later, someone will force you to use it." He hesitated, and then said, very gently, "You could lay it aside, young sir."

Jaufre had unbuckled the scabbard from about his chest and now he frowned down at it and the sword it sheathed. He looked up to meet Johanna's eyes. She said nothing, only waited for him to choose.

He drew his father's sword, handed her belt and scabbard, and turned. He thought he saw a trace of approval in the havildar's eyes, but later he would be equally certain he had imagined it. The havildar's approval was not so easily won.

"Yours is a weapon of the West," Firas said, pacing around him, hands clasped behind his back. "The Western warrior prefers a straight blade for hacking through heavy armor, wielded from horseback." He stopped to draw his own weapon. "My scimitar is of the East, also meant to be used from horseback, but shorter and used against a lightly-armored opponent, usually after the opponent's line has been weakened by archers."

He tossed Jaufre his scimitar. Jaufre caught it, just, in his left hand. "You will notice the difference in weight."

Jaufre tested both swords, and his eyebrows went up.

Firas nodded. "One on one, your sword will have the advantage."

"Until I meet someone with a longer sword," Jaufre said.

"Until then." Firas held up an admonitory finger. "You will have the advantage, that is, once you learn to use it properly.

An untrained soldier is more of a hazard to himself than he is to anyone else."

After Jaufre had nearly cut off his own hand and had gashed his own cheek, he took the havildar's warning more seriously.

But that would be in the future. This morning Firas had caused a thick post to be buried deep in the sand, and had Jaufre hack at it with a wooden practice sword, forehand and backhand, over and over, again and again, until Jaufre's arms felt as if they would fall off. "This post is buried behind the cook tents at each of our camps," the havildar said. "Half of each practice session will be spent at it."

Jaufre, sweat rolling down his face, the muscles in his arms burning, gasped out something that passed for, "Yes, havildar."

Firas then had Jaufre switch to his own sword and walk through a series of different movements: cut, thrust, parry, and right, left and overhead variations. There wasn't much finesse to it, as Jaufre soon came to realize. A sword was essentially a club with an edge.

Firas walked through each movement slowly, standing next to Jaufre and commanding him to mirror his own movements. Then he stepped opposite Jaufre and repeated those movements, meeting them with his own in mirror image.

After the work with the post, it was all Jaufre could do to get his sword to shoulder height, and Firas took advantage of every gap in his defenses, usually with a hard rap with the side of his blade on whatever portion of Jaufre's anatomy was convenient. There were many such gaps.

At some point during the following year, Firas stepped back and dropped his sword. "Enough for your first lesson, I think."

Jaufre blinked the sweat from his eyes and looked around to find that many of Uncle Cheng's guard had assembled in a circle. There were smiles hidden and smiles not and much nudging of elbows. Johanna, standing a little apart with her hands clasped over the sword's sheath as if she were praying, watched them with a face wiped unusually clean of expression.

"Tomorrow at the same time, young sir?" Firas said, producing a length of cloth and wiping his blade.

Jaufre took a deep breath and with trembling arms brought up his father's sword and wiped it on the edge of his tunic. He made a silent vow to acquire a clean cloth for cleansing his blade before their next practice. "Tomorrow," he said. It was all he could manage.

Firas inclined his head, a ghost of a smile on his face. "Until then."

Johanna, mercifully, waited until they were well away from the practice yard. "Where does it hurt?"

"Everywhere," he said. He'd meant it to be a shout but it came out as more of a groan.

She nodded, her suspicion confirmed. "Perhaps another visit to the baths."

It was good advice, despite its source, and he took it. He was marginally mobile when he awoke that evening, only to be nearly incapable of helping strike their yurt afterward. Johanna and Shasha broke their camp without comment, although there were meaningful looks. The night that followed, spent on camelback, was sheer agony.

Uncle Cheng at first skirted the Taklamakan Desert to the north, stopping at oasis towns and trading as they went. Shasha purchased cakes of indigo dye which she said would profit them well in Antioch and Acre, where they could buy kermes or carmine dye for trading farther west. Johanna found a merchant who specialized in antiquities and acquired a dozen flying horses made of bronze, all small, exquisitely made and of a portable size.

"Those aren't Han," Jaufre said.

"Who west of Kashgar will know that?" Johanna said. Her fingers caressed the mane of one of the horses. "And they are lovely little pieces in their own right. Who wouldn't pay a handsome sum to display one of these in their public rooms, to the envy of their neighbors and friends?" Her eyes took on a faraway look. "Perhaps I should find a marble carver. We could double the price if each one included its own pedestal."

"And it would be no strain at all on our pack animals to ask them to carry marble pedestals in addition to the solid bronze statues," Jaufre said cordially.

Shasha watched Johanna flounce off. Jaufre flapped a hand at Shasha's raised eyebrow and hobbled off in the opposite direction.

The feelings generated by discovery of the contents of Johanna's purse were prone to display themselves at odd moments. Shasha sighed and kept her inevitable thoughts to herself.

Jaufre's weapons training continued apace. The first morning he was able to block all of the havildar's blows, Firas introduced him to the shield, and then the mace, and then the flail, and then the axe, and then the lance. New muscles he didn't even know he had set up their individual protests. At which point Firas, obviously close kin to Father John's Christian devil, set the better swordsmen among the guards to attack Jaufre without warning, so that Jaufre found himself on alert at every moment of the night or day. Before long he was able to come out of a sound sleep, on his feet with his father's sword in his hand, and beat off an attack in the blazing sun of midday.

Johanna and Shasha, woken during the same attack, knew enough not to waste their breath in complaints, and perfected a quick roll to the wall of the yurt, beneath it and out, while the battle raged within.

None of the surprise attacks were half-hearted. One evening, as the caravan was being loaded and the camels were coming reluctantly to their feet, Jaufre blocked one of the havildar's thrusts and pushed through to touch the point of his blade to the havildar's tunic. He dropped his sword and stood back.

Firas, to Jaufre's infinite and inarticulate pride, saluted Jaufre with his scimitar. "You improve, young sir. You improve."

Félicien wrote a song about it and sang it at the campfire that night to loud acclaim. Jaufre's aches and pains lessened.

When they were near a city he sought out the hot baths. When they camped in caravansaries or on the trail Shasha rubbed him down with oil, strong fingers kneading at the hard knots of muscles bunched beneath his skin. After a while he had to find a seamstress to let out the shoulders and sleeves of his tunics.

One morning he was already laying face down on his bed, shirtless, his head pillowed in his arms, half asleep. He heard the flap of the yurt rustle and said sleepily, "Shasha?"

She didn't answer, and there was a long silence. Then her knees dropped next to him and he heard her rub oil into her hands. She laid those hands on his back and he knew instantly that they did not belong to the wise woman. They were strong, vigorous hands that kneaded the tension from his muscles every bit as capably as Shasha's would have, but instead of a massage this felt like a caress, like a prelude to love. He shifted when his body reacted, but he was anything but uncomfortable. He had wanted her for so long now, and for so long she had been unable to see anything but a brother when she looked at him.

He rolled to his back and looked up at her. Her hands had dropped to her thighs and her eyes were wide, tracing the curve of muscle and bone from his shoulder to his chest. His eyes followed the trail of golden down over his abdomen, and widened. She looked up at his face, startled. He made no attempt to hide what he was feeling.

Her lips parted and she leaned a little forward, and Shasha came into the yurt, oblivious to the tension, or making a good show of it. "Ah, good, Johanna, I see you've eased the pain of our wounded warrior."

Not quite, Jaufre thought.

Shasha, meantime, had her own agenda. The following morning after they pitched the yurt she drew the younger woman to one side. "Do you remember the herbs I gave you before you went to Edyk?"

Johanna colored. "Yes."

"You took them?"

142

"I did. Steeped in hot water every morning, as you instructed. They tasted terrible."

"Most effective medicines do, unfortunately. Edyk didn't object?"

"Edyk didn't know." Johanna looked away. "I made sure he was deep asleep each time."

"Good." Shasha nodded. "Good. You are pleased to be without child?"

Johanna was silent. Traveling the Road, having adventures, seeing all that there was to see, finding her grandfather, these were the things she was looking forward to.

Still, to have had Edyk's child… would have been most inconvenient. She didn't need a child to remember him by. Perhaps she would marry and have children one day, although that day was visible only through a rosy cloud in the distant future, with the father of said children an even less distinct figure. "Yes," she said firmly. "I didn't thank you, Shasha. I am very grateful."

"Good," Shasha said briskly, "then you will not object to learning to make your own." She led the way to a blanket she had spread behind their yurt, her herbs set out in small neat bags made of muslin, each marked with a Mandarin character. She sat down tailor fashion and motioned Johanna to join her. "This is pennyroyal," she said. "Take a pinch. Smell it. Taste it, a very little. When I find some of it growing I'll show you."

Dutifully Johanna pinched, smelled, tasted.

"This is mugwort," Shasha said, offering another muslin bag. She waited as Johanna went through the ritual. "Take either one dram of the pennyroyal, or one dram of the mugwort, but never both." She shook out a portion of the pennyroyal into her palm, demonstrating the amount. "Add one teaspoon of blue cohash. Infuse the herbs in one cup of boiling water and drink. Twice a day for six days, no more."

"And this will—"

The two women looked at one another, united in the eternal female conspiracy against the burden placed on them by nature.

"Will bring on a delayed menstruation," Shasha said, without expression. "You must pay attention, Johanna. If you are a week or less late, take the potion as prescribed. If it does not bring on your menses, Johanna, if it does not—" she emphasized those last words "—you must not repeat the dosage, do you understand? You must not. It could lead to uncontrolled bleeding. You could bleed to death."

Johanna took a deep breath. "I understand. But why tell me now? Edyk is five hundred leagues behind us."

Shasha was packing up her herbs. "There are other men in the world, Johanna." Her hands stilled and she looked up. "One in our own yurt."

Johanna went instantly scarlet, leapt to her feet and marched off.

13

Kuche to Kashgar

FIRAS' CHIEF ASSET for the job of havildar, so far as Jaufre could see, was the ability to instill fear into his subordinates. "Why do they fear?" Johanna said, sensibly, and Jaufre spent a few evenings loitering around the guards' campfire, participating in soft boxing competitions and wrestling matches and archery contests and taking care not to win all the time. "He's a Nazari Ismaili," he reported back.

Johanna and Shasha looked blank.

"From Alamut," Jaufre said.

Recognition dawned. "He's an Assassin?" Johanna said, thrilled. "Really? I've never met an Assassin before."

"Yes, well, try not to sound so delighted," Jaufre said dryly. "You may not have met one now. That sect died out over a hundred years ago. Or was wiped out, more like."

Johanna's brow puckered. "But Father said that Grandfather visited the Mountain, and might even have met the Old Man."

"Your grandfather wasn't always the most reliable source, as the honorable Wu Li himself admitted," Shasha said.

After that Johanna made a point of watching Firas at work when she could. She detected no outward menace in his demeanor, but he did have an indefinable presence that inspired respect, if not, as Jaufre claimed, fear in his subordinates. When he issued an order, it was followed, promptly and without question, and without his ever having to lay a hand on the hilt of the curved sword he wore at his side, much less drawing it from its sturdy leather scabbard.

"What were you hoping for," Jaufre said one evening, "that he'd kill someone right in front of you so you could see the gold dagger of the Assassin in action?"

Johanna put up her nose at his and Shasha's laughter.

From Kuche, Uncle Cheng had sniffed the horizon for weather and found it mild for the season, and so they crossed the Taklamakan to Yarkent at a brisk march that had them arriving in record time. There, Shasha traded nearly everything but the Mien rubies in their hems for spices, peppercorns from Malabar, nutmeg from the Moluccas, cinnamon from Java the Less, cloves from Ceylon.

When Johanna mourned the loss of the sables out loud Shasha held up a canvas packet, no larger than Jaufre's fist, plump with vanilla beans from Madagascar. "The annual salary for a Mosul doctor."

No more was said. Spices were small and light, and when Shasha was done two of their half dozen camels were packed to the saddle horns with the aromatic cargo. "The farther west we travel, the more valuable these will become," she said with satisfaction.

Uncle Cheng, too, was pleased. The risky desert journey had paid off in excellent profit for all, and the usual grumblings any caravan master heard daily had been replaced by smug smiles and fat purses.

They had been on the road ninety days, only seventeen of those days given over to trading, one day extra in Kuche for the races and their aftermath, the rest in motion. Uncle Cheng had pushed them hard but the journey had paid off in goods traded to their advantage. As they approached the walls of Kashgar the rubies of Mien remained securely sewn into their hems.

There had been no further attacks upon their yurt. They had glimpsed small groups of what they presumed to be raiders on distant hilltops, and the three of them might have had their suspicions about who might be with those menacing groups, but the size of the caravan and the number of guards had been enough of a discouragement, at least so far.

What happened after Kashgar was another story, one Jaufre worried over. They left their pack animals under Uncle Cheng's capable eye, mounted horse and donkey (Félicien accompanied them) and spurred ahead to arrive at the great east gate of the city two hours in advance of the rest of the caravan.

Which was where Johanna acquired her monk.

He was being beaten with a stick outside the gates, in a formally appointed punishment complete with magistrate, drum and enthusiastic crowd. The stick was large and smooth from much use. The strokes were slow and measured and delivered with the full force of the arm of a man as large and muscular as the convicted felon was small and thin. The man with the stick was stripped to the waist and sweating with effort. So was the drummer, a slender boy of ten who watched his stick rather than the flogger's.

The felon was also stripped to the waist, displaying a torso with barely enough flesh to cover his bones. His hair was black and raggedly cut, his skin a pale gold.

Johanna reined in, she could not herself have said why. Perforce, Jaufre and Shasha reined in next to her. Taken by surprise, Félicien had to haul back on the reins of his donkey who, recognizing the walls of the city as housing food, water and rest was reluctant to stop until he was inside them. He finally acquiesced in this change of plan, not without protesting bawls.

Johanna waited a decent time before addressing herself to the magistrate, an elderly, impassive man attired in the flowing robe of his office. His head was shaven, and two long, thin mustaches trailed down each side of his thick, sternly set lips. By not so much as the twitch of an eyebrow did he betray that he knew perfectly well whose daughter she was.

She knew him as well as he knew her, but she took her cue from his formal manner. "Greetings, honored one," she said. She spoke in Mandarin and received a blank stare. She repeated her greeting in Mongol.

"Greetings, lady," the magistrate replied in that language. "You are welcome."

"We have traveled far and seek a meal, a bath and a bed within your walls this night."

"There are many such within the walls of Kashgar."

"It is good to know. We have been many days on the road, and are tired and hungry." Johanna and the magistrate watched the stick descend again. "Perhaps, honored one, you would know of an inn where we might find cleanliness and comfort."

"All inns within the walls of Kashgar are clean and comfortable," the magistrate said, "but it is well known that the Inn of the Green Dragon bakes the finest naan in the city and airs its blankets twice-monthly."

"I thank you, honored one. To the Green Dragon we will go." But she made no effort to leave.

They watched the beating go on in silence for a moment. Félicien gave Shasha a questioning look. Shasha rolled her eyes in reply.

"What has this old man done, honored one," Johanna said, "that he should be punished so severely?"

The official gave a mournful shake of his head. "He has represented himself as a holy man, and accepted alms from the citizens of Kashgar. The law requires that such a one be beaten once for each alm."

Johanna lowered her eyes to show her respect and said, "Truly, a just and equitable law, worthy of the rulers of such a great city."

The magistrate bowed slightly, accepting the compliment.

Twice more the stick was raised and lowered against the man's shrinking back.

"He is not holy, then?"

The magistrate shrugged. "He drinks sulphur and quicksilver once a day. He says he is a hundred and fifty years old. This may make him holy in the city of Calicut, but not in the city of Kashgar."

The stick rose and fell. At last Johanna said, "It is not for this unworthy one to suggest such a punishment is unmerited, yet I have pity for the old man. Is there no way to redeem this sinner to the path of righteousness?"

The magistrate was silent. At last he said, "There is one way. If the offender be able to ransom himself by paying nine times the value of the thing stolen, he is freed and released from further punishment."

Another stroke fell.

"And nine times the value of the thing stolen is what, in this instance, honored one?"

The magistrate folded his hands beneath his sleeves and regarded his shoes, the toes of which were pointed, curled and embroidered with gold thread. "How can one value the honor of a city?" he said piously, and Johanna knew at once that it was going to be expensive. "This charlatan has trespassed on the faith of our citizens, has stolen the very trust out of their hearts. Fifty rials."

Johanna and the magistrate regarded the old man's bleeding back together in silence. "He seems such a little, insignificant man to have caused any great harm to a city as exalted as Kashgar," Johanna said finally. "But it is as you say, honored one, that where one offends, one should atone for one's crimes. Ten rials."

The embroidered toes of the magistrate's shoes raised as he rocked back on his heels in shock. "This charlatan has trespassed on the faith of our citizens," he said indignantly. "He has stolen the veneration and obedience due our own ordained priesthood. Forty."

149

"Twenty, and we will take him with us when we leave."

The magistrate watched two more blows fall. "It is done," he said. "Release him."

The man wielding the stick cut the thongs that bound the old man to the post. The boy with the drum looked relieved. The crowd was disappointed, and there were some rumbles of discontent and some dark glances cast their way.

Shasha slid down from her horse and reached for her basket of herbs. The old man warded her off with one hand and took three trembling, determined steps forward to stand in front of Johanna. "I am chughi," he said in solemn if unpracticed Mandarin. "You have done me service."

Stooping, he touched one finger to a pile of dry cow dung, straightened, and reached up to touch that finger to Johanna's forehead. North Wind danced a little in place, his refined nostrils offended by the smell coming off the old man. Johanna soothed him with a pat and the old man repeated the procedure with Jaufre, Shasha and Félicien, and then, pressing his hands together beneath his chin, bowed to each in turn. "I thank you."

Johanna, repressing a strong urge to reach for the nearest water sack, bowed in return. "You are welcome, old man." She indicated an old scar on his left cheek. "I see you bear the mark of the Khan. For what were you imprisoned?"

The old man smiled faintly. "Practicing religion without a license."

Shasha snorted. Jaufre raised one eyebrow. "You seem to make a habit of that, old man," Johanna said. "If we lend you our countenance and company in the days ahead, would it be possible for you to confine your activities to reflection and meditation?" She glanced at the magistrate. "At least until we are out of reach of the long arm of Kashgari justice?"

The old man inclined his head without answering and with unusual tact Johanna forbore to press him for a more definite answer. His face was without color and his golden skin seemed painted on over his high brow and cheekbones. "Very well, old man, you are welcome in our company. Will you take supper with us?"

"At the Inn of the Green Dragon?"

"How did you know?"

The old man shrugged. "You are strangers looking for lodging. You spoke with the magistrate. The magistrate's mother-in-law's brother owns the Inn of the Green Dragon."

Johanna repressed a smile. It was what one expected, after all. She would go to the inn and pay for a night's lodging for the group and then spend that night in the caravansary with Wu Cheng as usual. "May one know your name, old man?"

The old man smiled for the first time. "Call me Hari," he said, and fainted at North Wind's feet.

Shasha knelt beside him, saying practically, "The best thing that could happen. Jaufre, open the basket and hand me the packet marked 'Alukrese.'" She rolled a large pinch of dried leaves between her palms and let them sift down over the old man's torn back. "That will stop the bleeding and keep the wounds free from infection. When we get to the caravansary I will give him ground willow bark for the pain and valerian to put him to sleep."

"Will he be ready to travel by the time we leave?"

Shasha shrugged. "Who can say? That one—" indicating the receding back of the magistrate "—would have him so, and unless we want a taste of the stick for ourselves, it would be wise if he were." She covered the old man's back with a clean cloth and bound it lightly. She sat back on her heels and looked up at Johanna. "Why are we rescuing him, by the way?"

Johanna contemplated the face lying at her breast, lines smoothed from his brow and the corners of his mouth in unconsciousness. He looked much younger asleep than he did awake. Certainly nowhere near a hundred and fifty years old. "I like his face."

Shasha looked at Jaufre and rolled her eyes again. Jaufre shrugged.

They bore the old man to the caravansary while Johanna went in search of the Inn of the Green Dragon. She handed over an exorbitant fee for rooms she had no intention of occupying, accepted a piece of undercooked naan that she threw to the dogs, and arrived at the caravansary at the same time as Uncle Cheng.

"Ho!" he said upon seeing her. "You have picked up another stray, I see."

"She makes a habit of picking up strays?" Félicien said.

Shasha and Jaufre looked at each other, and then looked at him.

"Oh," he said.

They woke the next morning to find the monk sitting before the uncurtained window of their common room, directly in the rays of the sun, with his feet crossed on his lap and his hands palm up on his knees. He was humming: a deep, not unpleasant sound like the buzzing of a safely distant hive of bees. "Brahman is. Brahman is the door. Om is the glory of Brahman."

He continued to hum as they moved around him, elongating the oms into drawn-out syllables that lasted the length of a breath, which for Hari was very long, the m's seeming to vibrate against the very walls of the room. All of them were Mongol enough, at least by association, to have respect for holy men no matter to which god they bowed their head. After all, if the god graced Hari with good fortune, he might have a little left over for them.

When they were ready to leave, the humming ceased. He opened his eyes and smiled at Shasha. "By the vision of Sankhya and the harmony of Yoga a man knows God, and when a man knows God he is free from all fetters. I thank you for your care of me, mistress. I have rested well, and I am ready to start." He looked at Johanna. "Where are we going?"

"West, old man, as far as we can go and not fall off the edge of the world," Johanna said. "But we do not go for a few days yet."

The old man considered this in silence. "It is my life's work," he said at last, "to seek out new places, and the people who live there, and discover how and to whom they give their faith."

"Are you on a pilgrimage, then, old man?" Jaufre said.

"A pilgrimage?" The monk savored the word. "I am a seeker after truth, young master, wherever I may find it."

"So long as you do not seek after trouble at the same time," Shasha said.

"Trouble, mistress?" The monk looked amazed, as if he were not the one sitting there with the marks of a severe beating all over his back.

"Not your best idea," Shasha told Johanna.

"We will bring food and water," Johanna told the old man. "For now, it would be best if you kept to this room. Eat, drink, rest, sleep. Heal. Be certain you wish to join with us. Our journey will not be a short or easy one."

"No worthwhile journey ever is," the monk said, and formed his thumbs and forefingers into circles, closed his eyes, and began again to om.

On the street Jaufre said, "I will meet you at Uncle Cheng's fire tonight."

Johanna and Shasha watched him walk down the bustling street and vanish from sight around a corner, and proceeded on their way without conversation. They both knew where he was going.

When the pearl trade had increased, their trips had taken them more often east than west, and trips to Kashgar had decreased to one every two or three years. But no matter how long the time between visits, Jaufre never failed to ask for news of his mother in the souks and slave markets of the town. There had never been any word.

The two women wandered the market with purpose, looking for old friends, introducing themselves to new ones. Yusuf the oil seller had died the previous year and had been succeeded by his son Malik, who was desolated to hear of Wu Li's death. Son and daughter shared a half hour of gentle reminiscence that made them both feel better over their losses.

Shasha found a buyer for their cinnamon but his price was not high enough. "We will do better to wait for Tabriz, or Gaza."

"Or even Venice," Johanna said.

"Indeed," Shasha said, her voice very dry.

The livestock pens were thin, the herds not yet down from the summer pastures, but horses there were in plenty, and Johanna passed the word that she might have a nag with enough breath in him to stagger around a racecourse, provided it was a short one. This challenge was accepted in much the spirit it was given, and before long in their perambulations through the city they began to hear the rumor of a horse race the following day, and of a challenger to perennial favorite Blue Sky come new out of the east, prepared to lay waste to all comers.

"A formidable foe, it would seem," Johanna said gravely the third time they heard this tale. "Has anyone seen this challenger?"

"Oh yes, miss." The fruit seller, who was probably a tout on the side on race days, was anxious to assure her, and himself of her future bet. "Black as the night and fleet as the shooting star across the skies. Blue Sky has met his match."

"That is fast indeed," Johanna said. "I should definitely place a bet, then."

"Indeed you should, young miss. The odds on Blue Sky—"

"Yes, but I think I shall put my money on this unknown, black, did you say? Someone should, don't you think? To encourage future challengers. Otherwise who will dare to race against the formidable Blue Sky?" She placed her bet, paid for their oranges and moved on.

That evening when they met at Uncle Cheng's fire, Johanna met Jaufre's eyes. He shook his head, once, and she dropped her own so he would not see the sympathy there. Jaufre didn't want sympathy, he wanted news of his mother, and his bleak expression was enough to tell her that none of the slave dealers in the city had been able or willing to oblige.

The next day North Wind raced, and won. Johanna collected her winnings from the fruit seller, who gave her a wounded look but nobly did not complain, at least not within her hearing.

Sheik Mohammed met her as she led North Wind to his picket. She felt Jaufre stiffen next to her, only to be waved off by the sheik. "I renew my offer to purchase your horse," he said. "Again, name your price."

"He is not for sale," Johanna said. She was growing a little weary of the sheik. "Not for any price."

The sheik regarded her, his face as immobile as ever. "I could take him from you."

She laughed, and stepped to one side. "By all means. Try."

The sheik hesitated, and stepped forward to lay a hand on North Wind's halter.

North Wind met his hand with his teeth, closing them around his wrist. His two guards came fully alert, and this time it was Jaufre's turn to wave them down. "Johanna," he said, resigned.

Johanna smacked her hand against North Wind's side, and the great white horse rolled an eye in her direction, seemed to conduct an inward debate, and then almost with a sigh released the sheik.

He examined his wrist. Apart from some slobber and the red indent of North Wind's excellent teeth, it was intact. "I would speak with you," he said to Jaufre.

"If it's about North Wind—"

"It is, but it is not a subject I may discuss with a woman."

Johanna, fitting a curry brush over her hand, raised a shoulder in answer to Jaufre's raised eyebrow.

Out of earshot the sheik said, "Will she allow North Wind to breed with one of my mares?"

Jaufre grinned. "For a fee, I'm sure she would."

In the end North Wind bred with three mares over their last three days in Kashgar, two gleaming equine Arabian princesses belonging to the sheik and a third older mare belonging to a Kashgari noble.

"Honorable niece," Uncle Cheng said over their last dinner together, "you know that that horse will be a lure to every thief and robber and brigand from here to Antioch."

"They might try to steal him, uncle," she said, scooping up two fingers full of a delicious lamb pilaf cooked with plums. She licked her fingers and smiled at Jaufre. "But North Wind has a mind of his own, and formidable defenses. Even if they could steal him, I doubt very much that they will be able to keep him."

A circle formed soon after that, and the singing began. Johanna fetched the Robe of a Thousand Larks, mended with invisible stitches by Shasha's patient hands, and sang when her turn came. Jaufre, a pleasant baritone, provided a solid base note and Shasha and even Uncle Cheng made a pleasing counterpoint hum. Félicien joined in on the last stanza and then took his own turn, beginning with a song about a large white horse with fleet hooves and a nasty disposition that had everyone roaring and joining in on the chorus.

The sheik was there, not singing, and the sheik's son, looking as if he wished he could. His eyes strayed rather too often in Johanna's direction for Jaufre's taste. Johanna saw neither of their glances. Shasha watched them both from the corner of her eye, and then Firas joined them and raised a surprising baritone in a warrior's song, all clashing swords and thumping shields and wives and children left behind. The chorus, booming, rhythmic, sounded like an army on the march.

They sang until the moon rose, bright enough to cast shadows on the rugs covering the sand of the caravansary. They sang as it set, the shadows elongating into weird shapes that seemed to move with a life of their own.

As she sang Johanna looked at the windows of the apartments that ringed the second floor. She had stayed in all of them at one time or another, her mother and father in the next room, Shasha always in the bedroll next to her, Jaufre across the door, his chosen spot wherever they stayed. Her heart ached in her breast and tears filled her eyes. She blinked them away and returned full-throated to the song, a tale of a housewife, a tinker and a wronged husband.

The moon set on one horizon as faint golden light grew on another. Groups began to say their goodbyes and retire to their rooms and their yurts. Uncle Cheng sent for his teapot and poured for them all. The dark, fragrant brew was smooth and satisfying on the tongue. "Enjoy it while you can," Uncle Cheng said. "They don't drink tea in the West."

"Then we will introduce it to them," the irrepressible Johanna said.

"And make a profit on it," Jaufre said, and surprised, Johanna laughed with him, invulnerable and immortal in their youth.

Uncle Cheng sighed to himself. "You will trade as you go?"

"Yes, uncle."

"You have the names?"

"Grigori in Kabul, Hasan in Tabriz, Fakhir in Antioch, Eneas in Alexandria, Soranzo in Gaza." She touched the leather purse at her waist, and returned a grin to Shasha's glare.

Uncle Cheng noted the byplay without comment. Wise old Uncle Cheng knew her well enough to harbor his own suspicions. "And you have enough funds to be going on with?"

"More than enough, uncle." She didn't reach for the hems of her robe and trousers, just. "Father provided for us well." This time she didn't look at Shasha.

"Good." Wu Cheng nodded. "Good. I have a few more names you may find useful." He smiled. "And a bale of green tea to comfort you on your journey, and—" he turned to beckon to a servant, who brought forward a large bundle "—these." He unwrapped the bundle to reveal coats of black Astrachan lamb, fully lined with raw silk and fastened with black shell buttons and a sash of black brocade. Each coat fit beautifully, obviously tailor-made on Uncle Cheng's instructions. "Uncle," Johanna said. "I don't know what to say."

Jaufre stood very straight, the coat fitting him like a second skin, the black of the curly astrakhan highlighting the blue of his eyes and the gold of his hair. "It is a gift worthy of a prince, uncle," he said.

Uncle Cheng waved off their thanks. "It was Wu Li's choice to venture not beyond Kashgar, but often have I crossed the Pamir, and always, always have I been colder than a widow's—"

Shasha cleared her throat.

"Well," Cheng said. "Very, very cold." He looked at each of them in turn. "It will not be an easy journey."

Johanna thought of Hari, the mad monk, who she fancied she could hear omming from their rooms. "No worthwhile journey ever is, uncle."

Uncle Cheng laughed and shook his head.

Firas, still sitting with them, cleared his throat. "Wu Cheng."

Something close to a wince crossed the older man's face, as if he thought he knew what was coming and didn't relish it. "Firas."

"It has been my great honor to serve you these past two years," Firas said.

Wu Cheng sighed. "And your service has been more than satisfactory, havildar."

Firas bent his head. "I thank you, Wu Cheng, for that testimonial." He turned to Johanna and Jaufre but seemed to be speaking to Shasha. "You have heard your uncle speak well of me. It is my wish to return to the West. I wonder if my company on the Road would be acceptable to you, so long as our paths lie together."

"Why?" Johanna said, blunt as ever.

"Perhaps I do not wish to leave a task half done," he said, with a slight bow in Jaufre's direction.

Johanna looked skeptical.

"Perhaps I have been long enough in the east, and wish to return to the land of my birth," he said.

"The Old Man is dead and his people are dispersed to the four corners of Persia," Jaufre said.

"And I am one of them," the havildar said without resentment.

Johanna and Jaufre exchanged a quick glance, and as one they looked to Shasha. "Shu Shao?" Jaufre said. "What is your opinion in this matter?"

Shasha took her time, regarding her loosely clasped hands. "Why," she said lightly, "that Firas of Alamut is a man of good reputation and equable temperament, and a capable havildar as vouched for by the honorable Wu Cheng and as witnessed by each of us these past ninety days, and should be a welcome addition to our party."

"I thank you, Shu Shao," Firas said.

"He has left me a capable second-in-command," Uncle Cheng said. "And truly, my children, I will feel easier in my mind with Firas as your guide. He is quite deadly with that blade, you know."

Jaufre knew, but Johanna was still unsatisfied, until she intercepted a look that the havildar, unaware that he was being observed, gave Shasha. "Is Firas in love with Shasha?" she whispered to Jaufre.

He looked startled. "I don't know. Why?"

"I saw him look at her."

"Oh well, that clinches it."

"Jaufre, I tell you, it was that kind of look!"

He gave her a look of his own, and leaned in close. "Are you quite sure you would recognize a look of that kind if you saw one?"

Her lips parted as she stared up at him, and he heard with satisfaction her breath catch in her throat.

Félicien struck a jubilant chord that startled everyone and said, "I myself am on a westward trajectory. Might I join you as well?"

This had not been so entirely unexpected. Jaufre smiled and Johanna grinned, and the sun tipped over the horizon, flooding the courtyard with light. Cattle lowed, camels groaned, and North Wind sent out an inquiring whinny that had Johanna on

159

her feet and running to him. She returned in time to see the brighter stars begin to fade from existence, as savory odors began drifting toward them from the cook fire. Outside the walls, they could hear the city of Kashgar coming slowly awake.

Uncle Cheng stirred. "I must tell you a story, before we part."

"Naturally," Shasha said, casting her eyes upward.

"Yes, yes, I know," Wu Cheng said with unusual asperity, "the fat old man blathering on yet again to no purpose." He glared at her, and then at Jaufre, who sat up straight and felt guilty, although he couldn't have said why.

"You are setting out on a wonderful adventure, agreed," Uncle Cheng said, turning to Johanna, and the reproof in his eyes stilled the indulgent smile on her lips. "Why shouldn't you? You're young, you have strong bodies and sound minds. Like many young people, you crave new experiences, excitement, adventure. Not for you a safe life at home, I understand that, and thanks to Wu Li's fine example you are well versed in matters of trade. I have no fear that you will go hungry, no matter how far you travel or where your journey ends." He brooded for a moment.

"But I would tell you a story nonetheless. A cautionary tale, so that you do not go heedless into the west." He smoothed his palms over his trousers. "This story I heard long since, of a man and a time even longer past. He lived in Alexandria, oh, five hundred years ago and more. He was Muslim, and his name was Cosmas."

Jaufre leaned back against a saddle and Johanna, without thinking, leaned against him in the way she always had.

"It is said that this Cosmas constructed a model of the earth, in the shape of a large, rectangular box with a high, curved lid. The lid represented heaven, and as man would look down on it, so would God look down on his work. Do you see it?"

"I see it, uncle."

"Inside the chest there was a great mountain, and around this mountain moved the sun. Because the mountain was uneven

160

in size and shape, the rays of the sun shining down upon the earth shifted as the sun moved, making the days and the seasons unequal in length."

"Was heaven in the box?"

"There was Paradise," Uncle Cheng said. "From Paradise flowed four great rivers, the Indus into India, the Nile through Egypt, the Tigris and Euphrates to Mesopotamia. There were four peoples in Cosmas' world, the Scythians in the north, the Indians in the East, the Ethiops in the south, and the Celts in the west."

Johanna waited. When Cheng said no more, she said, "But where was Everything Under the Heavens?"

Wu Cheng looked at her, his expression sober. "It wasn't in the chest."

Johanna sat up. "Not in the box? Why not?"

"I don't know why not."

Johanna was unbelieving. "Was this Cosmas unaware of the existence of Everything Under the Heavens?"

Wu Cheng considered. "He may have been. He may also have been ignoring it, deliberately so."

"But how can this be?" Johanna said. "One cannot ignore Everything Under the Heavens. It just…is. Everything Under the Heavens, is, well, Everything Under the Heavens."

"Not everything," Cheng said. "Not even most."

Johanna didn't understand him, and didn't understand Cosmas, either, for that matter. "And to make the earth a box when everyone knows it is a ball? This is nonsense, Uncle."

"It is," Cheng agreed. "And then it isn't."

She looked at him accusingly. "You're as bad as Shasha, uncle."

"I am wounded that you would say so," he said gravely.

Shasha snorted.

"Johanna." The serious note in Wu Cheng's voice caused Johanna's smile to fade. He looked stern, even a little harsh. "Jaufre, yes, even you, Shasha, listen to me. If the Celts and the

Scythians and the Indians and the Ethiops think they share the whole world between them, and if they have thought that for five hundred years, and if for that long they have ignored the existence of Everything Under the Heavens..."

"Then," Jaufre said, "they will not wish to hear of the power and the greatness that we have left behind."

"No. They are also very jealous of their gods. You would do well to adopt, outwardly at least, whatever faith rules wherever you are."

Johanna thought of Hari, the monk at present eating their food and sleeping in a bed they had provided him, enjoying a freedom purchased by them. She had been ready to leave Everything Under the Heavens since she was old enough to walk, but for the first time she began to realize the dangers of doing so.

"Have you given any thought to where you will go?" Uncle Cheng said. "Other than simply west. Baghdad and Hormuz are not what they once were. Tabriz, perhaps?"

Johanna, Jaufre and Shasha exchanged glances. Jaufre would have said, Anywhere I might find word of my mother. Shasha would have said, As far away from the fell hand of the Widow Wu as possible. Johanna said, "Tabriz, certainly. Wu Li said my grandfather called Tabriz a crossroads of commerce. Then Gaza, perhaps. From Gaza we could take ship to Venice."

"You don't want to stop in Byzantium?" Jaufre said.

"Most of what was worth seeing in Byzantium," Uncle Cheng said, "is now in Venice."

14

Kashgar and the Pamir

"KERMAN?" HARI REPEATED. "In Kerman, unless the merchants be well armed they run the risk of being murdered, or at least robbed."

"Have you been there, old man?" Jaufre said.

The monk shook his head. "I have not, master. But I have traveled the road from India, and I have heard this said of Kerman many times. And before Kerman," he said dreamily, "I have heard of the plain of Pamir—so lofty and cold that you do not often see birds fly. Because of this great cold, fire does not burn so brightly, nor give out so much heat as usual, nor does it cook food so efficiently."

"Are you sure you want to come with us?" Shasha said pointedly.

He smiled at her. "Of course. Let us follow the chariot of Arjuna, whose wheels are right effort and whose driver is truth. Thus shall we all come to the land which is free from fear."

"Kerman, then," Jaufre said, bringing them back to the point. "The carpets there are said to be very fine."

"And Tabriz afterward," Shasha said.

"And then Gaza," Johanna said, and gave an impish smile. "And anything in between that looks interesting."

Firas and Félicien were interested auditors but contributed no opinions.

"Johanna?"

Johanna looked up to see Fatima standing in the doorway, an even more joyous smile than usual on her face. "Azar is here."

A slim young man in pants and tunic with a dark blue cheche wrapped about his head stood next to her, a shy smile on his face. He was older and taller than when they had seen him last, but then they all were, and they had no trouble recognizing her betrothed.

"Azar!" Jaufre leaped to his feet and they clasped hands warmly. Shasha pushed him to one side and took Azar by his shoulders. "You look well," she said, and gave him a gentle shake. She was displaced in turn by Johanna, who gave him a hearty embrace. He colored slightly, but he was definitely pleased to see them.

"We are coming with you to Kerman!" Fatima said.

Johanna was startled. "We only just decided we were going there."

Fatima gave that remark the back of her hand. "Father has heard of a new kind of grain available in the west, one that in the right climate can bear twice in the same season."

"Has Ahmed the baker become a grain merchant, then?"

"Who cares, so long as our time together is not yet done? Although—" Fatima managed to assume a stern expression "—we are not pitching our yurt anywhere near yours again. I tremble to think what would happen the next time you called on the North Wind for aid."

The four of them laughed.

Uncle Cheng had arranged for them to join a caravan headed for Kerman by way of Talikan, where they would trade for almonds and pistachios but mostly for salt. "It is said there are mountains of it," Jaufre said.

"What's so special about this particular salt?" Johanna said.

"It is said to be washed in the azure waves of the Gulf of Persia, and harvested by virgins at the dark of the moon."

Johanna raised an eyebrow. "Hard on the feet, stumbling around all those rock pools at night."

"Also said to be flavored with the blood of said virgins," Jaufre said, inspired.

"Oh, well, we should definitely buy some, then."

Besides the camels they had eight horses, one and a spare for each of them, and Félicien's donkey. Hari, too, had insisted on a donkey, purchased in Kashgar.

Sheik Mohammed and his son were also traveling west. The sheik told Jaufre they were returning to their home near Talikan, and offered escort, for a price.

He also renewed his offer to buy North Wind. Eventually he and Jaufre concluded terms for their journey that did not include the stallion, and when they emerged from the tent the old sheik further irritated Johanna by patting her cheek and saying approvingly to Jaufre, "Skin as smooth as mare's milk, my friend, and I have never seen such eyes, like the sky at sunrise. You should make your woman wear a veil, lest she tempt mens' thoughts into covetousness."

Jaufre smiled and bent his head without replying, and hoped he was going to survive the night, never mind the journey. Straightening, he saw the sheik's son's eyes drawn irresistibly to Johanna.

The old man was in love with the horse. The young man was in love with its rider. Jaufre squared his shoulders, feeling the reassuring weight of his father's sword against his back. Neither man would achieve his heart's desire on this trip.

They left Kashgar the next morning, since the heat of the day was easing as the year made its way toward fall. Uncle Cheng saw them off, tears unashamedly streaming down his cheeks. Johanna was the last of his family left to him. At the last moment, Johanna, similarly affected, said urgently, "Come with us, uncle!" She burrowed into his arms, her voice muffled against his tunic. "Who knows what wonders we shall find, far in the west! Come see them with us!"

He wiped his tears on his sleeve and patted her back before pushing her back. "I don't deny that it is tempting, Johanna, but I have merchants expecting cargo in Chang'an. Still, who knows? One day, perhaps, I shall follow."

With that Johanna had to be content. She mounted North Wind and kicked him into a gallop to catch up with her friends, where she reined in and stood in her stirrups to turn and look back for the last time. The large man in the sand-colored robes standing outside the great Kashgar gate raised his arms high above his head. She raised both of hers in return and cried out, something inarticulate, encompassing love, and loss, and farewell.

And then she faced west and nudged North Wind into motion again.

The white bulk of the Pamirs stood blunt and proud against the deep blue sky, on their left as they began to climb up. The way was all ridges and valleys and passes. The narrow trail was beaten down by hundreds of years of travelers' feet but no smoother for that. Rocks rattled down from the hills above, evergreen branches scraped their heads, and in places the trail fell abruptly to the bottoms of distant canyons where the way narrowed to a strip of ground barely wide enough for a camel to pass. Jaufre hooked the lead camel to Hari's donkey and let the sure-footed little beast lead the way. Hari walked behind, omming. He never seemed to be out of breath like the rest of them.

"Straight to heaven," Johanna said, panting.

"How long before we get to the top?" Shasha said.

Johanna touched the purse at her waist. "Father says forty days to the plain."

"Forty days!" It was only their third, and the path before them wound ever upward.

The people who lived between the ridges and in the valleys were few and secretive, and seen only in glimpses. They looked to be hunters, as they were dressed in skins. As the travelers soon found, if they did not mount a constant watch the mountain people were also expert thieves. Exhausted as they were at the end of each day, it was an additional hardship, to be always alert for theft.

When they met oncoming travelers, it was a mad, confused crush of swearing men and animals, jostling for place on the trail (no one wanted the outside edge if they were currently traversing a precipice, which they only too often were) and trying to avoid steaming piles of dung excreted by camels and horses and donkeys choosing to exercise their displeasure by the only means possible to them. There were no caravansaries along this stretch of the Road, and campsites were few, small and mean, lacking in fuel and often in water, which caused them to make camp earlier some evenings so that they could send out scouts to find the nearest stream. If another caravan was there before them, they slept between rocks and under trees at the nearly vertical sides of the trail, everyone out of sorts the next day from having spent the entire night trying not to slip down into whatever abyss they were camping next to. Arguments over who had laid claim to what campsite for the evening increased with altitude, and only Firas' calm, authoritative manner averted some outright clashes.

"I'm glad we brought him," Johanna said, when they were first into the next campsite that evening.

"Me, too," Jaufre said.

Johanna looked at Shasha. "Are you glad we brought him, Shasha?"

Shasha said nothing, but the next time her camel was in reach he took a nip at Johanna's knee.

There was none of the camaraderie that had existed on the crossing of the vast, flat plain they had left so far behind them. There was no singing around the campfire in the evening, as there wasn't much of a campfire and no one had any breath to sing with anyway. There was not even the comfort of light, as the twisting trail, the overhanging bluffs and the narrow valleys cut off the most wayward rays of the sun during the day, and hid the stars at night.

"No wonder Yusuf the Levantine charged so much for his olive oil," Johanna said one afternoon, toiling ever and ever upward. Like Jaufre and Shasha, she had donned her astrakhan coat very soon after they had begun to climb. She sweated beneath it as the trail rose, but if she took it off the sweat froze to her skin.

Félicien blew loudly into a large and filthy handkerchief. "I came by the northern way when I went first to Khuree. It was much easier."

They all wished he hadn't said that.

"We climb to the seat of heaven itself," Hari said, face raised beatifically to the sky.

Firas, like Hari, seemed impervious to heat and cold alike.

Thirty days into their climb, water would not boil, and even if it would you could stick your finger in it and not be burned. Game thinned out and the birds vanished altogether. They subsisted on dried fruit and nuts, and unleavened bread made from grain they carried with them, when they could find enough water to spare from filling their water sacks. They went thirsty before the livestock did.

Johanna kept North Wind behind her on the trail and picketed near them every night. He was better than a muezzin at sounding the call if someone smelling unfamiliar approached their camp, but she noticed that he ate less than he was used to, and drank every bucket of water dry.

They were all drinking as much water as they could find. It never seemed enough. One morning Johanna noticed that the others' voices were beginning to sound high and thin and somehow from a distance, even if they were standing right in front of her. Wu Li had written of this phenomenon in his book, but it was one thing to read of it happening to other people, and another thing – and very disconcerting – to experience in person.

Then, one day, she looked off the trail and beheld a sheep such as she had never seen before. He was very fat and bore a pair of enormous, curling horns that she recognized as the precursors of bowls she had seen in Kashgar. He baa'ed at her and bounded away, but they saw more and more of them as they climbed higher. That night they dined on fresh meat for the first time since they entered the mountains. Later that evening they also paid an extortionate amount to the herder to whom the sheep had belonged, who appeared, indignant and wrathful, at the very moment they were cracking the last of the bones for the marrow.

"Excellent timing," Jaufre murmured, and Johanna noticed he added a little to the requested sum. He saw her looking and grinned. "I admire professionalism in any endeavor."

And then the next morning Johanna woke to light, or at least more light than she had become accustomed to over the past month. The trail had begun to level out, and the tall evergreens gave reluctant way to dells of greensward, and then to pasture. They were able to ride again, and Jaufre unhitched Hari's donkey from the lead camel and Hari rode once more with his face upturned to the sun.

"Is this heaven, old man?" Jaufre said.

He smiled without opening his eyes. "It is very nearly nirvana itself, young master," proving that even holy men were subject to the ill humors of the trail.

Spirits rose up and down the line of camels, and soon Félicien had his lute out and was singing a bawdy song about a brute of a husband with a beautiful young wife and a handsome young lover, and the old hag down the village who spoiled everyone's fun. He sang it a second time in Mongol and a third time in Persian, and again in Frankish. He was out of breath and his voice didn't reach far but by the end they could hear snatches of chorus coming at them from up and down the line of camels.

Finally there came one evening when they camped at the edge of a fine, blessedly level pastureland that seemed to extend beyond the horizon, the rough trails and mountain ridges and the dark claustrophobia of the encroaching evergreens only a threatening green wall at their back. Tall mountains lined the horizon on every side with sharp, menacing peaks clad in white, but next to their campsite there was a clear lake fed by a bubbling stream, and even the fact that their fires burned small and sullen and threw off no heat whatsoever was not enough to stem the party's returning vitality. They had fresh meat again that night, and were ready when the sheep's owner materialized very nearly right out of the grass at their feet, rending his beard and crying out for redress. He got it, and a mug of lukewarm tea well sweetened with honey to send him on his way rejoicing.

Fatima and Azar joined them at their fire, Azar bringing his tambour and Fatima her finger cymbals. No one was in very good voice but they could gasp out the lyrics. It was sort of like poetry, Shasha said later, if poetry was chanted out to the rhythm of a drum and the clash of cymbals.

The sheik and his son joined them, too, solemn but attentive, light from the diminutive fire casting long shadows on their faces. A waxing moon rose above the horizon. Fatima and Azar disappeared arm in arm, whispering and giggling. Firas sat next to Shasha, dignified and silent, while she mended a large tear in one of Jaufre's tunics by the dim light of the campfire.

The sheik stirred. "Jaufre of Cambaluc, I would renew my offer to buy your horse."

"You do me too much honor, Sheik Mohammed," Jaufre said. "I am desolated to have to repeat my refusal."

From his picket nearby, North Wind whickered.

"Five thousand bezants," the sheik said, which was quite an advance on his last offer, and had the added advantage of being currency they wouldn't have to change when they arrived at last at the shores of the Middle Sea. They could tell by his expression he didn't see how they could refuse it.

Firas bent forward to look around Shasha, courteous and perfectly polite. "I believe you heard the young sir's answer, effendi."

The sheik was silenced, and seemed to sigh. He said something to his son in a low voice none of them caught and rose to his feet. "Then I must bid you goodnight." He sketched a small nod that was almost a bow in their general direction, and strode off.

With his elaborate headdress and his sweeping skirts, he always looked like he was leading a parade.

His son paused for a moment, his eyes on Johanna, as happened far too often for Jaufre's taste, and for Shasha's too, for that matter. "You will not reconsider?"

"I cannot, even if I would, sir," Johanna said, patiently for her. "If I sold him to your father I would be cheating him, because North Wind will not stay where I am not."

His dark eyes held hers for a long moment. "It is as you wish," he said, and turned to follow his father.

"It is as it is," Johanna said. "They'll have two foals out of the Wind, why do they keep asking for him as well?"

"Who wouldn't?" Félicien said cheerfully, and got to his feet. "I'm for bed. How long to cross this plateau, Johanna?"

"Twelve days, my father said," Johanna said.

"A quarter the distance, and it's flat," the goliard said with immense satisfaction.

Jaufre was still staring at the place where the sheik had sat. Johanna nudged him. "What is it?"

"I don't like his insistence on buying North Wind," he said, his mouth a hard line.

"He is very persistent," Johanna said, stretching her arms and yawning.

"It's more than that," Jaufre said.

Unexpectedly, Firas said, "I agree with you, young sir. We should keep a close watch on the horse."

Johanna laughed in mid-yawn. "I'd pay good money for a chance to watch someone try to steal North Wind."

She got up. Shasha assembled her mending and rose to her feet. "I, too, am uneasy," she said.

Firas looked at Jaufre. "You take the first watch, and then wake me."

Jaufre nodded.

"Thank you both for taking such good care of my horse," Johanna said with a mock bow. "Whether he needs it or not."

15

The Pamir and Terak Pass

AFTER SO LONG toiling up and up and farther up again, the rolling grassland was a positive luxury. The season was well into fall but the weather held and sunny day succeeded sunny day, although the sky seemed oddly leeched of color. There was fodder to spare for the pack and the riding animals, and plenty of water from snow trickling down from the high mountains, which reared up, jagged and forbidding, all around them.

"The roof of the world," Johanna said.

Jaufre, a practical man, stretched his hand up as if to touch it. "It's as if we are traveling beneath a clear dome."

They moved quickly now, all alone on this vast expanse of tall grasses, for it was late for them to be making this journey. They knew they were one good storm away from wading through snow piled as high as a camel's hump, and there was still a steep trail to descend on the other side of the high plain before they reached an altitude where the wind did not bite into one like a sharp knife.

By using every moment of daylight available to them, they made the top of the pass just after dark on the eleventh day, and everyone was too tired to do much more than wash down a handful of dried fruits and nuts and roll themselves into their blankets. They didn't even bother pitching the yurts, sleeping instead beneath that pale, open sky.

Sometime before dawn something woke Jaufre. The camp was silent but for the occasional grunts and groans of the livestock. There was no smell of woodsmoke so he was awake even before the cooks. Wide awake, and fully alert. Tense, even, although he could not immediately identify any reason why.

He raised his head. Johanna, Shasha, Félicien and Hari were all sleeping quietly.

Firas was missing, his bedroll tossed to one side, barely visible in the bleached light only now beginning to illuminate the eastern horizon.

Moving quietly, Jaufre got to his feet. He felt for his father's sword and strapped it to his back. He walked a short distance away to relieve himself, washed his face and hands in a pool of water just beginning to form a skin of ice, and went to check on North Wind. The great white beast was sleeping, strapped in a thick felt blanket. Jaufre felt a smile tug at the corners of his mouth. As tired as she must have been last night, Johanna had still first attended to North Wind. He ran his hand down North Wind's neck, and noticed that the big horse had lost some weight during their journey up and over the Roof of the World. The sooner they got back to sea level and a more civilized speed of travel, the better for them all. Jaufre was looking forward to the baths in Kerman.

There was a whisper of sound and something struck the back of his head very hard. The last thing he heard was an outraged whinny from North Wind.

He woke for the second time that morning from a ferocious headache that seemed to center right in the middle of his forehead. He blinked dazedly at the sky.

"Jaufre?" Shasha's voice was welcome but very loud. He winced.

"Can you sit up?"

He didn't know if he could. Hands tugged at him. Oh well, if he must. He sat up and vomited immediately, although there was very little in his stomach given that he had not broken his fast that morning. "What happened?" he said, blinking. Shasha's face blurred into two Shashas and then one again.

"Can you stand?"

He thought about it while listening to try to see what was going on beyond his currently lamentable range of vision. "If I have help."

She took one arm and someone else took his other arm. He recognized him. Félicien. Good. He was on his feet again. Also good, although his balance seemed to be questioning the vertical in a way it never had before. "Where is Firas?"

"I don't know."

"What's happening?"

"Look."

"What?"

Shasha's voice had never sounded so grim. "Look."

He blinked again. His vision cleared finally. He immediately wished it hadn't.

There was a hand, an arm, a leg, neatly severed from their bodies. He heard cries, cut off abruptly. Hard-faced men with bloodied swords stood in a circle around a group of people. He recognized Fatima's voice. She was screaming out Azar's name.

In the center of the circle Johanna stood alone, facing Gokudo. In one hand he held his naginata. He had Jaufre's father's sword strapped to his back and Johanna's purse now fastened to his belt. "As we agreed," he said to the sheik. "The horse is yours. The girl is mine," He grabbed Johanna's arm.

"No, she is not!" she said, and yanked free.

He grabbed her again and this time she screamed as loudly as she could. "North Wind! To me! North Wind!"

North Wind answered her loudly and there was the sound of trampling hooves and men's curses, but the sheik had evidently enough men to restrain even North Wind.

The sheik's son said, "Father."

The sheik made a motion with his hand. "A bargain is a bargain, my son." His son was silenced. His eyes met Jaufre's.

You die first, Jaufre thought.

Farhad reddened and dropped his eyes.

Gokudo began to drag Johanna away; a mistake, because she got her feet under her and tripped him. He almost fell and she was three steps away and moving fast when he caught her again. She fastened her teeth in his arm, and he gasped involuntarily. His face congested with fury and he hit her, brutally hard, knocking her teeth loose from his arm. She took immediate advantage of her mouth being free again. "North Wind! North Wind! To me!"

There was the sound of hooves striking and a man cried out in pain. This time North Wind sounded enraged. Come on, boy, Jaufre thought. He took a step forward, only to feel something sharp prod his back. He looked around and saw a hard-faced man with a grin on his face, holding a spear.

They were all of them being held at spear point, he realized. Shasha's face was twisted into a snarl and she looked coiled, ready to spring. Félicien was white to his hairline. He couldn't see Fatima or Azar or Malala or Ahmed, although a woman was sobbing somewhere nearby who sounded like Fatima. Hari was sitting on the ground with his legs crossed and his feet on his knees, eyes closed, omming, which Jaufre did not find useful. He heard Gokudo curse and looked around to see that Johanna had tried to trip him again, crying out, "North Wind! North Wind!"

This time Gokudo lifted her off her feet and carried her to his horse, to which a second horse was tethered. He threw Johanna up on the second horse and tied her hands to the pommel and her feet beneath its belly. She immediately kicked it in the belly so that it reared and plunged, the hooves narrowly missing Gokudo.

"Johanna!" Jaufre said. He would have gone to her, nothing would have stopped him, but he was seized from behind with arms like iron. "No, young sir, wait," a voice whispered in his ear. "Wait."

The man with the spear was laying on the ground, his blood spilling from a wide cut on his throat. So, Jaufre realized, were all of their guards. It had happened so fast and so quietly that, incredibly, no one seemed to have noticed what was happening behind them, their attention fixed as it was on the drama playing out in front of them. He looked at Firas, bloody scimitar in his hand, and found himself unable to utter a word.

Firas gave an approving nod and held up his hand, palm out. "Wait, young sir," he said in a low voice. "Wait."

Gokudo seized the reins of Johanna's horse and dragged him down with an iron hand and struck her again. Blood spurted and this time Jaufre could not help himself. "Johanna!"

Gokudo looked around and grinned. "Ah, young Jaufre. How nice that you woke up from your nap in time for me to say goodbye." He looked from Jaufre to Johanna and back again. "A little bruised but she will warm my bed nicely between here and Cambaluc." The grin widened. "You must know that Wu Li's widow has placed no conditions on her return to Everything Under the Heavens, other than that she be breathing."

Jaufre lunged forward and was restrained by hands like iron. Firas again, although Gokudo, flush with his triumph, perhaps also in anticipation of the joys of the night to come, didn't notice who was holding Jaufre back. The crowd had stepped forward over the slain mercenaries and had packed itself densely around Gokudo and Johanna and around Jaufre and Firas, occluding Gokudo's view and hampering his actions. Later Jaufre would realize they had done this deliberately: put themselves at risk out of respect for Wu Li and affection for Wu Li's daughter and foster son.

"Wait, young sir!" Firas' voice said in his ear. "Wait."

"Wait for what?" But something in Firas' voice made him stop struggling.

"Look," Firas said, a hand pointing over Jaufre's shoulder.

Jaufre followed the direction of that pointing finger, past the suddenly still form of the samurai, yet to climb on his horse, past the faces of the sheik and his son who looked as if all at once they felt less in control of the situation, past the hard-faced men with swords who were hastily cleaning them and putting them back in their scabbards, as if to show they had never drawn them in the first place, the various body parts scattered around them to the contrary. Some of them began to melt back into the crowd of caravaners, and shortly thereafter was heard the sound of galloping hooves.

"Look, young sir." Firas' voice was quietly insistent. Jaufre looked, and looked again, and then he didn't need Shasha's sharp indrawn breath to tell him his eyes were not deceiving him.

They had thought Uncle Wu Cheng's caravan was large, and so it had been. A thousand camels was a lot of camels, and the people necessary to feed and care for them and to pack them and drive them amounted to a respectably-sized town.

What was coming at them from over the eastern horizon was something else again.

It was a veritable wave of men on horseback, hundreds of them, thousands of them. The black wave filled the horizon from end to end, rank after rank after rank of them, holding their mounts to a disciplined trot, the silver ornaments on their saddles blindingly bright in the rays of the rising sun. As they came closer Jaufre could see that they wore leather coats wrapped and tied with sashes, calf-high leather boots, and helmets with horse-tail plumes. Each carried a bow and a quiver filled with arrows with different heads, and wore knives and swords thrust into their sashes.

On they came, and onward, never breaking stride, and the sound of that many hooves was the sound of approaching thunder. A black banner snapped over a man who rode a little in front of the rest of them.

Gokudo shouted and Jaufre looked around to see that Johanna had pulled her mount free of Gokudo's grip and was galloping toward the oncoming army. She shouted but she was too far away for them to hear her words.

"She has courage, the young miss," Firas said approvingly.

"What is she doing!" Félicien said. "Has she completely lost her mind?"

Shasha looked up at Jaufre. "Do you think—"

"Maybe," he said, his eyes straining to see the features of the leader, coming toward them at what felt at the time like an agonizingly slow trot.

He was so intent on the far prospect that he neglected the near, and jumped a little when Firas appeared in front of him. He had Jaufre's sword in one hand and Johanna's purse in the other. Numbly, Jaufre accepted the sword, and with a bow Firas offered the purse to Shasha, who accepted it with a long look that even Jaufre in this fraught moment could see promised a later reward.

He removed his sword from its worn leather sheath to see if it had come to any harm. It had not, and he slid it home again. No blood stained its blade, and he knew a burning shame that he had been taken prisoner without so much as raising a hand, let alone his sword, in his own or anyone else's defense.

He looked toward Gokudo, expecting to see his body laid out on the ground like the spearmen who had held them hostage but it was impossible to see over the heads of the crowd that had now surged forward.

He looked at Firas and found Shasha binding his arm. "Did you kill him?"

"Not quite," Firas said. "May I suggest, young sir, that you find North Wind and soothe him as much as you are able?" He nodded at the oncoming horde. "We do not want him to discourage any attempts at friendship the young miss might be making."

Johanna was reining in next to the man who appeared to be leading the army on horseback. He halted, and they seemed to be speaking. After a few minutes he pulled the knife from his belt and Jaufre froze, his heart thudding dully in his ears.

The sun flashed on the blade of the knife as it moved in one swift, clean gesture. Johanna's bonds fell and her hands were free. Jaufre breathed again. Johanna turned her horse and kicked it into a trot to match the leader's, and Jaufre went to look for North Wind.

He found the stallion restrained with a rope around his neck and another around each foot. Someone had even managed to loop one around his tail. Not that it had appeared to have helped them restrain the stallion. Two men were laying on the ground, one silent, one moaning in pain. Four men held tightly onto the remaining ropes as if terrified of what would happen if they let them go. They were right to do so, as North Wind's fury was incandescent. His ears flat, his teeth bared, with every plunge he jerked harder on the ropes holding him. As Jaufre came up he yanked one of the four off his feet, although the man scrambled up again immediately and scuttled out of the way of those deadly hooves. He would be free in the next moment and on a rampage that saw no difference between friend and foe.

"North Wind," Jaufre said in a loud voice.

The horse ignored him and plunged again. The end of the rope around his neck was tangled in his forefeet, and he was bleeding from where the ropes had scraped all four hocks. "North Wind," Jaufre said again, and in what was probably the bravest act of his life to date walked steadily forward, a hand raised, palm out. "North Wind," he said in Mandarin, knowing that the words were unimportant, that the tone was all, "North Wind, Johanna is all right. I will take you to her. North Wind, settle down, settle down now. Calm yourself, calm down, calm down now."

The ears stayed flat and the teeth bared but at least the stallion stopped plunging. Jaufre caught the eyes of the man North Wind had dumped on his back and gave a tiny jerk of his head, still talking to the horse. The man looked as if he might burst into tears of gratitude, and signaled to the other three men to follow his lead. He must have known something about horses in general for he did not just drop the rope: he laid it down slowly, and then backed up one step at a time. He was followed in lock step by the other three, and when they'd reached a safe distance they turned and ran. Wise of them. North Wind never forgot a smell, and when Johanna saw the state of his legs, the men would be in mortal danger from both of them.

Jaufre kept North Wind's attention on him. "North Wind, North Wind, North Wind, that's my boy, that's my good boy, be calm now, be quiet now, North Wind."

One ear came forward. Another. North Wind whickered and stretched out his nose to that familiar voice, and by the grace of the chariot of Arjuna, whose wheels are right effort and whose driver is truth, Jaufre had a bit of sugar in his pocket. He held it out in his left hand, just in case North Wind tried to take it off at the wrist, but the horse dropped his head and nuzzled his palm.

By the time he had calmed North Wind, Johanna came trotting up alongside the Mongol baron. Her hands and feet had been cut free and she had wiped the blood from her face, although bruises were already forming. Evidently her jaw wasn't broken because she was chatting as freely with the baron as she would have with Yusuf the Levantine over a particularly good press of olive oil.

Gokudo was still missing. Those men of Gokudo's still standing had been melting backwards even as the Mongol soldiers approached. The Mongol army took no notice, at least not yet. Everyone else stood stock still, watching Johanna approach at the head of an army with varying degrees of stupefaction.

"Jaufre, Shasha!" Johanna said. "Do you remember Baron Ogodei?"

"I would say I did regardless," Shasha said in a murmur, and raised her voice. "Of course! My lord Ogodei, very well met!"

"Lord Ogodei," Jaufre said, bowing. "It is an honor to meet you again."

"Hah! Not only the honorable Wu Li's daughter, but the honorable Wu Li's adopted son and the honorable Wu Li's adopted sister-in-law." He smiled benignly upon them. "Well met indeed. I had not looked to find such pleasant companionship on the Road this day." His eyes traveled across the assembled company, which now included everyone from the lowliest cook and camel driver to the sheik and his son, immobile in their voluminous white robes. As the baron's eyes fell upon them they seemed to recall themselves and immediately saluted him, touching their right hands to heart, lips and head.

He nodded and dismounted, revealing himself to be Shasha's height but twice as wide. His face was round and flat, his black eyes slanted up at the corners, and his skin was the gold of old coins. He was beardless but for two long mustaches trailing down to his chest, like those of Uncle Cheng. He looked to have spent every one of his thirty years in the saddle, bow and sword in hand, which indeed he had and which in part accounted for his rapid ascension up the ranks of the Mongol army.

Johanna brought her leg over the pommel and slid down into Jaufre's arms. For just a moment she leaned against him, and he thought he felt a fine tremble go through her body, but she straightened at once and went around her horse's head to the baron.

"I claim the Khan's justice, Ogodei of the Mongols."

He seemed to sigh. "Of course, Wu Li's daughter. Make camp," he said to his aide, who seemed a little bemused, probably at his commander taking what amounted to orders from a sixteen-year old girl. And not even a Mongol girl, at that.

Johanna turned to Jaufre, her face sharp with anxiety. "North Wind?"

"He's fine."

She looked around. "Where is Gokudo?" She saw Jaufre's sword. "Did you kill him?"

"Firas fought with him," Jaufre said. "He got my sword and your purse back, but he was wounded. Gokudo got away."

"He can't have gotten very far away," she said fiercely, and whirled back to Ogodei. While they had been talking, his horse had been led away, a yurt had appeared as if by magic, and a carpet had been laid before its entrance. Pillows and more carpets had been piled into a comfortable couch on the carpet, and thereon Ogodei took his seat. Someone hurried up with a tray holding a pitcher and a cup. Ogodei poured the cup full and drank it off. "Now, where is this villain for which you seek the swift and sure justice of the Great Khan, young Johanna?"

Johanna bowed. "He seems to have vanished, lord." Her tone of voice indicated her disbelief that Gokudo had done any such thing.

"Has he." Ogodei's eyes ran over the assembled crowd. "Has he, indeed." He raised his voice. "Who here knows the whereabouts of the Nippon mercenary who so cravenly attacked this caravan?"

"Is there a reward?" someone shouted, and someone else laughed.

Ogodei did not laugh. "There is death," he said mildly, "for anyone who aided his escape."

The caravaners, in a mood to celebrate their own escape from robbery, rape and murder, sobered at his words. Into this silence Fatima pushed forward to Johanna's side, her face tearstained, and said, "I add my demand for the Khan's justice against this man. He killed my affianced husband."

"Fatima!" Johanna cried. "Azar? Dead?"

A cold hand clutched hers. "Do not be kind, Johanna. I could not bear it."

The sheik, silent in the front row of the crowd, stirred and moved forward, in spite of the protests murmured by his son. He arrayed himself before Ogodei and bowed low. "I am the Sheik Mohammed, of Talikan. It may be that I have information useful to you." He waited.

"It may be that you do," Ogodei said, when it became evident the sheik had finished speaking. "I will not know how useful until you tell me what it is."

"It seems to me to be very valuable information," the sheik said.

Ogodei almost smiled, and did shake his head. "You Persians," he said. "You always have to bargain." His eyes narrowed and he leaned forward. "Mongols don't bargain. We take. We take? And you die." He let that sink in for a moment, and then leaned back. "You give? And you live." He waved a negligent hand. "Possibly."

The sheik was as cool as a lake on a calm spring morning, although people near him began sidling away. No one who had ever lived for an hour beneath Mongol rule doubted Ogodei's plain statement was anything other than simple fact.

Ogodei waited without impatience, until the sheik bowed his head, indicating an obeisance to a superior force, and gave a wave of his hand. His son vanished into the crowd, to return some minutes later with Gokudo, bound and under guard.

Johanna stepped forward. "This, lord, is the man who stole my horse and who tried to kidnap me."

Fatima pointed in turn. "This is the man who killed Azar of Kashgar, son of Kalal."

Displaying a fine sense of the dramatic, Firas came up leading North Wind, although the instant North Wind scented Johanna he shouldered Firas to one side and headed straight for her, people moving hastily out of his way. He sniffed her all over once, and then again, just to make sure, after which he threw back his head and whinnied a challenge to anyone who thought they could mishandle him so rudely and get away with it. Prudently, no one took him up on it.

"We have traveled these five days almost without stopping," the baron said, still mild. "We will join you here in your camp and refresh ourselves. While we rest," he said, looking at Johanna, "we will attend to the matter brought to our attention by the daughter of the honorable Wu Li." He looked at Gokudo, and though his expression remained amiable Gokudo seemed to shrivel in place. He turned from Gokudo to the sheik and his son, who looked wary but declined to shrivel. "We will meet in front of my ger to talk of these and other things when the sun is high."

They were dismissed. Two of Ogodei's soldiers sauntered casually over to stand on either side of Gokudo, while four more arranged themselves around the sheik and his son. There was a great bustle as the soldiers made their camp, yurts going up as if by magic, horses fed and picketed, and dried meat and skins of koumiss produced practically out of the air.

Hari was fascinated and walked among them, listening to them talk, now and then asking a question and listening intently to the answer. The soldiers tolerated him, but then Mongols were notoriously easy-going when it came to priests. They had so many gods already, what was one or two more? He ended his tour sitting before Ogodei, who questioned him closely about India, although Hari was more conversant with temples and gods than he was rulers and standing armies.

Johanna accompanied the others back to their campsite, North Wind following close behind. He wasn't ready to let Johanna out of his sight. She received her purse back from Shasha, made appropriate thanks to Firas, and tied it again to her belt. "Are you all right?" she said to Jaufre. "What happened to you? You were gone when the noise woke us. You and Firas both."

He reached a hand up to the back of his head and winced. "Something woke me up. I went to check on North Wind and I think that someone hit me on the head. What happened to you?"

Shasha found her pack and got out a smelly yellow salve that she smeared impartially on Johanna's cheek and Jaufre's crown. "The noise of the fighting woke us up, and then—"

"—and then he came," Johanna said, almost spitting out the words. "And he dared to put hands on North Wind, and then on me!"

North Wind still came first, Jaufre noted without surprise. "We were lucky today."

"Very," Shasha said.

"Very, very lucky," Félicien said, and the strength seemed to go out of his legs and he dropped the bedroll he was folding and slumped down on it all of a heap. "Traveling with you is more exciting than I'd bargained for."

Jaufre and Shasha looked accusingly at Johanna, who waved an airy hand. "Yes, well, at least you can't say it's been boring." She smiled as sunnily as she was capable of with the entire left side of her face stiff and swollen.

"What now?" Jaufre said. He sat down, too, feeling a little shaky himself.

Shasha, Firas and Johanna followed suit, and a brief silence fell as everyone took stock of their current circumstances and tried not to dwell on what might have been. After a bit Félicien went for water, and they built a fire, such as it was, and broke their fast with lukewarm tea, unleavened bread and dried fruit.

"I'd kill for a bowl of noodle soup," Johanna said. "Hot, hot, hot noodle soup."

"Never, ever say that again," Jaufre said. "Or at least not until we get down out of the mountains, where fire burns as it ought." The sun was warm on his back and Shasha had given him a powder in his tea that had eased the ache in his head. "What will Ogodei do, do you think?"

Johanna shrugged. She was putting a good face on it but she was clearly feeling her bruises, and the anger and indignation that had buoyed her thus far was ebbing. She yawned suddenly, her jaws cracking. "He was a friend of Father's."

"But Wu Li is dead," Shasha said.

Johanna nodded. "There are many witnesses to what Gokudo did. At the very least he is guilty of conspiracy, assault, theft. I asked for the justice of the Khan from Ogodei." She shrugged. "Perhaps he will give it. Perhaps he won't." She brightened. "I wonder where he's going. We could ask him for escort."

Shasha shook her head.

"What?"

"Johanna, I doubt very much if one of the generals of a

hundred thousand is going to offer the protection of his royal troops to such as us."

"He did for Father."

"Yes, well, and how many camels loaded with Cipangu pearls did we have with us on that trip?"

"We could tell Ogodei everything," Jaufre said.

Shasha was repacking her herbs but her head snapped up at that. "We have no proof."

"By all the round-eyed gods, Shasha. When did Wu Li in his entire life ever fall off of anything with a saddle?"

Johanna, who had been about to doze off, sat bolt upright. "What? What are you talking about?"

Jaufre looked at Shasha, who held his gaze for a long moment before sighing and dropping her eyes. "All right. Tell her."

Jaufre turned to Johanna, squaring up to her as if he were facing an opponent in a duel, which he might very well be. "I checked Wu Li's tack as soon as I could after the accident. His girth was cut through. Not all the way, just enough so that it would snap beneath his weight when he kicked his horse into a run."

The silence that fell over their little campsite was acute and uncomfortable. Félicien and Firas were asleep or pretending to be, and Hari had yet to return from his anthropological expedition into the Mongol horde. It was just the three of them. It had been just the three of them since Wu Li had died. "Why didn't you show me the tack?" Johanna said finally. She felt numb, and Jaufre's words were coming to her from a great distance.

"Because it disappeared from the stable right after I looked at it. I asked the stable master and he told me that Gokudo had collected it himself, saying it would be bad luck to keep it and that it must be destroyed."

This time the silence went on longer. Johanna's face was frozen, her eyes dazed, her body, usually a fountain of restless energy, immobile. Jaufre looked at Shasha, who raised a hand slightly as if to say, Wait.

"What else?" Johanna said.

He didn't answer at first, and she said more strongly, "What else did she do, Jaufre? Because there is something else. I can tell just by looking at you."

"I went to Wu Li's room as soon as we heard that he had died," Shasha said. "His eyes were red, and his lips were blue. He was smothered where he lay."

"She killed him," Johanna said.

"Gokudo killed him," Shasha said. "Wu Li was paralyzed only from the waist down. She wouldn't have been strong enough. He fought. There was blood under his fingernails."

"She killed him," Johanna said. "She killed him. Twice. Gokudo was only her tool."

Neither of them contradicted her.

When the sun was high overhead, they gathered again before the big round white ger with the black banner flying from its peak. Ogodei relaxed on his couch, an intricately woven carpet beneath him and a flagon of koumiss in his hand. "Johanna of Cambaluc, daughter of Wu Li, niece of Wu Cheng, you have asked for the Khan's justice."

Johanna rose, tall and proud and white to the lips. "I have, lord."

"Speak."

She kept it short, relating the incidents of the past night in full, pointing to Gokudo and the sheik in turn, ignoring the wounded look in the son's eyes. "He and they are guilty of conspiracy, my lord. They are guilty of assault and murder—three people are dead, including Azar of Kashgar, my dear friend and the betrothed of Fatima, daughter of Ahmed and Malala, also of Kashgar, and also a dear friend."

The baron quaffed koumiss. The smell of the fermented mare's milk was strong enough to reach Johanna's nostrils, and she repressed a sudden wave of nausea. She knew what she was asking for was just. She would not shame her father by asking for less than what was due his memory. "A dozen are wounded, some severely, and one woman was raped. I have no doubt more would have been had you not come upon us."

"Let us adhere to the facts of the matter, Wu Li's daughter." Ogodei said, pleasant as always. "If we venture into speculation we will be here until the snow falls."

Johanna bent her head. "It is my joy always to obey you, my lord." It was not merely an empty saying. When Johanna bent her head to Ogodei, she bent it to the power of the Khan in Cambaluc. "He conspired with the Sheik Mohammed to kidnap me and to steal my horse. We all heard him say so." She looked around and heads nodded vigorously in confirmation. "He assaulted me." She pointed at her face. "He announced his intention of doing more than that on the Road to Cambaluc." More nods. Gokudo had a fine, penetrating voice. Everyone had heard him clearly.

"Well," Ogodei said. "He is, clearly, guilty of all of these things, and of stupidity as well, since he did all these things and then convicted himself of them out of his own mouth." He drank koumiss and looked at Johanna. "What is the penalty he must pay, Wu Li's daughter?"

"His life," Wu Li's daughter said.

Gokudo made a sudden movement, and subsided when the Mongol soldiers at his sides reminded him they were there.

The baron raised his eyebrows. "You are not dead, Wu Li's daughter."

"Others are," Johanna said.

"You are not even much hurt."

"Others are."

"Your horse has been returned to you—he is very like a horse I bet on last winter in Cambaluc, did you know? A horse owned and raced by Edyk the Portuguese. Perhaps he is of the same lineage?"

"Perhaps," Johanna said through stiff lips. It was a warning, and kindly meant, but she could not stop, not now that she knew the whole story. "There is also the matter of blood guilt, lord."

Gokudo, unable to speak behind his gag, slumped a little between his guards.

The baron raised his eyebrows. "What blood guilt is this?"

"As I told you, Gokudo is a member of my father's household."

"Johanna—" Shasha said.

"He came there as bodyguard to my father's second wife."

The baron nodded. "Yes, I recall. The honorable Dai Fang."

"Not so honorable, my lord. She dishonored my father with Gokudo."

Gokudo came alive again, struggling and trying to shout from behind his gag.

This time the baron's eyebrows ascended all the way to his hairline. "You have proof of this?"

"The word of my foster brother and my aunt, and myself."

"Very well."

"By the observations of my foster brother, Jaufre of Cambaluc, my father's saddle was tampered with so that he would fall from his horse that day."

The baron looked at Jaufre, who nodded. The baron said, "But Wu Li lived beyond his accident, did he not?"

"He did, my lord. Too long, as it happened, because Gokudo and Dai Fang grew impatient, and smothered him in his bed."

Gokudo had managed to work his gag free. "Bitch! No one will believe your whore's words!"

"As attested to by my aunt," Johanna said steadily.

The baron looked at Shasha, who nodded in turn.

A murmur ran through the crowd, soldiers and merchants alike. Wu Li was well known to the Road, and those who traveled thereon. The baron suppressed a sigh. "So it is death you ask for, Wu Li's daughter?"

"It is death I am owed," she said. "And not just any death."

"Oh god, Johanna, no," Jaufre said beneath his breath. Next

189

to him Shasha closed her eyes and shook her head. Félicien looked at Firas, whose countenance was more than ordinarily mask-like.

"Give him the death of the carpet, lord," Johanna said clearly, raising her voice so that it could be heard.

There was an immediate tumult, not least of which came from Gokudo, who called her names until at a gesture from the baron one of his guards gagged him again.

The baron in turn rose to his feet. "It shall be so," he said, and the crowd, pausing only long enough to hear the words, shouted their approval, over and over again.

There wasn't a great deal of ceremony to it, and no waiting period. Gokudo was hustled to a flat space beyond the camp. Mongol soldiers mounted their horses and formed two lines with a clear lane between. A carpet was brought, the very carpet that had supported the baron's couch. Gokudo, cursing and struggling, was swallowed up by Mongol soldiers and when they saw him again he was rolled into the carpet. All they could see of him was a topknot of black hair.

The carpet was laid between the two rows of horses. The baron stood at one end and raised his arm. Another company of soldiers waited at the other end of the lane. When the baron's arm fell, they kicked their horses into a gallop. They thundered down the lane and over the rolled carpet. The noise was so loud from the crowd and the soldiers that nothing could be heard from inside the carpet, although Jaufre would have sworn he heard the man scream.

The baron's arm raised and fell again, and again the company of horses thundered down the lane and over the carpet. Again, the arm fell, and again the horses galloped, and again, and again. Red began to seep through the carpet, and they paused to unroll it to see if Gokudo was dead. He was unrecognizable by now, a mess of blood and splintered bone wrapped in a mass of quilted black cloth, but unbelievably the blood pulsing from many wounds indicated that he was indeed still alive.

Ogodei shouted something and his soldiers cheered and banged their bows against their shields. Two held open Gokudo's mouth and a third rammed it full of horse manure, of which there was by now a plentiful supply. The broken body jerked in a horrible, boneless struggle. They rolled him back into the carpet and thundered the horses over him another three times.

This time when they unrolled the carpet he was definitely dead.

The baron beckoned to Johanna, and she marched toward him on stiff legs, her back very straight, her chin very high, her face like stone. She wanted to spit on Gokudo's remains, but she could not bring herself even to look at him, and her mouth was too dry for spitting anyway. "Lord?"

"Is your call for justice satisfied, Wu Li's daughter?"

"I have received the justice of the Khan," Johanna said steadily, "and I am satisfied."

"And the sheik and his son, Wu Li's daughter? The samurai's co-conspirators? They have also gravely offended you. What to them?"

"I leave them to your good judgement, my lord," Johanna said. "So far as I know they are only thieves."

The expression on the sheik's face indicated that he did not view her words as a compliment, but he said nothing, and he stopped his son from speaking as well. He'd had dealings with Mongols before this, and he knew how little the Mongols wished for trouble with the Persians. They had other fish to fry.

"Thievery," Ogodei said pensively. "For a first offense, that usually means the sacrifice of the right hand."

Johanna swallowed hard, and repeated, "I leave their punishment to your good judgement, lord."

The baron approached her and bent his head so that his lips were next to her ears. "Did no one warn you, Wu Li's daughter, that vengeance can be as bitter on the tongue as it is sweet?"

By unspoken agreement Johanna and her party took their leave of the rest of the caravan, packing and riding away from that place of horror as quickly as they could. As they were leaving camp Fatima ran up. "Johanna!" She reached up and clasped Johanna's hand between her own and looked deeply into her eyes. "Thank you," she said.

Tears stung Johanna's eyes. "I'm so sorry about Azar," she said.

"He is avenged," Fatima said simply, and ran back to her parents.

The trailhead down was reached in less than an hour and Johanna was grateful that it was another narrow trail, so that they would have to go single file and she didn't have to talk to anyone. She had to stop once to vomit, and Shasha, who was behind her, said nothing.

Johanna wiped her mouth. "You should have told me."

"Before we left Cambaluc, do you mean? And what would you have done? Killed Gokudo? Killed Dai Fang? Tell me, Johanna, would we now be a thousand leagues from Cambaluc if you had done so? Or would we be locked in the same dungeon your grandmother died in?"

"You should have told me," Johanna said fiercely. "I am no longer a child, Shasha. You are no longer allowed to protect me from harsh realities of our lives."

Shasha threw up her hands in disgust and climbed back on her horse. Johanna grabbed a handful of North Wind's mane and threw a leg over his broad back, and they moved rapidly down the trail without another word.

That night they made a cold camp beneath the evergreen trees that had reappeared along the trail. No one spoke very much or slept very well.

At noon the next day the sheik and his men materialized out of the forest, surrounding them.

Johanna, too tired to be afraid, said, "Sheik, you are beginning to annoy me."

"He let you go," Shasha said. "Ogodei just—let you go?"

Félicien looked frightened and clung tight to his donkey. Hari said in a sterner voice than any of them had heard before, "Your god is named Allah, is he not? Would he approve, I wonder, of your attacking and robbing innocent travelers on the road?"

Firas said nothing and did nothing, sitting immobile on his mount.

The sheik ignored them both. "I will take the horse now."

Johanna laughed, an edge of hysteria to her voice. "Have you learned nothing, sheik? He will not go with you!"

"And I will take the woman as well," the sheik said, "since the horse will not go anywhere without her."

"No, you will not!" Jaufre said, reaching for his sword.

"I am sorry," Farhad said from beside him, and drove his sword into Jaufre's back.

He heard Johanna scream. Heard Shasha cry out. Heard Félicien say, "No no no no no!" Heard Hari om.

Felt himself falling.

Twice in two days, he thought.

Johanna, he thought.

And then the black rose up to engulf him and he thought no more.

16

"You are a samurai, are you not?" the baron said. "More specifically, a ronin, I believe it is called? A samurai who answers to no lord?"

Gokudo, bound hand and foot but demonstrably alive, gave a curt nod. His topknot was missing, as was his quilted armor, leaving him dressed in trousers and a simple tunic.

"I thought so," the baron said. "We tried invading Cipangu. Twice. You defeated us, both times." He smiled. "It takes a great warrior to defeat a Mongol army."

Gokudo, who had been shown the body of the hapless soldier who had been substituted for his own, said through dry lips, "Thank you, my lord."

"Yes," the baron said, "indeed, you owe me gratitude for your life. Such a bloodthirsty child she is, the daughter of the honorable Wu Li."

Gokudo spat out a hate-filled curse and called the ancestry of Wu Li's daughter into serious question.

The baron strolled forward and leaned down to say in Gokudo's ear. "The honorable Wu Li of Cambaluc was my very good friend." He stood straight again and kicked Gokudo once, very hard, between his legs. The guards standing around the inside of the ger laughed heartily.

Gokudo's mouth opened in a silent scream and he doubled up on the baron's carpet, scrubbed not entirely clean of blood.

"That is the last time you will insult him in my presence," the baron said pleasantly, "is that understood?"

Gokudo managed a nod.

"Good. I have no doubt his daughter was perfectly right. Such righteous wrath! She was a torch lit from within. If she were anyone else's daughter…" He looked down at Gokudo again. "No, you killed him, that much is certain, and your life is forfeit thereby. So is the so honorable Dai Fang's, if it comes to that. I shall have to see what I can do about that when next I return to Cambaluc."

The baron sighed. "There is an ineradicable stain on my own character for sparing you, and for sparing the Sheik Mohammed, who conspired with you, and indeed for sacrificing one of my own men in your place."

It did not appear as if that stain weighed heavily upon him.

"However." The baron's flagon had been refilled and he drank deep. He looked again at the bound man trying not to choke on his own vomit on the floor of the baron's ger. "It may be that I have a use for you."

"I cannot return to Cipangu, lord," Gokudo said, gasping for breath. "I will be slaughtered by my enemies the instant I step foot on shore."

Ogodei waved this comment away as inconsequential. "You have skills I believe I will find useful in many places," he said. "Come, get up."

A nod, and Gokudo's hands and feet were free and he was assisted roughly to his feet, where he stood, swaying. "Thank you, lord," he said, bowing as deeply as he was able without falling over.

Ogodei nodded, accepting fear and deference as his just due, and smiled. "You are ronin no more," he said.

"No, my lord," Gokudo said.

By the Shores of the Middle Sea

Book II of Silk and Song

I

Talikan, spring, 1323

JOHANNA HAD NEVER been so bored.

There was no lack of comfort in the harem, that was true enough. The blue-tiled floors had been built over a hypocaust, and were warm both winter and summer. So was the water in the rectangular bath that stretched the length of the main room. The silk cushions were large and comfortable, if a little gaudy in their brilliant red and orange and purple and green stripes, and so were the beds. The food was plentiful and most of it delicious, if the cook did have a heavy hand with sugar and spices. Each inmate had her own room and her own personal servant. The larger suites, assigned to the sultan's favorites, had their own kitchens, their own fountains and some their own heated pools.

There were no doors to these rooms, of course. Who knew what those women would get up to behind closed doors, if they had them?

They got up to plenty without them.

Concubines had been a feature of life in Cambaluc, too. Johanna's own grandmother had been concubine to the great Kublai Khan before being given in marriage to her grandfather, the honored Marco Polo. It was natural for men of power and wealth to accumulate women much as they did other possessions, as a way of measuring themselves against their peers and as a means of demonstrating their elevated status in society. More women also meant more heirs of the body, although Johanna, familiar with the stories of internecine warfare among the descendants of the Great Khan, wondered what any man needed with that many sons. Too many heirs only guaranteed long and extremely bloody fights over who would one day occupy the throne. Those fights inevitably spiraled out from court to city to countryside, and never ended well for the innocent bystander. Johanna's own grandmother had died in prison after one such dynastic disturbance.

But in Cambaluc, concubines could walk the streets unveiled, could shop in the markets, could visit their friends and relatives, could attend the horse races and bet on the outcome. They traveled, with personal guards of course, the number according to their consequence, but one saw them everywhere, Chinese and Mongol alike. The Mongol concubines could even own and ride their own horses. Here in Talikan, under the absolute rule of Sheik Mohammed, the only time the concubines left the harem was when the sheik called for their presence in his rooms for the evening.

With one exception.

The knock landed heavily on the other side of the great mahogany door, the sound echoing off the tiled walls. Before the second knock fell Johanna was on her feet and running. The third knock sounded and she was standing before the great door, fidgeting, waiting for Kadar, the chief eunuch, to deign to open it. He disapproved of Johanna's daily excursions to the stables and expressed his disapproval, in so far as he dared flout his master's will, by delaying as long as possible her departure.

She heard the sound of robes swishing over tile, and turned to see Kadar approaching with a deliberately unhurried stride. Concubines peered from behind him and whispered furiously among themselves, watching the Easterner with her odd-colored eyes, who had never been invited into the sheik's bed, not even once, be granted yet again this unheard of, this extraordinary, and some even alleged this blasphemous freedom. She didn't even wear a veil outside the harem!

After six months one would think her mornings out would occasion little comment, but no. Their lives were so monotonous and so entirely absent of event, they had so little else to talk about.

And she was here as a result of betrayal, kidnapping and blackmail. They might not speak of it directly, but they knew—and she would never forget. The sheik and his son and their men had ambushed her party on the trail down from the high pass through the mountains because the sheik had wanted North Wind, and because the big white stallion wouldn't go anywhere without Johanna.

She remembered again the blade of Farhad's sword sliding so easily into Jaufre's back, and closed her eyes against a wave of nausea. She took a deep breath and let it out, slowly. When she opened her eyes Kadar was sweeping past, and she stiffened her spine because it was a point of honor never to show weakness before the chief eunuch. A tall man of massive girth with a broad, impassive face clad in skin the color of tar in which no single hair could be found, he ignored her to shake back the elaborately embroidered brocade of his long, wide sleeves and draw the filigreed bronze bolt on the door. The bolt was more an ornamental badge of Kadar's office than it was any serious kind of deterrence to forced entry. The locks on the other side were far more substantial.

Johanna had refused all attempts to indoctrinate her into the Islamic faith, to the further scandalous twittering of the harem inmates, but she had embraced the opportunity to learn Persian, because another language was always a useful skill. When she discovered that Kadar meant "beloved" in that tongue she had been hard put to it to conceal her amusement. As with everything else in the harem, excessive mirth could draw unwanted attention.

The door began slowly, oh so slowly, to swing wide. Johanna was leaning forward, almost on her toes, every fiber of her being yearning toward the other side.

"Nazirah! Wait!"

A small, slim figure slipped through the crowd of women and rushed forward. She had dark flashing eyes, an infectious smile and a merry disposition. She reminded Johanna of Fatima, a childhood friend.

"Hayat," she said, striving to sound patient. "What is it?"

"Only this," Hayat said, seizing Johanna's hands in her own. "I need more indigo. Could you ask the guards to stop at the dyers' shed on your way back?" Hayat dimpled at Kadar. "You don't mind, do you, Kadar?"

Even the chief eunuch was not proof against Hayat's wiles, as indeed few of them were. Nevertheless he said sternly, "The master's orders are specific, Hayat, as you well know. Nazirah is to go directly to the stables and to return directly to the harem."

Johanna felt a scrap of paper transfer into her left palm. Her own closed over it. She gave Kadar a sunny smile that was not meant to be friendly and the chief eunuch was not so foolish as to take it so. "The dyeing shed is along the way," she said to Hayat. "If they have it, you will have indigo when I return."

She turned back to the door, smoothing back her braid and brushing the front of her tunic. In the process she slipped the scrap of paper into her sash.

With conscious ceremony Kadar bowed her through the doorway. Was the bow a little too exaggerated, a little over-elaborate? No matter. The door shut behind her with a thud that resounded off the blue-tiled walls of the harem's antechamber, vying with the trickling water of the inevitable fountain for precedence.

She felt rather than saw the two armed guards falling in behind her, fierce with scimitars and daggers. She knew the way by now and her pace quickened, until she was almost running again by the time she reached the next door. She didn't wait for the guards, she flung it open and burst into a walled garden. She threaded through roses red and white and pink and yellow— forever after she would associate the scent of roses with a feeling of imprisonment—and reached yet another door in the wall on the other side. She didn't wait for the guards to catch up with her, she hammered on the door with her fist. "Ishan! It's Johanna! Open the door!"

A horse's whinny, imperious and insistent, was heard, and Johanna laughed. "Ishan! Open the door before North Wind opens it for you!"

The door opened and Johanna shot through the opening as if she had been loosed from a bow. Still, North Wind was there before her.

Ishan, the stable master, was the only man in Sheik Mohammed's entire stables who could even marginally handle North Wind without injury. He was certainly the only one courageous enough to saddle and lead the stallion from his stall, and smart enough to flatten himself hastily against the stable wall as the great white stallion moved past him at a gait unsuitable for the relatively cramped quarters of the stable yard. She laughed again, caught a handful of mane and swung herself up on North Wind's back. He didn't stop as she settled into place, continuing on toward the double doors of the stable yard, his intent obvious. Either someone would open the doors or North Wind would go right through them.

Johanna was disinclined to slow him down. Indeed, she urged him on. She heard Ishan shouting and two brave or well-bribed souls ran for the gates and dragged them open just in time for North Wind to thunder through. She caught a confused glimpse of a man or men on horseback outside the gates and flattened herself on North Wind's neck. "Run, North Wind, run!" she cried, and felt his stride lengthen. The wind flattened her clothes against her flesh and tore her hair loose from its braid. The looming shadow of the palace walls fell away and they were at last gloriously out on the ribbon of sand groomed soft for the sheik's racing horses.

The trail ran next to a wide canal shadowed by date palms and almond trees, beyond which a horizon of undulating hills beckoned more alluringly than any line of hills on any horizon she had ever seen. Freedom. The hills seemed to whisper the word in her ears. *Freedom.*

In the sheer pleasure of the moment the rigid guard she held on herself at all times slipped, just a little. Jaufre. Shasha. How far beyond those hills were they? Had Shasha kept her promise?

Was Jaufre even still alive?

The great white horse, always sensitive to her moods, broke stride. She tightened her knees, banished thought, and bent over North Wind's neck again. Reassured, his stride lengthened and he ate up the track, a league and more of immaculately groomed sand filled with gentle rises and falls of ground and easy curves, meant to test and build speed and endurance. His gait never faltered, his spirit never flagged, and on his back Johanna felt that no distance was too great to travel so long as North Wind carried her on his back and her friends were at the end of the journey. For one precious moment, the moment she lived for every day, the moment that allowed her to possess her soul in patience for the other interminable hours she had to endure to arrive at it, she could imagine this was the day she would begin that journey.

And it seemed only a moment before the last of the palms flashed past. She sat up. North Wind's stride began to slow. After a few moments another horse drew level with them, flanks white with foam. It wasn't easy, trying to keep up with North Wind.

She knew without looking who rode the second horse.

North Wind slowed to a canter and at last to a walk. He was barely sweating. Johanna swung her leg over and slid to the ground, there to run her hands down his legs and pick up his feet to examine his hooves. He raised each foot obediently at a slight pressure of her hand.

"Still he obeys you as he does no one else," a rueful voice remarked.

She stiffened, and tried to hide it.

After a slight pause, which she did nothing to fill, the voice said, "He ran well today."

"He runs well every day," she said, and stood up to see Farhad's eyes gleam with satisfaction. It wasn't often that he was able to goad her into speech.

This was the time she craved most, to be alone with North Wind, or alone if she discounted the omnipresent guards. Farhad did not ride with them often, but he was always an intrusion when he did, and she made sure he knew it. Very well; if he wouldn't let her ignore him, she would attack. "Has your father reconsidered giving me rooms in the stables?"

"This again?" He sighed. "As I have told you, repeatedly, an unmarried woman is safest in the harem." He smiled at her.

She didn't smile back. He didn't dismount, not even to wipe down his mount. That was a task for lesser beings. "As you saw this morning, North Wind dislikes it when I am kept from him."

He smiled again. "He can still run. As you both just proved. It is all my father requires of him."

She had already thought of ways of making North Wind physically ill and claiming it as proof of the great horse's sickness of spirit, but she hadn't been able to bring herself to do it. Not yet. Although it might come to that in the end. She leaned against the stallion and he responded with a reassuring whicker, a comforting bulwark against Farhad and his most unwelcome attention.

The sheik's son gave a nod and his guards nudged their mounts into a trot and fanned out in a dozen different directions. A dozen, Johanna thought, interested against her will. When the sheik's son rode with her his guard was usually two men, no more, the same as her own escort. She looked more closely at the retreating figures and saw that they were not guards but scouts, equipped with water skins and full saddle bags. They were dressed in layers of sturdy clothing, cheches wrapped securely around their faces and heads so that only their eyes were showing, and they wore braces of daggers and swords. "Where are they going?" she said.

The sheik's son gave a negligent shrug. "To see what there is to see, merely."

205

She didn't believe him. There was a tension about his shoulders that she had not seen before. "Are we expecting trouble?"

He smiled, although the expression seemed forced. "How nice to hear you say 'we.'"

"Your father," she said thoughtfully, ignoring the provocation. "He is well again?"

Sheik Mohammed's son sobered. "He is not," he said. "The doctors fear the worst."

He looked at her, slowly, deliberately; all of her, from the crown of now-tumbled bronze hair to the hostile gray of her eyes and down, over slim shoulders, full breasts, narrow waist, and long legs. She was attired in the raw silk tunic and trousers she had worn from Cambaluc, which they had let her keep for riding. Kadar had forbidden her to wear them in the harem except when she was going to and from the stables.

The clothes, sturdy, unglamorous, workmanlike, did nothing to deter Farhad's attention. He wanted her. Johanna, no blushing virgin, saw his desire and recognized it for what it was. She did what she always did: she ignored it, vaulting again to North Wind's back. Again, the stallion was quick to sense her mood, and she felt the great muscles contract beneath her.

He would kill Farhad for her, if she willed it so.

Oblivious, Farhad nudged his mount to come up beside them, and dropped his voice to what he apparently had decided was an irresistible growl. "When you are my wife, Nazirah, when you are in my bed, I will keep you too busy to brood."

She faced forward and nudged North Wind into a walk. "Your father promised that I would be freed in his will."

"In his will," Farhad said, his smile fading. "Not in mine. And when I am sheik of Talikan, my will rules."

She gave him a considering look, carefully maintaining her own mask of polite civility. He was a young man, strong, not ill-favored and, inescapably, would one day in the lamentably near future be the most powerful man in Talikan. It would be unwise to offend him too soon, and if it came to that—here she swallowed and set her teeth—she could tolerate his attentions long enough to find a way, both to exact revenge for his treacherous attack on Jaufre and to find a way out of this silken trap.

Because if she didn't, Johanna would never see the outside of the harem again. The mere thought of that great wooden door closing between her and the rest of the world for the last time made her throat close up. For a moment she couldn't breathe.

Farhad saw her distress and mistook the reason. "Come, Nazirah," he said in a soothing voice, "surely the prospect isn't so bad as that. You—"

She turned North Wind and kicked him into a canter. Her guards scrambled to get out of the way and for the first time that morning she saw their faces. One of them was new.

But not, she realized, first with a shock and then with a thrill of mounting excitement, new to her.

The new guard was Firas.

2

Talikan, spring, 1323

JOHANNA SPENT AS long as she could in caring for North Wind after her ride – feeding him, watering him, grooming his coat, polishing his hooves – partly because his company was so much more acceptable than that of anyone behind the harem doors, and partly in hopes that the sheik's son would be called away before she finished. In this she was successful, emerging at last to find Farhad gone and the two guards waiting with varying degrees of patience to escort her back to the harem.

"Oh," she said, looking at Firas as if she was seeing him for the first time. "Where is Mahmoud?" she said to Tarik.

He addressed the area above and behind her left shoulder. In the entire city of Talikan it was by now well known that she did not share the sheik's bed, but one never knew what might happen in the future. She resided in the sheik's harem and she was subject to his will. At any moment the fancy could take him to sample this exotic, self-willed creature. She could end as his favorite—a wife, even. Thus no sensible man of the city of Talikan would dare trespass by addressing her with less than the utmost respect, but that didn't mean that Tarik, a deeply religious man, had to look at her face as she flaunted it with no veil before men not of her family.

Besides, she was the only person who could handle that very

afreet of a horse, and Tarik had won a month's salary on North Wind's last race. He answered her with civility, familiar to a demon though she might be. "Alas, Mahmoud is dead, lady. Inshallah."

"Dead?" Johanna was all polite incredulity. "What happened to him?"

A shoulder raised and fell. "He fell from his horse and broke his neck, lady."

"Now, how did he come to do that?" Johanna said, marveling. "I would have thought Mahmoud much too good a rider to be so careless as to fall from his own horse."

"Yes, lady, and so would we all." A note of condemnation crept into Tarik's voice. "Nevertheless, what is one to think when his horse returns riderless and a search discovers Mahmoud's lifeless body at the bottom of a cliff?"

"What else, indeed," Johanna said gravely, and turned to Firas. "And this is?"

"Firas, lady."

She nodded at him, schooling her features to courteous indifference while her heart beat so loudly it roared in her ears. "Well met, Firas," she said, in a voice, no matter how hard she tried to control it, not quite her own. "Let us hope you manage to stay on your horse."

"Let us hope so indeed, lady," Firas said, his face bland.

Bland, but for the merest hint of a wink.

A wave of relief and joy swept over her, so intense that her vision grayed a little. When it cleared she found his dark eyes still steady on hers, compelling her to composure. She could betray by neither word not deed that they were known to each other. It would be worth his life, and possibly even her own.

Jaufre lived.

He lived.

It wasn't safe to say any more in Tarik's hearing, who already appeared quizzical at a courtesy she had never displayed to her other guards, but she could wait. She had absolutely no doubt Firas would find a way to speak to her again. She was even, now that her heartbeat had steadied, a little curious to see how he'd manage it. "Tarik, I am done here for the day," she said, regaining her composure, with an effort she hoped she had masked. "I return to the harem by way of the dyers cottage." She had not and she would never call the harem home.

"Lady—"

Johanna turned her back on the protest Tarik felt obliged to make every time she deviated from a direct path back to the harem and strode off, letting them catch up to her or no as they wished. Follow they did, Tarik's whine degenerating into a grumble. Firas said nothing at all.

The dyers' shed was one of a row of artisans' cottages built against the thick, continuous wall two stories high that formed first a barrier around the palace, which was then enclosed by the city itself and by the city wall, twice as thick and twice as high. These craftsmen, each deemed the best in the city at their individual trade, had been granted their places inside the royal enclosure by royal warrant. In return they received a rent-free workshop and handsome prices for their work wherever they sold it, although the sheik had first right of refusal on anything they made. There was a saddler, a weaver, a cabinetmaker, a glassblower, a goldsmith, a jeweler, and more. A tanner was off by himself in a location predetermined not to waft any noxious fumes in the direction of the royal nostrils.

The dyer's shop was between the weaver and the herbalist. Johanna knocked once, and went in. "Halim, well met the day."

"Salaam, Lady Nazirah!" Halim, sleeves rolled back and red to the wrists with the blood of cochineal bugs, bowed as best he could. "It is a joy to see you well and flourishing. And that great white monster you persist in riding at peril of your very life and limb?"

Johanna, once more fully in command of herself, patted herself down ostentatiously, extracting Hayat's scrap of paper from her sash as she did so. The guards remained outside, but she was never careless on the errands she ran for Hayat. "I survive as you

210

see, Halim, and North Wind, too, is in fine health. You may bet freely and with confidence on his next race."

"Hah!" Halim said, grinning. "And that I will do, my lady." If Halim, like Tarik, thought it a scandal and an abomination for a woman to ride a horse at the public races—and that a stallion, no less!—he did not say so. Of course Tarik never said so, either, or not outright, nor did anyone else. The word of the sheik was law. Questioning that law had consequences, usually involving a whip, or even the edge of a sword.

The dyer's shop was sturdily built, and Halim was prosperous enough that his floor was tiled, but not so prosperous as to have his own fountain. Instead, a large urn glazed a deep blue was sunk into the floor up to the lip and filled daily by a small boy who came round with a donkey laden with sacks of water. The walls of the shop were white, with small, rectangular windows cut near the ceiling so as to let in the light and let out the heat. In spite of the messiness inherent in the craft of dyeing, it was scrupulously neat, with hanks of wool in various stages of drying looped over wooden trees as tall as Halim that surrounded vats of various sizes. The grate of a large brazier glowed with live coals beneath a large pot bubbling not quite over with a rich purple liquid.

It was a scene that looked both industrious and efficient, and indeed Halim was both. He was also a skilled smuggler.

"A lovely color, Halim," she said of the cochineal.

"Is it not, lady, is it not, indeed." Halim slid the bowl across the table for her to examine more closely.

Johanna tipped the bowl to admire the swirl of scarlet liquid, at the same time slipping the scrap of paper beneath it.

Halim slid the bowl back to his side of the table, hand beneath the table to catch the paper when it fell from the edge. "Is it the cochineal the lady Hayat is in need of this day?"

"It is not, Halim," Johanna said. "She hopes you have indigo in stock, a small amount only."

Halim made a wry face. "The lady Hayat will soon be setting up her own dyers' shed in competition with me."

"I think Lateef the weaver has more to fear," Johanna said with a smile.

They continued to pitch their voices to be heard beyond the cottage's walls, demonstrating to anyone within listening distance that there was nothing untoward or conspiratorial going on therein. "Let me see," Halim said, shifting boxes and jars and bags from the vast array on display. "Indigo, indigo, yes, I have some here." The lid of a cedarwood box was raised to display its contents, small square cakes wrapped in bright scraps of fabric and tied with dyed jute in elaborately decorative knots. Halim knew a thing or two about presentation and marketing.

"Excellent," Johanna said. "Could you spare two, most worthy Halim?"

"I believe I can," Halim said, and conjured a small silk bag with a thick bottom, into which he ceremoniously placed two cakes of the indigo. "Did you know, lady, that the flowers of the indigo plant are pink in color?"

Johanna, who had seen entire fields of indigo in bloom in Cipangu, widened her eyes. "No? Pink? Really? How curious, Halim, that a plant should camouflage its true nature in such a way."

"As you say, lady." Halim produced a length of jute and tied the mouth of the little sack with an even more elaborate bow. "I have often wondered how the first dyer discovered indigo's secret."

"Probably by accident," Johanna said. "A cut branch leaking sap on the leg of someone's trouser. Which then turns blue."

"But that would require the owner of the trousers to notice." Halim presented the bag to her with a flourish.

She accepted it, and felt the shape of the third item through the bottom of the bag. She beamed at him. "Thank you, Halim. Salaam."

"Salaam, Lady Nazirah."

There was no opportunity to speak further with Firas on the journey from the dyer's shop to the harem, and Kadar was of course waiting for her at the door. "Until tomorrow morning,

Tarik, Firas," Johanna said to Tarik, meeting Firas' eye with a very fleeting glance.

"Lady."

"Lady."

The door closed on their bows.

"Kadar," Johanna said with a pleasant smile.

No smile of any kind was returned to her, not that she had expected one. "You are late, lady."

"Am I?" She held out the little silk bag with a hand she was pleased to note was rock steady. "Would you care to examine the indigo Halim the dyer sends to the lady Hayat?"

He gave the bag a perfunctory shake and dropped it back into her palm. "We would be pleased to see you in proper clothing as soon as possible, lady."

She smiled again without answering and strode down the tiled hallway, eschewing the seductive, hip-rolling stroll of the harem inmate for the vigorous, ground-eating stride of someone accustomed to wide open spaces, one with no limits placed on her activities. It was a rebuke of him and of the constraints of his realm, and they both knew it. Johanna reveled in it. Kadar, she was sure, marked it down in the column of her sins. By now, it had to be a very long column.

She went to her room and changed into the hated harem clothing, the briefest of sleeveless vests and diaphanous trousers gathered at waist and ankle with, of all things, tiny bells. They tinkled as she walked. The sound was meant to be seductive, but all it meant to her was an easy alert to her location. Her feet might as well be bound.

At least she got to remove the bells once a day.

The veil she refused to put on. Instead she brushed her hair and reworked it into its single braid. She folded her riding clothes away, her hand involuntarily smoothing over the lumps in the hems of her trousers. She washed her own clothes herself, by her own hand, ignoring the scandalized looks of the other harem ladies and the reproving admonishments of the chief eunuch, saying only that they were made of a special kind of silk from her home and required a certain kind of care. She had no idea how long she would be able to continue to get away with such specious excuses.

She thought of Firas. Perhaps she wouldn't have to for very much longer.

It was quiet and still in her room, the only movement the slight breeze stirring at her window, the only smell a slight scent of roses, the only sounds the calls of doves. She stood very still in the luxury of this brief moment of private peace to remember that tiniest of winks that Firas had given her.

She had not grieved for Jaufre. She had refused to do so. If she had grieved him, then he would have been dead, and lost to her forever. She would not admit such a thing to be possible, and so it wasn't. Jaufre was alive, had been alive all these months, even though the sheik's son had stabbed him most treacherously in the back and left him laying in the middle of the trail, there to bleed to death.

Stay with him! she had shouted at Shasha, who was preparing to follow Johanna as the sheik's men crowded around North Wind, forcing him down the trail. In the ensuing mayhem created by one determined stallion, Johanna had managed to drop her belt and her pack. *Stay with him! Heal him! Make him live! Promise me!*

And Shasha, eyes stormy with rebellion, had cried out, *He will live. I give you my word.*

He was alive.

Jaufre was alive. The wink could mean only that.

For a moment, for one precious moment stolen from the unrelentingly public life of the harem, she let her proud head fall, let the hot tears fill her eyes, let her shoulder shake with silent sobs. All these horrible months, frozen in a state of unknowing despair, suffering the loss of her freedom and the absence and possibly the death of her family of friends, while at the same time aware of the absolute necessity of maintaining a facade of calm control in a place as competitive and potentially homicidal as a harem, she had allowed herself neither hope nor despair, only certainty, that Jaufre and Shasha were alive and on their way to Gaza. It had always been the plan that if they became separated, they would travel to Gaza and wait there for the others. It was all she had had to cling to.

Just this once, she let the tears fall. Just this once, she let herself realize how frightened she had been.

The tears stopped. She wiped her eyes carefully, raised her chin, and squared her shoulders.

There was no perhaps about it. Firas was here, which meant that Johanna was not long for the harem. She would admit no other possibility for that, either.

"Nazirah! Nazirah, you stand there daydreaming while the greatest weaving of my whole entire life sits waiting!"

She looked around and saw Hayat standing in her doorway, a hand holding the gauzy curtains to one side. The other woman's face changed when she saw Johanna's expression. "What is it? What's wrong?" She took a quick step forward and dropped her voice to a breath of sound. "Did Kadar—"

Johanna summoned a smile and shook her head. "No," she said, "no, nothing like that. I was missing—I was missing my family, that is all."

Hayat pounced on her hands and towed Johanna out of her room and down the hallway to her own room, larger than Johanna's and much more crowded with belongings. "You spend too much time on your own, Nazirah," she said. "It leads to brooding, which is unpleasant, unhealthy, and unattractive. Not this afternoon, however. This afternoon you will come and admire me as I weave."

"I'm not to admire the weaving?"

Hayat laughed, and the other woman in the room looked up with an annoyed expression, which cleared when she saw who it was. She dipped a pen into ink and bent back over the sheet of vellum. The lady Alma was always in the throes of another poem. Some of them were quite good, in Johanna's opinion, but she regretted the lady Alma's need to read them out loud to whatever audience was present at the time. Although she could only approve of anyone in the harem who took up an activity other than gossip and quarreling while waiting to be called upon to service their lord and master.

A corner of the room was dominated by a standing loom holding a half-finished tapestry three ells in width and at least that much in length. To one side of it, wooden stands were loaded with hanks of fine spun wools dyed in yellows and browns. A basin stood ready, filled with water, and Johanna handed over the little bag. Hayat opened it and took out one of the squares of dye and dropped it into the basin. She lit the brazier beneath and gave the dye an admonitory stir with a large wooden paddle. "There," she said, "we will leave that to be getting on with itself." She knotted the mouth of the bag again and tucked it into her belt, giving it to what all outward attention was an absent-minded pat. She smiled at Johanna and said teasingly, "Will you sit at my loom, Nazirah?"

It was the custom of the harem to rename all of its inmates at the time of their incarceration (Johanna never thought of it any other way). The sheik himself had bestowed the name on her, which she later learned meant "like," or "equal" and which she at first took as a joke at her expense. Later she realized he was sending a subtle signal to the other inmates, and most especially to Kadar, that simply because she was not called to the sheik's bed didn't mean she was not entitled to the same rights and privileges as the rest of the harem. Such rights and privileges as they were. When the anger had subsided, and whenever Farhad had been especially caressing on their morning rides, she wondered if his father knew of his son's interest in his "guest." If he did, it was possible that he had done his best, within the strictures of Persian society, to protect Johanna from that interest.

Although she resisted ascribing anything like benevolence to her kidnapper.

"I will not, Hayat," she said, as she had said every day since Hayat had first invited her to. Weaving was barely a step above embroidery, and Johanna had stringent opinions on learning anything to do with a needle and thread over and above the call of mending ripped out seams or darning tears.

Hayat laughed, a joyous sound very like bells ringing. Hayat meant "life," which was certainly appropriate, because Hayat was bursting with it, sometimes so much so that Johanna thought privately she would one day break right through the imprisoning walls from sheer exuberance.

Alma snorted, scraping busily at her vellum with a penknife. Alma meant "learned," given probably because of her ability to read and write. So far as Johanna had been able to discover, Alma was the only other member of the harem besides herself and Hayat who could.

"If the lady Alma is willing," Johanna said, "I would like to continue my writing lessons."

Alma looked up and smiled, brushing a strand of hair back from her face and leaving a smear of ink behind. "Of course, Nazirah," she said. "Especially as this pestilential poem has gotten hopelessly stuck."

Johanna did not ask how because Alma would have told her, at length. She curled up on a nearby cushion instead and Alma provided her with a sheet of parchment, almost transparent from being scraped and reused so many times. Spoken languages came easily to her, written ones less so, but Persian was infinitely less complicated than Mandarin and every bit as beautiful in written form. Every sentence looked like it should be framed and hung on a wall.

Today, Alma had chosen a poem by her favorite poet for Johanna to translate, working from a Uighur translation, which language Johanna had learned young and well from Deshi the Scout. "That way," Alma explained, "you can compare your translation to the poem as it was originally written in Persian."

Johanna surfaced hours later, hand cramped, shoulders stiff

with the effort of concentration, to the sound of a distant bell, accompanied by the patter of bare feet on tile. She looked up to see that the sun had set and that while she was absorbed in her work, a servant must have come in to light the oil lamps hanging from brackets on the walls.

"Let me see," Alma said, extending an imperious hand. It was said in the harem that Alma was the daughter of a king, an incentive to a trade agreement between the two kingdoms, and at moments like these Johanna was inclined to believe the rumor. She handed over the parchment.

"'Come, fill the Cup, and in the Fire of Spring,'" Alma said, "'The Winter Garment of Repentance fling/The Bird of Time has but a little way/To fly—and Lo! the Bird is on the Wing.'" She lowered the paper and smiled at Johanna. "Well done, Nazirah. Wait, let me read out the same verse in the original." She searched for and found a small book, parchment pages bound between covers, handprinted, a little faded but still legible. "Here, you read it."

Johanna read it slowly all the way through, the words in the original Persian lovely, graceful, as natural in flow as water moving downstream. The image of a bird on the wing worked powerfully on her in her present state of mind, and to distract herself she said, "This poet of yours? What did you say his name was?"

"Umar al-Khayyam," Alma said. "He was born not far from this very spot. He studied in Samarkand and then he went to Bukhara, where he lived out his life."

Johanna remembered seeing Bukhara in her father's book. It was north of here, a little north and west of Samarkand. It was a major city on the Road, known for its fine carpets.

"He was not only a poet, Nazirah; he was a philosopher who studied everything from the rocks on the ground to the stars in the sky." Alma's voice was reverential, and perhaps even a little envious.

"You would like to study the stars in the sky yourself," Johanna said.

Alma raised her eyes, an eager expression on her face, only to have it fall again when the arcaded ceiling got in the way. "They move, you know," she said in a low voice.

"What moves?"

"The stars."

Johanna looked at her, puzzled. "Of course they move, Alma," she said. Any dark night on the Road proved it beyond doubt.

"But some of them wander," Alma said. "I have read that it is so." Her face was the picture of yearning. She was a true scholar, a seeker after information for the sake of the information itself. "One must observe, over a period of time, to see them move. I had hoped to observe them for myself one day."

Johanna's brow creased. "From the garden, at night—"

Alma shook her head. "I asked. Kadar said no."

You shouldn't have asked, Johanna thought, but was just – barely – smart enough not to say so out loud. Accustomed to a life of freedom, in the harem it was an ongoing difficulty to master her tongue. If Kadar couldn't punish her, he could yet punish others in her place. "Perhaps the rooftop?" she said instead.

"There is no access to the roof from the harem," Alma said.

Alma was still called to the sheik's bed from time to time. It was the proximate cause of Johanna's smuggling activities.

Well. That was her excuse. Hayat had approached Johanna for help during Johanna's first month in the harem. "You walk from the harem to the stables every day," Hayat had said. "Halim's cottage is hardly out of your way."

Hayat's words, did she but know it, fell on fertile ground, as Johanna had lived that first month after her arrival in a state of bubbling rage. She was ripe for any act that directly or indirectly exacted revenge on her captor, even if it was only depriving him of children by at least one member of his harem, and she was utterly reckless of any consequences. It was another month before she gave any thought to what it was she was smuggling in, and another month after that before she asked. By then, Hayat and Alma were her firm friends, and she had seen with her own eyes how joylessly Alma responded to a summons from the sheik. Hayat had not been called to the sheik's bed since Johanna's arrival in the harem.

Thinking of all of this now as she gathered her parchments together, Johanna said, her eyes on her task, "Your master the sheik is known to entertain and sponsor philosophers here at Talikan. Perhaps he could be, ah, persuaded to access the roof for you." She quirked an eyebrow.

Alma tucked her ink and pens into an exquisitely carved sandalwood box. "Perhaps," she said slowly, her brow puckering. "It would have to be phrased in the right way..."

Johanna left it at that, contenting herself with imagining the expression on Kadar's face should such a thing be commanded of him by his lord and master. "Alma," she said. "How long have you been in the harem?"

"Eleven years," Alma said. "And ten months." She paused. "And sixteen days."

She stopped short of enumerating the hours and minutes. Almost twelve years, Johanna thought.

It had been seven years ago that Jaufre's caravan had been attacked on the Road, his father killed, his mother kidnapped and sold in the Kashgar slave market. She had not dared ask before, but the appearance of Firas that morning had woken her to the realization that her escape might be nearer than she had thought. And besides, she could trust these women. She dropped her voice. "At any time here in the harem, Alma, did you perhaps meet a Greek woman? She would have been older but lovely, dark hair and eyes. Her name was Agalia. She might have been called the Lycian Lotus."

Hayat's loom slowed. Alma met Johanna's eyes and said gently, "No, Nazirah. To my knowledge, there has been no one of that name in the harem during my time here."

Alma would not ask, Johanna knew, but she could feel Hayat's curiosity burning from across the room.

The distant bell sounded a second time, followed by another, larger patter of footsteps and many voices chattering. Hayat tidied away her bobbins and shuttles and racked her loom, and rose to stretch out her back. She checked the pot of dye. "Perfect," she said in a satisfied tone, and dropped in two hanks of undyed spun silk and addressed it in stern accents. "A beautiful blue you will give me, the color of the sky at dawn."

Johanna laughed.

Hayat looked around. "Hungry? I am famished!" She smiled at Alma, and Alma smiled back. Their gazes held, and Johanna, unnoticed, excused herself.

She had to admit that the privies in the palace were lovely, raised above their humble function with more tile and smooth seats, each separated from the others by a half wall, and so well constructed and maintained that the smell never became noxious.

She laughed silently to herself, sitting there alone in the dark. It was a measure of her dissatisfaction with her current position that the best thing she could find to say about it was that the necessaries were comfortable.

She thought of Firas, and decided that she would enjoy such comfort while she could, because very soon it would be back behind a bush on the side of the Road. She couldn't wait.

Back in Hayat's room someone had extinguished the lamps and the darkness of evening gathered in the corners. "Hello?" she said.

There was a scrabbling sound and a rustle of clothing, and first Alma and then Hayat came forward. Alma looked panicked, Hayat rebellious, and both women were flushed and rumpled.

She couldn't pretend that she hadn't seen, so Johanna bowed slightly. "Forgive me for disturbing you," she said, and passed on down the hall to the common room.

She had traveled the Road since birth and had learned at an early age that love came in many forms, and Shu Ming had been wise enough to instruct her daughter in the ways of the flesh. "Desire is a powerful thing, especially in the young," she had told Johanna. "There is no stronger urge to satisfy, except, possibly, hunger."

"And this is how children come into the world?" Johanna said.

Shu Ming had cupped Johanna's cheek and smiled into her daughter's curious eyes. "It is," she said, "and it can be so much more."

What Johanna found so offensive in harem life was that it contradicted everything her mother had taught her. There were at a rough head count a hundred women in the sheik's harem. For lack of anything better to do, Johanna had worked it out mathematically. Even if he distributed his favors equally, which he did not, even if to be fair he rotated each woman through his bed one at a time, the harem inmate would see his bed an average of three nights out of 365. If a harem woman was in need of a presence in her bed for purposes other than sleep, she would do best to cultivate a relationship with another member of the harem.

Which it appeared that Hayat and Alma had done.

Johanna remembered those three days at the summerhouse with Edyk the Portuguese, her last days in Cambaluc but one, and that one the day of her father's funeral. So much joy, attended by so much sorrow, the both to send her down the Road and out of Cambaluc and by the carelessness of fate to her confinement here in the harem.

She knew a sudden, fierce ache to feel again Edyk's hands touching her, his lips on her own, the intoxicating escalation of pleasure that led to such a bright, exquisite culmination of feeling in body and mind. What she had had with Edyk bore no resemblance to what the members of any harem experienced with their owners.

Shaken at how vivid those memories were, at the yearning they awoke in her own body, she went soberly into dinner, the sound of two pairs of slippers on tile close behind her.

If Hayat and Alma were discovered, they would be killed. Three months into Johanna's stay, one of the women had been caught with one of the eunuchs, who was found to be not so much a eunuch after all. The eunuch had been splayed like a fan in the courtyard, castrated, and disemboweled. The woman had been tied in a sack and thrown into the river. The screams of both lingered still in the thoughts of everyone in the harem for days afterward.

Which was, Johanna thought now, part of their purpose. If Johanna had found them out, someone else would. Spies were rewarded in the harem.

Perhaps they wouldn't be discovered, she thought, her step slowing as an idea struck her.

Perhaps Johanna would take them with her when she left.

She woke early the next morning and was dressed to leave her silken prison at the appointed time. Kadar, silently disapproving as always, met her at the door. Tarik and Firas were waiting on the other side, North Wind in the yard, and moments later she was riding the wind, her guards faint but pursuing. The sheik's son was not with them today and her spirit rose accordingly. She lay flat on North Wind's neck and cried out, "Run, North Wind! Run!"

North Wind needed no encouragement. He lengthened his stride and the almond trees and the date palms and the canal beside the track melted into a green and silver blur. The thunder of his hooves and the wind of their passage roared in her ears. She heard a voice crying behind her and ignored it for as long as she could. "Young miss! Young miss!" The voice changed. "Wu Li's daughter, stop that monster this instant!"

She sat up and North Wind's stride slowed. Firas came galloping up and reined in beside her, out of breath and evidently out of temper as well. "Did you not hear me calling you, young miss? We don't have much time, and we must speak!"

"Where is Tarik?" she said, looking around.

"His mount threw a shoe just outside the door to the stable yard," Firas said, adding no explanation as to how such a thing might have happened.

Johanna laughed. It was impossible not to.

"Yes," Firas said, "it is all very well for you to laugh, young miss, but we will be out of his sight for a very few moments only and if we are out of his sight for longer than that I will answer for it with my head! Please slow down!"

North Wind slowed to a walk. "Jaufre," she said. "He is alive?"

His expression softened. "He is alive, young miss," he said. "Jaufre is alive."

She turned her face away from him, battling once again for control. North Wind, always sensitive to her moods, moved uneasily beneath her, and she drew in a deep breath and sat up straight. "I saw you wink at me. I was sure that was what you meant, but—"

"He is alive, young miss, my hand on my heart," Firas said. "He lives. I wouldn't call him well, but I believe in time he will be."

"Where?"

"I left them in Kabul, but it was Shasha's intent to join the first caravan going to Gaza. She said that was the plan, if you became separated."

"It was," she said. "But Kabul is so near, and Gaza so far. We should go there." She looked hungrily at the rolling hills on the western horizon. They beckoned her even more strongly now than they had every morning she had ridden out. "We could go now."

"They would be after us in minutes," Firas said.

"We should go, Firas!" she said. It was agony, to feel the taste of freedom on her tongue and not be allowed to swallow. "We may never have a better chance! This isn't a tale of the Genjii, I'm not a princess and a magic carpet isn't going to appear to whisk us out of here! We should go! Now!"

"The sheik's men would be after us, and would catch us, in minutes," Firas said, his own voice rising in turn. He looked over his shoulder and lowered his voice. "We need some kind of distraction, something to draw their attention while we escape."

North Wind whinnied and tossed his head. Johanna could almost believe that he agreed with what Firas was saying.

"Besides," Firas said, "they may have already left Kabul. Indeed, it would be best if they had."

"Why?"

"Ogodei is coming, young miss," Firas said. "And Gokudo is alive, and he is with him."

Ogodei was the Mongol baron, the head of a force of a hundred thousand men assigned by the Khan in Cambaluc to patrol the western reaches of Everything Under the Heavens. Gokudo had been the mercenary soldier from Cipangu who had been her step-mother's lover and her father's murderer.

Johanna stared at Firas, shocked. "Gokudo! But he's dead, Firas, we all saw him put to death at Ogodei's word!"

"He lives, and he is now Ogodei's favorite captain."

"That cannot be true," she said hotly. "Ogodei was my father's good friend! He would not dishonor his memory so!"

"Gently, young miss, gently," Firas said. "I merely report what I hear on the Road."

Her brow cleared. "Then it is only rumor."

He looked at her, and her heart sank at the pity in his eyes. "I have also met refugees on the Road, young miss, from the cities and oasis towns that Ogodei and his army have attacked and destroyed." He pressed his lips together for a moment. "They are few in number, admittedly, but they almost all speak of one of the Mongol captains who wears black armor, who wields a tall staff with a curved blade. He is the fiercest of the captains, they say, with no mercy for anyone—men, women, children, the aged. He slaughters them all, at his master's bidding."

She stared at him, white to the lips.

"I believe Ogodei has determined to carve his own empire out of this part of Persia," Firas said. "And a ronin samurai from Cipangu would be a valuable asset to him in this endeavor."

But she was no long looking at him. "Young miss?" Something in her expression must have alerted him, and he pulled his horse around.

Tarik found them there when he came galloping up, staring

numbly at the bodies of all twelve of the scouts sent out by Farhad the previous morning.

They lay side by side in a neat row. Each one of them had been expertly flayed, castrated, and had had their genitals stuffed into their mouths.

3

Kabul, spring, 1323

IT HAD BEEN a cold winter, one snowstorm after another, followed by thaws and rain, followed by freezing temperatures that turned everything to ice, followed by more snowstorms. The people of Kabul emerged from their homes like pale, thin ghosts of themselves, blinking dazedly in the sunlight of longer days, not quite trusting in the warmer temperatures. Shutters and doors opened and remained so. Neighbors greeted each other with no memory of past quarrels and vied with one another in the clearing of communal toilets and fountains and streets, and in the cultivation of garden plots barely thawed.

The weeds around the dilapidated fountain in their tiny court-yard sprouted in a welcome show of green, and one day Félicien came home from the market with a basket of fresh strawberries. They devoured them on the instant.

With the sweet juice of the berries lingering on his tongue, Jaufre had the curious sensation of waking up. The room he was in seemed familiar and at the same time unfamiliar to him, small and square, and while obvious effort had been made to keep it clean the dirt bricks that formed the walls were crumbling beneath several layers of whitewash to form tiny piles of debris in odd corners. What had once been a small window had been inexpertly hacked into a larger one, and a roughly planed wooden sill recently plastered into place to form a seat. Light poured through it, illuminating the neatly rolled bedrolls in one corner and the packs heaped in another. There was a pot and a pan and four bowls stacked on a small table. A large brown urn stood next to one a size smaller, the mouths of both covered with plates. An unlit brazier sat nearby, next to a bucket of charcoal.

His own bedroll was arranged against the east wall of the room, out of the direct sunlight streaming in. Félicien, Hari, and Shasha were seated around it in a solemn half-circle, watching him. He stared at them in silence, and in silence, they stared back, all with the same expectant expression on their faces.

Félicien. A slim presence in a worn dark robe, a thin, beardless face with high cheekbones and a wide, thin-lipped mouth. A student, no, a goliard he called himself, from a country far to the west, who had been traveling the Road for years. There was a lute, well played, and a light, pleasant voice given to ballads about love and war. He collected coin in his bowl around the fire each night. He was a self-styled seeker after truth, who had joined their caravan… where was it? Chang'an? Yarkent?

He couldn't remember, and the inability to do so bothered him, so he let his gaze move to the next person. This name was slower in coming. Hari. Skin and bones barely clad in a length of saffron fabric that wrapped around his waist and over one shoulder. Dark, steady eyes that implied knowledge and experience, and an unquenchable need to gain more. The priest from the lands south of the Hindu Kush, whom they had first seen being beaten before the gates of Kashgar. He couldn't remember why.

And Shasha. Proper name Shu Shao. His foster sister, adopted by Wu Li. Trim and neat in her Cambaluc robes, and supremely capable at whatever she decided to set her hand to. A cook. A healer. A… trader.

A trader. Like himself.

It was Shasha who at last broke the silence. "Jaufre?"

"Shasha?" he said. He tried to sit up, and was incredulous to realize that he was too weak to do so unaided. Hari and Félicien each took an arm and Shasha tucked a bedroll between him and the wall.

Birdsong sounded from beyond the window. He took a deep breath and put a hand involuntarily to his back, where there was a dull ache in one spot. He prodded it with a cautious finger, but the ache was all there was. Why that was important he could not immediately remember.

"Drink this," Shasha said, putting a cup beneath his nose.

Perforce, he drank. The herbal decoction wasn't noxious but it wasn't delicious, either. Hari dipped a new cup from the large urn, which he was relieved to find was water, cool and fresh. Exhausted from the effort of draining it, he leaned back against the wall, his eyes closed. "Where are we?"

"Kabul," Shasha said.

"Kabul? But—" He frowned. Surely they had only just been in that great pass, high and flat, between the mountains of the Hindu Kush and the Tian Shan? No, coming down from it. He remembered the steep, crooked trail choked with pine and juniper, slippery with rockfalls, riddled with blind curves. A route perfect for ambush and attack.

He opened his eyes and looked out the window. A drape of gauze had been tacked over it, now drawn back to allow the sun to brighten the corners of this otherwise very dark room. A small, dusty courtyard lay beyond it, where he could hear a trickle of water. "Kabul," he said again, and despised how weak his voice sounded.

"Not Kabul, precisely," Shasha said. "More on the outskirts of it."

"Don't you remember, Jaufre?" Félicien said.

"Gokudo?" Hari said. "Ogodei? The sheik?"

"Johanna," Jaufre said, and shook his head, frustrated. "Where is she?"

A heavy silence fell. Shasha got up to refill his cup from the urn. "Have some more water," she said, offering it to him.

He shoved it away, spilling the contents on the floor. "Johanna," he said again.

"I'll get more water," Félicien said. He took the urn and left the room.

"Do you remember?" Shasha said.

He did remember it all now. It all came back in a rush of brief, too-vivid scenes. Shu Ming's death. Wu Li's remarriage. The secret departure from Cambaluc. Joining Wu Cheng's caravan at Chang'an. The months on the Road. Leaving the caravan in Kashgar to traverse the mountains through Terak Pass. The nearly successful attack by Wu Li's widow's paid thug, Gokudo. Their rescue by Ogodei, Mongol general and family friend. Gokudo's execution, Ogodei's parting gift. The trail down from the pass.

And then the sheik and his men. The sheik's son, Farhad. The sharp metal piercing his back. The shock and the subsequent searing pain. Falling. North Wind's angry neigh. Johanna shouting. And then the images faded to darkness.

"He stabbed me," Jaufre said.

"The sheik's son," Shasha said. "Farhad. Yes. In the back." She indicated. "Where it hurts. Does it still hurt?"

"It aches, but…" He felt his back again. The area was tender and his muscles protested. In sudden fear he raised his arms and lowered them, flexed them at the elbows, made fists and opened them. He threw back the covers. His feet and toes and knees, everything functioned, but his skin hung on his bones.

Félicien returned and he lay back, pulling his covers up. Félicien poured out another cup of water and this time he accepted it and drank it down, suddenly aware of how thirsty he was. He handed the empty cup to Shasha and said in a voice he hardly recognized as his own, "Tell me."

"Johanna, so far as we know, is with North Wind," Shasha said, answering the question she knew he wanted an answer to first.

"And North Wind is with Sheik Mohammed."

230

"Yes."

"And Sheik Mohammed is where?"

Shasha exchanged glances with Félicien and Hari. "All we know is that it is a place called Talikan."

"Do we know where Talikan is?"

Shasha hesitated. "As yet, no. Not precisely. But—"

Jaufre summoned up enough energy for a glare. "Why aren't you with her?"

Shasha glared right back. "Because I had my hands full keeping you alive."

"You should have gone with her," he said.

"And you should have known better than to turn your back on that poisonous little spawn of the sheik," she said smartly.

Hari raised his hands, palms out, smoothing the air between them, and spoke for the first time. "Gently, my friends, gently. Harsh words will not change our dilemma."

"How long?" Jaufre said.

Shasha met his eyes squarely and said, "Six months."

"What!" He sat up again and swung his legs to the side of the cot. Shasha didn't try to stop him, merely watched as he struggled to his feet. His legs would not hold him up, and worse, a wave of dizziness forced him back down, sweating and swearing in a breathless voice. He subsided as they rearranged his limbs and pulled the covers up over them again. "Six months, Shasha," he said. "In the name of all the Mongol gods, what is wrong with me?"

"You mean other than being stabbed in the back with one of those curved pig-stickers the Persians call swords?" She huffed out a breath. "It was everything we could do to keep you from bleeding to death on the spot. When I was marginally sure you wouldn't, we fixed up a litter and carried you down the trail. Firas scouted out a village and we took you there. It was filthy and in spite of everything I could do your wound became infected. You got through that, believe it or not, and then the village came down with typhus, which you also got."

231

"I don't remember any of this," Jaufre said faintly.

"You were delirious," Shasha said. Also coughing hard enough to bring up an organ, covered in red rash and complaining constantly of severe headaches, but she didn't say so. For a few horrible days she had been certain he was going to die, but she didn't say that, either. "You were delirious for a long time. Even after we left the village you were delirious off and on again." For months. "We brought you to Kabul because I thought we might find a doctor here who could help you."

"You left her behind," he said, his eyelids drooping, his voice even fainter now.

"She ordered me to stay with you," Shasha said. His eyes closed and his breathing deepened. "The last words she said were of you," she said in a softer voice. She smoothed his hair back from his forehead, and whispered, "She commanded me to save your life, Jaufre. And I promised her I would."

✡

That afternoon Jaufre woke to the presence of a man in a crooked turban and a once-handsome robe covered with unidentifiable stains, some of which had eaten right through the fine wool. "This is Ibn Tabib," Shasha said. "He is the doctor who has been treating you."

"Hah," the doctor said, beaming. He was Persian, short, dark of skin and hair, and of a cheerful rotundity. "It is good to see you back in your own body, young sir. It was start and stop there for a while, I can tell you." He had a brisk manner and deft but gentle hands. He peered into Jaufre's eyes and mouth, sat him up and prodded his wound, manipulated his abdomen, and placed his ear first against Jaufre's chest and then his belly. He pinched the flesh of Jaufre's upper arms and thighs between thumb and forefinger and shook his head over the result.

At last he sat back. "Well," he said. "How much do you know about your illness?"

"Nothing," Jaufre said. "How much do I want to know?" He was feeling better, and in spite of nagging fears concerning Johanna he was able to concentrate on the here and now.

"Hah! You make the joke! A good sign." The doctor settled onto a pillow, his legs crossed, sipping from a mug of sweetened mint tea provided by Shasha. Hari and Félicien had absented themselves from Jaufre's examination. "Well, you know how you were injured initially." Ibn Tabib cocked his head, his bright eyes inquiring.

"Someone stabbed me in the back with their sword," Jaufre said. "It's about the last thing I really remember." Although nightmarish visions of dark, dirty rooms and endlessly painful rides swam at the edge of his memory, interspersed by occasional glimpses of Shasha's face, pale and tired, her strained voice telling him to roll over, stay still, drink this.

"Hah," Ibn Tabib said. It was an utterance he made frequently, used to punctuate many different meanings. "Yes, indeed, young sir, you were stabbed, but either your assailant was particularly inept or he meant to do you as little harm as possible."

"What?" Jaufre looked at Shasha, who was regarding her tea with interest. "He meant to kill me."

"Then we must assume ineptitude, and praise Allah for it," the doctor said. "The blade entered your back, glanced off your ribs and slid someway between flesh and bone to come out more than a handspan later." He paused to consider. "There was a great deal of blood, of course, which led Shasha here to fear the worst. She bound up the wound to stop the bleeding and moved you to shelter as soon as possible, where she could look at it more closely. All very proper." He beamed at Shasha and raised his cup in salute.

Shasha thought of those nightmarish days before they found a village far enough off the beaten track to be reasonably confident that they might escape the notice of passing travelers, who might in their turn find what belongings Shasha and Jaufre and Hari and Félicien had left too enticing to ignore. She repressed a shudder.

"Unfortunately, by the time she was able to determine that your insides were, in fact, not at risk, infection had set in. She cleaned the wound as best she could and stitched you up—a very neat job, I must say. It's a large scar—two, in fact—but they will fade in time." He sipped tea. "There was nothing she could do for the infection but keep the wound clean and dose you with willow bark. You were in a very bad way for some time—"

Eleven of the longest days of Shasha's life.

"—and then your fever broke. You were on the mend when, would you believe it, the village you were in came down with an outbreak of typhus, which you contracted. So did the young scholar traveling with you."

"Félicien? He's all right?"

"Yes," the doctor said, looking at Shasha with an expression impossible for Jaufre to interpret. She stared back, impassive, until the doctor coughed and returned to his tale. "I understand that your priest got it, too, but his case was less severe. He tells me he has suffered this malady before, which may explain it."

"Is that all?" Jaufre said.

"If you don't count the food poisoning, the near starvation and dehydration because of your inability to keep anything down," the doctor said drily; "that was quite enough to be going on with, wouldn't you agree?" He nodded at Shasha. "You would have died three or four times at least, were it not for her, and for the devotion displayed by your other friends. Hah. Indeed, you are very lucky, young sir."

Jaufre looked at Shasha. A little color had risen into her cheeks. "Thank you," he said.

"I had to," she said. "I promised her."

He took a deep breath, and nodded once. What else was to be said could not be spoken of before strangers.

The doctor looked from one to the other. "Hah," he said, smacking his hands on his thighs. "It is not often that such a chapter of incidents leads to so happy an ending. I am very pleased with you, young sir, very pleased indeed. Now, as to your recovery." He bent a stern eye upon his patient. "You have lost perhaps a quarter of your body mass, much of it muscle.

You may not rise immediately from your sick bed and pick up your sword." Jaufre followed the accusatory finger to the leather scabbard that hung from a makeshift peg on the wall. "You have been ill for months. It will take weeks for you to recover your strength, and months to recover it completely."

Jaufre remembered the humiliation of failing to stand on his own feet that morning and felt his face grow hot.

"Hah," the doctor said, not without satisfaction. "So you have already tried. Good. I find empirical evidence always works best with stubborn patients, and soldiers are above all determined to prove their invincibility, young ones in particular."

"I'm not a soldier," Jaufre said. "I'm a trader."

Ibn Tabib ignored this. "Learn to stand again first. Then walking short distances." He raised an admonitory finger. "With aid, young sir. With aid. As you grow stronger, longer distances on your own." He looked at Shasha. "You may start him on solid foods, but bland, and in small amounts. Soups and teas for fluids, as much as he can swallow. A little wine once a day. Is the water from the fountain good?"

"Yes, effendi. We have all been drinking it. It is clear and cold and seems pure."

"Then water, too, as much as you can pour into him."

"Yes, effendi."

"Ha." The doctor rose fluidly to his feet. "Will I see you at my clinic tomorrow? Our patient from last week is returning."

Shasha looked up. "The young woman with the head injury?"

"Hah. Yes. It may be that we have saved her for many more years of abuse at the hands of her so detestable husband." They went out together, conversing.

Jaufre pushed back the bedding and heaved his legs over the side of the cot and looked down at his body. His skin, once a smooth healthy pink stretched over bunched muscle, was pale and loose. He pushed himself to his feet, grunting with the effort, and shut his eyes and clenched his teeth against the resulting wave of dizziness. He didn't fall. It was a minor triumph.

He opened his eyes again to see Shasha standing in the doorway, watching him. "With aid," she said.

He swayed, but shook his head at her when she took a quick step forward. She halted in mid-stride, and he lowered himself to the cot, the last few inches more of a controlled fall. "Tell me," he said. "All of it, this time."

"You should rest."

"Now," he said. "I remember everything that happened up until the time that son of a bitch stuck me. I heard screaming, and then—" he gestured "—nothing. Or not much."

"Let me make fresh tea." She served them both and sat down on a cushion opposite him. "You had fallen to the ground and were bleeding so profusely—" She took a deep breath and let it out slowly. "I got down to see to you. In the meantime, the Sheik and his men figured out soon enough that all they had to do was take Johanna and North Wind would follow."

She took another breath and said, with more difficulty, "She shouted to me as they took her. She ordered me, she commanded me, Jaufre, not to let you die. And I was the only one among us who had any experience with caring for the sick. I could go with her and let you die. Or I could let her go and you would live."

"And if I'd died?"

Her face darkened. "Don't you dare question my decision, Jaufre. Or Johanna's." She stood up and shook out her trousers. "Now, we get you well."

He stood up with her, slowly, shakily, but he was on his feet, without aid, no matter what the doctor had said. He knew a tiny spurt of triumph, and then he looked again at his sword, hanging from the wooden peg obviously placed there for it. He had been taking lessons from a master swordsman right up until the attack. He had been in peak physical condition. How long would it be before he was there again? How long before he could even raise his sword single-handedly? "Firas," he said suddenly. "Where is Firas?"

Shasha looked suddenly older and more careworn. "With Johanna."

All he could think of to say was, "Why?"

"Because I asked him to," she said. Before he could say anything else she said, "No, we have had no word. But he is with her. I am certain of it."

He closed his mouth on all he might have said. That Firas was new to their company. That they had no reason to entrust him with the well-being of one of their own, let alone when that one was Johanna. That he was Persian, like the Sheik, and could be counted on to sympathize more with a man of his own world than with a woman of Cambaluc, especially one who had abandoned the safety and security of home and family to hare off over the horizon on an adventure that a man of his culture would see as most ill-advised, not to mention scandalously unchaperoned. But Shasha was his sister in everything but blood and he would not willingly hurt her, no matter how great his fear for Johanna's safety. He cast about for another topic. "What assets do we have left to us?"

She looked relieved. "The sheik's men tried to take everything but Firas got away with my horse and Félicien and Hari on their donkeys, and one of the camels, the one carrying the spices. I've been trading them in the marketplace here for food and supplies." She cast an involuntary glance over her shoulder and lowered her voice. "I gave Firas one of my hems."

Johanna's father had left her a quantity of loose gemstones, mostly rubies, which the three of them had sewn into the hems of their garments before they left Cambaluc. Until now, they had had no need of them. "What did he say?"

"That it might be enough, but that he would return with Johanna regardless."

Possibly his judgement of Firas had been hasty. Possibly. "Have you spoken to Grigori?" Grigori the Tatar was Wu Li's agent in Kabul.

"I have," she said. "He recognizes Wu Li's bao, and he stands our friend. He found us this house." She gave a disparaging wave. "It's not much, I know, but all the better houses are too near the market. I thought it best if we could remain as much as possible unnoticed." She paused. "We are still too close to Cambaluc for my comfort."

"We have the bao?" He thought of the leather purse that never left Johanna's waist. "How?"

"We also have Wu Li's book." She smiled a little. "When they pulled her from North Wind's back, North Wind took exception."

Jaufre thought of the massive white stallion whose affections had fastened so oddly and inflexibly on the girl so much at the forefront of their thoughts. "I can imagine."

Her smile faded. "In the ensuing, shall we say, fuss? Johanna managed to drop her purse. They didn't notice."

"Was she hurt?" He heard the panic in his own voice, and tried to steady his heartbeat.

She shook her head. "I don't think so."

There was a momentary silence, fraught with memory. Twice in two days, he thought.

Shasha raised her head to look at him. "What?"

He realized he had said the words out loud, and his mouth twisted. "Twice in two days," he said. "First I let myself be knocked unconscious by Gokudo. Twenty-four hours later I let myself get stabbed in the back by Farhad. I was so amazingly useful."

Her eyes narrowed. "Self-pity is never useful, Jaufre," she said sharply.

He felt himself flush and looked away.

"We were all attacked," she said, with emphasis. "You, me, Johanna, Hari, Félicien. Even Firas. Johanna was kidnapped. Don't you dare be such a child as to think for one moment that you were alone in this, or that you alone could have stopped it!"

She realized that her voice had risen, and she got to her feet to take a hasty turn around the room. When she passed the door she caught a glimpse of a shadow on the other side. Félicien or Hari or both, keeping out of range. Intelligent of them.

She took a deep breath, centering herself with the intonation that began any practice of soft boxing. Root from below, suspend from above. Root from below, suspend from above. Her anger still flickered beneath the surface, but now it was under control. She returned to her seat.

"We have to go after her, Shasha," he said, and the agony in his voice was enough to cause her anger to evaporate.

"No," she said, not without sympathy, because she had suffered through her own guilt over remaining with Jaufre, no matter what promises she had made.

"We have to go after her, Shasha!" He leaned forward, groping for her hand.

"No," she repeated, in a voice much firmer than she felt. "We talked about this, Jaufre. We decided, even before we left Cambaluc, that if we were separated on the Road that we would make for Gaza. She will make her way there, too." And Firas, she thought. Whether he helped her escape or not, he would meet them there as well. He had promised, and Firas the Assassin was not a man to give his word lightly.

"Besides," she said, "we don't even know where Talikan is. We only know that it is the sheik's home. It could be as far as Baghdad, or as near as Balkh, but without direction we could spend the rest of our lives traveling every spur and trail of the Road and never find it."

He was silent for a moment. "It's not on Wu Li's map?"

She bit back a quick retort. Her temper seemed to be deteriorating in direct proportion to Jaufre's recovering health. "No," she said. "I looked, of course. We all examined every page before Firas left. There is no location of that name anywhere in Wu Li's book, and we asked in the marketplace before Firas left. The name is familiar to many, but it is no better known than any of the thousand and one sheikdoms scattered from Terak Pass to the Middle Sea. The more the Mongols retreat to the east and the

north, the more local warlords appear. You know this, Jaufre."
She made herself take a calming breath, and said more patiently,
"Which means that all we know is what we picked up in passing
from the Sheik's men during our time together on the Road. The
northeast of Persia. South and west of Samarkand. We believe."

"You believe," he said bitterly.

"Yes," she said. "It gives Firas a place to start, at least." Before
he could speak, before he could think up something even nastier
to say to her, she added, "The instant you are well enough to sit
on a camel, we start for Gaza with the first caravan of a decent
size heading west. We know where Gaza is. So does Johanna.
Wu Li had a factor there."

"Abraham of Acre," Jaufre said.

"If he's still there, we have the bao. Like Grigori, he will help
us. When she can, Johanna will meet us there. She might even get
there before us." Unlikely, but not impossible, she thought. She
took a deep breath and let it out slowly, preparing herself to give
him the worst news of all. "There is another reason we need to
start moving west, as fast as we can."

The tone of her voice made him look up. "What?"

"Ogodei." To her shame, her voice trembled. With an act of
will she steadied it.

He stared at her. "Ogodei?"

Her eyes dropped to her hands, which were curled into fists.
She straightened them, and smoothed one over the other; a
nervous, wasted motion totally out of character. "Ogodei has
brought his one hundred thousand down this side of Terak."

"Why?" he said, when she did not go on.

"He is…laying claim, I think is the only way to describe it.
He's marching up to the front doors of every walled city, of every
town and city of a size to make it worthwhile, and demanding
that they surrender. If they do, he lets them live. If they don't, he
destroys them."

"Destroys them?" Later he would think his prolonged illness
had slowed his ability to think rationally.

"Destroys them," she said. She put a hand to her mouth and then with what looked like a determined effort dropped it and sat up straight again. "Refugees arrived in Kabul over the past month. Pitifully few of them, and the stories are horrific." She made a poor attempt at a smile. "He seems to imagine himself the reincarnation of Genghis Khan himself."

"Is he acting on orders from Cambaluc?"

"I doubt it."

"Why?"

"Shidibala Gegeen Khan is dead, murdered. The news came earlier this month, when the trails over the mountains opened. I think Ogodei is taking advantage of what always follows a change of power in Cambaluc to set up his own empire."

Jaufre was silent, digesting this. "He was always ambitious, Wu Li said."

She nodded.

"Which cities?"

"Jaufre?"

"Which cities, Shasha?"

"While we were on our way here, he went first for Samarkand and then Tashkent, and from what they say didn't miss any of the oasis towns between. So far he's staying out of the mountains."

"So far?"

She met his eyes, and only then did he really see how worried she was, and how tired. "Rumor in the market has it that he is turning his attentions south."

"India?" he said.

She shrugged.

Realizing, he said, "And everything in between. Including Kabul?" Talikan? he thought.

"There's worse," she said.

He gave her an incredulous look.

"They say he has a new captain," she said. "A warrior, from a land far to the east."

He stared at her. "No," he said.

"He wields a tall staff, they say," she said. "One with a curved blade."

"Gokudo," Jaufre said, his voice barely above a whisper, and a chill chased down his spine.

4

Kabul, spring, 1323

IT TOOK A month for Jaufre to force himself back into health, or enough so that he could walk some distance mostly without aid. He never sat where he could stand, never stood where he could walk, and if he could only run ten steps before he had to stop, breathing hard, then he ran those ten steps. He had begun to practice form with Shasha every morning and again every evening, Félicien joining in, Hari off to one side chanting his interminable oms. Yesterday he had taken down his father's sword and practiced some of the parries and thrusts that Firas had taught him, no matter that after five minutes the yard had begun to revolve slowly around him and he'd had to let Shasha replace the sword because he could no longer raise his arms that high.

This morning Félicien had announced his intention of walking into the city to see if the first caravan of spring had arrived. "They say in the market that there should be one any day now," he said.

"I'll go with you," Jaufre said.

Félicien glanced at Shasha. "There isn't much to see," he said.

"Go ahead," Shasha said, waving a hand in airy dismissal. "Kill yourself."

When they had left, Hari said gently, "He is sick at heart."

"He is sulking," Shasha said, and stalked from the room.

The city of Kabul was a claustrophobic wedge crowded into a narrow valley, an unlovely jumble of square buildings constructed of mud bricks, interspersed with the inevitable neighborhood mosque. On all sides rose the sharp-edged peaks of the Hindu Kush, still clad in a receding layer of winter snow, leavened here and there by tiny patches of green. On closer examination those patches proved to be the smallest of terraced gardens jostling for place with granite outcroppings and small avalanches of broken shale, reclaimed from the mostly vertical landscape with waist-high walls made of loose, readily available rocks. The nearest arable land was far to the north, on the other side of the mountains, and those citizens of Kabul too hungry to wait for the first spring caravans to arrive with fresh fruits and vegetables scrabbled in the hard dirt to grow a few of their own. It was at best a vain effort, thought Jaufre, viewing the scraggly results of one such, but still they tried, toiling up and down the steep trails and stairs to their homes with sacks of water on their bent backs. Here and there a poplar bravely raised a spindly, trembling head.

"There isn't even a university," Félicien said, regarding Kabul with manifest disgust.

"There's a madrasa at the grand mosque, surely," Jaufre said mildly.

"Teaching religion. What of mathematics and rhetoric and philosophy?"

Jaufre, out of breath from their short climb, didn't answer.

"Look," Félicien said, pointing. "There is the caravansary. Such as it is." He led Jaufre through a cluster of one-storey buildings that formed their little neighborhood. Most of the men who lived there were employed in the construction of a new mosque not far away. Religion was the only industry that paid and paid regularly in Kabul. "They can't dig a well to water their gardens, but they can always find enough money for another mosque," Félicien said.

The women remained sequestered in their homes while their children too small to work played in the dirt outside their doors. A cloud of dust was already beginning to rise over the city and it wasn't even noon.

"An unlovely place," Jaufre said.

"It does not improve on closer inspection," Félicien said, and then clutched Jaufre's arm. "Look! Look, Jaufre, look there, you see!"

A cloud of dust, thicker than the one over Kabul, rose at the top of the pass leading into the city, and as they watched the first in a line of camels minced down the trail and approached the northern gate.

"Come, Jaufre!" Félicien said, his face alight with excitement. Jaufre couldn't blame him. His companions had not slept the winter away as he had and by now were heartily bored with Kabul and its environs.

They arrived at the caravansary at the same time as what appeared to be at least half the population of Kabul. When Jaufre saw what was in the caravan's train, he curled a lip in disgust. "Slavers," he said.

Félicien eyed him. "It's not illegal."

"No, just disgusting. Let's get something to eat while they sort themselves out."

Jaufre fended off an offer for ground testicle of sheep—"Guaranteed to rekindle the interest of the most indifferent lover, truly, sahib!"—and found a kebab vendor next to a fountain in an adjacent square. Jaufre, whose appetite had returned with full, pre-injury force, ate three of beef and one of goat's liver. Félicien had one of chicken. No vegetables, of course, but they found an old man with a fruit cart piled with last year's apples. They were wrinkled and a little dry but still sweet.

When they returned to the caravansary, the novelty of the first caravan of the year had worn off and the crowd had dispersed, at least until the merchants had offloaded their goods and set up their tents. Jaufre inquired for the havildar, and was introduced to a Gurkha named Rambahadur Raj who wore a kukri as long as his arm in a worn but well-cared-for leather sheath. He was a foot shorter than Jaufre but he stood with an easy assurance that reminded Jaufre of Firas.

"I am Jaufre of Cambaluc, havildar," Jaufre said, inclining his head in a show of respect. "This is Félicien of the Franks."

"Salaam, Jaufre of Cambaluc, Félicien of the Franks," the havildar said, bowing his head less deeply in return. "Let us retire out of the sun and send for tea."

"That would be welcome," Jaufre said, not lying.

They settled beneath the awning at the front of the havildar's yurt and discussed the weather until the tea came on a round tin tray. The havildar brewed the tea with his own hands, poured it into earthenware cups and handed it around with a plate of hard biscuits. He sat back with a sigh, blowing across the top of his cup. "I confess, it is a pleasure to be at rest."

Jaufre sipped. The tea was hot and heavily sweetened and scalded his throat as it went down. "Has your journey been a long one, then, havildar?"

"As long as necessary, Jaufre of Cambaluc, but certainly more interesting than usual."

Jaufre raised an eyebrow. "Bandits? Raiders?"

Rambahadur Raj grimaced. "Armies, more like."

"Kabul talks of armies as well," Jaufre said. "In particular of a Mongol army, come recently over the mountains from Everything Under the Heavens."

The havildar nodded. "If rumor is true, this army has a general who regards himself as the living reincarnation of the great Genghis Khan himself."

Shasha had said almost exactly the same thing.

"But you yourself are of Cambaluc," Rambahadur Raj said. "If rumor is true and he is a Mongol, surely he is known there."

"He is, if rumor is true," Jaufre said. "It is said his name is Ogodei. A Baron Ogodei was recently named to the head of a hundred thousand and posted to the West."

The havildar's eyebrow went up. "Possibly an attempt to move an overly ambitious lord from the seat of power?"

"Possibly," Jaufre said, and shrugged. "I don't pay much attention to politics, but it was said that the late khan was... cautious in the men he chose to hold office near to his person."

"Not cautious enough," the havildar said drily.

As the last khan's tenure had been less than two years, Jaufre could hardly disagree. "As you say."

"This Ogodei, rumor says that he is bent on conquest," the havildar said. "That if a city surrenders to him he will spare it, but that if it does not, he destroys it and kills all of its people, down to the last child."

Jaufre thought of his last sight of Ogodei, sitting at his ease on a pile of carpets before a yurt very like this one, drinking koumiss and watching with equanimity the death of one of his men by the riding of horses over his body. Next to him Félicien stirred, and he touched the boy's arm briefly in warning. It would not do to have it known that they knew Ogodei.

Besides, it was glaringly obvious that they didn't. If rumor did not lie, he had not, in fact, executed Gokudo, and there was no question that he had betrayed them to the sheik. "He is in the north of Persia now, if rumor is true," he said.

"If rumor is true," the havildar said, nodding. "But rumor also says that his army moves very fast. Samarkand fell in a matter of days, and he is said now to be moving south."

Where Talikan might, or might not, lie. Jaufre did his best to keep his face without expression. "You will be leaving Kabul soon, then."

"As soon as the merchants complete their business," the havildar said grimly.

"Where does your route take you?"

"Kerman, Damascus, and Gaza."

Jaufre nodded. "I see. As it happens, havildar, my party wishes to travel west," he said.

"Does it? And how many are in your party?"

"Four."

The havildar scratched his chin, staring off into the middle distance. "I have no wish to be discourteous, young Jaufre of Cambaluc, but in these unsettled times I would be remiss in my duty to the security of the caravan if I did not inquire as to your companions, and your business." The havildar's gaze was steady on his.

"Of course," Jaufre said. "We are merchants, late of the house of Wu Li, also of Cambaluc."

"Wu Li," the havildar said. "I have heard the name."

"My master was not accustomed to travel west beyond Kashgar, but he had a large network that extended as far as Venice," Jaufre said.

"News came down the Road some time back that Wu Li had died." The havildar's tone carried only mild inquiry, but his gaze was intent.

"Sadly, that is so. Early last year." Jaufre thought the wound scabbed over but something in his expression made the other man look away.

"My condolences on the death of so worthy a master," the havildar said, bowing, more deeply this time in respect of Wu Li's memory.

Rambahadur Raj made fresh tea and renewed their cups. "There was mention of a daughter," he said meditatively. "Is she one of your party?"

Jaufre unclenched the teeth that had snapped shut. "We left Cambaluc together. Of necessity, we took different routes on the Road. The intent is to meet again in Gaza."

"Hmm," the havildar said. "I can't seem to recall the name of Wu Li's agent in Kabul…"

"Grigori the Tatar," Jaufre said, and pointed. "He lives on the edge of the market, near the Grand Mosque."

"I am acquainted with Grigori," the havildar said. "The others in your party?"

"You have already met Félicien," Jaufre said.

"And what is it you do, young man?"

"I am a scholar, and a seeker after truth," Félicien said, not without pride.

The havildar grunted. "A full-time occupation these days. I wish you luck with it. Who else?" he said to Jaufre.

"Shu Shao, a healer and Wu Li's adopted daughter."

"Another healer is always useful," the havildar said, nodding his head. "That's three. You said you were four?"

"The fourth is…" Jaufre couldn't help making a face. "Hari of India. He is… chughi." At Rambahadur Raj's quizzical glance, he added, reluctantly, "A priest."

"A priest?" the havildar said, thoughtfully. "A proselytizer?"

"No," Jaufre said firmly, repressing the memory of Hari being beaten before the gates of Kashgar for practicing religion without a license. "He is, as is young Félicien here, a seeker after truth."

"So long as he doesn't seek after one truth to the exclusion of all others," the havildar said drily.

"He does not," Jaufre said, still firmly, and resolved to make the matter plain to Hari before they set out. "And the fee?"

"You will mount yourselves?"

"We will."

"Provide your own food and fodder?"

"Yes."

The havildar mentioned a sum, Jaufre reacted in horror, and after fifteen minutes they had agreed on a sum that Rambahadur Raj thought was too low and Jaufre of Cambaluc thought too high. A good bargain, sealed by a handshake.

"Consider you have been given the usual warnings against fire and quarreling with your neighbors," the havildar said.

"Of course," Jaufre said.

"As to our departure, as I said before. We leave the instant my merchants have sold their last sack of rice, their last bale of cotton, and their last slave." The havildar raised his voice. "Alaric!"

One of the guards, taller than the rest, detached himself from a group of men setting up tents. "Havildar."

"Meet Jaufre of Cambaluc. His party of four will be joining us when we depart Kabul. Jaufre of Cambaluc, meet Alaric the Templar, my second in command."

"Not a Templar, havildar," the man said in a long-suffering tone.

He was dressed in the ankle-length, belted coat and baggy pants with the gathered hems of the Persian, and at first that was what Jaufre mistook him for. As he approached, though, Jaufre saw that his face was long and his nose thin, and when he raised a hand in casual salute of the havildar his sleeve fell back and Jaufre saw a flash of paler skin and realized that the color of his face came from long exposure to the sun.

Most interesting of all, the sword that hung at Alaric's side could have been the twin of Jaufre's own.

5

Talikan, spring, 1323

"YOU CANNOT BE serious," Johanna said.

She was ignored, and in spite of the clear warning in Firas' eyes she went so far as to lay a hand on Farhad's sleeve as he brushed past her. "Farhad, if you fight Ogodei he will kill you, he will kill every single one of your people and he will raze Talikan to the ground. To the ground, Farhad!"

That morning, upon the discovery of the bodies, Johanna had sent Tarik back for the sheik, who had sent his son. Farhad had looked at the remains of his scouts and returned them all inside the walls of the city at once. The sheik had dispatched other scouts to confirm the story, and the men who came back all too quickly bore first-hand-reports of an approaching army infiltrating the valleys between the surrounding hills and laying waste to everything and everyone in its path.

"How soon will they get here?" the sheik said.

The first scout exchanged a glance with his peers. "An hour, my lord," he said. "Perhaps two. No more."

The sheik and his son, aided by a circle of grim-faced counselors, began immediately to lay plans for a siege. Now, an hour and a half later, they stood on the wall next to the great eastern gate, watching Ogodei's army spill from the hills onto the verdant plain between the hills and the city. Columns of smoke rose from farm buildings and villages.

Johanna wasn't supposed to be there at all, but she had taken advantage of the panic and confusion of the first moments of discovery to follow Farhad to his father's side. So far, everyone had been too busy to notice, or if they had, too distracted to order her back to the harem. "Look!" she said now, pointing. The Mongol army seemed to move forward like lightning, in horizontal bolts that covered terrifying amounts of ground in thrusts and forays. "They will be on the city in minutes!"

Farhad cast a casual glance over his shoulder and gave her an indulgent smile. "Calm yourself, Nazirah. Remember, we have seen this Ogodei. A bully, merely, who like all bullies backs down at the first challenge."

"A bully with a hundred thousand men, Farhad," she said. "And they are Mongols. It hasn't been that long since Genghis Khan laid waste to the Persian empire. You must have heard the stories." She thought of Halim the dyer, and of Alma and Hayat, and of Ishan the stable master. What Ogodei's men would do to them and their families would make death seem like a blessing. She tried to speak in conciliatory tones that would reach beyond the pride that formed such a strong barrier between Farhad and any reasonable viewpoint. "A bully, perhaps, as you say, but a bully with siege engines, and poisoned arrows, and fire bombs, and Ogodei alone knows what other horrors."

"I would match our walls against a hundred hundred thousand such men. We have withstood sieges before, Nazirah. There is nothing to fear."

His father was standing a few paces away and before Farhad could stop her she stepped in front of him, dropping to her knees to touch her forehead to the floor. "Sheik Mohammed, I beg you, for the life of your city and the lives of all its citizens, I beg you to hear me."

There was a sudden stillness in their immediate surroundings. No one in Talikan had ever seen Johanna offer anything but defiance to anyone within its walls, and her obeisance shocked them all into momentary silence.

The stillness gave her hope. "Lord, you have observed Ogodei with your own eyes. He was known as an ambitious man in Cambaluc, it was the reason he was posted to the West when he was named to his hundred thousand. He is a great admirer of the Great Khan, Genghis himself. It was suspected in Cambaluc that he views himself as a stronger ruler than any vying for power in Everything Under the Heavens." She was speaking rapidly, afraid that she would lose the sheik's attention. "He was a friend of my father's, who knew him well. From the words of my father, the honorable Wu Li, whose voice was respected from Cambaluc to Kashgar, I believe I divine Ogodei's thought. I believe that he wishes to build his own empire on the back of your own, and with that empire at his back to bring even Everything Under the Heavens itself under his rule. Perhaps even to challenge Oz Beg Khan in the north."

She raised her eyes and somewhat to her astonishment found the sheik looking directly at her. Encouraged, she said, "Lord, I beg you, I beg you on behalf of all the people of Talikan to treat with Ogodei. If you submit to his rule, he will spare you and your city." She swallowed. "If you defy him, he will destroy it, and every citizen in it."

He opened his mouth as if to reply, and then shut it again. "When they come," she said quickly, "the front troops will consist of every man, woman and child from surrounding towns and villages, as well as soldiers defeated in other battles whom they have taken prisoner. They will drive these before their own troops, forcing you to waste your arrows and bolts before Ogodei's own troops arrive at your gates with siege engines."

"We have no report of siege engines in the infidel's train," the sheik said.

"They will build them," she said. "Even now their engineers are razing the villages and towns they have captured for materials."

"Father," Farhad said, "she can't know any of this. And why would you listen to a woman who dares to speak in your presence of war anyway?" He seemed to recall where they were. "She should not be here. She is out of her place. Send her back to the harem."

It felt as if they were standing at the center of a large storm, surrounded by a whirlwind of frantic effort and only nearly contained panic. Johanna was conscious of Firas standing behind her, of Farhad one pace to the left, and of the sheik, tall and still in his white robes, the white band of his headdress casting shadow over his deep-set eyes. She hadn't seen him in over a month. He had lost weight. He looked pale and tired and she got the impression that he stood erect beneath the weight of his robe only with great effort.

He stirred. "My son has a point. How is it you know so much of the war tactics of the Mongols? Your father must have been foolish indeed to allow it."

"Lord, what does it matter!" she cried. "They are Mongols! Remember Baghdad! Remember Kiev! They have made an art of warfare! If you resist, they will destroy you, and Talikan, and every living soul inside its walls!"

The sheik listened as the echo of her words was devoured by the thunder of the approaching army.

In an agony of apprehension, she could only imagine what was going on inside his head. The Persians were a proud race, even now, hundreds of years after the fall of the empire that had once laid claim to everything from Khotan to Zaranj to Toprak Kala. Broken now into many separate pieces, walled cities and oasis towns separated by vast stretches of steppe and desert and truncated and isolated by mountain ranges, it was every community for itself. No leader of any community, no Persian and certainly no follower of Allah would find it easy to bend the knee to a barbarian horde out of the East.

But this man must, she thought desperately. He must.

He raised his contemplative eyes from her face and looked at his son standing behind her. "Perhaps it would do no harm to speak to them," he said.

Something seized her braid and she cried out in surprise and pain as she was yanked from her knees to her back. Farhad dragged her across the rough stone and dropped her in an unceremonious heap out of his way.

"You are old, father," Farhad said, "with an old man's ideas." And before anyone could say anything else, before his father could move out of the way, Farhad drew his scimitar and thrust it deep into his father's breast.

Johanna watched numbly as blood welled from around the blade and stained the front of his robes. His legs buckled and he crumbled to his knees before his son, in a parody of the Muslim observance of prayer.

Farhad withdrew his sword from his father's chest and flicked the blood from the blade. Johanna felt warm splatters on her face. "We shall not kneel before this infidel horde and beg for mercy," he shouted. "We will fight!" There was a ragged cheer, although there were more than enough men who did not cheer, who had heard Johanna's words, even if those words had been spoken by a woman. They were older men, she noticed with the part of her mind that was still functioning. The younger men looked excited and all of them had their swords out and raised in salute to Farhad. "And we will not just fight, we will destroy them utterly!"

He raised his scimitar over his head. A last drop of blood ran down the silver blade. "Allahu Akbar!"

"Allahu Akbar!" This time the response was larger and louder and longer.

"Allahu Akbar! God is great! Allahu Akbar!"

And with that, the transition of power was complete. Farhad began snapping out orders. Men leapt to obey.

Johanna tore her gaze away from the still face of the late Sheik Mohammed and got to her feet. "You are a fool, Farhad," she said fiercely, "and my only consolation is that you will know just how big a fool before Ogodei kills you!"

He looked over her head. "You, Firas, isn't it? See the Lady Nazirah safely back to the harem."

"Lord." Firas took her arm and force-marched her away. "You do our cause no good by calling him foolish in front of his men," he said in a fierce undertone.

"I would call him more than that!"

He gave her a hard shake. "Be still! This may be our chance."

Her vision, occluded by rage and fear, cleared at once. "To get away?"

"Yes, but we will have to do it before the city is surrounded."

"They will flank it," she said. "Ogodei knows me for Wu Li's daughter, he will know North Wind, could we not ride out to meet him and beg for the city's life?"

The glance he gave her was pitying. "Nothing you said to Farhad was untrue, young miss. If the city fights, it and all the people in it are forfeit. It is known that Ogodei has done the same to other cities ever since he came down from the Terak. He is building his own empire, and he will brook no interference. Besides, you have forgotten."

She looked at him.

"Gokudo," he said.

She halted at the top of the steps, and a sliver of unease shivered down her spine. "Gokudo," she said, although it sounded to Firas more like a hiss, and then they were both nearly knocked from their feet by a deafening roar of challenge that they could feel through the very stone of the walls of Talikan itself. As one, they turned and raced to peer over the side of the wall.

As far as the eye could see the plain was covered with men on horseback, mirrored armor glittering in the morning sun. Spears beat against shields and the shouts of a hundred thousand warriors joined in a deafening wave of sound. They were laughing, shouting, gesticulating obscenely at the men on the wall and above the gate. As more and more of them poured from the hills into the plain, Johanna saw more than one defender of Talikan grow momentarily still and pale beneath the sinking realization that there would be no defeating this massive army. Most of them had very probably never seen a hundred thousand men in one place before. Ogodei's force filled the plain in a broad wedge from canal on the right to river on the left, which left Talikan surrounded on every side they weren't bordered by water.

A ragged hail of arrows sailed over the walls and struck at Ogodei's front lines, filled with unarmed men, women and children who looked like farmers and their families. They fell, pierced by Talikan's arrows, and more were shoved forward to take their place. It was a plan designed to take the heart out of the fiercest defender, their own arrows killing their own people, and it did not fail of effect. An order was shouted, Farhad's voice, she thought dazedly, and another flight of arrows hurled themselves from behind the walls, striving for farther targets, most of them failing to find them.

"They are wasting ammunition," she said, her voice lost in the cacophony. Who knew that war was so loud?

She looked then for Ogodei, and picked out an unarmed man riding bareback, moving swiftly from the front of the force to a knot of men on a small rise well out of bowshot. The rider would be a courier, and she followed him as he bowed to the figure at the center of the knot. She pointed, and Firas pulled her hand back when an arrow sailed over her head too close for comfort. The Mongols were shooting back, but not in any concentrated way. They were saving their arrows, she thought. Farhad, if he had a brain in his head, would notice and act accordingly.

She had no hope that he would.

Firas put his mouth to her ear. "We must go!"

But then her eyes found Gokudo.

He was forcing his way through the throng gathering around the great wooden gates, which inside had four sets of massive wooden bars dropped into heavy brackets embedded into the walls. They looked formidable from where Johanna stood, until she looked again at the force on the other side of them.

Gokudo, the dull black of his quilted armor set apart from the sewed skins of the Mongols, looked more so, especially with the tall black spear with the curved blade held at his side.

Being told that he was alive when she had left him for dead so many leagues and months ago was one thing. To see him resurrected before her was like a body blow, and she bent at the waist, gasping for breath. Firas grasped her arm and drew her upright, preparing to pull her from the wall by force if he had to.

By some malign chance Gokudo chose that moment to look up. He saw her immediately, and there fell one of those odd, fleeting moments of stillness that come in the middle of even the bloodiest of battles. The world fell away, and there were only the two of them left, she staring down at him, he staring back up at her.

"Hah," he said, she could swear softly, although how she could have heard him if he hadn't shouted it at the top of his voice she would never know. "Wu Li's daughter," he said, and smiled when her white face flushed with gathering rage.

He made an odd bow in her direction and looked around him. As she watched, he handed off the naginata to pull a woman from those being held in front of the Mongol warriors. She was more of a girl, Johanna saw, she couldn't have been fifteen years of age. Gokudo forced her to her knees in front of him, pushed his thumbs into her cheeks to open her mouth, and used her thus, all the while his eyes never left Johanna's. The girl struggled and choked, her hands clawing ineffectually at his. He finished, wiped himself on her hair and threw her behind him, where she was fallen on by more of his men, shouting and laughing as they held her down and fell on her one at a time. This led to an orgy of rape at the front of the force facing the city, many of the women used a dozen, two dozen times, until they died of it, or had their necks snapped and their corpses left where they lay.

This, too, she thought dimly, was part of a deliberate plan, to instill disgust and hatred and above all terror into the defenders, to see Persian women so used and so dishonored by Mongols, to stir them to do something reckless and careless and misjudged, to allow ungoverned rage to open a breach in their own defenses through which Ogodei's forces could then pour. They had done it before. It always worked.

Gokudo was still watching her, oblivious to the arrows raining down all around him, none of them coming close enough even to wound, let alone kill. He seemed to be wearing an invisible cloak that protected him from all harm. She saw his lips move, and thought numbly that she could hear the words he spoke as clearly as if they were standing back in the courtyard of her father's house in Cambaluc. "I look forward to our next meeting, Wu Li's daughter," he said, and bowed again, and laughed.

"I told you to get her back to the harem!" Farhad said, and cuffed Firas across the face and was gone again. The evil spell cast by Gokudo that had held them frozen in place was broken. Without more ado Firas hustled for the stairs, Johanna's arm clutched in his as she stumbled behind him.

They had passed through the door into the garden when she again realized where they were. "Give me a weapon," she said. At his look she said, "There are no weapons in the harem other than those worn by the guards. Give me a dagger, something."

His hand went first to the serviceable dagger at his waist, and then from somewhere produced one smaller and slimmer knife in a thin leather sheath with straps. "This can be fastened beneath your clothes."

She slid the blade out. It was a narrow piece of steel that looked deadly even at rest. "Firas. What happens to the harem when the sheik dies?" When the news of the sheik's illness has reached the harem there had been rumors, of course, but Firas, a Persian man, would know.

They had reached the door between the garden and the court-yard that led into the harem. Firas spoke rapidly, in a low voice, one eye on the door. "It depends on the sheik's will, and on how much attention the sheik's heirs pay to his will."

Farhad was his heir, Johanna thought, and he had already told her his intentions.

"They can be provided for for life. They can be sold to other masters." He met her eyes. "They could all be tied into sacks and thrown into the river."

"They could be given to Ogodei's men for toys," she said, the horror of the scene at the east gate heavy upon her.

"So long as they lived," he said, and by the expression in his eyes she knew he was thinking of it, too.

They heard the twang of bows and the exuberant ululation of Farhad's warriors. "The fools," she said bitterly.

"Soon to be dead fools," he said. "I will be at the harem door just after twilight."

"I won't leave without North Wind."

Firas, a dignified man, would never do anything so obvious as roll his eyes. "Of course. I will saddle him before I come for you. And—the black?"

She shook her head. "The gray. He's smaller but he has almost beaten North Wind a few times." She hesitated.

"What?" he said with foreboding.

"If they will come, I will be bringing two others with me," she said.

Firas looked thoroughly exasperated. "Young miss! It will be difficult enough to get the two of us safely away!"

Johanna thought of the girl Gokudo had used before the gate. "I will not leave without them. Unless it is their will to stay."

"Can they ride?"

"I don't know. Probably not."

"Young miss!"

"We'll tie them on if we have to, Firas. Saddle two more horses."

Muttering imprecations, he reached for the latch on the door. She stopped him with a gesture. "What now?" he said.

"Halim. The dyer."

"What of him?"

"No. Just... warn him." Her eyes were pleading. "He is a friend to everyone in the harem. He smuggles drugs in when they are needed. Warn him. Please, Firas?"

He was relieved she didn't want to bring the dyer along, too. "I will do so, young miss."

"Thank you, Firas." There was another outcry beyond the walls, nearer this time, and deep enough for them to feel the vibrations in their feet.

"At dusk, young miss."

"We will be there, Firas."

He marched her up to the harem door, every bit the efficient, impersonal guard, and exchanged nods with the two standing before it. They both looked distinctly uneasy, which proved they weren't as stupid as Johanna had always assumed they were, and they broke protocol enough to say to Firas, "What is that sound?"

"It's an army, come to assault the city," Firas said, and then added without looking at Johanna, "A very large army."

"The sheik?"

"Is on the walls," Firas said, without specifying which sheik.

The guard brightened. "We will fight! Allahu Akbar!"

The second guard looked less enthusiastic but echoed, "Yes, we will fight, Allahu Akbar."

"Allahu Akbar," Firas said gravely in response, and nodded at the door.

The first guard recollected his duties and restrained his martial fervor enough to hammer on the door as the second guard drew back the outside bolts.

There was no response from inside. The guards exchanged a look, and hammered again. A third time produced the desired result. The inside bolts were drawn back and the door swung open the merest crack.

Johanna, who had an idea as to what must have happened, pushed past the guards and stepped inside the door, closing it firmly behind her and drawing the useless filigreed bolt across.

Hayat was standing there with an anxious look on her face.

"Where is Kadar?" Johanna said in a low voice.

"I don't know," Hayat said. "I was getting some tea when I

261

heard the knocking. When I came out, there was no one on the door."

"He knows," Johanna said.

"Knows what?"

"Come with me," Johanna said, and towed Hayat through the harem rooms to the little common room in back that Hayat and Alma had made their own. The other occupants of the harem were clustered in small groups, looking frightened. The sounds of battle were softened but not stifled in here.

"Nazirah!" one, braver than the rest, said. "What news from outside?"

"Talikan is under attack," Johanna said. "The sheik is preparing to fight." Like Firas, she did not specify which sheik.

There was an excited buzz and a few shrill screams and more questions but Johanna didn't stop. In Hayat's room, Alma had heard them coming and had risen to her feet. Her eyes were wide and her face was pale and she saw Hayat with relief. Hayat ran to her side and pulled her into a reassuring embrace. "It's all right, love, it's all right. Johanna is back, and all will be well."

Johanna wished she had Hayat's confidence. She beckoned both women closer, and dropped her voice to the merest whisper, conscious of listening ears clustering outside the open door. "Sheik Mohammed is dead. Farhad killed him." When they would have exclaimed she held a finger to her lips. "The city of Talikan is under attack by a force much too large for them to withstand. I know the man at the head of that force. He is a Mongol." Both women gasped. They had heard the stories, as indeed had everyone heard them, with the possible exception of that idiot Farhad.

She looked at the two women, her only two friends in the harem, the only two people she even marginally trusted within the walls of Talikan, and her heart sank. Alma was the daughter of a king and had been married to Sheik Mohammed as a means of ensuring a treaty. Hayat had been the daughter of a poor family who had sold her into slavery as a means of feeding the rest of their children. Neither had known anything in their adult lives but the useless luxury of the harem. "Can either of you ride?"

Alma looked scandalized, Hayat worried. Both shook their heads. Johanna took a shaky breath. "Do I have to explain to you what will happen when the Mongols attack the city?"

"No, Nazirah," Hayat said soberly. "No, you don't have to tell us." Alma shook her head, white to the lips.

"It may be that I can get you out," Johanna said, and held her finger to her lips when the other women would have exclaimed. "Dress in your warmest clothes." She surveyed the gauzy vests and pants of the two women and said, "Dress in all your clothes. Have you anything better to put on your feet than those slippers?"

"No."

No help for it. "Then wear what you have, as many pairs as you can fit over your feet. We'll try to find something better later." If there was a later for any of them.

"Where will we go?" Hayat said.

"We'll worry about that if we manage to get out of Talikan alive," Johanna said.

"What about—" Hayat said.

"The others?" Johanna said, and set her jaw. "I can't save them all. I might be able to save you. Will you come with me?"

The two women looked at each other for a long moment, and turned to face Johanna as one. "We will," Hayat said firmly. Alma, still pale, only nodded.

"It is well." Or she hoped with all her heart that it would be. "If we are caught, by either side—"

"We will come with you, Nazirah," Hayat said firmly.

"All right. Say nothing, nothing, do you understand? Nothing at all to anyone else. If you do they will panic and likely cause a riot and we will never get out of here." There was a noise like a thunderbolt far off, followed a few seconds later by a crashing boom somewhere in the city. Johanna thought she could hear the screams even through the thick walls of the palace. Judging by the cries in the harem, she wasn't the only one. "It has begun. Dress. Take nothing you have to carry, nothing that you can't fit into your pockets. You'll need your hands to hang on to your mounts. We will leave at dusk."

"What about Kadar?" Alma said. "The guards?"

Johanna's lip curled. "I am certain that Kadar is at present currying favor with Farhad," she said. Only one thing would absent Kadar from his office and that was his determination to keep it for himself no matter what the change of regime. "And we have a friend on the outside. I promise you, the guards will be otherwise occupied."

She left them rummaging through their belongings, speaking to each other in fierce whispers, and went back to her room. The first thing she did was pull the knife Firas had given her from inside her tunic and strap it to her forearm. She practiced pulling it a dozen times. It felt good in her hand, friendly, and deadly. She immediately felt much better dressed.

She stood still for a moment, staring hard at the walls that had been her prison for too many months now. She had the knife. She had her wits. She had Firas. She had soft boxing, which she had continued to practice each morning before the harem woke and each evening after it had gone to sleep, but it would be effective only in situations where there was ideally one enemy, two at most. Also an asset was the fact that she was a woman, a being perceived as incapable of fighting.

It would have to be enough. She would make it be enough.

Food, she thought, and water, and then rejected out of hand the notion of trying to find and pack anything. It would only draw attention, and they couldn't afford that. They would have to forage on the Road.

The stables should be deserted if everyone was fighting on the walls, and she had a fair idea of the average speed of Sheik Mohammed's horses. Firas could be depended on to choose the best and the fastest ones. If only Hayat and Alma could manage to stay on them.

She went through all of her belongings. She was already wearing her tunic and trousers. She stripped out of them and donned two vests scratchy with embroidery and two pairs of the gauzy harem trousers, then pulled her real clothes on over them. As always, she felt for the lumps in her hems, and wondered if she should remove two or three for bribes, just in case. She discarded that idea, too. Speed and surprise were all that would save them now.

She rolled some slippers and tucked them into her pockets, and wound several of the long, diaphanous veils around her throat, tucking the ends inside her tunic.

She looked around. The harem was a place singularly unsuited for preparing for long trips. A movement in the silvered mirror on the wall caught her eye and when she looked around she was astonished to find that she was smiling. Although there might be too many teeth to call it a smile. A snarl, perhaps.

Time to go.

It required every ounce of self control she had to wait in her room as the light faded from the sky. The sounds of battle didn't help. Ogodei's siege engines would now be at their destructive, deadly work. She'd only ever seen models and heard stories. It felt somehow as if she were in one of the stories now, as if she were one step removed from real life.

Muted sobbing could be heard from frightened women in rooms all over the harem. She set her jaw. There was nothing she could do for them. There was nothing they could do for themselves. From what Firas said, even if by some miracle Farhad did manage to beat off Ogodei's forces, with the death of Sheik Mohammed, their owner and master, their future was tenuous in the extreme.

The afternoon crept on, minute by agonizing minute. She tried to nap, but every time she closed her eyes she saw the girl at the gate, and she couldn't shut out the sounds of worried whispers and frightened cries at every distant boom and crash of the battle. None of them had as yet sounded so near as to cause her to fear for the disruption of her plans. Ogodei's catapults, it seemed, had yet to get the range of the palace. Certainly it would be a prime target when they did, and yet, was it her imagination or did the crashing sounds and screams seem to be moving away?

At long, long last, when her nerves had been stretched to the shrieking point, the shadows began to lengthen along the floor. A whisper of silk on tile, and Hayat and Alma drifted silently into the room. Johanna got to her feet and held out her hands. Hayat's hand was dry, her grip fierce. Alma's was damp and trembling. They held on to each other for a long moment, taking and giving courage. The two women were wearing multiple layers of clothes as she'd suggested, and, Johanna saw approvingly, had wound many scarves around their waists and throats and crossed them across their torsos.

Johanna led the way, slipping out of her room and down the corridor, seeking the shadows. Everywhere she looked clumps of women clung together, cowered in corners, huddled together in darkening rooms. If their passage was seen, no one had the courage to say so. Johanna's heart was wrung with pity for them, but she moved steadily forward.

The carved wooden door loomed up out of the shadows, its bronze fittings gleaming. Kadar was still nowhere to be seen. There were no eunuch guards on this side of the door, or anywhere else in the harem that she could see. If the fighting was going badly, every man with a weapon would have been conscripted to the walls and the gates.

Johanna laid hands on the bolt and drew it softly back. The door swung open.

She stepped forward into the courtyard, and her heart sank.

Farhad smiled at her. "Nazirah. How lovely to see you. Although you could be rather better dressed for the occasion."

He looked and sound supremely confident. He had brought only two guards with him. One held Firas' arms behind him and a blade to his throat.

Firas barely glanced at her. He looked less threatened than patient, and she took heart from that. Hayat and Alma had the sense to keep to the shadows behind her. "And what occasion is that?" she said, facing Farhad and trying to show no fear, although her knees had a tendency to tremble. So close, so close.

"Listen," Farhad said, holding a hand to his ear. They listened, and the sounds of war did seem to be diminishing. "We have beaten them back, Nazirah, as I told you we would. My men are even now in pursuit." His eyes glittered as they passed possessively over her body. "I would celebrate my victory."

"You pursued them?" Johanna said. "After they fell back? Your forces are outside the city walls?"

He strolled forward and put a caressing hand beneath her chin. He raised it to look her over in an appraising manner. "Of course. They have caused much damage and many deaths. They will pay for it. All of it."

"You fool," she said in a low, intense voice. "You fool, Farhad!"

There was a large whistling sound overhead, approaching nearer and nearer and while Johanna had never experienced anything like it she knew intuitively what it was. She opened her mouth to scream at Hayat and Alma to—

—and the projectile crashed through the roof. In the very brief moment granted to her for observation, Johanna saw that it was a large, heavy urn, stoppered with a round wood cover pierced with small holes and sealed with wax. And then it smashed into the floor and splintered into shards and slivers.

Inside there were snakes. Many snakes, of different kinds, with, Johanna saw at a glance, only one thing in common: they were all of them deadly. Time seemed to slow down. Johanna saw a cobra rear up and extend its hood, and strike seemingly at nothing. A knot of purple snakes with pure white heads uncoiled themselves and slithered in half a dozen different directions. Smaller adders with distinctive zigzag patterns flowed over each other and seemed to pull darkness with them as they slipped away.

Screams behind her said that members of the harem had been enticed into the entryway by the opening of the door, screams of fright and then screams of pain as they were bitten.

"You fool, Farhad!" Johanna said. "They have flanked the city!"

Farhad gaped at her and she leapt on his moment of surprise and inattention, pulling her knife and slashing it across his face. He flinched, but her blade caught his uplifted arm and left a growing red stain, and she knew a fierce satisfaction. He stumbled backward, tripped over a viper and went down to the floor.

She whirled. Firas had disarmed his captor, who was on the floor choking on his own blood. A man screamed and she whirled again, to see Alma with an adder held just behind its head, pulling its fangs from the second guard's throat and throwing it to one side. Their eyes met for a brief moment and Alma's face split in a feral smile.

A second missile crashed through the roof: another urn, this one filled with smaller pottery balls that burst into flame on impact. One burst at the feet of a woman whose flimsy clothes exploded into an instantaneous fiery veil. She screamed and ran, only fanning the flames and setting draperies and two other women alight. It was a horrifying sight, and Alma and Hayat were mesmerized.

"Go!" Johanna shouted. "Go, go, go!"

The four of them ran for the door to the garden, leaping over snakes and flames alike. The guards were gone and it was unlocked, and they charged through into the stable yards.

Ishan, the stable master, met them at the door. "Lady! What are you doing!"

"Get out of my way, Ishan!"

Instant comprehension flashed across his face. "You are leaving."

She pushed past him. "North Wind!"

The great white stallion already had his head over his stall door and he whinnied in response to the sound of her voice. She slipped the latch and he shouldered out, nosing her and nickering. Firas had succeeded in saddling him before he was taken. She tried to get her foot in the stirrup but North Wind kept moving. She hopped after him, clutching at the edge of the saddle.

"Here, lady." She looked around to find Ishan cupping his hand. She stepped into it and he threw her up on North Wind's back. She froze, staring down at him.

He held her gaze for a long moment, before telling Firas, "The gray, yes, and the little mare, but not the black. He will not carry you far, he has no stamina, no endurance."

He pulled saddle and bridle from the black and replaced them on a rangy chestnut who stepped nervously but delicately in place. Alma was put up on the mare, Hayat on the chestnut, and Firas mounted the grey gelding.

They all hesitated inside the door of the stable, looking at Ishan. "Come with us," Johanna said.

He bowed to her. "I am honored, lady, by your invitation. But my wives, my children..." A vague wave indicated the city's interior. "I must go to them."

Johanna bit her lip. "Get out then, Ishan, get yourselves out of Talikan as soon as you possibly can."

He bowed to her with his hand on his forehead. "Peace be upon you, lady."

"And upon you, Ishan," Johanna said. Impulsively, she held out her hand.

He took it in a firm, brief clasp, and smiled up at her. "Keep my horses safe."

They had never been the sheik's horses, not to Ishan. Johanna's throat was tight and her eyes burned.

The stable master went ahead of them to stand by the doors to the track that Johanna took every day, at the end of which only this morning, only hours before, Johanna and Firas had found the bodies of the scouts. "Are you sure?" she said to Firas.

"As sure as I can be, young miss," he said, gathering his reins. "If Ogodei runs true to Mongol tactics, he is at present bringing in two flanks of his troops to engulf the Talikan pursuers."

"I know," Johanna said.

He nodded curtly, leaning forward to check bridle, saddle and stirrups, and then moving to Hayat and Alma to check theirs. "Ogodei's troops are fully occupied at the main gate, which is almost directly opposite this one. This is our best chance."

Our only chance, Johanna thought. North Wind snorted and sidled beneath her. He didn't like the sounds he was hearing. The tension on the reins told her that he had the bit between his teeth. But then he was always ready to run, in peace or in war. "Alma, Hayat? Don't. Fall. Off."

Their faces turned to hers, Hayat's grim with determination, Alma's white with fear. But Alma had been the one to snatch up a venomous snake and use it as a weapon, and effectively, too. "Don't fall off. Just don't. We won't have time to stop to help you if you fall. Do you understand?"

They nodded mutely. Ishan had fastened their feet to the stirrups with quick lashings of what looked like spare reins. Their vests and pantaloons and scarves would be no protection and if they survived Johanna hated to think what the insides of their thighs would feel like. "Keep your balance." She attempted a smile that she feared was more of a grimace. "It's just like dancing."

Again they nodded, far too trustfully for her liking.

"All right," Johanna said. "Ishan, add to your goodness and open the doors to the track?"

He unlatched the doors and dragged them back. No invading force immediately poured in, which Johanna took to be a good sign. "God be with you and your family, friend Ishan!"

"Allah keep you and yours, lady!" she heard him say.

She bent low over North Wind's neck and kicked him sharply in the sides, and he went from a standstill to a full gallop in one pace. She heard the faint sound of hoofbeats behind her. Before her, the moon was near full on the horizon, vying with the last light of the setting sun opposite. The white sand of the track was easy to follow in the dusk. Behind them she heard yells and the sound of additional hoofbeats as a counterpoint to the thunder and smash of battle. All seemed to recede almost instantly but she knew better than to trust to that impression. She pulled a little on the reins, slowing him enough so that the other three horses could keep up.

Risking a look around she saw that Alma was being jolted from one side of her mount to the other, but recovering in time to pull herself back up again. Hayat had fallen too far to her left to recover. Johanna checked North Wind, and dropped back to reach out, grab Hayat's arm and dump her back in the saddle.

Something whirred by her face, and she looked around to see that their pursuers were a dozen Mongols armed with bows, presumably the guard set on the stable doors. Their ragged steppe ponies were no match for prize racing steeds out of Sheik Mohammed's stables. She turned to face forward and bent low again over North Wind's neck. He passed Hayat's mount and came up to Firas. "Archers behind us!"

"Really, young miss?" Even at full gallop, the wind whistling past their ears in one direction and the arrows past their heads in the other, Firas managed to sound sarcastic. "Thank you for drawing it to my attention. Look!"

He pointed at the canal beside them, and in it Johanna saw scum in it she had not seen that morning. "They've poisoned the canal!"

He didn't bother to answer, only pointed ahead. "We are making for that cleft, there, between those two hills, do you see?"

"I see!"

"There is water there, a small stream, where we can rest the horses." If they managed to lose their pursuers. He didn't say it, but they both thought it.

They didn't dare keep the horses at a full gallop for an extended length of time. She glanced again over her shoulder. The archers were definitely falling behind, and six of them had left the others and were making for the battle, either to apprise their commander of the escapes or not to miss out on their share of the women and the plunder when the city was sacked. Possibly both, and Johanna swallowed back the bile rising in her throat.

The city could not hold without a leader, and when last seen that leader had fallen into a seething mass of poisonous serpents. Johanna hoped in passing that three or four of them had bitten him. She had been a prisoner in Talikan, but she had been met with kindness from some of its inhabitants, all of whom would very probably be dead before nightfall. She thought of Halim the dyer, and Ishan the stable master, and the ornamental, useless women of the harem.

They pushed on as long as they dared, a league and a half, before reining in the horses to a walk. North Wind was sweating but only lightly, the other three horses more, but none of them had thrown shoes or picked up rocks in their hooves. Alma and Hayat both had tear-streaked faces, but no one mentioned that, or much of anything else. The rest of their pursuers had vanished, very probably now at the gates of the city with the rest of the Mongol forces.

They rode for another league, not speaking, before nudging the horses into a canter. They passed burned-out farms and mills, villages with no whole houses left standing, the bodies of men, women and children brutalized and butchered and left where they lay. With this fast-slow-fast pace, it was midnight before they achieved the notch between the two hills Firas had pointed out. They reined in to the incongruous sound of running water, a cheerful chuckle as it tumbled down in a series of rocky pools. Johanna slid from North Wind's back. He drank from the creek while she loosened his cinch and wiped him down with an armful of dry grass. She led him away before he drank too much and tethered him to a nearby tree.

Firas had loosened the ties that bound Alma and Hayat's feet to their stirrups and helped them down. Neither woman could stand upright at first, and they limped splay-legged to the creek, there to drop to their knees and drink deeply. Firas came behind with their horses and the chestnut gelding. Like Johanna, he didn't let them drink too much before leading them to a wizened tamarisk and tethering them to its lower branches.

They knelt next to Alma and Hayat and drank deep of the clean, fresh water, and then drank more, and rested for a few moments.

Johanna rose to her feet.

"Where are you going?" The restrained terror in Alma's voice caused Hayat to reach for her hand.

"To the top of that knoll. We should be able to see what is happening in Talikan from there."

Alma rose waveringly to her feet and pulled Hayat, protesting, up with her. Unaccustomed to drinking from creeks, they were both wet to their waists. "I want to see, too."

Firas joined them, following Johanna up over the small knoll. It was overgrown with some low-growing herb that emitted a cloud of fragrance with every footstep. Lavender, perhaps. She got to the top a pace in front and stood, catching her breath, as she looked across the long plain over which they had fled.

So far as she could tell by the moon's pale light, they were still not pursued, and it was plain as to why. At this distance, about five leagues, the sounds of human terror and agony could only be imagined, and she was grateful for that, but in a queer way it only more clearly defined what was happening there in her imagination.

Talikan lay in the bend of a wide river of the same name, the canal paralleling the path having been dug to irrigate the farms that filled the valley. The river lay at the city's back, the main gate at its front, and it was at the front gate that Ogodei had concentrated his attack. Two wooden towers on wheels stood near the walls, but not so near that the defenders could pour oil on them and light them off with flaming arrows. The catapults mounted on the towers continued to load and swing and hurl deadly projectiles inside the city's walls.

The great gates were burning, as were the walls on either side, the heat of the flames no doubt driving the defenders from the gate. "What is that?" she said.

"A ram," Firas said, as it crashed into the gates.

She nodded, numb.

Before the walls, two wide curves of mounted men rode toward each other, enclosing a comparatively pitiful force between them, the third force of Mongol riders closing the last arc of the circle. Talikan's defeat was nearly complete. She wondered if any city had ever fallen in less than a day before. She thought again of Halim, and Ishan, and the harem. "Do you think Ogodei gave the city a chance to surrender?" she said.

"I don't know," Firas said. "Given how soon he began the attack upon his arrival, it would seem unlikely."

"Why wouldn't he? My father said that Genghis Khan always gave cities a choice."

"Ogodei isn't Genghis Khan." She felt rather than saw him shrug. "Perhaps his men are hungry. Mongol armies are foragers, they feed themselves on the march. If that is the case, an outright defeat means less time between his men and the city's storehouses than negotiating a surrender. And a surrender presupposes that enough stores would be left to feed the city's people, which would be that much less for Ogodei's men." He sighed. "I don't know, young miss."

"How did they catch you?"

He shrugged. "We were not quite as discreet as we might have hoped, young miss. Tarik saw us talking and followed me to the stables. He saw me saddle the horses and sent for Farhad. They took me when I was on my way to the harem."

She nodded. "We were fortunate that Farhad thought he was safe with only two guards."

He almost smiled. "Yes," he said.

They watched as flame leapt from beyond the gates. It was impossible at this distance, but Johanna felt that she could hear it crackle, could feel its heat, could see the ravenous flames eat up everything in the city. "How do you bury that many people?" she said at last, her voice barely above a whisper.

"You don't," Firas said, and stirred. "Young miss. We must go."

"Yes," she said. "We must."

She turned her back on Talikan for the last time and the four of them slipped and slid back down the knoll to the little glen with its life-saving creek, where they surprised a massive striped cat who had come to the spring to drink. North Wind had broken the branch of the tree he had been tethered to and was pawing the ground, preparing to give battle. The tiger snarled at all of them impartially and slunk away into the night.

Hayat seemed frozen in place, until Alma burst into sobs. Hayat relaxed enough to put her arms around the other woman.

"I'll need a bow and arrows as soon as possible," Johanna said, and hoped no one else noticed how shaken her voice was. She was probably as frightened as Alma and Hayat, but the accumulated shocks of the day seemed to have left her temporarily numb to any new experience no matter how life-threatening.

Firas let out a long sigh. "We were lucky he wasn't hungry. He could have taken down any one of our horses. Or all of them."

Johanna looked at North Wind, still vastly annoyed at this disruption of his well-earned rest. No, not all of them.

"Here," Firas said, "this will make you feel better." He handed around bits of dried goat's meat. He had managed to pack a saddlebag, Johanna saw, and one water skin. "Chew it slowly. It has to last us for a while."

"We'll need food," she said, teeth working at the dried meat, which was very dry indeed. "And more water skins, and better clothing for them." She nodded at Alma and Hayat, who still stood together with their arms around each other, Alma's face buried in Hayat's shoulder, Hayat's own shoulders shaking. The tiger had been merely the last horror in a day filled with them.

"What do you intend to do with them, young miss?" Firas said in a low voice.

"That's up to them," she said in a hard voice that warned him away from further discussion of the topic. "Did you come this way when you came to Talikan? Is that how you knew of this spring?"

He shook his head. "I came roundabout, from the west. I am of Alamut, and so I said, and Alamut is west of here. But I asked questions in the guard house, and looked at maps, and listened to stories. Among these hills, higher up, is a small village that may be out of the way enough to have escaped Ogodei's attention."

"How much farther?"

"Ten leagues, twelve." He shrugged. "We should reach it before sunset tomorrow if we keep up this pace."

She thought. "You will occasion less comment if you go in alone."

He almost smiled. "And what will they say when I ask for women's clothing?"

"Don't ask for women's clothing, ask for men's," Johanna said. "Tunics and trousers and boots and cheches, if they have them. Tell them you were in the employ of the Sheik Mohammed, that you escaped the sack of the city and that you and your three men are running for your lives. They've lived this long this close to Talikan, if they still live; they will honor the relationship they had with the sheik. And they will be grateful for news."

She hoped.

6

Kabul, spring, 1323

"LAPIS LAZULI," JAUFRE said.

"Emeralds," Shasha said. She hesitated. "Copper? I've never seen so much copper for sale in one place as I have here in Kabul."

"Heavy," Jaufre said. "Depends on how much copper and how far we have to carry it. We should take counsel of Grigori the Tatar."

"One camel can carry five hundredweight," Félicien said. "The profit on that much copper ought to pay for the camel's feed with more than enough left over to make such a venture worthwhile."

The other three looked at him in some surprise. He reddened beneath their scrutiny. "I have been traveling with you for over a year," he said with asperity. "Even an idiot would have picked up a little knowledge by now."

Jaufre gave him a buffet on the shoulder that nearly knocked the goliard over. "You have fallen in with traders, Félicien. Who knows where it will end?"

Hari caught Félicien and helped him regain an upright position. "I have been speaking to the teacher in the madrasa," he said. "He knows of a man with a great store of maps, some old, some new."

Jaufre laughed. "Even the priest has succumbed to our wicked influence," he said, winking at Félicien, who reddened again. "I would look at these maps, Hari. Maps, old and new, are always valuable to someone. And light in weight." He paused, and exchanged a look with Shasha. "You are both continuing with us, then?"

"I am," Félicien said. "I have been five years in the East, and I would see the shores of the Middle Sea again."

"Hari?" Jaufre said.

"By all means, young sir," Hari said, bowing. "The Nestorian patriarch here in Kabul has told me that no seeker after truth can cease from looking until he sees Jerusalem."

"We're only going to Gaza," Jaufre said. "But Jerusalem, I'm told, isn't even twenty leagues away." He stood up, aware that Shasha's healer's eye was upon him and determined to betray by neither wince nor flinch that he was still very shaky on his feet. "Very well, then. I will go to the market and see what I can find in the way of a few decent camels."

Shasha rose, too. "I'll come with you. I want to see what the current prices are for lapis."

He held up an admonitory finger. "Don't buy until we know how many camels I can find. There could be nothing on the market but fifty-year old nags suffering from advanced blister." He felt for the purse at his waist. It was plump enough. He patted it and raised an eyebrow in Shasha's direction.

"If I am forbidden to buy," Shasha said tartly, "I have more than enough to see out our stay."

She'd been testy with him since he'd woken up that morning, and he had sense enough to realize that she was as worried about Johanna as he was, however determined they both were to keep it to themselves. Rambahadur Raj's news that Ogodei was moving south in what might be first Johanna's direction and then theirs was unwelcome and unsettling. "I have no right to forbid you to buy, Shasha," he said mildly. "I advise only caution in what we spend of our available funds. We have a long way to go, and I prefer food in my belly at regular intervals."

Félicien and Hari pretended not to hear either their squabbling or the subject matter, Félicien because he paid his own way with songs and stories and Hari because Jaufre was convinced he had no notion of the concept of money. Still, he had the knack of making friends, a good asset anywhere on the Road. Jaufre thought of Hari enthroned on a pile of carpets, deep in philosophical discussion with Ogodei on the plateau of Terak, and quashed the memory immediately. Johanna had still been with them then, and the farther he kept Johanna from his thoughts the better off they would all be. He fixed his thoughts instead on Gaza where they would meet again. Admittedly his mental wanderings overlay the prospect with a golden haze involving the two of them alone and with most of their clothes off. It was a vision enticing enough to move him forward.

But she would be there, with her clothes or without them. He would not, could not admit of any other possibility.

"I'll walk in with you as far as the storyteller's café," Félicien said, falling beside him. "There is a man from Turgesh who tells the most delightful tales of a Nasredden Hoja."

"Increasing your repertoire, young scholar?" Hari stood. "And I will return to the madrasa, to inquire after the man of maps. Young sir, is there a date for our departure?"

"Rambahadur Raj gave me to understand that we will be off at the earliest possible moment," Jaufre said. "There are…" He glanced at Shasha. "The times are unsettled," he said. "Rambahadur Raj wishes to outpace them."

They departed for the city in a body, separating at the Grand Mosque. Out of sight of the others, Jaufre allowed his pace to slow and silently cursed again his physical inability to walk even a league without having to mop the sweat from his face. He wondered gloomily if he would have to be roped to his mount on the Road, and made a mental vow that he would do no such thing, even if he slid from the back of his camel and was trampled beneath the hooves of the entire caravan for it.

He sought out the camel yard and looked over the stock. The

camel dealer singled him out as a young man of little experience and made his best effort to show him every sway-backed camel, horse and donkey with infected hooves and spavined knees he had in stock, most of which also exhibited bronchial coughs that splattered everything with yellow phlegm, including the dealer, whose robe showed signs of having endured the assault numerous times before.

Jaufre's acerbic comments on the kind and condition of what was on offer cast the situation in a different light, and the dealer led him round the back where animals in better condition waited in varying degrees of patience for purchase by their new owners. Jaufre found six camels whose teeth were not yet yellow with age, whose coats were thick enough to withstand both heat and cold, and who moved as if all their feet and the legs attached to them were healthy enough to last the distance to Gaza, or at least to the next city large enough to support a camel yard, where the sick, lame and lazy could be replaced.

They adjourned to the dealer's office and bargained over mint tea. An hour later Jaufre emerged feeling better than he had since he woke up, weak and enfeebled and bedridden. With the single camel Firas and Shasha had managed to liberate from the sheik's men, that meant they had seven head of freight stock, capable of transporting forty-two hundredweight of goods.

He next sought out the offices of Grigori the Tatar, who was a swarthy, stocky, taciturn man who said very little but whose sharp eyes saw everything. "Young sir," he said, rising to his feet. "The foster son of Wu Li honors me again with his presence."

"I thank you, Grigori the Tatar," Jaufre said, and tried not to fall onto the carpet-covered bench Wu Li's agent waved him to. Grigori sent for the inevitable mint tea and cakes, and Jaufre regained his composure and commanded himself not to think of his trembling legs.

Grigori offered brief commiseration again over the death of Wu Li, which Jaufre accepted with what he hoped was dignity, and wondered how to ask his next question. "Have you," he said, "had any messages from any other members of the house of Wu since last we spoke?" The thought of Wu Li's widow extending her clawed reach this far was unlikely but not impossible. It was lucky for them that she had not had time before Wu Li's death to gather all the reins of Wu Li's business into her hands. He thought of the tiny woman with the painted face and the gilded fingernails as long as her forearms, a being of infinite forethought and malice, brooding in Cambaluc on the wrongs she had suffered at Johanna's hands, and had to repress a sudden smile. And it had been lucky for them, too, that Johanna was such an accomplished thief.

"None," Grigori said. "Only yourself and Wu Li's foster daughter, young sir."

Jaufre nodded in acknowledgement, hoping his relief didn't show. "I went to the camel dealer you recommended," he said after the refreshments had been delivered. "When the camels are delivered and accepted, he will bring you a piece of paper with Wu Li's bao and an amount inscribed upon it." He handed over a pouch. "Of your kindness, please give him this as payment in full, less your commission, of course."

Grigori accepted the pouch and caused it to disappear somewhere about his person. "Young sir," he said. "You are lately come from the east. Is the news true? Are the Mongols once again on the march?"

"I believe it to be true, Grigori," Jaufre said. He hesitated. "If a much younger and less worldly man may presume to advise his elder in years and experience..." A minute nod gave him permission. "I know that the mountain passes between here and Persia are filled with fierce tribes who gave pause to Alexander and even Genghis Khan himself. And perhaps, even if Ogodei does make it this far, your city leaders will be wise enough to yield to him."

Not a muscle moved in Grigori's face but Jaufre got the distinct impression that his host had little faith in the wisdom of Kabul's leaders.

"My advice to my elder would be to look to his own," Jaufre

said. "And to do so sooner, rather than later." He paused, and stretched his back. The wound ached much less now, more of a phantom pain than a real one. As with Rambahadur Raj, he was not about to admit that he himself knew Ogodei. Absent proof, there was no reason for the Tatar to take his words as other than youthful braggadocio, and even if he was believed, he had no wish to become known as an authority. However, as a member of the family of Wu Li, he owed a duty to a retainer in that family's service. "The havildar of the caravan recently arrived in Kabul?"

"Rambahadur Raj," Grigori said. "He is well known as an able and prudent man."

"He is determined to leave Kabul at his earliest opportunity."

Grigori said nothing for a moment, and when he did speak again it was to talk of lesser things.

Jaufre made his farewells and went next to the caravansary on the outskirts of the city, where he found Rambahadur Raj overseeing the beating of an unfortunate man who, Rambahadur Raj said, had had the temerity to try to steal a horse that belonged to one of the merchants. His back was bloody when he was finally released, but he could stagger off under his own power and at least he still had both of his hands. Commonly the sentence for thievery had the right one lopped off. "But have you seen how many one-handed men there are in this city, Jaufre of Cambaluc?" said Rambahadur Raj. "I would not add to the city's burden of men who cannot work for their living. Not that this one did, but perhaps his sore back will remind him that there are less painful ways to earn one's keep." The havildar waved Jaufre to a seat before his yurt and sent for refreshments.

When they came, mint tea of course, Rambahadur Raj cocked an eyebrow. "You have news, young sir?"

"I do, havildar. My party will join you with three donkeys, six horses, and seven camels. If we can find reliable help, we will bring two and possibly three men to help with the livestock."

"A cook?"

"We have our own." At another quirk of an eyebrow, Jaufre added, "The healer, of whom I spoke before."

Both of Rambahadur Raj's eyebrows went up. "A healer and a cook," he said. "I would meet this paragon."

"You will, havildar. When do we leave?"

"In three days' time," the havildar said promptly. "Is that agreeable to you?"

"It is," Jaufre said. He hesitated. "I noticed when I was last with you," he said finally, "that you had a slaver in your train."

"I did."

"Will he be traveling with us?"

"No. He passes south, on through the mountains to Punjab." The havildar raised an eyebrow. "Do I understand you to have some objection to traveling with slavers, young sir?"

"My mother was captured and sold into slavery," Jaufre said bluntly, too exhausted to dissemble. "I would speak with him to see if he has heard of her."

"I see," the havildar said. "My sympathies, Jaufre of Cambaluc."

"I thank you, Rambahadur Raj. May I have the slaver's name and direction?"

"Ibn Battuta is his name. He is a Berber from Maroc, and a very young man to be such a successful trader, in my estimation. He had fully three hundred in stock when he joined us in Balkh."

"Three hundred!"

"As many," Rambahadur Raj said, nodding. "Although he did suffer some attrition through the mountain passes. Those Afghans." He shook his head, and observed Jaufre with a sapient eye. "You are prepared to defend yourselves, Jaufre of Cambaluc?"

"We are, havildar."

"Well, well, I doubt it will come to that." The havildar grinned. "Or what are you paying me for?"

Jaufre followed the havildar's directions and found Ibn Battuta established in a large house with an enclosed courtyard

283

near the slave market. He begged an audience of the doorman, an enormous Nubian who looked as if he could pick Jaufre up and break him in half with very little effort. Jaufre tried not to be envious of the man's obvious strength and excellent health.

He had used the name of Rambahadur Raj to gain entrance and so was not very surprised to be granted an audience. Ibn Battuta was indeed a young man, not very much older than Jaufre himself. Tall, slim, richly dressed, his manner was grave and somewhat avuncular, as if he feared his youthful appearance would cause people to take him less seriously and so was determined to make up the difference by assuming the manner of a man three times his age.

He was surrounded by pen and ink and pieces of parchment, but he set these to one side upon Jaufre's entrance and sent for refreshments. Jaufre already felt awash in mint tea, but he minded his manners and made no demur. Presently it was delivered by a slender girl dressed in the briefest of clothing, who fluttered her eyelashes at Jaufre.

"You like?" Ibn Battuta said, noting his interest. "A good price can be arranged."

Jaufre had a sudden vision of his mother in just such a situation and knew an instantaneous, consuming fury. It took him a moment to muster up a civil tone. "I am not in the market for a slave at present, effendi," he said, and waited until the girl had left the room to come to the point. "Effendi, my mother had the misfortune to be traveling in a caravan that was attacked by bandits. She was captured and sold into slavery."

"Unfortunate," Ibn Battuta said. As an owner and a seller of slaves and a successful one if these surroundings were any indication, he could hardly offer his condolences.

"Yes," said Jaufre. "She was Greek, with dark hair and eyes. Her name was Agalia. It may be that she was given the name of the Lycian Lotus when she was sold."

"When was this?" the slave trader asked.

Jaufre swallowed. "Seven years ago."

Ibn Battuta stared at him, startled out of his assumed stolidity. "Seven years! My dear young sir!" He strove to regain his composure. "I sympathize with your loss, but the thing is impossible. Surely you see that." He gestured with a hand that had never seen labor. "Do you have the name of the buyer?"

Jaufre shook his head. "I know only that he was a sheik out of the west."

"There are many such sheiks," Ibn Battuta said, not unkindly.

"I know," Jaufre said. "No such woman has passed through your hands, effendi? Or been offered you for sale? Dark, slender but well-formed. She would now be forty-one years of age. Agalia, or the Lycian Lotus."

Ibn Battuta shook his head. "I am very sorry, young sir."

Jaufre stayed just long enough not to be rude, and left.

He was exhausted by the time he got home. He stopped at the fountain to wash and drink long of the cool, refreshing water, and sat for a time on the edge of the fountain, gazing unseeingly into the water.

He had been asking after his mother in every slave market between here and Cambaluc, and the answer had always been the same. Seven years ago, the Road had swallowed his mother up and left nothing of her behind for him to find. She was lost to him.

Oh, he would keep asking as they traveled farther into the west. He didn't think he could stop himself, but he had to begin to accept the possibility that he would never find her. He hoped with all his heart that the man she had been sold to in the Kashgar slave market was a good master, and kind to her. She had been fortunate in her beauty and her intelligence. Certainly the price she had reportedly brought meant that she would be highly valued by whomever paid it.

He closed his eyes and let himself remember the sound of her voice in his ears, the feel of her arms around him, the laughter of his parents together.

He opened his eyes and blinked away tears. What was the name of Rambahadur Raj's second in command? Alaric? Alaric the Templar, the havildar had called him, seemingly in jest and definitely to the other man's displeasure.

Jaufre's father had been a Templar. And he had had a sword like Alaric's, the one now hanging from the wall inside.

He got up and went to stand before it, looking at it as if for the first time. He knew the names of the various parts of it now, as he had not as a child when it was all he had managed to save from the men who killed his father three days from Kashgar. A large pommel, set with precious stones. A metal grip covered in sharkskin, much less ornamental. An abbreviated guard. The blade itself, made of something very near but not quite Damascus steel, or so he'd been told by every smith he'd taken it to. The edge kept sharp for longer than any other blade he'd ever owned. He'd cut himself on it enough times.

Yes, Alaric's sword was very like this one.

And if his employer was to be believed, he was or had been a Templar. Jaufre did not know exactly what a Templar was, but he did know from his childhood memories that his father had been one too, before he had met and married his mother. Perhaps Alaric had known of him.

Perhaps he had known him.

If he had lost his mother, perhaps he could at least find out more about his father. Perhaps he had other family to be found, somewhere in the West.

Suddenly and thoroughly exhausted, he stretched out on his cot. He was instantly asleep.

Muted voices and the smell of roasting meat woke him at twilight. He blinked his eyes and found Félicien stirring something

286

in a copper pan under Shasha's direction, and Hari in a corner with his legs folded beneath him, chanting his oms.

Jaufre pushed himself to a sitting position. Shasha looked over her shoulder. "Ah. You wake, just in time for dinner. Well timed."

He rose to his feet, yawning hugely, and stumbled outside to use the necessary. Dinner was being served on his return, browned root vegetables baked in cabbage leaves and a skewer of goat's meat, this latter for all but Hari, who ate no meat. More of last year's apples followed.

It might have been the best meal Jaufre had ever eaten. It was amazing what a little forward motion did to improve one's appetite. He cleaned their few dishes and tidied their cooking utensils away and they gathered outside their door around a ring of small rocks in which a fire had been kindled. Smoke rose from similar fires in the little enclave of mud-brick buildings that constituted their neighborhood. The stars were winking into existence overhead and a three-quarter moon was cresting the peak of an eastern mountain.

"I found camels," Jaufre said. "Six of them."

"Six," Shasha said. "I did not think you would find half so many."

By her expression he could tell that she was mentally adding up all the goods she had found in the market that day and dividing them into seven loads. "I spoke with Rambahadur Raj, too. We leave in three days."

Félicien scratched with vigor. "Good. I don't believe I have stayed in a more pest-ridden place in my life."

"Did you find your man of maps, Hari?"

"I did, young sir, I did." Hari hitched his yellow drapery about himself, one shoulder bare as always. He seemed impervious to cold and heat alike. "He lives in a small room he rents from the mullah's sister. I went there, and what I found was curious, most curious indeed."

"He has maps?"

"He does, and all manner of other curiosities. He showed me

a very old memoir, almost assuredly a copy, of a treatise written by a Christian in Sinai. It is called *The Geography of Christ*, I believe he said, or something very like. It is written in a tongue foreign to me but he translated some of it. This writer claims there are only four seas: the Middle Sea, the Persian Sea, the Arabian Sea and the Caspian Sea. Even more strangely, he claims there are only four nations: the Indians in the east, the Celts in the west, the Scythians in the north and the Ethiops in the south."

Jaufre looked at Shasha. "He wasn't a Christian, Hari, he was Muslim. His name was Cosmas, and he was of Alexandria."

Hari looked surprised. "You have heard of this man?"

"We have. Our uncle told us of him, before we left Everything Under the Heavens. Cosmas constructed a box, he said, with a map of the world in it. His world. It evidently left out quite a bit. Or it was a very small box."

Hari meditated on this information for a moment. "The man of the many maps, his name is Ibn Shad, he says that the author of the book signs himself a Christian. And that he apparently was no scholar, as he has the shape of the world flat, longer by two than it is wide, and founded on their god. By which I took to mean held by him."

"Like Atlas," Jaufre said.

"Atlas?"

"A Greek god of whom my mother told me. I can't remember the full tale, but he misbehaved somehow and was condemned to hold the entire world on his shoulders for all eternity."

"A round world or a flat world?" Shasha said.

"Be cautious," Félicien said unexpectedly. "Especially after we arrive in the West."

They looked at him. "Cautious?" Shasha said. "But why?"

Félicien poked at the fire with a stick while they waited. "The god of the West, the god of my country, is a jealous god. Very jealous," he said, emphasizing his point with a vicious jab that made the sparks fly upward. "Philosophy exists only as it is relevant to faith. Therefore faith, in particular the Christian faith, dictates all philosophy, and only religious men can be scholars." Another poke, more sparks. "Map-making, for example, is not respected, and any western map I have ever seen is dictated by the texts of the Christian Bible."

Hari looked intrigued. "The Bible?"

"It is like the Koran, or the Upanishads, for Christians." Félicien's smile was crooked. "I believe I can even quote to you the exact verse that inspired Cosmas to his view of the world. 'Thou shalt make a table also of setim wood: of two cubits in length, and a cubit in breadth, and cubit and a half in height.' Exodus, chapter 25, verse 23." He said the words first in Latin, and then translated for them, adding, "The church frowns upon travel, too."

"Travel?" Jaufre and Shasha spoke as a chorus of disbelief.

Félicien's smile was wry. The shadows cast by the flickering flames fined down his features, making them appear almost delicate. "I quote from the blessed St. Augustine himself, now. 'And men go abroad to admire the heights of mountains, the mighty waves of the sea, the broad tides of rivers, the compass of the ocean, and the circuits of the stars, yet pass over the mystery of themselves without a thought.'"

"But—but—" Jaufre was spluttering.

"We are meant to stay at home, then?" Shasha said skeptically.

Félicien nodded. "So as to better contemplate the glory of god."

"Is god not in the mountains, and the waves, and the rivers, and the circuits of the stars, then?" Hari said.

Félicien sighed. "So I thought, when I left home, Hari."

"Do you no longer think so, young scholar?" Hari said.

Félicien raised his head, his eyes filled with fire. "Even more now than I did before, Hari. I left because what I wanted to study was forbidden me, and," he laughed a little, "because I had seen a text even older than your Cosmas' memoir, by a man called Solinus. He wrote two or three hundred years after Christ,

289

and the text had these marvelous illustrations of all manner of creatures, the dog-men in Ethiopia, in Tartary dolphins that can leap the masts of ships, the dread Basilisk of the Syrtis whose breath is fatal." He laughed again. "I found none of them, of course. But I found other things even more wonderful, built by the hand of god, and of man." He looked around the circle. "And I found friends."

"But—but—travel?" Jaufre said. "How are goods moved, then? Do they make everything they need themselves?"

"Oh, they trade," Félicien said, "every chance they get, and traders, perforce, travel. They are not much respected. Of course many of them are Jews, which makes it easier for the Christians to despise the profession."

"I have heard of Jews," Hari said, "but I have never met one. Tell me of them, young scholar."

"That," Félicien said, "is far too long an explanation to go into this evening. I will reserve it to while away the long hours on the Road between here and Gaza, good Hari."

"But—travel?" Jaufre said again.

Shasha poked him in the side. "Remember what Uncle Cheng said," she said. "We will do well to adopt the prevalent faith of whatever culture we happen to find ourselves in."

"Wise words," Félicien said, nodding.

"We don't go to mosque," Jaufre said. "And Hari says his prayers wherever we go."

"He says them in private," Shasha said, "and we don't shop on Fridays." She changed the subject pointedly. "I found a merchant who deals exclusively in good quality lapis, if his samples are anything to go by. It was very expensive, until I mentioned Grigori the Tatar. He then cut his prices in half, but I think they are still too high. I found a trader who deals in gemstones, too, but he would not speak with a woman. I think we should employ Grigori in both of these negotiations."

"Copper?"

She shook her head. "The prices are very high, I think because the mines close in the winter and the stocks are subsequently low in the spring."

"Well, we have seven camels. One is already loaded with spices—"

"Not as loaded as it once was," Shasha said. "I have traded perhaps half already."

"Why didn't you—"

She let her eyes flick down to their hems and back to his face. "I thought it would be best if it we were not known to have... special resources."

"We'll have to use them sometime, Shasha."

"To pay for our passage across the Middle Sea," Shasha said lightly. "We'll let Johanna decide, when she deigns to rejoin us in Gaza."

"You seem very sure that she will," Félicien said.

Shasha looked at him in surprise, but he was looking at Jaufre.

"Of course," Jaufre said, and there was that simple certainty in his voice that stopped any further comment Félicien might have made. He bit his lip and looked away.

Villagers began to appear in twos and threes: old women, young men, children up past their bedtime who had learned that song and story were to be found around the fire of the feranji. They brought naan fresh-baked that morning, and cool pomegranate juice in pails, and pieces of precious gaz, covered in spun sugar that whitened their fingers and mouths. Félicien got out his lute and struck up a lively tune that had evidently been acquired locally because everyone joined in on the chorus, and the rest of the evening was spent agreeably in song and story.

The next day Jaufre took delivery of the camels. Two days later they loaded ten hundredweight of first quality rough cut, jewel grade lapis, five hundredweights of dried fruit, another of almonds in the shell, a quantity of well-made copper pots and pans that Shasha had found at a bargain price at the last minute, and a small bag of emeralds that no one knew about except for Shasha and Jaufre and which never left the pouch Shasha wore next to her skin beneath her tunic. She had wanted to buy some of the famous pomegranates of Kandahar but reluctantly agreed when Jaufre pointed out that they would only spoil. Their store of spices was augmented by mint (of course), saffron and cardamom.

There was also a pack of twenty-five old and new maps rolled into a calfskin, as well as half a dozen bound manuscripts folded between sheets of parchment scraps, including Cosmas of Alexandria's *Topographia Christiana*, and that geographical flight of fancy by one Gaius Julius Solinus called *Collecteana rerum memorabilia*, which Félicien had mentioned and upon which the old man had assured Jaufre most of Cosmas' even more fanciful account was based. They were both copies, of course, and both in Latin. While Jaufre remembered very little of that language as laboriously schooled into him by Father John so many years before, since they were headed for a land of Latin speakers he was determined to learn it again so as not to be at a disadvantage when he got there.

He had exited the old man of the maps' lodging only to encounter Ibn Battuta on his way in. The slave trader regarded Jaufre's full arms with a sour expression Jaufre recognized as part envy and part annoyance. He brushed by Jaufre without a greeting, and Jaufre walked home with a step made lighter by having beaten the slave trader to the preferred pieces of the old scholar's stock.

✿

The afternoon before they would depart they moved down to the caravansary, accompanied by a gratifyingly universal bewailing on the part of their neighborhood. They pitched a new yurt near Rambahadur Raj's and settled in. Félicien, with his unquenchable curiosity, struck out immediately to see who would be traveling with them. Hari went with him to see who worshipped at which altar.

No sooner had they left than a voice called from the other side of the flap, and Jaufre stepped outside to find Alaric the Templar waiting for him. "Well met, Jaufre of Cambaluc," he said.

"Well met," Jaufre said, unsure of how to address the man, since he had protested at Rambahadur Raj's introduction. Jaufre was wearing his father's sword, being able to bear its weight again, barely, and Alaric's eyes went to it immediately.

"A fine sword," he said.

"My father's," Jaufre said.

"Do you mind?"

Jaufre drew it forth and presented it, hilt first.

Alaric, like Firas, handled the sword as if it were an extension of his arm, but he studied it with an intensity that seemed out of proportion to its existence.

"It is a style very like your own," Jaufre said.

Alaric glanced down at the sword at his side. "It is." He made a few passes with it before handing it back. "Are you a soldier?"

"I'm a trader," Jaufre said. "It is, alas, a profession that requires the occasional fight. I was studying with a sword master on the Road, before we became separated."

Alaric smiled, an expression that momentarily changed his long, sad face into something charming and attractive. "We practice, the men and I, at sunrise each day."

Jaufre wondered if all masters of the sword considered getting up before dawn as a requirement for a successful training program. "I would join you," he said. He hesitated. He didn't want to make excuses, but he didn't want Alaric and his men to think they would be seeing Jaufre's best effort on the morrow. Indeed, he knew a lively hope that raising his sword in a beginning parry would not leave him flat on his face. "I have been ill," he said at last, "and I am not yet entirely recovered. I'm afraid I won't provide much competition for you or any of your men."

"We'll take it easy on you at first." Alaric said. "But only at first."

Jaufre laughed, and the other man smiled again and then grew serious. "We will need every sword, Jaufre of Cambaluc," he said. "The mountain tribes that live along the pass between Kabul and Faryab are fierce and predatory. We fought off three attacks by bandits on our way here."

"And the times are unsettled," Jaufre said, "with the Mongols abroad again. Every strong man in every community is out to acquire as much as he can before the Mongols come take it all away."

"So young and yet so wise," Alaric said dryly.

"It is only common sense," Jaufre said, "and besides, haven't we all seen it before?"

Alaric's face resettled itself into its customary melancholic lines. "Indeed we have."

He paused for a moment to look long into Jaufre's face, long enough for the younger man to become restive beneath his gaze, and then abruptly bid him goodnight and strode off into the twilight.

Jaufre looked after him with a thoughtful gaze. There had been a certain pained recognition in Alaric's eyes when he looked at Jaufre's sword, and even more so when he looked into Jaufre's face, though Jaufre was certain that he had never met the other man in his life.

Had he seen Robert de Beauville in Jaufre's face, and Robert de Beauville's sword hanging at Jaufre's side?

✪

Jaufre slipped from the tent before sunrise the next morning, moving stealthily so as not to wake Shasha, who would have woken the entire caravan with her protests. He found the practice yard. Of course there was a wooden post. Firas' practice field had had one just like it. He sighed, and waited for Alaric and the rest to arrive. One of them was sure to have a practice sword.

An hour later, on legs that would barely hold him up, he returned to the site of their yurt to find it, mercifully, struck and packed away, along with their bedrolls. Shasha eyed him smolderingly but said nothing, while Félicien slipped him some naan and dried fruit. Hari was omming from his usual cross-legged position facing the rising sun. His eyes were closed but one of them opened to give Jaufre a quick head-to-toe survey before closing again. "Life is suffering," he intoned. "Blessed be the way."

Jaufre measured the distance between the tip of his boot and Hari's behind, but he didn't have the requisite energy.

All around the caravansary, men were shouting and camels were groaning as the caravan came slowly to life. Rambahadur Raj was everywhere, checking a girth, smacking the behind of a boy who wasn't moving fast enough with a pack, consulting with first one traveler and then another. He strode up to Jaufre and ran an approving eye over their livestock, their packs, and them. "Yes!" he said. "Someone who knows how to balance a load so it won't slip and pull the cursed camel off the trail!"

Jaufre gave a tired grin. "I was well trained."

"You were indeed, young sir," the havildar said. "Ready?" His quick eye had noticed the sweat drying on Jaufre's brow. He probably already knew the reason for it. There were no secrets in a caravan.

"Ready, havildar," Jaufre said. No excuses, for whatever reason, for this man.

"Good!" Rambahadur Raj said again, and turned to bellow, "Mount up! Mount up! Mount up!"

Jaufre swung his leg over the saddle and settled himself down. His camel was a male, about fifteen, with a thick coat that would do much to keep Jaufre warm on the trail, at least through the mountains. When they reached the desert, that would be another matter, but that was for tomorrow. Today, if felt good to be on the move at last.

Shasha was astride and her camel already on his feet, and as he watched she turned her head and looked toward the north.

Johanna, he thought with a pang. His camel came to its feet and he nudged it next to Shasha's. "Gaza," he said. "We will all meet again in Gaza."

"All of us?" she said.

He didn't know what she meant. "Yes, you, me and Johanna. All of us."

She shot him a glare that took him aback. "That isn't all of us, Jaufre," she said, and kicked her camel into a walk.

He stared after her, agape. Félicien came up beside him on his donkey, looking up into his face. "She sent Firas after Johanna, Jaufre," he said. "He may not have survived the attempt."

"Firas?" he said. "And Shasha?" His head swiveled around and he stared at the back of Shasha's unyielding head.

Félicien sighed and kicked his donkey into motion.

The camels picked up stride and became a long, undulating line that snaked slowly out of the city and up into the foothills. He looked at the line of mountains, crowned with the remnants of a hard winter's snow and ice. Johanna was somewhere on the other side of them.

It wasn't the first time Jaufre had been on the back of a camel, going in the opposite direction of a woman he loved. Then he had been ten years old. Now he was recovering from a wound and illness and evidently even more helpless than he had been then. His heart in his breast ached as much as his whole body.

Hari rose to his feet in a single fluid movement, shook the dust from his yellow robes, and mounted his donkey. "Do not dwell in the past, do not dream of the future," he said. "Concentrate the mind on the present moment, young Jaufre."

Jaufre would have glared at him, but he didn't have the energy for that, either.

7

Balkh, summer, 1323

THREE DAYS AND fifty hard leagues later, the refugees camped near a city mostly in ruins called Balkh—yet another city leveled by Mongols—and Firas prepared to go inside the city walls, such as they were, to find food and clothing for Hayat and Alma.

"You'll need money," Johanna said, and sat down on a tree stump and prepared to draw upon the Bank of Lundi for the first time.

"Wait," Hayat said, and unwound a veil to reveal a row of gold bangles that spanned her arm from wrist to elbow.

For the first time since they had fled Talikan, when all her attention was focused on flight, Johanna noticed that beneath the veils they had wound about their persons Alma and Hayat both were nearly dripping with gold and gems: around their arms, their necks, in their hair, tied to their waists in more veils. Alma produced a pair of opal earrings in an elaborate gold setting and handed them to Firas along with Hayat's bangles.

She looked up and smiled at Johanna's expression. "A woman's jewels are her own, Nazirah, even in the harem."

"So you needn't have hidden yours in your hems," Hayat said with a trace of her old mischievousness. At Johanna's expression, she said, "Oh yes, we knew. We all knew, Nazirah, the moment you would not allow the servants to wash your clothes. There are no secrets in the harem."

None in a caravan, either, Johanna thought.

All three women began to laugh, a little tremulously, and Firas collected the jewelry and vacated the area at once, before the laughter became hysteria. He was a perspicacious man. The moment he was gone, Alma's laughter changed to sobs. At Alma's first sob Hayat burst into tears herself. Johanna, more out of fear that she might join in than because the display of grief and relief made her uncomfortable, left them to hike up the rise that hid the little creek they had stopped beside.

Balkh sat near the open, west-facing end of a river valley between two arms of the Hindu Kush. They'd ridden hard and long over the northern arm, stopping to rest only infrequently, and Johanna thought that it was a good thing that Hayat and Alma had been tied to their mounts because the rough mountain trails were so narrow and so steep there would have been nothing to recover but the body if one of them had fallen off. Fear had carried them from Talikan to here, but both women were now paying for the hard ride, neither of them able to do much more than hobble once out of the saddle. Physical pain was probably one of the reasons they were both crying now.

She lowered her eyes from the mountains to the valley beneath, where a long, blue line indicated a river paralleling the course of the valley. On their side of the river, against the green of the valley she could see a small village or town. Opposite it, in the hollows of the hills behind, lay the ruined city of Balkh, whose proud history could be intuited from the amount of rubble left behind. Here and there small, habitable buildings that had obviously been built from materials harvested from the ruins showed signs of life in hanging clothing and wisps of smoke. She could just make out the tiny figure of Firas' mount picking his way between a tumble of white stone blocks that had once been part of a wall, and fragments of what might have been a gatehouse. He passed within, unchallenged.

She raised her eyes again and looked at the mountains they had crossed. It had been a nightmarish journey, as they had not dared to stop for anything but a snatched meal or a quick watering of the horses. They had slept by day and traveled by night, at considerable risk to both themselves and the horses. Ogodei and Gokudo could not have missed their escape, and they would have both known North Wind on sight, even at a distance, and known that only she could be riding him. Would they follow? She could not guess, but neither could she take chances with her life and the lives of Firas, Hayat, and Alma.

A scream from the hollow below spun her around. She leapt down the loose scree of the knoll and slid into camp in a scatter of loose gravel, barely managing to stay upright. There she found Hayat and Alma clinging to each other as they watched two young men, ragged and dirty, close in on their three mounts, which were cropping peacefully at a patch of grass next to the little stream.

The two men whirled at Joanna's dramatic entrance, and then relaxed. "Only another woman," one said, grinning. He affected a bow toward her and said, "Pretty lady, we mean you no harm. We only have need of your horses." The expression on the second man's face said otherwise as he appraised first her, and then Hayat, and then Alma.

"This great white stallion," the first man said. "Surely he would prefer to be ridden by a man?"

"I'm sure he would," Johanna said, her amiable reply hiding the fact that her heart was pounding in her ears. She waved a negligent hand. "Go ahead. Take him."

The first man laughed, excited, and tugged at the sleeve of his friend, turning his attention from the negligible women to the much more important horses. He caught at North Wind's bridle.

What followed wasn't pretty but it was certainly efficient. When it was over Alma helped Johanna bury the bodies and Hayat helped her to clean a still indignant North Wind's legs and hooves. Alma would always be more comfortable with dead men than live horses.

When Firas returned at sunset they didn't mention the incident, mostly because they were too tired to move camp. Firas had done well in the city, having acquired a complete outfit of clothes for both women, including sturdy leather boots that could be made to fit if they wrapped their feet in veils, and more importantly a bundle of naan, half a lamb, a sack of pomegranates, and dried meat, dried fruit and shelled nuts in enough quantity to sustain them on the Road for several days, or until they reached the next community with food for sale, no questions asked. He rigged a spit and they ate every scrap of the lamb without thinking twice about the bodies beneath the rocks not so very far away.

Johanna was secretly amazed at Alma and Hayat's acceptance of the presence of dead bodies so near their persons. By neither word nor deed did either woman betray any regret at their chosen path. They retired into a clump of trees to change into their new clothes, and proved adept at cobbling them to fit when the pants proved too long and the tunics too baggy. They needed help with their cheches, and the sight of Firas by firelight soberly winding material and tying intricate knots around both women's heads, and then instructing them in how he had done so, would stay with Johanna for many a day.

Firas had bought saddle bags and bedrolls as well, along with two small, belted daggers and one small sword, also belted, which he handed to Johanna. "Am I right to believe that you can be trusted not to cut yourself open with this?"

She smiled and accepted it. "You are. Although I am better with a bow. And better still at soft boxing."

He nodded. He had observed her and Jaufre practicing every morning. "Still, taking on two men alone is one thing."

She looked up from the blade, surprised.

"I can read signs, young miss," he said, casting an expressive look around the campsite. "The bodies are buried around that corner of rock, yes?"

"Uh, yes," Johanna said. They had moved away from the fire

and were speaking in low tones. Hayat and Alma had taken two of the bedrolls and retired to a rocky alcove out of the light of the fire.

"Good," he said. "It will keep the carrion birds away, which will keep them in turn from drawing attention to anyone who might come looking for them."

She shook her head. "They didn't look as if they were members of a tribe or village. Outcasts, perhaps, or—" she sighed "—perhaps more of the dispossessed from Ogodei's incursion into the west."

"There will be more," Firas said.

"Yes," she said grimly. "Hundreds more. If not thousands." She braced herself. "Tell me about Jaufre."

He answered immediately, as if he'd known the question was coming. "His wound was not as bad as it looked, but despite Shu Shao's best efforts it became infected. We took shelter in a village which came down with typhus while he was still recovering."

"He got typhus?" she said faintly.

"Yes, but he got over it," he said, "although he then contracted a case of what Shu Shao believed was ague." He told her the rest.

She could feel the fine trembling of her limbs and stilled it with an effort. "Why Kabul?"

He sighed. "I had traveled there before, I speak the dialect and I have friends among the tribes, so I was fairly certain of safe passage. Kabul is a large city where we would be able to find a doctor who didn't rely on astrology and camel urine to heal his patients. And..." He paused. "And Ogodei did not appear to me like a man who would stop at Terak. If he didn't, if he really is bent on conquest, he will come to Kabul regardless, but the mountains and the Afghans will slow him down, perhaps long enough for Jaufre to recover enough to stay on a camel. It was not the easiest route for someone in your foster-brother's condition, true, but I deemed it to be the safest."

"And did Shasha find a doctor?"

"Yes," he said. "I believe a good one. Your Jaufre was still alive when I left them, young miss." He let her absorb his news for a few moments, until he judged it time to direct her attention back to their present circumstances. "In the town today—"

Her head came up like North Wind on the scent of an enemy. "Yes?"

"There is another town across the river, where many of the residents of Balkh resettled when their city was destroyed, and where their descendants live today."

Johanna nodded. "I saw it from the top of the rise."

"There is some visiting and trading back and forth between the two communities, naturally—"

Johanna wondered what the old Balkh had that could possibly interest the new.

"—and I heard talk in the marketplace of a troop of men, arriving today across the river."

She stared at him, and spoke through dry lips. "It can't be. Not so soon. Not at the pace we have been maintaining. And we would have seen them coming!"

He raised his hand in a calming gesture, glancing in the direction of the other two women to see if they had heard. "Quietly, I beg you, young miss. We would not, in fact, have seen them coming. We traveled by night, if you recall, North Wind by day being a beacon bright enough to set the entire world aflame and have all of it running after us."

She thought he almost smiled. It steadied her, and she lowered her voice. "Did they say in the market who they were, this troop?"

"No," he said. He hesitated, and her heart sank. "But they said that one of them wears black armor and carries a spear curved at the head."

"Gokudo," she said, her voice the barest whisper. At first she could feel nothing but shock, but when she looked for it, she could see the tiny flickers of building anger gathering around the edges of that shock.

"There was no cover for us when we escaped, and we know at least six of the guards saw us the instant we escaped Talikan."

He hesitated again, and said gently, "It is in my mind that Ogodei would have been very pleased with the quick destruction of Talikan, and that afterward he would have been willing to grant his captain any wish he desired."

"Including coming after me," she said.

"Even that," he said, nodding.

She stood where she was, staring into the darkness. "We should separate, Firas," she said.

"No," he said.

"Firas—"

"No," he said more firmly. "I gave Shu Shao my word I would bring you back safely. I will not return to her without you."

"You can't do that if you are killed," she said tartly, "which you very may well be if you stay in my company."

"Even so," he said.

She took in a deep breath and let it out, thinking. "If that dog-fucking, frog-humping, son of a whore and a monkey is so determined to pursue us…"

He didn't so much as blink at her language. "Yes?"

She smiled, little more than a baring of teeth. "Then perhaps we should lead him where we want him to go."

"Yes?" he said again.

"It may be that I have a notion of how to rid ourselves of Gokudo once and for all. It would require going back into the mountains." She looked at the dark shadow where Hayat and Alma had hidden themselves. "Should we ride on tonight?"

He followed her gaze. "I don't think they can."

She agreed with him, and a rest for herself and North Wind and the other horses was necessary, too. Still, "They would if we told them they had to."

"They would. They have heart."

She was aware that this was high praise from Firas. "Tomorrow, then?"

He shook his head. "We still don't dare travel by day."

"Tomorrow night, then?"

"Tomorrow night," he said, and waited.

"I know how tired you must be," she said.

"How tired must I be to refuse to do what you are about to ask me?"

She looked up, startled, and his white teeth flashed in his black beard in the first full grin she had seen on his face. "Can you?" she said. "Cross the river and find out if it really is Gokudo, and exactly how many men he has with him?"

"I can," he said, "and I will. You will stand watch against my return?"

She nodded. "If we are not to travel until tomorrow night, we can sleep through the day." She looked again in the direction of the two women. "They need it."

He regarded her for a moment. "I ask again. What are you going to do with them?"

Her mouth quirked up in a half-smile. "And I answer again, that is up to them."

"Will you bring them all the way to Gaza?"

She shrugged. "If that's where they want to go."

"What kind of life will they have, two women on their own?"

"Well," she said, "they are more resourceful and have more stamina than I thought they would. And they certainly aren't penniless."

He didn't point out what Johanna already knew, that the two of them could travel much faster on their own. He didn't believe in wasting his breath. Instead, he melted into the night, and Johanna went to sit beside the small fire, pulling the blade Firas had given her from its sheath. It was rusty with disuse, and she found a whetstone and oil and a rag in Firas' pack and went to work.

"Nazirah?"

She looked up to find Alma standing before her. "My true name is Johanna," she said. "It would please me to be called that."

"Jo-han-na," Alma said. "Johanna. A difficult name to pronounce."

"Then it suits its owner," Hayat said, coming into the reach

304

of the firelight. "My true name is Miriam, which my family gave me before they sold me into slavery. I will remain Hayat."

"Mine," Alma said, "was always Alma."

The two women ranged themselves on the other side of the fire from Johanna. Both had taken the opportunity of running water to wash and tidy themselves, and neither one of them appeared weighted down by the scene at the campsite that afternoon. If anything, the cautious and hesitant manner that was the norm in the harem, where for one's continued safety and good health every word was presumed to have been overheard by those who did not wish you well, had disappeared. They spoke now in voices not loud but not hushed, either, and with the certainty that only the person they were talking to was listening. In spite of herself, in spite of her fears for Jaufre and her longing to see him and Shasha again, Johanna felt a corresponding lift in her own spirits. Those stifling months locked away from the world had worn on her more than she had known. Here she was free, to speak, to ride, to travel to destinations of her own choice.

To fight.

"We heard you and Firas talking," Hayat said.

Of course they had. "Do not concern yourselves," Johanna said, returning to her blade. "This is something personal, to do only with me, and Firas."

"Of course we will concern ourselves," Alma said sharply. "This man—Gokudo?—he wishes to kill you?"

"Afterward," Johanna said. She hesitated, and then told them of Gokudo and the girl at the gate.

A pregnant silence.

"I see," Alma said at last, and exchanged a look with Hayat.

"We would be dead now if not for you, Jo-han-na," Hayat said. "After what I imagine would have been a very long and painful time. We owe you our lives."

Alma looked up at a sky covered with stars. They lit her face with reflected glory. "And our freedom." She looked back at Johanna. "How can we help?"

305

8

East of Balkh, north of Kabul, somewhere in the Hindu Kush, summer, 1323

A FULL MONTH since Talikan, most of it spent traversing rough, precarious mountain trails, made all the more dangerous by traversing them at night, and Alma and Hayat were sitting much more securely in their saddles. Their skin was chapped and their hands were calloused and they were both much thinner and they'd probably never smelled quite so badly in either of their lives, but Johanna was more impressed every day by their strength and resilience. Neither of them had wavered in their determination to win their mutual savior free of her pursuer, and Firas and Johanna had yet to hear a complaint from either of them over hard beds or short rations.

They had camped the previous morning beneath a rocky outcropping that sheltered them somewhat from the day's rain. Firas had taken advantage of the storm to scout out their pursuers, and had returned at daybreak with the news that they were a day behind them. "A day, no more," he said, looking at Johanna.

She frowned. "I thought they would be nearer."

Firas removed his cheche, wrung it out and rewound it about

his head, tucking in the wet ends neatly. "I'm sure they would be desolated to hear that you were disappointed in them, young miss."

Hayat laughed, her unquenchable dimples still in evidence, grime notwithstanding.

"Still Gokudo and his twenty?"

"Yes, young miss." Firas sounded regretfully respectful. "None have dropped out."

Johanna nodded. "Do they know we are watching them?"

"No," Firas said, very firmly.

"You're sure?"

"I am sure, young miss. I have been very careful."

"Very well, then." Johanna reviewed their plans.

They had had considerable difficulty in finding exactly the right village to help them. Many were too small, without enough men. Others weren't poor enough, having staked out the only arable land in a day's walk and therefore capable of feeding themselves and their families without resorting to too much robbery. Some were simply apathetic from hunger suffered for too long, disinterested by malnutrition to any exertion.

She had begun to think that the fierce reputation of the Afghan hill tribes had been greatly exaggerated when they happened upon Aab, a small village at the confluence of two trickles of water contaminated by the effluent from the lapis mine at the head of one of them. "The mine is played out, young miss," Firas said, "and they are wondering if they should abandon their village to look for another."

A slow smile had spread across Johanna's face. "Were they thinking they would have to walk out?"

"They were, young miss, until I explained matters to them, and suggested our plan."

"And?"

"And the village elders would be pleased to assist us," Firas had said demurely.

"And us? Will they leave us alone afterward?"

"They can always attempt to take North Wind by force," Firas said.

After the village of Aab had agreed to join forces with them, they had had to backtrack two days to allow Gokudo and his men to pick up their trail again. Now they sheltered beneath this rock overhang, damp, shivering and content. The steep sides of the narrow canyon they were in were thickly covered in stunted cedars and junipers, twisted from wind and lack of sun. The stream that had carved it was narrow and deep and filled with boulders that had broken free of the cliffs above, and it was running very high from all the rain.

"Today, then?" Johanna said.

Firas gave no quick answer. The decision was too important to be made without thought.

"You said they were using the cover of the rain to advance," Johanna said. "They think to surprise us in our wet and cold misery." Her grin was fierce.

If she could be brought to admit it, which she never would, Johanna would have said that she had thoroughly enjoyed this month in the mountains. She had seen Gokudo, oh yes, but he had not seen her, and would not unless she meant him to.

"Today," Firas said. He looked down the narrow canyon. "We'll never find a better place."

They rose to their feet, and the three women stood patiently while Firas personally checked to see that all their weapons drew freely and that each had at least one edge that could cut. After which Johanna led their horses away and Alma and Hayat began to rummage in their packs for their harem clothing.

✧

Gokudo and his troop of twenty men, none of them known to him before Terak Pass, had been chasing a rumor of their objective for thirty days. Their diet had been hard rations, their beds, when they were allowed them, hard and rocky and cold and often damp, if not wet. The men vaguely remembered Johanna—they remembered North Wind much more clearly—and the others with her they neither knew of nor cared. They were with Gokudo because Ogodei, their ruler in all things, had ordered them to be.

Thus far, following Ogodei's orders had led to riches beyond imagining, their pick of beautiful women, treasure in the form of anything they fancied from any of the cities that had fallen beneath their swords, full bellies and whatever soft noble's bed they chose each night, so long as they hadn't burned down the noble's house first. But the last month had been a long, hard slog with no reward. They had been subsisting on wild game, ibex and urial and boar when they could find them, marmots and weasels and lizards when they could not, supplemented by wild fruits and nuts and fish from the mountain streams, which were not plentiful, the local villagers having cleaned them out when times were hard. And times in these mountains were almost always hard.

They had no thought of rebellion because they would follow Ogodei unto death, and anyone he named unto death as well. There was no thought of mutiny, and as yet none of them had questioned Gokudo's authority, not even out of his hearing. But they were cold, and tired, and hungry, a little annoyed that none of the mountain villages they had stumbled across in their peregrinations had anything to plunder. They were perhaps even a little impatient with the single-minded obsession of this foreign captain, which was to purse his quarry to what appeared to be the ends of the earth, no matter how long the journey, how remote the destination or how uncomfortable the weather.

It was in this mood that they turned a rocky corner of this narrow canyon and found a small stretch of smooth gravel next to the stream. Two women were kneeling next to the water, washing clothes.

It occurred to none of Gokudo's men to wonder why two very attractive women were washing clothes next to an isolated mountain stream, without male supervision, in the rain, or why in this weather and these rough surroundings they were dressed in the flimsy vest and baggy pants of the harem, which had dampened enough to cling enticingly to their curves. They were here, they were within reach, they promised some relief from the hard days past, and what fool would question such a gift?

Since rape was not best accomplished from the back of a horse, and since it was obvious that the canyon ended not much further on and that it appeared the people their captain had had them chasing for the last month had finally run out of places to run, half of them naturally dismounted. The two women dropped their wash, screamed convincingly and ran to the nearest cliff and began to scramble up, grabbing at stunted bushes, their frantic feet causing tiny avalanches of loose rock. Gokudo's men laughed and exchanged ribald comments as they started after them. There was no hurry.

"Gokudo!"

Their captain's head snapped up, eyes fierce. A feral grin curled one corner of his mouth.

Johanna sat on North Wind's back at the head of the narrow little canyon. Her bronze-streaked hair was loose around her head and curling damply in the rain. She wore her black raw silk tunic and trousers, the last clothing she would ever have from material that had been traded for by her father. At her waist she wore a sash made from the gauzy silk of a harem veil, blood red in color. Over it she wore a belt and scabbard.

Johanna had her blade out, and she'd choked up on North Wind's reins enough so that he danced impatiently in place. He was wet and hungry and tired, too, and disinclined to take any correction to his manners, which were wearing thin as it was. This mountain travel was all very well, especially as he had his favorite person on his back, but he was more accustomed to flat racecourses and the adulation of the crowds and the sooner he returned to them, the better.

"Did you want me, Gokudo?" Johanna said. She worked

hard to put a bit of a quaver in her voice, which wasn't difficult because she was terrified on behalf of Alma and Hayat, now engaged in pulling down half the cliff face in their manifestly desperate attempt to escape the attentions of Gokudo's men. "You certainly have been trying hard enough to find me!" She waved her sword with all the expertise of a ten-year old issuing a challenge to a playmate of equal years and experience. She was no threat to Gokudo and she was demonstrating it as blatantly as possible. "Because you have certainly been persistent in following me."

"And now I have you, Wu Li's daughter," Gokudo said, his voice coming out in a growling purr.

"Not yet, you don't!" she cried, brandishing her blade again even more clumsily.

Gokudo sat astride a steppe pony, the same animal that mounted his troop. "Come!" he said in his broken Mongol, raising his naginata. "We have them now!"

He kicked the sides of his mount and it began to pick its way up the side of the stream, avoiding rocks and holes with nimble sureness. Those of his men who were still astride, perhaps ten of them, followed.

Johanna wheeled North Wind and appeared to vanish around the corner of granite at her back. Gokudo urged his shaggy pony into as fast a gait as the terrain allowed.

He heard the sound of hooves plunking through water, and North Wind whinnied, high and loud. When he rounded the corner Johanna and North Wind were standing at the end of the canyon, boxed in on three sides by steep walls and the mass of green undergrowth hanging from them. The headwaters of the narrow creek cascaded down the rock face behind her in a small waterfall, where it splashed to earth to form the stream that rushed between them.

The rain was easing. Finally, things were going his way. "Yield, Wu Li's daughter," he said, his voice thick with anticipation. "Yield to me, and I will not kill you." Or not immediately, he thought. Not until Dai Fang insisted that he must, long after he bore this impudent, thieving bitch back to Cambaluc in triumph.

He slowed the pace of his pony, allowing it to pick its way without haste. Behind him the last of his men rounded the corner. The move effectively split his force in two, which he didn't realize until too late.

The hand of some fickle god parted the clouds at just that moment, and a slender ray of sunshine slipped through and fell in a golden shower on the girl and the horse, illuminating them against the green and gray background. It was so unexpected and the subsequent vision so striking that it halted Gokudo for a moment in something like awe.

It was just long enough, although it wasn't necessary. From their cover in the dense green growth, the men of Aab rose in a body, drew bowstrings and let fly. One of Gokudo's men was killed instantly by an arrow through the eye. Three fell from the saddle, clutching at arrows in their sides. One man took the measure of their hopeless situation at a glance and pulled his mount around to head back downstream and out of range as fast as his pony could carry him, riding right over one of his wounded comrades. In his haste his sleeve caught the edge of the rock corner and unhorsed him. When he landed he was immediately skewered with arrows. He screamed and groaned, and went still.

After the first volley, the men of Aab scrambled nimbly down the canyon wall, more arrows already fitted to their bows. Gokudo's men, in the act of reaching for the bow slung on their own backs, raised their hands in surrender. They were capable and knowledgeable warriors, veterans of many battles. If they had chosen to fight they knew they could have inflicted much damage on the men of Aab, but they could not have won the day. Ogodei had not commanded them to follow Gokudo into a situation that was certain suicide for them all.

Those that remained mounted were pulled summarily to the ground, including Gokudo. Some of the men of Aab began to lead the captured steppe ponies away at once, while others relieved the men of their weapons and, wounded and hale alike, kicked them stumbling downstream in the direction from which they had come. Half a dozen others grouped around Gokudo, arrows nocked and ready. He stood with his mouth half open in disbelief. From one second to the next, he had moved from a position where he had all the power, where he finally had Johanna in his hands to do with as he pleased, to a position where he had none and was entirely at her mercy. The change of fortune was impossible for him to immediately comprehend.

Nor did she intend to give him time to fully understand it. Beyond the corner Johanna heard shouts and screams and the clash of arms and the thrum of arrows even now diminishing.

She nudged North Wind into motion, and he picked his way down to where Gokudo stood. His naginata slipped easily from his slack grasp to hers, and she rested the butt on her foot. It felt heavy and cold and alien in her hand. "Bring him," she said over her shoulder, and she and North Wind continued down the little canyon.

Behind her, she heard a muffled grunt and the stumble of feet.

Around the corner, only two of Gokudo's remaining men were left standing and were being efficiently divested of their weapons. Like their fellows upstream, they did not resist. Firas was flicking blood from his sword, others were dispatching the wounded. Her eyes searched feverishly for Hayat and Alma, and found them just then rising from a crouch in a thick patch of brush halfway up the side of the cliff. "All well?" she said.

Their smiles were shaky. "All well," Hayat said.

Johanna nodded. The troop's horses had been attached to two leading reins and were being led downstream by two young boys. The men of Aab waited in a circle, exchanging contemptuous remarks on the caliber of soldier that had pursued their benefactors into the mountains. One of them laughed and said something to Firas, who wiped his blade clean and sheathed it again, and replied with a comment Johanna didn't hear. They all laughed this time. Gokudo's men, some of whom must have understood what was being said, stood with blank faces, motionless beneath the strung arrows.

All but one. "Bitch!" one of Gokudo's men said. "Cunt! Daughter and granddaughter of pimps and whores, may God curse them all! May you suffer in sixty thousand hells for all eternity!"

Johanna looked at him, puzzled at first, and then on an indrawn breath recognized the contorted features beneath the filth. "Farhad," she said.

Firas turned to follow her gaze. "Why, so it is."

There was little remaining of the elegant sheik's son. He wore a torn and tattered coat that looked from the stains as if it had been taken off a dead man who had taken a long time to die. His beard, once neatly barbered, was now a wild bush, and his hair hung greasily down from beneath a rolled cap that looked as if it harbored a healthy population of vermin. Two of the men of Aab were advancing with knives drawn, while Farhad's companions were trying to restrain him. He struggled, maddened, as he called more curses down upon her head.

Her head remained remarkably unbowed. "Not dead of snake bite after all, I see," she said pleasantly. "What a pity. How did you convince Ogodei to let you live, I wonder?" She paused and let her gaze wander over him insultingly. "Or maybe I don't. You used to be almost attractive." She smiled. "And Ogodei is known to be... liberal, in his tastes."

He was nearly sobbing and his eyes were wild. He struggled futilely against the hands holding him. "Daughter of pigs! May you give birth only to more!"

Firas walked up to Johanna, who brought her leg over the saddle to slide from North Wind's back. "The men of Aab want to know what they should do with the living."

She shrugged, indifferent. "As they wish."

"They don't want them among their own," Firas said.

"Well," Johanna said, "if they are inclined to set them free, Ogodei's men can return to their master. If they think he'll take them back after this."

"May you never know the father of your child!"

Her smile didn't reach her eyes. "But they'll have to walk."

Farhad was almost weeping. "Bitch," he said, "cunt that has seen a thousand cocks!"

"Come, Farhad," she said in a silken voice, "surely the prospect isn't so bad as that."

And with that echo of his own words in his ears, his companions dragged him away from her, shrieking more and worse imprecations to the sky.

"What are you going to do with that?" Firas said, indicating the naginata she still held.

"Which one is the headman of Aab?" she said.

Firas beckoned one of the men forward. He was older than the rest but still very fit, and he kept a wary eye on the curved blade of the naginata as he inclined his head in salute. He said something in a dialect Johanna hadn't had time to pick up. It was almost Persian, but not quite.

"Jibran complimented me on the success of my plan," Firas said. "I told him it was your plan. He offers you his compliments."

"Tell him it would not have succeeded without the courageous and able men of Aab," she said, and held up the naginata. "Tell him I would give this to him as a personal gift, in gratitude."

The headman's eyes widened and he replied vociferously, at extensive length and with sweeping gestures to an approving murmur from his men.

"He accepts," Firas said.

"I am pleased to hear it," she said. "Tell him it has one more task to accomplish before it passes into his hands. I would ask him, as leader of his tribe, to bear witness to that task."

Firas translated. Jibran squared his shoulders and replied with a long and complicated sentence that went on for five minutes, ending it with a bow and a flourish. All of his men bowed, too.

"He is honored," Firas said.

She turned and looked at Gokudo. He was on his knees in the middle of the stream, his hands bound behind his back. He was muttering to himself in his own tongue. Johanna had been to Cipangu with her father and while she was by no means fluent in Gokudo's tongue, she had spent enough time on the docks to realize that his insults were an order of magnitude even more insulting than Farhad's.

"Not here," Johanna said. "I don't want to get my feet wet. Or foul the water."

They hauled him up on the little gravel shoal where Hayat and Alma had been washing their clothes only minutes before.

She stood before him. "You dishonored my father with his second wife," she said in Mandarin, "and then you tried to kill him by cutting the girth on his saddle. When he didn't die quickly enough, at Dai Fang's order you smothered him in his own sick bed."

His muttering died away, and he blinked up at her as if he had just realized she was there. Behind her, she could hear Firas translating her words for Jibran and his men.

"My only mistake was in leaving justice for my father in other hands. Today, I rectify that mistake."

Johanna took a few practice swings with the naginata. Watching from behind and to her left, Firas motioned everyone farther back, which may have been an unusually superfluous gesture. Though she tried to hide it, it was obvious she found the staff heavy and the blade weighting its end heavier still.

He saw her set her jaw and square her shoulders. She choked up a little on the staff, but only a little. She readjusted her stance, moving her feet farther apart, bending her knees slightly, and adjusted the height of the blade to where it looked to Firas like she was aiming for the level of Gokudo's ear. Her torso twisted so that if she had pulled the naginata any more to her left she would have broken her spine off at the base, and commenced the swing. Its own weight brought the blade down to the height of Gokudo's neck just as the edge touched his skin. Her momentum and the weight and acute sharpness of the blade did the rest.

Gokudo's head bounced once with a meaty thud and rolled a few feet away, his face still looking a little puzzled. His eyes blinked rapidly six or seven times. His body crumpled into a disorderly heap. Blood at first fountained from his severed neck, then flowed, then streamed, then trickled, and then stopped.

The swing of the naginata pulled Johanna around almost as far to her right as she had begun it to her left, Firas noticed with professional detachment, so far as to pull her left heel from the ground. She let it, probably so it would look as if it was her idea, until the naginata's swing slowed and she was able to regain her authority over it.

She neatly reversed its waning momentum to bring it back level in front of her, and let it lay flat against her palms as she presented it to Jibran with a slight bow, the blade still wet with Gokudo's blood. Firas believed that only he saw the fine tremble in her arms.

Jibran looked at Johanna in silence for a long moment, and then bowed once more, deeply, respectfully, profoundly. As one, the men of Aab bowed with him. He accepted the naginata with due reverence and respect, and then he and his men began to melt rapidly down the canyon in the wake of the boys who had taken the horses, leaving Farhad and the other soldiers standing where they were, stupid with fatigue and shock, staring at Gokudo's severed head.

Hayat and Alma came up, having changed back into their traveling clothes and leading their horses. They looked at Gokudo's body. Alma shuddered. Hayat gave Johanna an approving nod. "All done here?"

"All done," Johanna said, and mounted North Wind.

As they passed down the canyon, Farhad lunged for Johanna, again calling down curses on her head and her line and her descendants until the end of time. Displeased, possibly by Farhad's intemperate language, possibly by his uninvited nearness, North Wind exercised the excellent muscles in his right hind leg to plant his hoof squarely in Farhad's belly. Farhad flew backwards and landed in the stream with a magnificent splash, where he lay gasping for breath.

Johanna gave North Wind's neck an extra pat. He gave his ears a nonchalant flick. They walked around the next curve of the canyon without a backward glance.

9

On the Road, summer, 1323

"TELL ME ABOUT the Templars," Jaufre said.

Alaric sighed. To Jaufre's ears it sounded a little theatrical. "First, I beg you, please rid yourself of the habit of calling me Alaric the Templar," the older man said. "Ram will have his little joke, but the farther west we travel, the more dangerous it gets."

"Why?"

"Because our order has been proscribed, by church and state."

"What church? Which state?"

"All of them," Alaric said gloomily.

"Since when?"

"That depends," Alaric said, and launched into a disjointed history frequently interrupted by strong personal opinions and bitter asides that lasted, on and off, for four days. They had come out of the foothills and were well launched upon the eastern edge of the aptly-named Emptiness Desert, and Rambahadur Raj had switched travel time from days to nights. Traveling across the great salt waste with the stars painting the sky overhead lent an otherworldly element to the tale, which might have been partially responsible for leaving Jaufre inclined to believe less than half of what he heard. It was all so very improbable.

The short version seemed to be that the Knights of the Temple was an order of warrior monks first established a little over two hundred years before by a Frankish knight named Hugues.

"De Payens," Félicien said, who kept close by during the entirety of the long nights of the tale of the Templars and evidently felt empowered to correct anything he felt Alaric got wrong.

Alaric, who had taken an inexplicable dislike to his fellow Frank at first sight, harrumphed and continued. "He went on crusade to the Holy Land—"

"Crusade?" Jaufre said. "Oh, I know, I remember my father talking about it. There's a shrine or, no, a city. Something near the western shore of the Middle Sea that—Christians, isn't it?—regard as belonging to their religion." Father John had spoken of it, he remembered. "Where your Christ was born," he said out loud.

"Everyone's Christ," Alaric said in a shocked voice, and this time Jaufre thought of Uncle Cheng. "His birthplace has fallen into the hands of the infidels. It is a holy cause to regain it."

"It was that," Félicien said, as if admitting an unpalatable truth. "But it was also driven by the need to re-open trade routes to the East." Jaufre couldn't see the goliard's lip curling but he could hear it in his voice. "Our noble rulers can't do without their nutmeg."

"It was a quest to reclaim the holy places where our Lord and Savior once walked and preached the Gospel," Alaric said frostily.

"It also gave the knights of Europe a new target to fight, instead of each other."

Alaric reared back so violently that his camel stumbled and protested. "My dear young student, as you say you are, you would do well to listen if you wish to learn."

"And Hugues de Payens…?" Jaufre said.

Alaric, very erect, said, "The evil Saracens—"

"Also known as the Seljuk empire," Félicien said to Jaufre. "Mostly Turkics."

"—were robbing and murdering pilgrims—pious, unarmed travelers to the holy places of Jerusalem, where—"

 320

"—once our Lord and Savior walked and preached," Félicien said in a sing-song voice, and grinned at Alaric's fulminating look, unrepentant. "And you say I don't listen."

Alaric harrumphed again. "The Holy Father on his throne in Rome—"

"Pope Urban II in 1096."

"—responded to these outrages—"

"As well as to a request from the emperor of Byzantium," Félicien said, "who was worried about the Seljuks knocking at his front door, and his back door, too, for that matter."

"—by preaching the First Crusade at the Council of Clermont."

"And Hugues de Payens…?" Jaufre said.

"Yes, yes," Alaric said testily, "that came later."

"How much later?"

"About a hundred years later," Félicien said, and he and Alaric fell into another wrangle about just when the Knights of the Temple had been officially established. As near as Jaufre could make out, the Templars were a volunteer force from when Hugues de Payens and his companions offered their services to King Baldwin of Jerusalem in 1113, but they weren't officially an arm of the Christian church until fifteen years later.

"So," Jaufre said, making a mental effort to sort all this into a timeline, "they protected pilgrims on the road to Jerusalem."

Alaric straightened. "It was our calling."

Félicien snorted.

"I beg your pardon?" Alaric said, the frost back in his voice.

"They were bankers," the goliard said. "And some of the richest landowners in Europe. And that is exactly why they no longer exist." Except as superannuated old fidgets like this one, his silence added.

"But—"

"They became too powerful, too rich," the goliard said. "It created a great deal of jealousy. Philip of France had borrowed heavily from them, and he didn't want to pay it back. And—"

Someone called for a guard and Alaric spurred away, gladly, Jaufre thought.

He saw Félicien's head turn as he watched the older man move down the line of the caravan. "And?" he said.

"And they lost," Félicien said. "They lost Jerusalem to Saladin in 1187. In 1291, they lost Acre, the last Christian outpost in the Holy Land. Eleven years later, they lost Ruad Island, most of the Templars who were there dying in its defense. In the end, they lost everything the Crusades had gained." He paused. "Well," he said, "at least everything they gained in the first Crusade. None of the rest of the crusades amounted to much."

"And when they lost the Holy Land, everyone turned against them?"

"How do you think the Crusades were paid for, Jaufre?"

"Oh," he said, after a moment.

"Yes," the goliard said, "taxes. The Christian world paid and paid and paid again to regain the Holy Land for those of their faith. Lords great and small from Italy to Spain to France to England bankrupted their estates financing this holy effort. A wasted effort, in blood and in treasure. I'm surprised the Templars lasted as long after the fall of Acre as they did."

Jaufre subtracted. "Twenty-one years."

"Fifteen," Félicien said grimly. "Philip the Fair arrested as many as he could lay hands on in 1307. Pope Clement held out as long as he could but Philip finally forced his hand at the head of an army. In 1314, with full papal approval, Philip burned the last Templar Grand Master at the stake in Paris, and it was all over."

Jaufre wondered where his father had been in all this. Alaric had given him to understand that Templars were monks and that they did not marry, but Jaufre himself had been born in 1306, four years after the fall of Ruad, a year before the first arrests and eight full years before the head of his order had been executed. "You don't seem all that fond of Philip the Fair," he said cautiously. "He was your king."

"He was my father's king," Félicien said, his voice devoid of his usual mockery. "De Molay, the Grand Master, cursed them both from his pyre. Pope Clement and King Philip, both. They both died within the year, and there hasn't been a king able to keep the throne of France beneath his ass for more than a few years at a time since then."

"And you think the curse had something to do with that?"

"You don't find the juxtaposition of events persuasive?" The customary mocking tone was back in the light voice.

"I'm not a superstitious man," Jaufre said.

He heard the shrug in Félicien's voice. "As you wish. They're still dead."

So are the Templars, Jaufre thought, but refrained from saying so. There was that in the goliard's voice that spoke of much unsaid, something personal, if he had to guess. Was there a Templar in Félicien's family, perhaps? Or a family bankrupted by taxes raised for a Crusade?

✧

At dawn, when they set up camp to sleep through the heat of the day, Jaufre took his sword to the guards' practice ground and whaled away stoically at the wooden post set up there. The men had at first teased him over his weakness and ineptitude, but his determination had eventually silenced them, and now when he was done they came forward to offer one-on-one practice. Slowly, too slowly, he was building his stamina and his skill back to where he might be able to beat a ten-year old child, if said child were armed only with a dinner knife.

He staggered back to collapse next to their campfire, and drank the entire bowl of soup Shasha handed him in one gulp, chunks of goat meat and all. She refilled it and handed it back without comment.

And so the days on the Road progressed, unchanging, monotonous, seemingly without end. The desert continued flat and salt, and Rambahadur Raj delayed their start a little longer each evening to allow the ground to cool before they set out across it. They had no trouble with raiders in this first leg of their journey. There weren't many people of any kind, the oasis towns few and far between, and the people of the caravan looked forward to Kerman in eager anticipation. Kerman was a storied city famous for carpets and turquoise and must certainly support a caravansary worthy of the name, with running water and public baths.

In this they were proven right, thankfully. Two mountainous ridges capped with late-melting snow hid the city from view until they were right on it, and at last they beheld the sprawl of red brick buildings, a vast expanse of peaked and arched and domed roofs rising up to a central fortress whose size awed them all into momentary silence.

"It's bigger even than the palace at Cambaluc," Shasha said.

"By half again," Jaufre said.

"It's not as tall as Chartres," Félicien said, and kicked his donkey into motion again.

The caravansary was large and spacious, with a fully functioning fountain and indoor plumbing. The stables were vast and the lush personal accommodations were better than Kashgar's. Jaufre and Shasha agreed to splurge on a suite of two rooms that opened onto a balcony over the central court, and they drew back the shutters so that the sound of water trickling out of the fountain would sweeten their sleep all night long.

Félicien leaned out the window and inhaled deeply of the scent of roses growing riotously beneath. "How long do we stay here?"

"Rambahadur Raj said his merchants want to spend a few days in trade," Jaufre said. "I wouldn't mind a look around the market myself." He looked at Shasha. "Should we buy some carpets?"

She answered his question with another. "I wonder what the going rate is here for lapis?"

"Did Wu Li have an agent in Kerman?"

She shook her head. "I think he bought most of his carpet stock through Tashkent."

"Wouldn't hurt to ask around," Jaufre said, and did so that afternoon, making the rounds of the market, which featured piles of carpets taller than he was arranged in long, straight corridors interrupted by spaces for the merchants to entertain opening offers.

"Wu Li of Cambaluc?" they said, doubtful. "I may have heard the name, young sir, but just sit here for a moment while I try to remember. My assistant will show you some of my finer carpets while you wait." A wink. "Very rare and fine, two hundreds of knots per finger, I assure you, you may count for yourself."

It would be an hour or more before he got away, and by the time he did there would be three or four other merchants clamoring for his attention. It was no wonder that he didn't notice the small, dark nondescript man who detached himself from a shadow near his fourth stop, and followed.

In the end they sold half of their lapis and could have sold it all but that Shasha wanted to see what the price was in Damascus. "Greedy," Jaufre said, and Shasha made a face at him while Félicien and Hari laughed. The copper pots went, all of them, at a twenty percent markup that was so easily swallowed that they were sorry he hadn't marked them up by half again.

Still, they had freed up loads on two of their pack camels and made serious inroads on a third. "I shall go down to the carpet bazaar," Shasha said the next morning, in the manner of Alexander announcing his descent on India, and she stalked off with Félicien in tow. The goliard would probably write a song about it.

"There is a Zoroastrian community here I wish to explore," Hari said in the manner of one anticipating the sight of a herd of exotic beasts, and he too was off.

Jaufre, on his own, went up to get as close a look at the fortress as he could without offending its guards, who were each large men, well armed, and looked very capable. He noticed towers rising up from the edifice, tall ones with perforations. Surveying the city, he saw many more, tall and short, rising up from buildings large and small everywhere. He bought a glass of fresh fruit juice from the cart of a friendly-looking vendor, who gave him a quizzical look in answer to his question. "Towers? Ah, you mean the bâdgir, the wind catchers."

Without further ado the vendor closed up his cart and ushered Jaufre around his city, displaying wind catcher after wind catcher and lecturing his new young friend extensively on Persian architecture, desert weather and prevailing wind dynamics throughout the year. He concluded the tour by bringing Jaufre to his favorite café and introducing him to all of his friends, who included an architect, two builders, and a philosopher of astrology who insisted on having Jaufre's birthday and birth place and who grew very sorrowful when Jaufre could provide him only with the former. Jaufre suspected there was something in the astrologer's glass besides tea, but no one said anything, alcohol being forbidden by Islam and all of his companions being good, observant Muslims.

He still hadn't noticed the small, dark man, who might have been made to order to blend into the woodwork, who sat at the back of the café and nursed the same carafe of pomegranate juice for three hours, impervious to the black looks of the waiter.

Jaufre and his new friends drank oceans of mint tea late into the night, swore eternal friendship, and everyone went home, Jaufre boring everyone back at the caravansary with an enthusiastic recitation of all he had learned that day. Balked of sharing by his companions' determination to sleep soundly off the ground for the last time for what would undoubtedly be many weeks, if not months, he attempted to enlighten the ignorance of his sparring partners the following morning at practice, and was soundly spanked for his pains.

Over breakfast, Shasha informed them that they had acquired a load of carpets and that she would need help loading them that afternoon.

"I have found a man of books," Félicien said. "He has so many he wishes to sell some of them to make room for more." He smiled. "Reluctantly."

"I don't know," Jaufre said, looking at Shasha. "Are they bound or scrolls? Bound books are bulky and heavy."

"They are also more valuable, pound for pound," Shasha said. "It can't hurt to look."

"In the souk they speak of a blacksmith who turns out fine knives," Hari said.

"Do you have his name and direction?" Jaufre said, and Shasha threw up her hands. "I'll go with you," she said to Hari, but raised an admonitory finger. "You must all be back in time to help pack!"

At the home of the man of books, Jaufre was surprised to find Alaric sitting cross-legged on the floor, mooning over an illustrated manuscript with brilliantly colored drawings of fantastical beasts, unicorns and dragons, and "Look, here, a parandrus. It is an animal that can take any shape, and so trick its enemies by becoming them, until they learn it too late to save themselves."

It was written in Latin and weighed as much as Jaufre's sword, scabbard and all. "What did you say it was called?"

"A bestiary," Alaric said, in the tone of someone describing a catalogue of heaven itself.

"So I see," Jaufre said untruthfully.

"Look," Alaric said, displaying a particularly magnificent illustration glittering with gilt, "a dragon! Have you ever seen such a dragon before, young sir?"

"About a million of them," Jaufre said truthfully, and when Alaric gaped at him he said, "Carved from ivory and jade of every color, painted on lacquered boxes and jars and vases, embroidered on tunics and tablecloths and robes of state. There are dragons on practically every flat surface of Cambaluc."

It was only a slight exaggeration, at that. He and Félicien stepped around Alaric for the next hour as they inspected the personal library of a man who, judged on its contents, had as much money as he needed to buy any book he wanted, and evidently he had wanted every book he ever saw. Jaufre found a manuscript called "Historia Calamitatum" by someone named Abelard, bound together with letters between him and a woman named Eloise. What he liked best about it was that it was written in Latin on the left-hand page with what Félicien told him was a French translation on the right-hand page. He could improve his Latin and learn French at the same time from this book, and he set it to one side, wondering briefly how it had wandered so far from its country of origin.

Alaric bought his bestiary and they bought half a dozen other manuscripts, Félicien falling in love with a collection of cansos by someone called Bernart de Ventadorn, who the goliard said was a famous singer a century before. Jaufre peered over his shoulder, saw text shaped like poetry, and retreated in a hurry. He had found a travel guide to Persia, illustrated, and a couple of scrolls that weren't quite ragged enough to substantiate the owner's claims that they dated from ancient Rome and were by the hand of Virgil himself, telling the story of Antony and Cleopatra. This said with a wink and a nudge, both of which mystified Jaufre, but he bought them, if for rather less than the seller wished to accept.

They were about to leave when Jaufre caught sight of another manuscript tucked at the back of a high shelf. He fished it out. The covers were calfskin stretched over wooden boards and it was bound together with five lengths of thin leather straps. Opening it, he realized that the binding was much newer than the manuscript, which was tattered and torn and had pages missing, some of them probably harvested for their illustrations. The text, neatly copied, was arranged in two columns.

He flipped through it and discovered that the remaining illustrations, though somewhat faded and with most of the gilt flaked off, were still perfectly legible. More than a few were stunning, faded or not.

He turned back to the beginning. "'Il Milione,'" he said,

sounding out the words. His eyes dropped farther down the page, and he almost dropped the book.

The Travels of Marco Polo. He couldn't read Italian but he was certainly able to puzzle out that much.

He heard a snort. "Marco Milione."

Jaufre looked around to see Alaric reading over his shoulder. "You're familiar with this book?"

"Who isn't?" Alaric snorted again, with contempt even more vast than he had the first time. "Marco Milione, that's what they call him," he said. "A liar and a braggart. If even a quarter of what he says is true, the world is a marvelous place, indeed." His tone indicated that he highly doubted it.

In a daze, Jaufre dickered only briefly over the price, although he would gladly have ripped out one of the rubies secreted in the hem of his trousers to meet any price the old bookseller set.

As they turned from the alley leading to the house, the small, dark man who had been following Jaufre ever since his morning among the rug merchants slipped from the shadows, knocked, and was admitted to the bookseller's house.

Back at the caravansary Jaufre drew Shasha to one side and showed her the book by Marco Polo. Like Jaufre and Johanna, the victim of sporadic tutoring in the romance languages by a Franciscan friar who had been more interested in converting the heathen than in educating them, she recognized the name and little else. She paged through the book, pausing here and there. "Could there be more than one Marco Polo, do you think?"

"Who traveled from Venice to Cambaluc, and spent twenty years in service to Kublai Khan?" he said. "I doubt it."

She gave an absent nod. "Wait till Johanna sees this. She'll be thrilled."

"I wonder..."

"What?"

"If he writes about Shu Lin. And Shu Ming."

The answer to his question would have to wait until they learned to read Italian. Jaufre bundled his purchases away, and he and Félicien departed immediately again for the armorer Hari had spoken of, where they found eating knives, skinning knives, fighting daggers, and the curved swords of the Persians, like the one Firas wore. They were nothing fancy, but they were well crafted and looked like they would hold an edge, so Jaufre bought a dozen of the eating knives and Félicien, a little to Jaufre's surprise, bought a long knife somewhere between a dagger and a sword, encased in a plain leather sheath. "Are you expecting trouble?"

"No," Félicien said, buckling the blade around his waist, "but that is when trouble always comes."

They returned to the caravansary, the sun low in the sky, to find everyone in an uproar of packing and cursing men and whinnying horses and braying donkeys and groaning camels protesting beneath their loads.

A little after dark, they set off. Félicien had his lute slung across his shoulder and as the city dropped behind them he began to play. Soon they were all singing along, or humming as in the case of Hari.

They sounded good, Jaufre thought, but not as good as if Johanna was with them.

The caravan had been increased by one rug merchant and a dozen camels. Among the handlers of the new camels was a small, dark, nondescript man who had demonstrated an ability with pack animals. He said so little that no one else with the caravan, if asked, could have said who he was or where he came from, or even what his name was, or what he was doing, other than traveling west.

10

Between the Hindu Kush and Baghdad, summer, 1323

THE MORNING AFTER Gokudo's execution, Johanna said, "Will you teach me the ways of the blade?"

Startled, Firas said, "Of the sword, do you mean?"

"Knife, dagger," she said. "Perhaps not the sword, or not your sword. I was not able to lift Jaufre's sword for any length of time, much less swing or thrust it." She swallowed, and added with difficulty, "I could barely raise Gokudo's naginata to do what needed to be done."

"You managed, nonetheless," Firas said, very dry.

"I wish to do more than manage," she said. "Yes, I practice form every morning, as I have most of my life, and it will serve to defend myself against unarmed attackers, so long as there are only one or two. I do well enough with a bow. But I have very little skill with the blade. The Road is a dangerous place, and the more ways I have to protect myself, the safer I will be."

Firas the Assassin, man of Alamut and master of the sword, inclined his head. "A worthy ambition," he said, somewhat to Johanna's surprise, because as a Persian Firas should have been appalled at the very notion of teaching such a thing to a woman.

The lessons commenced the following morning. At first Alma and Hayat only watched. After a few days, Alma came to

Johanna and said simply, "Hayat and I would like to learn to use a blade, too."

Firas shook his head but he didn't say no, and doubled the practice times to mornings and evenings. Johanna began to teach the other two women soft boxing. One evening, watching the sun sink down below the horizon as she stood post, Johanna became aware that Firas had joined them. Nothing was said, then or later, but from then on he joined them. He seemed to catch on quicker than either of the two women, but one day he heard Johanna say, "You don't have to pretend to be less able at this than he is, Alma."

"But he is a man," Alma said. "And our protector."

"The point is to be able to protect ourselves," Johanna said.

"From someone like Ogodei, or Gokudo?" Hayat said, skeptical and rightfully so.

"No one can protect themselves from an all-out assault by a full army," Johanna said grimly. "In that situation, the only recourse is to run, and we did. Or to conspire, which we also did. But one on one, there should be no reason—there will be no reason for us not to be able to defend ourselves from the harm that men would do to women when they are alone."

After that, Alma became much more difficult to confound at Four Ladies Work at Shuttles, of all the thirty movements of soft boxing the hardest to master. Hayat was left-handed—"Always an advantage in a right-handed world," Firas said—and proved to be quick and sure with a knife. When they passed a small town, Firas went into the market with a heavily veiled Johanna and found a slender, double-edged knife in a small belted sheath which he showed Hayat how to fasten to her forearm. Thereafter, he made her practice continually, until she perfected a draw so swift it was almost as if the knife sprouted from her hand.

Johanna was no match for Firas in upper body strength, but he made her practice with a heavy wooden practice sword for a month before he found a small sword in another market which weighed half of what the practice sword did. She discarded the first rusty blade he had bought in Balkh and blocked his first parry at their next practice with skill and quickness and even some ability. Her surprise and pleasure was evident, as was a burgeoning sense of pride.

He dropped his sword and stepped back. She dropped her guard. He leapt forward and with one circular pass disarmed her. Her sword flew from her hand and landed several feet away and a moment later the point of his blade pressed into the vein pulsing in her throat.

"Unless you are facing another woman armed with a sword, a highly unlikely circumstance, you will be facing armed men. They will not be Jibran, who is a man not so bound by Islam that he cannot recognize strength when he sees it, no matter the vessel. Nature has made men stronger than women. We will always have the advantage in strength, and most of the time in training as well." He dropped his blade and stood back.

She picked up the small sword and regarded it with a glum expression. "Then what is the point of all this practice?"

He could have pointed out that she had been the one to ask him to teach her. "Surprise will be your biggest advantage," he said. "No man will expect to face a woman with a blade. Even when they do, they will very probably laugh."

Her eyes flashed.

"Yes," he said. "Use their ignorance. It will be infinitely more powerful than any other weapon you could possible possess."

She looked from her small sword to his scimitar, which was twice as long and outweighed it by half.

"Don't allow the size of a weapon to intimidate you," he said. "The fact that you will be able to raise a weapon in your own defense will make them pause in sheer astonishment. Use that moment to your best advantage. Take time to think first, then act. Remember, your best weapon is up here." He tapped his head.

He looked at the three of them, weapons in hand, intent looks on their faces. They were committing his words to memory, and for a moment his heart failed at the thought of these women in a fight with real weapons against real opponents. An experienced soldier, an Assassin like himself or one of Ogodei's Mongols, one with years of training and the experience of many battles, could dispatch any or all of the three at one blow. Two, at the most. "Don't fight if you can possibly avoid fighting," he said. "But if you have to fight, win by whatever means necessary."

They were keeping to the less-frequented routes across central Persia. Some were so seldom traveled that they had to find elaborately circuitous ways around rockslides and fallen trees that had come down since last it had been used. The terrain was a continuous expanse of desert interrupted intermittently by low mountain ranges that ran more or less north and south. The narrow passes that led through these ranges required careful negotiation, populated as they were by tribes who regarded them as natural traps set by a providential god. Any travelers who attempted to negotiate them were regarded as fair game and their persons and their belongings as rightful winnings.

The women got their first chance to practice their newly-learned art against a band of men who leapt out from behind a heap of boulders that crowded a steep, narrow path with few trees and no water. The fact that their party was in a hurry to find the next stream or village with a well, whichever came first may have accounted for them not paying as much attention as they should have, because their attackers were not particularly stealthy. North Wind bellowed outrage and reared and plunged but the trail was so narrow that he was as much hindrance as help, and the men cascading down the rocks seemed like sixty instead of only six. Alma kept her composure, waited until one of the grinning men got close enough, and leapt from her saddle to land right on his chest, knocking him flat on his back. He let out a roar of triumph and started to tear at her clothes, but the roar ended in a surprised gurgle when her blade efficiently located the narrow space between his first and second ribs and slid easily straight on into his heart. He died staring into her eyes, a look of astonishment on his face.

Hayat let another of the raiders grab her leg and pull her from the saddle. She used his own strength to turn the motion into a somersault that vaulted her right over his head and came up standing with her knife in hand, which she sank in the back of a third man who was gaping at Johanna, fighting to stay on North Wind's rearing back. Hayat spun back to face her first attacker, who stared at her with his eyes goggling, unable to recover from his astonishment fast enough to live much longer than that.

When North Wind reared again Johanna slid down his back and over his tail, landing neatly on both feet, her blade out and her cloak looped around her left arm to form a felted shield. One of the attackers recovered his senses enough to slice at her with his dagger and she ducked beneath his arm and thrust her sword up into his belly, dodging back out of the way so his blood and guts would spill onto the ground and not on her.

The surprise of facing four warriors instead of one man with one sword and three helpless women worked, as Firas had predicted to Johanna, very much in their favor. He put his foot on the belly of the last man who had been standing and pulled out his sword, wiping it free of blood on the downed man's robes. When he turned, Hayat and Alma were rifling the dead men's purses and collecting swords and knives. "What are you going to do with those?" he said, indicating the weapons.

Hayat spared him a brief glance. "Throw them over the first cliff we come to, Johanna says, so their relatives will have to find new weapons with which to ambush the next travelers through this pass."

North Wind, scenting blood he hadn't himself shed and annoyed about it, stamped and snorted his disapproval until Hayat's mount whinnied his own dismay and North Wind nipped him firmly on the haunch in reproof. The only one allowed to complain was him.

"You knew they were there," Johanna said.

Hayat and Alma looked up. "What?"

"You knew they were there, Firas," Johanna said. "You didn't raise your blade until that last man was about to stab Alma in the back. You knew they were there."

"You will never learn to defend yourselves if you never have a chance to, young miss," Firas said, entirely without apology. "And if you had been paying better attention, you would have heard them from that stand of spruce trees a quarter of a league back. They displayed all the subtlety of North Wind at a gallop."

Johanna looked at Alma and Hayat. They looked back at her with sober expressions. She wanted to be angry at Firas, but he was right.

They remounted and went on their way, negotiating the rest of the pass with care and unmolested. Scouting ahead, Firas found a village among a few terraced fields, with a well, but Johanna said, "If it's the nearest village to the pass, the men who attacked us probably came from there. Let's go on."

Firas, who had been about to say the same thing, repressed a smile. They did, and as their reward found a small stream trickling over a rock shelf as they reached the bottom of the pass. Their horses gathered around the tiny pool, heads down as they lapped at the water, and Johanna shared out trail rations for her companions and hard grain biscuits for the horses.

Over the next few weeks Firas let Johanna take the lead more and more, stepping in with a quietly suggestive comment now and then when it seemed merited. Hayat and Alma, with a lifetime's training in deferring to the male, took longer to assert themselves, but soon began to contribute the occasional opinion as well. None of their comments were at first very useful, as their experience in both travel and survival was limited, but they were slowly progressing from merely doing what they were told. Firas revised his private estimate of their ability to survive on their own from zero to perhaps ten percent.

When a gang of thieves attacked on the other side of another pass, who were far more professional than the opportunistic villagers who had previously ambushed them, Firas fell back to monitor the fight, taking an active part only when one of his students became hopelessly outnumbered. The three women prevailed, although Alma received a wound in her knife arm and Johanna took an elbow to the face that left her with one eye swollen completely shut and both bruised in a steady progression of spectacular colors over the next week. Hayat was unscathed and smug about it, even as she tended to the other two women's injuries.

As a graduation exercise, it was definitive. Firas revised his estimate sharply upward.

The next morning he woke before dawn to find Johanna's bedroll empty. Their camp was in a rocky hollow beneath an encircling ridge, next to a clear mountain stream that gave off a peaceful chuckle that had lulled them all to sleep the night before. He found her on the ridge above, watching the lightening edge of the eastern sky, and took a seat beside her.

After a while she said, "I never killed anyone before."

He watched the horizon in silence. She wasn't speaking of the men she had killed in the two ambushes.

Presently, she said, "I wondered if I would be able to. I hated Gokudo for what he did, but this life, Firas, whatever Hari says, I believe this life is all we have. Even though I know, none better, what I would have suffered if I had fallen into his hands, his life was all Gokudo had. I took it from him."

He waited. There would be more.

The line of the horizon turned from dark blue to pale mauve. "I feel no remorse," she said, watching it. "I have had no bad dreams. I rubbed him out of this realm with a firm hand, and I didn't even worry about his blood on my trousers." She looked down at them, the raw black silk worn but holding up well to the rigors of the Road. "And now there are others to add beneath his name. And there will be more."

"And you want to know if you are a monster," Firas said.

She swallowed hard. "Yes," she said in a very small voice.

"You are not," he said.

Her spine seemed to stiffen a little from his matter-of-fact tone. "I want to believe that," she said.

"You can," he said firmly. "Regard this man. He acted to kill your father, not once, but twice, and was successful the second time. Affection and honor both called for his death. More, he professed his intent to harm your own person. You have the right to defend yourself from harm. Thirdly, there is the matter of justice." He considered. "In the fifth surah, it is written the life for the life, and the eye for the eye, and the nose for the nose, and the ear for the ear, and the tooth for the tooth, and for wounds retaliation."

She digested this. Organized faith had not been a part of her raising. She and Jaufre had taken some classes with Father John, a Franciscan friar who had made his way to the khan's court, who did his stern best to convince them in between Latin lessons that they were born sinners condemned to a fiery hell and that their only recourse was to adopt his faith, confess their every sin both real and imagined, and be redeemed in the eyes of what seemed to them to be a very vengeful and judgmental god. They had, at Wu Li's instigation, taken other classes with a Confucian scholar who was given to the pipe and who lectured them on the importance of family and education from the interior prospect of a rosy opium dream that admitted gods only as distant, cloudy outlines to be respected but not worshipped.

This regimen, overall, had been more productive of a healthy skepticism than blind faith. With a sudden shock of realization Johanna now realized that that might have been her father's purpose all along.

Whatever Wu Li's motivation, neither teacher had encouraged them to belief in an afterlife, and a life lived on the Road, at risk of lethal diseases, avaricious raiders, natural disasters and political upheavals, where your best help was an ear attuned to the most recent news, a lively sense of self-preservation and a fast mount, bred less dependence on faith and more on one's own competence and intelligence and ability to make friends. Doubtless many blameless citizens had fallen to their knees and implored God for salvation that awful day in Talikan. Equally doubtless, none of them had received it. She remembered the scene she had watched from the wall and repressed a shudder. No, she could not conceive of a faith that forgave behavior so wicked, so evil.

But this man, this warrior come so lately into their company, he had proved more than worthy of her respect and trust, and besides, she liked what his god was telling her, so she sat still and listened.

He turned to look directly at her. "It is written later in that same verse whoso forgoeth vengeance, it shall be expiation for him." She didn't like that as much, and Firas raised a hand. "Gently, young miss, gently. Here, I believe the Prophet revealed enough to merit this man's death. If you had shown mercy and let him live, would he have let you live, unharmed, as well? I think not, as I judge the words out of his own mouth. How many leagues did he pursue you over the trackless wastes of desert and rough trails of mountain? He would not have stopped. He could not." He sighed. "It was, young miss, truly, you or Gokudo. One would live. The other would not." He gave a faint smile. "Inshallah."

"If God wills?" she said.

"You are here," Firas said. "He must have willed it so."

She was silent again until the first sliver of gold lit the distant line of desert. She rose to her feet. "The others will be awake and ready for practice." She hesitated. "Does it show?" she said in a low voice. "On my face?"

Gravely, he inspected her countenance for traces of rabid killer set loose upon the world. "No," he said. "It does not."

Although, over the next weeks, he decided that perhaps it did show in some subtle ways. Not the act of slicing off Gokudo's head itself, no, she was not bent or haggard from guilt and certainly showed no signs of grief. But there was an added assurance in her stride, in the lift of her head and the straight set of her shoulders that he had not noticed before. It was as if she had discovered of what she was capable at need, and of surviving it – not easily, but with body and soul intact.

As they neared Baghdad they saw the ruins of the famous canals, pulled apart by Hulegu's forces sixty-five years before, leaving little but dusty ditches behind.

"Once canals encircled the city, filled with water from the Tigris and Euphrates Rivers," Alma said, very much in the manner of a scholar instructing the ignorant. "They were used for irrigation and some were even large enough for transportation. Some had to be crossed on bridges." She gazed around at the barren and bridgeless landscape, crossed by more dust-filled ditches that seemed to parallel themselves outward from the city growing larger on the horizon. She sounded disappointed. "I don't see why the Mongols had to destroy them. They could have used them themselves, couldn't they?"

"Hulegu was uninterested in occupation, mistress," Firas said, at his driest.

Like Ogodei and Talikan, Johanna thought, gazing at what was left of what surely had been a highly advanced system for the delivery and recovery of water. What makes some men build, and others destroy?

She was unaware that she had said the words out loud until Hayat answered her. "Men will always tear down what they didn't build themselves."

"What a waste," Johanna said.

They moved on.

It was four altogether different travelers from the ones who had escaped the sack of Talikan who trotted beneath the east gate of Baghdad one bright and dusty afternoon. They commanded the best rooms in the best inn nearest the gate and the best stabling for their horses. North Wind attracted much attention, as did the others, the sheik's racing bloodline having held up well over the leagues. North Wind had acquired a few scars on his legs but he seemed somehow bigger even than he was before: larger in stature, grander in manner, much more imperious in attitude. As long as they were in Baghdad, Johanna spent the hour after each morning's practice just brushing his coat, which

North Wind took very much as his just due. His ego had not noticeably diminished during the long journey, either.

There were baths nearby and that was their third order of business, after rooms and new clothes for all four of them. Alma and Hayat had to be very nearly forcibly removed from the bathhouse, hot water having been in short supply on the Road. They reassembled at dinner, scrubbed and shining, around a table they had neither to set nor to clear, loaded with dishes not cooked by their own hand over an open fire, nor killed and cleaned by them, either, for that matter. It was a nice change.

As their attendant brought a tray of sweets and a samovar of hot tea, Johanna sat back and took stock. Firas looked the same as ever: stoic, calm, fit, dangerous. He had taken advantage of the bath barber and his beard was newly trimmed and dark against the white wool of his jellaba.

Alma and Hayat, by comparison, were vastly changed from the women they had been. Gone was the pale, soft skin and plump forms so desired in the harem, replaced now by golden tanned skin and a fine ripple of muscle and sinew. The elaborate hairstyles had been replaced by single braids in imitation of Johanna's, the colorful, diaphanous costumes by hardworking linens and wools in creams and browns. Instead of falling instantly into studied poses of languor and invitation, both women sat comfortably erect, alert to what was going on around them. Their first response to a man in their midst would once have been instantly to seduce him. That reaction now was more a cool, measuring glance, mentally locating weak spots and formulating a plan of attack.

The word "seductress" did not instantly come to mind. Neither did "victim." Johanna wondered what they saw when they looked at her.

"How long do we wish to stay here in Baghdad, young miss?" Firas said, sipping his tea.

Johanna sipped her own tea and took her time answering. "It's been a long, hard summer," she said at last. "Let's take a few days to soak the dust of the trail completely out of our hair, and to gather the news and tour the souk." She smiled. "Who knows? We might find something there to interest the merchants of Gaza."

Firas stroked his beard. "I see no fault in this plan. The soldier is always better for rest and relaxation between campaigns."

"I have inquired after Wu Li's factor in Baghdad but I am told Basil the Frank no longer resides here," Johanna said. "Could you ask around—discreetly, of course—for the more honest jewel merchants in the city?"

Firas inclined his head. "It shall be so, young miss. I myself would like a look at the local armories, and, as you say, to hear the news." He stopped himself from saying more, but Johanna knew what was in his mind. Ogodei could well be turning his attention westward, and if that were so – and even if it were not – rumors of his approach would be rife in the marketplace. The oasis towns of Persia had for hundreds of years been an attractive target for avaricious warlords bent on plunder and acquisition, and the last time Mongols had arrived on Baghdad's doorstep it had not ended well for the city.

"I would like to see Baghdad," Alma said with a sparkle in her eye.

"It is not what it was since Hulegu sacked the city," Firas said.

"Even to stand in the ashes of the House of Wisdom would be a privilege," Alma said reverently. Behind Alma's back, Hayat rolled her eyes.

"Hayat?" Johanna said.

"I no longer smell and my clothes are no longer in tatters," the younger woman said with her dimpled smile. "I don't know that I have any right to ask for more."

And we are alive, her eyes said when she looked at Johanna. Yes, there was that, too.

While Alma toured the monuments of pre-Mongol yesteryear and communed with the spirits of philosophers past, Hayat in amused if a trifle bored attendance, Johanna plunged into the souk, which was something of a revelation. Until then Kashgar had set her standard for markets, but Baghdad's market was larger by half and much better organized and maintained. The streets were wide and clean, the booths were of a uniform size and shape, and the signage was large, easy to spot, and marked in pictures instead of words. Sometimes the signs bore actual items: a mortar and pestle for the apothecaries, a stool for the joiners, a scrap of damask for the weavers. The moneychangers were at the center, forming the heart of the market and the hub of the streets, although Johanna raised her eyebrows at the interest rates chalked on boards outside the various booths. There wasn't much to choose between them, which led her to suspect that rates were settled on well before the market opened in the morning.

But in the market itself, oh, there were all the goods here she had ever seen before and more; many more that she had not, or certainly not in these amounts. Where she had been used to seeing goods only of the East, here they were interlarded with goods of the West. A tall, heavyset man with graying blond hair and a taciturn expression held down a corner of the weavers' market with heaping piles of a heavy wool fabric with a thick nap that would surely protect the wearer from the hardest winter. In the spice market she found a root with no aroma, until it was peeled and grated, when it made her eyes water and induced a fit of sneezing, but was delicious with beef, or so the merchant selling it claimed. In the next stall she was introduced to a green herb that, when the leaves were bruised, smelled sweet and spicy at once, and when served in a sauce over a bit of lamb made a small explosion in her mouth that rivaled the taste of the curries of India. Every mineral from alum, for the fixing of dyes to zinc, which mixed with copper made brass was displayed for sale. Sandalwood, whose fragrance was so sought after by the ladies of Cambaluc and whose oil was so useful in the treating of wounds. Spices of all kinds from everywhere displayed whole in sacks and in their milled forms on round trays heaped into pyramids of yellow and red and orange and brown, dizzying passersby with their commingled aromas. Drugs and their every component part, wax, camphor, gum arabic, myrrh, and a selection of herbs that would have driven Shasha mad with avarice. Fruits fresh and dried, including grapes both red and white. Precious metals, especially gold and silver, in dust, coins, ingots and bars.

Her merchant's nose twitched.

There were chests made of a medium dark wood whose careful finish displayed a beautiful grain that she was informed resisted the teeth of insects of any kind or amount, a safe repository for her most precious clothes and draperies. She found no paper merchant worthy of the name, however, just a series of stalls selling the same vellum and parchment she had seen in every market after the Pass. One merchant glumly displayed an attempt at something made from wood pulp, and Johanna, amusement held at bay behind an expression of polite interest, wondered what the message would look like that would of necessity have to be written around the bits of wood embedded in it. There were some decent pens, but the ink was nothing like what she was accustomed to: thick, runny and indelible on skin, as she discovered when a drop fell on her hand. It would be days of repeated washings before it would disappear.

The silk she found overpriced, even if she had thought their selection was various and adequate, which she did not. Most of it, she was told, came not from Cambaluc but from Merv.

There were also gemstones from semi-precious to the rarer diamonds, although she saw no rubies as fine as the ones stitched into the hems of her traveling clothes. She found small round beads made of a forest green stone striated from dark to light, suitable for jewelry or embellishing clothing. The color reminded her of certain jades, although it was opaque rather than transparent. They were sold by the pound, sewn carefully into unbleached muslin bags.

Those beads were available in the stock of only one dealer in the entire Baghdad market, and he knew it. She made him an offer and he reacted in horror. He was a Muslim and told her candidly that he was surprised to see a woman trading like any man, but displayed no dismay at her presence and no reluctance to strike a bargain with her. He ordered tea and they settled down to it. An hour later they had agreed on a price for a tenweight, but discovered a further problem. The merchant would take only bezants, and Johanna had only taels and drachmas. She secured the merchant's word against a small coin acquired along the Road whose provenance they neither of them recognized but which was indubitably gold, and ranged forth in search of suitable currency.

Down the way there was a baker peeling fresh rounds of bread from his oven. She stepped up and paid for one in drachmas and received florins in change. She paid extra for a brush of oil infused with garlic and crushed herbs and devoured it on the spot, and waited for the next batch to come out of the oven to buy a second, less because she was still hungry and more because doing so was in some odd way homage to Ahmed, the market baker in Kashgar, and Malala his wife, and Fatima, their daughter and Johanna's lifelong friend. And Azar, Fatima's betrothed, who was so carelessly murdered by Gokudo in his attempt to kidnap Johanna on the Terak.

She felt anger well up inside her again, and willed it away. Gokudo was dead now, at her connivance and by her own hand. He had paid in full for the deaths of Azar and Wu Li.

Father, she thought with a pang.

She willed away the tears and plunged back into the crowded byways of the Baghdad marketplace in search of bezants. Bezants, as it happened, were hard to come by in Baghdad, for whatever reason, and her choice was either to go to the money lenders, despite their high fees, or lose her gold coin to the gem merchant. Instead, after some thought, she bought a length of brightly patterned silk that almost looked as if it could have been woven in Chang'an. Elsewhere she found a spool of gilt cord, and returned to the gem merchant in triumph.

The gem merchant, whose name was Mesut, regarded her purchases with a quizzical expression. "These look not like bezants, young miss," he said, stroking his beard. "Although I am old and I admit my sight is not what it once was, so I could be mistaken."

Encouraged by the twinkle in his eye, she said gravely, "You are correct, effendi, these are not bezants, but I believe you will find what you can do with them even more valuable." She indicated his stock, which was laid out on flat tables, the beads threaded into strings and the loose stones in wooden trays. "I see you also sell lovely pearls, as from the waters of Cipangu." She didn't mention that she herself had been to Cipangu, had dived with the pearl fishers there and could plainly see that his pearls were from another ocean entirely.

"I do," said Mesut.

"So, I see, does Karim, two booths down the way, and, if this unworthy one may say so without giving offense, his pearls look to be of much the same quality."

The twinkle became more pronounced. "One may," Mesut said. "Karim and I buy from the same wholesaler."

She nodded. "I see here also some trade beads, from Nubia, I would judge."

He nodded, curious now.

"But on the next street over Hafizah effendi also has Nubian trade beads, which look very much like your own."

"That is so."

She shook her head sadly. "And he is selling them at very much the same price."

Mesut smiled. "I suppose I could run back and forth between our stalls to make sure my beads are priced at less than his, but I confess the prospect does not appeal to me." He smacked his substantial belly with both hands, and in spite of herself Johanna grinned.

"No, indeed," she said. "Why waste your energy jumping about like a squirrel when there is a way to better entice the customer to your stall?"

"And what way would this be, young miss?"

She raised her brows and looked around, as several interested parties were loitering within earshot. Mesut followed her gaze, and said smoothly, "But we should step inside, out of the sun, young miss. I will send my daughter for tea."

"That would be most welcome, effendi."

She followed him inside to take a cushion next to the low table that occupied the back of his shop. After the tea came and they had refreshed themselves, Johanna cleared the table and produced the length of silk and the spool of cord. With her belt knife she sliced the silk into small squares and pooled strings from Mesut's stock of semi-precious stones, pearls and trade beads in the centers of them. These she folded over and tied with one of the elaborate knots she had learned from Halim the dyer in Talikan, what seemed now like a lifetime before. Baghdad's sophisticated marketplace required something grander than Halim's bright scraps of cotton, hence the silk. Halim was not here to hand-dye lengths of jute, hence the gilt cord. Halim the dyer, almost certainly dead, along with all of his family, and friends, and the entire population of his city with him.

With steady hands she pulled the triple bow into equal loops, and presented it to Mesut cradled in both hands.

He examined the bright, sparkling little package and cocked an eyebrow. "But how are my customers to see what is in the package?"

"Two ways, effendi," she said, "that choice being yours, of course. The first is that you, or perhaps your daughter" – this earned her a smile from the girl with the flashing eyes who had watched all this very intently from her father's side – "could learn this style of wrapping and wrap each sale as it is made."

"And the other?"

"Have the merchandise wrapped in individual packages before it is sold, but leave one string out for people to examine."

"Why should anyone assume that each package contains what is on display?"

347

"Why the name of Mesut, surely, effendi," she said demurely.

He laughed outright. "And so they should, young miss." He looked at his daughter. "What do you say, Rashidah? Are you willing to learn to tie string?" His belly shook as he laughed.

Johanna spent the rest of the afternoon teaching an eager Rashidah various ties and bows, and inventing a few on the spot. Rashidah came up with a design of her own that vaguely resembled the openwork crown on a minaret, and had the inspiration to thread one of the stones on the gilt thread so that it not only decorated the package, it alerted the interested as to what was inside.

After the heat of the day had passed, they brought out a few of the packages and placed them on display. If a crowd did not immediately gather, the gaily wrapped packages did disappear in gratifyingly rapid fashion, and before very long Hafizah effendi was seen to be loitering in the background. He wasn't quite gnashing his teeth but he was chewing on his beard, which Mesut said was a sure sign of agitation, and which Mesut seemed to find vastly entertaining.

Mesut was suitably grateful, discounting the price of Johanna's beads and accepting florins instead of bezants. He sent for more tea and cakes this time to cement the deal, and Rashidah joined them. Father and daughter were obviously fond of one another and Mesut treated Rashidah very much as an equal partner in the business. Again, Johanna missed Wu Li with a ferocity that almost occluded their next comments, but she surfaced in time to hear Rashidah's teasing remark about Mesut backing as good a horse in the next race. Miraculously, Johanna's vision cleared, and she cleared her throat. "Race?" she said delicately, fixing Mesut with what she hoped was merely a polite and not very interested eye.

Rashidah rolled her eyes. "Oh please, young miss, don't encourage him," she said, but she was smiling. "Sometimes I think he should have been a horse trader." She laughed. "There was news recently of some big white bruiser of a stallion new

348

come to the city, and there was nothing for it but for Father to ferret out its provenance."

Johanna looked at Mesut, who returned a glance limpid with innocence.

Rashidah looked from one to the other. "Father, didn't you say that the white stallion was ridden by a woman?"

Mesut sipped tea.

Johanna put her head back and laughed out loud.

And so it was, ten days hence, that Johanna found herself on North Wind's back as he ambled in his best unconcerned fashion onto the large oval racetrack outside the city walls. It was by far the most splendid track this side of Cambaluc Johanna had yet seen, laid with meticulously swept sand and lined with sturdy railings to keep the large and eager crowd from falling beneath the leaders' hooves and interfering with the proper running of a race. Vendors hawked fruit juice and pastries, and touts on makeshift stands shouted the odds to long lines of bettors.

It was a glorious day, not a cloud in the sky, and the temperature was mild. There had been four races before North Wind's, which was the last and evidently the biggest race of the day, and judging by the crowd's reaction possibly the year. The shouting reached near hysteria and the wall of sound caused even North Wind's ears to flick, one time.

Johanna took note of their competition. A fiery gelding on the inside nearly equaled North Wind in size, and judging from the crowd's cheers was the clear favorite. There were three other geldings, two more stallions and a roan mare, very small and dainty, her tail held at a coquettish angle, who was bridling and stamping and tossing her head. North Wind was placed squarely in the middle and right next to the mare. Johanna wondered how close the mare was to coming into heat. She could tell by the alert look of North Wind's ears that he was wondering the same thing.

349

There was no point in protesting to the race officials. Johanna was new to the racetrack and a woman beside. Mesut, their official sponsor, while a professional merchant of long standing and impeccable reputation, had no standing in Baghdad's horse world. The best she could hope for was that the mare's owner had misjudged the mare's condition.

The mare's rider looked at her and grinned. He didn't think so. Johanna returned a look of bland indifference and the grin faded. The riders of the other two stallions wouldn't meet her gaze. So. North Wind was meant to be distracted by the mare and by competing stallions while the favorite ran away with the race.

The gelding's rider was necessarily focused on controlling his plunging, sidling, rolling-eyed mount, who apparently couldn't wait to get out on the course. Johanna nudged North Wind with her knees and he clopped forward until his front hooves were planted precisely behind the starting rope and, as per usual, gave all the appearance of a horse who had fallen completely and soundly asleep.

There was a wooden stand to their right, holding a gaggle of greater and lesser dignitaries. The one who looked like an imam was invoking the smile of Allah upon this race. At least he wasn't calling down His wrath on Johanna's unprotected and female head. Mesut stood to the right of the stand, with Radishah, Firas, Alma and Hayat. Radishah was incandescent, Mesut only slightly less so. Firas looked resigned, as if he'd done everything he could to stop Johanna drawing attention their way in this public and imprudent fashion, and was determined to take his failure with outward composure. Alma was looking around her with an inquiring air, as if she had never seen such a thing as a horse race before in her life, which she very probably hadn't. Hayat had one hand on her dagger and her eye on a shifty-looking fellow who had insinuated himself next to them in the crowd. He saw Hayat looking at him, paled beneath his scruffy beard, and melted discreetly away. Hayat saw Johanna watching and dimpled delightfully.

The imam concluded his prayer. Everyone salaamed, and the imam gave way to the luminary Johanna presumed was the sheik of Baghdad, or whoever the sheik had delegated this chore to. He was a handsome elderly man in a resplendent turban accented by a magnificent sapphire the size of which convinced Johanna that he might actually be the sheik himself after all. He, a consummate politician, welcomed the crowd, praised the horses and their riders, made a joke at which everyone laughed heartily, gave a benign smile and raised a white silk handkerchief. Johanna took another wind of North Wind's reins around her hands and leaned forward, and at the motion felt him go absolutely still beneath her. She almost laughed.

The crowd went silent. There was no sound but the snapping of the decorative pennants in the wind. The white silk handkerchief dropped, and almost at the same moment the rope in front of the line of horses dropped to the track. Johanna kicked North Wind lightly in the ribs, and he exploded from a standing start that if she hadn't been prepared for could have snapped her neck. Within five strides her eyes had teared up and within ten her hair had torn free of its braid. Within fifteen North Wind's speed threatened to strip her from his back. She heard swearing, but only from a steadily increasing distance, until it was swallowed entirely by the thunder of North Wind's hooves. She never heard the roar of the crowd, all her attention on the strip of track she could see between North Wind's ears. The smoothness of his stride was such that he didn't even seem to touch the ground: it seemed to pass beneath them while they merely hovered above it.

The next thing she knew they were coming up on the first turn. North Wind moved steadily toward the inside. From the corner of her eye she saw the favorite, or rather the nostril closest to her, which she assumed belonged to the favorite. She was vaguely aware of his rider's arm rising and falling, and she realized that he had to be beating his mount. She felt a moment's brief pity. As if any horse could best North Wind, beaten or not.

North Wind slid in front of the gelding as if he were not even there, and by the second turn his tail was whipping just in front of the other horse's nose. Johanna risked a look over her shoulder and saw that he was North Wind's only real competition. The other three geldings had only reached the first turn. The mare had stopped dead in her tracks just before it, hind legs planted and splayed in traditional equine come-hither fashion. The two other stallions were fighting what looked like a duel to the death nearby, dangerously close to one of their riders, who appeared to have fallen from his saddle and hurt himself sufficiently that he couldn't move out of the way. Johanna tsked reprovingly and faced forward again.

After that it was a glorious, stretched-out, full-throated, league-eating ride, and North Wind didn't slow down when he crossed the finish line, either, but kept going. Johanna, who divined his intention, kicked her feet free of the stirrups in plenty of time and slipped from his back just before North Wind shouldered into the other two stallions, sending them staggering in opposite directions, and mounted the mare without further ado.

The mare braced herself against the onslaught and let out a loud, piercing whinny that sounded a little exasperated to Johanna, as if the mare was saying, "Well, and about time, too!"

Johanna was laughing before her feet hit the ground, and then she realized that everyone in the crowd was laughing, too, and the rest was madness.

Mesut laid on a celebration out of his shop in the souk that evening. There were the finest delicacies to eat and the finest juices and teas and coffees to drink. Everyone in Baghdad came, and Mesut welcomed them all beneath a new turban that grew increasingly askew. Rashidah was kept busy wrapping packages as her father's stock marched out the door as if on legs. Johanna arrived late to the party, waiting patiently until North Wind completed his assignation before leading him off to the stables to feed him and groom him and otherwise settle him down from his various exertions. Johanna did not stint on praise, although he already bore a distinctly satisfied air.

Mesut greeted her with a great welcoming shout that was repeated throughout the crowd. There were immediately a dozen offers to buy North Wind, and later another offer to pay a stud fee, made by a sheepish man Mesut identified as the owner of the mare in that afternoon's race. This offer she accepted.

Tumblers and dancers and singers, attracted by the noise and the prospect of donations to the cause, drifted in and launched into performances. Halfway through the evening a familiar song caught Johanna's ear and on impulse she stepped up and joined in, her mellow soprano filling out the chorus. The bowl that went round after that was overflowing, and Johanna won the head musician's heart when she refused a share. She took the loan of his gitar in payment instead, and sat herself on a stool beside the fire and sang a song about young love, a second about lost love, and a third about a man, his wife and a traveling tinker. She sang Félicien's song about wandering clerks and everyone joined in on the chorus.

She ended with the song about the plum tree, translating the Mandarin to Persian on the fly, and such was the poignant longing in her voice that the crowd was silenced, many of them listening with their eyes closed and more than one hiding sudden, inexplicable tears.

> White petals, soft scent
> Friend of winter, summoner of spring
> You leave us too soon.

She drew out the last note and let it fall, deep, down, into the well of memories that bubbled ever beneath the surface of her bright, impenetrable facade. In that instant she was ten again and back in the caravansary in Kashgar, singing along with Wu

Li and Shu Ming and Deshi the Scout, all of them dead now, and Shasha, who lived, she hoped.

And Jaufre, also ten, newly orphaned, hearing the song for the first time, and her watching the expression on his face the moment when he realized that the song was not about a plum tree, not at all.

Alma and Hayat watched in wonder from the sidelines. When Johanna, flushed and smiling, took her bows to a long, sustained applause, Hayat said, "She never sang like that in the harem."

"She never sang at all," Alma said.

"Because she couldn't?" Hayat said doubtfully.

"Because she wouldn't," Firas said, with a certainty that neither woman could gainsay.

The party broke up soon afterward, and no one noticed that the four of them were followed back to their inn by a man of determinedly nondescript appearance, who took up station in the doorway opposite for what remained of the night.

11

On the road to Damascus, late summer, 1323

TEN DAYS OUT of Kerman their caravan was hit by raiders, a group of some thirty or forty men, a number equal to or outnumbering their own troops of guards. They struck in the hour before dawn, just after Rambahadur Raj had sent out scouts to find them lodging or a campsite for the next day. Almost everyone was dozing in their saddles, not excluding Jaufre, but he woke in a hurry at the sounds of screams and the clash of arms.

He found himself standing on the ground beside his camel, sword in hand, and then running toward the cries of battle. There was no more than a thin band of light on the eastern horizon but his eyes were adjusted to the dark and he saw Alaric's distinctive white tabard almost immediately, surrounded by three men he could smell well before he came into blade's reach. Coming at a run from behind, he sliced into the back of one man's knee and used the force of the upswing from that stroke to thrust into the second man's shoulder. Alaric dispatched the third, who collapsed, screaming, as he tried frantically to stuff a rope of shining entrails back into his belly.

Jaufre saw Alaric's teeth flash in a grin. "Well met, young Jaufre!" which was all they had time for before they were attacked by a new group of assailants.

Their attackers were professionals who lived off the proceeds of passing caravans, but the disciplined guards led by Rambahadur Raj were their superior. The sun was well up by the time they were delivering killing blows to those wounded so badly there was no recovery for them, friend and foe alike. Afterward, Jaufre went a little way off the trail and was sick.

On his return Alaric handed him a flask without comment, for both of which Jaufre was most grateful. He rinsed his mouth and spat, and tried not to notice the severed fingers scattered in a little fan not an arm's length from his right foot.

The bodies of the raiders were thin, almost skeletal, and dressed in rags. Rambahadur Raj was directing his men to pile the bodies of the dead to the side of the trail, a ferocious scowl on his face. He stopped beside Jaufre and Alaric. "This is my fault," he growled. "I wanted to cut our time to Baghdad, so I took a shortcut. It has much less traffic, and this is the result."

Alaric shrugged. "Not the worst outcome, Ram," he said.

"We lost two men," the havildar said.

"They lost all of theirs," Alaric said. He clapped a hand on Jaufre's shoulder. "And our young friend here has been blooded."

Rambahadur Raj looked at Jaufre. "Is that so, then? Did he give a good account of himself?"

"He earned his feed," Alaric said, and both men laughed, heartlessly, it sounded like to Jaufre. He looked at the bodies being piled into an ever higher mound and thought he might be sick again.

Rambahadur Raj turned somber. "They were hungry."

"Starving," Alaric said, nodding. "Lucky for us. They had numbers, but in their weakened state they couldn't give as good an account of themselves as they otherwise might have. These hill tribes can be fierce when they are well fed."

The havildar said heavily, "I could wish they had chosen any other caravan but mine to ease their hunger."

And Jaufre realized he was not the only one of them to be affected by the growing number of dead in the mound by the side of the trail. Later, he watched as Rambahadur Raj oversaw the construction of a pile of foodstuffs not too near the burning pyre of the dead.

Their women would come, Jaufre thought, and along with their dead men they would find food for their children. He was comforted, a little, but not so much that he did not relive the encounter in his dreams.

They pushed on through that day and the following night to arrive at a small oasis town in a well-tilled valley. There was no caravansary but there was a large campsite with a well, and the members of the caravan were made welcome in the town. When the tale of the raiders was told there was much shaking of heads and sidelong looks. One of them, an elder with wise eyes and a wispy white beard, said, "Ahmed ben Eliazar."

"Ah." Many heads nodded around the circle.

The elder nodded his head, too. "He and his people have been preying on travelers through the high pass ever since we banished him, these ten years and more since."

Jaufre wanted to know why the man had been banished, but he intercepted a fierce look from Rambahadur Raj and subsided. That they didn't volunteer the information said enough. It would only have shamed them to have recounted a story that did not reflect well on one who had once been their own.

The elder looked around at the faces of his family and friends and neighbors. "We should send someone up into the hills for his women and children."

A man was dispatched forthwith.

The elder turned again to the havildar and this time bowed, deeply. "You have solved a problem we were not able to resolve for ourselves, Rambahadur Raj, and we are in your debt. Rest here a while. There will be no fees charged, and our water is your water for man and beast alike." He smiled. "And trade freely, if your merchants have a mind to trade. No taxes will be levied upon your people during your stay."

Already well disposed toward their havildar for his speedy

and able defense of themselves and their goods, Rambahadur Raj now soared in the caravan merchants' estimation and Jaufre foresaw a large bonus for him when they reached Damascus. Booths of scavenged poplar limbs and lengths of cloth were set up to form a tiny circular marketplace before the last camel was picketed. Women streamed out of the town and crowded around each vendor, talking and laughing and haggling. Children in high spirits tore around in games of tag and hide-and-seek, so happy and healthy and noisy that after a while Alaric muttered something about strangling them all in their sleep and took himself off. A juice cart appeared, a second cart with rounds of bread on it, a third with stuffed sheep's lungs and other delicacies. Félicien unrolled his rug and produced his lute. After a while a boy appeared with a tambour, and another boy with a flute.

It was a long way from the bloody morning the day before yesterday. Jaufre looked on the peaceful scene full of laughing people and to his horror felt tears sting the backs of his eyes.

"Here," he heard Shasha's voice say. "This way."

She led him stumbling to their tent, pushed him inside and shut the flap after him.

He fell on his bedroll and tears were arrested by a heavy sleep that rolled over him like a thick black blanket. If he dreamt he heard the sound of his blade slicing into human flesh, or heard the panicked, pained, disbelieving scream of the first man whose flesh he had sliced into, he did not remember it afterward. Not that first night, at least.

He woke again near dark, and saw that Shasha had left him a change of clean clothes. He took them to the baths in the town, small but adequate and fueled by a natural hot spring that had been brought down from the hills by an ingenious stone trough supported on a series of connected stone arches. He steamed away the rest of his aches and pains, suffered his cheeks to be scraped free of beard, and returned to camp feeling, if not exactly at peace, then once more calm and in control of his emotions.

Shasha met him at their yurt. "Come," she said, "there is

food, and drink, and dancing, and song this night." She smiled. "It has been so ordained by the imam, who has taken a great liking to Hari."

"God help us all," Jaufre said piously, and Shasha laughed. She set off and, after tossing his dirty clothing inside the yurt, he followed her.

A large fire had been built in the center of where that day's makeshift market had been, and members of the caravan and citizens of the town intermingled freely. To one side a dignified gentleman in immaculate white robes sat on a rich carpet, in earnest conversation with Hari, who with his thin yellow robe slipping from one shoulder looked distinctly underdressed by comparison. Félicien and his lute were accompanying a tenor with a gitar, the harmony forming a pleasing whole.

"How old do you think he is, anyway?" Jaufre said when Shasha came up with a tray full of lamb and onion kebabs.

Shasha followed his gaze. "Félicien, do you mean?" She arranged the tray and sat down next to him. "Why do you ask?"

"He is yet a beardless boy," he said. "Look at him. He must have left home at the age of ten."

"Some do," Shasha said. She looked at him and smiled. "You and Johanna were late bloomers."

He laughed and chose a kebab. The lamb was crusted on the outside, tender and juicy on the inside. He had never tasted better.

Later in the evening Alaric wandered into the circle of people who had formed around the fire. He had acquired a jug of wine from some illicit source and was very merry in consequence, while the elders of the town looked on with tolerant indulgence. It was not their way, but their way was not everyone's way. It was a very nice sort of town.

"Ho, Jaufre of Cambaluc," Alaric said, squinting. He offered out the jug.

Jaufre waved it away. "I've had wine. I don't like it," he said.

Alaric shrugged. "More for me." He drank, and wandered off again.

They all coped with the aftermath of battle in their different ways.

The conversation continued around them, the city fathers extracting the last bit of news from far and near that Rambahadur Raj had to offer. It wasn't long before one of them said, "Is it true, what we hear? Are the Mongols on the move again?"

The havildar looked grave. "I am very much afraid that it is," he said.

"Where?"

"In Kabul they said he was in Samarkand. In Kerman, they said he was in Kabul." Rambahadur Raj shrugged. "If rumor were truth, the Mongols would be advancing on a dozen Persian cities, all at the same time."

"In this case, perhaps rumor is truth," one of the men said bluntly.

"Even the Mongols don't number that many," another man said.

The first man turned his head and spat. "They settled away to the east, we know that. And we let them, and left them to breed. In a hundred years, who knows how great their forces have become?"

The eldest stirred. "It is said on the desert wind that this Mongol acts on his own for himself."

"Rumor, again."

"Perhaps. If true, however, invasion this time might not involve a horde."

There were muted chuckles at this dry comment. The first man flushed angrily and opened his mouth to speak further. He was elbowed into silence by the man sitting next to him, who said, respectfully, "Eldest, if they are coming, should we not prepare?"

The elder looked at Jaufre. "I am told, young sir, that you are of Cambaluc."

"Sir, I am," Jaufre said, bowing his head in acknowledgement, his heart sinking. He had no wish to be singled out, either as a repository of Mongol wisdom or as a target.

"Is all they say of the Mongol true?"

"Sir," Jaufre said again. He frowned a little, hesitating over an answer that would be both true and satisfactory to his listeners.

It was very quiet now around the fire, Félicien and his accompanists having scented an interesting conversation and downing tools so everyone could hear it.

"It is true," Jaufre said at last, and a sigh ran round the circle. Some looked frightened, others pugnacious. He met the eldest's eyes. "Almost all of what they say is true. If you fight, they will annihilate you to the last man, woman and child. Believe it." He paused. "If you yield—" there was an angry muttering and he raised his voice "—if you yield, yes, you will have to live under Mongol rule. But you will live."

He sighed. "If it comes to that," he said. "Your Bastak is small, and off the main routes. From what I saw in the market, you mine a little copper and a bit of turquoise, is this not so?" Nods. "You grow enough food in your fields to sustain yourselves, but not so much that you have entire grain houses filled to bursting and therefore irresistible targets. And your carpets, while very fine indeed, again are not so fine as to make Bastak the destination for an entire army bent on plunder." He paused again. "In short, eldest, if there is no reason for the Mongol to come here, he will not. He will go around you to find other, richer targets. If, against all logic, he does come…"

"If he does come, surrender, or die?"

Jaufre bent his head again. "I am afraid those are the only options, eldest. You cannot fight, because you cannot win."

There was more conversation after that, of course, the elders now mining Jaufre for every bit of information about Mongols and Mongol soldiers and Mongol strategy and tactics that he had. He did his best to comply, but he was weary before the fire burned low. He left them still in conversation there by the coals.

Most of the camp was asleep by then, and the town, too, but he felt restless. The southeast corner of the city's walls looked like it would have the best view of the valley. At the top of the stairs he found Alaric before him, legs dangling over the edge, jug in hand. "Ho, young Jaufre," he said.

"Alaric," Jaufre said. He saluted the sentry stationed at the corner, who nodded back, and sat down next to the ex-Templar.

The founders of Bastak had chosen their site well: a rise of ground with the western wall of the valley behind them, with a prospect that commanded a view of the valley from north to south. Moonlight limned the narrow peaks on either side and cast a pearly gaze on the irrigated farms that lined the Bastak River, a silver ribbon that wound between them.

"There is a structure made of arches," Jaufre said. "I saw it in the city."

"An aqueduct," Alaric said. "There is a pipe on the top which brings the hot water from the springs into the city."

"It looks very old."

"It should," Alaric said. "It was probably built by the Romans."

"They settled this far east?"

"And farther."

There was a promontory a short distant away: a triangular-shaped wedge of rock formed between the river where it came down out of the western ridge and a smaller tributary that rose to the height of the walls of Cambaluc. Bordered on all three sides by sheer cliffs, there were what looked like ruins on the top of it.

Alaric followed his eyes. "Ah, yes, young Jaufre," he said. "That is the Bastak that was. Their spring ran dry a hundred years ago. Or maybe it was a thousand." He belched. "And so they moved here." He hooked a thumb over his shoulder. "Young Adab here was telling me the tale."

Jaufre looked over his shoulder at the sentry, and saw a flash of white teeth in a dark beard. "They chose wisely, both times."

"It will do them no good when the Mongol comes," Alaric said.

"It is possible that Ogodei will not bother to come this far," Jaufre said.

"Or the Seljuks from the other side," Alaric said, and belched again. "But peace such as this is only an illusion, young Jaufre. You would do well to remember that. There is no safety, no security from ambitious men who lead their own armies."

Jaufre waited while the other man tipped up his jug. It was empty. Alaric tossed it aside and looked out over the valley with a glum expression. The jug rolled over the edge of the wall and a moment later was heard to shatter on the rocks below.

Jaufre let the silence grow for a few moments. Even the hardest and most cynical heart had to soften at prolonged exposure to this kind of pastoral beauty. Also, he was waiting for the alcohol to take full affect.

After a while he said, almost indifferently, "You recognized my sword when we first met in Kabul, didn't you?"

He felt the other man stiffen next to him.

"And since we have never met before, and since the sword came to me directly from my father, it follows that you might have known him."

Silence.

"Or heard of him," Jaufre said. "Robert was his name. Robert de Beauville."

An owl hooted, and was answered by the howl of a far-off wolf. The moon continued its serene passage above, flooding the landscape with light enough to read by.

Perhaps Alaric was inspired by that light, which illuminated so much of the dark places in the valley. Or perhaps he had decided that since Jaufre had been blooded and was, perforce, now a man that he was to be admitted to the confidence of other men. "Robert de Beauville," he said, and Jaufre felt the tension that had been coiled around his spine since Kabul relax, just a little.

"Tell me about him," he said. "Please."

"How much do you know?"

"That he was born in an island kingdom far to the west," Jaufre said. "That he was a Knight Templar, sworn to celibacy, but he married my mother. That he was a fine swordsman."

"How did he die?" Alaric's voice cracked on the last word.

Jaufre swallowed, half-forgotten memories of a caravan on a stretch of desert, raiders rising up as if materializing from the very sand. "He was working as a caravan guard, as you are," he said. "We were attacked. There were too many." He paused. "I was the only one who escaped."

"How did you manage to keep Robert's sword?" Alaric said. "That would be prime booty for bandits."

"I was beside him when he fell. He knew he was—He gave me the sword. Told me to bury myself and it in the sand. So I did. I waited until they were gone, and then I buried him." The horror of those moments, of listening to his father die and to his mother and the other women scream as they were dragged off, had never, would never fully leave him.

"Your mother?"

"They took her. All the women and children. We believe she was sold at auction in the Kashgar slave market a week after the attack."

A long silence this time. Alaric had to know how much Jaufre had left unsaid. "How old were you?"

"Ten."

Alaric's eyes closed and he shook his head. "You were lucky."

"Yes," Jaufre said, only now, seven years after the fact, able to admit that it was true. "I was found by a Cambaluc trader three days later. I would have died but for him. He adopted me as his foster son, and raised me as his own."

"You were lucky," Alaric said again. "Many on the Road are not so fortunate."

This time Jaufre waited.

After a while Alaric sighed. "Yes, well, why not. Surely we are far enough away, in space and in time, for the truth to be spoken out loud, here beneath the moon and the stars." He looked up at the sky and began to speak, slowly, even sorrowfully. It felt eerily like a confession.

"Robert de Beauville was born the fourth son of a Norman

noble who settled in western England. His father was not wealthy and with three other sons and two daughters to dispose of, Robert was left to find his own way. He took the Cross at the age of seventeen—"

Jaufre's own age.

"—and traveled to the East as a Knight Templar. We were both on Ruad when it fell." Alaric hesitated. "It would be five years until Philip sent out the order to have us all arrested, but Robert—" He shrugged. "The Knights fell with Ruad, he said. He said it didn't matter if it was our fault or not, that we would be blamed." He spat over the walls. "And he was right, of course, but then Robert was an old head on young shoulders and he usually was."

"You were friends."

Alaric shrugged. "We were comrades, for a while. Enough to exchange personal histories." He looked at Jaufre. "His vocation was more expediency than piety, I think. He was the youngest son, his father had provided for him as well as he could. But he was bitter at our failures." He sighed. "We all were."

"What happened after Ruad fell?"

"Most of the Knights were killed," Alaric said in a voice devoid of emotion, as if he were reading from an ancient text of events hundreds of years before. "I was wounded. Robert stripped us both out of our armor and pulled me through the water to a coracle he saw floating a little way out. There was no paddle, so he used his hands to get us to the mainland." He looked down at his own hands, turning them back to front and back again. "I was in a high fever and delirious by then. I don't remember much beyond what he told me afterward. Somehow, he got us off the beach, where we were most in danger of discovery, and found a hayloft to hide in. He cared for me until I was well enough to care for myself."

"And then you parted company?"

Alaric raised his head. "Not at once," he said. "We made our way to Antioch and hired ourselves out as guards on a caravan to Damascus. We had to eat, and all we had to sell was our skill with a sword. In Damascus, Robert met Agalia." He fell silent.

"My mother."

"Yes." Alaric brooded for a moment, and then seemed to realize that more was needed, and to give it freely was a better option than to have it demanded of him. "She was the daughter of a merchant traveling with the Damascus caravan. Robert—as I said before, Robert's vocation was less than devout. He had always struggled with the vow of celibacy." He added, reluctantly, "And she was very beautiful."

"And so they were married."

"Yes."

"And then you parted ways."

"Yes. I didn't believe Robert when he said the blame for the loss of Jerusalem would fall on our shoulders." Alaric's shoulders straightened and his chin lifted. "We Knights Templar were heroes, soldiers of God, anointed by the Pope himself. It was inconceivable to me that we could fall so far so fast. I wanted to go home, to see my family, to take up the Cross again in some other way, for some other purpose."

"And you went home?"

"Yes."

"What happened?"

"Oh, they greeted me with loud rejoicing and went straight off to kill the fatted calf." Alaric stared across the valley. "And the next day came the men of Philip the Fair, who may have been fair to look at but was not at all fair in his dealings with the Templars."

"Your family betrayed you?"

"My father, probably. His nose was ever up some royal ass." Alaric shrugged. "And he had not wanted me to take the Cross in the first place."

"You were imprisoned?"

"I was, in my lord of Agenois' deepest dungeon." Alaric grinned, his face bleached of color in the light of the moon. "For one night. I had a sister, a sister who rivaled Agalia for beauty, no less, and she… convinced the guard to allow her in to see me. He didn't even search her. She brought me two blades strapped beneath her skirts, and I fought my way out and ran for it."

Jaufre wondered what had happened to the sister, but thought on the whole it was better not to ask. "And returned to the East?"

"Yes." Alaric made a show of dusting off his knees. "And took up my present occupation." He hesitated, and looked at Jaufre. "I did ask after your father, and heard word now and then. I sent it back, as I could. But I never saw him, or Agalia again. I had no idea they had had a son." He paused. "But the moment I saw you, I knew. You are his image."

A prickle on the back of Jaufre's neck told him that there was more to tell of this tale, or at least of Alaric's part of the story, but he sensed that now was not the time to press for it. "Robert of Beauville," he said instead. "Is Beauville a place, then?"

"No," Alaric said. "Your father's father is or was a landless knight. He married disadvantageously—"

Jaufre translated that as his grandmother having no dowry.

"—and he pledged his sword first to Henry and then to Edward, mostly in France, as I understood Robert to say. France, you will come to understand, has been passed back and forth between the kings of England and the kings of France for a hundred years, and it's like to be a hundred more before they finally settle who has title to it."

"Edward I?"

"Yes." Alaric gave Jaufre a curious look. "Why?"

"He was—he came to the East, didn't he? In, what was it, 1270?"

"He was only a prince then, but yes," Alaric said. "Why?"

Jaufre shrugged. "No matter," he said, but he was remembering the history of Marco Polo as it had filtered down to him and Johanna all through their childhood. Marco Polo claimed to have met a Prince Edward of England in Acre on his way to Cambaluc. It was dizzying to think that it might possibly have been true. And if that was true, how much more might be? He thought of the book in his saddlebag. Not the dog-face men.

Alaric yawned, jaw cracking. "Me for my bedroll, young Jaufre." He pulled himself to his feet, moving lightly and surely while balanced on the edge of a wall quite a thousand hands in height, which argued just how drunk he was. Had he wanted Jaufre to ask him about Robert? If so, why?

Jaufre sat looking out over the silver fields and the winding river for a while longer, and then followed Alaric's example.

Neither man noticed the figure that detached itself from a dark corner and followed Jaufre back to his yurt.

They were attacked twice more before Damascus, and both times Jaufre blooded his sword. He wasn't sick again either time. He was glad he acquitted himself well, and knew a growing confidence in his ability to do so in future, but he had also learned that a life by the sword was not the life he would choose. Trading, buying and selling, the exchange of goods to the profit of both sides of the bargain, that was work for a man. And he didn't feel like a piece of him had died when he sold a copper pan to a cook or a Homeric scroll to a scholar studying the classics.

He wondered how long the attacks would continue before one of the lords and masters of the East would see fit to put the bands of raiders down once and for all. He wondered how trade could continue if they did not.

Of course if Ogodei, or some other powerful lord bent on conquest appeared on the horizon, the matter of itinerant raiders would be moot.

Damascus was a once-great capital of an independent empire that had dwindled into a regional capital ruled from Egypt by the Mamluks. It didn't look particularly downtrodden and it had a thriving marketplace, with an entire section of the city devoted to the blacksmiths and their forges. Damascus steel was a legend over the known world. A blade forged from Damascus steel was said to be able to cut a single hair dropped across it, and to be able to cut straight through other blades of lesser make.

Jaufre didn't know that he quite believed any of the legends, but as he made the rounds of the forges he had to admit he had seldom seen more beautiful blades. Some looked as though the makers had somehow replicated ripples of water on the surface of the steel. Others bore leaf-like striations that gave the impression they were about to sprout. The grips were made from every material, steel covered in sharkskin like his own but also made from antlers from oryx and ibex and one the dealer said was from a unicorn and told Jaufre with a wink that wielding it was guaranteed to enhance one's sexual prowess. There were handles made from every kind of hardwood that grew from Cambaluc to Eire, which Jaufre had never heard of, and even some from a kind of molded, hardened animal skin. There were blades with and without pommels and pommels with and without inlaid jewels. The hand guards of the swords were always of steel and as beautiful as they were useful. The daggers ranged from decorative to deadly and were always elegant, if you didn't count the cheap knockoffs made from pig iron one found in the less prosperous sections of the souk.

He decided not to bring out the knives he had acquired in Kerman. He had the feeling that the farther away he got from Damascus, the better chance he had of making a profit on them, or any profit at all. He did produce his sword in hopes of having its maker identified, but after much pursing of lips and shaking of heads, and not a few grudging compliments, no one recognized the smith's handiwork.

None of the steel production was on view, of course, as the process was regarded as proprietary and each smith was very protective of his own techniques, but Jaufre did find one artisan in a tea shop who was willing to talk about it a little. Producing Damascus steel involved something called folding, unexplained, and even more necessary was a steady supply of raw material from the East, somewhere in the Indus, unidentified, and, more recently from Persia, unspecified. Jaufre's new friend lamented the steady decline of said supply and prophesied the end of steel-making in Damascus, probably in their lifetimes, to the incipient beggaring of everyone in the trade and associated with it.

But blades of Damascus steel—knife, dagger, and sword—were still plentiful in the city's marketplace, if prohibitively expensive, and Jaufre wondered if the rumor of short supply had more to do with keeping the price up than an actual lack of raw material.

He spent the next day making the rounds of the slave markets and the dealers in human flesh. Most of them had the courtesy not to laugh at him, but none of them remembered Agalia or the Lycian Lotus or anyone who sounded like his mother. Or would admit to it, because how could anyone trust anything a slaver said?

He lay wakeful in their yurt that night, listening to the others breathe. Seven, nearing eight years ago now, his mother might or might not have passed through these same streets. She could be living yet, caged in some harem, vying for the attention of her master. Bearing his children. He might have half-brothers and sisters. It was not a thought that had previously occurred to him.

After another five minutes Jaufre gave it up and slipped from the yurt. There were a few coals left in their fire pit. He coaxed them back to life with a few bits of kindling and stacked on the wood.

Overhead, a sliver of new moon rose steadily from the horizon, almost but not quite eclipsing the millions of glittering stars. It was a sight he had never taken for granted. He and Johanna both had always recognized the beauty of the world in which they lived, and acknowledged the good fortune that had made them children of that most tolerant and encouraging man, Wu Li of Cambaluc, and his most gracious and loving wife, Shu Ming. He missed them both, but he missed Johanna even more. Her absence from his side, laughing, fighting, trading. Surviving.

It was an ache the proportions of which could, if he let it, subsume him completely. It was only at moments like these, when he was completely alone, that he allowed himself to conjure her face from the darkness between the stars, when he wallowed in the memory of every word she had spoken to him, from that first time in the vast aridity of the Taklamakan when she had brought him all upstanding and indignant out of his own self-dug grave by peeing on him.

He smiled at the memory, but the smile didn't last. Was she ahead of them on the Road, perhaps already in Gaza, or Jerusalem? Was she behind them, barely a day's ride ahead of Ogodei and Gokudo?

Was she even alive?

He was well now, fit, and able once again with his father's sword. And Johanna hadn't been missing as long as his mother. Perhaps it was time to backtrack. She might have left word with one of Wu Li's agents. And if North Wind were still with her, surely there would be tales to tell of a woman riding a white steed whose speed was only outpaced by the wind itself.

He had asked, of course. He and Shasha and Félicien and Hari, they had all asked, all along the Road, from Kabul to Kerman to Bastak to Damascus. There was still no word of woman or horse. But then, if they had escaped Talikan with North Wind, it was reasonable to suppose that the sheik would have been hot on their trail. Perhaps Firas was taking care to travel only along secondary routes, ones less traveled by those who would carry news of seeing them. That made sense to Jaufre and would explain the absence of news.

He felt comforted by the thought, at any rate. There was a rustle and he looked up to see Hari emerge from behind the yurt flap. The chughi shook his saffron robes in order, smoothed back his last wisp of hair, and assembled himself next to Jaufre in a complicated knot of knees and ankles. "Young sir," he said in a low voice. "It is a soft night." He looked up. "Such wonders we may see, if only we had the wit to look for them."

"You think people don't?" Jaufre said.

"'Make happy those who are near, and those who are far will come,'" Hari said.

"Buddha?" Jaufre said.

Hari smiled serenely. "That is a saying that comes out of your own adopted country, young Jaufre."

"I don't feel so young anymore, Hari," Jaufre said, and was horrified to feel tears pressing at the backs of his eyes. He restrained them by sheer force of will, and became aware that Hari had let his hand rest lightly on Jaufre's shoulder. As soon as Jaufre became aware of it, it was gone.

"Youth to adult is always a difficult transition," Hari said.

Jaufre gulped and tried to change the subject. "Was yours?"

Hari surprised him by laughing. "Oh, my very dear young sir! Difficult hardly describes it." He looked at Jaufre, still chuckling. "I was the only son. My duty was to marry and have many children and eventually take over the farm from my father, and see him and my mother safely into old age. When I was called, they were accepting, but they were never happy about it."

"Have you ever been back?"

Hari shook his head. "I am meant to go forward."

So far as Jaufre could see, Hari seemed at peace with his calling. Thinking of Johanna and where she might be and how he could find her, he said urgently, "How do you know, Hari? How do you know you are meant to go forward?"

"You desire to attain enlightenment, young Jaufre?"

Jaufre thought about it. "Insofar as I can come to understand myself," he said, "I believe so."

"Ah." Hari rearranged a fold of his robe. "Buddha said that you should steadily walk in your Way, with a resolute heart, with courage, and should be fearless in whatever environment you may happen to be, and destroy every evil influence that you may cross, for thus you shall reach the goal."

An answer, if not the definitive one he wanted, Jaufre thought. *Destroy every evil influence that you may come across.* He thought of Wu Li, who had taken Jaufre, an abandoned waif with no paternal or social claim, into his household without hesitation or reservation. Of Shu Ming, his wife, who had raised him like a son. He knew the face of goodness.

He thought of Gokudo, a mercenary, and of Dai Fang, a murderer. He knew the face of evil, too.

"You should be aware, young sir," Hari said, "that at this same time, the young miss walks her own Way as well."

Jaufre sat back, arrested. Hari watched him with a steady gaze, the flames of the fire flickering over his features, casting them now into shadow, now into light. "She won't be the same person I knew, you mean," he said.

"Nor will you be the same person she knew," Hari said.

Shasha, Hari and Félicien left Damascus for Jerusalem two days later.

Jaufre was with them.

12

October, 1323, the Holy Land

T HE CONVULSING WOMAN screamed again. She had a painfully loud and piercing scream which the rock walls of the cave only enhanced. Everyone in earshot cringed. Some cursed. And there were those who looked as if they would as soon murder the woman out of hand than endure another episode of her fits.

"This," said their guide, in full voice which was still amazingly although barely audible over the screams, "is the Mount of Temptation, where our lord Jesus Christ fasted for forty days, and was tempted by the Devil to throw himself over the cliff."

It wasn't the oddest thing Jaufre had heard during the last two weeks.

They had gone to Gaza first, arriving there six weeks before, taking their leave of Rambahadur Raj. The havildar ignored Jaufre's attempts to express his gratitude, instead congratulating him on Jaufre's rebirth as a full fighting man. "Not quite a Gurkha, no," he said jovially, clapping Jaufre on the back with a blow that would have knocked him to his knees were he still in his weakened state in Kabul. "But I believe you could hold your own with a Gurkha if it came to that, young sir!"

Alaric, too, took his leave of the havildar and seemed to consider himself a member of Jaufre's party thenceforward.

He said airily that he'd had enough of the high desert and, besides, he had a hankering to see Venice again. Jaufre thought with inward amusement that Johanna's habit of picking up strays seemed to have lingered on even when she was not with them.

Because, to his severe disappointment, they did not find Johanna waiting for them in Gaza. However, one of the first stories they heard in the taproom of their inn was of a great race in Baghdad, won by a white horse with a woman rider who flaunted her hair uncovered like a bronze banner.

There were other interested auditors of that news in the taproom that evening, among them two of Rambahadur Raj's muleteers. They had also left the havildar's employ at Gaza, and one or the other of them had kept Jaufre in sight ever since, while taking care to remain unseen themselves.

Jaufre barely managed to contain himself until they were safely behind the door of their room. "It was her! It has to be!"

Shasha, too, looked lit from within, although she said, "I wish there was some mention of who else was with her."

"Firas will be with her, of course he will be," Félicien said, who seemed surprisingly glum at the news.

Jaufre, unheeding, fought to control the sense of relief that nearly swept his legs out from under him. He found himself seated next to Shasha, with a cup of spiced fruit juice being pressed into his hands. Shasha put a finger beneath it and pushed it towards his mouth. He drank, and then drank again, deeply, and felt the better for it. He looked at Shasha and saw that she had tears in her eyes, and for a terrible moment felt a little shaky himself, big strong warrior that he was.

To have no news for so long, and then this. Johanna could so easily have been dead. What would have been even worse, they could so easily have never known what had happened to her.

Like his mother.

"Good news indeed, young Jaufre," Hari said, assembling himself into one of his complicated seated positions on the rug Shasha had spread out over the floor of their room. It had no

375

beds, but she had decreed it to be the least vermin-ridden of the six inns they had investigated.

Jaufre looked at Shasha. "We wait, then. She will come here."

She nodded. "She will." She smiled. "It was always the plan."

He smiled, and then he laughed, and drank off the rest of the juice. All would not be entirely well in his world until Johanna was within arm's reach, but the sun was going down on a day infinitely preferably to the day before, and all the days preceding it since the attack on the trail down from the Terak.

"It's a fine port city," Shasha said, "with good markets. We should turn over what we can of our own stock and lay in new supplies. When she gets here, she will want to get on the first available ship for Venice."

This brought an abrupt silence.

"Venice," Jaufre said. In the trauma of attack and separation and injury and recovery, he had almost forgotten the impetus for their journey, of much more importance for Johanna than for him. He and Shasha's prime motivation was to get themselves and Johanna out of the reach of Dai Fang, Wu Li's murderously ambitious second wife, as soon as humanly possible. Johanna, after growing up in a place that had vilified her all her life for her height, her coloring, her hair, her odd eyes, her very foreignness, had only wanted to find her grandfather, and acceptance.

Jaufre thought of the book he had found in Kerman, and of Alaric's familiarity with it. Of Alaric's disdain for it, and for its author. How many Marco Polos were there, who had traveled to Cambaluc and seen twenty years' service to Kublai Khan? If he was the same man, how kindly would he look upon the unexpected appearance of an unknown grandchild? It was one thing to celebrate great adventures thousands of leagues away, and another thing entirely to have one of those adventures land on one's doorstep.

He thought again of Dai Fang, of her inflexible determination to gather up the reins of Wu Li's trading empire into her own lacquered claws, no matter what it took, up to and including the premeditated, cold-blooded killing of her own husband. He could only hope that Marco Polo, also a merchant and as such someone who would value practicality and pragmatism above all other qualities, was not equally efficient in ridding himself of what could be a large personal embarrassment in the shape of his granddaughter.

None of these issues could be addressed until Johanna arrived, and not just in rumor but in flesh-and-blood reality. In the meantime, they had found lodgings in Gaza and settled down to wait with greater or lesser degrees of patience. Shasha disappeared into the bazaars for three days, and reappeared briefly to inform them that she had found an apothecary willing to mentor her in the mysteries of Middle Sea herbal lore. Félicien found a job entertaining at the largest local taverns.

After two weeks of this, Jaufre, edgy and snappish, and Alaric, thoroughly bored, greeted the arrival of two galleons from Venice full up to the gunnels with seasick pilgrims with positive relief. One of the galleons was captained by a cheerful rogue named Giovanni Gradenigo who wore a golden hoop in one ear and a black velvet jacket lavishly embroidered with gold thread. They met him by chance on the pier as he was overseeing the unloading and the housing and feeding of his miserable human cargo. He accepted their invitation for a drink and a meal at the quayside tavern and the three of them settled in around a corner table for the evening.

"I tell you, my new-found friends, for twenty years have I sailed the vast reaches of the Middle Sea, and yet never until now have I experienced a storm the force and fury of this one," he said, draining his tankard and refilling it immediately. "I thought we would break apart on the seas, which I swear by the Blessed Virgin's intact hymen were higher than the campanile of St. Mark's. My passengers...well. They are no sailors. Not," he added acidly, "that they took any comfort from my idiot crew, who behaved throughout as though we were headed straight for the bottom of the Middle Sea. Then a barrel of drinking water broke loose and rolled over the cook, who was trying to kill us anyway with the moldy biscuit he tried to pass off as ship's bread. I know he got a bribe from the vendor and I intend to prove it the minute we return. By the blood of Christ, this was a voyage bitched before it ever left the wharf in Venice." He drank more ale.

A plate of bread and cheese arrived, along with bowls of lamb stew. Conversation was temporarily in abeyance. Plate and bowls cleaned and tankards renewed, Gradenigo, much cheered—his was not a nature to brood for long—continued with his tale of woe. "We were meant to dock at Jaffa, but the weather proved as intransigent there as it had been in transit, so I brought us here. And now," he said, the omnipresent twinkle in his eye dying briefly, "here I sit in Gaza, a dozen leagues from my mules and my camels and my guards and my supplies. Which supplies I am sure the aforesaid guards began pillaging the day after I was due in port." He sighed, and cocked a weather eye at a passing barmaid with a pleasing waistline. He watched her out of sight and returned his attention to them, which included an appraising look at their weaponry. "But enough about me, my new friends. Yourselves, are you soldiers?"

Jaufre shook his head, but Alaric said, "Once, yes, but not now. We have been most recently employed as caravan guards."

"Say you so?" said Giovanni Gradenigo, sitting upright, and the rest was a foregone conclusion. Shasha, when they unearthed her at the apothecary's workshop, shrouded in a canvas apron with a large hole burned into the front of it, said only, "How long will you be gone?" He wasn't entirely sure she registered his answer.

Félicien made a spirited bid to accompany them, and won over the captain with an off-color version of his clerk's song. Hari gathered up his saffron robe in an authoritative manner and said he would accompany them as far as Jerusalem. Gradenigo threw up his hands and hired five other men in case the guards who were supposed to be waiting in Jaffa had wandered off, two of whom Jaufre vaguely recognized from their caravan.

Alaric greeted one by name. "Hussein! I thought that was you. You left Raj's caravan, too? You're as mad as I am, to leave such a good billet. No one from here to Kabul feeds you so well on the Road."

Félicien's presence turned out to be a blessing, as his lute and his voice became the only things that made the entire trip endurable. The Gaza muleteers were surly and uncooperative and Muslim to a man, which meant they were hostile to the entire enterprise of Christian pilgrimage from the beginning. They only deigned to sign on by a doubling of the going rate, which came directly out of Gradenigo's pocket. He did not suffer in silence. By contract, he was obliged to get the pilgrims to Jerusalem and back again to Venice or suffer the loss of his pilgrim transport license. Long experience of overseeing the said trade had led those authorities to provide for every eventuality, as well as inspectors stationed in Palestine – "Spies," Giovanni Gradenigo said, as if the word tasted of excrement – to ensure and enforce the safe, secure and successful passage of all who had paid a fee for such passage before embarking from Venice. Punishment for abrogating any one of the clauses in his contracts lay in the hands of the Venetian authorities, whose city derived much in the way of revenues from the pilgrim trade. Their judgment was sure and fell, and to be avoided by whatever means necessary.

The captain might make a good living but he had to work for it, Jaufre thought now, especially when – after taking in the sights of Jerusalem under the stern aegis of its Saracen authorities – the captain's group of pilgrims had decided on a side trip to visit Bethlehem, the River Jordan, which had required a tortuous descent down the face of a canyon on a narrow trail twelve leagues long, and the caves of Quarantana, where they were now.

The woman's screams continued unabated. She convulsed again and fell to the ground, her limbs jerking and twitching, where she rolled temptingly close to the edge of the cliff that fell to the rocks a thousand rods below. Since Jaufre had been given to understand that every Christian pilgrim who completed

379

the Jerusalem Journey was at death guaranteed a translation straight to their heaven, he didn't know but what he might be doing Mistress Joan Burgh a great favor if he helped her over the edge with the toe of his boot.

She was a woman in her fifties and not physically fit, and she wasn't supposed to be there at all, but when her companions had refused outright to help her climb that nearly vertical rock face, she had bribed a Saracen to carry her up. Upon achieving the top, she had been so overcome with ecstasy that she had fallen straightaway into the fit they were witnessing now.

Her companions, fellow pilgrims who had suffered Joan's presence all the way from England to this very spot, had explained at length to Jaufre and Alaric and anyone who would listen that they had been looking forward to visiting the caves without an accompanying one-woman chorus of screams, shouts, cries and exhortations. Jaufre, who had only had to endure Mistress Burgh since Jerusalem, felt a good deal of sympathy for them.

He met their guide's stern eyes, one Baldred, a Franciscan friar of middle age and miraculously even temperament, and went forward to pull Mistress Joan back from the edge. He took very little care for her comfort as he did so.

She rewarded him by grasping at his sleeve and shrieking, "I tell you the Blessed Virgin has baked bread for me in her own kitchen with her own hands!"

"Is there any left over?" he said. "I haven't had anything to eat since breakfast."

There were a few snickers and one outright guffaw.

"Sinner! You must repent, repent, before Jesus Christ our Lord!" Joan Burgh's eyes rolled back in her head and her body stiffened into a bow and she shrieked again. Jaufre dropped her unceremoniously to the rock floor of the cave and retired to the crumbling trail head in hopes that putting some distance between them would muffle the subsequent din. It didn't.

After that, Mistress Burgh was left to her visions and exhortations while her companions spent the afternoon exploring the caves where the saints had lived, seeing the remnants of a bed in a deteriorating piece of wood, a bookshelf in a niche carved into the rock wall above it. There was a faint painting here and there, only one or two with enough left to them to indicate some sense of the original whole. Some pilgrims surreptitiously chipped a shard from the altar of the chapel, others carved their names into the walls or wrote on them with chalk. Some got drunk on wine they had brought with them from Jerusalem. Some dickered with the few merchants who were hawking piles of dubious-looking relics they had hauled up the cliff on their backs in hopes of making a few coins from the pilgrims. "The little finger of the Blessed Virgin herself, I assure you, sir!"

Since the Blessed Virgin was alleged to have died thirteen hundred years before, Jaufre somehow doubted it. Besides, in the leagues from Jerusalem, if he had seen one bone from the little finger of the Blessed Virgin, he had seen a hundred.

A few of the pilgrims, the intelligent ones, he thought, had found an out-of-the-way corner in which to curl up in their gray cloaks, although it was hard to see how they could sleep, given the amount and volume of sound. Between Joan Burgh's continuous shrieking and sobbing, the drunken laughter, the surreptitious chink of blade on stone, the ever-louder prayers, and the steady increase in volume of conversation as the aura of holiness wore off the longer they stayed, there was no peace to be found on this barren hilltop. The Franciscan, Baldred, was holding a hurried Mass at the altar for those so inclined, and the rest of them lit tapers (available for sale) and tried not to stumble over scattered rocks and their own feet as they staggered around seeking out everything in the caves that looked even remotely as if it were once the site of someone doing something holy.

He became aware of Alaric's presence next to him, and looked around to see a disdainful expression on the Frank's face. "Peasants," Alaric said.

Jaufre didn't know what irritated him more, the emotional excesses of pilgrims like Joan Burgh or the supercilious superiority of the upper classes, with whom Alaric clearly associated himself. "Has this place no hold on your faith, then?" he said.

"I've been here before," Alaric said with the kind of weariness Jaufre could only describe as professional. "Many times. And I'd have had visions of the Devil, too, if I hadn't had anything to eat for forty days."

"Blasphemy!" shrieked Mistress Burgh. "Sinner! Repent, now, sirrah, before your soul is lost forever to perdition!"

"My good woman," Alaric said, looking down his nose, "look after your own soul, which will be in mortal peril if you continue to assault our Lord's ears in this cacophonous and most annoying fashion." His sword clanked as he stalked over to the altar, and bent his head in ostentatious obedience before Baldred's Mass.

From the cleft below Jaufre heard a feral roar, and he looked over the edge to see the distant undergrowth rustle. They had seen three lions in the leagues between here and the city, and a dozen wild boars who were the cause of their presence. He was hoping to descend in time to hunt for dinner, as the days in the blazing sun had spoiled all their food and all that remained to eat in his saddlebags was a boiled egg and a very worn pear, both of which were probably going rapidly bad. His mouth watered at the thought of some juicy roast pig, although he wasn't sure he would be allowed to eat one even if he caught one, since the Saracens were so set against the practice.

From the Holy Sepulcher in Jerusalem to the River Jordan, every second rock and tree was the site of an event in the history of the Christian faith. Here Jesus was arrested. There he wavered in his faith. That place was where he was crucified (whereupon much bewailing and cursing of the Jews, although after he learned the full story Jaufre thought the Romans didn't come in for near enough of their share of obloquy), and in there was where he rose from the dead. Here his mother lived with her sister Martha, both of whom lived not far from another Mary, this one a prostitute whose home had been replaced by a chapel, which in turn was now a goat byre. Next to this riverbank in those waters was Jesus baptized by John. This saint scourged himself here, another saint's eyes were pierced by arrows there, and that one was thrown to the wolves, professing his faith until his tongue was torn out.

It all sounded overwrought and highly exaggerated to Jaufre, who wished the heir to one of those wolves would appear now and make for Joan Burgh. "Your faith is very violent," he said to Félicien.

"I warned you," Félicien said. He looked glum, but then the pilgrims had forbidden him from playing his lute during the entire journey. It was sacrilegious, they told him, disrespectful of our Lord's suffering and resurrection.

A particularly loud and sustained screech made them both jump.

By now the pilgrims were exhausted from days of tramping through the dusty desert, weakened by a subsistence diet of eggs and fruit, when the hostile Saracen villagers would sell anything to them. There was little enough water to drink and none at all with which to wash and they could be smelled long before they were seen. When the last one of them had finally managed to scramble down the cliff—Mistress Joan employing the same Saracen farmer to carry her back down—they were all relieved to hear that the group would rest for the night next to a small spring nearby. Most of them were too tired to eat, which relieved Gradenigo, who said frankly that they would be lucky to find enough fodder for the animals to get them back to Jerusalem, never mind enough food for the pilgrims. Normally this would provoke outraged mutters and threats of retribution involving authorities in Venice, but tonight the pilgrims were too tired to bother.

Back to Jerusalem they went the next morning, clattering through Jericho on their way. They remained only one night in Jerusalem, long enough to collect Hari, who had spent the intervening two weeks there in the collection of unknown faiths. A representative of each appeared the following morning to see him off. Jaufre had never seen such a collection of old and wizened men.

They departed for Jaffa, where Gradenigo hoped the weather would by now have allowed his two galleons to meet them there. Alas, Jaffa was bare of ships, and with much cursing Gradenigo booted his increasingly sulky and recalcitrant charges back down the coast road to Gaza. They were all relieved, captain, guards and pilgrims alike, when they came over a rise to see the buildings of the bustling port outlined against the deep blue waters of the Middle Sea, and the small forest of masts bobbing there. The pilgrims, hungry, filthy, sunburned, exhausted, their gray robes in tatters and their sandals in need of resoling, altogether a sight fit to make their mothers weep, straightened up in a body and hustled down the road as if Gaza was their home village and there was a hot meal and a loving welcome waiting for every one of them. Which there wasn't.

Mistress Joan Burgh of course shrieked at the sight of the port town and their ships and nearly fell from her donkey in ecstasy. No one moved to catch her, since Father Baldred had been left behind in Jerusalem and could no longer shame them into it. Regrettably, she recovered her balance, resettled herself in her saddle, and moved back into the line of trotting beasts. "The blessed Lord Jesus is guiding me home! O, such riches he has in store for me! Surely to God I am anointed for sainthood in this world and destined for the Kingdom of Heaven in the next!"

"We'll all be sainted for having survived travel with you, mistress," someone said, and there was laughter, although it was much better humored now than the malicious laughter directed at her at the Cave of Quarantana.

Jaufre found himself kicking his horse into a faster gait, leaning forward in the saddle. Félicien and Alaric began to fall behind.

His eyes squinting against the brilliant sun, Jaufre tried to make out the figures gathering at the northern gate of the city. Word of their coming had gone before them, and Shasha met them inside. She met Jaufre's eyes and shook her head.

He scowled.

384

Alaric sidled up and said in a low voice, "Jaufre, for the sake of us all, will you please find yourself a woman and have done with this unseemly pining?"

Jaufre turned his back on the Templar and went to help shepherd their flock into an inn while Gradenigo rode ahead to the quay to check on his galleons. Mistress Joan slid from the back of her mule and dropped to her knees and raised her arms to the sky, eyes closed, singing a hymn which would have sounded better if she'd been able to carry a recognizable tune. The other pilgrims, long inured to this behavior, gathered their belongings and stepped around her to stream into the inn, where in a triumph of hope over experience they looked forward to hot water for washing, a hearty meal, and a vermin-free bed.

Mistress Joan continued as she was, where she was, and Jaufre, alas, lost his temper. "Will you, mistress, for the blood of this sweet Christ you adore so much, be STILL!"

There was a momentary, and somewhat respectful, silence from everyone but Mistress Joan.

An hour later, Gradenigo reappeared, full of wrath at the dismasting of one of his galleons by an early fall storm that had swooped in with great gusto on the very night they had left. His crew had botched the replacement so badly it would have to be done over again from the beginning. "By Christ's bones, gentlemen," he said indignantly, "I have to do everything myself!"

Jaufre, brooding over his ale, made no reply.

Alaric cleared his throat and said, "How long will your departure be delayed, captain?"

"A week at least," the captain said.

Alaric nudged Jaufre and said in a low voice, "Didn't you say you wanted passage to Venice? Perhaps by the time the captain is ready to sail, your Johanna will have arrived."

Félicien paused in the act of raising his tankard. "Or perhaps she will never arrive."

Jaufre glared at him. "You don't have to sound so pleased at the thought, sir."

Félicien was unabashed. "We haven't seen her for a year, Jaufre," he said. "Who knows who this woman is now?"

Hari had said much the same, he remembered. A year was a long time. They had not spent more than a day apart since they had met as children, outside Kashgar, seven years before.

It was a legitimate, if unwelcome, question. Clearly he was not the same man she had left behind on the trail down from Terak Pass. Who would Johanna be?

13
Gaza, October, 1323

IN BAGHDAD, AN astute Firas arranged for them to leave with a caravan en route for the port of Gaza. He explained, not unreasonably, that he didn't want the Baghdadian euphoria over North Wind's month-long winning streak to erode into ennui and jealousy, which could lead to attempts at retaliation by those citizens who had bet against the stallion and lost. Everyone agreed that this made sense and started to pack.

The man who had been following them presented himself to the caravan master shortly after Firas' conversation with that same gentleman and asked for employment. He appeared trim and fit and wore weapons that looked well used and well tended. It was two hundred leagues to Gaza. Since the Seljuks paid more attention to law and order within their cities than without, the way grew more fraught each year, and the caravan master was pleased to have another blade to safeguard their journey. When asked, he named several well-known caravan masters as previous employers and said they would give a good account of him. This caravan master didn't bother to check. Few ever did.

Back on the Road, city and farmland gave way again to desert and the trip devolved to a forced march. The merchants in this caravan were headed single-mindedly for the coast and transport west, as it was growing late in the year and everyone wanted to get home before being caught at sea by the first winter storm. It was mid-October when they passed through the ruins of Jaffa and headed south down the coast on the last leg of their journey. The sky was clear and blue and the temperature unseasonably warm and the general mood improved with every league.

"Fresh droppings," Firas said, pointing. "We are not the first on this road this morning."

Indeed, they arrived less than an hour behind the travelers ahead of them, who were dismounting in the yard of the caravansary. Johanna was looking eagerly around them for any sign of Jaufre, of Shasha, of Hari, Félicien, anyone familiar to her.

"Johanna!"

Her head whipped around, a beaming smile spread across her face as she searched for the man who called her name so urgently. She found him. Her smile faded to a look of blank astonishment.

"Johanna!" A different voice, from a different direction. "Johanna!" She blinked, dazed, to see Jaufre thrusting through the crowd, his face bright with joy. "Johanna!"

"Johanna!" the first man called again.

Her hands went slack on the reins and North Wind moved restively beneath her. She slid bonelessly to the ground, grasping his saddle to remain upright.

Jaufre reached her first, his blue eyes blazing. "Johanna!" He half-raised his arms and realized her gaze was fixed on something over his shoulder. He turned to look, and went still.

The stocky young man, clothed in nubby dark blue raw silk and a round cloth cap, smiled all over his brown face. "Johanna," he said again.

"Edyk," she said, in a high, silly voice.

"I don't understand," Johanna said.

She had looked happy but bewildered at first sighting Edyk.

Jaufre could understand the bewildered part, but the happy? Not his chief emotion, certainly. Now he saw that her happiness had faded a little, and was meanly pleased.

Shasha had arrived at the caravansary and taken in the situation at a glance. She scooped them up in a body and moved them bag and baggage to their lodgings, a small house in a side street with kitchen and necessary in the yard out back. They sorted themselves out in groups, Jaufre and Shasha, Firas nearby, Félicien and Hari, Alaric a little apart, Alma and Hayat close together but not so close that they would get in each other's way if they had to draw their weapons.

Johanna and Edyk stood in the center of the room, staring at each other. Edyk raised his arms as if to embrace her, and then looked round the room at the eight pairs of interested eyes trained on them. His arms dropped. "Johanna," he said, a break in his voice.

"What are you doing in Gaza, Edyk?" Johanna said.

Hari had been right, of course, and Félicien, too—damn him—this Johanna was not the girl Jaufre had last seen a year before on the trail down from Terak Pass. He couldn't quite lay his finger on the difference. She seemed not just older but taller. It wasn't her appearance so much as it was her attitude. This woman was confident, disciplined, in command of herself. He saw the short sword hanging at her side. Where by all the Mongol gods had she gotten that? And could she use it? *You carry a sword*, Firas had told him, a year ago and more now. Sooner or later, someone will force you to use it.

He glanced at the Assassin, who looked just the same. Or perhaps slightly more taciturn, if that was possible, and just as communicative, which was to say not communicative at all. He appeared to be waiting for an answer to Johanna's question. Shasha stood next to him, and she, too, waited for Edyk's answer. She looked troubled, which was not what Jaufre would have expected given the long-awaited reuniting of their party.

Hari and Félicien were eying Alma and Hayat. The two

women wore sturdy men's clothing and also carried weapons, one a slim dagger, the other a short sword. Both women showed signs of recent outdoor life, but there was an indefinable air of refinement about them in spite of their travel-worn state.

Alaric stood near the door, pretending not to be there at all in hopes that no one would notice and throw him out before they got to the juicy bits. His eyes lingered on Jaufre for a moment, registering the younger man's unhappiness, traveled from him to Johanna, paused to consider, and then moved to the young man in the round hat. From his expression, he was not impressed.

Edyk the Portuguese, merchant and trader, veteran of many journeys along the Road, husband of two and father of three and Johanna's lover in a three-day goodbye before they had left Cambaluc, colored and shuffled his feet. "Perhaps we could speak privately."

Jaufre opened his mouth and felt rather than saw the look Shasha threw him. He shut it again.

"Just tell me what you're doing here, Edyk," Johanna said with a trace of impatience. Jaufre noticed nothing loverlike in her voice.

Edyk noticed that, too, and it was obvious that he was much less pleased about it. Undoubtedly he had also noticed the other changes in Johanna, which measured from Cambaluc to Gaza had to be even more remarkable than the changes incurred from Terak Pass to Gaza. "Well," he said falteringly. "Well. She sent me, of course."

Jaufre ceased to breathe. Shasha went very still. The others exchanged uneasy glances.

"She?" Johanna said, very quietly into the silence that had fallen on the room.

"Your honorable stepmother," Edyk said. "The widow Wu Li." He paused, and added hesitatingly, "Dai Fang?"

There was a long silence, as Edyk looked increasingly confused at the lack of response. Jaufre heard a distant drumming sound, which he took to be the thud of blood in his ears.

"Dai Fang sent you to Gaza?" Johanna said at last.

"She wanted me to find you and bring you home," he said. "She said she needs your help to continue your father's business. She understands that all young things are restless and seek adventure, but that it is time for you to come home now and take your place at her side." He looked around the room again, and took a step forward and dropped his voice. "You know it is the dearest wish of my heart that you will obey her in this, Johanna. We could marry. I promise I could make you very happy."

Edyk didn't know that Dai Fang and Gokudo had murdered Wu Li, Jaufre thought. Because they hadn't told him, before they left.

Perhaps they should have.

"Dai Fang sent you to Gaza," Johanna said.

"Yes," Edyk said.

"To find me," Johanna said.

"Yes," Edyk said. "Johanna, what is it?"

"To bring me home," Johanna said. She looked at Shasha and laughed. It wasn't a pleasant sound.

"Who came with you?" Jaufre said.

Edyk turned, a flash of anger in his eyes. "No one. Chiang only. Not that it's any business of yours."

"She would have had him followed," Johanna said to Jaufre. It was the first thing she'd said to him.

Jaufre found the hilt of his sword in his hand. "She would," he said. The drum of blood in his ears sounded louder.

"How would she have known about Gaza?" Shasha said. "That we would come here?"

Johanna, considering gaze fixed on Edyk's increasingly irritated expression, said, "It's the main port for Venice in this area. She would surely have heard enough stories of my grandfather from Wu Li. She couldn't know for sure, of course, but…" Her voice trailed off.

Shasha held up her hand, and such was the authority in the gesture that all conversation stopped. "Listen," she said.

At first Jaufre could hear nothing, and then he realized that what he had taken for blood thumping in his ears was actually the sound of many feet approaching their front door at a run. Firas was first to draw, Johanna and Jaufre not far behind him and Hayat, Alma and Alaric following suit at almost exactly the moment the door was kicked in.

It bounced off the wall with a loud thud. Six men burst inside, weapons drawn. Three were obvious professionals with hard, unemotional faces, the other three paid bravos, who wore broad grins at the prospect of murder and plunder.

They paused when they saw that at least some of their so-called victims were ready to meet them with blades of their own, but only momentarily. The three professionals charged directly for Johanna. Alaric engaged the first bravo while Hayat tripped one of the others. He staggered and regained his feet and parried her blow hard enough that she staggered into the wall and dropped her knife. Another knife appeared immediately from her sleeve and a third from her belt. It was enough to give her attacker pause and in that brief second Alma tucked herself into a ball and somersaulted into the back of his legs. This time he fell. Hayat was on him before he could recover. Both of her blades flashed, silver first, then red.

"Wait!" Edyk said. "What?" He stood where he was, incredulous, staring as the battle raged around him.

Upon the unceremonious entrance of their six attackers, Félicien had stepped expeditiously to the rear of the room, holding his precious lute up and out of danger. Hari joined him, hands clasped before him and a stern, declamatory prayer issuing forth condemning all acts of violence against one's fellow beings and prophesying the certain return of all so engaged as cockroaches in their next lives. Shasha stepped neatly through the door into the back yard, where she remained, watching Johanna with an expression of increasing wonder.

For all three professionals had converged on her foster sister, whose sword was up and deflecting the blows aimed at her in a positive blur of defensive parries. Shasha cast a quick glance at Firas, and was reassured when she saw him, scimitar drawn. He was watching Johanna, too, with what she would later realize was a critical gaze, like a teacher watching a promising student during her final examination.

But Jaufre leapt forward, to deflect a slashing cut that would have struck Johanna's arm off at the elbow. She parried her second opponent's thrust, at which he looked fleetingly surprised before he barreled in again. She was only a woman, after all.

"What?" Edyk said from behind her. "What!" He had not so much as drawn his dagger.

Alaric's bravo had had some training and he gave the ex-Templar some brief cause for alarm, especially in the crowded confines of a room where the walls had a tendency to get confoundedly in the way. Ah. He parried the incautious thrust and slid the point of his sword forward to slide between two ribs and straight on into the heart. The bravo's eyes widened in surprise and he fell, dead before he hit the ground.

Alaric stood back, wiped his sleeve across his forehead and looked around in time to see Jaufre take a cut on his left forearm. The ex-Templar watched approvingly as Jaufre ducked to avoid the return sweep of the blade, dropped to lean his weight on his free hand and kick the other man in the knee. The man shouted and staggered back against the wall next to Félicien, who nudged Hari. Both of them moved farther down.

The man managed to stay upright and to hold on to his sword and shoved himself away from the wall to slash at Johanna, catching her a glancing blow on her right thigh. The cloth of her trousers parted beneath it and so did her skin. Blood welled up and at the sight of it Jaufre went a little mad, hacking at the man with brute force and no finesse.

Unseen behind him, Firas clicked his tongue.

"What?" Edyk said. "What?"

The man fell back beneath the fury of his assault and Jaufre finished him off with a blow to his head. He didn't bother to watch him fall. A glance found Johanna still on her feet, and some of his rage abated, although it whipped up again when one of the others lunged at her.

Hayat pulled out her knife, wiped it on the tunic of the man she had felled and rose to her feet, holding out her hand to Alma. Alma gave the body a contemptuous kick in the face on her way up. He rolled over with a groan and lost consciousness. He was crippled if he lived. If he died, no matter.

"Well done," Firas said, who had yet to raise his weapon in earnest. "But please to remember that demonstrations of emotion are best left until the battle is won." The third bravo, smarter than the rest, was still hesitating in the doorway, his smile quite gone. Firas stepped over the body at Hayat's feet and said conversationally, "I think you should put down that sword, don't you?"

The bravos had been hired as a distraction, sacrificial lambs meant to draw attention while the professionals went after the real target. The third bravo realized this a beat after Firas had, and about two beats after the second of his friends had gone down. In the next moment he surrendered his sword and begged for mercy. Firas accepted the weapon, shook his head over its imperfect balance, and shepherded his captive out of the way.

That left the two professionals, the one currently hammering at Johanna and the one at his back, holding the others off while the first one finished off Johanna. That was the plan, at any rate. Later Jaufre would marvel at how little apprehension he felt. He watched the other man with slightly unfocussed eyes, the man's movements overlaid by the same ones made against him so many times by Firas and Ram and Alaric. He could see them coming, almost predict them as the other man moved. His opponent was older, had trained longer, had vastly more experience, but he had not had Jaufre's teachers. The end came suddenly and without any warning to anyone except Jaufre, who had been aiming for that particular target from the moment they had engaged. His opponent dropped his sword, looked down at the slashing cut that had opened him up from waist to shoulder, and could only watch as Jaufre's blade came on a backswing and sliced opened his throat. He fell with a look of vast astonishment on his face.

Behind him, Johanna's opponent hacked at her with increasingly desperate blows, as if he knew his only recourse now was to overpower her by sheer brute force. It wasn't a bad plan, but she foiled it by parrying the latest blow while pulling her dagger, stepping unexpectedly inside his guard and sending the dagger's blade into his belly. She twisted hard and yanked up.

"Uh," he said. He dropped his sword and looked down in disbelief, staring at the blood and bit of slippery intestine that pushed out of the jagged wound. His hands went to his wound in a vain effort to push the blood and guts back inside. The strength went out of his legs and he went to his knees and then down to the floor, Johanna's dagger pulling itself free with the movement.

From start to finish the fight had taken no more than ten minutes. And, Jaufre realized, it had all been very quiet. None of the yelling, screaming, cursing that had accompanied every fight he'd ever been in until today. There had been clangs of metal and thuds of feet, and of bodies, but nothing loud enough to alarm the neighbors.

Of course, he thought. Dai Fang's instructions would have been to kill Johanna and to bring back the bao and the book. Loud noises would have brought the authorities down on them, and subsequent explanations would have been most inconvenient to the conspirators. City fathers were not as a class generally complaisant to mayhem and murder committed on their streets. Explanations, and possibly detention while those explanations were made would have been time-consuming.

Dai Fang, unable to trade without the bao, had to be running very low on time, and assets, by now. Jaufre smiled to himself. How very unfortunate.

Johanna went down on one knee to speak to the man she had dropped. "How long have you been following me?"

"Johanna," Jaufre said. "We need to bind your leg."

She ignored him, her attention on the man laying at her feet. "How long?"

His breathing was labored and stertorous. "Not you." He coughed, and gave a faint nod in Jaufre's direction. "Him. I picked him up in Kerman." He coughed again, and gasped. A full loop of intestine pushed out between his fingers. "But there were three of us, and we had a detailed description of all three of you. And the horse was easy enough to find, once you raced him in Baghdad. Sharif picked you up there. Bilal followed him, in case he found you first." Another faint nod, this time in Edyk's direction.

"Hussein," Alaric said. At Jaufre's look the knight said, "He was a muleteer in our caravan. I recognize him now. And," he added, in growing indignation, "he came with us to Jerusalem, in Gradenigo's employ."

"Yes," the man said. He mustered enough energy to smile up at Johanna, blood bubbling now from between his lips. "Who expects a woman to be armed? To fight? To win? I will be a laughingstock to the end of my days."

"Who hired you?"

"I never knew the name. The money was good, though." Another cough, followed by several rattling breaths, and a long, slow expiration. The man's chest ceased to rise. At least he had not had to suffer his humiliation for long.

Jaufre looked around. All three professionals were dead, and one of the bravos. A second bravo was badly wounded and the third was sitting with his legs crossed and his hands folded on top of his head. He looked terrified but unhurt. Shasha was binding a scratch on Alaric's forearm, and Alma had a spectacular black eye coming up. Other than that, plus the cut he had taken on his arm and the wound on Johanna's thigh, they seemed to have come off without injury.

It is always a mistake to underestimate your opposition, Jaufre heard Ram saying, and he smiled again, openly this time.

Johanna cleaned and sheathed her sword and smiled back at

Jaufre with a fierceness he recognized, as it matched his own. "Whatever are we going to do with all these bodies?"

✷

"She sent me after you," Edyk said slowly, making a visible effort to understand. "And she sent them to find you, too."

It was some time later. The room had been cleared and Firas and Alaric had disposed of the bodies under cover of darkness. No one asked where. The wounded bravo and his lone surviving companion had been dealt with, too, and again, no one cared enough to ask. The room had been scrubbed clean of spilled blood but the smell of it lingered in the air. They took rough seats placed around a splintery table beneath a cedar tree in the back yard, and Shasha had put together a scratch meal of fruit and bread and cheese. They were all downing copious amounts of hot, sweet tea, although Alaric was trading off with wine that he was drinking directly from a clay bottle.

"She sent me after you," Edyk said dully. "I didn't know she sent them, too." He looked up. "I believed her when she said she only wanted you back to help her run your father's business."

"The last strike of the dying serpent," Jaufre said, and laughed.

Edyk's voice rose. "But you knew when I told you that she wanted to kill you. Didn't you? Didn't you!"

"Yes," Johanna said in a level voice. "Yes, I knew. She killed Wu Li, Edyk. She and Gokudo." She looked at Jaufre, and at Shasha. "Gokudo is dead."

By her hand, it was understood, by them if not by Edyk. Jaufre watched her with an appreciative gaze. He wanted to hear the story but it could wait, now that she was well and truly back. Or someone was. Johanna had been first his savior, then his sister, then an object of desire, but this was the first time that Jaufre had seen her as a companion in arms. He was a welter of emotions, beginning with incredulous delight, gratitude, lust, and, oddly, a kind of wariness. He had no idea what to expect next.

He found himself looking forward to it.

"Do you have my purse?" Johanna said, looking at Shasha.

Shasha unfastened it from her waist and handed it over. "I kept them safe for you."

Johanna smiled. "I knew you would."

She opened the little leather bag and brought out Wu Li's bao, the jade cylinder inscribed on one end in raised characters, and the tiny jade pot filled with the red paste the seal was dipped it before impression. "This is why she wants me back, Edyk," she said. She pulled out the small, leather-bound book. "And this. It's not because she wants me to run Wu Li's business with her. It's because she can't run it without these, and I took them from her when I left."

Edyk looked from the bao to Johanna with a kind of horror. "You stole Wu Li's bao?"

She tucked everything back into the purse without replying.

"She can't run Wu Li's business without it, Johanna."

"I know," Johanna said, and smiled. Jaufre warmed to that smile.

Edyk appeared less enchanted. "What have you become, Johanna?"

"She has become a warrior," Alma said.

"Strong," Hayat said.

"Able to defend herself when attacked," Alma said.

"And capable of exacting revenge where it is merited," Hayat said. Edyk looked at her, his eyes wide, and her lip curled. "You have no reason to fear, little man. You are no threat to her, and therefore stand in no danger from us."

Alaric snorted, and drank more from his clay bottle.

"Hayat." Johanna's voice was warning. Hayat sniffed and subsided.

Johanna turned to Edyk. "Go home, Edyk," she said, her voice much gentler now. "There is nothing for you here."

His hands half rose in entreaty, and fell again. "What do I tell her?"

Johanna shrugged. "Whatever you wish. Tell her you couldn't find me. Tell her I'm dead. Chiang has always been discreet, you can rely on him to say nothing. Dai Fang will never know, and she has no reason to fear you. You'll be safe from any further attention on her part." She rose to her feet, and perforce, so did Edyk.

"But—" It was obvious that Edyk the Portuguese had followed more than Dai Fang's instructions to Gaza. He had also followed his heart. That heart had loved a young girl once, high in the hills above Cambaluc, in a cabin next to a lake, in the springtime when the plum trees were in bloom. He looked for any trace of that girl in Johanna's face, and could not find her.

"Go home to Jade and Blossom, Edyk," she said, not unkindly. "They will be missing you."

Edyk stumbled twice on his way out of the lodging. Firas put a helping hand beneath his elbow and saw him safely back to the caravansary.

Exhausted, the company made up their beds for the night and rolled into them. Introductions and plans could be made on the morrow. When Firas returned, the lamps had been doused and all were deeply asleep.

All but one. A hand met his in the darkness and drew him into the yard. "You returned," Shasha said. "And you brought her back to me."

"She is your family," Firas said. "Which means she is now my family, too." He traced her features with his fingertips. "You were ever in my thoughts during my absence, Shu Shao of Cambaluc."

Her hands came up to his shoulders. "As you were in mine during yours, Firas the Assassin."

He heard the smile in her voice, and laughed soundlessly.

She had spread their blankets in the farthest corner of the garden.

The others might have had more comfortable beds, but Firas and Shasha enjoyed theirs much more.

14

Gaza, November, 1323

THAT PILGRIM HERDER and charming rogue, Giovanni
Gradenigo, fell in love with Johanna at first sight. Of course
North Wind succeeded her immediately in his affections, and he
had nice things to say about the purebred Arabians, late of the
Sheik of Talikan's stables, too. Like everyone else who first made
North Wind's acquaintance, he offered Johanna a fortune for
him. She let North Wind discourage him, too, which the stallion
speedily did. Gradenigo took it well, partly because no bones
had been broken.

The good captain had his mast re-stepped and re-rigged four
days following the arrival of Johanna and company, after which
they were forced to wait two interminable weeks for a favorable
wind. His pilgrims, thoroughly bored with the delights of Gaza's
bazaars and women, were impatient to depart. They said so, in
steadily increasing volume, and with mounting threats to inform
the authorities of his malfeasance once they were back in Venice.
There were some truly colorful phrases that polyglots Johanna
and Jaufre were quick to commit to memory. English was a great
language for oaths.

Johanna and Jaufre and Shasha used this period of waiting to
catch up on the past year, whose events seemed so distant and
yet so immediate in retrospect. Jaufre and Shasha listened to

the tale of Talikan with sober faces. Shasha's detailed account of the torturous journey from Terak to Kabul and Jaufre's slow recovery leached the color from Johanna's cheeks. The tale of Gokudo's pursuit and his eventual death was met with a silence that was almost awed.

"Good," Shasha said at last.

Jaufre raised Johanna's hands to his lips and kissed them, one after the other. "For Wu Li, twice over," he said.

Johanna colored and pulled her hands free, ostensibly to drink more tea.

Jaufre produced the book written by Marco Polo he had found in Kerman, and watched Johanna leaf through it, her forehead puckering. "Have you told anyone why we're going to Venice?" she said.

He shook his head.

"Good," she said. "Let's keep it that way. At least for now."

"Why?"

She was slow to answer. "I'm not sure," she said finally. "We don't know what's waiting for us in Venice. If my grandfather lives there still. If he is even still alive. If he is in or out of favor with the authorities."

"Gradenigo might know all of those things."

"Let's not ask him." Her smile was fleeting. "Something tells me the good captain likes gossip too well. Word would fly ahead of us the moment we docked." She touched the leather purse at her waist and her smile faded. "Remember what it was like in Cambaluc. Remember what my father always said."

"That it was always better to be unknown at court than known," Jaufre said.

She nodded. "Let us go to Venice anonymous and un-announced."

She looked at Shasha, who nodded agreement.

"Very well," Jaufre said.

401

In the meantime Alaric became slowly accustomed to the idea of women warriors, especially after Hayat and Alma working together managed to dump him on his backside during a practice session. He looked on their joining morning practice with a less condemnatory eye after that, and he was certainly less smug when he faced them across a practice blade.

Not by so much as a quiver of a cheek muscle did Firas show how much he had enjoyed the scene. But then he was feeling very mellow these days.

Félicien took to the two women immediately, and they to him, Alma in particular because he was a student, Hayat because he was eager to learn all the songs she knew. Hari questioned them most stringently on the role of women in Islam. Alma struck up an instant friendship with Shasha who, like Félicien, she regarded as a fellow acolyte in scientific matters.

When the question was asked, it appeared that the entire company was traveling to Venice, each for their individual reasons. Johanna was going to Venice, and Shasha was going with Johanna, and that meant Firas was going, too. No further comment was made. None was needed. Everyone had seen the bed in the yard.

"I seem to have acquired a taste for travel," Alma said, and Hayat shrugged. "Where Alma goes, I go." She and Firas were very alike in that way.

Alaric had already declared his intention of returning to his homeland, ignoring Félicien when the goliard said beneath his breath, "To see if it has cooled down enough for him to go home, more like."

Félicien, too, had declared a state of homesickness. He looked at Jaufre when he said it, although no one noticed but Shasha and Hari. "It's been five years," he said. "I can't stay away forever."

Hari said simply that he had no option but to move forward as his calling bade him. He was on a lifetime voyage of exploration, and a little thing like a vast sea would not stop him. Besides, he had been told of an enormous temple in Rome, dedicated to the Christian god... "Wait until you see Chartres," Félicien said.

402

"Eight then," Giovanni Gradenigo said when he was informed, adding up figures. He looked up with a broad smile. "Seven ducats each. That includes bed and board, of course."

This provoked the expected outrage, as forced intimacy with the pilgrims had taught them that seven and a half ducats was the going rate for the round trip from Venice to Jaffa and back again, weevily hardtack and sour water included. They beat him down to two ducats each, if they provided their own food. Shasha, who had volunteered to go among the pilgrims to treat their aches and pains, had had an earful of what kind of board Gradenigo provided and laid in stores accordingly. Further, she had prescribed a large dose of valerian tea every night for Mistress Joan, which seemed to promote a quieter attitude. Jaufre claimed, not without credence, that Gradenigo owed them all a reduction in fare for that alone.

Then there were the horses. Since four of Gradenigo's pilgrims had died en route, three on board ship and one in Jerusalem of the bloody flux, he bundled extra pilgrims into the second ship to make room for North Wind and the three Arabians on the first, although he charged them a fortune for it. Johanna would entrust food and water for the horses to no one but themselves, so it wasn't as expensive as it could have been.

Meanwhile, they waited for a favorable wind. "We could sacrifice a virgin," Félicien said. When the wind finally came—with all the Gaza virgins still accounted for—Gradenigo bundled everyone on board post haste and set sail before it could change its fickle mind.

Of course their group found themselves on the same ship as Mistress Joan. Of course they did. Johanna only hoped she wouldn't frighten the horses.

On the voyage she found herself most in company with Jaufre, who had a disturbing habit of watching her with a smile in his eyes. It had been a long year apart and they were both much changed, but now that she was back in his company, she remembered clearly the feelings for him that she had only just begun to discover before they were parted. The kind of feelings she had once had for Edyk.

And then he had been attacked, stabbed in the back and for all she knew killed, as she had been dragged off against her will. She knew an enormous relief that Jaufre had survived, and thrived, as well as an astonishment at the maturity—and the competent swordplay—of the man who had taken his place. But she felt as if she hardly knew him now. She felt, unbelievably, shy, a thing she had never felt before in her life, and something it had taken a while for her to identify.

And then there was Edyk. Seeing him had been a shock, if not for the reasons she might have expected. He was older than she was by several years, a more experienced merchant and traveler, and vastly more experienced as a lover. And yet in Gaza he seemed so young and comparatively innocent. It was as if their positions had been reversed, and she was now the elder and wiser and by far the more experienced of the two.

She had been happy to see him again, and she had gone to see him off when he left Gaza to return east because she could not bear to part with him on bad terms. But in the end, it was with a very faint fond remembrance that she watched him ride through Gaza's north gate. It had not been nearly as easy for her to leave Edyk at the summerhouse the previous spring.

"Do you want to take North Wind with you?" she had said, dreading the answer.

Edyk smiled. It was only a slight smile, but still, he did smile. "He would not come. And even if I compelled him, he would not stay with me." The smile grew wider. "I should never have let you help with his training."

They both laughed a little. He had said much the same before she left Cambaluc. His hand caressed her cheek briefly, toyed with a bronze curl. Then his smile faded and he kicked his mount viciously in the sides and galloped away from her for the last time, followed by the ever-faithful Chiang, who had pretended not to have seen Johanna at all.

She should feel sad, she told herself. But mostly what she felt was relief.

✧

It was a violent crossing, the previous lack of wind compensated for by one violent fall storm after another. The two ships were brutally pushed along a course that more resembled the trail of a snake that the wake of a boat. The storms had the virtue of making it a quick passage, at least, and of drowning out the shrieking and exhortations of Mistress Joan en route. Johanna and Jaufre, wise to the ways of sea travel since childhood, remained on deck for the entire five weeks, one standing watch while the other slept, fending off the attention of crewmen interested in what might be in their pockets.

They saw few other ships. "I thought anyone who sailed the Middle Sea was at grave risk from pirates," Johanna said one day when the captain was passing.

A gust of wind tore at the sails and rattled the rigging so fiercely that for a moment she thought the whole mass would be torn loose and carried away, leaving the ship at the mercy of the storm with no means of propulsion or control. The ship listed sharply and a wave of water came over the gunnel to soak them both to the skin.

Gradenigo laughed and pushed his wet hair out of his eyes. He had to shout to be heard above the wind. "Signorina, no pirate in his right mind would be out in this weather!"

Except for the mandatory stops at Candia in Crete and Modon in Greece, when everyone staggered on shore for an hour of fresh air and a surface that didn't move beneath their feet, the rest of their party stayed below in their single cramped cabin with their heads over the communal commode. The resulting aroma only increased their nausea and multiplied the rats. Firas and Shasha were unaffected, and joined Johanna and Jaufre on deck, where they held hands longer and more tightly than strictly necessary to keep their balance against the heaving of the ship. Johanna reserved comment. She was, amazingly, learning discretion.

Several more of the pilgrims died mid voyage and their bodies were buried at sea in accordance with the rules as set out by the captain's contract. There were moments when Alaric, Alma and even Hari wished most heartily to have been one of them.

✿

They disembarked with relief for the last time, on the Grand Canal in Venice one cold, gray morning in early November. Stabling for the horses provided for and bags left at an inn Gradenigo recommended, the first gondolier they hailed said, "The Polo palazzo? Of course."

They climbed gingerly into the long, narrow boat and penetrated the heart of the one of the stranger cities they had ever visited. Most of the streets were canals connected by bridges, and Johanna wondered if this was what Baghdad had looked like before its canals had been destroyed by Hulegu. There were few signposts and many people, all talking and gesticulating at a great rate. There were shops filled with every kind of merchandise and they caught quick glimpses into open doors of dazzling arrays of silk and gemstones and spices.

Their gondolier pushed them along with a long pole he went up and down hand over hand, more often than not ducking when they passed beneath the bridges, which did not seem to have been built with gondoliers in mind. After thirty minutes' worth of twists and turns down waterways that all looked—and smelled—the same to them once they got off the Grand Canal, he decanted them at the foot of a bridge on one of the smaller canals. He pointed at a massive double door made of wood set in the front of a grand stone house, accepted payment and a tip that Shasha thought was extortionate, and shoved off in search of his next fare.

"It doesn't look like a building occupied by a family out of favor," Jaufre said, inspecting the elaborate carvings on door and columns.

Johanna wiped her sweaty palms on her tunic, that same tunic made of the raw silk dyed black that her father had brought back from his last trip to Kinsai. It showed its many leagues: Cambaluc to Terak, Terak to Talikan, Talikan to Baghdad, Baghdad to Gaza, Gaza to Venice, and the doorstep of her grandfather's house. She wore the tunic now like a badge of honor.

They gathered behind her, her fellow travelers, her compatriots, her friends. Her family. With them at her back she could do anything. Even knock on her grandfather's door.

She stepped forward, raised the large brass knocker and rapped the wood with it twice, three times. The sound echoed beyond the door. After a few moments footsteps were heard. The massive door swung back.

She and Jaufre had seized the few calm moments at sea to use Captain Gradenigo and those of his crew amenable to bribes to amass a rudimentary knowledge of Italian. What she said now had been carefully rehearsed, over and over and over again.

"Good afternoon," she said. "My name is Wu Johanna, late of Cambaluc in Everything Under the Heavens. I am looking for Ser Marco Polo. Is this his home?"

The man who had answered the door was obviously a servant, and an upperclass one if the quality of his clothing and the loftiness of his manner were any indication. "It is."

He offered no further encouragement. Nonplussed, she said, "Well, I'm glad we have found the right place." He did not return her smile and she lost interest in further politesse. In a manner even loftier than his own, she said, "Could you please inform your master that his granddaughter wishes to speak with him?"

"Ser Polo lies on his deathbed," he said. "And the occupants of this house have no time to spare for ragamuffins off the street purporting to be relatives."

And he shut the door in her face.

THE LAND BEYOND

BOOK III OF SILK AND SONG

I

Venice, December, 1323

THE BEST THAT could be said about winter in Venice was that
the colder temperatures suppressed the smell of the canals.
There was, however, no known advantage to the constant fogs
that lay heavily on the Laguna Veneta, ghostly tentacles of which
slithered up the canals to enfold the city in a chill embrace that
no hearth fire however large could ease. After nearly two years
spent traveling the Road, most of the journey spent in dry desert
country where a day without a hot sun glaring down just meant
that night had fallen, it took some getting used to, especially in
the location Johanna currently occupied.

Which was the minuscule square fronting Ca' Polo, with lesser
buildings crowding the sides. She had found an alcove created
by the uneven joining of two of these, bought a dark, hooded
cloak that enveloped her head to foot and melted into the shadow
created there, from where she observed the comings and goings of
the Polo family. By the end of each day the encroaching fog had
soaked her from shoulder to knee. It was a wonder she hadn't
come down with inflammation of the lungs. More irritating still,
watching the house had been productive of very little in the way
of information. Her grandfather, Marco Polo, lay on his deathbed,
but that much she had heard from the supercilious steward who
had closed the door in her face the day they had arrived in Venice.

The two older Polo daughters and their husbands were the first people she identified, though she only saw them once and each couple for the exact amount of time specified by duty and no more. They arrived by private gondola, attended by personal guards, wore sumptuous clothes that shouted their worth from across the square and wooden pattens on their richly embroidered shoes to keep their feet up out of the mud. They were not noticeably grieving as they left.

She didn't see anyone who looked like the third daughter, Moreta. She didn't see the wife, Donata, either, but that was more understandable.

✝

Summarily dismissed from the door of Ca' Polo, the second order of business on that day of their arrival in the Jewel of the Sea was to look for lodgings for the company, man and beast. Johanna found North Wind and the other horses stabling across the lagoon in Marghera, a brief boat ride away so that she could still see him and ride him every day. The farmer never raised so much as an eyebrow at Johanna's dressing in trousers and riding astride, and for that alone she would have paid him twice the silver penny he had asked for his fee.

She kept her ears open while engaged in these homely occupations, and by keeping silent learned a good deal. Venice was ruled by a Doge, one Giovanni Soranzo, eighty-three years old, a leader with the majority of the merchants of Venice solidly in his camp. This appeared to be less due to the remembrance of the martial exploits of his youth, when he conquered Caffa during the last war with Genoa, than for the rare ability to keep the peace on the Middle Sea. As every marginally competent merchant knew, peace was good for business. In the eleven years since Soranzo's ascension, Venice had made treaties with Byzantium, Sicily, Milan, Bologna, Brescia, Tunisia, Trebizond and Persia, which had greatly facilitated the movement, not to mention the security of sale goods. Doge Soranzo had also presided over the opening of trade with England and Flanders, which either inspired or was inspired by the building of a new kind of ship, called a merchant galley. It was wider and longer than existing ships, and was propelled by both sail and by 200 oarsmen. The oarsmen were free men, and armed, so that upon attack the galley could muster 200 more men to its defense. She went down to the Arsenal to see several upon the ways, and even saw one of them launched, and was impressed with the nimble way the craft took up the wind in its sails and its speed over water when it did.

Along with the rest of Venice they all spent extended periods down at the Arsenal, watching the galleys being built, and they never missed a launch. Jaufre wasted a good deal of time figuring the payload per galley, and came to the conclusion that it was roughly equivalent to that of six hundred camels. Respectable, he thought. Given a competent captain, favorable weather, and no war breaking out between any countries with coastlines, a trader could make a reasonably good living. Always supposing the ship didn't sink. Remembering the rough passage from Gaza in November, Jaufre could only imagine that they did with a frequency that would put said merchant out of business and probably into the poorhouse, if not debtor's prison.

In a month she and Jaufre and Shasha were roughly fluent in Italian, the lingua franca of the Middle Sea, and Johanna practiced her fluency by sidling up to groups of Venetians and eavesdropping on their conversations. Whenever someone mentioned the name "Polo," her ears pricked up. One day a group of lawyers were trumping each other's stories of bad clients. Marco Polo had figured in several of those stories, either as claimant or defendant. It seemed that her grandfather was somewhat litigious in nature. She was smart enough during these intelligence forays not to draw attention to herself, drifting off when anyone looked her way, but gossip along with trade goods was the fuel that powered Venice, and it was amazing how much information

413

she managed to acquire on the inmates of the Polo palazzo, or, as it was known more familiarly, Ca' Polo.

Upon his return from Cambaluc, or Cathay as the Venetians would have it, her grandfather, his father and his uncle had had some problems re-establishing themselves in Venetian society. This accomplished, chiefly by the generous giving of fabulous gifts brought with them from the East, his father and uncle resumed their positions as merchants in good standing. Marco enlisted in the Venetian war on Genoa and was captured in the Battle of Curzola.

She asked Félicien where Curzola was. A visit to the Biblioteca Marciana and he reported back. "It's an island in Dalmatia. There was a huge battle there twenty-five years ago, between Venice and Genoa. Venice lost."

Johanna nodded. That much she'd gotten. "My grandfather was taken prisoner there. It's where he wrote *Il Milione*."

"Ah."

"What?"

"He didn't write it, exactly."

"What do you mean?"

"He dictated it. A man from Pisa, name of Rustichello, shared his cell. He wrote down your grandfather's stories and published them in a book." Félicien paused. "And then about a hundred others copied it and printed it, too."

Johanna looked at him, and he held up his hands, palms out. "Don't believe me, go look for yourself. Any bookstall will have a used copy, I promise you."

Venice boasted on average one bookstore per canal, and that was just between bridges. No bridge itself was worthy of the name unless it bore at least one bookstall itself. She sampled a dozen between their lodgings and the Grand Canal and it was as Félicien had said: copies of her grandfather's *Il Milione* were readily available, some in readable condition, many not, and all, it seemed, copied by a different hand and bound by a different publisher. Oddly, as many copies seemed to have been published in French as had been in Italian. "Of course," Félicien said matter-of-factly. "French is the language of romances."

Johanna compared pages of a few of these diverse editions side by side and found very little uniformity of text between them. Some copyists appeared to have even inserted their own narrative, real or imagined, into her grandfather's.

One thing was sure: everyone in Venice had heard of *Il Milione*. It came as a shock to Marco Polo's grand-daughter that almost everyone thought it was a fabrication from start to finish. Johanna, increasing her written Italian and French, was working her way through the fairest copy she could find of the earliest possible date of original publication, side by side with a French edition, and noted that the more fabulous of the tales her grandfather had been careful to begin with "Men say." On the facts, facts she knew to be true from her own experience, he was unassailable: what was for sale where, local craft specialties and trading practices, regional social norms, distances between cities. He wrote of gunpowder, and spectacles, and coal, and paper money, all of which she had noticed were taking hold here in Venice.

"You have to wonder," she said to Shasha that evening.

"What?"

"If my grandfather brought spectacles back with him. The recipe for gunpowder." Johanna shrugged. "All of it. Everything he wrote about."

It was a useful book for a merchant, *Il Milione*. But then, she thought, her grandfather was a merchant, after all.

And he lay dying at Ca' Polo. It was common knowledge throughout the city that his wife waited only for the drawing of his last breath before dancing in the streets.

Because of course he had married. Of course he had. The fortune with which the Polos had returned had bought him a good match with one Donata Badoèr, daughter of a wealthy merchant. The midwife Johanna had this tale from over a mug of wine in a taverna off of St. Mark's Square told her, "I delivered all three of their daughters. She told me after the birth of the third one that he sold all of her dowry for himself." The midwife, a stout woman with a red face, nodded emphatically. "There was a farm, and a house, and—" She waved an expansive hand and belched. "Property," she said. "And he sold it, every bit of it. If you ask me, she never forgave him. I'd bet you a hundred ducats that she'll do everything, short of holding a pillow over his face—" Johanna flinched but the midwife, busy with her wine, didn't see it "—to see him out of this world as speedily as possible." She belched again. "Traipsing back home after twenty years' absence with a hatful of tales that would shame the devil himself. A liar, a braggart, and a fool, to think he would be believed when he came home. He probably spent the whole twenty years he was gone in Byzantium, collecting the stories of real travelers to try out on the gullible in Venice." She snorted. "Although Venetians will believe anything. As *Il Milione* well proved."

"Three daughters," Johanna said indifferently, did the midwife but know it displaying an admirable hold on her temper.

The midwife eyed her empty mug. Johanna signaled for a refill and the woman drank half of it down in a single gulp. "Three daughters, yes," she said, dabbing daintily at her mouth with the hem of her sleeve. "Fantina, Bellela, and Moreta. The first two are married."

"And the third?"

The midwife drained her mug. "Moreta? They have yet to find her a husband. She still lives at home."

Back in her shadowy corner across from the Polo residence, Johanna reviewed the information she had gleaned from a month's worth of eavesdropping and bribery, and wondered after all if she shouldn't just march up to the front door and try to force an entrance. Even being turned away a second time in ignominy would be better than standing in this thrice cursed fog. She shifted her sodden cloak in a vain attempt to find some part of it that was dry, and jumped at a noise that sounded like a muffled squeal.

She looked around to behold an urchin, her hair a mess of ink-black curls clustering around a small face with a determined chin, a mouth pressed into a defiant line, and dark brown eyes, narrowed and glaring in an effort to project pugnacity and fearlessness. She couldn't quite bring it off, and Johanna wondered what her own face looked like at that moment. She straightened her expression, not without effort. She touched the purse at her waist, containing her father's book and the squared cylinder that was his bao. As always, the touch comforted her, and today it calmed her, too. "And who are you?" she said.

The chin came even more into evidence. "You're standing in my spot."

"I beg your pardon?"

"This is my spot. You can't take it. I'm here all the time, and everyone who lives on this square knows me."

And tossed her a coin from time to time, Johanna thought. Beggars the world over had their pitches. The girl's rough homespun cloak was worn and too short and her face and hands looked as if they had not seen clean water in days. "Ah," Johanna said. "My apologies. You weren't here, so I thought it was unclaimed." She didn't mention that she'd been here off and on for a month unmolested.

"It isn't."

"I see that now." Johanna paused. The girl couldn't have been more than eight years old, nine at the most. "Perhaps I could rent it from you."

The girl scowled. "Rent it?"

"Yes." Johanna searched her pockets and produced a silver coin whose place of origin she did not immediately recognize and which could have been a solidus, an aureus, a denari, a bezant, a florin or something else altogether, because making change in Venice was like that.

The girl snorted. "I take in double that most mornings."

Johanna doubted it. "I'm sure you do," she said nevertheless. "One now, and another like it at the end of the day." And then, struck with an idea, she said, "And two more like it every day, if you will stand watch here and take note of everyone who comes and goes to Ca' Polo. You know which one is Ca' Polo?"

With infinite scorn, the girl said, "I know all the palazzos in Venice."

"It is agreed, then? I will meet you here at vespers each day. You will tell me everyone who came and went through that door, and I will pay you two silver pieces."

"For how long?"

"For as long as I say." Among other advantages, having someone else watch Ca' Polo would free up enough of her time so that she could get over to see North Wind more often. Unused to being pent up in a paddock, he was already getting restive, and made his displeasure known to her by dumping her off his back at least once per visit.

The girl hesitated. "Very well." She snatched the coin from Johanna's hand and ran, her wooden soles clattering over the cobbles and the surface of the bridge as she vanished from view.

The encounter nearly caused her to miss the man who slipped out of the door opposite, but not quite.

He was short, with bowed legs. He was dressed in the fashion of Venetian men, a sleeveless tunic buttoned over a long-sleeved chemise and loose-fitting breeches, but when the hood of his cloak fell partway back from his face she caught her breath. He had a heavy brow, narrow, uptilting eyes, a short, flat nose and golden skin. A long, wispy mustache clung perilously to his upper lip and trailed down both sides of his mouth.

He was a Mongol. He had the look of Deshi the Scout, dead in the same cholera epidemic that had taken her mother that dreadful year in Cambaluc.

He pulled up his hood against the rain and hurried off. She slipped from her corner and followed.

He made several stops, one at an apothecary, one at a book-seller, and one where he walked all the way to the Rialto bridge to seek out a particular sweets seller, from whom he purchased a quantity of small, hard candies flavored with lemon.

Halfway back to the palazzo, she waited until he had drawn almost even to a small taverna and increased her pace to catch up with him. He shot her a cursory look and halted in his tracks, staring at her with eyes slowly widening, as if in recognition.

"Steppe rider," she said in Uighur, "you are far from home."

Still he stared, and made no reply.

Very well, it appeared shock tactics would best carry the day. She squared her shoulders, raised her chin, and said, "I am the daughter of Shu Ming of Cambaluc, who was the daughter of Shu Lin, also of Cambaluc, and the wife of the Venetian traveler, Marco Polo. I believe you serve my grandfather." She gestured at the taverna. "Shall we sit, sir? You must have questions. I know I do."

She gave a polite bow and stepped forward. Perforce, he fell back, and soon found himself inside a snug room where a bright, crackling fire gave at least the illusion of warmth. Johanna saw them seated at the most private table in the darkest corner of the taverna, regrettably far from the hearth, and the alewife bustled forward with a clay pitcher of mulled wine, two battered but clean pewter mugs and a plate of bread, cheese and olives. Johanna tipped her lavishly, conveying with a jerk of her head the private nature of her business. The alewife, a diplomat in coif and apron, retired behind her serving counter and never looked in their direction again.

Johanna filled their mugs. "My name is Johanna," she said. She held one of the mugs out to him.

He hesitated before accepting it. "Peter," he said eventually.

She raised an eyebrow. "Peter?"

"In Venice," he said, "I am Peter."

She wondered how old he was. In the best Mongol tradition, his face was ageless, the skin smooth, the fold of his eyelids confounding the lines at the corners that might have given her some indication. The countenance he presented was bland, but his eyes, alert and interested, gave him away.

"You recognized the name of Shu Lin," Johanna said. "Perhaps you knew her."

He said nothing.

She fortified herself with a drink. "As I said, I am her granddaughter. She was wife to Ser Polo, who served the Great Khan for twenty years. The gift of her person was a mark of the Khan's favor, or so it is told in my family."

"Is it?"

She felt a spark of anger at his evasion. "It is," she said with emphasis. "From this union came my mother, Shu Ming. She married Wu Li, a merchant of Cambaluc and a friend to Ser Polo. I am their only child."

"Wu Li," he said. "What is any respectable father about, to let you travel unescorted so far from home?"

She smiled a little. "You should talk."

"I am a man," he said, but mildly.

Her smile widened. "You are a Mongol," she said. "You don't make the mistake of underestimating women."

He was surprised into a laugh, turned into a cough.

She let her smile fade. "My father is dead," she said. "As is my mother. I left Cambaluc to travel to the West."

"To find what family remained to you?"

It was at least in part the truth. "Yes," she said.

"Wu Li," he said, musingly. "The son of Wu Hai, perhaps?"

"Yes."

His gaze was straight and piercing. "The Honorable Wu Hai was a great friend of my master."

She felt the knot in her belly begin to ease. "Yes. He married my mother to his son, after my grandmother died."

"Ah," he said. "Shu Lin…"

"…was dead by that time. The circumstances of her death were not… pleasant."

420

Now she had his full attention.

"Explain," he said.

For a servant he possessed a great deal of innate authority. She told the tale without emotion, distant enough from her now that it caused her no pain.

"And Wu Hai turned his wife out of doors for the betrayal of Shu Lin and my master's daughter?"

"His entire household, except his son, my father, whom he married to Shu Ming."

There was silence as Peter the Mongol absorbed this information. "And you wish to see your grandfather."

Her heart seemed to leap into her mouth. She took a deep breath. "I do."

"What do you want from him?" he said. "He lies on his deathbed."

"So I have been told," she said. She sat back in her chair. What did she want from her grandfather? She had traveled almost two thousand leagues to find him. What now did she want to say to this storied man, this legend whose blood she carried in her veins?

"Perhaps," she said slowly, "it is what he might want from me." She met Peter's eyes. "News of his wife and daughter. The knowledge that he has a grandchild."

"He has other grandchildren," Peter said. "And if he would have wanted news of Shu Lin and Shu Ming, he could have sent for it."

She swallowed. He was brutal but he wasn't wrong. "You think he won't want to see me, then?"

"I don't know," he said, surprising her with his frankness. "He is not…" He lingered over his next words. "…himself much of the time now."

Her turn to say nothing.

"But it is possible that his daughter might wish to meet you," he said.

She looked up. "Which one?"

"Moreta," he said, and again his eyes dwelt on her face with something she recognized as fascination. "The youngest daughter, who is still at home." He smiled. "You may find you have something in common."

2

Venice, December, 1323

SHASHA HAD FOUND them a suite of rooms on the first floor of a house on the Rio del Pontego del Tedeschi, midway between the Polo mansion and the Ponte di Rialto, the bridge that crossed the Grand Canal. Jaufre was fairly certain that Shasha's major incentive for hiring these particular rooms was that each one had its own hearth. By far and away their biggest expense so far was fuel, but no one complained. They were all afflicted by the cold.

Shasha had set up a stillroom on the ground floor and was combing the various fairs and markets for herbs new and old. Soon the first floor was perfumed with the aroma of simmering herbs and spices. One thing—possibly the only thing—Venice had for sale at a reasonable price was glass vials and bottles. Shasha bought them in bulk empty and sold them full of lotions, potions and tinctures of her own devising, effective if the traffic through her stillroom was any indication. Hers was a going concern before Christmas.

She and Firas were sharing a room, which surprised no one, not after their reunion in Gaza. "Almost a honeymoon," Jaufre told Johanna, who either ignored or was oblivious to any hidden meaning in the remark. But then Johanna was gone so much of the time those first days in Venice.

Alma and Hayat shared another room, also to no one's surprise. Alma appeared determined to seek out and interrogate every human being with a claim to scholarship, however tenuous, within the authority of the Doge. Her only complaint was the lack of clear skies at night, the worse for astronomical observations. She ran into less opposition because of her sex than Jaufre would have expected. Possibly her harem-cultivated beauty was responsible but he thought that the curiosity that burned with such a genuine fire effectively negated her gender. Certainly she was unstoppable as a seeker after truth, as the philosophers of Venice deemed it to be, and she was rarely turned from their doors.

"She is determined to make up for all the time she lost in the harem," Hayat told him. Hayat's free time was spent in practice with Firas, who had commandeered the attic of their rental for his own private salle and filled it with mats and practice swords and staffs. He was insistent that the group maintain their fighting edge, honed by two years on the Road. They all had bruises, excepting only Alaric, whose Templar training was too well-learned and too long ingrained to allow for dropping his guard now.

Alaric had attached himself and his sword to the salon of an expatriate from Paris, a Messire Roland, who made a good living spanking the young Venetian whelps of wealth and privilege who harbored the laughable illusion that they could wield a sword in workmanlike fashion or, they were soon given to understand, in any fashion at all. Alaric gave lessons in the broadsword and drank his pay in a series of local tavernas, seemingly determined to betray the vows of his former order insofar as temperance and sobriety were concerned. But then the Knights Templar had been disgraced and disbanded and their leaders burned at the stake in Paris almost a decade before, so it wasn't as if he would be damned for it.

Now and then he invited Firas to join him in an exhibition and charged admission. "He is much too fond of his wine," Firas told Jaufre privately.

"I am not his mother," Jaufre said with an edge to his voice.

Firas gave him a keen look from beneath suddenly frowning brows and said no more, leaving Jaufre a little ashamed of his curt reaction.

Hari had gathered up his yellow robe and vanished behind the walls of the San Giorgio Monastery, where he had by means best known to himself become the bosom friend of the abbott. He surfaced occasionally to take tea with his companions, or to stand in rapt witness to one of the many gorgeously-costumed processions to St. Mark's Basilica. He was an object of great curiosity to the children of the city, who would trail in his saffron-clad wake and gather round in an intent and strangely ridicule-free attitude whenever Hari stopped to take speech with anyone he thought looked interesting.

"Which is almost everyone," Félicien said. "No citizen of Venice is safe from our monk." The goliard had taken himself and his lute to the largest of the local inns and was there to be heard singing songs of the Princess Padmini and the night it rained emeralds, and telling floridly embellished tales of the hedonistic life lived in Cambaluc and Kinsai. Very little exaggeration was necessary to enthrall his audience, which swelled as his fame spread. Before long he began to receive invitations for private concerts in canal-side palazzos. "Not since l'Alouette du Sud have I heard such a voice," Jaufre heard one grizzled old Frankish roué claim.

"One would think Venetians would be a little more sophisticated," Félicien told Jaufre when this was reported back to him, "but every fish bites at some bait, I suppose." And spoiled his supercilious tone with a jingling shake of his full purse and a wide grin.

"Who is l'Alouette du Sud?"

Félicien gave an airy wave. "A singer not quite as talented as myself, it would seem."

Jaufre, for his part, had watched the rest of them pursue their various interests only briefly before seeking after his own. He had thought he would do this in company with Johanna, but when he approached her she said, her mouth in a grim line, "I am going to see my grandfather." She was facing him but her gaze was fixed somewhere beyond him. "Although right now I'm going to visit North Wind."

"I could go with you," he said, but she was already out the door, her footsteps moving firmly and briskly away. It took everything in him not to pursue her, but then what would he do if he caught her? She was not someone moved easily from her purpose.

He had loved her for most of his life, this tall, slim, vibrant girl with the long bronze braid and the gray eyes that sparkled with life and the full lips so quick to smile. First their youth and then Edyk the Portuguese had kept her from seeing him as more than a friend and foster brother. But then came that moment in the yurt on the Road when he had watched her finally become aware of him as a man.

And then Gokudo and Ogodei and Sheik Mohammed had conspired to separate them for a year, and Edyk, damn his eyes, had reappeared in Gaza as they were about to take ship for Venice, and yes, he understood that there was unfinished business between them but by all the demons dwelling in the Christian hell, how long was he supposed to wait? There were other women in the world, after all.

But none like Johanna, a voice inside him said.

A voice next to him said, "Patience."

He looked around to see Shasha standing next to him. "Patience," she said again.

"I've been patient," Jaufre said through his teeth. "No one has ever been as patient as I have been." He looked away, the words wrenched out of him. "It's just that...she seems so indifferent, Shasha."

"Not indifferent, Jaufre," his foster sister said. "Just preoccupied. Until this business with her grandfather is settled, she won't have any attention to spare for anything else." She touched his arm. "It's what brought us here, after all. And we did follow her, willingly."

He took in a breath, held it, and then expended it again on a long sigh. "Patience," he said.

"Patience," she said. "For just a little longer."

After all, they both thought, by all reports the old man was dying. How long could he be about it?

"I suppose I could use the time to find us a place to sell our goods," he said. "A storefront on a short lease." He had thought that he would be about that task in company with Johanna, but he was entirely capable of doing so on his own. Entirely.

She smiled, understanding very well his unspoken words. "You could do that. You might want to get to know Venice a little better first. And the Venetians."

He began his research on the docks, watching ships arrive and load and unload. It was one thing to peruse the posted bills of lading. It was another thing to talk to the sailors and the dock-hands who actually laded the cargoes. There was always some master who thought he was smarter than the merchant officers posted the length of the Grand Canal. He was almost invariably wrong, which made for amusing entertainment, but that was another story, too, one fit for one of Félicien's more picaresque stories. Jaufre wanted information, good, solid numbers and facts, and the best facts were those he could observe for himself.

Venice was a city of merchants. Everyone who lived there was a member of or made their living by association to the merchant class. If they weren't shipping, they were buying. If they weren't buying, they were selling. If they weren't selling, they were building ships to transport more goods. Even the omnipresent priests were in business for themselves, selling indulgences or pieces of the True Cross.

Venice sold lumber – what they didn't use themselves at the Arsenal building their own ships – and metal ore, and cured skins. They bought gold and silver from the mines of Germania, or did during the brief lulls between the dynastic skirmishes of the Wittelsbachs and the Hapsburgs, when the trade routes to the mines were safe to travel. They bought as much wool from England as they could and were always clamoring for more, as England, Jaufre soon learned, grew the best quality fleeces. The Venetians bought enormous quantities of fabric from Flanders in multiple weights and a degree of fineness that Venetian weavers would have loved to have woven and sold themselves without recourse to a middleman, but for the scarcity of raw wool. They bought and sold at immense profit luxury items from Constantinople, the storied capital of Byzantium, everything from magnificent pieces of gold jewelry inlaid with enamel and set with gemstones to massive classical statuary that was allegedly antique. "Everything in Byzantium is for sale," one Venetian merchant told Jaufre in a rare moment of expansiveness. "For a price."

There was also, inevitably, a brisk market in slaves, brought to Venice from Gaul and Britannia to be sold to Muslim traders. Most slave auctions were held indoors, due to the inclement winter weather, with only known traders admitted. He had bribed his way into three of these and had bolted from the third auction before it was a quarter over to be sick against the wall of the auction building. He straightened, trembling, gulping in fresh air, or air as fresh as Venice could provide.

He thought he had made his peace with never seeing his mother again. His mother, captured by slavers when their caravan had been attacked on the Road between Kashgar and Yarkent when he was just ten years old. His father had been killed protecting Jaufre, and his mother, along with all the other women of the caravan, had been kidnapped and sold in Kashgar. Jaufre had spent a lifetime looking for her. She would be in her forties now, if she were even still alive. She had been beautiful, he thought, although he knew a child's memories of a beloved parent were always suspect. He hoped, fervently, that they did not lie in this instance, because beauty invariably fetched a higher price in the slave market, and a higher price meant better treatment.

He suddenly wanted Johanna beside him with a ferocity that eclipsed all else. She alone understood. She alone could offer him comfort. She alone would have flayed him living for attending the slave auction in the first place.

"Are you all right, young sir?"

He turned to see an attractive young woman wearing a servant's coif and carrying a basket over her arm. Her eyes were kindly and concerned. And appreciative in spite of his condition.

Wrong woman, wrong time, wrong place. "Thank you, mistress," he said, trying to look as if he were. "Something I ate."

"Or drank?" she said, and shook her head with a smile. "There is a well around the corner, open to all. Rinse out your mouth and wash your face." She rummaged in her basket and presented him with a handful of leaves. "And chew these afterward."

She went off, and he became aware of the smell of mint rising up from his hand.

He did as he was bid and then forced himself to concentrate on the rest of what was on offer on the Rialto. Venice had no land to cultivate, and so imported everything it ate and drank and wore. Vegetables, meat and grain came from Tuscany, brought daily by boat from the port of Mira. Venetians made the best bread he'd ever eaten, as evidenced by the multiple bakers' carts clustered together in St. Mark's Square, but they grew none of their own grain. A glass industry thrived on Murano, one of the other islands in the lagoon, but they exported the best of what was produced there and drank Nebbiolo imported from Valtellina in thick, heavy-bottomed mugs made of a glass so impure it was barely translucent. Shasha's vials and bottles, he remembered, were serviceable, not exemplars of the glassblowers' craft. The cloth that came in bolts from Flanders, the tailors and sempstresses of Venice labored long into the night making into richly embroidered robes for Venetian patrons. Very little of the finer cloth imported to the island city made it off the wharf again.

There appeared to be a street market somewhere in the city every day of the week, not to mention a fair celebrating either a saint's day, some of the more obscure events from the 1204 Venetian sack of Byzantium that resulted in the four bronze horses on top of St. Mark's, or the arrival of just about any ship bearing goods for sale. Jaufre thought of the Kashgar market, held at the eastern edge of the Pamir Mountains every Sunday since the birth of Mohammed, but only every Sunday. Venice was one entire city-sized market, a trading fair open every day of the week, dawn to well past dusk, including saint's days as celebrated by the local church. Indeed, the church was one of the Venetian merchants' best customers, an inexhaustible purchaser of silken vestments, gold plate, incense, and the knucklebones of saints. If Christ had had as many fingers as Jaufre had seen for sale between the Holy Land and the Grand Canal, He would have had more arms than the Hindi goddess Durga.

He kept that last observation strictly to himself. Venice was also a city of churches, sporting on average one per canal, and everyone went to church at least on Sundays and many of them attended services once a day. Jaufre, accustomed to Persian cities dotted with mosque towers issuing forth the call to prayer five times a day, still had never encountered such a priest-ridden society. He minded his manners, and enjoined his companions to do the same. Félicien emphatically endorsed this warning, and even Alaric bestirred himself enough to say, "Best to draw no attention our way, of any kind, religious or not."

If you were not in a mood to buy or sell, a very rare occurrence in Venice, there was plenty more to keep you entertained. Along with the usual puppet shows and dancing troupes and singing groups, Jaufre saw a man juggle flaming brands while walking on tall sticks. Another man swallowed a sword, and a third put his head into a lion's mouth, although the lion had no teeth left to speak of and seemed supremely disinterested in anything but the next gobbet of meat thrown his way. There was an elephant tethered on one of the few green spaces of Venice, down by the Arsenal, upon which his owner sold rides for a bit of silver. There wasn't a line. In a large cage on the Grand Canal, near St. Mark's, you could pay to watch an enormous snake unhinge its jaws to swallow his prey, usually a stray cat someone threw into the cage. It inspired only revulsion, and a futile wish to rescue the cat.

After a week of sightseeing he went looking for a storefront. He quickly discovered that rents for commercial property in Venice were astronomical. Rooms the size of a shoebox looking out on the Grand Canal rented per month the equivalent of a round-trip passage to the Holy Land. Chastened, he readjusted his ambitions and was rewarded by a literal hole in the wall half-way between their lodgings and the Rialto bridge. Two wooden flaps comprised a wall that separated the stall from the street. The top half opened upward and was held up by a wooden pole to form a roof. The bottom half folded in half to form a counter, hinged on one side and latched on the other so he could get in and out. Both folded back into the wall and could be locked by means of a substantial wrought iron hasp. His first purchase was a bronze padlock with a key the size of his eating knife. He didn't know how effective the combination would be at keeping out burglars but it was certainly ornamental.

The street wasn't a main thoroughfare, and his new neighbors were merchants in only a small way, but there was a promising bustle to the foot traffic, and there was a taverna four doors down that offered a superior daily special, usually featuring chicken, some of Venice's excellent bread, and a variety of noodles that reminded him very little of the noodles he had eaten daily in Cambaluc but were indisputably noodles nonetheless.

Empty, with his arms extended straight out he could almost touch both walls of the space. He laid one of their precious Kerman carpets on the floor, hung a few oil lamps chosen for their clear glass lenses, and filled the three walls with shelves. He spent the next two days hauling and displaying all of their trade goods.

When he was done he stood back and looked at the result with a pride tinged with regret. They had had a half a dozen camels loaded with trade goods acquired between Cambaluc and Kashgar during their time with Uncle Cheng's caravan. All but one had been lost to Sheik Mohammed's forces, who had ambushed them on the trail down from Terak Pass, with the tacit aid of that renegade Mongol general, Ogodei. Who might, from the latest reports, be knocking next at the doors of Baghdad.

He rearranged a few things on the display shelves, the better to catch the eye. When he had been healthy enough he had acquired another half-dozen camels in the Kabul livestock market, and they had bought and sold from their backs from the Hindu Kush to Gaza. There were papyri, manuscripts and books bought in half a dozen cities across Persia. There were small, exquisitely made silver pocket knives from Damascus. There were strings of smooth malachite beads glowing with green and cream striations from Baghdad. There was a pile of intricately woven, brightly colored carpets from Kerman, a smaller pile than he would have liked but their quality instantly recognizable to the educated eye. Jaufre was determined to sell to none other, which was why the rugs were the most expensive items in his store. To alert shoppers to his most valuable commodity, he hung a wooden sign that jutted out at right angles from the wall that displayed a gaudy carpet with tassels on both ends, painted for him by Alma, who was enthusiastic enough with the gilt so as to make the sign very nearly glow in the dark. Jaufre was sure this was what had caused the first sign to be stolen the first night it was hung. The second sign was more restrained.

There were a few of the bright copper pots and pans left from the smiths of Kabul, those that Shasha had not given as thank-you gifts to hosts who had shown them hospitality on the Road. Jaufre regretted the loss of trade goods but never questioned Shasha's decision to do so.

He half turned, as if to say to Johanna, "Remember Bastak, the town we came to, the one after the bandits ambushed us in the pass?" And then he remembered that Johanna had not been with them during that adventure, that she had indeed been on an adventure of her own, one that resulted in a woman he barely recognized.

She wasn't here with him now, either. His lips tightened, and he deliberately turned his back on that thought. He folded his hands and smiled at the small, curious crowd that had gathered as it became evident he was about to open for business. "Good gentles, step forward, please. I am Jaufre of Cambaluc, and I bring goods to you from Damascus, from Kashgar, from beyond the fabled walls of Cambaluc itself." And with a sweep of his hand, "I am happy to answer all your questions, for truly a fascinating story lays behind every object you see here."

The story was always what put the sale over the top, and productive of stories in return, which were always useful. The more they learned about this new continent they had traveled to, the better able they would be to navigate it safely. "Yes, madam? Ah, that item, yes. It is a seal from ancient times. Indeed, madam, it is in truth a seal, the personal seal of a priestess of Memphis. Allow me to show you." He flattened a lump of damp clay and rolled the tiny cylinder in it, pressing firmly and allowing only one rotation. "You see? A goddess with a lamb at her feet...Yes, indeed, it is very tiny."

The woman, too vain to admit she couldn't see details that small, was convinced by the admiring murmur of her fellow shoppers. She bought the seal as a gift for her mother and went on her way rejoicing. Others immediately stepped up to take her place.

3
Venice, December, 1323

"THE YOUNGEST DAUGHTER, *who is still at home,*" Peter had said. "*You may find you have something in common.*"

Like a face, Johanna thought.

They met at the taverna where she had met with Peter the first time. It was convenient for both their lodgings and the alewife remained as professionally disinterested in her clientele as she had been previously.

Moreta Polo sat across the table looking as startled as Johanna felt. The other woman was older than she was, shorter than she was, her hair was darker and straighter and her eyes were brown, all of which Johanna found comforting, because otherwise any third party looking on would have called them sisters. The same straight nose, the same high cheekbones, the same wide mouth, the same firm chin. Moreta's skin was pale and creamy where Johanna's was a faint gold, and Johanna's teeth were better, but for the rest...

"No wonder you looked at me so oddly when we met," she said to Peter.

Peter was sitting back from the table with his arms folded, his expression a carefully maintained blankness.

The other woman found her voice. "Of all my father's fabulous fables," she said to Peter, "of course this was the one he chose to leave out. It is so like him."

"You believe I am who I say I am?" Johanna said.

Marco Polo's daughter looked at Marco Polo's grand-daughter again. Moreta wore a loose gray wool dress with a wide belt heavily embroidered in gilt thread with beautifully wrought flowers and leaves. Her cloak was hooded and though she drew the hood back from her face the better to see, she did not remove the hood entirely against the unlikely event someone might recognize her. She had also, Johanna noted, taken care to sit with her back to the room.

When Moreta didn't speak, Johanna said, "My name is Wu Johanna. I come from Cambaluc. Your father is my grandfather." She folded her hands on the table, sat back and waited. Almost she bristled, but not quite.

Moreta gulped, unused to such plain dealing. She fidgeted with her mug, toyed with a piece of cheese, and looked up. When she spoke, Johanna's singer's ear noticed that her voice was pitched much as Johanna's was, low for a woman but clear. "I would think that anyone looking at us would know we were somehow related." She saw Johanna's surprise, and Johanna was surprised further at the gleam of mischief she saw in Moreta's eyes. "What, did you expect me to deny you? It would be hard to do, on the face of it."

Her small joke made Johanna smile. "It would," she said.

"You are definitely a Polo," Moreta said. "There is a resem-blance, even, between you and my sisters." She hesitated. In a softer voice, she said, "Is it all true, then?"

"Is what true?"

Moreta gestured. "All of it. His travels. The tales he told in his book." She shrugged. "A city of twelve thousand bridges."

Venice had only a little over three hundred. "Kinsai," Johanna said. "A city south of Cambaluc. I haven't personally counted all of its bridges myself, but it has a lot of them. Canals, too."

"Girls who dive for pearls, off the shores of some island nation in the East?"

"I have dived with them myself," Johanna said.

435

Moreta raised a skeptical eyebrow.

Johanna shrugged. "I dove with the pearl fishers of Cipangu. I even brought back pearls. No, before you ask, I can't prove it. You either believe me or you don't."

The other woman gave what she probably thought was a surreptitious once-over. Venice was cosmopolitan enough that Johanna was able to wear her own clothes with a cloak overall, but Moreta Polo was probably thinking that a woman in trousers who wore a knife in her belt would be capable of anything. "Dog-headed men?" she said tentatively.

"I don't know where he got that," Johanna said. "I've never seen any dog-headed men myself. I've been reading his book for the first time recently, and—"

"You hadn't read it before?"

"I didn't even know it existed until two months ago," Johanna said. "What he says he actually saw himself seems accurate. It's when he starts repeating what someone else has told him that he gets into trouble."

Moreta sipped her beer. "When he was still able to go out," she said, "people would laugh at him behind his back. Children would follow him, calling him names. 'Milione! Milione!'" She looked up. "You know what they meant?"

"A thousand lies," Johanna said. "Or something like that. A play on the title of his book. They called him that in the streets?"

Moreta nodded. "More or less." She reached for a piece of cheese and folded a piece of bread around it, concentrating on the task with all her attention. "You appear to have traveled a great deal."

"My father was a trader. My mother and I traveled the Road with him."

"The Road?"

"All the roads, east and west, north and south of Cambaluc. Or Cathay, you call it here. There are many, east to Cipangu, south to Ceylon, north to Khuree where the khans hold their summer courts. East to Kashgar. And Venice."

"And you got to go with him." There was envy in Moreta's voice. "I've never been out of Venice." She must have seen pity in Johanna's eyes, because she squared her shoulders and ate an olive. "Could you," she said, and stopped. "Would you mind telling me about your grandmother?"

Johanna raised an eyebrow. "Your father's first wife, do you mean?" she said pointedly, and then was sorry when Moreta blushed. She had dumped herself on the woman without warning, had removed her from the side of her father's deathbed, no less, and had received nothing but courtesy in return. She refilled their mugs from the jug and sat back. "I never knew her. She died when my mother was very young." She took a deep breath and let it out slowly. "She was a gift from her father to the Great Khan, Kublai Khan. The Khan in turn gave her to your father." She saw the appalled look in Moreta's eyes and said without emotion, "It was the custom once a year for the barons to send their most beautiful maidens to the Great Khan. It was a measure of how high your father stood in the Khan's favor, that he would receive such a gift. It was the greatest of honors." She drank warmed wine to moisten a mouth suddenly dry. "When he left Cathay, it was to escort a princess to her marriage with a Levantine prince. The Khan would not allow Shu Lin—"

"That was her name?"

"Yes, Shu Lin. Her daughter, my mother, was named Shu Ming. Your father was a favorite of the Khan, so the Khan held Shu Lin and Shu Ming as hostage against his return. Wu Hai, a merchant of Cambaluc, was a great friend to your father, and agreed to take them into his own house until he, Marco, could send for them."

"What happened?"

Johanna didn't look at Peter. "The Khan was ill when your father left. When he died, there was the usual scramble for power. Which always involves treachery and betrayal of some kind, which is always visited upon the most innocent of victims. Shu Lin… died. Wu Hai married Shu Ming to his own son to protect her."

Moreta digested this. "And you are their child."

"Yes."

"And my father's grandchild."

"Yes."

Moreta shredded a piece of bread into crumbs, and spoke without looking up. "Peter says you want to see him."

Johanna's heart missed a beat. "I think the question is more, does he want to see me?"

Moreta sat up, as if she had made a decision. "He's very... fragile, at the moment." She hesitated. "He is as much out of his senses as he is in them, these days." Her eyes met Johanna's. "But you should see him. And he should see you." She glanced at Peter, who had sat silent throughout their conversation. "It will not be easy. My mother—"

Something shifted behind Peter's eyes.

"Yes," Moreta said, "my mother will be difficult."

Johanna mentioned nothing of the midwife's tales. "But not impossible?"

Moreta's chin firmed. "No. Not impossible."

✠

Johanna watched Moreta and Peter vanishing into the fog that had shrouded the city in a mournful, dripping blanket, before turning to wend her way homeward herself. She was checked by a wraith the size of a half-measure of oats, who materialized out of the mist and fixed her with an accusing stare.

"Girl, you are an afreet in the flesh," Johanna said.

"I don't know what that is," the girl said, her glower melting the fog between them, "but it doesn't sound very complimentary."

"It's not," Johanna said, beginning to walk.

"I expect to be paid for today, even if you already found the people you were looking for."

"Of course." She dredged up a saying Hari had picked up in the Holy Land. "The laborer is worthy of her hire."

"What's that mean?"

"It means you labored for me, I owe you, I'll pay." Johanna dug around in her pocket and produced two silver pennies. She hesitated before dropping them into the outstretched palm. "Where do you rest tonight?"

The glower became even more pronounced. "I live at home."

"Yes."

"With my parents."

"Oh, yes?"

The girl looked away. "Well, with my father. My mother died when I was born."

"Oh."

"My father says it's my fault."

Johanna was silent, and something in the quality of her silence seemed to compel the girl to say more.

"He can't bear the sight of me."

"I'm sure that's not true."

The girl shrugged. "He tells me so often enough."

"So you sleep in the streets."

"Sometimes."

Johanna stopped in front of their lodgings. "How about tonight, you don't?"

✝

For a wonder, everyone was home for dinner, even including Hari.

"And who is this?" Shasha said

"This is—" Johanna looked down at the girl. "What is your name?"

The girl hesitated. "Tiphaine."

"Tiphaine," Johanna said, sounding out the three syllables.

The girl nodded, looking a little sullen, as if she had only accidentally told the truth and already regretted it.

"Well then, Tiphaine, these are my companions. This is Shasha, my foster sister, and Jaufre, my foster brother. Here is Alaric the Frank, and Firas the—Firas of the Alamut, and Félicien the goliard. Hari is a chughi, a priest in his own country, and here are Alma and Hayat, scholars of Persia. This is Tiphaine, everyone. She has come to share our meal."

Shasha looked at Jaufre and rolled her eyes behind Johanna's back. He grinned, but said to Tiphaine, "I hope you're hungry. Shasha always cooks enough for a cohort." He found her a bowl and a spoon, ladled in a generous helping of chicken stew thick with root vegetables and gravy, and cut her a chunk of the hearty bread still warm from the baker's oven two doors away. And then everyone pretended not to notice as the girl pretended not to wolf it down. She managed to wait until everyone else had at least gotten their spoons dirty before she looked instinctively at Shasha for permission, who smiled and nodded at the kettle. Tiphaine refilled her bowl to the brim. That disappeared a little more slowly. The third bowl she slowed down enough to actually taste the ingredients. "Good," she said.

Shasha cut her another thick slice of bread and handed it over without comment.

✝

In the middle of the night Johanna felt the call of nature and reached under the bed for the chamber pot. Instead she found herself clutching a handful of hair, which squealed in a distressing manner. "What—?"

There was a quivering silence, and then a small voice said crankily, "It's Tiphaine. Who else?"

Johanna realized she was still holding on to the girl's hair and let go. "I didn't hear you come in." In fact, she distinctly remembered the girl taking her leave of them after dinner. She felt for the pouch beneath her pillow. The hard shapes of her father's book and bao reassured her through the soft leather. "We locked the door behind you. How did you get back in?"

The girl snorted. "You call that a lock?" There was an ostentatious rustle as she flounced in place on the floor and began to breathe heavily through her nose.

The next morning Johanna found Tiphaine curled up in bed next to her, her face looking younger than ever beneath its layer of grime.

Everyone was poker-faced as they broke their fast the next morning, but Johanna noticed that no one left before they saw what happened next.

"How long have you lived in Venice, Tiphaine?"

The girl crammed another fistful of last night's bread into her mouth and spoke indistinctly around it. "All my life. I was born here."

"So you know it well?"

The dark eyes flashed. "There is no one who knows it better!"

"And the people who live here?"

The small but defiant chin raised. "Point to anyone on any street and I will tell you their name and the names of their parents and where they live and where their parents live and what house they look to and what they had for dinner." She met Johanna's mild look with a challenging stare.

Johanna held her gaze for a long moment, and then turned to look at Shasha, who sighed but was not entirely successful at hiding the smile tugging at the corners of her mouth. "Does the child have a home? Parents?"

"She claims a father." Johanna looked back at Tiphaine. "Well?"

The small face looked mutinous.

"If we're going to take you on as—" Johanna cast about in her mind for an appropriate job title "—courier, your father will naturally want to see that all the appropriate requirements are met."

The small brow wrinkled. "Courier?"

"Dragoman. Messenger." Tiphaine's face remained blank and Johanna said, "Page?" Although she was not entirely certain pages existed outside royal courts.

But Tiphaine's face cleared. "Page," she said. "I could be your page."

"But we cannot offer you employment without your father's permission," Johanna said.

✝

It was one of the darker, dirtier dwellings in one of the darker, dirtier sections of Venice, near a defunct foundry off the Rio della Misericordia. Leftover slag from the foundry's workings was piled everywhere and it was impossible to walk there without collecting soot to your knees.

Tiphaine's father worked out of a storefront that made Jaufre's look palatial by comparison, located beneath the surface of the street, reached by steep, narrow steps that looked hand-hewn and which were difficult to negotiate because of the jumble of what might have been merchandise and what might have been trash piled everywhere. The one window was boarded over. The wooden door was so warped it was hard to see how it could close.

There was a front room for business and a back room for living, if you could call it that, as it consisted of a single pallet, a brazier with one broken leg propped on a cobblestone, and a saucepan that looked as if it hadn't been washed since the birth of Christ. The piles of goods continued inside, some stacked so haphazardly that they stepped warily in case of an accidental avalanche. There were bales of faded and tattered clothes, pots and pans strung together by their handles, dull knives and a box of wooden, bronze, and silver spoons thinned from years of use. One corner was devoted to remnants of what might once have been books, loose stacks of pages in a higgledy-piggledy heap. Jaufre could smell the mold coming off them from three feet away, and kept his distance. Other items were less identifiable.

Some attempt had been made to lighten the dark interior with lamps, but they were so few in number and like the saucepan had not been recently—if ever—cleaned that Johanna could barely make out the gentleman who stood inside. He said something brusquely in a language previously unknown to her, and Tiphaine answered in kind, indicating Johanna with the wave of a hand. "This is Mordecai the Jew, my father," she said, and stepped back, Jaufre thought not coincidentally out of the reach of her father's arm.

The old man, bearded and filthy and who simply could not be as old as he looked and have fathered a child Tiphaine's age, looked at Jaufre and said in roughly accented Italian, "My daughter says you wish to take her as your servant."

"I do," Johanna said.

"She is healthy and strong and not uncomely," the man said to Jaufre. "How much will you pay?"

Johanna felt Jaufre go rigid next to her and dropped a warning hand to his arm. "She is very small to be so strong," she said mildly, and named a price. This provoked the usual outrage. Fierce bidding culminated in coins exchanged, Johanna somewhat hampered with producing them by the restraining hand she must at all costs keep on Jaufre's arm. She produced a document that laid out the terms of Tiphaine's employment, on which Mordecai would not place his mark until she produced another coin, and they were done.

"Get your things," Johanna told Tiphaine.

"There is nothing here I want or need," Tiphaine said, and led the way out the door and up the stairs, as careful to kick everything off the steps on the way up as she had been careful not to kick anything off on the way down. At no time during the meeting had Mordecai looked directly at his daughter. He made no farewell to her now, nor she to him.

Halfway home she said suddenly, apparently to no one, "It would have been better if my mother had lived."

Another bridge, another canal, and she said, "It would have been different if I'd been a boy."

And that was the last word Tiphaine ever said about her family.

✝

Scrubbed (a process Tiphaine vociferously resisted, right up until the moment Shasha picked her up bodily and deposited her into the tub), her hair ruthlessly combed (her eyes were watering by the time Shasha had judged her curls were in as much order as was possible), and clad in new skirt, tunic and belt, with a new cloak overall and sturdy, made-to-order boots on her feet, Tiphaine looked like a new and far more respectable person, but she was still dissatisfied, apparently. She fussed at the shoulder of her tunic, and looked at all their tunics one by one with a gathering frown.

"What?" Johanna said, inclined to be amused rather than annoyed. Certainly the girl's spirit had not been broken by her unfortunate beginnings. "What are we missing here?"

Tiphaine pressed her lips together but couldn't hold it back. "You—we have no badge."

"Badge?" Johanna said, repressing a smile at the girl's quick correction.

"House badge. A—an emblem that signifies what house or company we belong to."

There was a brief silence. "She's right," Jaufre said slowly. He looked at Johanna. "Almost everyone who comes to my stall and certainly every male wears a badge of some sort sewn to their clothing."

"The Venetians only?"

He thought about it, and shook his head. "Sometimes it signifies what ship's company the wearer belongs to. The Doge's guards have uniforms, of course. A few of the nobles' servants have livery, but not all."

"It's customary," Félicien said. "Everywhere, for soldiers' companies, craft guilds, city officials."

"An identifier," Shasha said, nodding. "Something that will show the authorities we have friends, should one of us get into trouble."

Jaufre didn't look at Alaric, who would have been voted most likely of their group to get into trouble. Alaric, as usual looking

444

a little hungover, was hunched over his morning tea as if it were his last hope of survival and was not thus far contributing to the conversation. "And it'll help us fit in," Jaufre said. "If everyone wears a badge, we should wear a badge, too."

Johanna looked at Tiphaine and smiled. "Well, you've started something now. What kind of a badge should we have?"

"Bright colors," the girl said instantly. "That you can see from across the street."

"Just colors?"

"No," she said. "There should be a shape, an animal or a— a tool."

The discussion which followed lasted over three days and was the subject of vigorous debate. Everyone had an opinion. Alaric surfaced long enough to say it should be a sword crossed on a shield. No, Félicien said, everyone would think they were a mercenary company, arms for sale. A lyre, he said, that was the thing, or a harp. Or perhaps both. Or maybe a flute, everyone recognized a flute. So they were a troupe of jongleurs now, Alaric said. He'd brush up on his tumbling.

They decided on red and yellow for colors since they were the imperial colors of Cambaluc, the pigments were easily obtained and they were bright enough to satisfy Tiphaine, who seemed to be in charge. Images suggested for the figure ranged from Alaric's sword to Félicien's harp to Shasha's suggestion of a willow leaf. "You've all been dosed with it enough times," she said. Alma suggested a quill pen, Hayat a dagger, and Johanna, of course, held out for a white horse at full gallop. Which would be fine if they were a guild of ostlers, Alaric said.

"Why not a sun?" Hari said one evening. "It shines down upon us all."

"Not in Venice," Jaufre and Johanna said in the same moment. They smiled at each other.

"Ordinary," Alma said, without much feeling one way or the other.

"Universal," Hari said.

445

"It doesn't mean anything," Félicien said, frowning.

"Inoffensive," Hari said.

"Simple to draw," Hayat said.

"Easy to recognize at a distance," Alma said.

"And leaves the center free for any additions we might like to add later on," Shasha said thoughtfully.

"Um," Tiphaine said.

They looked at her and she flushed. "Oftentimes we are made to wear a gold star on our clothing," she said.

"A gold star?"

"Who's we?"

"Jews," Tiphaine said.

It took a moment for everyone's ideas to readjust. "And that would be bad," Jaufre said slowly.

"Jews are held to be…"

"Unclean," Alaric said, almost with relish. "They killed Christ our Lord."

Tiphaine glared at him.

Alaric bristled. "They did crucify him. It says so in the Bible, which is the word of God made manifest on this earth."

"'Away with him: Away with him: Crucify him. Pilate saith to them: shall I crucify your king?'" Félicien's voice was soft. "'The chief priests answered: We have no king but Caesar.'"

"And that makes Jews the whipping boy wherever Christ is worshipped?" Johanna said.

Félicien glanced at Tiphaine and nodded.

"Sunnis and Shias," Hayat said with a sigh. Tiphaine looked up, surprised, and Alma said, "Both of Islam, but they follow different prophets descended from Mohammed."

"Which means they can and do kill each other for any reason," Alma said.

"Or none at all," Hayat said.

"All heathens," Alaric said, but without heat.

"Does that mean—" Tiphaine hesitated. Her face was pale and she looked strained.

"What?"

The girl sat up straight, firmed an already firm jaw and glared at Johanna. "Does that mean I can't stay?"

Johanna smiled at her. "Do I not hold your contract?"

Everyone looked away as the girl collected herself. She spoke first. "Very well," she said, very businesslike. "Not a sun, because it looks too much like a star. What, then?"

Johanna looked at Shasha and then at Jaufre, and they knew before she said it. "This," she said, and opened the leather purse that was always at her waist. She produced a rectangular rod half a handspan long and a small round pot, both carved from dark green jade. Alma found a scrap of vellum and Johanna uncapped the pot, revealing a red paste, a little dry and flaking after two years of disuse. She touched the end of the cylinder into the paste and pressed it against the vellum. She held up the result for everyone to see. "Three Chinese characters," she said. "My family name, and the character for trader, and the character for honest. It was my father's bao. You would say, seal." She frowned down at the imprint. Mandarin characters were not known for their simplicity or lack of flourish. "Perhaps one of the characters would be enough. 'Honest,' or 'trader.'"

"Trader," Jaufre said.

It felt right to all of them, even Alaric, and Alma was put in charge of construction with Tiphaine supervising. The resulting badges were of calfskin scraped thin, cut into circles and dyed red. Alma embroidered each badge with their device in gold silk, and sewed them to everyone's outer garments. They looked good, distinctive and professional, and very shiny.

"When someone asks us who we look to, what do we say?" Tiphaine said. When no one answered she said, spacing the words out as if speaking to the very slow of wit, "What is our name? The name of our compagnia? Someone is bound to ask."

Johanna looked at her and said, "Sometimes I think I might have made a mistake, hiring you on."

The girl gave an impudent grin. "You know I'm right."

...rtunately, and dreaded more days of wrangling.

"...wu Company," Jaufre said. He looked at Johanna and raised an eyebrow.

She looked at Shasha, who smiled. Johanna blinked away unexpected tears. "Wu Company it is."

Tiphaine wasn't finished. "And what does our compagnia do?"

Johanna's eyes roamed over the members of the company. Two traders, a healer and cook, an assassin, a knight, a monk, a goliard, an amateur astronomer and her what? Assistant? Guard? Companion? Lover? All of the above. And now, a page. "Anything anyone will pay us for," she said, and smiled. "Short of robbery and murder."

4

Venice, winter, 1323–1324

Tiphaine's first task in her official capacity as Wu Company's page was to carry messages between Johanna and Moreta. She and Peter would meet as they browsed the goods in Jaufre's shop, or when Ca' Polo sent for medicinal herbs which Moreta now purchased from Shasha and had delivered by Tiphaine.

Shasha was beginning to make a modest name for herself as an herbalist, to the point that the line of people trailing down the street from their lodgings provoked a complaint from their landlord. Jaufre found her a space one canal down where she set up shop and where the line became even longer. Firas unilaterally dedicated himself Shasha's deputy and took on the task of assessing injuries and disease in order of necessity. There was a boy with a broken arm, accompanied by his mother. There was a young woman who wouldn't meet anyone's eye and who wouldn't talk to anyone except Shasha and who would only talk to her alone. There was a leper swathed in bandages and a blue robe, which failed to hide that he was in the last stages of that dread disease. There was a tall man with a wispy beard, an angry boil on his left buttock and the melancholy air of one to whom disaster and disappointment were boon companions. "He reminds me of Alaric," Shasha said to Firas.

There were also the usual tittering girls looking for love potions and the men looking for spells to curse their neighbors' crops. One woman was so insistent that Firas finally said solemnly, "They say that if a woman spits three times into the face of a frog, that she will never conceive again," and watched with some satisfaction as the woman immediately adjourned, presumably to the nearest swamp. He wished he could have followed her, just to watch.

The rest Firas purged from the line of prospective patients with smart dispatch and a pithy reminder that Shasha was a healer, not a sorcerer. The last thing they needed in Venice was a reputation for witchcraft.

He dealt with the leper more gently. "Then you cannot help me?" the leper said, his mouth hidden by the stained cloth wrapped around his face.

"No," Firas said. "Allah will decide when to call you to him, my friend. Leave that decision to Him."

"He has had little enough time to spare for me so far," the leper replied, and left on what remained of his heavily wrapped feet.

For a man with a runny nose and a cough Shasha prescribed sage leaves, rubbed and placed inside the nostrils. A housewife had cut her hand on a knife, and Shasha stopped the bleeding with an application of cobwebs.

The boy's injury was more serious. Both bones in his lower left arm were protruding through the skin, the ends fractured. The skin around them was already dark red and hot to the touch. He was in great pain, although he bore it better than his mother did. Shasha soaked a sponge in a distillation of herbs and placed it over the boy's nose. A few moments later, the strain eased from his face and he slid into unconsciousness.

His mother tried for the sponge for herself. Shasha slapped her hand away without looking up, manipulated the bones back into place, splinted the arm and bound it firmly. She measured out ground willow bark. "He will have a fever," she told his mother. She placed a hand on the boy's forehead, which already felt too warm. "Make him a clear broth and put a pinch of this into the bowl, morning, noon and night. Do not give him solid food, no meat, no bread, until the fever goes away. Only liquids, watered wine, small beer, broth. A little warmed mead in the evening, if your purse runs to it. Do you understand?" The mother nodded, but Shasha repeated her instructions once more to be sure. "If the wound begins to smell bad, if the skin of his arm turns dark, you must bring him back at once."

She and Firas stood watching the woman walk away, packet clutched in one sweaty hand and all her anxious attention on the face of the boy in her arms. "The wound is already infected," Shasha said. "That arm will very probably have to come off."

There were cripples who begged in every market place, using their lost sight or lost limbs to fill their bowls with alms. It was not a future either of them would wish on anyone, let alone the brave little boy who had just left them.

"I could use some puppy tongues," Shasha said.

Firas looked at her. "What?"

"The tongues of dogs have special properties. They heal their own wounds by licking them. Often dried puppy tongues, ground to powder and sprinkled on the wound of a man or a woman, will heal it as well."

"And am I supposed to find these puppies, kill them, and remove their tongues for you?"

"Yes," she said. She stretched the kinks out of her back. Firas kneaded her shoulders and knuckled the muscles down either side of her spine, and she groaned her relief.

"Well, then," Firas said. "Are we done raising the dead for today?"

"Mistress," a voice said.

They turned to see the tall man with the boil. He'd propped himself up against the outside wall of the house because he was unable to sit, Shasha remembered. "Ah yes, the boil," she said. Like most healers she had a tendency to call people by their afflictions. "Come inside."

451

He followed them inside the stall with a halting gait.

"Drop your hose," Shasha said, "and bend over."

With the air of one inured to indignity, he did so. The boil was the size of a large grape. Shasha stood well back when she lanced it, and as a result got very little of the resulting expulsion of pus on her apron. She stepped forward again to press gentle fingers against the dark, angry skin around the boil until the flow of pus and serum was replaced with good red blood.

"That hurts," the man said, more in resignation than in distress.

"I know," Shasha said. "It can't be helped." The wound drained, she applied a paste made of turmeric and a square patch of clean cloth that stuck to the paste. "Try not to dislodge the dressing, and try to keep your weight off that cheek for the next few days."

The man stood up and pulled his hose up over his buttocks in gingerly fashion. "I thank you for your care, mistress." He indicated his worn appearance. "As you might expect, I cannot pay you." He nodded at the taverna down the street. "I serve at that establishment. The owner is a woman of generous heart. May I offer you a mug?"

"Are we done?" Shasha asked Firas. He nodded.

Jaufre, home from work, met them at the door. "Where's Johanna?" he said, his inevitable greeting.

"With North Wind," was the invariable reply, and he accompanied them to the taverna. Hari, sighted on the street with his usual comet's tail of children, was hailed and joined them. It was a bustling place: a low, dark, rectangular room with a fat woman sweating in front of a large fireplace as she wielded a wooden paddle to slide round loaves of bread from a cavernous brick oven, an even fatter man dispensing enormous tankards of ale from a succession of barrels, and what was obviously their daughter. She had neither the size of her father nor the heft of her mother but had ample charms for all that, well displayed in a red gown cut low over her breasts and of a length that flirted with her ankles. She served them ale and tiny cakes made of very thin pastry layered with honey and crushed almonds. Shasha took careful note of the construction and the ingredients.

"Allow me to introduce myself," said the man, with as much dignity as he could perched half on and half off the bench. "I am Jean de Valmy, born in Provence of Alys d'Arly and Didier de Valmy. My parents died when I was very young, and I was apprenticed to the Knights Templar."

They introduced themselves, and Jaufre was niggled by the certainty that he had seen Jean de Valmy before.

"Your eyes," Jean de Valmy said hesitantly to Shasha.

"These are how eyes are made where I come from," she said.

"And where would that be?"

"Cathay."

"Cathay!" Jean de Valmy's eyes lit up. "Is it true that jewels rain from the skies in Cathay?"

"Only when the moon is full for the second time in a month," Shasha said gravely. "The next morning one must wade through emeralds ankle deep. It's a nuisance to clean up and very hard on the street sweepers, who receive an extra ration of wine that day for their trouble."

Jean de Valmy eyed her uncertainly, and she relented. "People in Cathay are born, and marry, and have children, and worship, and honor their ancestors, and visit tavernas very like this one, and eat cakes and drink wine with their friends, and grow wheat for bread, and pay taxes, and eventually die, just as the people do here." She smiled. "Our eyes are differently made." We certainly bathe more frequently, she thought but didn't say.

Jean de Valmy considered her for a moment longer, and turned to Hari. "And yourself? I see your eyes are different even from your companion's."

"Ah," Hari said, and Shasha settled back to enjoy herself as she always did when the subject of Hari's background came up, as it was never told the same way twice.

He did not disappoint her this time, either. "I was born to my mother, whose name I do not know, to a father who never knew me, many thousands of leagues distant, on the banks of the Ganges, one of the four great rivers of the world, and the spiritual home of my people."

"Who are your people?"

"We are chughi. We live long, doing little, seeing much, shunning possessions, increasing our knowledge of life so that one day we may ascend to the next level."

"The next level of what?"

"Of consciousness."

"You're awake now," Jean de Valmy pointed out.

Hari smiled again and finished his wine. "There is awake, and there is awake, my friend."

Jean de Valmy looked confused, as well he might. Heredity and inheritance was everything in his culture, and he could only dimly conceive of another to which both were shrugged off as inconsequential. "How long have you been from home?"

"Nearly five years now. And yourself?"

Jean's naturally dismal face fell into even more mournful lines. "Thirty years. My Templar master brought me on crusade." He sighed. "It wasn't as I had imagined it as a child. Few battles, little swordplay, even less opportunity to gather riches, as one is promised when one goes to war. But there were rewards. We were very busy. There was constant coming and going between the Holy Land and Paris. We sent home much gold and silver from Africa, cloth from the East, the swords and armor of Damascus, the horses of Arabia. It was a good life, certainly a profitable one, and as I can read and write, I was useful to my master, and he was pleased with me."

"What happened?"

"We were proscribed, and it became dangerous even to be who we were."

"Why?" said Shasha, exchanging looks with Jaufre. They had heard bits of the Templar story from Alaric, but another perspective on the same tale was always informative.

Jean de Valmy shrugged. "I was never told the full story.

It was said that the Knights Templar were devil worshippers, that our kiss meant death, that we worshipped a black cat called Bahomet. We began to be imprisoned. Some of us were even burned at the stake. We no longer exist as a group. It is still death for a Templar to return to France."

"Yet you survived."

"Because I have not returned to France," Jean said patiently. "Although I miss it, I do. I have a great desire to visit the home of my childhood. I was very happy then. My mother was as beautiful as Helen of Troy, and my father as strong and brave as Ajax himself, and the food—" He kissed his fingers. "But such is the lot of us all, to be separated from that which makes us happy, to live out our lives as best we can in the eternal hope that upon death we will be translated unto heaven and be reunited with those we love."

"'There is no certainty in worldly matters,'" Hari quoted, nodding his agreement, "'and no perfect happiness; good is mixed with evil, and virtue with vice. One must endure, and endure with grace. That is the true test.'"

Jean's brow furrowed as he attempted to translate this into his kind of sense. Jaufre wanted to tell him not to bother. Eyeing their badges, de Valmy inquired after their provenance. "Wu Company," he said, when they had explained. "The young man, the goliard who sings. He wears such a badge, does he not?"

"Félicien?" Shasha said. "Yes. He is a member of our company."

"Ah," de Valmy said, stroking his chin. "You are a very diverse company. A goliard. A healer. A trader. A monk." He looked at Firas, turban ever on his head and short sword ever at his side, and forbore to comment further.

And then Jaufre remembered where he had seen de Valmy before. The Templar had been the old roué who had compared Félicien to a songbird after de Valmy had heard Félicien in performance.

The group parted with expressions of mutual esteem later than evening and Jaufre would have had no cause to think further on the elderly Frank until the following week, when Shasha suffered a visit from the priest of the local parish. Father Amadeo was a lean, fidgety man who wore a perpetually startled expression and spoke with all the consciousness of a man who had God and, more importantly, the church on his side and whose authority was therefore indisputable. "I have received a complaint from a member of my congregation, mistress, regarding unchristian practices taking place in your shop." Further speech revealed Father Amadeo to be a traditionalist who believed that pain and suffering were his congregation's lot in life, and that anyone who eased the pain of broken limbs or boils was regarded as suspect and their work very probably inspired by the devil.

Shasha and Firas exchanged a glance and knew in an instant the instigator of this clerical visitation. Jean de Valmy must have made a complaint in hopes of some reward. From his emaciated appearance he would likely have done so for as little as a full meal. "A broken limb or a boil isn't the work of the devil?" Shasha said. "And is it not a healer's duty to alleviate suffering if God has given her the skill to do so?"

Father Amadeo went away unsatisfied. Jaufre could practically smell the wood burning at the stake. He sent immediately for Hari, who answered the call with alacrity and marshaled his unlikely forces from the monastery. San Giorgio's infirmarian, a pleasant, rotund gentleman by the name of Brother Luca, paid Shasha a visit a week later, chaperoned of course by Hari. They enjoyed a comfortable conversation over tea that ranged from the relative efficacies of willow bark infusion taken orally over mustard seed plasters applied topically for joint pain, although Brother Luca held out for a large helping of olive oil taken internally on a daily basis and massaged into the skin weekly as the most sure relief. But then he was Italian, and in Venice olive oil was known as the mother's helper and used for everything from keeping a woman's skin young to oiling the hinges on a door. If he hadn't held out for olive oil, it would have been garlic, which he did in fact recommend for the common cold. Ingest enough of it, he told Shasha, and the smell alone would keep off even the most determined of the ill humors that assailed mankind.

Leave was taken with compliments all around and Brother Luca extended an invitation to Shasha to visit the herbarium at the monastery and make herself free of its stocks, and another invitation to Alma to meet with Brother Uberto, the monastery's precentor, who shared Alma's interest in the movement of the heavens. Nothing further was heard from Father Amadeo, and Shasha was free to pestle her herbal concoctions, tuck them into squares of parchment tied with string, and send them off to Ca' Polo or anywhere else she liked.

They congratulated themselves on their near escape from the flames of the Inquisition but Jaufre, ever cautious, made a point of attending mass at least once a week. The incense wasn't any worse than your average temple function in Cambaluc and he already had the ability to look attentive while his mind was quite elsewhere. The when to sit, stand and kneel took longer to learn. Father Amadeo looked upon his presence in the congregation with a very sour expression, which was not alleviated by the generous donation Jaufre left in the collection plate at the end of every service.

✢

Messages from Johanna frequently accompanied Shasha's concoctions to Ca' Polo. Moreta sent messages back with less frequency, and the year had turned before Johanna got the one she most wanted.

She and Tiphaine were sitting in their lodgings, not speaking, when Shasha, Jaufre and Firas returned home.

"What news?" Jaufre said, looking from one to the other.

"Tomorrow morning," Johanna said, without meeting his eyes. "Moreta says morning is when he is at his most alert, and most himself."

There was a brief silence. "Are you sure you want to do this, Johanna?" Shasha said.

Johanna gave a laugh that was half-sob. "Want to do it?" she said. "Rather, I must."

She felt rather than saw Jaufre and Shasha exchange looks over her bent head. She held out her hands and felt each of them clasped, Jaufre's hand warm and calloused, Shasha's warm and soft from the cosmetic cream she made herself of oil and beeswax and dried lavender. "Must," she said again. "I must do this."

✝

Peter met her at the servants' entrance. Ser Polo's house was dark and gloomy and like all Venetian palazzos belied its magnificent exterior by being disagreeably dank inside. The servants' stairway was ill lit and narrow. Johanna followed Peter on tiptoe, one hand touching the damp stone wall for reassurance. Her heart seemed to be beating unnaturally loudly in her ears.

At the top of the stair he paused, one ear to a door. The door opened inward without a squeak—she wondered if he had been busy at the hinges with olive oil that morning—and they found themselves at the end of a broad hallway, the length of which ended in a much broader stair with elaborately carved marble bannisters. Up which the invited guests were escorted, no doubt.

The hallway was wainscotted to the ceiling in some dark wood hung with varnished portraits lit by candle sconces. Already difficult to make out, they were made more so by their subjects being painted in dark clothes against dark backgrounds. They all seemed to be wearing the same dour, disapproving expression, too, and Johanna felt a most inappropriate bubble of laughter rising to the back of her throat.

Peter gave out with a delicate clearing of throat and at once one of the doors opened a crack, throwing a bar of light across the tiled floor. Johanna felt herself being taken firmly in hand and steered down the hall and through the door, which closed behind her with a thud of finality that sounded to her admittedly feverish imagination like the closing of the door to a tomb.

Moreta was standing there and the three of them stood stock still for a moment. Johanna could tell that the other two were listening hard, so she listened, too. She heard nothing.

"Did anyone see you?" Moreta said.

Peter shook his head.

Moreta seemed to relax. "Good." She looked at Johanna and attempted a smile. "I'm sorry, but if my mother sees you…"

When her voice trailed away without offering any horrible outcomes, Peter said diplomatically, "She will be displeased."

Moreta huffed out something between a snort and a laugh. "Indeed she will." She looked at Johanna. "I'm sorry. I couldn't tell him. I just… I couldn't."

There was a stir across the room. "Moreta? Daughter?"

It was an old man's voice, thready and dry. It came from a wooden bed shrouded in brocade curtains and canopy, dark blue in color. A clothes press stood in one corner, and one wall was completely covered with a set of shelves cluttered with pottery and porcelain. Johanna recognized a few blue and white bowls that had surely been made in Shinping. A small chest sat next to the bed. On it sat a candelabra, a pitcher, a squat, stemmed glass and various glass bottles. A bit of paper sat scrunched up on one corner. The container of Shasha's last potion, possibly.

Moreta went to the bed and leaned over the man lying there. "Father?"

"Ah, daughter. Some water, of your goodness. My mouth feels most dry."

Moreta poured from the pitcher and leaned over the bed with the stemmed glass in her hand. A moment of silence, and then an "ah" of satisfaction. "Thank you, daughter."

She leaned down and Johanna could hear the press of lips against cheek. "Father," Moreta said in a low voice, "there is someone here to see you."

"Who is it?" the thready voice said. "Peter?"

"Yes, Peter," Moreta said. "And someone else, too." She stood back and beckoned to them.

Peter stepped forward, Johanna following in his wake on legs whose knees felt very peculiar. They stopped at the side of the bed.

"Peter." The voice was stronger now, and Johanna looked at her grandfather's face for the first time.

His features were sunken, his beard grizzled, but his dark eyes were fixed on Peter's face with a look of pleasure. "Peter, my old friend. It is good to see you."

Moreta made as if to say something. Johanna saw Peter touch her hand briefly, and she was still again.

"It is always good to see you, master."

The old man shifted in his bed, lips tightening momentarily in what Johanna took to be discomfort. "I have been laying here thinking of the old days, Peter, in the court of the Great Khan, and on the steppes of the tribes, and in all the lands we traveled. Do you remember the unicorns, Peter? Not like horses at all, thick-snouted and short-legged and broad-bellied, with skin like leather, and two horns, Peter, two, not one as the old tales would have it."

"I remember the unicorns, master. Ugly creatures, and dangerous."

There was a snorting sound from the bed that took Johanna a moment to recognize as a laugh. "No maiden I ever met would have allowed such a creature anywhere near her lap."

He gave that snorting laugh again and this time choked and coughed. Moreta poured him some water and held the glass once more to his lips. He gulped it down and the choking subsided, although he gasped for air afterward. "Thank you, daughter."

Moreta murmured something in return, and Johanna thought she saw tears in his daughter's eyes as she turned to replace the glass on the stand.

"I did not tell half of what I saw," the old man said. "I could have written another book, and more." His fingers plucked at the sheets. "I should have. Il Milione! I'll 'Il Milione' them!" He subsided into mutterings.

There was a brief silence. "Father, there is someone else here to see you this morning."

"Oh?" The old man half-raised his head, peering through the gloom. "Make them come closer. It is so dark at this time of year."

"Here is Johanna, father," Moreta said, motioning at Johanna to come forward. She hesitated before adding, "Johanna of Cambaluc."

"What? Cambaluc?"

Johanna found she could hardly speak around the heart in her mouth. "It is true, Ser Polo."

The raspy voice strengthened. "Nonsense!"

"Indeed, I was born in Cambaluc, Ser Polo." She swallowed. "I am—I have traveled many leagues to come to Venice, over roads with which you and Peter would be very familiar."

A withered hand gestured. "Come closer."

She leaned in between the bed curtains to meet the faded, watery eyes of the old man. To her surprise he seemed alert, his gaze sharp and penetrating, at least in that moment.

For a few moments neither said anything, while behind her Moreta and Peter seemed to hold their breath. After a long moment, he spoke. "Shu Lin?"

There was dead silence in the room, until Johanna managed to say, "I am her granddaughter."

The hand fell back. "Tell me." His voice was stronger and very harsh.

"Do you remember Wu Hai?"

"Of course I remember Wu Hai," the old man said testily. "The best friend a man could have. I committed Shu Lin and Shu Ming into his care when I left Cambaluc." A brief silence, into which the dying man seemed to read reproach. "The Khan would not let me take them with me when I left," he said, a little querulous, perhaps even a little pleading. "What happened, after I was gone?" When Johanna didn't answer immediately he raised his voice. "What happened?"

"Shhhh, father, shhh," Moreta whispered, glancing at the door. "Mother will hear."

The remonstration quieted him immediately, which told its own tale. "What happened to Shu Lin, Johanna of Cambaluc?"

Johanna swallowed. "She died not long after you left, Ser Polo," she said. "It doesn't matter how. Wu Hai married Shu Ming to his son, Wu Li. I am their daughter."

"But if you are Shu Ming's daughter—"

"Yes, Ser Polo. I am your granddaughter."

There was a charged silence. "Shu Lin's granddaughter," he said at last. After a moment, he said in a stronger voice, "My granddaughter."

"Yes, Ser Polo."

The ghost of a smile flitted across his face. "I believe the proper way to address me is 'Grandfather,' young lady."

Johanna felt an answering smile, a little trembly at the corners, spread across her own face. She had not expected such instant acceptance. "Very well. Grandfather."

"Tell me of your life," the old man said.

And for the next hour Johanna did just that. She told him of her birth in Wu Li's house and of her childhood on the Road. "He took you with him?"

"He did, grandfather, myself and my mother, both of us." Before that silence became too uncomfortable she said, "We traveled to many of the places you wrote of in your book. To Kinsai, the city of many canals—"

"Canals!" the old man cried. "Hah! More canals than Venice itself! I was governor of Kinsai for three years, you know."

Johanna didn't remember that in any of the stories told to her by her paternal grandfather, but then Wu Hai had died when she was still very young. She spoke instead of the journeys south into the Indus and Mien and from there the quick trips across the water to the islands where the spices grew. He questioned her closely about the kind and quality of nutmeg, clove and cinnamon, and then, exhausting that topic, he said, on an inter-rogatory note, "In Mien the finest rubies are found."

Johanna smiled, and told him the story of Lundi, the man

with the dhow they had met in Kinsai on her last trip with her father. She glanced at Peter and Moreta, and leaned forward to whisper in the old man's ear about the rubies that had fallen out of Lundi's turban.

He laughed again, and choked again, and was again revived with water, mixed with a little wine. Peter gave him a lemon drop and he sucked on it ruminatively. "Did you only go south, then?"

"No, grandfather, we went east, too, as far as the islands of Cipangu, the land of the Nihon. I dove with the pearl fishers there." She smiled. In this company, only he would know the pearl fishers were always women, who dove dressed only in a cloth wrapped about their loins. She thought it impolitic to say that she herself had donned this attire.

"Hah," he said, an answering smile on his face. "And the islands to the north? The ones where those large salt water weasels are so plentiful?"

"No, we did not go so far. There was no need, as the Nihon traded in them."

"Ah," he said reflectively. "Their fur makes the best coats and hats. If you could have cut out the middleman…"

"The honorable Wu Li was of much the same mind, grandfather, but we didn't have long enough in Cipangu for investigation. The Nihon's pelts were of the finest quality, and expertly cured."

"How much profit in Cambaluc?"

"Before transportation costs, almost fifty percent. The Mongols love good furs."

He grunted. "So you traveled with your father, your mother and you."

"Until he died, yes." She willed her voice not to tremble. Old griefs should never be visited upon new friends, or old friends for that matter. "My mother predeceased him by a year." She did not go into details and he did not ask. Old people were uninterested in any suffering but their own. "When he died, I left Cambaluc."

"On your own?"

"Even I am not so foolhardy, grandfather," she said. "No, I travel with friends."

"And you all came to Venice together?"

"Yes."

"To what end?"

She didn't answer.

He raised up shakily on one elbow. "What do you want, granddaughter? What do you want from me? A letter of recommendation to the merchants guild? An introduction to the Doge?" A rumble of a laugh. "I'm afraid my credit is such that neither would do you any good." A tinge of bitterness crept into his voice. "Not from Il Milione. The man of a thousand lies."

"Father—"

"Did you think I didn't know what they called me behind my back, daughter?" The old man sank back to move restlessly beneath the covers. "I did not tell half of what I saw," he said again, "for fear that I would not be believed. No, granddaughter, I see no use in my bringing you to anyone's notice in Venice." He paused and added, "Your Italian is appalling. Practice until you are fluent before you try to do business in this city." He shifted again. "I have no coin about me, but—"

"I have sufficient unto my needs, grandfather. I need nothing from you except—" here she hesitated "—except perhaps your—your regard."

"My regard, is it?" His voice was beginning to slur. "You have that, then, for what it's worth. Lean down so that I may see you once more."

She did so, tears she had not expected pricking at the back of her eyes.

"I'm sorry," he whispered. "I never tried to find out what happened. I was—I think I was afraid." He swallowed and fell back on his pillow. "And ashamed."

Well he should have been, came the unbidden thought, but again, she forbore from speaking it out loud. He was dying. What good would it do?

She felt a light touch on her elbow, and turned to see Moreta nodding toward the door, an anxious expression on her face.

Johanna straightened and took a long and what would probably be her last look at the old man, who had fallen fast asleep with the suddenness of the very ill and the very old. She had a feeling they would not meet again. "Goodbye, grandfather," she said, and followed Moreta out of the room.

In the hallway Moreta said, still in a whisper, "It's been a long time since I have seen him so alert and animated and—" she hesitated "—alive."

"And I," Peter said, his shuttered Mongol features as close as Johanna thought they might ever get to an expression of approval.

"May I come again, do you think?" Johanna said.

"Who is that!" A voice, harsh and demanding, called from the head of the stairs.

The three of them turned to behold an older woman at the head of the grand staircase, staring at them from a swarthy face which might have been attractive but for the perpetual scowl that had left deep creases between her eyes and at the corners of her mouth. "Moreta! Who is that woman?"

As if they had rehearsed it, Peter took Johanna by one arm and hustled her toward the servants' stairs. Moreta walked toward the woman, her hands held out in calming fashion.

"It's no one, mother, a—"

"Who is she? I won't ask again!" The sound of a ringing slap.

"Merely another healer, mother, who thought she might have something to ease father's joint pains—"

The sound of another slap, and as Johanna was shoved through the stair door she caught a glimpse of Moreta half-turned from her mother, one arm raised in her own defense. "I told you, we've done all we can! The Lord God visits only so much pain on us as we can endure, and endure he must, like—"

The door shut on the rant and Peter galloped Johanna down to the bottom of the stairs and shoved her out into the street.

"I'll send word when there is news," he said and closed the door. Johanna walked away as fast as she could without running, the hood of her cloak drawn closely about her face in case anyone was looking out the windows of Ca' Polo.

✛

"As well as can be expected," was Shasha's verdict.

"You're sure no one followed you when you left?" Jaufre said.

Johanna nodded. "I took care not to come directly home," she said. "I stopped for a meal on the way, and went to the market. I saw no one twice."

"Good." Jaufre sat back and crossed his arms. "Donata Polo doesn't sound like a pleasant person."

"No," Johanna said definitely. "She isn't." She remembered the black-visaged presence at the head of the grand staircase, whose rage and jealous resentment could be felt all the way down the hall as something nearly palpable. "From what Moreta has said, and what my grandfather said this morning, I think she's something of a despot, too."

"Abusive?"

She nodded.

"Murderous?" This from Jaufre.

In fact Donata Polo reminded her somewhat of Dai Fang. Selfish and vicious. "I don't know," Johanna said. "Possibly. Dangerous, certainly."

Jaufre gave Johanna a considering look. "All right," he said. "You've done what you came to do. Now what?"

She sighed. "I'll see him again, if it is possible. His wife will only be more suspicious from now on, and he is very ill." And his wife is determined he shall stay that way, she thought.

"So, we're in Venice," Jaufre said. "You've met your grandfather."

"So now what?" Shasha said.

"Good question," Johanna said, making a face. She fiddled

with a string unraveling from the hem of her tunic. "I know, this was all my idea," she said without looking up. "And you two have never tried to—to—"

"Talk you out of anything?" Shasha said, and exchanged a look with Jaufre, who laughed.

"What would be the point?" Jaufre said. "This was the destination you chose for us. We could come with you, or you would go alone."

"You make me sound like—like—"

"Foolish?"

"Stubborn?"

"Spoiled rotten?"

Johanna flapped a hand. "All that and more," she said. Her smile was crooked. "You still came with me."

"Yes, well." Jaufre looked at Shasha. "It wasn't as if we had someplace better to go."

"We don't now, either," Shasha said. "But I don't much care for the idea of staying here past the winter."

"Well," Johanna said, and cocked a brow. "We are still traders."

Jaufre shrugged. It didn't need answering, if it was even a question.

"And we haven't seen all there is to see here," she said. She felt for the square, leather-bound book in the purse at her waist. "And my father's book is not yet complete. There are new roads to see and to write down in it."

Jaufre and Shasha exchanged looks. "Obviously," Jaufre said.

"Without question," Shasha said, smiling.

Johanna felt a matching smile spread across her face. "Then I say we gather up a pack train of—asses, I suppose, as camels don't seem to have successfully crossed the Middle Sea, more's the pity, and horses are too expensive to feed to be used for pack animals. We gather as much information as possible as to the kind of goods that are most in demand to the north of Venice—"

"Spices," Shasha said.

"Small items, to pack as much as possible into as small a space as possible," Jaufre said. "Jewelry, gemstones, small antiquities."

"Seeds," Shasha said.

"Sugar?" Jaufre said.

Shasha shook her head. "Too bulky, and they cultivate honey here. Venetian glass?"

"Big pieces will be too heavy, and too breakable," Jaufre said. "Vials for potions and tinctures, perhaps." Shasha nodded. "Coral, amber, ivory, worked or unfinished. Small pieces, nothing larger than would be suitable for a belt buckle."

"And spices," Shasha said again, in case either of them hadn't heard her the first time.

Johanna looked at the two of them for a long moment. "And we leave when—"

"Spring," they said together.

Johanna nodded. "After the snow melts and the ground dries out."

"I'm told there are high mountains to the north," Jaufre said, "but also that there are hard but negotiable passes through them."

Johanna laughed, as anyone who had been through the Tien Shan would do at the mention of other, de facto inferior mountains. "No plans to stay put, then?" she said.

"No!" they said in unison, and this time all three of them laughed.

"We should acquire an agent here, though," Jaufre said thoughtfully. "If we are to continue trading, we will need a source of goods from the East, and Venice appears to be the acknowledged source of foreign goods for trade in these parts."

"May, then," Johanna said.

They looked at each other. "May," they agreed.

✠

Later that evening Jaufre came to Johanna's room. She looked at him, and, unbidden, the tears began to gather and fall. He gathered her up in his arms and lay down with her on her bed, and held her all night. Once she said, "It's not as if I really knew him."

His heart beat strongly and steadily beneath her cheek. He stirred, and said, "It's not Ser Polo you weep for, Johanna."

"Who, then?"

His smile was barely visible in the dim glow of the embers of what was left of the fire in the little fireplace that graced her room. "You weep for Wu Li, and Shu Ming, and the life you've left behind. Ser Polo was the last link left to that old life."

She listened to the beat of his heart beneath her ear. "Do you still think of your mother, Jaufre?"

He remembered the women being stripped naked at the slave auctions down on the Grand Canal. "Always."

"I wish we could have found her for you."

"So do I."

They fell asleep then, holding each other until morning, when the watery daylight leaking through the small window high up on the wall stirred Johanna to consciousness. She stretched luxuriously, feeling a sense of wellbeing at odds with the emotionally taxing experience of the previous day.

Jaufre stretched in turn and blinked up at her. "Good morning."

"Good morning," she said. "And thank you." Impulsively she leaned down to give him a quick kiss.

He was instantly awake, one hand behind her head and another around her waist. He rolled them over so that he was lying on top of her, one leg sliding between hers, as he deepened the kiss.

Shock kept her frozen in place for one moment, and then another, and then another, until she realized that her shock had passed and that her hands were moving up his back, kneading the warm, firm flesh beneath the rough nap of his tunic. His lips moved across her cheek and down her throat and she gasped when he pulled her nightshirt down her shoulder, exposing her breast. Her nipple hardened instantly and his lips were there, suckling, rubbing with his tongue.

She heard breathless, whimpering, mewling sounds and realized they came from her. Her body was arched from head to toe, she had one leg wrapped around him and she was rubbing up against the hard ridge of flesh between his legs with a need she only dimly remembered from the time by the lake with Edyk. This need seemed far more urgent, more—more necessary.

He raised his head. His blue eyes were narrowed, his golden hair tumbled. "Johanna," he said, his voice rougher than she'd ever heard it.

"Jaufre," she said, in—disbelief? Wonder?

"Johanna," he said, this time in unmistakable satisfaction, and felt for the drawstring at her waist.

The door to the room opened. "Johanna, you must come—oh."

The door closed again. After a moment came a knock, and Shasha's subdued voice from behind it. "Johanna, Peter is here and asking for you. You'd better come." A brief pause. "I'm sorry." Footsteps moving away.

Johanna stared up at Jaufre. "I'm sorry," she whispered in her turn.

Jaufre was the son of one ex-soldier and the friend of two others, and he had lived his entire life within earshot of muleteers, camel handlers, grooms and ostlers. These were not people known for moderation in language, and every curse he had learned was on display and at full volume as he extricated himself from Johanna's bed and fumbled his clothing into place.

Her face heated when she saw that his trousers were halfway down his legs and that it was she who must have made that happen.

He looked up and saw her expression and snarled, "Say 'I'm sorry' one more time, do!" He yanked his trousers up and stormed out.

She gaped after him. "Jaufre," she said. "Jaufre!"

He did not return.

She stood up and stared around the room as if she'd never seen it before. And then she got dressed and went out into the common room, where Peter sat, his face ravaged with grief.

He looked up at her and said, "He's dead. Early this morning." He swallowed. "He wasn't in pain and he wasn't alone. He just—left."

5

Venice, spring, 1324

THE EFFECTS WERE barely noticeable, at first. Through January and February custom at Jaufre's stall began to fall, but no more than his fellow stallholders on the street. At first he thought it was due to the usual drop-off of business after the Christian festivities in December, during which a great deal of money had been spent by the citizens of Venice not only at his stall but at every vendor in the city, large and small. By March, when the rise in temperature and increase in daylight brought more custom to the stalls around him and less and less to him, he began to wonder.

When he mentioned it at dinner that night Firas and Alaric exchanged glances. "What?"

"Master Roland told us he's been having trouble selling tickets to the next exhibition," Alaric said.

Jaufre frowned. "The last time I was there for practice, he told me that the salle was too full during the afternoon to accommodate non-paying guests. He told me morning hours would be best."

"Morning hours being when there are fewest people there."

Firas looked at Shasha. "And Shasha has had little call on her for potions and tinctures of late."

"Custom has been falling off since late January," she said, troubled.

"Well," Félicien said lightly, setting aside a bowl of stew he had barely touched, "not to chime in on this tale of woe, but I have been—uninvited—from performing at the Inn of the Four Horses."

"What!"

"Why?"

"You draw more of a crowd than any other performer in Venice!"

"That's not all, I'm sorry to say," he said, glancing at Shasha. "I'm afraid Father Amadeo has been inveigling against the devil again."

"In Shasha's name?" Firas said, his voice hard.

"No," Félicien said. "Not yet. Just generally expounding on the notion that man is born to suffer, and that anything that interferes with that suffering is the work of Satan himself and should be shunned by all true faithful." He glanced at Hari and added, a little mockingly, "However much we stand in the favor of the abbott at the monastery of San Giorgio, it appears we shall not, after all, be impervious to the scourge of Father Amadeo's tongue."

"I have heard nothing of this during my visits there," Hari said, looking troubled.

"January," Jaufre said, looking at Johanna. "I don't know. What happened in January?"

No one except Shasha knew for sure why Johanna blushed to the roots of her hair, although they all had their suspicions. "My grandfather died in January," she said, willing her color to subside. Her eyes widened and she looked at Shasha. "And Peter came to tell us so." She thought for a moment, and looked at Tiphaine. "Will you take a message to Ca' Polo for me?"

The girl bounced up. Between the new clothes and the regular food, she looked a handspan taller than when Johanna had first brought her home. "Of course," she said briskly.

"Delivered directly into Moreta's hands if possible, and if not, Peter's. No one else."

"Certainly."

It took three days for a reply. "She will meet you at the taverna at none."

✝

Alas, perhaps blinded by his grief, it appeared that Peter had not been as careful as Johanna had been in seeing that she was not followed when she left Ca' Polo. "My mother," Moreta said, and grimaced. "My mother," she said again, and stopped again.

Johanna thought of the frighteningly enraged woman standing at the top of the stairs at the end of the corridor when they had come out of Ser Polo's room. "It's all right," she said.

Moreta's head came up and she said hotly, "No. It isn't. She had Paolo follow Peter to your lodgings when I sent him to you with news of Father's passing. Then she wouldn't rest until she knew everything about you."

"Does she know—"

"Yes," Moreta said. "I don't know how, because Peter didn't tell her, and she hasn't said a word to me about you, and I'm the only other one who knows." Her brow creased. "I can't understand why."

"Can't you?" a voice said, and startled, both of them turned to see Donata Polo standing there in her luxurious dark robes with not a fold out of place. She was attended on her right by a serving woman who looked every bit as censorious as her mistress and on her left by the man who had shut the door so decisively in Johanna's face on the day of her arrival in Venice. He looked very pleased with himself.

The three of them bore a distinct resemblance to the statues on the temple walls she had seen in Mien as a child, glaring of eye, thunderous of brow, prepared to smite the unworthy. Although with fewer arms.

The taverna's keeper, yet again proving her worth, became

absorbed in the examination of her stock of pitchers and mugs, one at a time, inspecting them for flaws.

"Can't you?" Moreta's mother repeated, looking from her daughter's face to Johanna's and back again. "I see. I see, indeed. A bastard of your father's, looking for largesse. Well, we know how to deal with your kind."

The temple statues of Mien had frightened her. This woman did not, perhaps because she had known another woman very like her in a prior life. Johanna rose to her feet, shaking Moreta's hand from her sleeve. "A granddaughter, certainly," she said, stepping forward and perforce causing Serra Polo to step back, which didn't please her. Unfortunately, Johanna was taller than she was and she couldn't glare down her nose at the younger woman. "I ask nothing of you, Serra Polo. I want nothing from you. I came a long way to meet my grandfather, and I merely wished—"

Serra Polo looked at her daughter. "I had not thought to suffer such disloyalty in my own house."

Moreta closed her eyes for a moment. "He was pleased to see her, Mother."

"Pleased! Pleased! I will say what pleased your father and what did not! You thought to bring this stranger, this—this adventurer, this pretender to the house of Ca' Polo, and make your father's last days on this earth a living misery!"

"He was pleased to see her, Mother, and to hear news of the—" she hesitated and cast Johanna a quick look of apology "—friends he had left behind."

"Friends," Serra Polo said with awful sarcasm, and swept Johanna with a look from head to toe that was far from complimentary. "Friends, indeed."

Johanna allowed a smile to cross her face. She ignored another desperate tug at her sleeve and said, "Obviously a great deal more than friends."

Serra Polo was quick to hear the deliberate mockery in Johanna's voice, and anger stiffened into outrage. Before she could say anything else, Moreta got to her feet. "It's time we went home, Mother."

"But before you do," Johanna said, "call off your dogs. I am no threat to you." She raised an eyebrow. "Or to your inheritance."

"I know nothing of dogs," Donata Polo said inaccurately, and swept out of the establishment, followed by her minions, everyone satisfied at having the last word.

Tomorrow, Moreta mouthed at Johanna, pointing at their table, and followed.

Johanna turned to look at Peter, who had sat still and unperturbed through the encounter. "Well?"

His eyes held the hint of a smile. "My master left me well provided for in his will. I dance to no one's tune but my own, now."

She sat back down and gestured at the taverna keeper, who miraculously remembered she had customers. She bustled over with a new pitcher of small beer and whisked away Moreta's mug so there was no sad remembrance of absent friends. "What will you do now?" she said.

His shoulders lifted in the merest shrug. "It depends on what she does next." She remained unidentified but not unknown. "Moreta was the only member of that household who had any value for my master. If she needs me, I will stay."

If he was allowed to, Johanna thought. "Will you go home, otherwise? Do you miss the wind on the steppes so much?"

She couldn't be sure but she thought he might almost have smiled, if he didn't have a racial reputation for stoicism to live up to. "What is home to me now," he said with a sigh.

It wasn't a question, so she didn't try to answer. "Lacking other options..." She hesitated. "You could join Wu Company."

He surprised her with a laugh, a deep, rumbling sound pleasant to the ears. His eyes positively twinkled and he said, "I don't know that I have it in me to chase another Polo halfway around the world, mistress."

She grinned at him. "All I can promise is that it won't be dull."

He looked at her for a long moment. "I will think on it."

✠

"Your very existence is an affront to her," Moreta said the next day. They had met at the taverna and Moreta had said that since there were no more secrets left from the Grand Canal to the Rialto Bridge they might as well go to Johanna's lodgings. Shasha made them comfortable with hot tea and sweet biscuits and settled down in a corner with mortar and pestle, there to grind ingredients and eavesdrop.

"Your mother appears to be harboring what seems to us to be a disproportionate amount of rage," Johanna said. "And is occupying herself in venting it all on us."

"My mother is a very angry woman. She's been an angry woman all my life, and she is better at holding a grudge than anyone I've ever met. Paolo spends all his time ferreting out information for her, I believe just to fuel more slights and grievances. It is a way of life for them both, now." Moreta sipped her tea. "This is wonderful," she told Shasha.

She bit into one of the biscuits, and Shasha held up a hand. "Not as wonderful, I know," she said ruefully. "My friend the baker turned me from his door before he taught me all his secrets."

"It's simple," Moreta said, "double the butter."

Shasha was pleased. "Thank you, lady."

"Moreta, please."

"But we have given her no call to hold a grudge," Johanna said.

Félicien was teaching Tiphaine how to finger chords on his lute, with Hayat and Alma interested auditors. Jaufre and Firas were attending to the ongoing conversation, thus far taking no part in it. Hari was as yet persona grata at the monastery and Alaric was out, probably drinking somewhere in a taverna. He wasn't going to be able to afford it for very much longer if Donata Polo did not soon relent. One of the potential benefits of her enmity, Johanna thought.

"She needs no reason," Moreta said. "My father offended her by spending her dowry the first year of their marriage." She paused, and added meditatively, "I really think she might have killed all three of her children in the womb in revenge, could she have found a way."

A discordant jangle of lute strings, and Johanna looked around to see that Tiphaine was realizing that there were worse things in the world to be than a motherless child.

"My sisters married as soon as my father could arrange dowries for them. I…" She sighed. "I didn't want to leave him."

"Will you have to live with your mother now?" Alma said, exchanging an appalled look with Hayat. The harem was looking better to them all the time, Johanna saw.

Moreta's smile was grim. "Yes, but in his will my father settled my dowry upon me, for my own use. I have already an apartment set aside at Ca' Polo, and I have my own friends. I shouldn't have to see more of her than I can bear." She drank tea. "But you."

"Yes?"

Moreta looked around the room. "You must leave Venice. All of you."

"We always meant to," Johanna said. "It was never our intent to settle here."

"Yes, but—" Jaufre said.

"What?"

He spoke to Shasha. "I'm having difficulties acquiring an agent for us, and even more difficulty in acquiring sales goods. Not to mention which…" He looked at Firas.

"No one will sell us pack animals," Firas said. "I've been down to the livestock market and the merchants are all very pleasant, some even cordial, but all of their stock is spoken for." He stroked his beard. "They say they can sell us none for fear that this year's gray cloaks will go unprovisioned."

Translating "gray cloaks" to "pilgrims," Johanna said, "But that's nonsense! There are all the donkeys in the world at Gaza,

478

and Jerusalem." Moreta was shaking her head. "Is your mother's influence so strong in Venice, then? She doesn't sound like a friend who would be that welcome on anyone's doorstep."

Jaufre snorted out a laugh but his head was turned away when Johanna looked at him. She knew a flicker of temper, then. She hadn't meant she was sorry, she couldn't ever make love with him. She'd only meant she was sorry they'd been interrupted (and she had been, teeth-grindingly sorry, ready to kill Shasha sorry). But try as she would she had been unable to corner him alone anytime these past two months to say so. He seemed to positively enjoy nursing his grudge and feeding its flame wherever possible. Donata Polo could take lessons.

The thought made an involuntary smile cross her face, which of course he turned his head at the last moment to see. He looked suspicious immediately, because of course she had to be laughing at him, didn't she, even if he was sitting there doing nothing. She hid a sigh and turned back to Moreta.

"She doesn't have to be friends with anyone to have influence, Johanna," Moreta said. "She just needs to be born into the right family, one that has lived here forever and is related by blood and marriage to all the other right families. Since the day Paolo reported back to her, she has been spreading the word, palazzo by palazzo, canal by canal. Your morals are suspect, your faith nonexistent—"

"I go to Mass every Sunday!" Jaufre said, sounding aggrieved. His regular attendance to Father Amadeo's services certainly wasn't for pleasure.

"—and worst of all, your coin is not to be trusted. Venetians will do well to neither sell to nor buy from you, to avoid socializing with you – indeed, better they should turn aside rather than touch shoulders if they meet you on the street." She nodded at the badge on Johanna's shoulder. "You made yourselves so easily identifiable with your compagnia insignia, too. She didn't even have to describe you individually. No member of Wu Company may trade in Venice."

There was an edge to Johanna's voice. "And because Donata Polo says it, it must be so?"

"Well." Moreta drank tea. "It's not quite the law." She looked up from her cup. "Yet."

It was silent in the room as Moreta held out her cup for a refill. "That really is marvelous tea, Shasha. Where did you get it?"

"We brought it with us," Shasha said. "I have seen none for sale here in Venice."

"What a pity."

"We have our living to make," Johanna said. "We are traders by profession. Where else can we buy goods to sell, if not in Venice?"

"And how do we get those goods anywhere," Firas said, "if we can buy no pack animals?"

"Especially if they decide to burn us at the stake first," Félicien said.

Moreta sat back, her cup filled. She did not look as downcast as the rest of them did, Johanna noted, or as indignant as Johanna felt. "You have an idea," she said.

Moreta sipped her tea. "Perhaps." She looked at Johanna. "What you said to my father that day." She hesitated, looking at the others. "About the pearl fishers of Cipangu."

"Yes?" Johanna said, mystified.

"Is it true, what you told me? That you dove with the pearl fishers?"

"Yes," Johanna said.

"You dove, and brought back oysters, with pearls in them? So you have the knack of finding small objects at depth?"

"Moreta—"

"The Wedding to the Sea!"

Moreta nodded at Tiphaine. "That is my thought."

Everyone in the room who was not Venetian looked askance at one another. Tiphaine bounced to her feet, black curls flying, all eagerness to explain, and Moreta waved a hand for her to be about it. "It's an annual holiday, the Feast of the Ascension! The Patriarch blesses a golden ring, and then there is a grand procession of boats from the Basilica of St. Mark to the Church of San Nicolò on the Lido, with the Doge and the Patriarch and all the nobles dressed in their finest silks and velvets. And there is music, and jugglers, and stilt walkers, and dancers, and acrobats—"

"Any horse racing?" Johanna said, sitting up straight.

"Horse racing?" Tiphaine frowned. "No. I don't think so. I've never heard of any."

"Oh." Johanna slumped, losing interest. She had a large bruise on her right hip from the expression of North Wind's continuing displeasure the previous day. If horses could talk, he would have heartily endorsed any idea that got them back on the Road as soon as possible.

"But oh, it is such a fine sight to see, the costumes are so beautiful, and they throw coins—" She caught herself, and added haughtily, "For the street urchins to catch, you understand. Not for respectable citizens."

"Of course not," Johanna said, to an accompanying murmur around the room.

"Then the Doge on el Bucintoro—"

"El Bucintoro?"

"His barge, oh, wait till you see it, it is the most magnificent boat ever built, all gilded with gold! It is from el Bucintoro's deck that the Doge throws the blessed ring into the sea, so that La Serenissima renews her vows once again to the sea that gives us our livelihood." She clasped her hands and stood in rapt silence.

"Yes, well," Johanna said, a little at sea herself, "that sounds most romantic, and, ah, a spectacle to behold. But I don't quite see what—"

"The instant the ring goes into the sea, Johanna," Moreta said, "Venetians strip off their clothes and dive after it."

"What?" Johanna thought of the filth she saw every day in the canals, of the opaque green of the waters. "By all the Mongol gods, why?"

Moreta smiled. "Because whoever recovers the ring lives tax free in Venice for the next year."

The silence that followed this statement was profound.

"I dove with the pearl fishers, too," Jaufre said.

"I dove deeper and brought back more pearls," Johanna said.

"That is true," Shasha said, a little reluctantly, and later Johanna would take her to task for that.

"Shasha, that was Cipangu, where all the ama are women."

"Because they're better at it than the men!"

"But this," Jaufre said, glaring at Johanna, "is Venice, where women doing anything but having babies and minding their homes and going to church is frowned on. You think Serra Donata has them whipped up against us now! I can only imagine what they're going to say when you strip down on the side of the Grand Canal to dive in!"

"But with two divers, our odds of recovering the ring increase," Shasha said, stepping in neatly to avert the imminent conflagration. She looked at Jaufre. "The waters of Venice are not exactly the waters of Izu, which I remember as clear right down to the bottom. I doubt the bottom of a Venetian canal has been seen in a thousand years."

Johanna and Jaufre subsided, seeing the sense of this. "When is this feast day?" Johanna said.

"May," Moreta and Tiphaine said together.

"Two months," Johanna said. "Can your mother starve us out by then?"

Moreta smiled. "Probably not. And you can always take the ferry to the mainland to buy foodstuffs, if you have to. But you have to stay in Venice, because only those resident in Venice on the day itself may dive for the ring." She set down her cup. "And you will need a sponsor, someone from one of the first families, because only such are eligible to dive. That I cannot help you with." She grimaced. "In fact, if my mother got wind of it, she would make it her new mission in life to see that you never acquired such a sponsor."

Johanna and Jaufre looked at each other, animosity forgotten for the moment. "Gradenigo," they said at the same time.

"Which one?" Moreta said.

"Giovanni Gradenigo," Jaufre said. "He was the captain of the ship that brought us here from Gaza. He told us, very grandly, that he was a great-nephew of a doge of the same name."

"Gradenigo," Moreta said thoughtfully. "I haven't met this Giovanni, but a Gradenigo was our last doge but one, memorable chiefly because he got Venice excommunicated again."

"Again?"

"Unfortunately. The family's influence lessened somewhat after his death, but there is a younger one of the house named Bartolomeo who is known as a coming man. Yes, the Gradenigos might do, so long as there is no association between our families of which I am unaware. Will he do it?"

"From his conversation I think he would welcome the opportunity." Jaufre grinned, and Johanna watched, fascinated, as the dimples creased his cheeks. It seemed like years since she'd seen them. "So long as he gets to wet his snout."

"Ask him," Moreta said. "And soon."

6

Venice, May, 1324

"A RE YOU ALL right?" Shasha said in a low voice.

"I'm fine. I just wish they'd get on with it."

It was late May, forty days after Easter Sunday. The air was warmed by a sun in a pale blue sky for a change unobscured by clouds, but Johanna couldn't stop shivering.

From the size of the crowds on the quay and the amount of boats in the Grand Canal there wasn't a Venetian left at home that morning. The cathedral of St. Mark's held a crowd whose overflow packed the piazza in front of it. From the loggia above the portico the four great bronze horses that Venice had looted from Byzantium a hundred years before reminded everyone of Venice's might and reach. Johanna never saw them but she was reminded of Uncle Cheng's observation that everything worth looking at in Byzantium was now in Venice.

She sighed, and shivered again. Almost two years and so many leagues away, that infinitely warmer evening in Kashgar. Where was Uncle Cheng now? En route somewhere, no doubt. If the rumors about Ogodei settling west of Terak were true, if the renegade Mongol general had decided himself satisfied with the territory he had overrun to date, Uncle Cheng could be arriving in Kashgar itself, selling silk and buying bronze. Mongols, however acquisitive of territory, never underestimated the necessity and profitability of trade, and whatever else Ogodei did to gather territory beneath his banner, he would do nothing to obstruct the free passage of goods and merchants. Uncle Chang and his livelihood would be safe.

The sound of thousands of Venetians on holiday forcibly returned her attention back to the present. Impossibly the great buzz of shouts and laughter increased in volume when the massive doors of the cathedral finally opened wide to disgorge the Patriarch, the Doge, the Senate, the heads of all the guilds, the legate from Avignon and the ambassador from Paris walking together as if joined at the hip, any noble with rank enough to squeeze themselves inside for the service. Everyone was wearing every necklace, tiara, and ring they possessed. The cumulative glitter was painful to behold.

In contrast, Johanna and Jaufre wore belted robes of brown fustian that muffled them from head to toe. They looked, she thought, like something you might find down the privy hole after a harsh winter on short rations.

Fortunately, no one was paying them any attention. "The cloth of gold times the nobili in this procession would provide enough sail for five sea-going vessels," Giovanni Gradenigo said irreverently.

"There's a song in that," Félicien said promptly, and for all Johanna knew set about writing one in his head that minute. He'd been on the nearest street corner earlier, playing his lute and singing songs about farting peasants, lovelorn knights and cuckolded husbands, to the sniggering delight of a gathering crowd. His smooth soprano was as mellow as ever, a voice that never broke or missed a note, to which the growing pile of coins in the hat on the cobblestones in front of him could attest.

Hymns sung loud if untunefully, accompanied by drums and trumpets, were drowned out by the bells of St. Mark's, which by themselves were loud enough to jar the teeth from your head. The procession from the church was preceded by banners and crosses and the teeth and toe bones of saints in gilt boxes held high on elaborately decorated litters, and was followed by a crush of Venetian citizens following behind, all determined to miss no detail of this day when Venice once again tied the very sea herself to the city in holy matrimony.

"Impressive," Jaufre said, sounding amused, and Johanna knew he was remembering the processions of Cambaluc, which for richness of regalia and self-importance of its dignitaries outshone this one by a mile.

Tiphaine snorted. "This is nothing," she said grandly. "You should see Corpus Christi Day. All the reliquaries are out on Corpus Christi Day."

The procession made its stately way across the piazza to the Grand Canal, where el Bucintoro waited, heavy with paint and gilt and silken hangings and golden figurehead. Unconsciously Johanna held her breath as the highest were shown tenderly on board and settled themselves into luxurious seats, and the gilt ship sank in the water beneath the accumulated weight of all that might and majesty. When they were all aboard, if the water did not quite overlap the gunnels it certainly nibbled at them. If it hadn't been flat calm, if there had been even the slightest chop, Johanna would have had every expectation that el Bucintoro would have swamped before they were an arm's length from the dock.

The sailing master barked orders, lines were loosed and the golden vessel separated from the quay in the stately fashion befitting its august cargo. Both lines of oars sliced into the water at precisely the same moment. A mighty shout went up from the quayside and from boats large and small crowding the waterway, whose number Johanna estimated in the hundreds.

"All right, it's time, get in," Gradenigo said, and Johanna turned to scramble into the nimble craft tied next to them, Jaufre right behind her. Shasha and Firas were left on the wharf, Shasha anxious and Firas as enigmatic as ever. Alaric, looking painfully sober, stood next to them, with Alma and Hayat, hands clasped and looking concerned. Even Hari had deemed this occasion worthy of an absence from the monastery. He smiled benignly, to see their comrades set forth on a mission as foolhardy as it was unquestionably futile. Certainly no one cheered as Gradenigo pushed them off. Their new badges flashed in the sunlight, bearing the flamboyant, full-sailed ship of the Gradenigo Azienda. Tiphaine had objected most vehemently to Wu Company's badge being removed, however temporarily, for the remainder of their stay in Venice. Johanna suspected that the girl wanted any glory to be reflected back to its proper source. If any glory there was to be had.

"Where's Tiphaine?" Johanna said suddenly. A movement caused her to look around. "Tiphaine! I told you to stay on the quay!"

A small face with a mutinous expression looked back at her from the stern and said nothing. A muffled sound was heard and Johanna said dangerously, "Jaufre, don't you dare laugh."

"Wouldn't think of it." Jaufre stared off in the middle distance with a bland expression on his face.

Gradenigo and a short, wiry man Johanna recognized from the voyage from Gaza wielded an oar each as they joined the grand procession of what looked like anything that had a reasonable chance of floating, from a bathtub on up to a cog. Most of them were oar-driven but Johanna saw a few small skiffs rigged with jibs darting recklessly before, between and behind the much larger vessels that made up the bulk of this unwieldy fleet, and giving rise to not a few curses bellowed as only sailors can, especially when the big ships stole the wind and the sailboats became momentarily becalmed between two fast-approaching and much larger hulls.

Their own vessel was made of cedar planed suicidally thin and formed into an open, narrow shell with two thwarts inside to sit on and two oar-locks in which to rest the oars, and that was all. The draft was so shallow that with all five of them inside it rode low enough to sink if anyone so much as inhaled. The three passengers were enveloped in a fine spray raised by the oars but she had to admit that the little boat skimmed over the water like a bird in flight, overtaking and passing laboring craft as if they had been frozen in place, passing so close to others that you couldn't have inserted a feather between them, shifting course so rapidly that they shipped water over first the port side and then the starboard and then the port side again, until they were close, too close if the shouts from above were any indication, on el Bucintoro's stern. There Gradenigo laid off a few lengths and used his oar only enough to maintain their position.

"There," he said with evident satisfaction. He saw Johanna's expression, mistook it for admiration, and sent her a cocky grin.

Johanna blew out a breath and looked at Jaufre, who was also grinning. Over her shoulder she heard Tiphaine laugh out loud. She wiped her face on her sleeve and forbore to comment.

"Don't do that," Jaufre said, catching her hand. "You'll wipe it off."

The procession came to a halt, or as much of a halt as the tides and currents would allow. The flotilla came together in a cluster about the Doge's barge. Gradenigo fended off a couple of pretenders to their position, vigorously enough to cause said pretenders to hastily right their craft before they went under. A larger craft tried to muscle its way in but Gradenigo held his ground, Johanna thought by sheer force of will, because this wooden leaf they were barely floating in certainly had no tonnage capable of offering any threat. The current hymn, rising from the ships at sea and the crowds on shore, came to a ragged, triumphant crescendo and broke off, and in the following breathless silence the Doge rose to his feet and made his way to the side. They weren't more than a couple of arms-lengths from the hull of el Bucintoro and she could see his lined face clearly. He was smiling.

"Get ready," Gradenigo said.

"Are we too close?" Jaufre said in a low voice, rising to his feet, hands at the tie of his robe.

"He's an old man, how far can he throw?" Gradenigo said.

The old man's arm raised and Johanna saw the tiny gold ring in his hand, illuminated for just an instant by the rays of the morning sun. She stood, the little craft rocking beneath her feet, and shed her robe next to Jaufre. Everywhere she looked men were tearing at their clothes, on boats, on shore.

Her robe fell next to Jaufre's in the bottom of their boat. They were attired in tunic and trousers and slippers, white for better visibility underwater and wound close to their bodies in strips of more white cloth covered with a thick layer of grease. Johanna's hair was caught back in a long braid and it too was slicked over with a layer of grease, as was every exposed bit of her skin. Shasha had rendered the fat of two sheep for enough to encase her and Jaufre both during their dive.

A tiny gold object sailed over the gathered flotilla, actually bouncing off the grasping hand of a young grandee attired in velvet, who leaned too far out of his boat and toppled into the water a moment after the ring hit the surface.

"Go, go, go!" Gradenigo said, a moment before a mighty shout went up from the assemblage.

Johanna, who had been taking deep, whistling breaths from the moment they had stopped moving, brought her hands over her head and dove over the side, conscious of Jaufre's slicing into the water next to her only a second later. Even with all the practice dives they had made over the past month, it was gaspingly cold. Johanna blinked her eyes to clear them, pulled her head down and kicked hard and pulled harder with her arms, heading for her best guess as to where she might find the ring.

Something grabbed at her foot and she kicked hard, half-turning to see a bearded man in shirtwaist and hose hanging off her ankle. He was grinning, or he was until Jaufre took a handful of his hair and yanked, hard. An explosion of bubbles from his mouth and Johanna's ankle was free. She felt someone else take hold of her braid and yank and she was momentarily arrested in her dive, until a moment later Jaufre was on him. Her attacker's fingers were already slipping from the greased braid but Jaufre shoved two brutal fingers up his nose and a cloud of blood obscured his face. He screamed and air bubbled out of his mouth and he struck for the surface.

Jaufre pointed, and she followed the direction of his hand and took a precious second to reorient herself. Was that a flash of gold? She pulled herself down with all of the strength in her shoulders and arms, putting all the muscle in her hips and legs behind her kick. The deeper the water, the darker it was. If the ring fell below a certain level she'd never see it. If it reached the bottom she would never find it. The pressure was building on her ears and in her lungs and she began to let out air, one tiny bubble at a time, in measured beats. The water became colder still, almost paralyzingly cold the further down she dove, the farther behind she left the weak spring sun.

There! A flash, and she kicked and reached out, and, disbelieving it even as it happened, her hand closed around something hard and tiny and round. She pulled up and someone grabbed her braid but again, Jaufre was there and this time he didn't bother with nostrils, he grabbed between the man's legs. The man tried to scream, there another explosion of bubbles, and Johanna was free. She kicked for the surface, her lungs burning now, it was too long since she'd done this, she was out of practice, but she could not inhale, who knew the filth that she would bring into her body, and then there was the drowning, no, and then yes! She broke the surface, the force of her kick propelling her out of the water as far as her waist, and Gradenigo was there and he had her arm, the one with the fist clenched tight around the ring that would make all their fortunes.

Another shout went up, this one loud enough to be heard at the doors of Everything Under the Heavens itself, although this might have been partly due to the fact that Venice realized that a woman had retrieved the ring this year.

She collapsed on the bottom of their tiny eggshell of a boat and used the rest of the air in her lungs to blow out her nose and gasp, "Jaufre?"

There was a splash and a gasp and a sleek head surfaced. Gradenigo and his crew grabbed him by the hair and the seat of his trousers and lifted him on board, although Tiphaine went over in the process. Gradenigo grabbed the back of her tunic, lifted her out of the water, shook her vigorously and tossed her into the stern.

"Did you get it?" Gradenigo said to Johanna.

"Did you get it?" Jaufre said.

"Did you get it?" Tiphaine said, pushing her soaking curls out of her eyes.

"Did you get it!" the crowd bellowed.

"Quick," Gradenigo said, "your robes."

When they were decently swathed once again in brown fustian, Johanna's braid tucked inside, Gradenigo helped her to her feet. She kept her knees loose so as to keep her balance in the rocking boat. She did not want to go back into that cold, dirty water, not ever again. Above her, a row of heads crowded the side of el Bucintoro, one of them, she saw fleetingly, belonging to the Doge himself.

She rolled the ring forward to hold it between thumb and forefinger and then, her fingers cold and numb, almost dropped it, to the accompanying, deliciously horrified gasp of everyone watching. But the grease on her hands was so thick the ring stuck to her fingers. She raised her hand over her head, and the sun, which seemed to have increased in strength and brightness in the moments she had been gone from it made the golden hoop glitter like the finest diamond ever pulled from the sands of Nubia.

This time the shriek was loud enough to be heard at the door of Heaven itself.

✠

There was some grumbling about the winning diver's sex and nationality, not to mention the unfair advantage of the grease.

Gradenigo, backed by his family's name and especially by the vocal and public support of his cousin Bartolomeo, his family's coming man, overbore it. He could indeed conduct business in Venice tax free, for a year beginning from the day of the Wedding to the Sea. "He wants to meet you, by the way."

"Meet who?"

"All of you," Gradenigo said, "but especially Johanna." He winked. "He admired your diving costume. As did all of Venice."

"I assume he admired mine as well," Jaufre said in a silken voice.

"All of you," Gradenigo said hastily, "the entire Wu Company is bidden to dinner at Ca' Gradenigo on Saturday next. Bring your best stories, because he will expect you to sing for your supper. But now." He smacked his hands together. "Let us construe." He cocked an eyebrow. "How would you feel about leading a shipment of goods to Lyon?"

"Where is Lyon?" Shasha said.

"And what's there?" Jaufre said.

"A city in France about a hundred and seventy leagues west of Venice," Gradenigo said, "and a trading fair in France where the House of Gradenigo has a permit to buy and sell."

"Who trades there?" Johanna said.

Gradenigo smiled. "Everyone."

Firas raised an eyebrow in Shasha's direction. "That certainly sounds comprehensive," she said, and Johanna hid a smile.

It was as well that the dinner with Gradenigo's cousin didn't take place until the following Saturday, as it took that long to get all the grease off.

On Monday they met again with Gradenigo on the Grand Canal. "You will be coming with us to Lyon?" Jaufre said.

"Are you mad?" Gradenigo looked horrified. "The first sailing of pilgrims takes place next week, and besides, I am building my own merchant galley down on the Arsenal and I'll want to be here when she launches. You will be on your own, my friends."

Johanna and Jaufre exchanged glances. They preferred it that way, but— "And you'll trust us with your cargo? You may never see us or it again."

Gradenigo grinned. "Considering that I don't have to share a year's worth of profit with the Doge? You could plunge over the edge of Mount Genevre and I'd never miss the income. Enough of this now, come with me."

They followed him to a large warehouse of solid construction secured by a padlock the size of a newborn babe. Venice liked its locks large. Gradenigo led the way inside. "What will you have? Greek antiques from Rhodes? This is said to be the head of Athena by no less than Praxiteles."

"Definitely not," Jaufre said, and Johanna said firmly, "Much too bulky."

Gradenigo shrugged. "Ah well, if I can't sell it here, it will go with the rest of the marble to Rome and be burned into lime. Sponges from Calymnos, then? Olive oil from Kerkyra? A Gozurate mat, perhaps? See the leather, both red and blue, and the birds and beast embroidered in gold. A fine piece, worthy of any lady's bower."

Johanna caught sight of a bundle of cloth and caught it up. "Silk from Chinangli! Where did you come by this, when the roads to the East are overrun by the armies of Barka Khan and Hulaku and Ogodei?"

The Venetian smiled. "If there is a market for such a thing, a way will be found to supply it."

Gradenigo led them deeper into a labyrinth that appeared to contain a sample of all the riches of the known world: cloth from Flanders, silk from Lucca in Italy, leather from Spain and North Africa, furs from Germany, spices, wax, sugar, alum, lacquer again from the East, grain, wine, dyes, cotton, flax from Egypt. In the stables behind the warehouse Gradenigo housed horses and livestock from Gaul to Africa. In one small room, reinforced, this one locked three times over and heavily guarded, he kept gold and precious stones.

"Anything anyone could ever want," Johanna said.

He looked at Johanna, fingering his beard. It was clear that he wondered at her lack of awe. She looked down at the hems of her trousers and repressed a smile.

The arrangements were straightforward. Gradenigo drew up a commenda, which set out the details. The investor, Gradenigo, would supply the goods and take three-quarters of the profit. The merchants, Johanna and Jaufre, would put up the other quarter, take possession of the goods for trade, and do the transportation and selling.

Reading it, Jaufre said, "We have a free hand, then."

"Yes," Gradenigo said. "It is up to you what you do with the goods and where you go to sell them. When you return, however, you will note that you must make a detailed and fair statement of profit and loss."

"And if we didn't?"

Paolo smiled. "Surely it's obvious. If you wish to continue in trade, you must cultivate a good reputation among the investors. If you do not, if you are suspected of dishonesty, trickery or thievery, no investor will ever back you again."

"I suppose you investors talk to each other." Jaufre didn't make it a question.

Gradenigo's smile widened. "Of the honesty and dependability of merchants, most certainly. Of the trade itself…" There was no need to complete the sentence.

"Spices," Shasha said, ignoring Johanna's grin. "Pepper, and nutmeg."

Gradenigo grimaced. "I'm low on spices. See Tomasso on the Street of Spices, tell him I sent you and that I expect his very best price or I send you to Enzo instead."

"Paper?" Jaufre said doubtfully.

Johanna shook her head. "Too bulky, too heavy, too subject to damp."

"But it fetches an excellent price in Lyon," Gradenigo said, and waved off their protests. "Don't discount it immediately, is all I ask. Perfume?"

They settled on spices, perfume, glass vials always in demand for oils, potions, unguents and tinctures, pearls and such other gemstones as Gradenigo had in stock, and since they agreed on oil in spite of its weight and the bulk of its jars they decided they might as well include paper in their trading stock, after all.

"What do you want us to bring back?

"Wool," Gradenigo said. "And if you run across any gold or silver ingots going cheap…" He laughed at their expressions. "Wool," he said. "I'll be happy if you bring back nothing but packs and packs of wool, preferably English wool." He stroked his beard. "When my new ship comes off the ways, I may look for a route to bring English wool directly to market in Venice, without having to pay out extortionate fees to all those overland middlemen." His eyes gleamed. "I could start my own house, independent of my family."

Johanna and Jaufre and Shasha managed to spare a few moments to lay in their own goods. Jaufre, from his experience on the Rialto, specialized in jewelry for the discriminating – and wealthy – buyer, along with his usual store of manuscripts, scrolls, and books, too, in spite of the space they took up. Johanna found a dealer in antiquities down on the Grand Canal who had never heard of the Polos and was happy – for a price – to help her lay in a good stock of curiosities, including two chess sets made from ebony and ivory, one fashioned after the court of Genghis Khan and complete with long mustaches, the other made in the image of a Persian court, with the pawns made in the forms of dancing girls, which Hayat examined critically. "The maker of this set hadn't been within a league of a harem."

While the three of them were stocking their pack train, Hayat, Alma, Hari and Félicien took the opportunity to visit Padua, where Alma had heard there were some fine frescoes. They returned aglow with discovery, or at least Alma did, and Félicien was busy writing a song about the experience so Johanna assumed he was aglow, too. "Giotto, he's the artist, we wanted to meet him," Alma said. "But he was away in Assisi, alas."

Behind her back, Hayat rolled her eyes.

Alma looked at Johanna imploringly. "Are you sure you don't want to go to Rome? There are many examples of classical architecture there that I would like to see."

"You didn't see enough Roman ruins in Palestine?" Jaufre said, remembering his time as a pilgrim guard with a shudder.

✝

In two weeks they were ready. Their last night they held a farewell dinner in their lodgings, to which they invited Moreta and Peter. "It's good you are leaving," Moreta said. "My mother is so angry that you managed to circumvent her ban that I think she might be thinking of hiring assassins."

Johanna shrugged. "That's all right, we've got one of our own."

Firas sighed. "So discreet, young miss, as always."

They ate well, drank well, and sang road songs, and were generally happy to be once again on the move. "All of you?" Moreta said, her eyes lingering on Tiphaine, who scowled back.

"I'm going with them," she said fiercely. "She bought me. She has to take me."

Johanna raised her hands helplessly at Moreta's look.

Moreta looked at Alma and Hayat, who sat close together on the bench the other side of the table. "And yourselves?"

Alma smiled. "I was too long held in one place. I am not done moving yet."

"Where she goes, I go," Hayat said.

"And you, boy," Moreta said to Félicien. "You have quite a following in Venice. You could make a good living here, in spite of my mother. Especially now that you stand in Gradenigo's favor."

"I have learned all the songs I can in Venice, lady," Félicien said.

"And you, sir knight?"

"I, too, am a Frank, lady, and have been long gone from home." Alaric burped.

"And you go with them," Moreta said to Shasha, and to Firas, "And you go with her." She smiled.

"And we go wearing our own company's badge," Tiphaine said, proudly displaying hers, which had once more replaced the Gradenigo ship.

Johanna looked at Peter, who sat a little back from the rest. "And you, Peter? Now that your master is dead? Will you be leaving Venice?"

"I will, young miss," Peter said, and acknowledged the shadow of sadness that passed briefly over Moreta's face. "But not north. I will be going east, with Captain Gradenigo's next shipload of pilgrims. I have a wish to die with the wind of the steppes once again in my ears."

"The latest news says that Ogodei still holds much of the area west of the Terak," Johanna said.

"He is a Mongol," Peter said. "I am a Mongol. He will let me pass."

She felt for the lump at her waist, the jade cylinder of her father's bao, the square solidity of his book. They were the only things left to anchor her to her beginnings.

"I will hate to leave you behind," she said.

He smiled. "Look forward, young miss," he said. "Your grandfather always did."

✛

They took two boats over to the mainland at dawn the next morning, where their pack train awaited. Johanna heard a piercing whinny and a demanding stamp of hoofs, and ran to North Wind to bury her face in his mane. First he leaned against her, and then he tried to step on her foot. It had been a trying winter for both of them.

"Here," Jaufre said, cupping a hand. She placed her foot in it and he tossed her into the saddle. To him her smile was as radiant as the sun just breaking over the horizon. He couldn't stop the answering smile from spreading across his face.

Impulsively, she stretched out her hand. He caught it in his own, and they stared into each other's eyes. Or they did until North Wind did a combined hop-skip-and-jump, skittering like a foal, and broke into a trot. Johanna leaned forward to pat him on the neck. "On the Road again, North Wind!"

His stride lengthened into a smooth canter. She looked over her shoulder, laughing. "Well? Come on, everyone! Let's go!"

7

Lombardy, summer, 1324

THEY SOON DISCOVERED that travel in Europe was nothing like travel in Cathay, or in Persia for that matter. The Road was marked by steles built by the Great Khan. Each of the cities along its many routes had clean, well-maintained caravansaries for travelers and their livestock, or at the very least campsites, all of which came under the protection of the cities who built them and, not coincidentally, charged fees for their usage.

Here there were few roads worthy of the name, even fewer of which were signposted and of those few almost none were reliable. Lodging was a free-for-all of inns, all of them independent businesses and most of them verminous. There was no oversight from the various cities next to whose walls they were built, and there was no oversight from the city fathers, which left travelers prey to assault, robbery, and sometimes even murder.

On the other hand, the string of cities from Venice to Milan presented multiple opportunities for trade. Wu Company neglected none of them.

Verona boasted forty-eight towers and a ruler of martial temperament who was constantly at war with his neighbors. But he was also vitally interested in his fellow man and no sooner had word arrived in his court of visitors from storied Cathay than members of Wu Company one and all were summoned before him. They washed off the dust of the road and arrayed themselves in their finest clothes and sallied off to entertain as best they could the honorable Cangrande della Scala, ruler of Verona and various surrounding subjugated cities as well. He had a lantern jaw, intelligent eyes and was of medium height, with the broad shoulders and muscled arms of a man more comfortable with a sword in his hand than a scepter. They had been required to leave their weapons in the outer chamber but one of his aides whispered in della Scala's ear and his eyes lit up. "Let us see these swords of yours, my friends."

These were sent for forthwith and a great deal of time was spent examining and discussing the weapons. Della Scala was a little disappointed in Jaufre's smiling insistence that he was a trader first and a warrior only at necessity. Della Scala and Alaric got on much better, especially after he sent for wine and other refreshments for his guests. He did have a few questions about Cathay and even more about Ogodei when they let fall that they knew the Mongol warrior. He stroked his beard as he listened to Johanna describe in flat, unemotional terms the siege and ultimately the utter destruction of Talikan as she had witnessed it the year before.

"A man to be reckoned with," della Scala said, some moments after she had finished.

"My lord," Johanna said, and hesitated.

"Speak freely, and without fear," he said. "You are my guests."

Having been steeped in the history of the eternally treacherous battles of the court of Everything Under the Heavens from birth, she doubted that meant much.

But Alma spoke up. "Mongols are not to be reckoned with, my lord," she said. "An opponent has two options. Submit, or die to the last man, woman and child. If a city resists his forces, when the Mongol wins, and he almost always does win, my lord, he will then send in teams of men to kill every last living survivor. Those few he allows to remain alive are usually soldiers he conscripts into his army." She paused, and glanced at Hayat.

"My friend and I were citizens of Talikan, and we saw these same things with my own eyes, so I know them to be true."

There was a brief, appalled silence, and then Jaufre said smoothly, "Of course it is not a decision that any Western ruler would have to face, my lord. Ogodei and the Mongols are thousands of leagues to the east, with many strong nations and an entire sea between."

"Of course," della Scala said, a twinkle in his eye. "You have a singer of songs among you, I am told."

"We do, my lord," Jaufre said, effacing himself, and Félicien came forward, lute in hand. Della Scala motioned for a stool to be brought and the goliard disposed himself to play a tune involving a farmer, his wife and a traveling monk that had the court roaring their appreciation.

When Félicien finished his impromptu concert della Scala said, "I understand you have a magnificent white stallion in your train."

"We do, my lord," Johanna said.

"I would like very much to see him," the lord said, and Johanna perforce went to fetch North Wind from the inn outside the city walls. Della Scala's eyes lit up, as so many pairs of eyes had lit up before during their travels. He ran his hands over the stallion's back and legs, Johanna keeping North Wind on a very short rein for fear he might nip the royal buttock for its owner's presumption.

"Some scarring of the legs, I see," the lord of Verona said.

Johanna thought of the weeks in the mountains of the Hindu Kush. "We have ridden some rough trails together, my lord."

He stood back and gave the stallion a critical examination, nose to tail. "Is he fast?"

She said blandly, "He has won a few races, my lord."

Della Scala looked at Johanna, a question obvious in his eyes, and she said, hurriedly, "Alas, my lord, North Wind suffers no one on his back but me."

The royal eyebrow raised. "You? A woman?"

She forced a smile and shortened the rein even more when North Wind moved restlessly. "Even so, my lord. We formed an attachment when he was very young."

North Wind snorted and tossed his head, shortened rein be damned.

Della Scala grinned. "I daren't risk my own dignity," he said conspiratorially, "but…" He cast an eye around the courtyard. "Piero! Come here. Try out this fine steed's paces."

Piero, a young noble in a velvet tunic lavishly embroidered with gold thread and silken hose, swaggered into the center of the courtyard. "Of course, my lord."

Johanna felt the tension on the rein slack as North Wind went very still.

Every member of Wu Company stepped as far back as they could without actually leaving the courtyard. The courtiers and their ladies, in their innocence, pressed forward for a better view. Johanna took a deep breath, exchanged a pregnant glance with Jaufre, and offered an arm to della Scala. "The sun is very hot this morning, is it not, my lord? Allow me to find you a bit of shade."

The corners of the royal mouth quirked but he took her arm and she urged him to a place where the city wall cast the most shade and was coincidentally as far from the action as she could put him, halfway up a flight of stairs leading to the top of the wall. "Your view would be best from here, my lord." She kept the sentence as much as possible to a suggestion and not a plea.

The lines around his eyes crinkled, but he said solemnly enough, "It would indeed. I'm obliged to you for your courtesy, Serra Johanna."

She watched long enough to see him gain a stair higher than North Wind could kick and hurried back to the stallion. Jaufre relinquished the reins, his face preternaturally sober, and didn't need her nod to remove himself from the area forthwith.

"Ser Piero," she said. The young man looked fit enough beneath his pomaded locks, and she gave a mental shrug and handed over the reins.

North Wind's nearside ear flickered once. Other than that, he remained motionless.

Piero eyed North Wind's broad back. "It is a style of saddle with which I am unfamiliar." He shrugged. "Ah well." He grabbed a handful of North Wind's mane and vaulted up onto the stallion's back.

Johanna took a few quick steps away. There was a still, silent moment when the world seemed to hold its breath, including North Wind. He remained motionless for just long enough for the young lord to gather in the reins and kick the stallion in the sides.

It wasn't a kick really, more of nudge, the merest hint even, perhaps, but North Wind had been confined for six months on a farmer's paddock and he had not just regained his rightful rider and his rightful place on the Road to put up with this sort of nonsense. He reared on his hind legs, standing almost upright, and not bothering to break a sweat over it, either. Piero let out a startled yelp, almost lost the saddle but managed to hold on with his legs. North Wind came down on his front feet, hard. Piero managed not to be pitched over the stallion's head, just. North Wind kicked up with his rear legs, so high that Johanna, alarmed, thought for a moment the stallion would allow himself to tumble over into a somersault. Piero held on through that, too, although he lost a stirrup.

North Wind huffed out an impatient breath and without further ado lay down and rolled over. Amid a cloud of curses Piero got his leg up and out of the way just in time. Credit where credit was due, he tried to hang on to the reins but when the stallion began rubbing his back in the dirt like a dog, hooves in the air, he threw up his hands and retreated to a chorus of catcalls and jeers.

Johanna looked around and found della Scala next to her, tears of laughter in his eyes. "Your North Wind has run some races, you say?"

"A few," Johanna said demurely.

Jaufre, hearing this, said to Shasha, "So, not leaving tomorrow morning after all."

The lord arranged a race for two days later. North Wind looked over his competitors with manifest contempt and would have humiliated them all if Johanna hadn't held him back a little. When they crossed the finish line to the roar of the crowd at a gait a little too close to a trot, she brought him to pass before the lord's viewing stand, where she caught a satisfactorily heavy purse, and bowed her thanks.

She raised her head to see him speak to Piero, standing at her elbow, and was ready when the young lord came to their lodgings that evening. They remained in Verona for another week while North Wind serviced two of the lord's favorite mares at a fee which included board and room that even Jaufre said was handsome.

✦

From Verona they travelled to Brescia, still recovering from the siege of 1311 by Henry VII, now Holy Roman Emperor, and Bergamo, which city either was or was not currently under the jurisdiction of Milan, it was never made quite clear. They found nothing to delay them in either place and so pressed on to Milan. There, after fifty years of Visconti rule, the city seemed more stable than warlike Verona or subjugated Bergamo, and much more prosperous. The guilds were thriving, particularly the craft guilds. Of those, the weavers held sway, and Jaufre and Johanna spent as much time as they could observing the weavers at work, or such work as the proprietary guilds would allow. The first question they were asked everywhere was "Do you trade in wool?" When they were asked where they were going, the first comment was always, "Write to us if you get as far as England. I'm in the market for as much of the finest wool as I can get. The best prices, I promise you."

The seemingly endless dynastic struggles between France and England, Jaufre learned, had the wool trade in a constant state of flux, frustrating grangers in England as much as it did weavers in Milan, and putting a high demand – and a higher price – on fleeces of every grade. He began a running tally of names and places, just in case. No wonder Gradenigo was thinking of testing the wool trade by water.

When they identified themselves as being from Cambaluc, there were similar questions about the availability of silk in commercial quantities, but none like so urgent as the inquiries over wool. "They get all the silk they need from Lucca and Florence," Johanna said. "And Venice. Venice has been cultivating the worm for two centuries now."

Jaufre nodded. "The consensus seems to be that the finest wool comes from England."

She looked at him. "Are we specializing?"

He shrugged. "I wouldn't mind seeing where my father was born."

She smiled. "Then we should go there."

She turned on her heel and walked off down the street. He ran to catch up. "I didn't mean this very minute."

She laughed over her shoulder. "No, this very minute I mean to see that all is well with North Wind."

He followed her to the stables of the large inn. North Wind had his head over his stall door, looking in her direction every bit as much as if he'd been expecting her, and not waiting too patiently, either. Johanna let herself in his stall and crooned to him, offering an apple in recompense for the horrors of solitude the great stallion had had to endure during their hours apart. She found his brush and began to curry his already perfect coat. He whickered out a long, pleased sigh.

Jaufre hitched the door closed and leaned against the wall, arms folded. Johanna looked around and saw him watching. "What?" she said, smiling.

Deliberately, he pushed himself off the wall and stepped forward to stand in front of her, keeping his gaze locked with hers. He heard her breath hitch and was glad of it. The horse was too close for her to back away and he was glad of that, too.

"I was just thinking," he said, raising a hand to brush back a curl that had escaped from her braid.

"What? She sounded breathless. "What were you thinking?"

Both hands came up to cup her face. "That I was jealous of the horse." He lowered his face to hers.

"Oh," was all she had time to say before he kissed her.

It was like this every time, he thought somewhere in the dim recesses of his mind where rational thought still held marginal sway. He touched her and it was as if he'd been enveloped in flame. One touch and he had to, he must fill his hands with every curve of her flesh, trace every hollow with his lips, sometimes he felt he would be satisfied by nothing less than eating her alive. All the finesse of North Wind at stud, that was as close as he could come to describing it.

It wasn't as if she was struggling, some part of his mind noted. Somehow they had found themselves up against the stall and her legs were wrapped around his waist and when he managed to pull enough of her tunic down to find her breast her back arched and she whimpered. Her hands raked at his back, one slipped between them. Her hand closed around him and he groaned and raised his head to kiss her again.

They should do this someplace else, he thought as he reached for the drawstring of her trousers. She deserved better than being tumbled in the straw of a stall. Of North Wind's stall.

He raised his head. "If we do this is that bedamned horse going to take exception?"

"I'll risk it."

He gave a half laugh and then groaned again, but this time because they heard voices approaching the stable. A moment later they heard Shasha say, "The stallion is just down here, my lords."

When the group arrived at North Wind's stall Johanna was currying him as if her life depended on it and Jaufre was raking straw in much the same manner. Shasha took one look at the both of them and turned to the half dozen nobles with an affable smile. "This, good gentles, is North Wind, of whom you have heard so much, and his owner, Johanna of Wu Company and Cambaluc."

Johanna paused long enough to give a slight bow in their direction.

"North Wind can be, shall we say, a little temperamental—"

Johanna nudged the stallion and he woke up enough from his pleasurable doze to whinny loudly and snap his teeth.

"—so perhaps we could adjourn to the public room of the inn to discuss matters further? Thank you, thank you, yes, just across the courtyard, and his owner will join us there."

When the voices had faded they looked at each other. Jaufre thought Johanna looked most marvelously disheveled, and Johanna thought Jaufre looked seriously disgruntled. "I'm sorry," she said helplessly, and then gulped, remembering the last time she apologized to him. They stared at each other for a long moment, and then Johanna couldn't help it: a tiny giggle erupted, another, and then they were both laughing so hard they could only stand by leaning against the stall. North Wind, indignant at this lack of sangfroid, or perhaps hoping for another apple, gave Johanna a vigorous nudge with his nose, and she staggered forward into Jaufre's arms again.

"I didn't mean I was sorry," she said, when she could speak again. "Then or now."

"I know," he said, resting his forehead against hers. "I was feeling—interrupted."

"So was I, and that was what I was sorry for," Johanna said, with feeling.

He raised his head. Blue eyes met hazel. "I can wait."

"I can't," she said.

In an heroic act of self-sacrifice, he pushed her a little away. "Go talk to the lords."

She took a step away and then as if in the grip of some irresistible force stepped back. A little shyly she laid her hands on his chest and looked at him. "This thing, it is going to happen between us."

507

"Yes," he said. "Yes, it is. Thank all the gods."

"This is what you've always wanted? Even so long ago as Cambaluc?"

"Yes."

She looked at her hands, flat against his tunic, and looked up again. "I didn't know. Until that time in the yurt, after Kuche, I didn't even—how could I not have known?"

It wasn't a question so he didn't attempt to answer it, but in truth he had no idea how she could not have known. He had known, almost from the moment that he had fallen asleep behind her on her camel, his arms around her waist, his head on her shoulder. Well, perhaps not that soon – she was only ten years old at the time – but it was difficult now to remember a time when he did not love her.

She could not sustain the intensity of his gaze for any longer and dropped her eyes again to his tunic. "Could we—I don't— it's not that—" She huffed out a laugh. "I seem to have lost my ability to put words together and have them make sense." She met his eyes, if fleetingly. "With Edyk, I was saying goodbye. I knew—well, I thought I would never see him again. I'd known him my whole life, longer even than you. I loved him, and I wanted him, and I couldn't leave him without—without—"

"I understand," he said, not without effort.

"Do you?" Another fleeting glance. "With you, it's different, it's less—less—" She cast about for the right word. "Friendly."

Unbelievably, he found the ability to laugh. "Good."

"Truly? Because we are friends, too, Jaufre. Wu Li took you in and made you my foster brother. I have always loved you that way. Friends, and, and... comrades." She was silent for a moment, and then said with difficulty, "This—what I feel now is different."

"Friendship is how it begins, sometimes," he said. He cupped her face in his hands. "We'll take this however you want to, Johanna, but understand me now. I love you, and I want you in all the ways a man wants a woman."

She flushed. "I want you in all those ways, too."

His heart thudded in his ears. "Good," he heard someone say hoarsely, and swallowed hard. "Good." With every ounce of self-control he possessed, he dropped his hands and stepped back. "The gentlemen are waiting. You had better go talk to them before Shasha comes looking for you."

She looked the same way he felt, hungry and impatient, but she knew he was right. "Later, then," she said around the lump in her throat.

He smiled. "Later."

The Milanese nobles found North Wind's owner a little distracted, and later they congratulated each other on the very favorable stud fee they had been able to negotiate. That was not North Wind's owner's reputation. Shasha, when she heard of it, was less than complimentary.

✛

Alaric was waiting for Jaufre when he returned from the stables to their rooms on the first floor, intent on seeking out the landlord to see if there was an additional room available. If there wasn't he would find one in another inn, and he was dwelling on the possible and protracted activity to take place within when Alaric, annoyed, spoke his name in a louder voice. "What?" he said. "Oh. Alaric. I'm sorry, I wasn't paying attention."

"You certainly weren't," Alaric said severely. "I must speak with you."

"Is it important? I—"

"It is very important," Alaric said, and waved him into their private common room, small but comfortably appointed. "Sit down."

Alaric himself did not sit, taking up a stance in front of the fireplace, hands clasped behind his back. Coming out of his romantically-inspired fugue state, Jaufre noticed that the Templar looked remarkably sober. Thinking back, he realized that Alaric had been so since their last days in Venice.

"There is someone I want you to meet," Alaric said.

"Fine," Jaufre said. "Invite him to dinner. Shasha always cooks enough for—"

"—for a cohort," Alaric said. "Yes, yes, I know. We must go to him."

"Why?"

"He is cloistered."

"A monk? Where?"

"In Butrio."

"And Butrio is—?"

"About seventy leagues south of Milan."

"Seventy leagues," Jaufre said. He only hoped it hadn't come out as a scream. "That's three or four days' travel. Each way."

"This from the man who came all the way from Cambaluc."

Jaufre reddened beneath Alaric's disbelieving eye. It wasn't the distance, it was that he'd had other plans for how he would be spending the next four nights and they hadn't involved sleeping rough with Alaric.

"He knew your father," Alaric said.

That, unfortunately, did get his attention. "This monk?"

"He was a Templar, in our company. When we were disbanded, he took his vows and retired to the monastery in Butrio." Alaric stared off into the distance.

"Was he with you at the fall of Ruad?" Jaufre said.

To his surprise, Alaric's expression darkened. "Yes," he said, and stood abruptly. "North Wind will be busy in Milan for the next week, which will give us time to get there and back again before Wu Company departs for Susa. Will you come or not?"

Every part and fiber of his being was screaming no. "I'll be ready in an hour," he said, and sought out Johanna and lay the matter before her.

"No," she said instantly, brow darkening, and then she said, "This monk knew your father?"

"Alaric says so."

"And he brings this to you only now?"

510

He reached for her hands and pulled her close, some part of him marveling that he finally, at long last, after what felt like forever, had the right to do so. "It's only a week."

"But—"

He kissed her. "You could spend the time finding a yurt," he said. "One just big enough for the both of us. For when we're between inns."

She relented a little. "I suppose I could do that."

He kissed her then, and she kissed him, and neither of them gave a thought to holding anything back. When they finally broke apart they were both trembling. "Does Alaric know if this monk is even still alive?" she said, her voice so rough he hardly recognized it.

He hadn't asked. "He seemed certain."

She took a deep, shaky breath. "Go, then," she said. She even laughed.

"What?"

"Just that I find it extremely annoying that North Wind's love life is better than my own."

His response to that left her certain that he'd broken at least two of her ribs. "Go," she said, breathless, half laughing, half crying. "And Jaufre?"

"What?"

"Ride fast."

Jaufre forced himself to let go of her. In the courtyard he said to Alaric, "Let's get out of here before Hari finds out we're going to a monastery."

✝

For speed, they took two of the Arabians that Firas and Johanna had liberated from Sheik Mohammed's stables during her escape from Talikan. Jaufre pushed the horses hard enough that Alaric complained. Jaufre's only response was to press on even harder.

Félicien complained, too, but he was uninvited and so ignored by both Jaufre and Alaric. He'd returned to the inn in time to see them saddling the horses, inquired as to why, and volunteered himself as the third member of their party. Jaufre didn't care, all his intent focussed on getting there and back again as quickly as possible, and though Alaric huffed and puffed he made no serious objection. Félicien dashed into the inn for his kit and into the stable for a mount and was now riding in their train on a rented nag, gitar slung over his shoulder. Whenever a hill slowed down their passage he brought out a wooden flute he had acquired in Venice and practiced. Its plaintive wail did seem to calm the horses.

They passed through a fertile plain where flourishing farms and manors jostled for place with dense alders and tall elms, an occasional poplar and willow, grove after grove of olive trees, and a deciduous tree with a straight trunk and dark green leaves that Jaufre recognized as an ironwood tree, common in Everything Under the Heavens. Alaric called it a hornbeam and dismissed it as of no consequence. They splashed through innumerable rills, streams and rivers, all of them seeming to flow south and east. "They flow to the Po," Alaric said. "All the water here does."

They clattered into the village that was neighbor to the hermitage just before dark on the third day. Their steaming mounts were led away by an ostler, all agog at this unheralded visitation by two knights accompanied by their own minstrel. Jaufre managed not to laugh when he was so addressed but Alaric straightened up as if he'd heard a trumpet fanfare and paraded into the common room, hand on the hilt of his sword and looking loftily down the length of what was after all a very long nose.

The innkeeper, a man of some dignity himself, was deferential without being obsequious. He bowed Alaric to the best table, flapping his apron at the two men who already occupied it, who gratified him by springing to their feet and finding another table without comment or complaint. Félicien's gitar might have had something to do with that, because after a meal of hearty stew, bread and an excellent cheese, one of them approached the table and asked humbly if the lord's minstrel might favor them with a song or a story.

Jaufre looked around and saw that the word had gone forth. There were no longer any empty seats and there were more people leaning against the walls. Ah well, country folk must find their entertainment where they could, and the hermitage, so far as he could tell as they had approached it at dusk, was in an isolated spot that could not have seen much traffic.

"I don't expect there will be many coins in my cap from this crowd," Félicien said in an undertone.

"Be kind," Jaufre said. "It's not every day one has the privilege to hear the song of a young goliard who has traveled all the way to Cathay and back again. Especially in a town this size, this far off any main road."

The room was dimly lit by a few fat candles in sconces and the light of the fire on the hearth, but he thought the boy blushed. He wondered again if Félicien had even been out of swaddling clothes when he left home. Other than admitting to being a Frank, the goliard had steadily ignored any other questions as to his life before he had joined their campfire and company one evening somewhere between Chang'an and Dunhuang. Or possibly Dunhuang and Turfan. "Sing," Jaufre said. "They may not have much to give, but you do. And they will talk of this night for years to come."

The goliard struck a chord and did as he was bid, and before long a bashful young man appeared with a small drum to beat out the time. A tonsured monk brought a wooden flute to play high while Félicien sang middle and the gitar sang low. There were songs of the Road, marching songs and marrying songs. Songs of love lost and love found, songs of battles lost and won. Many Jaufre recognized and many more he did not, but then the goliard had the gift of the true entertainer, the ability to divine what his audience wanted to hear and to give it to them in a key they could hum along to.

The next morning they were up with the dawn, or Jaufre was, the need to be back in Milano at Johanna's side riding him hard. Félicien didn't stir but Alaric followed him downstairs to break their fast in the common room, the site of last night's concert. "Enough!" Jaufre said, cutting the knight's grumbling short. "You wanted to make this journey and you wanted me to meet your friend. Let's go meet him and be about our business."

They presented themselves at the door of the monastery, an imposing edifice built of square blocks of local stone. There was an arcade surmounted by a second storey with a row of rectangular windows, a church with a vaulted ceiling supported by pointed arches and painted with luminous frescoes, and a low dormitory attached to the main building. There was a thriving garden and an orchard filled with fruit trees.

The knight rang the bell hanging outside the main door. It was answered by the same tonsured monk who had accompanied Félicien on the flute the night before. Jaufre had thought that the purpose of a monastery was for its inmates to be sequestered from public life but the ways of Christianity were still a mystery to him and he made no comment. The monk, who introduced himself as Fra Lamberto, greeted them with enthusiasm, heard out Alaric's request, and shook his head. "I will ask," he said, "but Brother Donizo rarely speaks to anyone these days." He saw Alaric's look and shook his head. "No, no, he is well, at least in body." His brow creased. "It is his spirit which suffers, and nothing I nor Father Matteo say can ease him." He cast a shrewd glance over the two of them. "Perhaps you can," he said thoughtfully. "Oblige me by waiting a moment, do."

He rustled away and returned shortly. "Come with me."

They followed him down the arcaded passageway, each of the column's capitals carved with fearsome animals or human figures writhing in the worst the Devil could do to them, a sight guaranteed to keep you at your prayers. They entered the long, low building and proceeded down a corridor of many doors, entering the last one on the right. "Brother Donizo? Brother

Donizo, I have here two visitors for you." He stepped inside and motioned the others to follow.

It was a tiny room, scrupulously clean and sparsely furnished with a cot and a niche in the wall with a statue Jaufre recognized as the most prevalent Christian saint, the woman in blue with the child in her arms. The statue was delicately made and really beautifully colored, perhaps by the same hand that had created the frescoes in the church. Before it knelt a man clad in the same rough spun brown robes as Fra Lamberto. His hands were clasped in front of his face, his eyes were closed and his lips moved soundlessly.

"Brother Donizo?"

The man on his knees looked up finally, blinking, as if the light from the eastward-facing window hurt his eyes. They were a light blue, so light that for a moment Jaufre thought he was blind. But those blue eyes looked first at Fra Lamberto and then traveled to the knight standing at his shoulder, and widened. "Alaric?" The monk stumbled to his feet and had to be caught by Fra Lamberto before he fell. "Alaric!" He reached out, weeping, to grasp Alaric's hands in his own. "Alaric! You came! You came at last!"

✠

They sat outside in the sun, Fra Lamberto fetching watered wine and a plate of bread and olives and then tactfully leaving them alone. Jaufre sat a little apart, watching the other two men. Brother Donizo had stopped crying but he was still incapable of complete sentences. "Alaric. After all this time, I—When we parted, you—I never expected—It's been so long—"

Alaric patted his arm and muttered soothing nothings, and plied Brother Donizo with watered wine. After what felt like a very long time to Jaufre the monk pulled himself together and attempted a smile. "And who is your companion, Alaric? I'm sorry, my boy," he said belatedly. "I am a little overcome. It has been so very long since I saw Alaric, you see."

"You know his face, Gilbert," Alaric said, watching the monk closely.

"No, I—" The blue eyes widened. "No! Robert? But how can this be? He left us when—"

"Yes, he left us," Alaric said, interrupting the monk. "He married afterward, Gilbert. This is his son."

"His son!" There was a long moment of profound silence as Brother Donizo, or Gilbert, stared at Jaufre. "He saved us. He saved us both. And how we repaid him, Alaric. How we repaid him."

"He didn't want it, Gilbert. He didn't want any part of it."

The monk made a gesture of repugnance. "I know, but—"

"What did you do with it, Gilbert?" Alaric said softly.

"What's 'it'?" Jaufre said, his head whirling at the thought that here was someone else who had known his father. "What are you talking about?"

Gilbert sought Alaric's eyes. The two older men looked at each other for a long moment. "He is truly Robert's son?" the monk said.

"Show him your sword," Alaric told Jaufre.

Jaufre pulled his sword from the sheath he wore on his back, and handed it to the monk, who received it reverently. His grip was sure and practiced, for a monk. "It is Robert's, of course," he said, his awed voice barely above a murmur.

"Yes, it belonged to my father," Jaufre said, losing patience. "What of it?"

"You didn't tell him?" Gilbert said.

Alaric's face was like iron. "Some of it. Not all."

In that moment both men looked considerably older than their years.

8

Lombardy, summer, 1324

THERE HAD BEEN four of them after the fall of Ruad. Alaric and Robert, Jaufre's father, yes, but also Gilbert, a Frank like Alaric and now the man known to them as Brother Donizo, and a fourth man, Wilmot of Bavaria. The son of a wealthy mason with social ambitions, his father had bought Wilmot his knighthood. "Like Robert, it was what he could do, not what he wanted to do," Gilbert said, sounding rueful.

Ruad, the island redoubt of the last of the Crusader outposts in the Levant, had been given by the Pope to the Templars in 1301, who would hold it until it was overrun by the Mamluks two years later. The ordinary troops had been slaughtered to a man and the surviving knights shipped off to prison in Egypt, where most of them starved to death.

"It was Robert," Gilbert said. "The four of us would have been caught, too, but for Robert." He gave Jaufre a sober look. "I owe your father my life." He looked at Alaric. "We all do."

"Why?" Jaufre said. "How?"

Gilbert looked at Alaric and sighed. "Robert was much more long-sighted and realistic about the future of the Templars in the East."

"About the future of the Templars, period," Alaric said.

"That, too," Gilbert said.

Confusion is rampant at the end of any sack, they told him, which he already knew from Johanna's account of the fall of Talikan. Confusion at the fall of Ruad was compounded by Ruad's location. "An island," Gilbert said. "And we were hopelessly outnumbered. In 1301, when Ghazan didn't come when he said he would—"

Alaric spat. "Mongols," he said, the word itself an epithet. "Never trust them."

Jaufre thought of the Mongol Baron Ogodei, and didn't disagree.

"Yes, well, when the Mongols didn't come, Robert told us it was over." His smile was wry. "We didn't believe him, of course."

"Wilmot did," Alaric said.

"But you and I didn't," Gilbert said. "Our faith was still strong. We believed in the righteousness of our cause, that the Holy Land was meant to be under Christian rule, that we would triumph over the Saracen savages and that God Himself would appear in our vanguard to lead us with flaming sword back to Jerusalem." He closed his eyes and shook his head.

Jaufre let the silence linger for just as long as he could bear it and no more. "But my father…"

Gilbert opened his eyes, looking upon the flourishing garden as if uncertain how he'd come there. "I think he was planning our escape from the moment Ghazan's forces retreated. The week before Ruad fell, he went up to the walls to look over the situation and when he came down he gathered the four of us together and told us that we had to leave. By that time, none of us needed much convincing." He looked again at Alaric. "I'm going to tell him. All of it."

"Confession is good for the soul," Alaric said.

"So they say," Gilbert said. "At any rate, I have never confessed this to anyone else, but I am going to now, to Robert's son." He turned to Jaufre and straightened where he sat. Clad in rough homespun, his hair tonsured, he nevertheless somehow had the faint air of the knight he had once been, with all the strength and pride that came with the oath and the office.

"There was a room," he said, "where they kept what remained of our treasury."

Jaufre stiffened. Gilbert noticed, and gave a wry smile. "Yes. The structure of our lives was crumbling, and all we had to hold us together was Robert's determination that we would survive. How, we asked ourselves, we who had always had our meals and roofs and clothes and armor and weapons provided for us, how were we to live?" He sighed. "But I won't make excuses. Alaric and I decided to help ourselves to some of it before we left. In all the confusion we thought it would never be missed, that we would never be noticed." A short laugh. "Our mistake. There were others, equally interested in the remnants of the Templars' treasure." He glanced again at Alaric. "Alaric was wounded in the escape. Wilmot would have left him behind, I think, but Robert insisted."

Jaufre tried to imagine it, the noise, the shouting, men wounded and dying, the boats landing on the beaches, the walls breached, the enemy pouring in.

"The fort was burning by the time he got us down to the beach. He'd hidden a small boat among the rocks. We buried our mantles and armor in those same rocks and got in the boat and pushed off. Halfway to shore we were seen and capsized. God, I have never seen such a hail of arrows. They might be heathens but the Saracens are excellent shots. I can only attribute to the protective hand of God Himself that only I was hit." Gilbert put a hand to his leg, massaging the memory of an old wound. "Wilmot took me and Robert took Alaric and they managed to get us ashore and into hiding. He found us food and medicines and tended us until we were well enough to travel."

"And the treasure?"

Gilbert laughed shortly. "We should have drowned with the weight of gold and silver we were carrying with us, Alaric and I. Wilmot and Robert would have killed us both when they discovered it, if we hadn't needed it so badly, to pay for the food and medicines."

"And afterward?"

Gilbert shrugged. "Robert and Alaric went to Antioch to seek work as caravan guards. Wilmot and I went to Byzantium and took ship for Venice. I came here." He glanced at Alaric. "It was what I had always wanted."

"You talked about it enough," Alaric said.

"Yes, I suppose I did. I imagine that is how you knew where to find me?" Alaric nodded, and Gilbert sighed. "Wilmot left me here and went north, he said to seek work as a mason at Chartres. They're building a cathedral there."

"They've been building it for a hundred years," Alaric said sourly.

"Then Wilmot should have been successful," Gilbert said. "I have seen or heard nothing of him since."

There was a weighted moment, and then Alaric, as though the words were forced from him, said, "Where is it?"

Gilbert looked up. "Where is what?" he said blankly.

"The rest of the treasure. Where is it?"

"Where is—" Gilbert's face cleared and he turned a look composed equal parts of realization and sympathy on the man who had once been his brother in arms, his co-conspirator, his fellow thief. "It is here, Alaric," he said gently.

"Where?" Alaric looked around the garden. "Is it buried somewhere?"

Gilbert sighed. "Come with me," he said, rising to his feet.

They followed him about the monastery until the bells rang for vespers. There was a great deal to see, the handsome church and the arcaded cloister they had seen before, a chapter room large enough to accommodate all the community at Sant' Alberto's, lay and clerical. There was a many-roomed novitiate, spare and scrupulously clean, a library of well-filled shelves that made Jaufre's palms itch, and a scriptorium with cunningly arranged skylights that introduced much-needed light on the work of monks laboriously copying out more manuscripts. There was a large kitchen, an infirmary, two guesthouses, one for men and one for women, and a large and well-tended herb garden that Jaufre wished Shasha could see. The vegetable garden and the orchard they had already seen. "There is also a leper's hospital," Gilbert said, with a wave of his hand that indicated the hills at the back of the monastery.

Alaric had followed Gilbert on this tour of Sant' Alberto's facilities with a steadily decaying patience. Now he said, "Where is it, Gilbert?"

Gilbert met his eyes with a slight smile. "I told you, Alaric. It is here."

"You gave it to the monastery," Jaufre said, a grin spreading across his face.

"What!"

Gilbert smiled again. What with his confession to Jaufre of the truth of their escape from Ruad and his confession to Alaric of what had happened to the rest of the Templar treasure, he was looking years and years younger. "Yes," he said happily. "I put it to work here. It seemed best."

Alaric seemed unable to speak. When he did he was barely coherent. "I—we trusted you! How could you—you—you false friend! You thief!"

"You could have taken your share with you when you went east with my father," Jaufre said. "Why didn't you?"

Gilbert chuckled. "Because he was following Robert and Robert wouldn't have countenanced it."

Alaric shouted something incomprehensible to the sky and stamped off into the orchard, scattering monks as he went.

He seemed to have calmed down by the time they gathered in the refectory for dinner. Jaufre thought he detected what might even have been a trace of pride in the eyes that appraised the long, well-polished oak table and the finely woven tapestries that warmed the stone walls.

And later that evening, when the other two supposed him asleep in his blankets, he heard the low-voiced conversation. "You are weary, and heartsore, Alaric," Gilbert said. "You could stay here. You should stay here. I won't guarantee you will find peace here. I haven't." A brief pause. "Although perhaps the possibility of it, now. We could use a good blacksmith. You were always handy around a forge."

Alaric grunted, and Jaufre wondered if he would be returning to Milano alone.

But then Alaric said, slowly, "No. Perhaps, one day. But no, not now. Not yet."

"What are you looking for, Alaric, that you can't find here?"

"Goodnight, Gilbert," Alaric said. "We'll say our goodbyes in the morning."

"Alaric. Why did you come seeking the treasure? Why now, after all these years?"

A loud snore.

A sigh, the light of the candle snuffed, and the slap of the monk's sandals as he let himself out of the guesthouse.

✝

As promised the next morning Gilbert stood at their stirrups to wish them goodbye and godspeed. "Thank you, my boy," he said to Jaufre. "I am glad that Robert went on to have some happiness in his life. Your mother sounds like a fine woman, and I can see for myself that they had a fine son."

"Thank you, Brother Donizo."

The monk took courteous leave of Félicien, and moved to Alaric. He reached up a hand and they clasped arms for a long moment. "I hope to see you again in this life, Alaric."

"As God wills." Alaric smiled. "Brother Donizo."

A league or so onwards Jaufre motioned to Félicien to drop a little way behind and said to Alaric, "You've never struck me as one who hankered after riches, Alaric. Why seek out Gilbert and the treasure now?"

They rode in silence for a few moments. "Because," Alaric said. He swallowed and turned to look Jaufre full in the face.

He looked miserable, and ashamed. "Because it was all I could do to provide for Robert's son." He faced forward again. "And it turned out I couldn't even do that much."

He kicked his mount into a canter and moved ahead, leaving Jaufre staring after him, mouth open.

✝

They traveled as quickly back as they had come, wringing the last ray of sunlight out of the day before stopping for the night. The closer they came to Milano, the more Jaufre became preoccupied with thoughts of Johanna, and of all the wonderful things they would do together, some of them even with their clothes on. For the first time he wondered where they would settle, where a home that would suit them both could be found, and then all he could think about was the house they would live in, and the room that would be theirs, and the bed in that room. Would they marry? In what faith? Children. Shasha would stay with them, and Shasha staying meant Firas would stay, too. Firas was a fine man, a good fighter, loyal, intelligent, able. He could wish for no better brother-in-law.

The others? He didn't know. After the revelations of Sant' Alberto, he couldn't predict what Alaric would do. Tiphaine was with them for the duration, that was certain. He grinned to himself. She might even be their first child.

They stopped to water their mounts at the ford of a small stream. Jaufre was just pulling at the reins of his horse to keep him from drinking too much when movement caught the corner of his eye. He looked up and they were surrounded at spear's point by a company of ten men, mounted. He reached for his father's sword and found his hand knocked away, replaced by the point of a sharp point pressing into his neck. He went very still, his empty hands raising in surrender. He heard an oath and a thud and turned his head to see Alaric on the ground, glaring up at his attacker.

"Yes, yes," said his attacker, very brisk, "suffice it to say we are outlaws and villains, but we have no interest in you and will take none if you give us what we want without resistance, after which we will be on our way and you on yours."

Alaric used his horse's stirrup to pull himself to his feet, his face red with rage. "You would leave us disarmed, on foot, on a road where—"

"We don't want your weapons or your horses, good sir," said the knight, as the circlet around his helm indicated he must be. He raised his head and smiled at Félicien.

Something in the quality of the goliard's silence made both Jaufre and Alaric turn to look at him. He was still astride his horse, sitting very still, his face whiter than Jaufre had ever seen it. "Don't harm them, my lord," he said. "Please."

"That, my dear Félicienne, is entirely up to you."

Félicienne? There was something odd in the pronunciation of the goliard's name. Jaufre looked at Alaric and saw dawning revelation, succeeded by furious anger. "Félicienne! Félicienne?"

Their attacker was politely incredulous. "You didn't know?" He looked from Alaric to Jaufre and back again. "Truly? You didn't know?" He threw back his head and laughed so hard he seemed in danger of losing his seat. "Oh my dear Félicienne! You have fallen in with fools!"

The goliard waited for the knight to stop laughing, and met his eyes with a calm that seemed to Jaufre to be very hard won. "How did you find me?" he said again.

"Oh, my very dear." The knight laughed again. "If you will persist in singing where people can hear you, eventually someone will recognize the dulcet tones of l'Alouette du Sud, famed all over Provins for her voice, and her poetry." He looked over his shoulder. "And sooner or later, that someone will remember the very generous gifts waiting for anyone who could lead me to her."

Jaufre saw Alaric follow his gaze, and did the same. An older man dressed in bright new clothes lurked behind the spearmen. "Jean de Valmy!" Alaric spat out the name.

Not since l'Alouette du Sud have I heard such a voice. And Jaufre felt certain more was intended by the oh-so-casual comment, *The young man, the goliard who sings.* He had no very certain idea of what was happening here, but he knew one thing. "You treacherous, sarding whoreson," he said.

The older man reddened and looked away.

"I hope your new hose are easier on your boiled ass than your old ones were," Alaric said. "Betrayal must pay well."

The knight kicked his horse until it was alongside Félicien's rented nag. "That is a very unworthy mount for you, my lady wife. Allow me." He stretched out an arm.

Wife?

Félicienne didn't move. "If you don't harm them, I will submit to you, willingly."

"By God, you will. I seem to remember missing out on my wedding night." This last was said with an odd twist, and Jaufre saw a flicker of revulsion cross Félicien's face.

"I give you my word, here and now, witnessed by your men, that I will not run away again, that I will share your bed, that I will bear your children without complaint." Jaufre, watching her, thought she might be sick over her saddle there and then, but she was not, and continued to speak in a strong, steady voice. "I will do all these things. But you must let them live."

The knight laughed. "Do you imagine you have a choice?"

Something like pride flickered in Félicien's dark eyes. "I escaped from you once before, if you remember, my lord."

"I do remember," the lord said silkily. "I don't make the same mistake twice, be sure, lady wife."

Félicienne raised her chin, but Jaufre could see her hands trembling on her reins. "You have to sleep sometime, my lord."

The lord stared at her for a long moment, and then burst out laughing again. A merry gentleman, indeed. "Florian!" he said, still laughing. "Call off the dogs and go on ahead. I will follow."

"My lord—"

"God's balls! Do you think I can't manage a green boy who

can't even get his sword out of its sheath in time to use it and an old man long past his prime who should be dreaming by his fire? I, Ambroise de L'Arête?"

"No, my lord."

"Very well, then. Get you gone."

The point pressing against Jaufre's neck disappeared. Something warm trickled into his collar. There was some signal unseen by Jaufre, and the troop wheeled its mounts as one and moved down the road at an orderly trot, with L'Arête's lieutenant leading and Jean de Valmy falling in behind, head sunk beneath his shoulders. Jaufre only wanted the opportunity to strike it off.

"Well, my dear?"

Her eyes sought Jaufre's. "Tell Johanna and Shasha and Hari—tell all of them goodbye for me."

"It's true then?" he said, disbelieving. "You're a woman? And this man's wife?"

A tremulous smile. "And my thanks to them, from the bottom of my heart. And to you, Jaufre."

She grasped the knight's arm and was hoisted behind him. With the loose end of his reins he lashed at the two loose horses and sent them crashing through the undergrowth in different directions. Jaufre's mount neighed and sidled and made an abortive attempt at rearing.

"My lord—"

"My very dear lady, they are fortunate I don't kill them both for having traveled in your company unchaperoned." The knight nodded in their direction. "Gentles. We should not meet again." His smile was thin, and there was a wealth of meaning in the way he sheathed his sword. "Really. We should not."

He kicked his destrier into a trot and then into a canter, and Jaufre and Alaric watched as they disappeared in the wake of the troop of spearmen.

9

Milano, fall, 1324

"Félicien is a girl?" Tiphaine said.

"Not just a girl, a married woman," Alaric said, who appeared not just surprised but outraged at the revelation.

"No beard," Jaufre said. He'd been thinking about it all the way to Milano. "I kept thinking he was just too young to shave."

"I never saw him shit," Alaric said, toasting the room with his wine and drinking deep. "Should have known right then. Unnatural, a man never shits."

"He never removed that awful robe," Alma said, her nose wrinkling. "I offered once to wash it for him and he thanked me but said he preferred to wash his own garments."

"Dirt can be a useful disguise," Hari said. "People do not care to look too closely at the unwashed."

"He never said much, either," Alaric said. "Except when he was singing."

"Didn't want to draw attention," Hayat said. She looked at Alma. They knew what that was like.

"He looked so young," Jaufre said again. "I kept thinking he must have left home at ten."

"Félicien's a girl?" Tiphaine said.

"I don't understand how we didn't know this," Johanna said.

"He—she was with us for almost two years. How could we not know this?"

"Well," Shasha said, and exchanged a meaningful look with Firas, and Hari cleared his throat and refolded a section of his orange robe into an elaborate pleat.

Johanna stared at the three of them. "You knew? The three of you knew and you said nothing?"

"It was her business," Shasha said.

"It was our business, too," Jaufre said with, "especially when she's got some crazed lord for a husband chasing after her. He could have killed us both." And would have, if she hadn't traded herself for them. The memory seared him like a burning brand.

"Why did she run from him, would be more to the point," Shasha said. "He was so young. She. She was so young. She couldn't have been more than a child when she was married to him. Obviously she disliked her situation enough to run as far and as long from it as she did." She looked around the room. "And what are we going to do about it?"

Alaric choked over his wine. "Do? Do? He's—she's his wife! You don't interfere between a man and his wife!"

"He was with us almost since we left Cambaluc," Shasha said, eyes on Johanna.

"She lied to us!" Alaric said. "We owe her nothing!"

"Alaric!" Jaufre's voice cracked like a whip. "She bargained herself for us, traded herself for our freedom. There was nothing to stop him from killing us and burying us there. No one would ever have known."

Alaric's gaze dropped and a tinge of color might have crept up the back of his neck. Still, he said, "We don't even know where he took her."

"We have a name," Jaufre said. "Ambroise de L'Arête."

Alaric fired up again. "And they're nobility! You saw the circlet he wore on his helmet!"

Shasha, startled, said, "Is this true?"

528

"And they were my lord and my ladying it all over the place," Alaric said, triumphant.

Jaufre's face was hard. "It doesn't matter. She sacrificed her freedom for our own. She didn't want to go with him, Alaric. Surely you saw that for yourself."

"She's his wife," Alaric said. "She has no choice in the matter."

Johanna took a deep breath and let it out slowly. "We have other obligations."

Jaufre whirled around. "By all the Mongol gods! That we do, and first among them is—"

"First among them, Jaufre, is our obligation as merchant traders to carry the goods in our care to the trade fairs in Lyon, as we contracted with Ser Gradenigo to do."

He stopped short, breathing hard.

"Further," she said, as calmly as she was able, "Lyon is the crossroads for commerce in this part of the world. Everyone who buys and sells goes through Lyon, which means—"

"—news of everyone," Shasha said, jumping in because Johanna was right and she didn't want her to have to take all of Jaufre's fire when he realized it. "Our best hope for finding news of Félicien is to go to the place where the most news circulates."

Jaufre's breathing, loud in that silent room, began to slow down.

Firas stepped in. "Do we stick to our planned route?"

"I think so, yes," Shasha said. "Perhaps we move more quickly now." She looked around. "Does anyone have any other comments or observations?"

Alma exchanged glances with Hayat, and said, "We'll revisit this discussion in Lyon, yes?"

Alaric snorted.

"Of course," Shasha said before Jaufre could say something that this time would alienate everyone in the room instead of only five or six of them.

"North Wind had his last appointment in the duke's stables this morning," Johanna said. "I have accepted no more offers."

This time Jaufre snorted, and followed that by leaving the room. The door did not quite slam behind him.

"Wait," Shasha said, when Johanna would have gone after him. "Give him time to cool down."

"I didn't know he cared so much for Félicien," Johanna said.

"I don't know that he did, or does, young miss," Hari said. "What I believe he objects to most is the way she left us." He gave a faint smile. "Suppose it had been you? Or Shasha?"

"Or even yourself," Firas said.

"Or even my unworthy self," Hari said, unperturbed by the mocking note in the assassin's voice. "It would be unwise to be too quick to judge. Like so many travelers before her—" his eye excluded no one in the room "—the young woman evidently had reasons to be far from her native land."

There was a brief, freighted silence.

"Then why did she return here with us? She must have known the risk." Johanna paused. "Alaric? What was it you said that man—her husband called her? The Songbird of the South?"

"The Lark of the South," Alaric said, his voice soft now. He repeated it in French. "L'alouette du Sud."

"You come from the south," Jaufre said. "Are you familiar with this name?"

Alaric drained his mug and refilled it from the pitcher on the table. "I've been in the East for so long, home might as well be a foreign country to me. I have heard all the same news that you have heard of my homeland, and in none of it was there mention of this—lark." He drank and gave the hearth a malevolent stare. "Old man sitting beside a fire," he muttered. "Who's past his prime?"

"Félicien's a girl?" Tiphaine said.

✠

Johanna paused outside the room Jaufre shared with Hari and Alaric. The room they had shared with Félicien. She raised a hand as if to knock, and let it fall again.

She slept alone that night in the room she had acquired for the two of them. The next morning she found him in the stable yard, where he already had their pack animals assembled. He was evidently prepared to drive all of them single-handedly to the warehouse where their goods were stored and load each of them himself. "Jaufre."

He spared her a glance. "What?"

"We should probably lay in a few supplies for the trip," she said, trying to keep her voice reasonable. "There are very few towns of any size between here and Lyon and we still have to get over the Alps."

"I sent Shasha out at daybreak. She knows what we need."

"Jaufre." She caught his arm as he finished tacking up one donkey, only to have him pull free and move on to the next. "Jaufre, we'll never be able to leave today."

He yanked hard on a cinch, and the donkey gave a bray of protest. "We are leaving today."

"Jaufre—"

He rounded on her so ferociously she actually backed up a step. "We will leave today, Johanna. Or I will, alone."

He wasn't interested in comfort, only action. She waited until he'd turned back to the donkey, and then stepped forward to begin tacking up the next one.

By noon Shasha was back, trailed by a dozen street urchins Tiphaine had each bribed into carrying back a mountain of supplies. Everyone helped, even Alaric. They were loaded by sext and an hour later they were on the road west.

Jaufre set the pace and the plain of Lombardy seemed to roll away beneath them of its own volition. They found campsites near water sources, living as much as possible off their own supplies, showing arms and attitude when they thought a display of force advisable. "I don't want any trouble," Jaufre said, "but by Mohammed's hairy ass I want to look like we could cause a lot of it if needs be."

Alaric's eye brightened at the prospect, but they were for the most part left to themselves. They saw more pilgrims than any other kind of traveler, gray-robed and en route for Venice and Jerusalem. Dame Joan was still vivid in their memories and they all expressed their silent gratitude to whomever might be listening that these pilgrims were going in the opposite direction.

Les Alpes rose steadily before them, tall and sharp-edged and snow-capped. The pass through them was called Moncensio in Lombardy and as they would discover, Mont Cenis on the other side. The trail switchbacked suicidally up from the plains but when they achieved the pass Johanna said to Shasha, "Not quite Terak, is it?"

Jaufre heard her. "Let's just hope there are no surprises waiting for us on the other side."

"Always with the cheerful prospect in view," Firas said, but he said it for Shasha's ears alone.

The pass was quite beautiful, ringed with white peaks and blue lakes. Going down, the trail felt less likely to fling them from the side of the mountain into the ravine beneath. It was August by then, with the bright, pitiless sun leeching the blue from the sky. The temperature rose as the elevation fell and made everyone snappish. Firas, scouting ahead, found a campsite near a trickle of water barely large enough to suit their needs. They picketed the livestock, and Johanna led North Wind downstream and let the cool water trickle over his hooves. He nudged her, and she produced a bit of apple. He munched contentedly.

A splash behind her and she turned her head. "Jaufre." Her heart rose at the thought he might have followed them.

"Don't go too far away from the others," he said. "It might not be safe."

North Wind nosed at her pocket and she smiled a little. "I think I'm safe enough."

"Don't forget, I've seen a time when even North Wind wasn't enough to keep you from harm."

"Jaufre," she said when he turned. She splashed over to put

her hands, a little shyly, on his shoulders. "Jaufre," she said again. She leaned in to kiss him.

She felt a flash of undeniable awareness go through him, felt an instant of yielding, felt his hands on her arms tighten for a moment. And then he used them to push her away. Not roughly, but firmly, and with finality. "Not now, Johanna," he said. "I can't think of anything until Félicien is safe again."

She stood for a long time, the water gurgling around her feet, staring before her at nothing in particular. Then North Wind snorted and she went to lean up against his vast, comforting bulk, before he nudged her again and she remembered she had a curry comb.

✠

The inchoate jumble of city-states and personal fiefdoms and royal dominions that formed the chain of mostly Frankish states stretched from the Middle Sea north to wherever the Holy Roman Empire began. Mostly they spoke French, albeit with regional accents that tested everyone's polyglot abilities to the maximum. It was fifty leagues from Mont Cenis to Lyon. The first half of it was mountainous, but they made up the distance on the rolling plain that succeeded the mountains and were taking the ferry across the Rhône three days later. Wu Company had about five minutes to appreciate the setting, a city crowded between two rivers and two hills, prosperous and bustling and ready to do business with anyone regardless of race, color, creed, nationality, gender or diet, before Jaufre called them together, his voice pitched low so as not to be overheard.

"Shasha, find us a place to stay. Firas, a place to stable the livestock. Johanna, find the Gradenigo agent. Alaric, you're with me."

"And where are you going?" Johanna said it but they were all thinking it.

"I want to see the inside of every inn and tavern and tour every market inside and outside the city walls. I want to know what people are saying. I want every scrap of news and gossip going. The rest of you keep your eyes and ears open. If you see two men talking to each other on a street corner, I want to know what they were saying. Drop Ambroise de L'Arête and l'Alouette du Sud into the conversation whenever you think you safely can, but don't let it come back on us. I don't want him to know we are coming."

He and Alaric, his expression indicating he was anticipating the taverns, vanished into the crowds of people moving through the eastern gate.

"Good thing this seems like a nice place," Johanna said, in not quite a growl.

Shasha raised an eyebrow at Firas.

"He is certainly focussed," he said, and shrugged. "At least it's warmer and drier than Venice."

Alma was gazing at an edifice on a hill. "I wonder if that's a university?"

Hari, standing next to her and gazing likewise, said, "Or perhaps a church?"

Tiphaine, who had disappeared from their train when they arrived at the outskirts of the city, came trotting up. "Did we want to stay inside or outside the walls?"

"Outside, I think," Shasha said. She looked again at Firas. "I imagine our lord and master would not like to be locked behind gates if he wanted to leave in a hurry."

Firas laughed.

"Very well," Tiphaine said, impatient, "there is a large inn called The Sign of the Black Lion this side of the south gate. It is large enough for our party and it is spoken well of in the city. There is a stable nearby. I don't know if it's large enough for our needs. We'll have to go see."

"Is it indeed?" Firas said. "Very well, young miss, let us seek out this inn." They went off, Tiphaine marching importantly at the assassin's side.

Johanna slipped from North Wind's back. "Evidently I'm off

to find one Phillippe Imbert, Ser Gradenigo's agent in Lyon. As I have been bid." She tossed the reins to Shasha. "Don't let him bite anyone."

"Johanna."

She looked over her shoulder, her jaw very tight.

"Try for some understanding."

"Oh, I do understand," Johanna said, and departed.

"Of course you do," Shasha said, and warned Gradenigo's stallieres to mind the pack animals and their merchandise carefully in this throng of people, and issued a dire warning as to what would happen if any of them slipped off to the Lyonnaise fleshpots before they were given leave to do so.

✝

Phillippe Imbert was a smooth-talking Frank, his robes made from the finest fabrics in the richest colors and his beard clipped in the latest fashion. He had an eye for the ladies and he certainly had an eye for Johanna. It took a while to convince him that Gradenigo of Venice would send a woman to deal for him, even with Gradenigo's letter in hand as evidence. "Ser Imbert," Johanna had to say at last.

"No, no, Sieur Imbert on this side of Les Alpes," he said, laughing.

"Sieur Imbert," she said through her teeth, "while I'm flattered by your attentions, as what woman with blood in her veins wouldn't be—" and fluttered her lashes, because after all it was nice when someone demonstrated appreciation for her feminine charms, even the wrong someone "—I speak truly when I say my companions and I are come to Lyon this day with goods new even to the wharves of Venice. Of course, if you are too busy—"

He was merchant enough to react immediately to the implied threat. "No, no, dear lady, heaven forfend, never too busy—"

But he didn't entirely believe her until he met her the next morning at the warehouse Shasha and Firas had managed to secure for storage space. The quality and variety of the goods was wholeheartedly approved of. Sieur Imbert was anxious to receive the goods and since Johanna, but especially Jaufre, was anxious to be rid of them, matters proceeded apace. Afterward Jaufre said, "We should pay off the stallieres and send them home, and sell the pack animals."

Johanna looked at him in surprise. "But Jaufre—"

"We don't know how long we'll be gone, once we go," he said. "There's no point in paying for five men and fifty beasts to sit around and eat their heads off."

"We're not returning to Venice, then," she said.

"No, we're going after Félicien. How many times do I have to say so?"

She stared at him, eyes narrowing. "Only one more time," she said very gently, and turned and walked away.

Shasha, watching, saw him take a step after her and visibly make the decision not to. Instead he turned on his heel, collected Alaric, and headed back into the city. "I could kill them both with my bare hands," she said meditatively.

Firas chuckled. "I'll bury the bodies."

"Done."

Johanna and Shasha wrote out a statement of profit and loss for Gradenigo, to be left with Sieur Imbert along with the earnings they had accumulated along the way. Sieur Imbert made himself of further use by recommending a farmer a league from Lyon who would be willing to stable North Wind and the other Arabians, and Johanna worked off some of her temper by moving the horses there that afternoon. North Wind's general magnificence had already raised some comment in Lyon and the sooner he was out of sight the better.

✠

"L'Arête is a château fifty-five leagues south of here," Firas said.

"Blade is what l'arête means in French," Alaric said. "Or edge."

They were in their sitting room at The Sign of the Black Lion, surrounded by the remnants of dinner. Their voices were pitched low in what Johanna thought an excess of caution. The noise from the common room downstairs was muted, and footsteps could be heard occasionally in the passage outside the door, but it was a solid door and Lyon was a town that took a group like theirs in stride.

"It's also what the Château L'Arête looks like," Alma said. "In the library at the monastery, where Sister Eliane was kind enough to grant me entrance, there is a map of the region. I made a copy." She produced a roll of vellum very much in the manner of a conjuror pulling a coin from an urchin's ear, and it was greeted with the same kind of acclaim now. She unrolled it with a flourish and they weighted the corners and perused it with attention. Johanna felt instinctively for her father's book, opened it to its furthest written page and began to scribble on the page after Lyon.

"It's rudimentary, as you can see," said Alma, "but here is Lyon and it is in the north – see the indicator here, that says that Paris is in this direction – which means that everything this way is south. Here is Le Puy, and Pradelles. Florac. Avignon where their grand imam lives. And here, east of Avignon, is L'Arête."

They followed her finger as it traced the journey. "The river," Jaufre said. "It goes almost all the way. We could hire a boat here in Lyon."

"And get off in Avignon," Shasha said, tapping her finger on the city.

"And walk the rest of the way," Alaric said with a grimace.

"Easier to hide from view without horses," Firas said.

"Look here," Alma said. "These illustrations around the edges? They show the major cities and castles in the area of the map. This one? This one is L'Arête."

The drawing was the size of Johanna's palm, and it was clear that Alma had spent the most time on it of all the drawings. It showed an abrupt, skyward thrust of rock capped with towers and walls made of the same rock. One tiny road crept back-wards and forwards up one side and the rest was given to sheer vertical cliff. "And how do we get inside that?" she said.

"It doesn't show," Alma said, "but Sister Eliane, who comes from Provins, says there is a village at the top, a village outside the castle walls."

"So we could get that far," Firas said. "And then, perhaps, reconnoiter."

Be best if we didn't get ourselves killed in the interim, Johanna thought. She glanced at Jaufre and left the thought unspoken.

"How far?" Jaufre said. His face looked hollowed out, almost haunted. "How far from Avignon?"

"As you can see, many of the distances are not marked, so I asked Sister Eliane." Alma looked up and around at the circle of faces. "She said not more than seven leagues."

Jaufre pored over the map. "It does not look to be rough country."

"The Blade will be sure to make it rough enough if he catches us on his ground," Alaric said.

"He won't hurt Félicien, will he?" Tiphaine said in a small voice.

Shasha gave her a smile that she hoped was more reassuring than she felt. "No."

"Why?"

"Because he needs her." Shasha looked at Johanna.

"She's the daughter of the last lord of L'Arête," Johanna said. "Who was improvident enough not to have a son, and so when Ambroise started making incursions onto L'Arête lands the old lord bowed to the inevitable and married him to his daughter, his heir. The old lord died almost immediately thereafter. Some say naturally, some say by Ambroise's design." She shrugged. "But then his reputation is so bad, they would say almost anything."

"You didn't see him," Jaufre said.

"And the daughter?" Shasha said quickly.

"Disappeared the day of the wedding."

"How did she manage that?"

538

"There are a lot of stories," Johanna said. "The one I liked best was that she escaped in the company of a band of troubadours who had been summoned to L'Arête to help celebrate the day."

They all thought about that in silence for a few moments, remembering the slim young goliard in his rusty black robe, sitting cross-legged by a campfire, head thrown back in lusty song, his flat black cap open side up on the ground in front of him. He'd gone home coins to the good most nights. He could write songs as well as sing them, and accompany himself on almost any instrument that came to hand: lute, gitar, flute, hautboy, even the morin khuur, that odd instrument so loved by the Mongols, strung with horsehair and played by dragging more horsehair strung on a bow across the strings. It had always sounded like a cat in heat to Johanna.

"What was her name?" This from Alma. "The daughter's?"

"Aceline Eléonor." Johanna paused. "Félicienne." She sighed. "Aceline Eléonor Félicienne de L'Arête."

"It's true then," Hayat said, and at a look from Jaufre, added, "You have to admit, Jaufre, it is a tale fanciful enough to keep a sultan's interest."

He couldn't deny it. Instead he said, "Ambroise?"

"He calls himself The Blade, which tells its own tale." Firas' lip curled. A man was frightening in and of himself, and no fanciful name, no matter how exaggerated, would make him more so.

"His reputation with the church is bad as can be," Hari said. "The priest of his church is one of his own choosing, and the monks say he is no priest, either. None of his people are obliged to attend services, and he, ah, redirects the church tithes into his own coffers." He paused. "Which I must say is what they find most objectionable about him, although they say also that no woman's virtue is safe within his borders, and any man's life is forfeit. It is rumored that for fun he shoves people who have displeased him off the castle wall to see if they can fly." He paused again. "One of the monks called Ambroise the devil on earth."

There was a momentary silence, not untinged with respect. When these faith-ridden people called someone a devil, it was not a condemnation to be taken lightly.

"All right." Jaufre stood up and began to pace back and forth. "Back to Ambroise. We know what he looks like, we know where he lives, we know he thinks he is a khan on the order of Ogodei."

"What's a khan?" Tiphaine said.

"A king," Shasha said.

"A tyrant," Jaufre said. "We can't attack in force because we don't have a force, so stealth is our only option."

"There is some news lately from the south," Hayat said. "In spite of the fact that people don't like to talk about him, it is said in the marketplace that he has found his runaway wife – and the heir to L'Arête – and brought her home in triumph."

"It is also said in the marketplace that the Lark of the South sings no more," Tiphaine said.

There was a brief silence.

"People don't mind so much talking about her," Tiphaine said, with a cautious look at Jaufre, "at least about her before she married the Blade. She was famous for her beautiful voice. Her father hosted a great celebration of jongleurs and troubadours and minstrels every year at L'Arête, and she would sing with them."

"There is a long and noble tradition of chansons de geste in Provins," Alaric said, who had an eye on Jaufre himself, "going back before Queen Eleanor. Her son, Richard the Lionheart himself, wrote songs. I remember songs by a duke in Aquitaine, more by a countess in Die."

"At any rate, our Félicien is definitely this same Aceline Eléonor Félicienne de L'Arête," Jaufre said. "And is our friend and companion, and requires our help." He removed the weights and rolled up the map. "I'm going down to the waterfront to find us a boat going south."

10

Provins, October, 1325

"NORTH WIND CAN'T come," Jaufre said that evening. "He will draw attention. He always does."

"The farm where they are now will suffice. I'll ask Phillippe to keep an eye on them." Johanna only hoped the big stallion wouldn't come after her if he decided she'd been gone too long. It wasn't as if he hadn't done it before. "What about a boat?"

"I found one that will give us deck passage," Jaufre said.

"For how many?" Firas said.

"What do you mean, how many?"

"Exactly what I said," Firas said, unperturbed. "Alaric?"

"Certainly," Alaric said with hauteur. "I would not allow my companions to travel into danger alone."

"So three of us. Who else?"

"Me," Shasha said.

Hayat and Alma exchanged long looks. "We're going," Hayat said.

"I don't know how much use I will be, but I believe I must witness this story through to its end," Hari said.

"You will have to put off your chughi robe, Hari. We need to draw as little attention as possible."

Hari nodded agreeably. "Of course, young master."

"I'm going," Tiphaine said.

"No, you most certainly are not," Johanna said.

Tiphaine glowered. "I most certainly am, and there is nothing you can do to stop me."

"You think not?"

"I know not! If you leave me behind, I will follow you, and I will help rescue Félicien! She's not just my friend, she's a member of my compagnia! She wears my token!" Tiphaine pulled at her tunic to display the insignia of Wu Company on her right shoulder, brave in red and gold.

"Yes," Johanna said. "Yes, of course she does." She looked up to meet Jaufre's eyes. "It's unanimous, then. Nine passengers."

But later, when the others had dispersed about various tasks and they were alone, Johanna said to Shasha, "What are we doing, Shasha? We're not warriors, we're merchant traders."

Shasha looked at her with a serious expression. "You would leave your friend in such hands?"

"No, but marching into the middle of her husband's army wouldn't be my first reaction, either."

"We don't know that he has an army."

"We know he has a company of mounted spearmen. Some of us are going to get hurt, Shasha. Some of us may die."

"And if it was you? It was you, in fact, and not so long ago, either."

Their eyes met. Shasha had sent Firas for Johanna when Johanna was a prisoner in Talikan. She might not have escaped Gokudo if Firas had not come for her. She might now be prisoner in her stepmother's house in Cambaluc, subject to mistreatment no less degrading and humiliating than what Félicien was no doubt experiencing right now. She had not been angry to see Firas, she had been ecstatic.

All the tension that had existed between her and Jaufre since his return from Sant' Alberto fountained up and something inside her seemed to break beneath the pressure.

Shasha saw it in her face. "Here now," she said, drawing Johanna down to a cushion by the hearth and pulling her into a comforting embrace. "Here, now." She rocked them both back and forward, and made no mention of the hot tears soaking her shoulder.

"I never thanked you for sending Firas after me, Shasha," Johanna said, snuffling miserably into her foster sister's tunic. "I am the most selfish and ungrateful person who ever lived."

"Nonsense." Shasha patted her and continued to rock. "It's not that you don't want to save Félicien, Johanna," she said. "It's that you'd rather Jaufre didn't want to save her quite so badly."

Johanna didn't deny it. How could she, when it was true?

✠

They reduced their belongings to the bare minimum, storing the excess with the ever-resourceful Sieur Imbert, and at dawn boarded the barge on which Firas had procured them deck passage. It was a long, wide boat with a nearly flat bottom, made for ferrying goods up and down the Rhône from Genéve to the shores of the Middle Sea.

"There's no sail," Johanna said, and then subsided when the boatmen tied their bowline to the stern of another barge almost exactly like it, which was in turn tied to the barge ahead of it, and so on for a total of six. The lead barge was harnessed to a team of horses on shore, as was a spring line from each of the other barges. A boy who looked younger than Tiphaine had the lead horse on a rein and led them down a well-worn path on the edge of the river bank. The lines took up the slack between horse and barge, the horses strained briefly against their harness, and they began to move slowly down the river. "It's been a dry summer," Firas said. "The barge captain says that normally there is enough current that they can float down in good time, but not this year."

Each barge was piled high with goods, and each carried deck passengers as well. There were two horses in one of the barges, and Johanna tried hard not to be resentful at leaving North Wind behind. North Wind was an army in and of himself. Besides, she already missed him.

The water lapped contentedly at the hull and the landscape passed slowly by. Here, it was mostly tall grass interrupted by the occasional drainage ditch. They passed fields with the harvest grouped together in shocks, waiting to be winnowed, and other fields where serfs were already beating the grain against cloths spread on the ground. A high, thin layer of clouds muted the usual ferocity of the southern sun, and an unusual air of peace and tranquility settled upon the company. It was the first moment of inaction they had experienced since Jaufre and Alaric's return from Sant' Alberto.

"I've been thinking about how we get into L'Arête," Johanna said.

Most of them had made comfortable nests against and among the bales and bundles on deck, but this statement brought everyone into an upright, attentive position.

She smiled a little. "It's not that startling," she said. "Alaric has told us that troubadours are a tradition in Provins. What could be more natural than for a group of troubadours to be traveling there?"

"The Lark of the South escaped the first time with a band of troubadours, we've been told," Alaric said dryly. "I don't think the Blade is going to look too kindly on the breed. Besides, I can't sing."

"You don't have to," Johanna said. "I can, and so can Shasha, Hayat and Firas. Hari can hum. Alma can play a flute."

"Not very well," Alma said. "I haven't practiced since Talikan. I don't even have a flute with me."

"We'll buy you one in Avignon," Johanna said. "It'll come back to you."

"I can sing, and kept a decent beat on a tambour, too," Jaufre said.

They all gaped at him. "What?" he said, a little defensively.

He really didn't know, Johanna thought, marveling.

"Jaufre, you can't go," Shasha said when it became clear that Johanna wasn't going to.

"What! Why not?"

"Because Ambroise has seen you, Jaufre," Firas said, "and in Félicien's company, too. He will know you again. You and Alaric, neither one of you may go with us to L'Arête. It would probably be best if both of you waited for us in Avignon. In fact, I'm not at all sure we shouldn't put the both of you off at the last stop before Avignon." He paused. "Or perhaps you should stay on board until the next stop after Avignon. The last thing we need is for someone to describe you to de L'Arête or any of the twenty of his men who have also seen you."

✚

They were still arguing about it five days later when they docked at Avignon. "I can dye my hair and my skin," Jaufre said. "I could give myself a tonsure and dress in a habit."

"Yes, a Christian monk would be traveling with a troupe of troubadours," Shasha said.

"Why not?" Jaufre said. "We've already got a Buddhist one."

"So far," Firas said, "we've got one good idea on how to get into L'Arête. We haven't talked about how we're going to get out again."

They were speaking in low voices, crowded into the only room they'd been able to find in the most flea-ridden inn farthest from the city gates. Not that the inn wasn't noisy enough to drown out any conversation. Their door looked out onto the kitchen, which abutted a yard where the cook pitched out excess offal and left it to be fought over by stray dogs. The only way to breathe without vomiting was to keep the door closed, which made the room almost unbearably stuffy. And to Shasha's indignation they were paying more for a night there than they had for a week anywhere else on their entire journey from Venice.

Avignon was the seat of the Christian Popes, and the city overflowed with papal officials, petitioners noble and common, ambitious priests and prelates from England to Venice looking for advancement, servants, flunkeys, sycophants, bootlickers and hangers-on. Perched on a hill on the edge of the Rhône, the massive stone wall that surrounded the city seemed barely strong enough to contain the many towers that sprouted from inside it. They were all topped with banners and standards and pennons standing straight out in the harsh wind blowing out of the south that the locals called the mistrau. The banner flying from the tallest towers on the tallest hill of the city bore the crowned keys of the Pope himself.

The nobles were the worst, of course, as they never traveled alone and their enormous entourages were each determined to prove how much more important their liege was than anyone else's. That afternoon, in the time it took to find shelter for the night, Johanna saw three street fights between servants dressed in different liveries.

"Young men with swords," Shasha had said with a sigh.

Scarcely were the words out of her mouth when a young man with, yes, a short sword at his waist shouldered past her, followed by three of his fellows, all four clad in similar blue and green livery. The last to shove past her jostled her with enough force that she was knocked off balance. Firas caught her and set her back on her feet.

"Watch where you're going," this gentleman said over his shoulder.

"Watch yourself!" Johanna said.

As if she had rung a bell the four swerved around and came back to array themselves in a line in front of Johanna and the others. "Did I hear a mouse squeak?" one said, wriggling a finger in his ear. His friends laughed heartily at this sally.

Another stepped forward and had the temerity to flick the badge on Johanna's shoulder. "And to whom might you belong, my pretty?"

"Myself," Johanna said.

He had a spotty face with dark eyes and a full head of dark hair. "Oh ho, this one has teeth," he said, evidently vastly amused. He snaked an arm around her waist. "And how does your master let you out alone, my pretty?"

"I have no master," Johanna said. She even smiled when she said it.

Jaufre stepped up and by a feat of legerdemain managed to insinuate himself between them. He smiled down at the gentleman from his superior height and said, "We littles aren't worth the trouble, my lord."

The gentleman wasn't a lord and if they hadn't known that before they would have known it soon afterward by the whistling and stomping and catcalls of his companions. When the commotion died down enough to be heard Jaufre said, "We're but lowly merchants, my lords—" including them all in a deferential bow "—grubbing about with buying and selling. No one you could wish to dirty your hands on."

It was obvious the four of them were greatly tempted to give Wu Company a drubbing just on general principals. Then again, eyeing this oddly well-armed company, some instinct for self-preservation told them to live to fight another day. When they had achieved a safe distance they called a few insults concerning merchants and traders and took to their heels, disappearing into the crowd, which had barely taken notice of the entire encounter.

After which Jaufre rounded on Johanna. "Unnoticed and if possible, barely seen," he said in an infuriated whisper. "Did I not make myself clear?"

✠

Remembering it now, Johanna allowed her gaze to dwell on him, pacing back and forth between them and the single, tiny window placed high up on the wall of their stuffy little room. Even on the barge he had been constantly in motion, bow to stern and back again, earning more than one reproof from the crew, who offered to set him ashore where he could walk behind the horses. On occasion he took them up on it. Once she had accompanied him, pacing beside him, saying nothing. It was the only comfort thus far that he would accept.

There was a fumbling at the door and Johanna was halfway to her feet, hand on her knife, in company with almost everyone else in the room, when Tiphaine tumbled into the room. "He's here!" she said, eyes bright, breast heaving.

Shasha put her finger to her lips and Johanna said in a low voice, "Who's here?"

"Him!"

"Him who?"

Tiphaine all but stamped her foot. "Ambroise! The Blade! The man who stole Félicien!"

In two strides Jaufre had Tiphaine by both elbows. "Are you sure? How do you know it's him?"

She wrestled free and this time she did stamp her foot. "It's the talk in all the markets! He's here to petition the Pope about something, I couldn't find out what, but he's got a company of ten men with him."

Jaufre spun around, his face lit with a fierce excitement. "That's ten men not at L'Arête," he said.

"We need more information," Firas said, a warning note in his voice. "How long will it take him to get his audience with this Pope of theirs? As you can plainly see, there are many in line in front of him."

"Lines!" Jaufre stared at him incredulously. "You think this is about lines, about who got here first! It's about whoever offers up the most coin! We saw that in Venice!"

We saw that in Cambaluc, Johanna thought. It was the same the world over, evidently.

"By the sheerest of luck," Jaufre said, "we have been given an opportunity here, Firas. We must take it. We leave tonight."

His force of will nearly had them all trooping for the door, until Alaric spoke. "Wait," he said.

He'd been sitting in the darkest corner, wrapped in his cloak, a pitcher of something cradled protectively in his lap. Now he set the pitcher carefully to one side and rose to his feet. It was easy to dismiss this man as negligible, to define him by his sour attitude and the drink ever to hand. But in this moment, as he rose to his full and not inconsiderable height, Johanna was faintly surprised at the presence and the authority he managed to gather around him.

"We have followed you on this ridiculous quest to rescue your lady fair," he said to Jaufre, "even though I warned you how it would be from the beginning. She is his legal wife, in the eyes of God and under the law of the land. She has been with him long enough that the marriage has undoubtedly been consummated. She could even by now be with child."

He stepped out of his corner and into a stray ray of the day's last light. He looked most stern.

"Now you want us to follow you into L'Arête itself, which is by all the accounts one of the most inaccessible châteaux in Provins. A place with one small road traversing the face of a sheer, vertical cliff face some furlongs in height. The same cliff face, I would point out, that surrounds the entire castle. There is one gate, we are told barely large enough to admit one man at a time, and that man must be walking, not riding. It is unassailable, Jaufre, possibly even impregnable, and since we don't muster an army at our backs, we are not capable of settling in for a prolonged siege. I have no intention of allowing you to lead us recklessly to our deaths in a quest that is hopeless, not to mention unlawful, to begin with. And we don't even know if she wants rescuing." When Jaufre would have spoken he held up a hand. "I know, I was there. She did not want to go with him, but in this world, Jaufre, this world to which she willingly returned, I might add, she had no choice. She is his wife. She lives on his sufferance and under his authority. And she knows it, Jaufre, if you don't."

549

It was as many words as Alaric had ever put together in one speech without slurring them or burping an interruption. Sheer astonishment held them speechless for a long moment.

"I agree," Shasha said, breaking the silence. She met Jaufre's furious and somewhat wounded look without flinching. "For one thing, we should try to discover if Félicien is here with him."

Jaufre opened his mouth, and closed it again. It was clear he hadn't thought of that, but then none of them had.

Tiphaine frowned. "I heard no word of her."

"We must be sure," Shasha said. "There is no point in racing off to L'Arête to rescue Félicien if she isn't there."

"Agreed," Firas said in his calm way. "Alaric, Jaufre, you will remain here tomorrow, out of sight of Ambroise and his men. The rest of us will go into the city when the gates open and glean what information we can. We will meet back here at nightfall to take stock." He held up an admonitory figure. "Remember not to get caught inside the gates. If you do and we decide to leave tomorrow night, you will be left behind."

✠

The next morning Johanna headed straight for the palace, a massive stone edifice with multiple towers, many doors including the main, columned portico, and staircases large and small that led up or down labyrinthine passages. A bell that she was certain could be heard in Lyon clanged every quarter hour and brought everything to a momentary, wincing halt.

She ordered a cup of small beer from one of the many taverns scattered around the edges of the palace and disposed herself at a table tucked into an alcove that had an excellent view of the palace's front door, which appeared to accommodate most of the traffic. A discreet bribe to the host and she was left alone.

The Place des Papes was teeming with people of every station, although the crowd was dominated by religious. They were all dressed head to toe in black, which must have been stifling on such a hot day. The higher prelates were easily identified: their garments were of the finest quality fabric, fit the best and were for the most part the cleanest. None of them could take a step without a citizen, lord or commoner, catching their sleeve and whispering in their ear. This was almost invariably followed by something passing by hand from one pocket to another, and the cleric taking himself a few more steps down the Place, there to repeat the experience.

A lucrative business, religion.

There were many carts selling foodstuffs and religious souvenirs. More than one cart was upset by groups of young men engaging other groups of young men dressed in differing livery, a repetition of the scene they had witnessed outside the city the day before. In all instances the vendor was left to pick up the pieces and reassemble his business as best he could, with no assistance, no recompense and no apology. It didn't seem to discourage any of them, or their customers, who waited at a distance until the young hooligans had swaggered on, and then gathered again around the resurrected cart.

A lucrative business, but a labor-intensive one.

The bell in the tower thundered out one o'clock and when her bones stopped vibrating Johanna ordered a plate of bread and cheese and another cup of small beer. The bread was freshly baked and hearty and the cheese a kind she had never seen before, hard with blue striations. It was several steps above the Mongol byaslag she was used to, and she was settling in to enjoy it when another commotion drew her attention. She was vastly unsurprised to see two groups of young men scuffling together, to encouraging shouts from the crowd and heartfelt curses from the vendors. One dressed in silver and black threw another dressed in red and blue against a cart selling roasted hazelnuts. The cart went over and the brazier scattered coals and nuts, causing everyone nearby to dance out of the way. The hapless vendor bleated his distress and scrambled after his goods.

This time a priest came forward, a man whose lack of height

was more than compensated for by the bulk of his brawn. He reached into the welter of flailing limbs for an ear each and banged their heads together, hard enough to have Johanna cringe just a little in sympathy. He then stood them on their feet, not letting go of their ears, and looked around the circle of staring faces. "I'm sure all you good Christians have something better to do with your time than stand around watching a couple of foolish boys—" he banged their heads together again for emphasis "—beat up on each other for no good reason other than the colors they wear."

Such was the priest's authority that the crowd found something better to do immediately, and the priest let the two boys go and strode off, followed by many an admiring glance, not least Johanna's. When she looked again for the two heroes, still staggering, she found the one in black and silver had been helped tenderly to a table in the very tavern at which she was sitting, and had been joined by his fellows.

They were all four of them handsome young lads, not a day over twelve, fair of face and form, dark of eye and hair, with fresh complexions and erect carriages. They were almost similar enough to have passed for brothers. Johanna wondered if they'd been chosen for their looks, a matched set to enhance their lord's consequence.

The table was also near enough that their conversation was clearly audible to her, and their first words held her transfixed. "My lord Ambroise will not be best pleased if he gets to hear of this. He told us to mind our manners in Avignon."

"At least until he gets what he wants from John," another said.

"God's balls," the third said, "we'll be here, until Christmas."

"What does he want from the Pope, anyway?" the fourth said, and found his already abused ear soundly boxed by the first. "Ouch! What did you do that for, Bernart?"

"Because, Guilham, my lord does not want his business bruited about the streets," Bernart said, looking around, and Johanna made sure her face was over her plate when he looked her way. "If you cannot learn discretion, perhaps you do not belong in his service."

Guilham, his face red with anger, lurched to his feet and stumbled away. Most fortuitously, he stumbled in Johanna's direction, and more fortuitously still he tripped over a stool and fell face forward on her table, knocking over her cup of small beer and breaking the cheese plate.

She sprang to her feet with an exclamation of dismay. "Sir! Are you hurt?" She picked him up and set him on his feet again, where he stayed, none too steadily. "Here, let me help you." She made a show of brushing the bread crumbs from his tunic, waiting for him to raise his head. When he did, she gave him her best smile. "Are you well?" she said. "Perhaps a drink to refresh yourself." She contrived to sit him on a stool, the very one he had tripped over, and motioned to the host, who arrived posthaste with a pitcher this time of small beer and another, larger plate of bread and cheese. She poured the boy a cup, broke off some of the blue-veined cheese and put it on a piece of bread and served him so, with yet another smile as an appetizer. He was still blinking from the first one.

"What, Guilham, and who is your new friend?"

Johanna looked up with all the surprise she could muster showing on her face. "Gentlemen?" She took in their livery with an awed glance, and looked at Guilham. "Ah, I see. You are comrades. Please, join us."

They did, Bernart looking her over very frankly. She knew what he saw: a young woman dressed for the road in well-made clothes who didn't look hungry enough to sell herself by the hour. She did wear insignia, the characters of Wu Company, on her shoulder, which meant she was not without protection. Still, she was alone, and this led him into error. "A professional lady, is it? Perhaps you can find time to, ah, fit all of us in," he said, elbowing one of the others, who sniggered dutifully.

"Sir," she said, in a voice she copied from one of the khan's wives at Cambaluc, chill enough to freeze the small beer pouring out of the pitcher, "you labor under a misapprehension. I am a trader, a merchant in fact, and my company even now sets up our stalls in the marketplace."

Bernart wasn't quite convinced – after all, no respectable woman went about in public without at least one servant to lend her consequence – but he was willing to play along. "Where are you from?" he said. She looked him in the eye and said firmly, "Cathay."

He laughed. She did not. The other three boys leaned forward. "Cathay? Truly?"

She produced another dazzling smile, directed this time impartially around the table of eager faces, not neglecting Bernart. "Truly."

After that all she had to do was simper, and tell some of the more sensational tales from her grandfather's book. She ordered more small beer and two more platters of food, because food was a guaranteed way into the confidence of boys of this age. In combination with the admiring attention of an attractive older woman, it proved irresistible. "Where are you gentlemen from?" she said, refilling their mugs with a generous hand.

They responded with names of four different Frankish-sounding places. She eyed their uniforms. "Yet you all wear the same livery."

"We are in service to the Lord of L'Arête," Guilham said.

She produced a look of abject admiration. Her mouth might even have dropped open. "Truly? You serve at a noble court?"

They preened as only boys on the verge of manhood can. "Indeed," Bernart said, with what he imagined was just the right amount of hauteur. He was so very young. They all were.

"Imagine!" she said. She dropped her eyes and said modestly, "I'm merely a trader, a traveling merchant, you know. I've never even been inside a nobleman's house." She paused to let the difference in their stations sink in, and then said, with hushed reverence, "Is L'Arête a, well, a castle? No, really?"

She had learned a great deal indeed by the time the bell

sounded vespers and a shadow darkened their table. They looked up, to behold an older man wearing their colors in richer fabrics: a man with a strong, hard face and heavy gold around his neck and on his fingers. "So, gentlemen," he said, "you have found a friend. How nice."

Johanna looked at Guilham, and saw his face had gone white.

"I believe we were to have met before none in the Rue Peyrollerie," their lord said. There was a leather whip coiled at his waist, and he allowed one hand to toy with its end, which had more than one tail. "And yet I find you not there, but here." He affected a slight bow toward Johanna, his eyes flickering over her person, noting the quality of her clothing and her badge and then dismissing her in the next moment. "In charming company. Which would no doubt provide its own excuse. For some other, less demanding lord."

Such was the paralyzing force of Ambroise's tongue that Johanna thought for a moment none of the four boys were ever going to be able to move again. She wasn't all that sure about herself.

"Gentlemen," he said. "With me. Now."

The last word cracked like the whip at his side would have, and there was a clattering scramble that knocked over all four stools and a babble of apologies, directed not at her but at their lord. They were really afraid of him, Johanna saw, and it was manifestly obvious that the lord Ambroise enjoyed their fear.

At that moment another quarrel broke out on the other side of the square and everyone turned involuntarily to look. She took advantage of the confusion to slip away into the dusk and was so late she nearly got her robe caught in the city gate as it closed behind her. There she was pounced on by an infuriated Shasha. "Where have you been all day?"

"Gathering information," Johanna said airily. She grinned. "And meeting the lord of L'Arête."

"What!"

They gathered back at the inn, crowding into the cramped room and speaking only so loud as to be able to hear themselves over the roistering going on in the common room next door. Someone had foraged for better food than could be had from their landlord and they sat in a circle around a roast chicken and a rice and shrimp dish seasoned with saffron, and apples and cheese to follow, talking as they ate. When they were done Shasha passed around a damp cloth for them to wipe their hands and faces.

"So," Johanna said, summing up. "Félicien isn't with them. She was left at home, I would imagine under close guard of those of his personal guard he didn't bring with him. Ten of them, according to the boys."

"And how long does he remain here in Avignon?"

"The boys don't know. One of them said they'll stay as long as it takes to get what Ambroise wants from Pope John."

"Do they know what he wants?"

Johanna gave an impatient shrug, but said, "They think it's something to do with his wife. He married her for L'Arête, but it sounds as if their church has to formally invest lordship in Ambroise. Because she's the heir. Something like that, I didn't really understand all of it, and I couldn't ask too many questions or they would have become suspicious."

"Perhaps this Pope was named in Félicien's father's will," Alaric said. "He might have stood as her guardian, should she be yet unmarried at the time of her father's death."

"But she was."

Alaric shrugged. "Lords tend to secure their succession by soliciting the endorsement of the marriage of their heirs by the most powerful lord of the land. In these parts, that's the Pope." He shook his head. "L'Arête sounds like a rich property, and Provins is a rich region. Any liege lord would want the allegiance of the lord of L'Arête, if only to be able to tax its profits."

"The point is that Félicien is in L'Arête, and right now, this minute the lord isn't," Jaufre said. He sounded as if his patience was fraying.

"Under heavy guard," Alaric said, without much hope.

556

"Those boys?" Johanna said. "They are terrified of him." She raised her eyes to look at Jaufre, and knew the same thought was in their minds. And if the lord of L'Arête gave his pages cause to be terrified of him, how much more cause would he give his runaway wife? "There used to be five of them. Five pages. I gather one of them died recently."

Jaufre made an impatient gesture. "Sad, if true, but what has that to do with us?"

Firas was quicker. "Did Ambroise give him flying lessons?"

"They wouldn't say specifically, just that he died." She paused. "They are terrified of him," she said again. "I've never seen such fear."

"And if L'Arête has left orders from its lord not to admit troubadours?"

"The boys did not say so. And Ambroise isn't home."

"But how will we get out again?" Alaric said, a little querulously.

"We can't know that until we see the place," Firas said.

"I've found someone who knows the way and is willing to guide us," Jaufre said.

"Someone trustworthy, I hope?" Alaric said.

"Someone for hire," Jaufre said. "He has a boat and will bring us across the river and then guide us to L'Arête." He looked around at their faces. "We leave tonight. And Alaric and I will be accompanying you to L'Arête."

"What!"

"By the round-eyed Christian god—"

"Jaufre—"

"Jaufre, please be reasonable."

"You'll get us all killed!"

"Wait," he said. "They won't know us. Trust me."

His smile was thin but it was the first smile any of them had seen on his face since Sant' Alberto, and it was enough to silence them long enough to listen to what he had to say.

11

Provins, October, 1325

W HEN THE BELLS rang lauds they donned packs filled with the bare minimum of food and necessities and crept out of their room, picked through the offal-strewn yard and down to the river's edge where a small, open boat waited for them. "This is Pascau," Jaufre said in a low voice.

The boatman, of middle age and wary mien, gave a curt nod and motioned them into the boat without further delay. They were almost too much of a load for it, and Johanna was sure they were all thinking of how many boats they'd almost swamped to date during their journey west, and if this was going to be the last one. Pascau stood in the stern, wielding a single oar with an offhand competence that was marginally reassuring.

Their passage across the river was swift and silent and unwitnessed so far as they could tell. The current left them considerably downstream on the opposite shore, but there was a neat moorage which hid the boat beneath a dense thicket of willow that argued steady usage.

There was a small clearing up the bank beneath more willows. "Sleep here," Pascau said. "Leave at first light."

They wrapped themselves in their cloaks and made themselves as comfortable as they could on the bare ground. At dawn they broke their fast with bread and cheese and were off across a flat landscape of stubbled fields lined with tall plane trees. The day was gray, with a mist that hung low to the ground. They kept to the shadows and slept rough the next night, too. The second morning found them approaching a collection of rock piers in fantastic shapes.

Pascau gestured at the rocks. "The Valley of Hell."

"Cheery," Hayat said.

"Welcoming," Johanna said.

Pascau's face, set in uncommunicable lines, didn't change. "No sense of humor," Hayat said.

Rosemary, thyme and lavender grew in thickets from every available crevice, perfuming the air with their scents, long limbs grasping at the carelessly-placed boot. Shasha walked in a permanent crouch, rubbing leaves here, plucking branches there. The plane trees had given way to cypress, and here and there olives trees had scratched together enough dirt to make a living. All the trees were stunted and twisted and leaning southeast beneath the eternal abuse of the mistrau, and rocks, herbs and trees clustered so thickly together as to make the way very difficult. From the brief glimpses they caught of it, the trail would have made their journey a little easier, but not so much that they dared risk encountering other travelers by taking it. The mist had lifted and the late autumn sun blazed down without mercy and everyone's clothes were damp with sweat and grimed with dust. Altogether an unprepossessing group, Johanna thought, looking them over. No self-respecting castle would let them in the door.

At mid-afternoon Pascau came scrambling back down a rocky incline and motioned to Jaufre. They held a brief, hurried consultation. "He says L'Arête is over this rise," Jaufre said. "He says we must go carefully if we don't want to be seen."

"I don't want to go at all," Alaric said, but it was the barest grumble and easily ignored.

"He's found a spot on the ridge covered with rosemary grown very tall," Jaufre said. "We are to crawl into it and be very careful not to crawl out the other side."

When they had climbed and crawled and slithered into place, they could understand Pascau's caution.

"In truth, a very blade," Firas said, after a long, awed moment of silence.

A massive stone of brilliant white, the southern end pointed, the northern end squared off, L'Arête appeared to have debarked from the mountains behind it to set sail on the flat plain below. Its sides were one continuous face, so smooth they looked planed by the same giant hand. Wave-like curls of vegetation clustered thickly all around its base, through which a single narrow road crept back and forth. Anyone on the road would have a sheer and certainly injurious, if not fatal drop on one side of them going and coming.

"They must have water up there," Firas said. "They could never withstand a siege otherwise."

"There is a small river in the valley below," Alaric said, craning his neck.

"If they were under siege they would never be able to get to it," Hayat said. "And it would be easy to poison." Johanna knew she was thinking about the river upon which Talikan had been built. Ogodei's first action had been to poison it.

"How high is the rock, do you think?" Shasha said.

"Five times the height of the towers of St. Mark's, and that's just the rock," Firas said.

Everyone's eyes raised to what grew from the top of the rock.

On a ledge close to the summit many tiny houses had been carved from the white rock of the precipice and roofed with orange tiles. Above them was the castle.

Johanna swallowed.

It increased the height of the freestanding ridge by a third. There were a dozen towers of varying sizes and shapes, sides pierced with multiple arrow slits. The towers were connected by a thick, high wall, built from more white rock. The wall was topped with a battlement defended by a parapet. Even at this distance she could see movement through the crenellations in the parapet. Guards. Ten spearmen that they knew of, but how many more?

Inside the wall roofs of buildings could be glimpsed, including a large square keep. Another wall ran around the village to connect with the castle wall on either side. Because of the differences in elevation the doors into both were easy to identify. Neither looked welcoming.

L'Arête wasn't just impregnable. It was unassailable. All its defenders had to do was lock the doors and rain down death on their enemies with mangonels, one of which was in plain view on the south end of the prominence.

They slid back down and gathered in a circle beneath a clump of cypress. Even Jaufre looked shaken.

"How are we going to get in there?" Alma said.

"How are we going to get out again?" Alaric said.

Jaufre squared his shoulders. "We go with Johanna's plan. We're an itinerant band of troubadours, looking for a place to sing for our suppers."

"And if the Blade discovers our presence?" Alaric said.

"He's not here," Jaufre said.

"And we'd best be gone before he returns," Firas said. He nodded at Pascau, who was sitting apart from them, an expression of stolid indifference on his face. "Have you paid him yet?" By prior arrangement they spoke only Persian among themselves.

"No," Jaufre said, affronted. "He gets paid when we return safely to the Avignon side of the river."

"Is he coming with us?"

"No. He says he'll wait here."

"Tell him you'll double his fee if he comes with us," Firas said. "Firas—"

The assassin shrugged. "It's the only way to be sure he won't hotfoot back to Avignon and sell us out to Ambroise."

"He could sell us out to them instead," Alaric said, jerking his head in the direction of L'Arête.

"They'd kill him, too, and he knows that," Firas said, and

561

looked at Jaufre. "Either he comes with us or someone stays here to see that he doesn't run off. I nominate you and Alaric."

Jaufre looked back in the direction of the castle. "We'll wait till morning. Come around this ridge in plain view like we have nothing to hide and nothing to fear." He looked at Tiphaine. "How is your juggling coming along?"

✠

The guards at the gate were bored. The cloudless morning promised another blistering day in this unusually warm fall, and since the lord was away their attention to their duties was not perhaps quite what it ought to have been. They flirted with the village girls, opined on the past excellent harvest with the villagers, and speculated on how the war was going in the Low Countries, or was it Bavaria? At any rate, a war somewhere they weren't, where soldiers other than themselves reaped the spoils of battle in gold plate and jewels and women willing or unwilling, it mattered not.

They didn't hear the flute at first, and when the beat of the tambourine registered they didn't rush to the gate, which stood wide open to facilitate what little breeze there was. It wasn't until Tiphaine, dark curls caught up in one of Alma's gauzy, glittering scarfs, strolled through the gate, juggling three rag balls as if she'd been born to it, that they realized the defenses of L'Arête had been penetrated. Before they could sound the alarm the invading force resolved itself into a small troupe of traveling troubadours. They relaxed, although the sergeant of the guard, when summoned, looked apprehensive and muttered something about the lord not liking it.

"He's not here, is he?" one of the guards said. They'd all heard the story about the lord's lady eloping with a different group of troubadours on her wedding day, but she was back, wasn't she? The reputation of the Lord of L'Arête was so fearsome that they saw little enough in the way of travelers. They hated

Ambroise as much as they feared him, especially after that poor little tyke had been thrown from the wall. The half of Ambroise's personal guard who had remained behind when their lord went to Avignon had left the day before to inform the boy's parents of his death, although to be sure they wouldn't tell them how he had died, or why. However the parents reacted, the show of force would keep them in line. It wasn't the first time they had performed such a task, and it never failed in its effect. It would also occupy them for at minimum four days including travel time.

So they were bored, and feeling a little rebellious while not under their lord's eye. "Come on, sergeant, have a heart," one of them said, eyeing Alma, who smiled at him and put a little extra into the sway of her hips. "One night. What can it hurt?"

Tiphaine melted the sergeant's heart by tossing him her balls one after the other, and darting in to catch the one he dropped before it hit the ground, neatly catching the other two when he tossed them back and returning all three into a simple fountain. The sergeant laughed and the guards applauded, and the townsfolk came out of the houses lining the tiny street that wound uphill to the square, situated, very conveniently, directly outside the gate into the castle. There, Johanna and Jaufre came forward and with a graceful bow to the assembly launched into a spirited rendition of one of the very first songs they'd ever heard Félicien sing.

O wandering clerks
You go to Chartres
To learn the arts
O wandering clerks
By the Tyrrhenian
You study Aesclepion
O wandering clerks
Toledo teaches
Alchemy and sleight-of-hand

O wandering clerks
You learn the arts
Medicine and magic
O wandering clerks
Nowhere learn
Manners or morals
O wandering clerks!

It scanned and rhymed in French, thank goodness, even Provencal French, and their voices blended together well, and if they sang a trifle loudly, why, they had their way to make in the world and could be pardoned for a hearty sell. Besides, the song went over so well that by the middle of the last verse everyone was chanting along, the last "O wandering clerks!" bellowed out by guards, villagers and soldiers peering through the crenellations from the castle parapet above.

Johanna bowed again and fell back, deferring to Jaufre, who stepped up. His hands and face had been stained a deep brown with walnut juice and his blond hair was hidden beneath a long dark scarf knotted elaborately in the way of the Tuareg. Alaric's skin was likewise stained and he had condescended, at Jaufre's insistence and not without the inevitable grumbling, to leave his sword behind and to be dressed in yeoman's clothing. When he remembered he stooped to disguise his height. She only hoped it would do.

"Good gentles, thank you for your kind attention and applause for our humble offering," Jaufre said, pitching his voice to be heard over the castle walls. Indeed, the people standing in front of the crowd fell back a little from the force of it. "We are Jerome's Jongleurs, late of Venice, Jerusalem and Persia—" he let his voice drop dramatically on that last "—and with your kind permission we will entertain you with a show this evening beginning at dusk, here in your beautiful place de la cité." He flourished another bow, Johanna feared to the imminent hazard of his headdress, but by some miracle it remained upon his head.

"I am that selfsame Jerome, and here—" indicating Johanna "—is the lovely Jeanne of the East, who will sing you stories of the wonders of Cathay, the mirrored roofs of Cambaluc, of the Great Khan himself, and of Princess Padmini, and of the night it rained emeralds." He winked.

An anticipatory murmur ran around the crowd.

"Mohammed of Alamut, student of the Old Man of the Mountain Himself, will dazzle you with tricks of the sword!"

Firas stepped forward, too dignified to bow to people so infinitely beneath him. They had of course left all their long weapons behind in Lyon, but they all wore short swords, although the women wore theirs in light scabbards strapped to their backs beneath their clothes. The sword Firas wore was slightly curved, not quite a scimitar but similarly shaped, and he drew it now and tossed it up into the air, where it spun three times and fell hilt first neatly into his hand. There was a rumble of appreciation from the guards.

"Zubadiyah, late of the harem of the Sultan of Bagdad and valued student of Giotto of Firenze will draw your likeness in charcoal!" Alma insinuated herself forward, hips rolling in the best harem-approved manner, to the point that one goggle-eyed man had his head thumped by his indignant wife and was subsequently towed home by his ear. A charcoal sketch on a piece of vellum that had been scraped so many times the sun shone through the illustration it bore was held high in her hands as she circled the square, although when asked later hardly anyone and certainly none of the men could have said what the illustration was.

"And the lovely Umayma will tell your fortunes as they are written in the secret stones of Damascus," Jaufre said, dropping his voice again as Hayat stalked out and fixed the crowd with a bleak and intimidating eye. She had been the hardest to convince of her role when they had planned this mad scheme on the journey from Lyon to Avignon, and she was privately terrified that the first fortune she told would get them all killed.

She didn't know that her demeanor alone convinced everyone with a penny in their pocket that some austere and unforgiving deity had blessed the intimidating Umayma with the seeing eye, and all of them determined on the spot to have their fortunes told that evening.

There was a bit of applause following Hayat's introduction and into the middle of it tumbled Tiphaine, regaining her feet with ease and commencing a fountain with three apples the fruit vendor had not known were missing until Tiphaine caught them all, bowed, and strolled over to return them to him. Charmed, or perhaps mindful of the ripple of laughter from his fellow villagers, he gave her one, and she winked at him and bit into it with gusto.

Born to the part, Johanna thought.

"We meet again at dusk, good gentles," Jaufre said, bowing again. The crowd began to disperse, chattering eagerly – with the master it had, L'Arête probably saw such distractions only rarely, something Johanna had counted on when she made her plan – and the headman and the sergeant of the guard stepped up to begin negotiations. Non-resident duties – a tax one paid to reside inside the gates for a night – and stallage – the right to offer one's wares, or as in this case a performance within that city – were both reasonable, as both gentlemen planned on attending the evening's entertainment. Inquiry brought the information that the lord was not in residence. "How sad that we shall not be able to entertain him," Jaufre said, trying his best to seem so.

The sergeant, mistaking his meaning, grinned and clouted him on the shoulder. "Never fear, good Jerome! Entertainment such as you provide is not easily come by in L'Arête. The people here will reward you well."

"His family is with him?" Jaufre said casually. "His knights and their ladies?"

The sergeant's bonhomie dimmed. "There is only his wife remaining, and I doubt she will attend," he said dryly.

"A pity." Jaufre bowed and effaced himself to rejoin his

566

companions. "She's here," he said in a low voice. "The sergeant confirms it."

They refreshed themselves at the communal fountain in the center of the square and retired to an unoccupied corner out of the sun. They piled their bedrolls and packs and Alma and Hayat went off to see what could be had in L'Arête in the way of charcoal and scraps of paper, parchment or vellum. A sullen Pascau subsided beneath a large plane tree, attended by a vigilant Alaric and an ever-smiling Hari, who maintained a constant flow of gentle conversation. Pascau did not look to be greatly attending.

Tiphaine went off with them and returned before they did, looking as if she would burst if she couldn't speak. Jaufre and Johanna retired with her to a shadowy corner.

"Ambroise's personal guards are gone off somewhere!"

"Quietly," Johanna said, smiling over Tiphaine's head at a curious housewife.

"The spearmen, Johanna, they're gone, off to some manor east of here." Tiphaine's eyes were blazing. "They won't be back for at least three days and perhaps as long as a week."

Johanna looked at Jaufre and saw that his eyes were blazing, too. "Our luck is in," she said, "but we stick to the plan."

Tiphaine looked up at the wall of unbroken white rock stretching above them. "Do you think she heard us?"

"Someone will tell her," Jaufre said, with more confidence than he felt.

"Will she know it's us?"

"She wrote the song we sang, Tiphaine," Johanna said. It was the only way they had been able to think of to get word to Félicien of their presence. She only hoped it worked.

No one contacted them during the afternoon, but they hadn't expected it. Even if Félicien was free to move about the castle, even if her close guard had been raised, she would most probably have a servant with her at all times, and that servant was in the pay of Ambroise. She had given Ambroise her word not to leave again but that didn't mean he believed her.

Félicien had to find her way out of the castle, because otherwise they were going to have to find their way in, and then find Félicien's room, and somehow get in and out of the room, castle, castle gate, village, village gate, down the precipitous path without being either stabbed, shot by the castle archers or pulverized by the mangonel.

But first she had to know they were there. Johanna looked up at the wall and saw faces peering at them over the parapet, but not the face they most wanted to see.

People began filtering back to the square well before dusk, blankets and cushions in hand along with food and drink. Jaufre had marked off a half-circle of space next to the castle gate where normally nothing was allowed, the gate remaining clear of detritus at all times as a matter of security. But for this special occasion, with the master away, the sergeant of the guard had allowed himself to be persuaded. He had also been persuaded to allow a couple of rough tables to be set up and their legs lashed together to provide a rudimentary stage.

Jaufre and Johanna with Shasha, Alma, Alaric and Hari started off with what had brought them their crowd: a repeat of Félicien's wandering clerks song. That went over well, some of the village folk were even joining in the chorus. Johanna only hoped that Félicien heard it the second time if she hadn't the first. They followed it with a drinking song.

When I see wine into the clear glass slip
How I long to be matched with it;
My heart sings gay at the thought of it:
This song wants drink!
I thirst for a sup; come circle the cup:
This song wants drink!

The last line was more shout than song and from that moment the audience was theirs to do with what they would. After a dozen songs the musicians rested while Tiphaine juggled and tumbled and was impudent to the audience and Alma drew portraits for anyone with a penny to pay. This was very popular and the coins in the little bowl passed by Tiphaine while small in denomination were large in number. The sergeant, who had commandeered a seat in the very front, gave Jaufre a gratified nod, and Jaufre bowed in acknowledgment. Alma took up her flute and accompanied Shasha on a song about a traveling artist and a farmer's wife, which went over as well as any song about a farmer's wife and a traveling anyone did.

The others retired, leaving Johanna the stage. She sang a song of strange things culled from her grandfather's writings, of the stones that burned, of the tribe with tails. She sang of Aijuruc, daughter of Caidu, a warrior of the Bright Moon who refused to marry anyone who could not defeat her, and lived unmarried to the end of her life in her father's kingdom far beyond the mountains of Salamander. She sang of Ferlec, where the first thing they saw in the morning they worshipped for the rest of the day, and the resulting disasters this odd custom caused. She sang of the pearl fishers of Cipangu, and the enchanters of Tebet, and of the monks of India, who caused ropes to climb to the sky and then climbed them to vanish into the air. Her voice had never been able to reach as high as Félicien's but she could write songs every bit as well, and she had not spent all that time reading the different versions of her grandfather's book in vain. Her audience showed their appreciation with generous applause and much coin.

For the second interval Hayat, adorned by an elaborate turban made from one of Alma's spangled harem scarves, of which she apparently kept an infinite number wound about her person beneath her clothes, settled onto a rug and told fortunes with the storied Secret Stones of Damascus. The Secret Stones of Damascus were a handful of smooth agates recovered from a tiny beach between Lyon and Avignon, one dark in color, the rest light. On the river they'd all worked with Hayat to come up with a plausible set of stories that could be altered to fit anyone.

Her fierce and forbidding aspect led everyone to regard her with some trepidation, and added that much more weight to the fortunes she told. It helped that, in Hayat's fortunes, every man's crop or business would prosper, every married woman would bear a male child next, and every maiden would marry a man both handsome and kind.

In the break after Hayat's fortune telling Johanna noticed two women standing just inside the gate to the right of the stage. One was dressed in gray, the other in black. Both wore cloaks in spite of the warm evening, their hoods pulled forward so as to shadow their faces.

She nudged Firas, who was nearest. "I saw," he said, his lips barely moving. He drifted off to stand near Jaufre, who was doing his best to look everywhere but at the gate. If you didn't know him, perhaps you might not notice, Johanna thought. Perhaps.

By now the audience was in an excellent mood, beating time in a body to a trio of marching songs that evoked the spirit of the Road. Johanna sang in her mellow contralto of Princess Padmini and Ala-ud-din, and women wept. She sang another about the night it rained emeralds on the steps of the palace in Everything Under the Heavens, and men sighed with envy. What they could do with a fistful of emeralds.

Their last song was the plum tree song, the first song Jaufre had ever heard sung by the Wu family, with Wu Li keeping time on a small skin drum, Shu Ming plucking out the tune on a lap harp, their voices melding with Johanna's and Shasha's and Deshi the Scout's.

> White petals, soft scent
> Friend of winter, summoner of spring
> You leave us too soon.

The lyrics, which were not at all or not only about a plum tree, had as powerful an effect translated into French and performed

570

before this audience of villagers and castle guards as it had had on Jaufre in the caravansary in Kashgar so long ago. They had taught it to Félicien, who had sung it with them over a thousand leagues of Road and more, and who was standing now just inside the castle gate, close enough to them to join in. She didn't.

He found himself swallowing back tears, and felt Johanna's touch, gentle and fleeting on his hand. He turned his head to look at her, really look at her for the first time since Milano. The moon had risen and flooded the square with light, and she looked so beautiful to him in that moment that she seemed almost not of the same world he inhabited.

Their eyes held for a long moment of absolute stillness, that ultimate accolade of the professional performer, and then she smiled, and applause crashed over them, shouts and whistles and clapping of hands and stamping of feet. Before it had quite ebbed the troupe launched once more into "O Wandering Clerks," this time everyone joining in, Jaufre, Johanna, Shasha, Firas, Alma, Hayat, Hari, Alaric, and of course Tiphaine, who sang louder than any of them. By then almost everyone in the audience was letter-perfect in the chorus, if not the lyrics.

The bowl Tiphaine passed during the last chorus came back gratifyingly full. The villagers dispersed and the castle folk returned to their lodgings or duties and the troupe gathered in a tight knot in their shadowy corner, ostensibly to refresh themselves and take their own rest before departing the following morning.

"Did you see the two women standing inside the gate?" Tiphaine said.

They all had. Jaufre tore off a chunk of bread and ate it mechanically.

"They left just after the plum tree song," Shasha said, her voice low.

"The sergeant will never consent to us staying another night," Alaric said.

"And he would be right not to," Hari said. "Ambroise could return at any time."

"The spearmen he left behind could return at any time, too."

"She has to come to us," Johanna said.

Jaufre shot her a look but said nothing.

There were still some villagers moving around the square, extinguishing braziers and packing up vending carts for the night. Several of them drifted over to offer thanks for the show. A slight woman in gray hovered in the background until the rest had left. She kept casting nervous glances at the guards, as if the moment they looked her way they would arrest her just on general principles. "Alma," Johanna said in a low voice. "Hayat."

Hayat picked up a jug of watered wine and Alma four cups and they sauntered over to the gate and engaged the two guards in conversation. The massive wooden gates were closed now, and undoubtedly barred from the inside. There was a smaller door, sized for one person, in one of the larger doors, but no one could use it without being challenged by the guards, two more of which were very probably stationed on the inside.

The woman in gray came closer, her manner tentative, if not outright terrified. The hood of her cloak was pushed back enough that they could see her face. Her features were fine but lined and drawn, her figure thin to the point of emaciation. "Who is the one called Jaufre?" she said in a voice barely above a whisper.

No one could move or say anything for a moment, and then Jaufre began to surge to his feet. Firas' hand on his shoulder pressed him firmly back down. "And who asks, milady?"

The woman cast another look over her shoulder and stepped forward to speak rapidly in so low a voice she could barely be heard. "It is not safe for you here. The lord is expected back at any moment. You must go." She half-turned, as if to leave.

"Who says this, lady?" Jaufre said, straining against Firas' hand.

She cast another glance at the gate. All the guards' attention was on Hayat and Alma. She turned back to Jaufre and spoke quickly. "The one who wrote your song. You are in grave danger. You must go."

"Lady, tell us only this. Does she truly wish to stay? In her own heart?" Alaric stirred and Jaufre quelled him with a single, ferocious glare. "Please speak truly. We have come a great distance to see to her well-being."

"You must go," the woman said. "You must go, and she must stay. It is the way of things."

"Tell her," Jaufre said, "tell her that we won't leave without her." He shoved Firas' hand off his shoulder and came to his feet, the better to issue edicts. "She must come with us when we leave tomorrow morning."

"If she doesn't come, we won't leave, and then we will all die here together," Johanna said. She met Jaufre's glare without flinching. "Tell her that, milady."

"I must return before someone notices I'm gone," the woman said, a panicked look on her face.

"Return?" Firas said. "How? The gates are locked and barred for the night."

Johanna looked at the gates dwarfing the figures of Alma and Hayat and the guards. "Milady? Is there another way out of the castle?"

✝

The morning dawned bright and a little chilly, a welcome relief from the heat of the day before, but it wouldn't last. From the heights of L'Arête one could see a layer of insubstantial mist collecting in the hills and hollows of the mountains west and north of the castle, making the weird shapes of the rocky spires look horrifyingly animate and inherently evil. The farmlands to the east disappeared into an accumulating haze.

The troupe, packs shouldered, had arrived at the gate just as it opened and were taken fond leave of by the guard stationed there. One pulled Jaufre aside and confided a new joke that might make it into the next show, and he laughed and slapped the fellow's back and slid a penny into his hand. He hailed the other guard and retold the joke, with embellishments, and the three of them roared with more laughter.

The two guards did not notice that the troupe had increased by one, a slender figure wrapped in a gray cloak emerging from the morning shadows to mingle with them as they passed through the last gate. Hayat slipped an arm around her waist and pretended to be whispering something in her ear. Tiphaine skipped along on her other side, juggling her rag balls, and the rest of them moved back and forth, changing places continuously to create a confusion to the eyes. Alaric took the lead with Pascau firmly in tow, so the boatman noticed nothing untoward, not at first.

They moved down the little road that switched back and forth across the face of the mountain. "More slowly, if you please," Firas said, waving over his shoulder at a group of children hanging over the village wall. Everyone tried to but it was difficult not to break into a run. The lack of cover made them imagine arrows trained on their backs from every direction. It was a positive relief when they reached the top of the hill across the valley and turned to wave their goodbyes for the last time before disappearing around a corner and down the other side.

"Félicien, what—"

"Not now!"

"She's right," Shasha said. "To the river as fast as ever we can."

"Who is that?" Pascau said, noticing for the first time that they were now eleven, not ten.

"It doesn't matter," Jaufre said. "Lead us back to the boat and get us across to Avignon."

Pascau looked alarmed, as one who lived seven leagues from L'Arête might well be. "A gold florin over and above your pay and you'll never see us again," Firas said.

The mention of gold was enough to soothe the boatman's anxiety, at least for the moment, but Johanna thought that the sooner they were out of Avignon the better.

They force marched all that day and all of that night, again keeping to the shadows beneath the trees, this time in fear of meeting Ambroise on the road coming back. They stopped only to eat of their remaining meager rations and relieve themselves, and reached the river before noon the next day. Pascau, possibly motivated by the thought of the gold florin that waited for him on the other side, possibly just wanting to be well rid of these dangerous passengers, rowed them across with a will.

"Find us a boat going upriver," Jaufre said. "Preferably one leaving today." Tiphaine, Firas and Alaric scattered. The rest of them repaired to an inn with a common room large enough to lose themselves in and ate the first hot meal they'd had in days. Johanna, eyes adjusting from the blazing sun to the cool darkness, saw the servants bustling round with laden trays and slopping pitchers through a faint veil of incredulity. They'd done it. They had penetrated the defenses of L'Arête itself and come off scathless. She turned her head to look at Félicien. And they had rescued their comrade.

Félicien leaned back against the wall, the gray hood drooping around her face. Johanna thought she had her eyes closed but couldn't be sure. Everyone else was looking at Félicien, too. Félicien had yet to say how she had come to join them and they had no idea how soon the alarm would be raised in L'Arête. Perhaps it already had been. Perhaps a guard was even now galloping for Avignon with the news for his lord.

Meanwhile, they were back in Avignon, and in a room full of loud conversation they were an oasis of silence. It was occasioning a few looks. Johanna cleared her throat and smiled. "This is good bread, isn't it," she said, tearing into a piece with her teeth. "And excellent small beer."

"I, uh, don't know when I've tasted better," Hayat said.

"We should ask for the name of their brewer," Hari said, a man who to Johanna's certain knowledge had never touched alcohol of any kind.

"Do you think it will rain tomorrow?" Alma said brightly.

✝

It was Tiphaine, of course, who found them a boat going in the right direction, departing the following morning. They took a room and spent a tense night during which no one got any sleep.

Ambroise de L'Arête was still in Avignon. "He's staying in a house near the palace," Tiphaine said. "On the rue Pey—" She stumbled over the word.

"The Rue Peyrollerie," Johanna said.

"That's right," Tiphaine said, surprised. "How did you know?"

"He mentioned it," Johanna said. "When he came for the boys."

"You've seen him, then," Félicien said. She was curled in a corner, as much apart from the rest of them as possible in the cramped space. It was the first time she had spoken since they had left L'Arête.

"Yes," Johanna said. "Here, in Avignon, before we left for L'Arête. I, uh, met his pages, and I was still with them when he came for them."

Félicien gave a sound that was nothing like the lighthearted laugh they were used to hear from her. "Pages," she said.

"Yes," Johanna said slowly. "The four boys who wear his livery. Guilham. Bernart. I don't remember the names of the other two."

She waited, they all did, but Félicien said nothing more.

The next morning they waited in their room until there was just enough time to get from the inn to the quayside before debarking, and slipped outside in twos and threes so as to attract less attention. It was a market day and the streets were already crowded with carts and stalls and it seemed the entire city of Avignon had come outside the walls, determined to enjoy the unseasonal weather while it lasted. All the better to be lost in a crowd, Johanna thought.

They had reverted to their travel clothes, tucking away all vestiges of the troubadours who had entertained L'Arête so well.

They moved at a slow, steady pace, determined to avoid attention and keeping their eyes on the ground except when necessary for navigation.

Which was why they almost walked straight into Ambroise de L'Arête. Walking with Jaufre and Félicien, all the warning Johanna got was a glimpse of black and silver. She stopped dead in her tracks. The bullish body dressed in incongruously elegant attire, topped by that leonine head, moved through a crowd that knew instinctively to give way before it. The four pages followed, towed irresistibly in his wake, but Johanna wasn't looking at them. She was looking at Pascau, whose arm was grasped firmly in Ambroise's hand, and who looked like he already regretted his bargain.

They were headed in the direction of the quay. Johanna caught the arms of her companions and began to steer them around Ambroise's route and on toward their destination.

"What?" Jaufre said. He'd felt the tension in her grasp.

"Ambroise," she said, breathing the name through stiff lips.

Félicien started, but she said nothing and she didn't faint.

They made their way forward, the crowd thinning as they reached the wharf, not daring to look behind them, although there was a spot between Johanna's shoulder blades that had commenced a furious itching – one she was sure that both her companions were experiencing, too. She wondered where the others were and if they'd seen Ambroise. Of them so far he knew only Jaufre, Alaric, Félicien and, perhaps, Johanna herself, although she had effaced herself that day in the Place des Papes as soon as humanly possible. But Pascau knew them all. Her step quickened in spite of herself. She had no desire for flying lessons from the Lord of L'Arête.

"There," Jaufre said, and she looked up to see the mast that Tiphaine had told them to look for. She was a little river freighter, with a broad, shallow hold and a single mast. The square brown sail was being hauled up as they approached, and she saw with relief Shasha's face peering anxiously over the rail, Firas at her shoulder. They allowed their pace to quicken. When they got to the boat they didn't bother with the ladder: Jaufre caught up Félicien and tossed her up into Firas' waiting arms. Johanna was already halfway up the ladder when Firas was setting Félicien on her feet, with Jaufre close behind her.

As they achieved the deck a rotund, authoritative individual cracked out orders, lines were loosed and they slipped from the quay into the current.

"This way," Shasha said, and led the way forward to the bow. The rest of their companions were already there. No one, wisely, was hanging over the gunnel to see if Ambroise was in sight on the dock.

Félicien subsided to the deck with her back to the mast. She kept her head down and her face covered by her hood.

"Félicien—" Jaufre said.

"Not now," she said, and such was the urgency in her voice that they left her alone.

"Give her time," Shasha said, patting Jaufre's shoulder.

The sail luffed and then caught the mistrau and billowed out with a crack, to be quickly close-hauled by the crew. Downriver traffic adhered to the western side of the river, leaving the center and the eastern side to the upriver traffic. Their course was a series of short tacks, a continual back and forth against the wind. The ship's crew was kept constantly on the hop, and Wu Company stayed in the bow and kept out of their way.

Between the current and the mistrau, their speed upriver was kept to not much more than their speed downriver had been, but they were away, blessedly out of Ambroise's reach. With the relaxation of tension they were overtaken by a sense of extreme fatigue and spent most of that first day dozing with their heads pillowed on their packs. Except to relieve herself in the half barrel provided for deck passengers, Félicien kept to her position at the mast. No one had much to say. Alaric sat facing forward in the bow, his back to the rest of them, stiff with disapproval.

"But at least we could count on him when we needed to," Shasha said to Firas. It was late the third evening.

Firas grunted. They were laying on her cloak and wrapped in his, looking up at the stars in the night sky. Night showed fall's true colors with a considerable drop in temperature and everyone was wearing all the clothes they had brought with them.

Someone moved and Shasha raised her head. "It's Félicien."

"Shasha—"

She patted his arm and followed the girl. Alaric had rolled himself into his bedroll and was snoring slightly. Félicien was standing in his place in the bow. Shasha came up to stand behind her. "Félicien."

"Shasha."

So hard and cold was her voice that Shasha was at something of a loss as to what to say next. "Are you well?"

A brittle laugh. "As well as can be expected." A pause. "Why did you come?"

Shasha smiled a little. She could smile, now that they had satisfied Jaufre's mad obsession, and now that they were all safe. "Jaufre would not allow us to rest until you were free once more."

"The fool!" Félician whispered. "All of you, such rash and reckless fools!" She turned and put back her head, and the same moon that had shone down on them in the courtyard before the castle of L'Arête shone down on her face now. She looked as if she had aged twenty years in the months they had been apart. "I traded myself for you, Shasha. For all of you. The only thing that kept me in L'Arête was the thought that you were free."

"He understood that, Félicien. But he could not accept it. And neither could we."

"He will come for me," Félicien said, and then she gave that humorless laugh. "Ambroise. He will come for it."

"And we will deal with that when it happens," Shasha said.

"Fools," Félicien whispered. "You are all fools. And soon to be dead fools."

"How did you get out?"

Félicien sighed. "The same way I did before. There is a secret passage from a place hidden near the kitchen. It exits in the shrubbery near the outer gate, very close to where I joined you. My father said it was built by his grandfather. Ambroise knows nothing of it."

"It's how you joined the troubadours?"

"I didn't leave with them. I just left at the same time they did. I hoped Ambroise would think to follow them instead of looking for me."

Shasha wondered what had happened to the troubadours. "And the woman who came to us?"

"Laloun? She is my maid. She was still at L'Arête when I— when I returned. I tried to make her come with me but she said where the guards might not notice one, they would be sure to notice two. She's pretending to be me, keeping to my room until someone discovers her."

Shasha thought of the thin, terrified woman in the courtyard of L'Arête. "She must love you very much."

Félicien made no reply.

"I see that you have need to relieve yourself quite often, and that you have been sick over the side, more than once," Shasha said. "Are you with child?"

Félicien shuddered. "Laloun believes so," she said, the hard, cold note back in her voice. She looked at Shasha, eyes black as the night around them. "Can you get rid of it for me?"

Shasha was silent for a moment, and not because the question was unexpected. "There are certain herbs," she said. "They are very dangerous, and they don't always work."

"I don't care if they kill me," Félicien said. "I want this devil's spawn out of my body as soon as ever you can help me to do so. Or I want to be dead." That cold, bitter laugh again. "Either will do, and perhaps the one is more attractive than the other."

There was nothing to be said to that, at least not at present. "The pages," Shasha said. "What did you mean when you spoke of them in that way?"

"Ambroise doesn't like women but he needs an heir to secure his position as lord of L'Arête," Félicien said. "He likes boys.

580

Little boys. His pages are all chosen for looks and age. The instant one turns thirteen he is dismissed back to his family with a handsome reward."

She choked and clapped her hand to her mouth. She turned abruptly to face forward again, taking in deep, cleansing breaths of air. Behind them, Shasha sensed an alertness in the company, although they neither moved nor spoke. Alaric had stopped snoring. They were all awake, and listening. It was as well, because Shasha didn't think Félicien could have told her story twice.

"He couldn't—he could barely—he had to bring in one of the boys and—God, I hate him. I hated him touching me. It makes me ill. The very thought of it disgusts me. It always has. I don't know how any woman can bear it."

"You could have become a nun," Alaric said.

"Or I could have had myself locked in a dungeon for life and been done with it!" Félicien said, almost shouting.

Prudently, no one else offered commentary.

Félicien bent forward from the waist and was suddenly and comprehensively sick over the side. Shasha rubbed her back until she straightened, wiping her mouth on a corner of her cloak. "Afterward, the boy vomited, and Ambroise took him outside to see if he could fly. Do you know what that means? Do you, Shasha?"

"Yes, we know."

"Their parents must have heard something," Félicien said. She sounded exhausted now. "A messenger came from them, demanding the return of their son. It's why Audouard took the rest of the troop to their château, why they were gone when you came, why the guard was so lax." She began to laugh, half hysterical. "Little Roubin died so I could escape. Isn't that funny, Shasha? Isn't it?"

Shasha moved forward to take Félicien in a secure embrace that ignored every effort to throw it off. "Sit down, Félicien. Sit down here, and take comfort. You are with us now. Free once again to determine the course of your own life."

"I won't be free until you rid me of this incubus in my belly."

Félicien spoke no more, her confidences at an end. Soon she dozed off, jerking and whimpering now and then in her sleep. Shasha went back to her place at Firas' side and was grateful for the warmth of his body to take the chill from her flesh.

Johanna could not sleep, eyes wide and staring blindly up at the starry sky.

By his breathing, Jaufre lay wakeful, too, throughout all of that very long night.

12

Lyon and environs, late fall, 1325

THEY DEBARKED AT Lyon with due haste and went directly to Sieur Imbert's. He came forward to kiss Johanna's hand and smile warmly into her eyes.

"Sieur Imbert," she said, allowing it. "Well met."

"Sieur Imbert? Surely it was Phillippe the last time we met?"

She had the grace to blush. "Phillippe then. Forgive our manners, but we are in something of a hurry."

"You are returning to Venice?"

They had discussed this thoroughly on the boat. Félicien—she would not answer to any other pronunciation—had told them, and repeated herself with bitter emphasis. "He is coming. He is right behind us. He won't stop. He wants this—" she clenched her fist and struck herself in the belly, not gently "—he needs it to reinforce his title to L'Arête, and he won't stop until he has possession of it again." Her face twisted. "And he won't want to have to go through a second time what he went through to get it the first."

She had paused, and then turned abruptly and was sick over the side. Other than a little water she had been unable to keep anything down, and she seemed to grow thinner and paler with every passing hour. She wiped her mouth on the hem of her cloak. "He is coming." She looked at Jaufre and said angrily, "I traded myself for you! And look how you treated the gift of your lives!"

Jaufre opened his mouth to respond but Firas said, "Did Ambroise travel to Avignon with only the ten spearmen?"

Félicien frowned, her near hysteria arrested by the assassin's calm manner. "I don't—no. He took Florian. And the four pages, of course." Her lips twisted. "John likes his vassals to put on a bit of a show."

It took a moment for them to realize that she meant Pope John.

"With Ambroise, that makes twelve armed, experienced men." Firas was silent for a moment, hands on his belt, a calculating look in his eyes. Presently he said, "I believe Félicien is correct. Ambroise will be coming, and he won't be coming alone." He looked around with a slight smile. "Well, we are not exactly toothless ourselves, and he won't expect any of the women to be able with arms, so we may even have a slight advantage."

"I know something else he won't be expecting," Johanna said.

Alma and Hayat looked at her, and then at each other. "No," Hayat said. "No, he won't."

Firas looked at Johanna. "Oh. Ah. Yes. I had forgotten. Very well. We need a plan."

"We can't go back to Venice," Johanna said. "This trouble started there and followed us here." She paused. "What happened to Jean de Valmy? Did anyone see him at L'Arête? Or in Avignon?"

"Ambroise killed him just after we left you, rather than pay him the rest of his Judas price," Félicien said drearily. "They dragged his body into the woods and left him for carrion."

It might be the one action taken by Ambroise de L'Arête that they could all approve of. Johanna wondered what had happened to Pascau. "We can't return to Venice," she said again. "This trouble could follow us back to Gradenigo. We owe him too much to take the chance."

"There are merchant fairs north of Paris," Firas said. "I have heard people speaking of them."

"We have nothing to trade at present," Johanna said.

"Chartres," Alaric said.

"Where is Chartres?" someone said, and someone else said, "Why Chartres?"

"A hundred leagues, maybe a little more," Alaric said. "North and west of here. And because I have a friend there who may be able to advise us."

Jaufre glanced at him but held his peace. From the conversation between Alaric and Gilbert, he wouldn't have thought that Alaric and Wilmot would have much to say to each other, or that a stonemason would be especially able to advise them on matters of trade. "Everyone I've talked to since we stepped ashore in Venice wants wool," he said. "By all accounts the best wool comes from the north. Let's go look for wool."

Afterward, Jaufre wondered at the spark of satisfaction he saw in Alaric's eyes when the group decided on Chartres. Much later, he wondered if Alaric's irritation at riding to Félicien's rescue might have been less because he disapproved of their violating the sanctified bond of marriage than because they were riding in the wrong direction.

"Ambroise will come," Félicien said in a hopeless voice. "He will kill you all."

"No," Johanna said. "No, Félicien, he won't." She leaned forward and grasped Félicien's hand. "He won't. Trust me, Félicien. Trust us. Firas? Let's work on that plan."

"Indeed, young miss," Firas said. "Let's."

✠

Here in the present, in Lyon, Johanna smiled at Gradenigo's agent and said, "No, Phillippe, not Venice. We thought we'd try our luck in the north."

Firas, Jaufre and Alaric retrieved their weapons from Sieur Imbert's warehouse and spent a day giving everything in their armory a new and sharper edge, in case the plan went awry. Shasha

585

scoured the markets for supplies. Alma and Hayat returned to the convent to inquire after maps apropos to this journey. Hari went to the cathedral to insinuate himself into the bosom of the clergy there and perhaps acquire some names of brother clergy in Chartres who might look kindly on visitors from Outremer.

The next morning Johanna and Tiphaine walked to the farm where their mounts were stabled, some two leagues south of town. North Wind caught Johanna's scent on the mistrau and they heard him trumpeting half a league away. Dusty, hungry and thirsty, Johanna broke into a trot, bypassed the farmhouse and went straight for the paddock in which the great white stallion was stamping up and down. The fenceposts around him were made from sawn lengths of tree trunks buried deep in the ground, which explained why he was still inside them. Johanna undid the latch on the gate and North Wind thundered up and whickered and whiffed down her neck and back and sides and around her waist and between her legs and under her arms until, laughing uncontrollably, partly from relief that he was still here, she caught a handful of his mane in one hand and vaulted astride. He went from a standstill to a full gallop and she wound her hands in his mane and flattened herself against his neck and let him go. Behind them she could hear Tiphaine whooping and shouting. Her eyes blurred with tears, not all generated from the wind forceful enough to blow the braid out of her hair. Félicien was free, none of their company had died in L'Arête, and she was on North Wind's back again. In this moment it was more than enough.

After what felt like a league at a full gallop she judged it safe enough to pull North Wind into a canter and turn him back toward the farm. As she approached she saw the farmer and his wife and two children gathered outside the front door of their farmhouse. Tiphaine was perched on top of a fencepost, waving her scarf over her head. The farmer was grinning, but his wife and children looked as if they'd bolt inside at the first opportunity.

Johanna stopped at a safe distance, or as safe as North Wind would ever be, swung her right leg over and slid to the ground on legs that trembled just a little. Her smile trembled just a little, too.

"That big one, he thinks he is so tough," the farmer said, coming forward, "but he missed you. He pined for you, I swear it."

"I pined for him, too, Glaude."

He grinned again. "He would have been all the better for a gallop every day, but no one had the courage to try to get on his back."

She stepped back and ran her hands down the stallion's flanks and legs. "He looks well, very well indeed. I am grateful for your care of him."

Glaude shrugged. *"C'est normal."*

"And the others?"

Glaude shrugged again. "Eating their heads off." He cocked his head. "One of my mares came fresh while you were away. I put the black to her."

Her turn to shrug. "You had my permission." Her turn to cock her head. "Not North Wind?"

He shook his head. "She is small, my Celestine. I would not burden her with a too-large foal." He jerked his head at North Wind. "He could smell her. He wasn't happy."

Johanna laughed. "I can imagine."

The wife came forward, a little fluttery, one wary eye on North Wind. "Please, come in and refresh yourselves."

They adjourned to the farmhouse, which was old even in these parts, and small, snug and immaculate. A sharp word and both children scurried to lay the long table in front of the hearth with bread and cheese and olives and a pitcher of water. "The water is good," she said, "we have our own spring," and took a drink to prove it. Everyone sat down and ate heartily. At last Johanna sat back with a sigh. "That was wonderful, Magali. Thank you."

The housewife beamed, and cuffed her son, who was pinching his sister. "Outside, the pair of you, and feed the chickens." She refilled Johanna's cup and her husband's, and bustled about setting her kitchen to rights.

"Glaude, I wonder if you have room here somewhere for ten of us. Perhaps tonight, and definitely tomorrow night and perhaps for a third night, but that would be all."

He considered. "We have not beds enough—" a wave of his hand indicated the farmhouse, which was not large "—but there is a loft in the barn. It is clean, and there is hay to make your beds. And you may use the spring, of course."

Johanna smiled. "Hay beds are a luxury for the likes of us. Can you feed us, too? We will be happy to pay."

They agreed on a price, and Johanna spent the afternoon going over the horses and their tack, which was in better repair than when she had left it behind. She remonstrated with Glaude, who waved a hand and said again, *"C'est normal."*

Perhaps rendering kindness to strangers was normal in this part of the world, Johanna thought. She was immeasurably soothed by the notion. No one joined them that evening and after a hearty dinner of pottage and bread Johanna sang and Tiphaine taught "the children" (as she referred to them) how to do a basic fountain, which she did not see fit to tell them she herself had only learned how to do not three weeks before. Everyone went to bed pleased with themselves.

The rest of Wu Company arrived in good order the next day at mid-afternoon. Félicien had new clothes in unrelieved black, tunic and trousers and cloak, and tough new boots. When her hood fell back Johanna could see that she looked far from well, and as soon as she dismounted she went to the edge of the trees and was sick.

Jaufre was watching her with a worried expression. "She's been continually ill," Shasha said. "I don't know how far or how fast she is going to be able to travel."

"Is this normal for pregnant women?"

"Not to this extent, nor of this violence, not in my experience. She has diarrhea, too."

"What?" Johanna said, when Shasha seemed reluctant to say more.

Shasha drew Johanna to one side and lowered her voice.

"I consulted a midwife in Lyon. She says there are cases, very rare, of pregnant women who suffer excessive, constant vomiting and diarrhea throughout the first months. It frequently leads to miscarriage."

They looked at Félicien, still standing at the edge of the trees, bent over, shoulders heaving. Jaufre approached and said something they couldn't hear. They did hear Félicien tell him to go away, and so did everyone else.

"Miscarriage?" Johanna said.

"Yes," Shasha said. "Even, in extreme cases, the death of the mother as well."

"Is there nothing you can do?"

"The only thing that might help would be to confine her to bed. She would want to know why."

Their eyes met. Johanna said nothing. There was nothing to be said. They had to leave very soon, whether Félicien could travel or not, and if Shasha told Félicien what might happen, Félicien would be the first of them on a horse.

✠

They stayed two nights at the farm and woke the morning of their departure in the hour before dawn and were riding out of the farmyard before the family had woken. Johanna left a pouch filled with coin on the sill of the window next to the door, and sent a silent wish for good fortune to follow Glaude and Magali and their children always.

There was a well-traveled road near Glaude's farm that ran north to Paris but they had decided to keep clear of the road and so struck out through the forest, made up of mature trees with broad canopies of leaves turning gold and orange and red. There was little undergrowth, certainly nothing like the choked countryside around L'Arête, and the horses had no trouble picking their way.

It was a cool morning beneath clear skies, and after so many days without rain the ground was hard as iron. They kept to a brisk walk and gradually the land began to rise. Firas was riding ahead and Alaric behind, and both came cantering up when the party emerged on a knoll covered in sweet grass and a tiny spring bubbling up out of the ground. The sun was well up by now and they dismounted to break their fast.

And that of course was when Ambroise sprung his trap, catching them out of the saddle, weapons sheathed, food in hand.

They emerged out of the tree line: the lord of L'Arête, Florian, ten mounted spearmen and four boys who rode two to a horse and looked cold, tired, and terrified. The men held spears at the ready. No one had bothered with bows, Johanna noted, probably because arrows occasionally went anywhere and the count's lady was among them.

Ambroise was dressed in the same black and silver Johanna had seen him in in Avignon, with additions. The sword at his side did not look the least bit ornamental and his neck, shoulders and arms were thick with muscle, statement enough that he knew how to use it. He wore a round helm with a nose guard and a cuirass, both of black steel polished to a dull gleam. He rode an immense black destrier who was curried to a fare-thee-well, tacked up in black leather and whose hooves looked oiled that morning.

Together they formed a single weapon that gave every appearance of being unstoppable, invincible, ultimately lethal. It was a first blow struck before the battle had even begun.

A veritable Prince of Darkness, Johanna thought, an appearance deliberately designed to intimidate and if possible frighten.

North Wind snorted and sidled and she realized that her hands had tightened on his reins. Her heart was thumping in her chest hard enough to escape and run away on its own, and she didn't seem to be able to catch her breath.

Yes. It was possible.

She took a deep breath and walked forward to stand next to Félicien. Behind her North Wind stamped his displeasure.

Jaufre had his sword out before Alaric and Firas, but only just. Johanna, Alma and Hayat did not reach for theirs.

"I'll go with him," Félicien said. She sounded tired.

They ignored her, spreading into a half circle that would have looked rehearsed to anyone paying attention. Johanna and Félicien hung back. Alma, Hayat and Hari scattered to the sides of the clearing but did not go so far as to disappear into the trees.

"My dear Félicienne, you most certainly will go with me, but it will avail your companions nothing," Ambroise said. "You gave me your word, you broke it, and I, as you well know, always pay my debts in full." Ambroise pulled his sword and nudged his mount forward. "In fact it will give me very great pleasure to dispatch them one by one myself, while you watch."

Jaufre stepped into his path and his sword was dealt a contemptuous blow that had it flying from his hand. He tumbled back just out of the reach of Ambroise's sword. Firas fell back into a guard stance and was similarly dealt with, and Alaric as well, although this was the part of the plan they had had the most trouble getting Alaric to agree to. "You never learn, old man," Ambroise said.

Alaric regained his feet and glowered.

Now Ambroise was facing Félicien, and Johanna.

Johanna said, she hoped clearly over the thundering of her heart, "You may not have her, Ambroise."

"Ah yes, the lady in the Place des Papes," Ambroise said. His smile bared his teeth and no more. "You made only one mistake. Well, two, actually. You stayed around long enough for me to notice you, and you wore the same sigil as your friends there." He gestured at Wu Company's badge. "It wasn't difficult to find word of that sigil, and of you, in Lyon, which led me directly to Sieur Imbert." His smile was thin. "He was persuaded to tell us all he knew very quickly indeed."

Johanna knew a pang of remorse and then a flare of anger. "You may not take Félicien again," she said again and stepped forward, well within reach of Ambroise's sword.

"Johanna—" Jaufre said.

The count laughed. "Too little, too late, boy. Your lady friend appears eager to go to her death." He drew back his sword to strike with an almost lazy gesture. Johanna dodged the edge of the blade, just, tumbling forward to come perilously close to the destrier's front hooves. She screamed. She screamed very loudly and very impressively. The destrier, uneasy, began to dance. A hoof struck and pain flashed up her arm. She screamed again, this time in good earnest, and kept rolling forward so that she was directly beneath the black war horse. She kicked out at his legs, connecting about half the time. The destrier stumbled and Ambroise cursed. Johanna kept screaming.

North Wind had had a trying few months. He had been force marched over the Alps from Milano to Lyon with no chance to stretch his legs in a race. In Lyon he had been imprisoned on a farm, where, to add insult to injury, when a mare came into season no one had availed themselves of his superior services. His human had gone away and left him for an unconscionable amount of time, the longest they had been separated since leaving Cambaluc. Behind a fence even he couldn't break down and it wasn't for lack of trying.

He'd just got her back, and now she was screaming. He'd just gotten her back and someone or something was trying to hurt her.

Enough.

Before Florian or the spearmen or the boys or Ambroise himself could react, North Wind yanked up his picket, which had been knocked only loosely into the ground to begin with, and sounded a thunderous challenge. Anyone who had ever seen him race would have recognized the standing start that was his signature. One moment he was standing still, looking half asleep, and the next he was charging forward at full speed. He roared a challenge that could have been heard back in Lyon, terrifying the rest of the horses, theirs and Ambroise's alike. It didn't help that none of Ambroise's men, or indeed Ambroise himself expected any resistance from a bunch of money-grubbing traders. This was supposed to be a simple slaughter and a reclaiming of property.

Instead the horses plunged, reared, plunged, neighed, and plunged again, bucking and twisting, their instinctive desire to get away, to get right away right now, as far as they could get as fast as they could go. Two of the boys fell off. One of the spearmen nearly did. Two of the spearmen's mounts got their bits firmly between their teeth, yanked the reins from their riders' hands and crashed through the trees to disappear. The rest of them were fully occupied in trying to bring their terrorized mounts under control.

Johanna waited until the very last moment, trading a few more kicks with the destrier, and scrambled from beneath the destrier's belly and rolled clear. The others of her company were following suit with promptness and agility. North Wind thundered down on Ambroise, who raised his totally inadequate sword in a pitiful semblance of defense before the great white stallion slammed into the black destrier and knocked him completely off his feet. He fell heavily on his side with a thump that shook the ground and set a few branches swaying. He lay there, wheezing his astonishment.

Ambroise barely got his leg up out of the way in time and staggered to his feet. He raised his sword to the great white stallion rearing before him. North Wind treated this puny defiance with the contempt it deserved, and broke Ambroise's sword arm with his left front hoof and cracked Ambroise's breastbone with his right front hoof. Ambroise's sword fell from a suddenly numb hand. Ambroise fell on top of it.

North Wind dropped to all fours and did something Johanna had seen him do only once before, in a little campsite south of Talikan when two men had thought to take advantage of three unarmed women. He hopped. He hopped straight up into the air and came down on all four feet, landing directly on Ambroise. One hoof missed altogether, one sheared off an ear; the remaining two landed directly on his chest. The sound of cracking ribs echoed around the clearing.

North Wind hopped again, bellowing his outrage. This time his rear hooves landed on Ambroise's pelvis. Ambroise screamed, louder even than Johanna had.

Possibly affronted by a noise made by someone else other than himself, North Wind hopped a third time. Both front hooves landed on Ambroise's face. There was a crack and a sort of a splash and his skull split and his brains and blood splattered across the grass, to lay glistening red and gray in the morning sun.

The lord of L'Arête's screams stopped.

North Wind snorted and turned to find Johanna. Finding her, he sniffed her all over. She smelled like herself, although she was pulling rather hard at his mane to hold herself up. No matter. She was well, which meant all was well in North Wind's world. He raised his head and bugled his triumph, terrifying all the other horses a second time. Satisfied, he dropped his head and nudged Johanna to scratch behind his ears. She did so, noticing in some dazed part of her mind that her hand was shaking. She did not look down at his hooves. She looked up instead, to see Tiphaine peering from behind the trunk of a tree at the edge of the clearing, her dark eyes enormous. Johanna fought to bring a smile to her lips but they were trembling, too.

Ambroise's men got their horses back under control and stared at the broken mess that had been their leader with white faces. "You—you did that on purpose," one of them said.

Jaufre, who was, like Firas and Alaric, back on his feet, sword at the ready, said baldly, "Yes." He recognized the man as Florian, Ambroise's lieutenant.

"We will kill you all," Florian said.

"You can," Firas said, stepping forward. "But we won't go easily."

"And we'll be sure to take some of you with us," Hayat said. She was flanked by Alma and by Johanna, who stepped around North Wind to stand with them, all three with swords drawn.

L'Arête's men looked at them askance. They were only women, of course, but one similarly trained couldn't help but notice the easy assurance with which they held their weapons. They appeared, incredibly, to have had some past experience, and if there was one thing a soldier disliked, it was unknowns in battle. It was the unknowns that would get you killed. These women looked like they knew how.

"But why should it come to that?" Hari said soothingly, coming forward and smiling his warm smile at the lieutenant. "You're Florian, aren't you?"

Such was Ambroise's reputation that Florian had not seen this much naked steel arrayed against him in a long time. He had forgotten how the edges gleamed in the sun. He felt the sudden uncertainty in the men at his back. "Yes," he said.

"You were the lord's second in command?"

"Yes?"

"And..." When Florian said nothing Hari tut-tutted, and said kindly, as one explaining something to a child, "And there is no one left in L'Arête above you in rank?"

Realization dawned on Florian's face. "No," he said. "No. There isn't." He hesitated, and looked at Félicien.

"You must press your claim without me," she said. "I will never return to L'Arête. In this company, before these witnesses, I renounce all claims to L'Arête and its attendant properties." The finality in her voice convinced them all, even Florian. "One thing, however."

"What?"

"What happened to Laloun, my maid? She put herself in my place so that I could escape."

"She is locked in the dungeon, awaiting my lord's return."

Félicien gave a thin smile. "There will be no flying lessons for her, Florian. Let her go."

He stared at her.

"That is my price," she said. "Let her go, and you will never see me again. I will never contest with you for the title of L'Arête.

It is yours. Do with it what you will. All I ask is that you let Laloun go."

He wavered visibly. Hari pressed Félicien's words home, even walking forward to stand within weapon's reach and staring up into the lieutenant's face, his expression calm and serene and wholly without fear. "Go directly back to L'Arête and see things secure there. Then go to the Pope and demand title by right of conquest. If you go to him first, he can then give it away to anyone he wants, so don't give him the opportunity. Take L'Arête and hold it for yourself, and then ask for his blessing."

There was a brief silence where no one moved.

"If you're going to do so, you'd better do it now," Jaufre said.

"Indeed," Firas said, and went so far as to sheathe his scimitar and tuck his thumbs into his belt. "Who knows what has happened in L'Arête in your absence? Another man could be thinking the same thing." He glanced at the pages. "There are those with motive enough."

Florian followed his gaze to the boys, and his mouth set in a grim line.

"Let Laloun go," Félicien said again. "Give her a horse and money and tell her to make for Lyon and Sieur Imbert." She hesitated. "You didn't kill him, did you?"

Florian gave a short laugh. "There was no need. He told us everything we wanted to know almost without our asking."

"As we told him to do," Jaufre said, determined that the Blade's men understand that this morning had been a trap into which they had ridden all unknowing.

When they were working out the details of their plan, Firas had said, "Ambroise will not consider us a threat. We will use that arrogance to our advantage." They had waited to be sure that Ambroise had had enough time in Lyon to track down Sieur Ambert, who had instructions to give them up as soon as he was asked. Firas and Alaric had scouted ahead to find the most suitable place to be ambushed in, and had withdrawn back to the farm, there to wait another night so that Ambroise and his men could set their trap, all unknowing that a different trap had already been set, for them.

"What if they decide to take us at the farm?" Johanna said.

Firas had shaken his head. "This isn't his territory. Remember Sant' Alberto. He chose to ambush Félicien somewhere without witnesses. He will do the same here."

"I don't want Glaude and his family hurt," she said.

"They won't be," Alaric said. "Firas is right, Ambroise will wish to draw as little attention as possible to the fact that he lost his wife a second time." He looked at Johanna. "Are you sure North Wind will react as you say?"

Johanna, Firas, Alma and Hayat had only smiled.

Now, Florian flushed darkly, and Jaufre was satisfied. "Then let us go our separate ways in peace."

Florian hesitated for a moment longer, but only a moment. "Audouard! Retrieve Ambroise's body and find something to wrap it in."

What was left of L'Arête was rolled into in one of the spearmen's bedroll and tied across his saddle. Bits and pieces persisted in falling off until they tied both ends of the bedroll with strips of hide. The lieutenant tied the reins of the destrier to his saddle and, with a long, last look at the members of Wu Company, Hari smiling benignly, the rest grim and determined, moved out. The two unhorsed boys scrambled back on their mounts and kicked them into a trot. The last Johanna saw of them as they disappeared into the trees was Guilham's astonished face as he twisted round in his seat behind.

"What happens to them?" she said.

"If Florian really wishes to hold L'Arête, he'll send them back to their parents," Alaric said. "Otherwise he will have in his keeping four excellent excuses for sieges. Especially if their parents are at all ambitious."

"I expect they'll be glad to go," Johanna said.

His gaze was somber. "I expect so."

13

Chartres, winter, 1325–1326

THE FINE WEATHER broke the next day. The heavens opened up and it rained day and night. Their clothes were wet, their bedrolls were wet, their horses were so wet they steamed. Every inn they came to was already packed to the rafters with people seeking shelter and they slept outside more often than not. They all had colds, and Félicien was still sick all day every day and throughout most of her nights.

The terrain was easy enough and the road well marked for a change, but the hundred leagues to Chartres felt like a thousand. They were twelve days in transit, and of course the rain started to taper off their last day en route. The next morning dawned, if not clear then at least with high clouds and blessedly no rain. The forest had given way to rolling fields of stubbled grain. At noon Shasha said, "What's that?" and they followed her pointing finger to the massive stone spires rising up from the horizon, as if to knock at the very doors of heaven itself.

"That would be the cathedral," Alaric said, spurring up from the rear. Firas returned from scouting ahead to confirm that they had, indeed, reached their destination. A feeling of mild exhilaration swept over the company; even Jaufre, who had spent the journey with his chin on his shoulder, could relax a little. He didn't trust Florian to keep his word. Félicien was too great a prize.

"Are we Wu Company again," Tiphaine said, "or are we still Jerome's Jongleurs?"

"Wu Company, I beg you," Alaric said in a tone so dry it surprised a laugh out of the rest of them. The farther north they traveled, the lighter of heart Alaric seemed to become. It was a pleasant change.

Chartres was a small, prosperous town clustered around its crowning glory, the cathedral, an immense and awe-inspiring edifice of stone surrounded by flying buttresses and surmounted with two towers in two different styles. The town around it bustled with inns and taverns, and shops selling everything from cockleshells to shards of the True Cross. One busy agent was organizing pilgrimages north to Notre Dame in Paris and south to Santiago de Compostela in Galicia, with a sideline in the same to Jerusalem, via Venice.

"I feel right at home," Johanna said.

They found a comfortable, commodious inn with excellent stabling and settled in with a sense of relief. Jaufre investigated the state of his trouser hem and went off to find a gem dealer who might be interested in purchasing a ruby, since Chartres was too busy a town for cheap lodgings. Shasha disappeared for the entire day and returned that evening with an elderly woman with a severely curved spine who walked with the assistance of two sticks. She had wise eyes and a quiet, calm manner. They vanished upstairs for an hour and then the old woman came down alone and left, the sound of her sticks on stones tapping off into the distance.

Johanna went softly up the stairs and down the hall and knocked on the door. "Shasha? It's Johanna."

"Come in." Félicien turned her head on the pillow and gave a weak smile. Shasha was lifting a covered chamber pot in preparation for emptying it outside. "I'll be right back," she said with a smile. As she brushed by Johanna, she murmured, "See if you can get her to talk."

Johanna shut the door behind her and brought a stool next to the bed. Sitting down, she said lightly, "I won't ask how you're feeling."

"Please. Don't."

There was a touch of ruefulness in the reply that sounded more like the old Félicien. Encouraged, Johanna smiled. "What do you want? Peace? I can go away again."

Félicien reached for her hand. "No. No, please stay." Her eyes were sunken, her face white and drawn. The skin of her hand felt hot and dry to the touch.

Johanna looked at the tray of food on the table next to the bed. "Haven't managed to eat anything?"

"I can't keep it down. Most annoying."

"I would imagine."

They sat in silence for a few moments. Félicien kept hold of Johanna's hand. "I can't believe you came for me." For the first time in speaking of it, her voice held wonder and gratitude.

"It was Jaufre," Johanna said. "He knew the right thing to do from the beginning."

"I was—fond of him, you know."

Johanna blinked. "Jaufre?"

A faint smile. "Yes, Jaufre. The man so in love with you that other women might as well not exist." She shifted and winced a little. "Especially women dressed as men."

"I thought—"

"What, that I didn't like men? Well, I didn't, then. Until I met him. He is just as all the songs say. 'A parfit gentil knight.'"

Johanna had thought of Jaufre in many ways but as a knight was not one of them. "I didn't know."

"No, and nor does he, and don't tell him." The bed creaked as she shifted again. A drumming began on the roof. "Rain, again. I'm glad we're inside and dry."

"So am I," Johanna said with feeling.

"You have a lovely singing voice, Johanna."

"Thank you. So do you." She hesitated. "When we were asking after you, we heard you had a nickname."

600

Félicien smiled. "L'Alouette du Sud," she said.

"Yes."

"My father said I was born singing. My mother died when I was born, and I was all he had, and my voice pleased him very much. He hired many teachers for me, from Avignon, Lyon, Nice, one all the way from Paris. And when I was growing up, every troubadour and jongleur and minstrel and poet passing within a hundred leagues of L'Arête knew they could find a meal and a bed there. All my father asked was that they sing for me, and to let me sing with them." Her eyes closed and she swallowed hard and breathed deeply several times. "One of them gave me that name."

"It...sounds like a good childhood."

"The best." Félicien sighed and opened her eyes again, the nausea passing for the moment. "And then I grew up, and my father decided I must marry."

"Why Ambroise?"

"He was strong enough to keep me safe, or so my father thought." A soundless laugh. "He was looking forward to grand-children. And then he died, and I tried to break the betrothal. Ambroise showed up with his troop, forced me in front of a priest. I ran." She was silent for a moment. "At least he's dead. He won't hurt anyone ever again."

She looked at Johanna. "You know what I'd like?"

"What?"

"For you to find a lute or a gitar for me. I'd like to teach you some songs."

Their eyes met.

"All right," Johanna said in a low voice.

She met Shasha on the landing, and it was a good thing she did because her eyes were filled with tears and she tripped on the top step. Her foster sister caught her before she fell down the stairs. "Johanna! Be careful! I don't want to have two patients on my hands." She took a closer look at Johanna's face and put down the chamber pot. "What is it?"

Johanna took a long, shaken breath. "Félicien thinks she's dying, Shasha. Is she?"

Shasha folded her hands and frowned down at them. "I don't know." She raised her eyes. "She isn't improving, certainly."

"What did the old beldame say?"

Shasha hesitated. "She said," she said at last, "she said that she had known only a very few women who suffered this badly during pregnancy. And that all of them had died."

Johanna swallowed. "She wants me to bring her an instrument, and let her teach me songs."

Shasha's face cleared a little. "Good. If she takes an interest in something other than her condition, perhaps it will help."

Johanna was a little shocked. "Shasha! She has been most grievously hurt!"

"Well, and so have others been hurt, and hurt worse," Shasha said, a trace of anger in her voice. "And recovered, and gone on to live useful lives. So could she."

"Could she?"

Shasha pressed her lips together. "Perhaps. I don't know."

"Can you not... help her?"

"If by help you mean help her abort her child, I fear that at this stage anything I did would only make things worse." She sighed. "I told her so, and she told me she'd rather be dead than carry what she persists in referring to as 'it' to term."

The next day Johanna went out into the town and found a music shop that sold instruments, and spent far too much on a beautiful lute made of walnut polished to a rich gleam, inlaid with mother of pearl. She bore it back to the inn, and her first lesson commenced that evening. Félicien, propped up by many bolsters and rolled blankets, sat up, her back to the headboard, and cradled the lute in her lap. "Well, now, what first, I wonder. The dawn song, perhaps. It's always been my favorite. Yes, the dawn song."

Every day Johanna attended Félicien in her room and learned all of the songs the goliard had in her repertoire, joined by other members of the company or not. Some songs Johanna had heard many times, like "O Wandering Clerks." Others were completely new to her, and she could only marvel at Félicien's capacity to remember each note and every word of what appeared to be every song she'd ever heard, and be capable of retrieving them at will.

"Where did you learn all these? You couldn't have learned them all sitting at home in L'Arête no matter how many troubadours your father imported for you."

The goliard's smile was reminiscent. "I picked up some Latin from a defrocked priest I traveled with for a time, and I read everything I could get my hands on."

"Such as?"

Félicien shrugged. "Forgotten scrolls in a letterless lord's solar." She strummed a few plaintive notes. "An illuminated manuscript at a monastery where we spent the night." This time the lute sounded like a monk's chant. "A good jongleur can memorize three hundred lines of poetry after only three hearings. I don't know that I ever got that good, but the more I memorized, the more easily rhyme came to me. Almost everything is written in rhyme, you know: religious tracts, scrolls on the cultivation of wheat, a chatty little pamphlet on how to get and keep a husband. All in rhyme. Paper is so scarce."

It wasn't in Cambaluc. Not for the first time, Johanna deeply regretted not learning the art of paper making before they had left. She didn't trust that her memory would be as good as Félicien's. "Where else did you find songs?"

In Montpelier Félicien had met Beatrix, the lady of the local castellan, whose husband went on crusade. "'If I had gone with him, I would have been only a wife,' she told me over a fine dinner," Félicien said. "'Here,' she said, 'I am castellan of my own keep.'"

"I have heard of this Beatrix," Alaric said, disapproving. "She disinherited her son in favor of her daughter and granddaughter."

"Good for her," Shasha said, earning an indignant look from the Templar.

"It was Beatrix who first showed me Geoffrey of Monmouth's *History of the Kings of Great Britain*. I promptly wrote a song of Igerna's rape by Uther and she was horrified. She said Igerna was willing, that Geoffrey of Monmouth made that very clear." Félicien's lips twisted. "Of course, Geoffrey of Monmouth was a man."

No one said anything.

Félicien took a deep breath and struck a presentation chord. "And then at the puys, the gatherings when all the jongleurs come together, we would all sing our songs and learn each other's. I've borrowed from Polyhistor stories of people who sacrificed to Apollo by dancing barefoot over hot coals, of pythons that grew long and fat by feeding from the udders of milk cows, of lynxes who urinated topazes, of the dog-headed Simeans of Ethiopia, ruled by a Dog-King."

She laughed, a little guilty, her cheeks flushed with real color for the first time in days. "Once, a local priest denounced me for singing a song of romantic love between a knight and his lady, what he condemned as pagan practices, 'fit only for the ears of the devil himself.'"

"What did you do?"

Félicien's smile was sly. "I substituted the Virgin Mary's name for the name of the lady in the song, and all was well."

Alaric actually laughed. "You should have been burned at birth, my lady." Alone among all of them, he refused to revert to calling her Félicien.

"Then," Félicien said, "there was a tale of a knight who pretended to be deaf and dumb so his lady would be assured of his discretion and take him into her bed." This time she laughed with them, and then her face went white and Johanna got the night jar up in position just in time. She washed Félicien's face with the damp cloth always at the ready. No one said anything. They were all too used to it by now.

"The songs I liked best were the ones the jongleurs wrote about themselves," Félicien said, her eyes closed. "Ottar the Black made the mistake of dedicating a poem to the daughter of King Olaf, was condemned to death for his presumption, and gained his reprieve by singing the king's praises on the way to his execution. 'A song without music is a mill without water,' he was quoted as saying, and troubadours from the Danube to the Nile promptly acquired that line for songs of their own. They are great thieves, the jongleurs and the troubadours; they steal lines, verses, entire songs without fear and without shame."

Félicien's eyes opened. "It is a great honor, you know. It means the other singer likes the work." She smiled. "Besides, you know the story. Why did God make thieves thieves and jongleurs jongleurs?"

"The thieves had first choice," Johanna replied by rote, and smiled back at her friend, though her heart was breaking.

Félicien insisted that Johanna teach her her songs, too. "There isn't much point," Johanna said. "When I sing of China, such tales are treated as fine fables, though hardly true."

"It's only because your songs dare to imply that the Chinese culture is far more advanced and superior to the European," Félicien said, and Johanna laughed.

More months passed: December, January, February. In the beginning Félicien was well able to reach and strum all the chords, but as winter progressed she was reduced to plucking out individual notes. Her flesh shrank as her belly grew incongruously in contrast, a hard, firm lump beneath the bedclothes that if nothing else provided a good platform for her instrument. She could no longer rise from her bed unaided, and the company formed the habit of spending their evenings in her room. Alaric and Firas brought tack in to be mended and swords and knives to be sharpened; Shasha mixed dried herbs and put them in packets; Alma painted. Hayat had bought a lap loom and was weaving a scarf of blue silk and green wool, a lovely thing. She had refused to have anything to do with weaving since they had left Talikan, as it was too much a reminder of endless tedium of the harem. It seemed she had decided it was time to take it up again.

Tiphaine roamed the town for delicacies to tempt Félicien's appetite, and when Félicien couldn't eat them ate them herself.

Jaufre looked in, but could never bear to stay for long. Félicien's eyes no longer followed him from the room. Mostly she looked out the window.

One evening when they had left Félicien to try to sleep, Shasha said, "The infant hasn't moved in days. I think it has starved to death."

Johanna thought of the skin and bones that were all that was left of Félicien's body and wasn't surprised. "Could that help Félicien? Now that she only has herself to nourish?"

Shasha leaned against the wall and shook her head. "If it had happened sooner, perhaps."

"Shasha? Is she truly going to die?"

Shasha's face twisted. "I should have helped her as she wished me to."

Johanna put her arms around her foster sister. "And if she had died, you would never have forgiven yourself." She felt hot tears soak into her tunic. Her turn to comfort now.

Hari took up permanent residence in Félicien's room, violating his chughi rules to spend his nights with a woman. They teased him about it, gently, which he took with a smile, and remained where he was. Sometimes he and Félicien spoke through the night. Sometimes they simply shared the silence.

One day Johanna came to the door of the room. It stood ajar, and she paused when she heard the voices inside. "Peace comes from within, young goliard," Hari was saying. "Do not seek it from without."

"I don't, truly I don't, Hari. I found my peace in freedom, and I lost it again because I didn't want to leave the company of people who had become my friends. Who had become more family to me than my own."

"Do you wish, then, that you had not met us on the Road?"

There was a long pause, but then Félicien said, "No. No, I don't."

"Good. Happiness never decreases by being shared."

"Hari?"

"Yes?"

606

"What happens? Afterward?" What might have been a sob. "I have never been what one could call religious, but I am afraid I have sinned greatly, and that I will be punished for it."

"Do you wish for a priest, young goliard? There is a parish church here, with a priest I find to be kindly and intelligent. I could—"

"No, he will only make me confess, and I don't want to confess to a stranger. And I don't need to be forgiven by any man."

"If it would give you ease—"

"It wouldn't."

A long silence. "Buddha says that even death is not to be feared by one who has lived wisely."

A choked laugh. "There are many who would say I have not lived wisely, not at all."

"Yourself included?"

Another long silence. "No, Hari. No. At the very least, I have lived, and I would not have been able to do so had I remained at home." Johanna could hear the smile in her voice. "I would not have met you. The man who now shares my nights."

In March the days lightened, and lengthened, and came one evening when it was warm enough to leave the window uncovered, when the scent of new grass was in the air, when birds returned from the southern reaches filled the room with song, when Félicien said to Johanna, "Wear your robe tonight."

The robe in question had belonged to Johanna's mother, a robe that she had packed carefully and brought with her all the way from Cambaluc, her most precious possession. It was called the Robe of a Thousand Larks and it was made of heavy gold silk, with wide sleeves and a wide skirt that, after Johanna had unpicked the hem and let it down, just reached to her feet. It was embroidered in silk thread with a thousand larks in all their yellow, orange, red, green and black glory. In between the larks wound brilliant flowers on green vines and black branches.

It was a glorious example of the spinner and the weaver's art, and Johanna looked glorious in it. Félicien stared at her from her emaciated face with its sunken eyes and cheeks. Her hair had begun to fall out and Shasha had taken to wrapping her head in one of Alma's harem scarves, the only color about her now.

Shasha had summoned them all to attend Félicien that evening and they had all obeyed that summons: Firas, Alma, Hayat, Hari, Alaric, Tiphaine, even Jaufre, who stood in a corner, his arms crossed, his face in shadow.

"Sing the dawn song," Félicien whispered.

Johanna struck a chord, and the sadness of lovers about to be parted was repeated in the features of her face, the gleam of her hair in a last stray beam from the setting sun, and above all in the husky contralto tones of her voice.

Ah, would to God that never night must end,
Nor this my lover far from me should wend,
Nor watcher day nor dawning ever send!
Ah God, ah God, the dawn! how it comes soon.

The glittering of the brilliants sewn on the Robe of a Thousand Larks captured the little light in the room and threw it back tenfold, so that amethyst lilies and ruby roses seemed to sway in a gentle breeze, and nightingales' wings flickered in flight.

Sweet lover come, renew our lovemaking
Within the garden where the light birds sing,
Until the watcher sound the severing.
Ah God, ah God, the dawn! it comes how soon.

She looked up from the lute to see Félicien's drowsy smile, saw her eyes close, heard the rattle of breath in her breast. She handed the lute blindly to someone and kneeled to take her hand. Shasha came to kneel at Félicien's other side, and the rest of them gathered round, as Félicien the goliard, also known as Aceline Eléonor Félicienne de L'Arête, also known as l'Alouette du Sud, slipped from her earthly vessel, and left it, and them, behind.

14

Chartres, spring, 1326

THE DAY AFTER they buried Félicien, Johanna stood in the yard of the inn and closed her eyes in repugnance against the brightness of the day. The sun felt warm on someone else's skin, not hers. She felt numb and oh so tired, and beneath it all there was a tiny core of molten anger, anger at Ambroise, at Florian for abetting Ambroise, at Shasha for not being able to cure Félicien, at Félicien for dying. That anger was encased for now in a hard layer of ice but its distant warmth was at present her only comfort. One day soon it would perhaps break free of its icy shroud. One day.

She heard North Wind give an inquiring whinny. Soon, she would take him out for gallop. Soon. This afternoon, perhaps. Tomorrow. Next week.

She felt the others assembling around her, and opened her eyes to see that they were all there, gathered around Hari.

Hari had been an exemplary member of their group since Johanna had rescued him from a potentially fatal beating before the gates of Kashgar, where he had been arrested for preaching without a license. He never again forced his religious beliefs on an unsuspecting populace, or at least not in a manner that rebounded adversely on their company. Upon their arrival in any city, his first action was to seek out the religious community and disappear for days. Imams and priests, rabbis and patriarchs, monks and nuns, scholars and pedagogues, all were of abiding interest to Hari, and evidently none were proof against the chughi's air of mild inquiry, which was all he ever displayed. When Johanna had asked him what he was doing, he smiled and said, "Listening." Once when Jaufre asked him where he was going he had replied only, "Forward."

He had put off or covered up his yellow robes with clothing more suited to the current climate, but there was no hiding the yellow skin that clung so closely to the high cheekbones, or the tilted eyes, or the shaven head. He would always be other so long as he stayed in the West, but he seemed unconscious of the second and third looks cast his way, and none of them could deny the air of gentle authority he exercised. People did what he told them to as a matter of course. Not excluding themselves.

And so here they were this morning, emerging pupa-like from their winter cocoon, burdened with heavy grief at the loss of their comrade, and for the first time in all their time together uncertain of where they were going, or even why.

"Come with me," Hari said.

They followed him, dispirited and unquestioning, through the winding streets of the town and up to the cathedral. It was after morning services but before the line of pilgrims had begun to form to see the holy relic, and they passed unhindered and unchallenged between the two towers, under the royal portal and down the center aisle. There were a few people at their prayers and someone cleaning the candleholders on the altar, but for that they were alone. Any scrape of the sole or whisper floated up and was magnified by the impossibly high, vaulted ceilings, carved with fantastical shapes and painted with bright colors.

"Stand here," Hari said. They stood, nine abreast where there should have been ten. They had passed rapidly from light into dark and they closed their eyes to let them adjust.

It was the first time Johanna had been in the cathedral itself, although she had been to its Christmas fair, looking for something, anything to cheer Félicien this past December. What had she bought? A puppet, she remembered, and she and Tiphaine had made it dance on the bedspread, and Félicien had laughed, back when she could muster up enough energy to laugh—

"Look up," Hari said. "Look up, now."

Obediently they opened their eyes and looked up, and were assaulted by a blaze of colored light shining through windows that on every side reached for the sky, for the heavens, for the stars themselves. Crowned figures royal and religious, common folk wielding axe and saw and scythe, burghers making and merchants selling, saints ascending unto heaven and angels on outspread wings, mother and babe, mother and man, mother and sacrificial son. Green vines like emeralds and roses like rubies and borders like amber and stars like diamonds twined about the figures, creating a jeweled setting for an already almost blindingly dazzling display.

Dumbstruck, they drifted in ones and twos from window to window, necks craned, eyes straining. Only Alaric and perhaps Hari understood half of what they were looking at, but somehow they knew that they were reading a book, a book that could tell them the history of the culture of the land in which they now stood. Of course, Johanna thought, of course, in a land where so few people could read, of course the church must have a way to imprint its legends on the lay folk, who after all could not spend all of their time listening to sermons. Here was their story, all their stories, written in light and color, for everyone to see and remember. But it was more than just a book of the church: it was a book of the people as well, kings to commoners. You knew where you were in society, who you were when you came here. Here there was certainty. Here there was clarity. Here there was comfort in the regular order of things.

She found herself standing next to Jaufre, and glanced at him. He too was staring up, absorbed, this time in a tall, slender column of glass showing a tree springing from one man's groin in the bottom panel and ending at the top in another man crowned with seven doves. "Their Christ?" he said.

"Yes," she said, in an equally hushed tone. "It's almost enough to make me believe."

He shook his head. "They're barely civilized enough not to shit in their own drinking water, and then they build something like this."

Alaric had come to stand by them. "You know why they built it, don't you? To bring in pilgrims to spend money in the town. It's why all cathedrals are built."

Jaufre looked at him. "You don't even believe that yourself." A thought struck him. "Wilmot. I completely forgot. Is your friend here?"

Alaric shook his head. "I've asked. If he was here, it was only briefly, not long enough to make an impression on any of the residents. No one remembers him."

It was past noon when they emerged again, feeling half-drunk on the wonders within, to find pilgrims lining up to view the Sancta Camisia, allegedly the tunic Mary wore when she gave birth to Christ and the cathedral's most precious relic. Behind the pilgrims a man was perched on the edge of a fountain, a bound trunk on the ground below, open to reveal a sheaf of forms. Another man displayed a writ of some kind upon a red velvet cushion. Even at a distance they could see that the writ was most wonderfully decorated with great scrolls and flourishes, and the cushion was no less wonderfully decorated with elaborate embroidery in gold thread and gold tassels. It was very gaudy.

To one side a flock of men in clerical black stood with their hands folded piously beneath their cassocks, crucifixes gleaming upon their breasts. Behind them a huge wooden cross had been raised and draped with a banner.

Alaric caught his breath and crossed himself.

"What is it?" Jaufre asked in a low voice.

"That banner is the banner of the Holy Father himself," Alaric said, murmuring a prayer and crossing himself again.

"Of Pope John in Avignon?"

"The same."

"What's going on?"

"I don't know."

Everyone appeared to be waiting for the bells in the tower to stop ringing. When they did, the crowd surged forward, hands held out, usually with coins displayed in them.

"I have here your passport to Paradise!" the man on the fountain cried. "One quarter florin saves you seven years of penance! Have you committed the mortal sin of carnal knowledge of your mother or your sister? Poor Christian soul! Step up, place your coin in the bowl of the Holy Father! You will receive a letter of remission of your sin, and if the Holy Father forgive it, then God must also. Step up! Did your father die unshriven? Poor Christian soul! As soon as the coin rings in the bowl, that soul will fly straight from Purgatory to Heaven! Step up!"

They stepped up in a body, crowding around, fighting for place. Even a few pilgrims broke rank, perhaps tired of waiting for Mary's attention. A third man counted the money as it dropped into the bowl with one hand, and handed out forms from the chest with the other.

"I thought you said you had to confess your sins to a priest," Johanna said to Alaric. "That was why they wouldn't let us bury Félicien in one of their graveyards."

"And that you couldn't be forgiven your sins until you had done penance for them," Shasha said.

"Usually on your knees in church," Jaufre said.

Alaric's mouth was a thin line of disapproval.

"Is it not said, 'Who fears not, God, Thy gifts to take and then Thy ten commandments break, lacks that true love which should be his salvation?'" Hari quoted piously.

"Amen," Jaufre said heartily, and was seconded by a chorus.

Alaric scowled. "Let's get out of this crowd."

They let him lead the way home because none of them could keep their faces straight.

Life was not all tragedy, Johanna thought, and people were not all of them evil. For every Ambroise there was a Hari and a Firas and a Jaufre and yes, even an Alaric. For every Chartres Cathedral built to the great glory of church and state by the hand of man, there was a man offering you an opportunity to buy your way into heaven.

No, not all tragedy. Johanna felt the numbness that had enveloped her upon Félicien's death begin to ease, and when she next drew breath the scents of spring were rich in her nostrils.

And Félicien?

She was unaware she had said the words out loud until Jaufre answered her. "Félicien would have written a song about it," he said.

She looked at him and saw that he was smiling. "And not a nice one."

Even Alaric smiled.

✝

That night Shasha conspired with their landlady, with whom they were by now on quite good terms, and produced a feast of roast chicken and a heaping bowl of root vegetables mashed with butter and herbs, and another bowl of fresh-picked strawberries for dessert. Johanna couldn't remember the last time she had eaten anything that tasted as good.

They cleared away the debris and returned the dishes to the scullery, and came to roost on the fenced paddock that currently housed North Wind. He trotted directly up to Johanna and nosed her so impatiently that she nearly fell off the rail. She climbed back up and produced a wizened excuse of an apple excavated from their landlady's cellar. North Wind snorted down the front of her tunic and after a little fake dissembling deigned to accept the tribute.

He ambled away, munching, as the other three Arabians and the rest of their mounts fell in a respectful distance behind. He still had that scar on his right foreleg from that time in the Hindu Kush, when they ran from Gokudo until they caught him. There was another on his left hindquarter, a rope burn suffered from one of Sheik Mohammed's men.

She looked around at her human companions. They were all scarred in one way or another, too.

"So," Shasha said. "What do we do next?"

It so happened that they were facing north. Johanna saw Jaufre raise his head and stare off at the horizon. "I'd still like to find a good source of wool," he said. "Good quality fleece would fetch a fine price both in Lyon and in Venice."

Alaric was picking at his teeth with a twig. "They do say," he said, "that the best wool comes from England."

"Do they," Shasha said, eying Alaric narrowly. There had been something suspiciously studied in his statement.

He returned a glance of limpid innocence and spread his hands. "So I have heard. I've never been there myself, of course."

Johanna wondered what wool cost in England. It had been an expensive winter. She herself was down to two rubies, one sewn into the hem of each leg of her trousers, the last of her patrimony, the last gift she would ever receive from her father. As for coin, there was precious little of that left in any of their pockets.

"Then perhaps we should go to England," Jaufre said.

Alma and Hayat exchanged glances. "What?" Jaufre said.

"Well," Hayat said. "Where is it?"

"North," Alaric said. "And west. And we'll have to cross La Manche."

"The channel? What channel?"

"It's what they call where the ocean travels between Normandy and England." He looked at their blank faces, and added kindly, "Normandy is also north."

"There's a university in the town," Alma said to Hayat.

"And where there is a school, there will be a library," Hayat said, with resignation.

"And where there is a library, there will be maps," Alma said, with satisfaction.

"How far to this channel?" Firas said.

Alaric shrugged. "Fifty leagues, perhaps?"

Johanna looked at him, at his purposely diffident air, and thought that he knew down to the rod how far it was to the channel.

"And how long a voyage to cross it?"

"If the weather is fine, a day or less."

Their last voyage, a storm-ridden journey across the Middle Sea, was strong enough in everyone's memory to be relieved to hear it, even if they didn't quite believe that any sea voyage could be quite that easy. Tiphaine, never having been on a ship, was enchanted at the notion and bounced on top of the fence, to the imminent danger of them and the railing they were sitting on. "When do we leave?"

"As soon as possible," Alaric said.

"Why?"

"It's spring. In two months' time, or when the ground dries out, whichever comes first, armies will begin to march. It would be best to be gone before that happened."

"Which armies?"

"All of them. Did you think all those ships were being built in Venice only for trade?" Alaric grimaced. "The English kings have been fighting with the French kings ever since Henry II died. All this—" he waved an inclusive hand "—or much of it once belonged to the English, by marriage portion of Eleanor of Aquitaine. They've been losing it a piece at a time to the French ever since, but they're very tenacious, the English. There is nothing they love so much as a vain hope, and they are more than willing to sacrifice any number of lives to it."

That last came out a little acidly. "You know them well, in spite of never having been there," Shasha said.

"There were many English among the Knights Templar." He nodded at Jaufre. "His father was only one of them. My suggestion is that we sail from Harfleur. It's a smaller port than Calais, with fewer ships to choose from, but it's closer to us. And farther from the Low Countries."

"The Low Countries?"

"Someone is always fighting over or fighting with the Low Countries," Alaric said. "They are very rich, and so present tempting targets to anyone with a large enough army. We would be much safer avoiding them altogether, even though it will be a longer sail from Harfleur."

"Fifty leagues," Shasha said, sliding to the ground. "Say a week's travel—what is the way like? Should we go supplied, or will food be readily available for purchase on the journey?"

"We begin practice again every morning," Firas said. "If we are going where armies march—"

"Armies march everywhere, all the time, Firas," Alaric said. "And we are not an army, in and of ourselves."

"Nevertheless—"

"A ship! We're going on a ship!"

They moved off, chatting animatedly. Johanna found herself alone with Jaufre for the first time in months. She hesitated, looking at him.

"What?" he said.

"Is looking for wool the real reason you wanted to go to England?"

"Oh, well…" He looked a little self-conscious, which was better than the open, gaping wound that had been living with them lately. "I suppose I would like to see the land my father came from."

"Will you look for his family? Your family?"

He shook his head, more definitely this time. "No. They are nothing to me." He looked at her. "Johanna."

Something in his expression made her heart skip a beat. "What?"

"I'm sorry." He took in a breath and blew it back out again. "It's late to say it, and if you have a shred of self-respect you won't accept it, but I am truly sorry."

She didn't pretend not to understand. She surprised them both when she said baldly, "Did you love her?"

He looked first surprised and then confused. "What?"

"Did you love her? Félicien? I thought you—I thought we—" She couldn't go on, her throat closing over the words. She looked away, unable to bear the sight of his face when he said "Yes."

"Johanna. Johanna, look at me." A large hand raised her chin and she willed back the tears to meet his eyes. They were so blue, and so dear. "Of course I loved her," he said, and her heart plummeted. "No. Listen. Listen to the rest. Listen to all of it." He put his hands on her shoulders and pulled her towards him. She went, step by hesitant step. "Of course I loved her, as I love them all—" he jerked his head at the group now entering the inn. "—the whole annoying, irritating, infuriating bunch of them. They are my comrades, as Félicien was my comrade."

"But she was more than that," she said.

He squeezed her shoulders. "I lost my mother the same way, Johanna."

She looked up, startled, and he smiled. "I didn't think I'd have to explain this to you of all people. My mother was kidnapped and sold into slavery when I was ten. I never saw her again, but I never stopped looking for her." He raised his head and stared into the distance with blind eyes. "I went to the slave auctions in Venice, Johanna. I watched women being stripped to their skins, their mouths forced open to show their teeth; filthy, grinning old doctors produced to attest to their virginity."

He gave a shaky sigh. "I was sick. Worse than Félicien on the worst day of her illness. I barely made it outside." He looked back at her, his eyes very bright. "I swore to myself, then and there, that I was done looking for my mother. I swore to accept the fact that she had gone beyond my reach. That my memories of her were all I would have. All these years of looking for her, and I finally realized. I wasn't ever going to find her. I wasn't ever going to rescue her. The last word I would have from her, the last sight of her I would see would be from that morning on the Road, three days from Kashgar. When we woke, and broke our fast with tea and dried fruit, and she made a joke when I brought in a bag of dried camel dung for that night's fire."

She felt tears sting her eyes. "It's not a bad last memory." She thought of her own mother's death. But she had been there, holding her mother's hand as she died. She hadn't seen her mother disappearing around a street corner in every city between Cambaluc and Venice for the last ten years.

She looked at Jaufre. "And then Félicien was taken."

"Yes, and it was my mother all over again. She was taken, and I could do nothing to stop it. I might as well have been that ten-year old boy again, utterly useless, utterly ineffectual. I couldn't let it go, Johanna. I couldn't let her go." He searched her face. "Do you understand?"

She thought back to those days and weeks following Félicien's taking, when Jaufre had seemed so maniacally focussed on getting Félicien back, allowing nothing and no one, not even his friends and comrades' doubts and fears to get in his way. "We could have been killed, Jaufre," she said. "All of us, not just Félicien."

He gave a short, explosive laugh. "Don't I know it! Looking back I can't believe I did that. But I had to." He looked at her again. "We had to. We had to rescue her, because we could. We could not have left her there, with him."

She thought of Félicien, laying on the bed in the room upstairs in the inn, wasting away to a skeleton, her hands growing ever more frail on the strings of her lute. How much more terrible would those days have been, had they been spent in L'Arête? "No," she said. "No, we could not."

He looked relieved, and then doubtful. "Does everyone feel the way you do?"

She pushed him away gently. "That is something you must talk to them about. Each and every one of them, Jaufre, from Hari to Tiphaine. Make your peace with them, or it will blight us all going forward."

He drew close again. "And us?" he said. "Did I blight us, too? Did I lose what we could have been, too?"

She gave a sudden, blinding smile. "You don't get rid of me that easily, Jaufre of Cambaluc." She kissed him swiftly on the corner of his mouth. "Félicien died free, and she died among friends, among people who loved her." She drew back and looked at him with steady eyes. "All that we did, all that we endured, all that we dared. It was worth it."

She ran after the others.

He watched her go, the lithe girl with the bronze braid and the golden skin, running easily across the yard to disappear inside the inn.

One thing he hadn't told her, one thing he might never tell her, was what he had felt when she tumbled beneath the belly of Ambroise de L'Arête's destrier, to deliberately place herself within range of the dangerous hooves of a trained war horse. A terror greater than any he had ever felt seized him and for a moment he couldn't move, he couldn't speak, he could do nothing but watch to see if the destrier trampled her to death. Such was his concern to keep Félicien free of Ambroise that when they had made their plan, when Johanna had insisted it was the only way to provoke North Wind into action, he had not thought what it would mean.

She could have been injured. She could have died. Surely she knew that, and much sooner than he had. And she had done it anyway.

He looked about himself with new eyes. Their world over the winter had slowly contracted to the room in which Félicien lay dying. But here, outside that room, there was sun, and blue sky, and trees and shrubs going from bare limb to fat buds overnight, and pollen gathering in yellow drifts on roadsides, and farmers laboring in the fields, and calves and lambs mastering insubstantial legs to totter in search of mother's milk. He saw gray-cloaked pilgrims on the road, eyes fixed on the towers of the cathedral, burning with the hope that the Holy Mother would grant their wish for a son, a cure, forgiveness, grace.

Inside the inn his friends waited.

And then he closed his eyes and gave devout thanks to whomever was listening for the luck of a fool such as he.

15

England, summer, 1326

THEY WERE AWAY three days later and at the coast of Normandy a week after that. The route was well signed, the roads were dry, the weather was delightful, the inns were plentiful and welcoming, and, refreshingly, no one they met was trying to kill them. Jaufre spent time riding with each of them, making his peace. Alaric was acerbic, Firas calm and might even have been a little amused, and Shasha read Jaufre a lecture about reckless behavior, regardless of how worthy the cause.

"We could do nothing less for a friend who wished to be free of the harem," Alma said, and Hayat nodded her agreement.

"'Friendship is the only cure for hatred, the only guarantee of peace,'" Hari said, and smiled his wonderful smile.

"Did you hear when North Wind landed on Ambroise's head?" Tiphaine said. "Crack! Squish! That'll teach him to mess with Wu Company."

They crossed the river Seine at Tancarville and followed it down to its mouth, where the town of Harfleur presented a bustling picture of energy and industry. "They're starting a merchants' association here," Tiphaine said, returning to the inn where they had procured rooms for the night. "Perhaps Wu Company should make ourselves known to them."

"Perhaps," Jaufre said, looking at Alaric, just entering the common room. The Templar had been dispatched to find them passage across the Channel, and from the sour expression on his face he had not been successful. He sat down and called for a pitcher of wine but it was seen that he drank abstemiously, at least for him, and ate heartily of bread and cheese and a heavenly bean stew flavored with bits of chicken and sausage and a lot of garlic.

The inn was close to the waterfront and catered to a clientele of merchants, traders and ship's captains. The conversation was certainly animated but it never got too loud, bargaining for freight and rates was conducted briskly and professionally. Like the city itself, the inn appeared to exist to do business.

Alaric pushed back his plate and refilled his cup. "I have not found us a ship," he said. "It appears that Edward's wife is cuckolding him with one of his lords, and she has betrothed their son to the daughter of Hainault. She's brought him over to meet the girl. A smart man's money is on Isabella's primary purpose being to use the daughter's dowry to finance a rebellion against him." He saw blank looks surrounding him. "Edward, king of England. Isabella, his wife. Edward, their son. Hainault, one of the Low Countries everyone is always fighting over. And I'm sure," he said, staring glumly into his wine, "that ineffectual bastard Charles probably has an incompetent hand in this somewhere." He saw their looks again. "Charles IV, king of France."

"You speak of these great people with great familiarity," Firas said.

Alaric snorted. "I do, don't I."

"More to the point, what does this have to do with being unable to find transportation to England?" Jaufre said.

Alaric sighed. "All the Harfleur ships are in Calais, looking for work transporting the royal party across this summer. Invasions are good for the transportation business. You can charge anything you like and they have to pay."

"Not all the ships, surely," Shasha said.

Alaric studied Johanna. "I assume we need a ship big enough to bring along the livestock?"

"You are correct in that assumption," she said.

"Well, then." He raised his hands in a gesture of defeat, and let them drop again. "There is one possibility I have yet to explore."

"What?" they said in a chorus.

"I'd rather not say. I'll leave tomorrow at first light. I should be back by nightfall. If not, the day after."

✛

They looked for him the next day, and the day after. On the third day he rode into the stable yard as they were assembling in the common room for dinner. He had a glorious black eye and he chewed as if some of his teeth were loose.

Nobody said anything until they were finished. Alaric poured a cup of wine, filled his mouth and held his head on one side for a moment.

Shasha cleared her throat delicately. "I don't know that that will do any good."

Alaric swallowed. "I don't, either." He put both arms on the table and leaned on them. "Jaufre."

"Yes, Alaric."

"You remember I told you about my sister."

"Your what? Oh." One night he had sat on the wall of Bastak and watched the moon travel across the sky as Alaric told him about Jaufre's father. Not all, as it turned out, but some, and some of Alaric's own history as well. "Your sister," he said. "The one who, uh, convinced the guard to let you go when your father betrayed you."

"You never asked what happened to her."

"No." Not that he hadn't wondered.

"We were… separated after the escape." Alaric swished the wine around in his cup. "She came here."

"Here? To Harfleur?"

"Yes." Alaric sat up and drained his cup. "She has a ship, big enough for us and the horses, too."

Jaufre looked at Johanna, who looked at Shasha. "And will she take us to England?" Shasha said.

Alaric felt tenderly of his jaw, and winced. "For a price," he said. "For a price. She'll be landing us in one of the smaller ports. She doesn't—" He thought for a moment, and then said, "She has no charter for any of the larger ports."

Johanna might have seen the suspicion of a smile hovering around his mouth for a moment, and then it was gone, too soon for her to be sure.

✝

They paid their charges at the inn the next morning and were off with a clatter of hooves, turning right out of the yard and trotting down the road that ran next to the river. The river widened and the trees of the high ground became marshlands covered with tall reeds, but the path stayed hard and dry. They reached their destination by sext, the sun high in the sky. By then the other side of the river was lost in the fine mist rising from the surface of the river.

It was a good-sized village clustered around a single dock stretching out into the water. Moored on either side were two ships. Both had single masts with square sails rigged between mast and boom. The hulk was round-hulled, the cog flat-bottomed. The hulk had a round stern and a side rudder. The cog had a square stern with decking built on the inside around three sides, and a center rudder controlled by a capstan.

A woman stood in the stern of the cog, watching them come. As they approached, Jaufre saw that she was tall and thin, long of face, with dark hair and eyes. The similarity was unmistakable, but unlike Alaric the lady crackled with energy. "Are these yours?" she said.

"They are," Alaric said.

"Well, get them aboard before we miss the tide."

Introductions were deferred until the horses were loaded into

624

the hold, where stalls had been created by boards bolted to the hull. Posts formed a center aisle. "Hobble them," the captain said, peering down from the deck. "I don't want one of them to take a notion to kick holes into my hull in mid-channel."

The horses were duly hobbled and backed into their stalls. North Wind's indignant trumpeting could probably have been heard in Harfleur. He knew all too well from his only other sea passage how uncomfortable being under sail could be, and he did not take kindly to the feel of a deck rising and falling beneath his hooves again. Johanna held his head and soothed him while more boards were slotted in to form gates. They went further and ran a line over the horses' backs, in case they took it into their heads to rear. A couple of bales of hay were tossed between the two ranks of stalls. North Wind calmed and deigned to lip at it.

Johanna gave him a last reassuring pat and went up on deck. The lines had already been loosed and the downriver current was parting them rapidly from the dock. Gulls screamed overhead and Johanna saw a pod of porpoises surface and blow and dive off their bow, backs gleaming wetly in the sun. At mid-river the captain said, "Set sail!" The large square of canvas raised and shook itself out and bellied gently before the offshore breeze. Through it all the sunlight on the river was bright enough to blind, and it was warm even out here on the water. Jaufre murmured in Johanna's ear, "It can't be this easy, surely?"

She laughed and turned, leaning on the rail. "Hush. The gods will hear, and make us suffer."

They stood like that, smiling at each other, for a good long while, and then in mutual unspoken agreement turned and watched as they left the mouth of the river and Normandy behind. "So," he said finally, "what do you reckon? A pirate?"

She looked over her shoulder at the captain, who stood, arms folded, behind the helmsman at the capstan, legs spread in a stance that took the small swell beneath their hull with ease. She was dressed much as they were, in tunic and trousers, a wide sash of some dark red material wrapped twice around her waist.

As they watched Alaric approached the stern, and the captain's arms dropped and she advanced to the steps he was approaching, where she planted her hands on her hips and glared down at him. He halted immediately and returned to where the rest of the company was gathered amidships. "I don't think they parted well," she said thoughtfully.

"No," Jaufre agreed.

"What do you think happened?"

"Nothing he's proud of," he said, keeping Alaric's confidence. "Or he wouldn't have let her give him that black eye."

The downstream current and the outgoing tide took them out into the Channel, and there a nice strong offshore wind took over. The swell was minimal, with no chop at all. The cog slipped through the water like North Wind down a race track, leaving a wake of frothing foam behind them.

The captain spoke to the helmsman and took to the deck in a single bound. Jaufre and Johanna joined the others as she reached them. "All right," she said briskly, "if the wind doesn't change we might make landfall before dark. Alaric told you that you will be set ashore in Cornwall? The south of England," she amended when she saw their blank expressions. Her language was cultured and refined, its timbre and accent much like her brother's. "It's a rocky, barren coast but the harbor is good, if small, and well sheltered, and there is a place for you to stay the night. Not an inn, but I—do business with the owner there. He's a genial soul and welcomes travelers. The agreement was half up front, half upon delivery, and I will expect payment in full before we land you." She nodded and marched back to the helm.

They ate bread and cheese and last year's pears for lunch, and then Jaufre took his courage in his hands and ventured to approach the aft deck. "Captain?"

She turned her head and saw him standing at the foot of the stairs. She hesitated, and then nodded permission. "Yes?" she said.

He smiled the smile that the ladies of Cambaluc had considered his secret weapon. The captain did not visibly melt. "I wondered how often you made this passage," he said.

"As often as I have paying customers," she said. "Why?"

He cast an appraising glance over her craft. "I make the length to be some sixteen rods?"

"Seventeen," she said.

"And the beam, one and a half?"

"One and three-quarters."

"Making your payload—"

"Four thousand hundredweight."

"Very nice," he said. "Big enough to make a good living, not big enough to be too enticing a target, and fast enough—" he glanced at their wake "—to outrun all but the most serious trouble."

She smiled; reluctantly, he thought, but she did smile. "What is your interest in my *Faucon*?"

Falcon, he thought. An apt name, as falcons were swift and elusive. Also predatory, but he preferred not to dwell on that at the moment. "I'm a trader," he said. "I'm always interested in the means of transporting goods."

She eyed the hilt of the sword looming over his shoulder. "A trader."

"Yes, a trader," Jaufre said firmly. "Where you are landing us, do you call there on a regular basis?"

This time she laughed. "Say rather, on an irregular basis," she said.

"Do you ship fleeces?" he said. "Wool?"

"Often," she said.

"And land them at your village?"

"It's not my village," she said, "and no, I land English goods at Harfleur. There is no point in unloading my cargo at the village and then paying someone to haul it all the way to a buyer, now, is there?" Her voice was mocking.

"None at all," he said. "How do the Harfleur wool merchants find the quality of your fleeces?"

"English wool is much prized by merchants all over the continent," she said.

"I know," he said, "I've heard nothing else since Venice. English wool seems to be universally regarded as the finest wool there is." He meditated for a moment. "If an ambitious trader—"

"Such as yourself," she said, a faint smile lifting one corner of her mouth.

"Such as myself," he said, returning her smile, "if such a trader, new to the ways of England, was desirous of buying and exporting wool, how would he go about it?"

Still smiling that faint smile, she shook her head. "Don't even think it, young sir. The fees will be astronomical. You'll need a charter from your local lord to do business. Every shire and city you pass through will levy a tax. There will be export fees, and the port fees—" She shook her head again. "No, young sir. For a stranger, a man new to England, one with no connections, such a thing cannot be arranged."

He was somewhat dashed by the certainty in her voice, and then rallied. "And how would one avoid some, or all, of those obstacles, captain?"

She smiled warmly. "Why, however would I know that, young sir?"

When she laughed he laughed with her.

When he rejoined the others, Johanna raised an eyebrow at him. "We were discussing the wool trade," he said. "What can I say? It's been months since I bought or sold anything that wasn't for our own consumption. Time to start thinking like a trader again."

They rolled up together in his cloak and fell asleep, protected by the gunnels from the sharper sea wind, comforted by the warmth of the last rays of the setting sun, lulled to sleep by the gentle swell of the ocean.

It was dark when they woke. Jaufre sat up and Alaric said immediately, as if he'd been waiting for him, "The wind changed. It took longer to get here than the captain estimated. We'll land at first light. Go back to sleep."

Instead, Jaufre got up and went to stand next to Alaric, who was leaning on the rail. "How did she end up here?"

Maybe the concealing dark inspired in Alaric the urge to confide, as it had that night in Bastak. "Angelique got me out of the dungeon, but we were pursued. Her horse went lame. I panicked and left her behind." When Jaufre would have spoken he held up a hand. "Don't. There is nothing you can call me that I haven't called myself over the years. There is no word, no epithet, no curse bad enough." He gave a laugh that was more like a groan. "If Robert had known, he would have called me all of them and invented some new ones, too."

Memories of his father were so dim and far off now. Jaufre knew he looked like him: height, hair, build, eyes. He remembered a deep voice and a rich laugh, and large, calloused hands over his on the hilt of the sword he now carried. But he liked the man Alaric spoke of. The man who would never leave a comrade behind, let alone a sister.

Water lapped at the sides of the cog. Jaufre thought he could see the dim outlines of land off the beam. They appeared to be standing off a coast. "How did she end up here?" he said. "And how did you know where she was?"

Alaric sighed. "When we were in Avignon, I sent a message home. What was my home. To our old priest, who was always a good friend to the two of us. He was the one who got us our horses." He took a deep breath. "I didn't know if he would reply, but he did. In not very kind terms. Oh, nothing less than I deserved, and I knew it. But he did tell me to look for Angelique in Harfleur, as the captain of a ship, and her own ship, no less." His voice was rueful. "Our father disowned her when her part in my escape was learned, but she had a lover, a Dane, a ship's captain – this ship. She eloped with him, and she sailed with him. He died four years later, after which the crew accepted her as their new captain. She settled in Harfleur, and eventually wrote to Father Étienne that she was alive and well."

"Is she a pirate?"

"What? No! What makes you think that?"

There was a smile in Jaufre's voice. "She is so far as I can see unattached to any guild or association. She moors in a small village inconvenient to offloading merchandise in Harfleur, but very convenient to hide any cargo she cares to ship from prying eyes. She lands in a foreign port so small—" he gestured to where he could hear the surf hissing against the shore "—it is completely dark at night."

Alaric sighed. "You are entirely too observant, and in that, young Jaufre, you are very like your father, indeed." He paused. "Not a pirate, no, but a smuggler, I fear."

"And used to using her fists in a fight?"

"Indeed, and able to use them to give me a proper welcome. Now get some sleep. It will be dawn soon."

16

England, summer, 1326

THE DAWN BROKE on clouds gathering over a steep coast, colored sullen orange to deep red. They were reflected against the oily, steadily increasing swell beneath the *Faucon*'s hull. "Yes," the captain said, "let's get docked now."

She brought the ship in close enough to what looked like an uninterrupted shoal that her passengers held their collective breath, and then a ray of sun broke through the clouds to illuminate a narrow channel. The *Faucon* threaded it with easy confidence.

Inside the reef was a small, half-moon bay, with a narrow edging of golden sand on the left and an outcropping of rock on the right that formed a natural breakwater. There was a man-made rock pier, patiently chipped to a broad level surface just long enough to dock one ship the size of the *Faucon*. The shore dropped so steeply here that there was room to spare for the ship's draft at any tide, and there were men waiting to catch their lines.

A gangplank was laid of deckboards and the horses led up from the hold in short order. There was a stable with a small paddock halfway up the bluff into which the horses were turned, while the passengers followed the captain up a twisting path to a large building that backed against the cliff. It was square and solid and made of the same black rock as the pier. Johanna, looking over her shoulder, saw the *Faucon*'s crew lading bundles and boxes to the end of the dock and vanishing around a corner. She wondered if she'd missed a warehouse built at the water's edge.

The heavy wooden double doors of the keep opened at their approach, and the captain took two strides and embraced the man standing in the opening. He was half a head shorter than she was and an arm's length broader but she nearly raised him off his feet. He let out a booming laugh and pulled her down into a loud, smacking kiss. Jaufre nudged Johanna and they looked on, grinning, as Alaric looked at first startled, then revolted, and finally resigned.

They trooped inside, where the first floor of the stone keep was taken up by one enormous room. A set of stairs climbed the back, north-facing wall, in which a great stone fireplace was set with a stack of logs that burned with a welcome warmth. Next to the fireplace a door opened out the back, through which wafted the enticing scent of baking pastry. Two long tables had been set up in the center of the room, benches on either side and a chair at the head of one of them. "Sit!" their host boomed, his deep voice echoing off the stone walls. "Sit and break your fast." His French was rough but perfectly understandable. He sat in the chair and had the captain sit on his right. "And who are all these lost waifs seeking shelter from the storm?"

As if in counterpoint thunder cracked in the distance. "Me, for one," the captain said dryly. Her crew pattered inside and closed the doors behind them before taking their places at the second table. At some unseen signal servants entered from the door at the back bearing platters of large, crescent-shaped pastries stuffed with minced onion, root vegetables and some kind of meat, well spiced – Johanna watched Shasha take a bite and immediately begin cataloguing the ingredients – and pottery mugs of small beer.

"So? Who are these people eating at my table? Or is it a mystery again?" Their host winked.

"It is not a mystery, so far as I know," the captain said, "but first I should perhaps introduce you to them, Hugh. Allow me to make known to you one Hugh Tregloyne, the master of this keep." She made a graceful gesture with one hand. "Your guests may introduce themselves."

One by one they went around the table and did so. Alma and Hayat were examined pretty thoroughly and Tiphaine would have been chucked under the chin if she had been within arm's reach. If Tregloyne's gaze rested on Alaric's face a little longer than on the rest of their faces, and if he looked back and forth between Alaric and Angelique, and if he drew any conclusions, he was tactful enough to say nothing. Oddly, his gaze lingered longest on Jaufre.

"So," he said when they were done. Lightning flashed outside the back door, thunder rumbled again, and rain followed immediately, an instantaneous deluge that stopped almost as soon as it started. "All the way from distant Cathay. Welcome to Glynnow." His voice mocked without being offensive. "What would such world travelers want with Cornwall, then?"

They looked at each other. "Well, sir," Jaufre said, "we are interested in wool."

Tregloyne stroked his chin. "Buying or selling?" He heard Jaufre out, and at the end shook his head, much as the captain had. "The tax will eat you alive, young Jaufre. Every city and town you travel through will levy a charge, and the ports!" He threw up his hands.

"How do the graziers feel about all these taxes?" Jaufre said.

Tregloyne snorted. "How do you think? And the local merchants and traders as well. But there is no other way to get their goods to market."

"What if we camped between towns?" Jaufre said. He looked at Angelique. "And what if we shipped from a small port, with whom we had negotiated a reasonable shipping and lading tax, hired locally for lading, and contracted a favorable rate with a single ship to transport goods?" He let them think about that

633

for a few minutes. "It would remain a small business, obviously. Although I know a Venetian trader with his own ship who might be able to find his way to Harfleur, the wind and gods providing."

The captain sat up. "Who would that be?"

"Giovanni Gradenigo, of the family Gradenigo," Jaufre said.

"I have heard the name," the captain said. She looked at Jaufre with growing respect. "A sea route to the wool markets in Venice, avoiding the overland fees and expenses, would greatly increase your profit. Always supposing this Gradenigo's price for transporting it could be kept to a reasonable amount."

"I believe it could," Jaufre said. "Captain Gradenigo has a wish to build his own business, apart from his family's." He thought of their crossing of the Middle Sea. "And he is a fearless sailor."

"Better an old sailor than a fearless one," the captain said dryly.

They sat in silence for a few moments. "A business small enough not to attract attention," Tregloyne said.

"Obviously," Jaufre said with a smile. "A place called the Shropshires has the best wool, or so I'm told. How far is it from here to there, and how bad are the roads?"

Tregloyne sat forward, his interest now fully engaged. "The condition of the roads I can't tell you," he said. "I've stayed close to home these last few years. The road used to be good from Exeter on, but the royals have been very busy trying to stab each other in the back and they're not particular about trampling who gets in their way betimes. I can give you a few names, though, if you wanted to look for yourself." He thought, frowning. "You would want to make for Ludlow," he said at last. "It's in the heart of the Shropshires, about seventy leagues from Launceston, the nearest market town, which is eight leagues from Glynnow. Before making any firm plans, I would recommend that you travel the route, and talk to such graziers as might be interested, and examine the quality of their wool. Do you know anything about wool?"

"I know where it can be sold at a profit," Jaufre said. He

smiled at Shasha and Johanna. "And I know all the ways it can be fiddled to seem to weigh more than it does."

Tregloyne let out his booming laugh. "I'll just bet you do, young Jaufre of Cambaluc." He saw Jaufre's look and said, "Yes? What is it?"

Jaufre hesitated and glanced at Alaric. "I just wondered if perhaps you had heard of a family called de Beauville."

"De Beauville," Tregloyne said, eyes fixed on Jaufre's face in a disconcertingly intent stare. "De Beauville. There was a family of that name. Expatriate Normans, granted land by Henry III, or perhaps it was John Lackland. The property was outside Launceston, I believe."

Jaufre swallowed, his mouth suddenly dry. "'Was?'"

"There were four sons, as I recall," Tregloyne said, matter-of-fact. "One of them was shipped off to the Templars." He glanced at Alaric. "The first died at Stirling. The second died at Methven. The third died at home of the bloody flux." He shrugged. "All died without issue. Their father made some effort to find the fourth son and return him home to take up his father's estate and provide it with heirs. It came to nothing, unfortunately, and he died soon afterward. The estate reverted to the crown."

Jaufre let out a breath he hadn't known he'd been holding. "Did you know them? Any of them?"

Tregloyne shrugged. "The elder son, to nod to on market days. He was a short, fierce fellow, dark-featured and very bellicose." His eye again wandered over to Alaric. "Much like his father, and two of his brothers. The fourth son was tall and fair. Were they some relation to you, young Jaufre?"

A hand slid into his, and Jaufre felt Johanna's presence warm and solid next to him. "Possibly. It doesn't matter now," he said, a wry twist to his mouth. "Not if they're all dead."

"If you could prove your parentage," Tregloyne said, "the estate—"

Jaufre cut off the words. "I couldn't, and I wouldn't. And besides, I'd rather attract as little official attention as possible."

"Oh? Is there something I should know?"

Jaufre smiled. "No, sir, I do assure you. We have left behind no unpaid debts, and no enemies." He looked around the table. Everyone stared soberly back. No living ones, that was. Except perhaps for Dai Fang, and one could not imagine Wu Li's widow ever leaving Cambaluc, and certainly her reach would never extend as far as England. "It's just that any business is better conducted as far from the official eye as possible. It won't be possible forever, of course – we will require our own charter eventually – but I'd like to keep as many hands out of our pockets as possible."

"Understood," Tregloyne said. "And, young Jaufre, if you manage to put together enough of a supply chain to fill a ship the size of, oh, say the *Faucon*—" He grinned at Angelique "—Glynnow would be a port willing to keep its lading tax—what did you call it—reasonable."

Calling a one-ship dock a port was something of a stretch, Jaufre thought, but they would see what the numbers added up to before they made any firm decisions. Still, he liked Tregloyne, and Angelique felt like someone they could do business with. Wu Company could do much worse.

That evening they gathered around the fireplace and sang and played for their host, to such effect that he was moved to enthusiasm. "God's teeth, are you sure you're merchants? You sound like professional minstrels!"

"We learned from the best," Alma said.

"The best taught you well," Tregloyne said. "Now let's have that drinking song again," and he beat time on his thigh from first verse to last. "You know," he said, when they were done and everyone was quenching their well-earned thirst with watered wine, "a group of traveling minstrels is welcome everywhere."

He met Jaufre's eyes and nodded. "Every village and town and city, every manor and castle. In the towns, you could time your performances to market days, when all the farmers and graziers come in to trade. A man is always eager to pass the time of day with travelers. It's the only way to get the news."

They digested this in silence for a moment. Jaufre, looking around the table, saw no serious objection to the idea, although Alaric did cast up his eyes.

Next to him, Johanna stirred. "Tell me, sir," she said, "do the English race horses?"

✝

Their host and the captain retired up the stairs, Alaric averting his eyes from the spectacle. "Well?" said Jaufre. "What do you think?"

"If we go in telling the truth, we should be prepared to be hanged at the first crossroads we come to," Firas said.

Shasha nodded. "There will be strong, entrenched interests vested in keeping things the way they are. Our plan will be money out of their pockets, and they won't like it."

"Perhaps…"

"What, Hayat?"

"Tregloyne said we'd be welcome at manors and castles, too. If we could gain the sponsorship of a lord—"

"But then he'd want his share of the profit," Jaufre said.

"So will Tregloyne, and so will Captain Angelique," Hayat said.

"But they'll earn their share." Jaufre scrubbed both hands through his hair. "It's like being nibbled to death by ducks."

"We don't own a ship," Firas said, "and even if we did we don't know how to sail it. We don't own a port, on either side of the Channel. We were never going to be able to do this alone."

Jaufre made a rueful face. "No." He looked at Hayat. "We'll travel to this Ludlow, by way of Launceston. We'll keep our eyes and ears open, and if we see someone who might help us—"

"And who we think won't hurt us," Alaric said.

"Then we'll see." Jaufre shook his head and gave a short laugh. "It's a good idea, Hayat. It's just that we've been independent for so long, with no ties."

637

"Gradenigo—"

"He had no power over us beyond our contract," Johanna said. "Accepting a lord's protection would be different."

"Especially when he finds out we can sing," Tiphaine said, yawning.

Jaufre ruffled her hair. "And that you can juggle."

✠

They bedded down around the hearth, but Jaufre found himself too restless to sleep. He got up and went to the back door, whose bar was more easily raised than the immense oak beam across the front doors, and slipped outside.

The square house had been built on the right side of a swift-running stream set between steep banks. A footpath led up the side of the stream. He followed it and in a very short time gained the top of the cliff that ringed the little bay. The moon was nearly full and the sky was cloudless now and the sea calm, so that he could see every slab, every pillar and pinnacle of rock as it rose out of the water, the tiny white ruffles of foam on the rocks, and the sand of the little beach. The bare mast of the *Faucon* barely bobbed as the ship sat sedately next to the rocky pier. From here, in the moonlight, it was easy to see the channel between the two rocky pillars the captain had guided their ship so confidently and competently through that morning.

In this light, from this angle... he squinted. Those two rocky pillars looked almost manmade, or rather as if their original forms had been at least in part deliberately shaped by the hand of man. He wondered how long Tregloyne's people had been living at Glynnow, and how long ships had been landing goods here.

There was mostly grass and a few shrubs on the cliff. Too much wind for trees, perhaps. Farther up the stream he saw a clump of houses clustered on both sides of it, and some turned earth beyond them. Where Tregloyne's people lived, probably.

There was a sound behind him and he turned to behold Johanna standing before him. She had undone her braid, leaving her hair a mane of ripples and curls, each one kissed by moonlight. She was carrying their blankets over her arm.

His heart began to thud against his ribs.

She smiled, and turned to shake the blankets out and lay one neatly on top of the other. She turned back to him, waiting.

He stepped forward to slide his hands around her face. "Johanna."

"Jaufre."

"Are you sure?"

"I am," she said, and raised her face.

He kissed her, sliding his arms around her and pulling her in so tightly that she uttered a slight protest. He loosened his hold immediately. "I'm sorry," he said. His head dropped back, his eyes closed, his blood pounding in his ears. "I have wanted you for so long. Loved you for so long."

"I know that now," she said, tracing his lips with a fingertip. "I'm sorry I was so silly."

"I should have said something sooner."

"I should have known."

"It almost killed me when you went to Edyk."

She raised her head at that. "I'm not sorry I went to him, Jaufre. I won't ever be sorry. I loved him, too. If he had wanted me to, I would have been with him again in Gaza."

"I know." And he had known, and it had nearly killed him to say nothing then, too. "I wanted you to come to me."

"And now I have."

His heart seemed to have lodged somewhere up in his throat. He was so hard he couldn't bear the touch of clothing against his skin. "I don't know if I can go slowly."

She smiled. "We'll go slowly," she said. "Later."

She stepped back and her hands went to her girdle. It fell, and so did her tunic, and her trousers. She stood naked before him: proud, perhaps a little shy.

He couldn't get out of his clothes fast enough, and then finally they were laying together on the blankets, skin to skin, and he finally had his hands on her, on the golden skin turned silver in the moonlight, on the breasts like apples, on the curve of her belly, on the curls between her legs. He knew her so well, had known her most of his life, and still there were mysteries to be found. The creamy taste of her skin on his tongue. The velvet of her nipples. The sweet curve of her hip. The length of her legs, thigh, knee, calf, down to her ankles and back up again, lingering, savoring, feasting.

She was moving restlessly beneath him now, reaching for him. He caught her hand and held it down, and slid his fingers between and up. She was ready for him, hot, wet, clutching at him, trying to draw him in. He exulted in it, wanted to shout it from the top of the cliff. Oh yes, she was ready.

She would be more so. He found the place and rubbed, gently but firmly, with the tips of his fingers. He heard her gasp and he looked up and saw her head raised, watching him. She saw him watching her, and arched her back and opened her legs more.

Johanna exulted in the feel of Jaufre's hands on her where she had imagined them to be ever since that yurt in Kuche. She couldn't catch her breath. She raised her hips and pushed against his hand. "Harder," she said, and she could hardly recognize her own voice. "Harder, faster, oh, Jaufre, oh—" Her hips thrust, raising her body into a bow of flesh and bone straining toward that one glorious end.

She fell back, panting, and he settled in between her legs. "Take me in your hand," he said, and she could hardly recognize his voice, either.

She reached between them and closed her hand around the hard, hot length of him. She had watched covertly from time to time, curious, trying to imagine what lay beneath his clothing: if he was like Edyk, or different. He was both, she discovered now, like and different, and he was Jaufre, which made him something else altogether, something more. She tightened her grip and it was his turn to throw back his head, eyes closed, mouth tight. He was wet at the tip and she rubbed it with her thumb, and his breath hissed out. "Johanna," he said, and she shivered at the sound.

She rubbed the tip of him against her, up and down, up to the place that was the seat of all this frenzy of need, down to where he would come inside her, up again, down.

"Johanna!"

"Jaufre," she said, but it was almost more of a growl, and she brought him down again and inside her. He held very still, weight on his elbows, looking at her. She could feel him inside her belly, inside her veins, inside the blood pumping through them. She felt hot all over and cold all over and hot all over again. She wanted more. There was more and she would have it. She raised her legs and wrapped them around his waist, and catching and keeping his eyes she raised her hips, driving him all the way inside. She pulled back, slowly, agonizingly, and he groaned and closed his eyes. "Johanna. Don't. Don't—"

She grabbed his hair in both fists and said, "Look at me. Look at me!" She pulled him inside her again, and now he took up the motion, slowly, steadily, watching her, wallowing in her, rejoicing as she reached for her pleasure.

"Wait," he said.

"You wait," she said.

"Not yet," he said, "no, Johanna, not yet, not yet—"

He thrust forward for what he was afraid would be the last time and felt her clamp down on him and arch beneath him and heard her cry out his name, and for the very brief space of time granted to him before he followed, he thrilled to the knowledge that it was him giving her that much pleasure.

She felt the base of her spine melt in a burning rush and heard him call her name in a half-shout, half-groan, and felt a rush of power that he had wanted her so much and had waited so long and that it was so very good for both of them.

They lay together, a messy, sweaty tangle of repletion, and watched the moon travel a little farther across the night sky, as the sea chuckled and gurgled against the rocks below, as if nothing special had happened here on this little patch of grass. She smiled to herself.

When he got his breath back he raised his head to look at her. Her eyes were closed and there was a smile on her face. "All good?"

Her smile widened and she opened her eyes and looked at him, a goddess in the moonlight. "All great."

He dropped back with a relieved sigh. "I was afraid I was going to have all the finesse of North Wind at stud."

"You didn't," she said, "but we can work on that."

✠

The next morning Shasha took one look at them and brewed Johanna a cup of her special tea, the same tea she had served her when Johanna went to Edyk. "It's not a guarantee, you understand," she said, "but it works with most women most of the time." When Johanna only smiled she said anxiously, "You understand that what you're doing is what makes babies, don't you, Johanna?"

Johanna burst out laughing.

17

England, summer, 1326

IT WAS A golden summer. Everywhere they travelled in England, people remarked on it. At every village and town, people paused from their work to stand and bask in the sun, as if they were afraid that it would wink out in the next moment. "Forty years of wet misery had we," one Devonshire farmer told them. His broad face was creased with an almost personal resentment. "Bad harvests. No harvests. People eating each other they be so hungry. The winter snow bury the county for months, and the summers the rain come down like it be poured out of a pitcher that never emptied." He closed his eyes and raised his face again to the sunshine. "This be back now. For a while now, maybe. We be enjoying it while we can."

When they weren't drinking in the rays of the resurrected sun the English were toiling in their fields, sowing grain and corn, pruning and espaliering fruit trees, working night soil between rows of vegetables and across fallow fields, pitching every spare scrap of food to the pigs and the chickens, frantic to make up for the previous hungry years, and constantly terrified that the sun would leave again and the rain return and all their work go for naught.

The halcyon weather was of far more interest than the royal to-ing and fro-ing across the Channel and the countryside, but one thing was abundantly clear across all levels of society. The English felt they had been taxed beyond endurance, and what was worse, to no purpose. Such careful inquiries as to more profitable markets for wool that Jaufre felt safe enough to make were greeted everywhere with interest, if not outright enthusiasm. Further, many of the people he spoke to lay blame for a generation's worth of drought, flood and famine squarely on the doorstep of the ruling family, whose fraternal disorder since the reign of Edward Longshanks had clearly roused the wrath of God Himself. God had visited His displeasure upon the English with forty years of drought, flood, blizzards and famine, and defeat after defeat in the continual war with the Scots culminating in the shameful battle of Bannockburn. Everyone, it seemed, had a brother or a son or a nephew killed at Bannockburn, and what had they died for, indeed, when ever since the bloody Scots raided the border at their whim?

The eating away of Plantagenet properties on the continent by the French was also an issue. Everyone knew how vastly inferior the French forces were to the English. There could be no other explanation than God's personal displeasure. To be taxed for war was duty owed to the king, this was understood. But to be taxed for losing foreign wars on every border and front (and now those thrice bedamned Glendowers were stirring in Wales), to be taxed for wars the English lords were fighting against each other, domestic disputes that led only to more domestic disputes and to the turning of good English fields into abattoirs, this was not so well understood, or so well tolerated. It was in many cases resented enough to create discontent among even the lowest laborers in the fields. It was as yet only a rumble, as examples of rumbling rotted in cages hung from every city gate and castle wall and crossroads post, but it was there if you listened for it. The royal family and the noble families clearly did not bother to listen, and that unconcern caused equal discontent.

But meanwhile the sun shone down, and the rain fell in plentiful amounts it seemed only after nightfall, and seemed always to end before dawn. Given this kind of encouragement it was no wonder the land responded. Never had Wu Company seen such a lushly growing countryside, such greenly growing fields, such a profusion of wildflowers. Every ewe had a lamb and often two, every cow a calf, and the amount of chicks in every farm yard was a hazard to navigation. Nor were they alone in marveling at the pastoral scene set before them, because there were English adults living who had seen nothing like it before in their lives, and who could not help but gaze about themselves in wonder.

Jaufre was aware that his own happiness at loving and being loved by the object of his affections colored his perception of everything he looked at, but he tried, he truly tried to look at his surroundings with a merchant trader's clear, practical eye. Was it his fault that all of England looked as if it had been dusted with gilt?

They made love everywhere they could find a moment to themselves: in a hayloft, behind a barn, one memorable time in a lord's solar, on the lord's very bed, while the rest of the troupe entertained the lord and his household in the great hall below. "We could probably be beheaded for this," Johanna said, flushed and scrambling into her clothes.

"Only if we get caught," Jaufre said, snatching a kiss.

Tregloyne had been correct in that a troupe of traveling minstrels would be welcome everywhere. No farmer was so anxious over his crops in this extraordinary year that he could not bring his family into the village for an evening's entertainment. No city burgher was so concerned over the price of pepper that he would allow his neighbors and fellow merchants to attend such an event without him, and possibly from his absence infer that his business was so fragile it required his constant presence. The ladies of the wealthy and the nobility heard their servants speak of the wonderful singing troupe, some members of which had come from as far away as Cathay and Persia, and summoned them for command performances in their halls. Firas with his scimitar, Shasha with her tip-tilted eyes, Hari in his yellow robes,

Alma and Hayat with their groomed beauty, Tiphaine with her tumbling curls and juggling fountains, even tall, spare, aloof Alaric, these would all have been oddities had they been traveling on their own, to be regarded with circumspection and treated with caution. In company with Jaufre and Johanna, the young lovers, they were romantic and mysterious but not dangerous.

The one snag was the languages, which seemed to change by the league. Even their facile ears and nimble tongues were put to the test in the battle between Cornish and Devon and Welsh and whatever it was they spoke on the English side of the Welsh border, where even Johanna admitted defeat. Fortunately, almost everyone spoke French in some fashion, from baron to freeman and even a few villeins, and on the rare occasion when they did meet with total incomprehension a translator could always be found.

And, Johanna discovered to her and North Wind's immense gratification, not only were the English vitally interested in horse racing, there seemed to be a racetrack outside every major town. The stallion took on all challengers with enthusiasm. He hadn't raced since Milano and he was eager to stretch his legs and show these inferior English nags the speed a horse with his august lineage considered a winning pace. Gentlemen arrived in groups to inspect him, and to arrange more races for him, and to make appointments for their mares. Some of the mighty were so enraptured that they might have been inclined to exercise *droit du cheval*, had Johanna not been so very obliging about renting him out to stud, and had North Wind not himself held such decided opinions on allowing anyone other than Johanna on his back.

They traveled first to Launceston, where they held their first performance at the livestock fair. From there they went east to Exeter, where they were lucky enough to encounter a fair whose grounds had a stage for rent. From Exeter they went north to Bristol, a seaport with as much bustle as Venice, which boasted a healthy shipbuilding industry and an energetic wool trade, and where the amount and variety of seafood outran their experience even of Venice. "Our competition," Firas said, from where they stood watching the loading and unloading of ships at very nearly a run, with more ships lined up in the channel waiting for their turn.

Jaufre grinned. "No. Pretty soon we'll be their competition."

North of Bristol they detoured around Berkeley, where they had heard the castle was being sacked by one of the Despensers, a king's favorite. This detour brought them deep into the Cotswolds, a farming shire whose cottages were built of a uniform golden stone cut into perfectly square blocks. When they saw the first one Alaric murmured something to himself and went forward to examine the wall of the cottage.

They dismounted. "What is it, Alaric?" Jaufre said.

"Wilmot's father did work like this," the Templar said, running his fingers down the impossibly straight lines and angled corners of the stones. "There is no mortar, do you see? It would take a mangonel to break down this wall."

A farmwife came to the door, her children peering from behind her skirts, but when she saw the party had women in it she relaxed. She spoke enough French to invite them to water their mounts at the horse trough that was a feature of every farmhouse they passed and asked if they would like a meal of bread and cheese and radishes, with fresh fruit to follow. It was late in the day and soon her husband and her eldest son came in from the fields and they were invited to camp near the house. His name was John and hers was Mary and they were happy to share their dinner pottage, and in gratitude for their hospitality Johanna staged an impromptu performance, signaling Tiphaine to bring out her rag balls. Alma produced her charcoal and a precious piece of her stock of parchment to make a sketch of the entire family which was much admired. Firas and Alaric staged a fierce mock duel and of course then the eldest son had to hold the sword of the victor, which of course required instruction, and then Hayat gave the children a ride on the Arabian she had been riding since they'd stolen him out of Sheik Mohammed's stables.

They were seen off with thanks the following morning and rejoined the road at Tewkesbury, where they tarried for a week at the behest of the local lord, who had taken a fancy to having every mare in his stables who might be even peripherally interested topped by North Wind, and then left for Birmingham, which rivaled Bristol for size and was a city of artisans and craftsmen, boasting products from the hands of the finest wood workers any of them had ever seen. Jaufre was tempted to switch cargoes, but as Shasha pointed out, fleeces could be folded flat and bound together many to a bundle, whereas chairs and chests manifestly could not.

From there they went west, deep into a verdant country of forested hills and rolling farmland, where every second person they met was a grazier, a farmer of sheep. Jaufre's knowledge about wool grew exponentially, and he bored everyone at dinner on the best breeds to produce the finest fleece to be spun into the best wool fabrics. They avoided Ludlow, Shropshire's largest town, as it belonged to the Mortimers and Roger Mortimer was reputed to be Queen Isabella's lover and about to aid her in invading England. The Despenser sacking Berkeley could easily make Ludlow Castle his next stop. The members of Wu Company did wonder if the impending civil upset would interfere in a major way with commerce, but after forty years of internecine warfare the English themselves were inured to the prospect. "They always be fighting," one grazier said with a dismissive wave of his hand, "but they always be needing clothes to wear and food to eat, too, and I don't see no fine lady milking her own cow nor no fine lord tending his own sheep."

Thus far they had avoided any encounters with the warring factions, although there was rumor and conjecture on every tongue. Alaric especially was avid for all the news he could get. All knew that Queen Isabella and Roger Mortimer, in company with her son, Edward Duke of Aquitaine and the heir to the throne, had gathered together on the shores of Holland, together with a group of Dutch and German mercenaries, prefatory to invading England and wresting the crown from the king's head. Another rumor had it that Charles of France was mustering his own invasion force from Normandy, although Alaric let out a mighty snort when he heard that. Throughout the summer one force or the other was held to be landing at, alternatively, Portsmouth, Hastings or Dover, with a critical minority holding out for London itself.

As to which of the factions should win, no one would commit themselves, high or low, city or country. It was agreed that Edward had been an ineffectual king with a dangerous predilection for all the wrong friends. However, no one thought – or said out loud – that Isabella and Mortimer could manage the kingdom any better. "They be taking the coin out of the land as fast as ever they could, whoever they be," said a farmer outside of Worcester, "and putting none of it back in again. It make no matter to us which royal ass sits on a throne in London." There were grave nods from his friends, one of whom went so far as to spit and say, "Most of them know not even which way is west," which raised a laugh.

There was a faint hope that Edward's heir, the Duke of Aquitaine, might be an improvement over either, but he was only a boy, thirteen or fourteen, wasn't it? He would be surrounded by those same lords who had bankrupted the nation with their petty jealousies and revenges until his majority, or until he gathered together enough powerful lords of his own to oust the old ones, and then it all started over again.

"These folk hold no illusions about their overlords," Firas said one evening.

Alaric opened his mouth to say something, and closed it again. Johanna saw, and wondered what he had been about to say, and why he had thought better of it.

They reached Bristol again in mid-September, and were still there when they heard that Isabella and Mortimer's forces had landed at Orwell in Suffolk. They had intended to move on the next day to Glynnow by way of Plymouth this time, but they waited instead to hear the news. A few days later it came with a group of men under arms, who told them that London and many of the larger cities were in a state of anarchy, everyone in a panic and no one in authority. The king was said to be in flight into the west before the march of Isabella's army, much enlarged by English nobles defecting to Isabella's side. He was expected momentarily in Bristol itself, and the troop of men stationed here, led by one Lord Dundry, were king's men, and were there to meet him.

Shasha began packing immediately, but even all of them working together couldn't outpace a king in full flight and they were coming up on Bristol's south gate just as the royal party clattered through. The heavy wooden gates shut behind them and the bars thudded into their brackets with finality.

The royal party was a pitifully small group of men. The king rode at their center, barely visible over the heads and shoulders of the rest of them, but the roar of the crowd said he was there. Jaufre swore beneath his breath. Johanna squeezed his hand. "It's all right," she said in a low voice. "We don't know any of these people, we'll just—"

"Wilmot!"

It was Alaric, shouting out the name.

A stocky man in full armor, mounted on a destrier, swiveled his head as much as he could. "Alaric? God's nightgown, Alaric, is that you?"

Alaric bounded forward and practically yanked the man from his saddle, and then they were both pounding each other on the back, tears streaming down their cheeks.

"Wilmot," Alaric said, choking over his and still pounding his friend on the back, although the other man's armor must have hurt his hand. "I saw Gilbert in Sant' Alberto. He said you were in Chartres. I looked for you there."

"I was there," Wilmot said, disengaging himself and giving a hitch to his cuirass. He looked around and waved at someone in the men surrounding the king. They clattered on without him, and Alaric led the way back to their inn, where Shasha was just in time to reclaim their room.

They commandeered the largest table in the common room and ordered food and drink. "Why did you leave Chartres?" Alaric said. "Gilbert said that you intended to go there and take up your father's trade."

"I went there," Wilmot said, and paused. He was a stocky man with a thick neck and heavily muscled arms that tested the sleeves of his tunic. "I went to the cathedral, and prayed."

Jaufre was watching Alaric, who was wholly enthralled, intent on Wilmot's every word. "Yes?"

"A voice came to me, and told me that I was a soldier, and that I must not yet put up my sword. I must find a worthy cause, and fight for it."

At that, Alaric did raise a brow. "Edward?"

Wilmot flushed a little. "It wasn't Edward exactly. It was Robert." He met Alaric's eyes squarely. "Robert saved our lives after Ruad. Robert was English. So I came to England and offered my sword to the king." He refilled his cup and drank deeply, and set it down again with an explosive thump. "Well, God's bones, Alaric. You've been to Chartres. You've seen the cathedral. If anyone was ever going to hear voices, that would be the place."

They both laughed.

"And you?" Wilmot said.

Alaric glanced at the other table. "I went home, and I was not made welcome, so I returned to the East and offered my services to a much less exalted personage, but he paid well and on time." He gestured. "That's where I met my friends."

Wilmot looked at the circle of interested faces. He blinked at Alma and Hayat, indisputably women but dressed and, God above, armed like men. Hari with his thin, ascetic face and his yellow robe. Firas, unmistakably a warrior, if most certainly not a Christian one. Shasha, with her foreign features set in such a bland expression that one could express no surprise or aversion. Johanna, who earned an appreciative look. Tiphaine, an urchin

651

with curly black hair who had no place at this table. His gaze came to rest on Jaufre, who made no effort to hide his curiosity. Wilmot's eyes widened, and Johanna saw his hand tighten on his cup.

"No, Wilmot," Alaric said. "Your eyes do not deceive you. This is Jaufre. Robert's son."

Wilmot stumbled to his feet, staring. Jaufre, not knowing what else to do, stood up, too.

"I knew your father, boy," Wilmot said.

"I know," Jaufre said. "I've heard the story."

A wintry smile. "All of it?"

Jaufre glanced at Alaric. "I've met Gilbert, too."

"Ah." Wilmot took a deep breath and let it out on a long sigh, and sat down again. His eyes saw something over Jaufre's shoulder. "By the great good lord, boy, is that your father's sword?"

The great sword was leaning against the wall, since it was so long Jaufre couldn't sit properly with it. "It is."

"He gave it to you?"

"He—" Jaufre hesitated. "He died in the East. He left it to me."

"Damn," Wilmot said, with feeling. "I'm sorry to hear that, boy."

"Jaufre," Jaufre said. It had been a long time since he'd let anyone call him boy.

A trace of amusement crossed Wilmot's face. He jerked his chin at the sword. "Do you know how to use it?"

"Yes," Jaufre said. "Not very well, though."

Wilmot shook his head and exchanged a glance with Alaric. "Do you know who gave it to your father?"

"No," Jaufre said. "Who?"

"Wilmot—" Alaric said.

"Your grandfather," Wilmot said. "Before he sent your father off to join the Templars."

"Oh." Jaufre thought of the story that Tregloyne had told him of his paternal relatives. They hadn't sounded like the kind to give a disposable son so costly a gift. "That was kind of him."

652

Wilmot gave a crack of laughter. "Aye, that it was, boy. And if you're not very good at using it, you should get better." His face set in grim lines. "As soon as possible."

"I'm not a soldier," Jaufre said, meeting his eyes steadily. "I'm a trader. I'm about to go into wool."

"Then give up that sword to someone who can use it," Wilmot said, frowning.

"No," Jaufre said. "It's all I have left of my father. It stays with me. If I have to use it, I will."

Wilmot refilled his mug and sat back. "Is that what you've been doing, Alaric? Setting up as a wool merchant with this—this—"

"We are Wu Company," Tiphaine said. She thrust a thumb beneath her badge and pushed it out. "As you can plainly see by our badge."

Wilmot, nonplussed, stared at the Chinese character. "Oh." He cleared his throat. "Yes. Plainly."

"Furthermore," Tiphaine said, nose in the air, "we are also minstrels. We have performed in some of the highest houses in the west of England, and all of the villages and towns." She thought. "And most of the fairs, too."

"I see." Wilmot stroked his chin. "Are you any good?"

Tiphaine bristled. "We are very good indeed, sir."

"Well. In that case, you had better come and perform before the king after his evening meal."

Everyone sat up with a jerk. "I don't think—" Jaufre said.

"We're not really—" Johanna said.

"It's a great honor, of course, but—"

Wilmot stood up. "Excellent. His majesty's troubles are many. He could use a little distraction. I'll send for you this evening, then."

18

England, autumn, 1326

THEY HAD NO occasion to see Bristol Castle on their way north other than as a menacing outline against the sky. It was perched on a hill on the edge of the river Avon, with a moat fed by the river. A formidable curtain wall ran inside the moat and was interrupted by towers. Inside the curtain wall was a massive keep guarded by two sets of doors which had to be challenged and opened sequentially and the entrants inspected by a host of nervous guards in various liveries who looked as if they'd rather not admit anyone at all. They were ushered into a great hall: a large, rectangular room with tapestry-covered walls and tables and benches ranging around three sides. The longest table stood on a platform at the far end of the room.

Wilmot came forward to meet them. "Excellent," he said. "His Majesty was most pleased to hear of the evening's entertainment. The past few days have been an anxious time for him." He gestured and a few stools were brought and set far too close to the king's table for Wu Company's comfort.

Close up, the king was seen to be tall and spare, with blue eyes and thinning fair hair, and looked oddly familiar to Jaufre, although he couldn't think why. His gaze was a little vague, and Jaufre wondered if he were shortsighted. He had deep pouches beneath those eyes, due to worry or drink or both. Probably more of the latter, Jaufre thought, as the royal nose was a little swollen and red-veined. Well, he was about to lose his throne, or so it seemed. Reason enough to drink.

His attendant lords and retainers looked collectively strained, edgy, almost on tiptoe, as if the next loud noise would have them either reaching for their swords or bolting for the stables. From their demeanor, Johanna thought that the stables would be the preference for most of them.

"You have his majesty's permission to sit in his presence," Wilmot said, and retired to lean his shoulders against an ill-executed tapestry depicting Vincent at work with his pickaxe digging the Bristol Channel while his brother Goram slept in his chair.

The king condescended to address them directly. "Yes, indeed, sit and play something..." He hesitated. "Play something lively for us."

They arranged themselves before him, Johanna on a stool with Félicien's gitar, Jaufre standing behind her with a tambour, Alma next to her with a flute, Hari with a lap harp he had learned to play that summer from a Welsh harper they had encountered in Oswestry. Shasha, Firas, Hayat and Alaric stood behind them and Tiphaine, who was developing a rather nice alto, stood next to Hari. Johanna struck the opening chords without consulting her fellow minstrels but they had all known what their first song would be from the moment the king had spoken.

O wandering clerks
You learn the arts
Medicine and magic
O wandering clerks
Nowhere learn
Manners or morals
O wandering clerks!

After a summer of command performances, they had learned to meld their voices together into a mellifluous whole in which the lyrics were clear and understandable to the farthest ear, accompanied by music that intensified the rich emotion they brought to each song. They had learned to stay in a chord that suited their collective reach. They had learned that they had a gift for comedy, as manifested now. Even the king was chuckling when they came to the last line, and before the last note died away Johanna launched into the drinking song they had sung at L'Arête, and again in Glynnow, the one Tregloyne had so enjoyed the night they landed in England.

When I see wine into the clear glass slip
How I long to be matched with it;
My heart sings gay at the thought of it:
This song wants drink!
I thirst for a sup; come circle the cup:
This song wants drink!

The king laughed outright at the end of the song and thumped the table with his tankard. They followed this with half a dozen more songs, and by then the tension that had been so clearly felt on their arrival had as clearly eased. The king leaned forward and said, "Our good Wilmot has said that some of you are from the East. Is this so?"

Jaufre looked around and saw that he had been chosen as spokesman. He rose and bowed low. "It is, sire. I am Jaufre, the foster son of Wu Li of Cambaluc of Cathay. This is Johanna, daughter to Wu Li, and Shasha, his foster daughter. Hari is a chughi from the Hindu Kush. Firas—" probably best not to say the word "assassin" in this company "—is a Saracen warrior of Alamut. Alma and Hayat are Persian scholars." Because, well, they were, or Alma was, and he didn't want to go into the whole harem topic in this company of men who were used to getting anything they wanted by just reaching for it. "Alaric—"

Unexpectedly, Alaric stepped forward and made obeisance. "Sire, I am Alaric de Claret. My father was Regnault de Claret.

We were presented to your father in Marseille in 1270 by Blaise of Agnois, who was our liege lord."

The king looked a little appalled. "A nobleman's son, and a sworn man? How came you to be a member of this company?"

Alaric, amazingly, did not blush for shame. "I was a member of the Knights Templar, sire. When they... ended, I was still in the East and had to make my way home. I met my friends in Kabul, and we have traveled together ever since."

The king shook his head disapprovingly. "It has ever been our thought that our brother, Philip the Fair, by God's grace the ruler of France while he still lived, was, er, over-enthusiastic in his persecution of the Templars. Our sympathies are with you, Alaric de Claret."

Alaric bent his head. "I thank you, sire," he said. "May I also make known to you the son of a fellow Templar, Jaufre de Beauville."

"De Beauville?" The king frowned. "I thought he said his name was Camelot."

Jaufre, ears burning, inwardly forming the intention to kill Alaric stone dead at his very first opportunity, rose to his feet, tried to hide the tambour, and executed a clumsy bow. "Cambaluc—" he sounded out the syllables "— is where I spent my formative years, your majesty."

"Your father was a Templar, too?"

"He was, my lord. He died in the East some years ago."

"De Beauville," the king said ruminatively. "De Beauville. There is something familiar about the name." He waved a hand. "It will come to me. Now, one more song, I pray you, and then we should all seek our beds this night." He smiled wanly at the man sitting next to him: a stocky, dark-browed man younger than he was. "I doubt few easy nights will be vouchsafed any of us in future."

None of the men in the king's party looked appreciative of this reminder that the king's wife's forces were even now bearing down on them from the east.

"The dawn song," Johanna said, trying to relax the spine that had gone rigid at Alaric's introduction. Royalty was notorious for bestowing favor or blame at its slightest whim. It was much better and far healthier to avoid either. She was furious with Alaric. She plucked a string with fingers she willed not to shake, and sang alone, accompanied only by instruments. There was a moment of silence when she finished, and then the king led the applause. "You have a lovely voice, my dear," he said.

Johanna bent her head. "Thank you, your majesty."

The king sighed, his eyes wandering around the room. "I only wish there were more of mine to hear it, but alas, I believe Isabella landed with so few men because all the support she needed was already here."

That was awkward however you looked at it, and no one knew quite how to reply.

The king smiled. "But that is melancholy talk, after such wonderful entertainment as you have lightened our cares with this evening. I thank you. Wilmot! A purse for, er, Wu Company."

This surprised them all, but they bowed their thanks and backed out of the great hall. As they left, Johanna thought that Edward's eyes followed Jaufre, but it might have been her imagination. She fervently hoped it was.

Firas tossed the purse to Shasha, who weighed it appreciatively in one hand. "Generous of the gentleman. I wouldn't have thought he had coin to spare, especially in his situation."

"Who was that black-browed man sitting next to him, who scowled at us so ferociously?" Hayat unconsciously reached for the short sword that usually hung at her side. It was forbidden to carry arms into the presence of the king.

"Not a music lover, I fear," Hari said.

"The current favorite, the younger Despenser, I would imagine," Alaric said. "The eldest did not seem to be in evidence."

Johanna managed to fall a little behind with Alaric on the way back to their inn. "Did you mean that to happen?" she said.

"What to happen?" he said.

"All of it," she said. "You have been pushing us north ever since Avignon. Did you always mean to meet with the king? And to bring Jaufre to his notice?"

"It doesn't seem to have harmed him any," he said.

"Kings and princes are omnipotent and capricious," she said. "It's a bad combination, and it's never wise to draw their attention. Don't do it again, Alaric."

Wilmot met them at the inn a little later, and he and Alaric took a seat by the hearth in the common room, talking well into the night.

The next morning they woke before dawn, packed, saddled their horses and led them down to the south gate. There had been some apprehension that with Edward in residence and hostile forces approaching the gates would remain locked, but they opened at dawn as usual. Wu Company was first out and proceeded south at a fast trot. At the top of the first hill, Alaric reined in and looked back at the castle, the royal standard flying defiantly from the tallest tower. "'The sins of my youth and my ignorances do not remember,'" he said. "'According to thy mercy remember thou me: for thy goodness' sake, O Lord.'"

He crossed himself and sat with his head bent for a moment, and then with a grim expression kicked his mount back into a trot and caught up with the others.

✝

They clattered south as fast as they could without damage to the horses, and the first week of October were welcomed by Tregloyne with open arms, and a few days later with more restrained enthusiasm by Captain Angelique. "It will be my last trip for a while," she said. "The Channel becomes even more unfriendly than usual at this time of year."

They sat down to a council of war. Jaufre recounted all the information he had gathered from the graziers he had spoken with and the interest he had received in an alternative method of shipping and selling their fleeces. Enough were willing to take a chance on the unknown – and the possibly illegal – to fill the *Faucon*'s hold many times over.

"This is what I propose," Jaufre said at last, looking at Tregloyne. "I would build a house and a warehouse here on your property, for the purpose of running a summer caravan between Glynnow and the Shropshires. We would keep to the smaller villages. This can be done, as the villages are never very far off the main roads. There would still be fees and taxes, of course, but much lower fees and taxes than if we went city fair to city fair as the other merchants do. We would transport the fleeces here, and ship them to Harfleur on the *Faucon*."

He looked at Angelique. "I will write to Captain Gradenigo. When last we spoke, he had the intention of trying to establish a route by sea between England and Venice. They have a new kind of ship they call a merchant galley. It will sail farther in rougher weather with larger cargoes."

"Why Harfleur?" Tregloyne said. "Why not Calais? It's much closer."

"From everything I have heard so far, every power in this part of the world spends all their time either invading the Low Countries or planning to. Harfleur would be a much more peaceful port to cultivate. And they just started their own merchants' association, which you should join immediately, captain."

She shook her head. "They won't let a woman join, shipowner or not." She looked at Tregloyne.

He laughed, his great belly shaking. "It seems young Jaufre here is going to solve all our problems."

"Problems?"

Tregloyne leaned forward, his broad face intent. "Do you intend to settle here in Cornwall, Jaufre?"

Taken aback, Jaufre said, "I mean to start a business here, certainly."

Tregloyne shook his head. "Not what I asked you. Come with me."

He led the company down to the rock pier where the *Faucon* was docked, but turned left before the pier and followed a path around an outcropping. At first it looked as if they were heading straight into the rocky cliff, and then they saw that the cliff was made of two immense slabs of granite, one in front of the other. The path led around the first slab and between it and the second. There they halted and stood, gaping.

It was an enormous cavern, well above the tide line and remarkably dry. Over the years rows and rows of shelves had been laboriously chipped into the walls. In the center of the cavern, bundles, bags and boxes were stacked in orderly fashion, including, Jaufre noticed, a few bundles of fleeces. He rubbed one of them between his fingers. While not as fine or as well cured as those he had seen in Shropshire, they would still fetch a good price across the Channel. Tregloyne noticed what he was doing and said, "Yes, we farm a few sheep ourselves down here in Cornwall. If my people knew there was a market for more, they might improve their breeds."

Jaufre crossed his arms. "What are you proposing?"

"You don't have to build a house, or a warehouse," Tregloyne said with a wave of his hand. "You have all the storage space you need here, and all the living space you need in my keep."

"You want us to move in with you?"

Tregloyne laughed, the sound booming off the cavern walls. "Tempting as that sounds, no." He looked at Angelique. "I have longed to see what lays beyond my own shores for some time," he said, "but I could not leave my people." He looked back at Jaufre. "If we came to an agreement, you would be factor here, and responsible for the care of the people of Glynnow."

"Making sure they don't starve, is that what you mean?" Johanna said.

"That and more. You will look after their interests, represent any of them if they run into trouble with the sheriff in Launceston, which does happen now and then, or if someone takes it into their heads to encroach on any of their lands. They would look to you, and tithe to you. You would be, in effect, their lord."

Daunted, Jaufre said, "I don't know, Tregloyne. How many people look to Glynnow?"

"A hundred and three," Tregloyne said promptly.

"A hundred and three!" Jaufre looked at Johanna, at Shasha, at the rest of Wu Company. There were only nine of them, and that many had on occasion felt more than enough. And they were all pretty self-sufficient, too, if it came to that. The prospect of having a hundred and three people dependent on him was daunting in the extreme.

"Possibly a hundred and four, if Mistress Melwyn has finally given birth to her first. She's been in labor for a full day and night, poor lady."

Jaufre was speechless.

Tregloyne nodded placidly, as if that was what he had expected. "I can see you're a bit overwhelmed. Let's go back to the house and have some cider. Fresh pressed, from our own trees. You won't have seen them: they're farther inland than the village, in a little valley that protects them from the wind."

When they would have turned to leave the way they had come, Tregloyne said, "No. This way."

He walked back into the cave where the shadows were darkest and seemed to disappear. Jaufre, approaching, put out his hand; where there should have been rock wall there was nothing.

Tregloyne's voice came out of the darkness. "There is nothing to fear." A scrape of flint and a spark, and the master of Glynnow was seen to be holding a torch now ablaze, looking at them with a grin on his face.

"Where does this lead?" Johanna said.

"Follow me and find out," Tregloyne said.

The tunnel was long and narrow and so dark that Tregloyne's torch did not reach very far. Jaufre heard Alma say something, sounding a little panicky, and heard Hayat reply in a soothing murmur. The tunnel ended in a flight of narrow, lumpy steps carved from the rock. They went up, and up, and up some more, until they finally emerged on the cliff above the house, blinking in the light. The exit was concealed by a hawthorn bush that had been allowed to run wild, and they were all scratched and a few of them bleeding by the time they were aboveground again.

The exit wasn't far from where Jaufre and Johanna had come together the first time, and he looked at her to see her smiling at him.

"The Romans mined tin and silver all up and down the coast in these parts," Tregloyne said. "This tunnel was part of one such. We, ah, repurposed it to our own uses. There is another exit halfway up the cliff, nearer the house. I will show it to you later."

He led the way back to the house. As they neared the door, Shasha said, "I know something of the healing arts, sir. Might I offer my help to Mistress Melwyn?"

"We would take it most kind in you," Tregloyne said. "Hicca!" A young boy came trotting up. "Show Mistress Shasha to Mistress Melwyn's cottage, and fetch anything she needs."

"Yes, Tregloyne."

Shasha took her pack and she and the boy vanished up the path next to the stream.

The rest of them followed Tregloyne inside and sat down to pitchers of cider and a dinner of whole roast pig and a vast bowl of mashed turnips. "Here it is, Jaufre," Tregloyne said, as the table was cleared. "You have to belong somewhere. You may have already noticed that our island is a contentious and violent place, and one needs to know who one's friends are. Jaufre of Glynnow has a much better chance to form friendships and associations and partnerships with the English than does Jaufre of Nowhere in Particular. Jaufre of Nowhere in Particular, especially if he is going into competition with the local merchants, will carry no weight with the authorities who are, inevitably, bought and paid for by those same merchants."

"You barely know me," Jaufre said feebly. "Why would you trust me with the care of your people?"

"I'm used to summing up men and women pretty quickly," Tregloyne said, with a sidelong glance at the captain. "It comes of living on such a chancy place as the Cornish coast." He smiled. "I like you. I like your friends. I especially like how your plans will bring prosperity to my people. They could use some." He held up a hand. "Don't worry, I'll spend this winter with you, to make you known to Glynnow and to see you into the way of things. But next fall—" he looked at Angelique "—next fall it is my wish to leave with Angelique on her last trip of the season."

He drained his cup and pushed himself to his feet. "I will leave you to discuss this. It's not a decision to be made without due consideration, and you will have more questions. We will talk again in the morning."

He and Angelique ascended the stairs, and the company gathered around the hearth. Jaufre's head, for one, was whirling. "Well," he said. "What do you think?" He looked at Johanna.

"I think I like it here," Johanna said. "I think you do, too." She jerked her head in the direction of the dock. "And I think here we have easy access to a ship if we need to feel the Road beneath our feet again."

"What if they sail away and we never see them again?" Tiphaine said in a small voice.

"They won't," Jaufre said, tousling her hair. "Tregloyne will want to check up on how I am doing my job, and Angelique makes her living on the freight she ships in and out of Glynnow. But even if they did, why…" He smiled. "We'd build our own ship. Or have Ser Gradenigo build one for us." He looked around the circle, every face dear to him. "What do you think?"

Hayat frowned. "I think I spent too many years locked up in a harem. I've only had a taste of freedom. I don't think I'm ready to settle down."

"Or me," Alma said.

"Or me," said Hari, not unexpectedly.

"But this could be home for you," Johanna said. "You could come back whenever you wanted, stay as long as you wanted."

"I like the sound of that," Alma said, smiling at her.

"I wasn't intending on leaving forever," Hayat said.

Hari bowed his head. "There is much still to be learned here."

"Angelique will have to build a warehouse on her side," Jaufre said, thinking. "And I must write to Gradenigo immediately. Perhaps I should even go to him myself."

"I will take your letter to him," Firas said. "Shasha will want seeds to grow her own herbs, and a larger supply of spices if she's going to be ministering to the needs and ailments of an entire village."

"You're staying, then?" Jaufre said.

Firas nodded. "If Johanna is staying, Shasha is staying, and if Shasha is staying, so am I." He smiled. "I'm already half a merchant. I might as well become a whole one."

19

England, winter, 1326–1327

FIRAS, ALMA, HAYAT and Hari departed with Angelique two days after Tregloyne had made his offer. Alma, Hayat and Hari were bound for Paris. Firas would accompany them that far before moving on to Lyon and then Venice if the mountain passes were open to travel.

"Ask Imbert if Laloun ever showed up," Johanna said. At Firas' blank look she said, "Félicien's maid?"

Firas' face cleared. "And if she has?"

"Make an offer of employment. Alma and Hayat could use a maid." At his expression she said impatiently, "Fine; if they don't want her bring her here, we'll find a job for her."

Firas salaamed deeply, hand to heart, lips and head. "All shall be as you desire, mistress."

She picked up a roll and made as if to shy it at him. He went out, laughing.

Jaufre, Johanna, and Shasha settled in to plan an English extension of the Road, and Jaufre began his study of how to be a lord under the tutelage of Tregloyne. "Not a lord," Tregloyne told him. "God's teeth, save me from that, I'd be taxed to death and have to take up arms at the king's behest to boot. Master of Glynnow is what they call me, and what they'll call you."

At first Jaufre was certain they wouldn't. They were a taciturn bunch, these Cornishmen, and unwilling to put their trust in strangers, no matter whether Tregloyne vouched for him or not. Grunts were the usual response to his attempts at conversation, and when it wasn't grunts it was Cornish, which was worse.

He didn't force things, and instead let his company speak for him. Shasha spent part of every day in the village, administering tonics and tinctures and dressing wounds and splinting the occasional broken limb. Alaric had hired two of the more likely Glynnow lads to help him maintain their small armory, and had begun to teach them how to use a small sword, which, when they went back to the village and told the tale, had the entire male population of the village there the next day. Tiphaine was ever attended by a covey of small children who wanted to learn to juggle, and after a while she started teaching them songs from Wu Company's repertoire.

Johanna kept herself busy with North Wind and the rest of their string. This was a good land for horses, covered in rich sweet grass, and as the summer's travels had taught her horses were highly valued in England not just for transportation and war but for entertainment. She broached the notion of planting more oats and lucerne with the villagers, and was met with a receptive ear. She brought the men of the village into the stables a few at a time to introduce them to North Wind and to discover if there might be some among them with the gift for horses. She found a boy, Talan, who could be relied on to muck out stalls and replenish feeding troughs when he was supposed to. Then one day she found Talan's younger sister, Kerra, in North Wind's stall, currying him with long, slow strokes. North Wind was so annoyed by this invasion of his personal space that he was sound asleep. Johanna engaged brother and sister as permanent stablehands on the spot.

When they discovered that Cornishmen were natural stonemasons Johanna hired some to expand the stable. When the Arabian mare who had traveled with them all the way from Talikan came into season she planned to put North Wind to her.

The resulting foal would be the beginning of their own breeding stock.

Shasha hired more men to build a high-walled garden in which to plant her herbs, aided in its design by Jaufre, who remembered the walled garden at Sant' Alberto. She hired boys to bring in topsoil for the garden by the basket, hauled on their shoulders from a vacant farm inland, and then set them to working seaweed harvested from the beach into the soil.

Johanna got wind of the vacant farm and went to look for herself. She came back full of plans for a practice track and badgered Tregloyne to seek out the holder of the title to see if he would sell. He did, he would and for a pretty cheap price, too, and Johanna found herself in possession of a nice piece of flat land where most of the rocks had long since been harvested for fences. She got two men from the village to clear the undergrowth that had begun to creep back in after the farm had been abandoned and then set them to building a dirt oval from one corner of the lot to the opposite corner. The village carpenter built a wide, wooden rake according to her specifications and each morning the dirt of the track was groomed. While the weather held she was out there every day, exercising each horse in turn and, when he insisted, North Wind twice a day.

Before midwinter the horses were snugly housed and the walled garden was ready for planting in the spring. Improvements to the house were in the planning stages because, Johanna told Jaufre, she was not prepared to spend their lives sleeping in the same room as the rest of Wu Company.

"Or not sleeping," he said, sliding his hands around her waist and kissing her.

When she could speak again she said, "Oh well, there are always the stables."

"So there are," he said, and tossed her up in his arms and carried her out the door.

Tregloyne, accompanied by Alaric, disappeared inland for a month, and returned in time for Christmas, barely beating the first winter storm to the door. He handed Jaufre a scroll tied with a red ribbon.

"What's this, then?" Jaufre said. It was a long document, written in Latin side by side with a French translation. His eyes ran down the document, and his jaw dropped. He read it a second time, and a third, before he looked up, dazed. "You adopted me?"

"All legal according to the laws of the land. Keep that in a safe place and should someone try to come the lord over you, pull it out. It was the best thing I could think of to keep you and this place safe."

Jaufre carefully rolled the document back up and retied the ribbon. Johanna, watching, smiled to herself. Jaufre liked Tregloyne a great deal. It was warming to know that that feeling was returned.

Alaric had brought back news of the wider world. "Edward and the few followers he had left fled into Wales. The queen said that since he'd left the country their son should take the throne, and he did so on October twenty-sixth."

"He was right then," Johanna said. "The queen didn't have to bring anyone with her. All her supporters were already here."

"Waste no sympathy on Edward of Caernarfon, as he is now to be styled," Tregloyne said. "Twenty years we had of him, and in twenty years there was neither peace nor prosperity in the land. He had a positive genius for befriending the one person who was most guaranteed to inflame the nobles into rebellion, and to inflict more suffering on humbler folk than they have any right to bear."

"He looked tired, when we sang for him in September. Maybe he's glad to be rid of the crown. What have they done with him?"

"He's at Kenilworth, they say."

"And the men who were with him?"

"The younger Despenser was dragged through the streets of Hereford by four horses, and then hanged from a fifty-foot scaffold so everyone could see – and so could he, because he was not quite dead as they cut off his cock and balls and threw them into a fire burning below." Alaric's voice was flat and even.

"His entrails and heart were pulled out and also thrown into the fire. One hopes he was dead by the time his body was lowered to the ground to be butchered into quarters." He paused. "It is said that the crowd whooped for joy during the entire display."

Even Tregloyne looked a little ill at this.

"His head hangs now in London. The elder Despenser was likewise disposed of in Bristol, the day after the new king was proclaimed. They sent his head to hang on the walls of Winchester."

Johanna shuddered, and thought of Gokudo before the walls of Talikan. "And Wilmot?"

"I can discover no news of him." Alaric looked drawn. "It may be that he held so minor a post in the king's household that he escaped punishment. After all, they couldn't kill them all."

Tregloyne snorted.

At Christmas they held a celebration at the house for the entire village, and put on a performance for which Johanna brought out the Robe of a Thousand Larks, which alone elevated her to the role of goddess in the dazzled eyes of the villagers. Who were then doubly astonished when their new master stepped up with a tambour and joined his pleasant baritone to her smoky contralto. Shasha and Tiphaine provided an admittedly high baseline that nevertheless had everyone tapping their feet. These Cornish could dance, too, as they discovered in short order, and it was a merry evening that ended in gifts for all which Tregloyne had brought back with him from his trip to Launceston. They roasted a whole cow and a whole sheep and Tregloyne had brought sugar back from the Launceston shops for the baker to make iced cakes. There was a barrel of hard cider, but only one, and it wasn't enough for anyone to become too jolly.

Jaufre watched everything Tregloyne did very carefully, storing away information against the next Christmas celebration, when Tregloyne would be gone and Jaufre would be expected to host his own feast. Tregloyne read his intent expression correctly and roared with laughter. "You will make a fine Master of Glynnow, my boy, never fear!"

After the new year Johanna called for the carpenter, this time to remodel the first floor of the house. As it existed it was little more than a copy of the great room below with the addition of a garderobe, which at least obviated the necessity of chamberpots. There was one bed and one clothes press and one stool and one fireplace that was built into the existing chimney. The roof of the first floor was much lower than that of the great hall and therefore more amenable to walls, as well as much easier to heat. She was able to create eight rooms separated by walls made of woven lathes and a plaster compounded of sand, straw and clay found in deposits along the coast which the local people used for pottery. She set the carpenters to making beds, and found a local woman to sew mattresses and fill them with straw and sweet smelling herbs. She was determined to have their own weavers in Glynnow as soon as possible, but for now most of the beds were without blankets.

The rooms smelled of sawdust and lavender when they were done. There were room and beds enough to house all of Wu Company when they were all at home.

When they were all at home. Johanna wondered what it would be like, to live in one place all the rest of their lives, and knew a cold feeling in the pit of her stomach. She took the feeling to Jaufre. "We must find another Jaufre," she said.

"What?" Jaufre was hunched over Wu Li's book, calculating from Johanna's drawings of the past summer's journey through England where they should be and when during the following summer's buying trip, so as to produce some kind of schedule for Captain Angelique.

"We've spent our whole lives on the Road, Jaufre," she said.

"What?" He looked up.

"We've spent our whole lives on the Road," she said. "We don't know how to live in one place."

He closed Wu Li's book and put it down carefully. "I thought you liked it here."

"I love it here," she said. "I'm coming to love the people here, too, and the land is beautiful. But it won't be enough to satisfy me my whole life long, or you, either." She laid a hand on his arm. "You need to find another Jaufre, and train him up as you are being trained. A trustworthy man from the village, known to the people here."

"Another Jaufre," he said. "To take the reins when we are gone away for a time."

She grinned. "Someone, preferably, who won't usurp us in our absence."

He took it to Tregloyne, who saw the sense of it at once. "You'll be gone every summer on buying trips. You'll need someone sensible in authority while you're gone then, too. Let me think on it."

Shortly thereafter Shasha announced, "No one in Glynnow can read or write."

She looked at Tregloyne, who raised his hands. "And for what would they be needing that, lady?"

"They at least need to know how to sign their names," Shasha said severely.

"They can make their mark like everyone else," Tregloyne said.

So Shasha started a school for the children at the house most afternoons, beginning with writing their names. She taught them in French, because it was the language of trade from Ludlow to Venice. Some of the children were very quick to learn their letters, some not so. The quicker ones she began to teach their numbers, too. If they were going to be members of a merchant's company, they would be that much harder to cheat if they were in possession of both skills.

During a spell of fine weather in February Alaric made another trip to Launceston: for salt for the kitchen, he said, but really for news, as they all well knew.

While he was gone Angelique took advantage of that same fine weather to make a quick trip from Harfleur, carrying spices, dried fruits, bales of linen, wool and silk, and Firas.

Shasha stood at the top of the path, watching the assassin take long strides toward her. They disappeared into their new room and were not seen again until the following morning, both ravenous with hunger. Alma and Hayat and Hari sent their regards from Paris, where Alma had discovered the existence of a library even larger than the one in Venice and had, according to Firas, been translated straight to heaven. Hayat had found a swordsman who didn't disdain teaching a woman and a weaver of silk who was willing to take her on as a paying apprentice. Hari had disappeared inside the cathedral of Notre Dame which in Firas' opinion, while magnificent, did not hold a candle to Chartres.

The Alps having proved passable, Firas continued on to Venice. "I found Ser Gradenigo at home," he said, "and he is very excited about this venture of ours. His new ship is scheduled to be launched in May. He had me meet with the weavers' guild, and they, too, are very excited at the prospect of getting their hands on English fleeces without having to pay excise taxes on them from Dortend to Cenis to Ravenna."

"And Laloun?" Johanna said. "Did Sieur Imbert have any word of her?"

Firas smiled at her. "He did. She is working in his house. I spoke with her, and she is happy there." His smile faded. "She was very sorry to hear of her mistress' death, but she told me to say that she was glad she did not have to die in L'Arête."

"Any news of L'Arête?" Jaufre said.

"There is rumored to be a new lord of L'Arête," Firas said, "but nothing more than that. Except—"

"Yes?"

Firas toyed with his mug, making them wait. "This new lord seems less inclined to teach his tenants how to fly." He looked up, smiling beneath his beard.

"Do you think the new lord is Florian?" Johanna said.

"Who knows?" Jaufre said, pushing himself to his feet. "And who cares?" He gave Firas a brief smile and went out. Johanna watched him leave but stayed where she was.

Alaric returned home a few days later with a long face. "Parliament assembled at Westminster after Christmas, and insisted that Edward be replaced by the Duke of Aquitaine.

It was done on January twenty-fourth, and the new king crowned on February first." He shook his head.

"The old king was a bad king, and bad for England," Tregloyne said.

"Perhaps," Alaric said, "but the new king is barely fourteen years old. It is Isabella who rules England now, with her lover Mortimer at her side."

"What have they done with the old king?"

"He is imprisoned in Berkeley Castle, under the closest watch."

"They should kill him and be done with it," Tregloyne said.

Alaric was shocked. "He was anointed by God!"

"Proof positive that even God can make a mistake. He's a constant danger to the new king, a point of rebellion for every noble who lost out in the new order. There are always some who back the wrong horse and are then aggrieved and scheming for revenge and redress. Pah."

"Tregloyne," Johanna said, "I have often wondered why there is no priest in Glynnow."

Tregloyne's smile was broad and sharp. "Why, lady," he purred, "it is simple. There is no priest in Glynnow because there is no church in Glynnow."

Johanna laughed. Alaric looked perfectly appalled.

Spring arrived like an invading army, if possible even more aggressively than the previous year, pushing aside the melting snow with vigorous shoots of green grass and brightly-colored wildflowers. Brambles sprouted a profusion of roses red, pink and white, swarmed over by bees drunk on nectar. Hawthorns budded in the hedges and the blooms perfumed the air with an aroma that was said to smell like a woman in need. Shasha harvested the flowers and the berries from one tree for the distillation of an excellent tonic for an unsteady heart, and then allowed herself to be seduced beneath it – all in the name of the study of medicine, she assured Johanna, who noticed that Shasha had had recourse to her special tea herself.

Johanna and North Wind spent most of the daylight hours

together and Glynnow became accustomed to the sight of the bronze-haired young woman clinging to the back of the great white stallion, the two of them galloping at full speed across the grass-topped cliffs of the coast. It was scandalous, to be sure, a woman on a stallion and that woman in trousers besides, but the people of Glynnow were learning to take a certain pride in the eccentricities of their new master and his woman. They certainly weren't ordinary.

✠

Captain Angelique returned with the *Faucon*, and they gathered at dinner that evening to set out the details of the summer's buying trip and fix dates for *Faucon*'s departures, hopefully with a hold full of high-grade fleeces.

"I know there is an excellent livestock fair at Launceston," Jaufre said, "but then we'll have to feed the pack animals all the way to Ludlow. I think we should wait and buy our pack animals there."

"You know what they'll cost in Launceston," Tregloyne said. "You have no idea what the prices will be in Ludlow."

"Even if they're high, we'll have saved on feed and pasturage en route."

"And we'll be able to travel faster going north," Johanna said.

"Are we Wu Company, or Jerome's Jongleurs?" Tiphaine said.

"Wu Company," Jaufre said firmly, and relented a little when the girl looked disappointed. "We can perform if the price is right, but we pick and choose and we don't wear ourselves out singing. We're traders first."

Tiphaine sighed.

"Who runs things here?" Firas said.

"Ah," said Tregloyne, and beckoned to a small man with dark hair and eyes, calloused hands and an air of quiet authority. "This is Kevern. He is the headman of the village, and a carpenter by trade."

675

Johanna nodded. Kevern was responsible for most of the work done on the first floor of the house.

"He's a Glynnow man back ten generations. Everyone knows him and everyone trusts him, including me. And—" Tregloyne winked "—he has a large enough family that he's happy for the extra income."

"How big?" Shasha said.

"Thirteen," Kevern said, not without pride.

"Talan and Kerra among them?" Johanna said, Talan having said that his father worked with wood.

He nodded.

"And Cador, I believe," Shasha said. "He's one of my best students."

"So we leave Glynnow in good hands," Tregloyne said, rubbing his own together. "How soon can we be off?"

"The sooner the better," Captain Angelique said.

"The merchants of Harfleur anxious for our wool?" Alaric said, almost genially.

"Better," she said, and produced documents that guaranteed sales at a set price per bale that made Jaufre smile. "No limit on amount," she said, pointing.

"Well done, sister," Alaric said, sounding almost respectful.

Captain Angelique actually smiled.

It seemed spring in England could cure anyone of anything.

"Do we take North Wind?" Shasha said.

"Can anyone stop him from coming?" Jaufre said.

Johanna laughed.

✠

They set forth the first week of June, this time with Tregloyne in tow who having seen little of his native land beyond Exeter, was anxious to see more of it before he set off with Captain Angelique to explore foreign lands. They performed as minstrels when the purse was right, and accepted those races for North

Wind when those requests were made by those too powerful to refuse, but otherwise Jaufre was insistent that they move up the road with all dispatch. They took one detour for Alaric, passing near Berkeley Castle, where Edward of Caernarfon was imprisoned, and where they asked as many questions as they dared. Most were too wise to say anything, but one older farmer did say, "Oh, aye, they have the old sodomite locked away up there. No one has seen him since they brought him in, but there is talk he won't be there long." He gave them a significant wink, downed his mead and went on his way.

"A rescue attempt?" Jaufre said in a low voice.

"Not much of one if the local people are already talking about it," Alaric said, looking disgusted, and went off to find the tavern where the castle guards drank, because there was always such a tavern in a fortified town. It was the one nearest the gate, called, imaginatively, the Crown and Castle. He returned late that evening to their campsite after they were all asleep.

"No news of Wilmot, then?" Johanna said tentatively the next morning.

Alaric shook his head.

They hastened up the road to Worcester, where there was a fine livestock fair that was able to supply all their needs. They led this much longer caravan to Ludlow and its environs – "Now it feels like we're back on the Road," Jaufre said, grinning – and spent the next eight weeks going from grazier to grazier, collecting fleeces as they went. They prospered so well that Jaufre began to wish they'd bought twice as many pack animals, but Johanna overruled him. "Better to sell all we have than have more sitting around mouldering in the cave," she said. "Besides, we don't know how many donkeys the Launceston livestock fair can absorb."

As it happened, the Cornish tin mines further west were always in need of more donkeys and they were able to dispose of their stock for a penny more per head, which even Johanna admitted was a triumph. They reappeared in Glynnow on the first of September to find that nothing had burned down and no landless lord had appeared to seize the estate by force. Kevern's chest swelled when he reported the size of the harvest, and animals and villagers alike were healthy. Everyone fell to with a will to transport the bundles of fleeces to the cavern below, there to await shipment to Harfleur and possibly even trans-shipment to Venice, if Gradenigo had managed to find his way up the coasts of Spain and France to the correct port.

Jaufre, without prompting from Tregloyne, declared a holiday and held a harvest festival. Mead, wine and small beer ran like water and there was a whole roast pig and small mountains of fruit pasties. The company sang songs not yet heard by the villagers and Tiphaine startled them all by conducting a choir of village children performing "O Wandering Clerks." Hearing those shrill young voices raised in that particular song took Johanna straight back to Kashgar and the first time she had heard Félicien sing it, dressed in her black robe and cap, her head thrown back, her high, pure voice rising up and reaching out and enveloping them all in song. She had to close her eyes against sudden tears. She felt Jaufre's arm come around her and opened her eyes to see that his were wet, too. "We will not forget her," he said.

That night Jaufre said, "I love being on the Road, wherever it leads us, but it's good to come home, too. For one thing, we don't have to work so hard to find a place where we can be alone." He closed the door of their own room firmly behind them, and dropped the bar into the brackets.

Johanna reached for her braid and began to loosen her hair, her heart beating high in her throat. Was it like this for every woman and every man who came together? Perhaps she should ask Shasha.

He walked toward her, pulling his tunic over his head, pushing his trousers down and kicking them to one side.

Perhaps not.

He reached up and replaced her hands with his own, unplaiting her braid and tousling the bronze-streaked hair into a wild

678

mane. She shook it back from her face and raised an eyebrow, waiting. He smiled and reached beneath her tunic to yank her trousers down and pushed her on the bed. He thrust into her without waiting and she cried out at the shock, but she was ready for him. He reached between them and rubbed and she made a sound deep in her throat and tried to move her hips. He wouldn't let her, holding her down, rubbing that place where all the pleasure came from. She whimpered. She begged. She pleaded. "Jaufre. Move. Please. Move."

"No," he said, his voice a deep growl, and he shoved her tunic up and sucked a nipple hard into his mouth, and all the while he was this hard, hot, unmoving presence within her and all the while his thumb was rubbing, rubbing and she tried to move and couldn't. She reached up and caught the hair at the nape of his neck in her hand, forcing him to look at her. His eyes were slits, his lips drawn back, his neck corded. She smiled, a feral, predatory smile, and contracted her muscles around him.

He very nearly shouted. "Ah! Johanna! That's not fair!"

"Move," she said, her turn to growl, and he did then.

They lay together in an exhausted tangle, watching the last of the light leave through the tiny window in the thick stone wall. "Yes," she said, her voice slurred from pleasure, "it is nice to come home."

He laughed and nuzzled her neck. "It almost doesn't feel real." When she raised her head and looked at him, he said, "I've thought of this, of us like this, for so long." He traced the line of her spine. She arched involuntarily, and he smiled. "It's still hard for me to believe this is real."

"Some people take a lot of convincing." She touched his face, tracing his eyes, his nose, his lips, threading her fingers into his hair to pull him back to her. "So was it worth the wait?" she said against his mouth. When he didn't answer at once she rolled on top of him, caging his hips in her thighs and shoving his arms back against the bed. His sex stirred against her and she smiled. "You are at my mercy," she said. "Answer me, or be destroyed."

679

She looked flushed and triumphant and rumpled and he'd never seen anything so beautiful in his life. Best of all she was naked and in his bed, and so was he. "I don't know," he said. "Maybe I'll take destruction."

✠

A thunderous knocking woke them well before dawn. "What?" Jaufre said, feeling for the sword that hung always within reach before his eyes were half open.

"Who is it?" Johanna said, awake and alert in an instant and already pulling on her clothes. She heard doors opening and other voices, and when she had their door open everyone else was already in the hall and making for the stairs, and everyone was armed. "I knew things were going too well," she said to Jaufre in an undertone.

"Nonsense," he said, stealing a quick kiss before leaping the last three steps into the great hall. He strode to the door and said in a loud voice, "This is Jaufre, master of Glynnow. Who disturbs our rest at this hour?"

Tregloyne, last down the stairs, smiled.

"Wilmot, friend to Alaric de Claret. I must speak with him."

Jaufre looked at Alaric, who stood next to him with his sword drawn. "Is that his voice?" Alaric nodded.

They unbarred the door and Wilmot stumbled in. He was alone and distraught, and they immediately barred the door again behind him. Shasha stirred up the fire on the hearth and heated some wine and Wilmot drank it gratefully. He looked thinner than when they'd seen him last, and his clothes were worn and shabby. "What's amiss, Wilmot?" Alaric said. "Is it the king?"

Wilmot nodded as Shasha refilled his cup. "They're going to kill him."

"Good," Tregloyne said, but he said it beneath his breath and only Shasha heard him. She gave him a speaking glance.

"There have been three attempts to free him," Wilmot said,

"one in April, one in July, and one just this month that nearly succeeded. Isabella and Mortimer will no longer tolerate his presence. It is too dangerous to them."

"What are you going to do?"

"I'm going to get him out of Berkeley and across the Channel to the continent. You said you had a ship. Do you know when it will call here next?"

"No, but soon," Jaufre said. "The captain knows we have goods to carry to Harfleur at this time of year."

"Harfleur?"

"It is the *Faucon*'s home port."

Wilmot brightened a little. "Harfleur is still small enough that we may escape notice. Will you arrange passage for us?"

"How many?"

"The king and one attendant."

"Is there money?"

"There is, more than enough. I'll explain later." He looked at Alaric. "I'm sorry, Alaric, but there is no one else to ask. I need your help to get him away."

"There was no need to ask, Wilmot." Alaric stood up, his shoulders squared, his chin high, his expression that of one who had heard the trumpets sound one more time. "Of course I will go with you."

"So will I," Jaufre said.

"What?" Tregloyne said.

"What!" Johanna said.

"It's forty-five leagues to Berkeley," Jaufre said, thinking out loud. "Four to five days—"

"If we can get there in four," Wilmot said, "the king's keepers will be away overnight in Bristol."

Tregloyne regarded Wilmot, clearly wondering how Wilmot had arranged that.

"Four days," Jaufre said, "provided we camp and carry our own food. We'll take the Arabians. They're the best over distance, and God knows they're used to a hard pace."

"Jaufre!"

"You heard what was done to the Despensers, Johanna. Can we really leave that man, that tired old man who listened to us sing with so much pleasure, who rewarded us so handsomely, to that kind of end? When we could have helped to prevent it?"

"You can't be serious," Shasha said flatly, and next to her Tregloyne, arms crossed over his chest and a glower on his face, gave a most emphatic nod.

"Shasha, listen—"

"No, Jaufre. You listen to me. I have followed the two of you halfway around the world, and make no mistake, I don't regret a moment of it, but after five years we have finally come to rest. I can plant a garden and begin my book of herbal remedies, and—and perhaps begin a family." She glanced at Firas. He smiled at her. Visibly heartened, she turned back to Jaufre. "You can build your wool business. Johanna can start her breeding stable. For a full year we have been making a home for ourselves here in Glynnow, and now you want to hare off on some idiot mission to rescue a man whose rule, by every report we have ever heard, this adopted country of ours is well rid of? You want us to think of what happened to the Despensers? Let's think for just a moment of what they will do to you if they catch you!"

She had been gaining in volume as she spoke and by the end she was standing on her feet with her voice ringing off the stone walls. She paused, breathing heavily and glaring at Jaufre.

"Besides," Tregloyne said, leaning forward, "you are the new master of Glynnow, or had you forgot? You have responsibilities here, people depending on you here. Or did I go through all that legal nonsense for nothing?"

"I don't take up those responsibilities in full until you leave," Jaufre said.

"And if you are killed during this ridiculous rescue attempt? If you don't return?"

"Then you'll have to find another Jaufre."

Tregloyne's face a turned a dark red. "God's nightgown, mayhap

I should find another Jaufre now, if the one I have is determined to risk his life on such a foolish and dangerous and useless mission!" His voice boomed so loudly it created its own echo.

For the first time since she'd known her, Johanna saw that Tiphaine was afraid, and tried to give her a reassuring smile. It wasn't much of a success, because Tiphaine flinched away from it and went to curl up in a ball next to the hearth, studiously ignoring the ongoing argument.

"That is of course your choice, Tregloyne," Jaufre said, so politely and in so comparatively calm a voice that Johanna for one realized there was no moving him from his purpose. Her mind raced for a solution, and found only one.

Into the fraught silence Wilmot, who was looking at Jaufre with an expression Johanna could not quite interpret, said softly, "There is much of your father in you, boy."

"The name's Jaufre, not boy," Jaufre said curtly, and turned back to Shasha. "Alaric and Wilmot were friends of my father's. My father can't help them. I can."

Shasha gave a sound very much like an infuriated cat. Tregloyne growled.

"Very well," Johanna said. "If you're going, I'm going, too."

As one, all the men turned to gape at her. "Oh, of course," Jaufre said scathingly. "On North Wind, I suppose. Whom no one will notice as we gallop over the countryside, or recognize as the reigning racing champion of all England!"

"I'll darken his hide with dirt, and need I remind you that North Wind is an army in and of himself?" Johanna said. Her voice was as calm as his had been when he faced down Tregloyne. "Jaufre, if you thought being together meant I stay at home like a good little girl while you ride off on some Sir Gawainish quest, you much mistake the matter. Being together means being together, no matter the journey or the destination or the danger." She crossed her arms. "We are together, truly together, sharing everything, going forward from this moment. Or we are apart. Choose."

She stood before the fire on the hearth: slim, vibrant, willful, determined. He knew her well enough to know that she meant exactly and precisely what she said.

"You can't bring a woman," Wilmot said, who looked horrified at the prospect. "We have to move fast. She'll slow us down, and if there's a fight we'll have to protect her."

Alaric cleared his throat. "I'm sorry, Wilmot, but I'm afraid they come as a set." And he smiled at Johanna, the first time in all their acquaintance he had ever done so. "And I promise you, she won't slow us down, and you will not have to protect her in a fight."

Jaufre couldn't help it. He laughed out loud.

Johanna laughed too, and ran upstairs to get her belt, boots and short sword.

✠

They rode by day and by night, stopping only to rest the horses before pressing on again. Alaric was reminded of the ride from Sant' Alberto to Milano and over the mountains into Lyon, with Jaufre nagging them on every step of the way. This time it was Wilmot pushing them, but there was no need because everyone was in a hurry for different reasons. "For one thing, the *Faucon* is expected any day," Jaufre said, "and I don't want Edward sitting around Glynnow waiting to be discovered while he waits for transportation."

They went around Launceston at night and avoided Exeter altogether, eating dried meat and fruit and feeding the horses on oats they had brought with them. Covered with dirt to color his white hide, North Wind was in excellent form, nipping at the rumps of the others when he felt they were going too slow. "By Christ's holy bones," Wilmot said on the second day, "he can practically talk," and there was no further grumbling about women slowing them down.

The fourth day they passed Bristol near enough to see the castle on the hill and the glitter of sunlight on the Avon. When they approached Berkeley it was coming on sunset. Wilmot led them to a thicket of trees clustered below the high walls far enough out of earshot of any guards patrolling the crenelated wall. There was a large round tower, looking solid and impenetrable. "That is where he is being held," Wilmot said, pointing.

"Is the front door the only way in?"

"No." Wilmot hesitated. "Jaufre, if you and Johanna could provide a diversion, Alaric and I can get the king out of his cell and outside the walls."

"What kind of diversion?"

"Draw the attention of the guards to the front gate."

"How?" Jaufre said.

Wilmot smiled. "You had no problem getting and holding the attention of the king the last time you met."

Johanna looked at Jaufre and smiled. "Well," she said. "It worked at L'Arête."

✠

"Did you hear that?"

"Hear what?"

"I could swear I heard someone singing." The guard peered over the wall.

A woman strolled up the road to the front gate like she owned it.

I came riding into a land on a blue goose
There I found marvels
A crow and a hawk catching pigs
A bear hunting a falcon and flies playing chess
A stag spinning silk and if this is true
A donkey makes hats

Her voice was a fine, warm, contralto. She looked up to see them peering down at her, and smiled at them. "Ho, my fine gentlemen," she said, "have you a few coins for a hungry minstrel? I promise to sing for my supper, and sing well, too."

They came through the small door cut into the larger one and gathered round to hear her sing. What was the harm, after all? Their lords and masters were away and their prisoner was safely tucked away. They might have hoped for other favors in addition to the serenade, but Jaufre put paid to that notion. He looked muscular, protective and like he knew how to use the short sword at his side.

He was also her accompanist, keeping time on two sticks he'd picked up in the forest. They could have taken him at a rush but some of them would have been hurt in the process, and besides, she sang so prettily, they just wanted to listen to her. She sang the drinking song, and the song of wandering clerks, and the song about the farmer's wife and the traveling tinker, and a Mongol marching song, and a song about a knight and his lady love. She sang for what felt like hours but was probably only one and perhaps a little more, before Jaufre heard an owl hoot three times from the trees to their left and poked Johanna in the back with one of the sticks. She finished the verse of the current song with a little trill and a bow and a beaming smile that set all of them aglow. "Thank you for your kind attention, good sirs. Your generosity will make the difference between my husband and I going to bed hungry or not this eve."

Jaufre doffed his cap and passed it around. The guards were generous within their means, and Johanna felt badly for fooling them, and for the punishment that would undoubtedly be coming to them in the morning. Jaufre returned with a respectable clank of coin and she thanked them warmly again, and sang her way down the road and out of sight.

She looked at Jaufre. "It can't be that easy."

A shout was heard behind them.

"No," he said, and hustled her toward the thicket, where North Wind stamped his impatience and where they found Wilmot and Alaric with a man they scarce recognized as the king

686

who had commanded their performance. Gaunt, almost bald, he managed a smile that only made him look more like a death's head. "Good people, I thank you for the timely rescue."

"You got yourself out, sire," Wilmot said, "now we have to get you away."

Edward of Caernarfon cocked his head at the steadily rising clamor coming from behind the castle walls. "Indeed."

Jaufre unbuckled Johanna's sword and handed it back to her. She put it on while he untied his father's sword from North Wind's saddle and slung it over his shoulders. It wasn't a sword a poor minstrel would wear, and it would have been a curiosity and possibly a temptation to the castle guards.

They mounted without further ado, the king behind Wilmot for the first leg of the journey. Wilmot and Alaric had wrapped their horses' hooves in rags to muffle the sounds of their passage. The horses sensed the urgency of their riders, especially North Wind, who snorted and sidled impatiently, but Johanna kept him on a short rein, patting his neck and whispering soothingly into his ears. They moved at a forced walk, ignoring every instinct to break into a mad gallop, picking their way downstream through the forest, letting the trees hide them as long as possible.

"The king got himself out?" Jaufre said to Wilmot.

"Indeed, and slew the porter at the door who would bar his way," Wilmot said.

Jaufre and Johanna exchanged a glance. The death of one of the castle's men would make a hot pursuit that much more certain, particularly if the porter had friends among the guards. North Wind's pace quickened, and the other horses followed suit.

It had taken them four days to get from Glynnow to Berkeley. It took them nine days to return, with Jaufre fretting and swearing beneath his breath every day they had to remain hidden in dense thickets and rocky caves and one memorable evening in the middle of a moor that on every side threatened to suck them down to their deaths. The king took turns riding with Wilmot, Alaric and himself. Johanna brushed dirt into the stallion's hide every morning after they made camp, and every evening he ghosted his way over the countryside. The only people they saw were two young lovers trysting in a hay stack, who took one look at North Wind and ran screaming into the night.

For his part Jaufre lived every moment of the journey in the fear that Angelique would have come and gone before they got home. It had been easy to be caught up in the excitement of the rescue, but in the aftermath he was very much afraid that Tregloyne had been right, that his action had been foolish beyond permission and that he had risked the lives not only of every member of Wu Company but of Tregloyne, too, and everyone else in Glynnow for that matter. The farther south they traveled, the less triumphant he felt. Shasha had been right, and he had known it when they quarreled that last evening. After all, he had said the same many times himself. He was a trader, not a warrior.

He compensated by sleeping very little during that fraught journey, remaining awake no matter who was on watch, doggedly seeking out the least-traveled paths with the most cover, constantly alert to the possibility of anyone picking up their trail. He took it upon himself to check the horses at the beginning and end of every day, for fear that one would pick up a stone or cast a shoe or suddenly go lame. Days he sat with his father's sword drawn, laying across his lap, ready at need to defend himself and Johanna to the last drop of blood in his veins. Which it might come to, he thought bleakly.

But either they were very clever or very lucky, for they saw no one who looked like they might be interested in the king's whereabouts. Alaric in particular could not account for it, and was inclined to be indignant. "A royal prisoner escaped, and no hue and cry?"

"Under the circumstances," the king said dryly, "I will forgo the honor." He had held up remarkably well on the journey, unflagging and uncomplaining, although it was evident that he was unused to rough travel and was exhausted and half faint from hunger, as indeed they all were.

They reached Launceston at last. They stopped well out of town and Alaric went in on foot for food. He came out without food, stumbling in his haste to impart the news. "They are saying that you are dead of an accident, majesty," he told the king. "They say the warders cut your heart out and sent it to the queen as proof. Your body is to be buried in Gloucester Cathedral."

"What?"

"What!"

"But—"

"They lied," Johanna said. She looked at Jaufre, a smile spreading across her face. "The guards. They lied."

"Very probably at Maltravers' instigation," Wilmot said, thinking out loud.

"Maltravers?"

"The queen made him responsible for the king's person," Wilmot said. His mouth curved into a small, satisfied smile. "He is even now undoubtedly shaking in his boots imagining what Isabella and Mortimer would do to him if it became known the king had escaped his custody while Maltravers was off whoring in Bristol, never mind while guards under his command were humming along to an itinerant minstrel."

"Whoring?" Alaric said.

Wilmot shrugged. "One of his mistresses lives in Bristol. Maltravers is the veriest of dogs. It was easy enough to arrange."

"That's why no one is looking for him," Jaufre said." Or for us." He felt dizzy, and held a hand out to lean on a tree that was across the clearing, and then Johanna was there beside him, warm and solid. He looked up to see her grinning at him.

"Not yet," she whispered in his ear. "Wait to faint until we get home."

He let out a short laugh and pulled his scattered senses together.

"They took the porter's heart and sent it to the queen as proof," Alaric said in an almost awed voice. "And the porter will be buried in Gloucester Cathedral."

The king started to laugh. He laughed until he could no longer stand and Wilmot helped him to a seat on a fallen tree, where he laughed still more, clutching his belly and rocking back and forth.

Wilmot was distressed. "Majesty. Majesty, please, be calm. Be calm, sire."

Johanna thought His Majesty was in the first stages of hysteria, aggravated by hunger and fatigue, and wondered what the protocol was for slapping a king. Edward did calm, eventually, although occasional chuckles erupted like hiccups as they remounted and left Launceston behind. He was in much better spirits during the last leagues to Glynnow. They detoured around the village, wanting as few witnesses as possible. Along the cliff they rode and down the path to Tregloyne, where Tregloyne himself waited with a scowl on his face. The king dismounted. He was moving a little stiffly, but he looked less like a death's head and more like a man who might live to see the next day.

"Has Angelique been and gone?" Jaufre said.

"Once," Tregloyne said. "She should return shortly."

Jaufre went limp with relief.

"I tell you, Jaufre, I did not look to see you again alive," Tregloyne said. "And now that I do, I am not sure that I rejoice in the sight of you."

Jaufre held up a hand. "Peace, I beg you, Tregloyne. You cannot damn me any more than I damned myself all the way here from Berkeley."

Before Tregloyne could start in on him, Johanna said, "Have you heard the news, Tregloyne? Edward of Caernarfon is dead. They have sent his heart to the queen as proof."

Tregloyne scowled, looking from her to the king and back again. "What is this nonsense then, mistress Johanna?"

So they told him, and Tregloyne stared, dumbfounded, and then a rumble began in his chest that erupted in a braying laugh. He laughed until tears started from his eyes and then he laughed some more. They watched him, grinning, not least the king.

"Well," Tregloyne said, wiping away tears, "if I am to entertain royalty uninvited, I'd best get on with it. This way, sire."

He bowed the king into his house and gave him the spot closest to the fire and called for a blanket to wrap around his shoulders, and mulled wine and the inevitable pasties from the kitchen. Johanna returned from stabling the horses in time to polish off the dregs in the pitcher and the crumbs on the tray.

"Why, I know you," the king said to her, as one coming awake after a long sleep. "You sang for me. In Bristol, wasn't it?" He looked at Jaufre. "And you, too. And you, Alaric—Alaric de Claret, isn't it?"

Alaric bowed.

The king stared from one face to another. "You're not even English," Edward of Caernarfon said at last. "Not even Wilmot. Why would you do this for me?"

"Good question," Tregloyne said to Shasha, but he said it in a low voice that only she could hear.

"I did it because I took an oath to serve you, majesty," Wilmot said.

Jaufre glanced at Johanna. "We did it because Wilmot said they were going to kill you, and we could not bear to have someone who was so kind to us so unkindly used, if we could help it."

"I did it because my friend asked for my help," Alaric said. "And because my father was your liege man, which means I am, too."

The king smiled and shook his head. "You ran a dreadful risk."

"God's balls and that they did," Tregloyne said to Shasha, angry all over again.

"There is something you should know, sire," Wilmot said. "Something we have not had the time to discuss."

"What is it, good Wilmot?"

"Your escape was arranged by your son, sire."

There was dead silence. "My son?" Edward said at last.

"Your son, majesty. He had me brought to him after you were taken in Wales, and bade me watch you wherever you were taken and report back to him on your condition and the manner of your keepers. When I heard of Mortimer's plot to murder your majesty, I rode to him and told him. He bid me arrange for de Berkeley and Maltravers to be called away to Bristol that night. Any guard is always lax absent supervision, no matter how well trained they are. You found it easy to get to the postern unobserved, I imagine."

Edward looked a little deflated at the thought that he might not have escaped under his own power after all.

"Majesty, forgive me for speaking so frankly, but your son bade me tell you he cannot guarantee your safety. His mother and Mortimer rule all. Later, when he gains full power, it may be safe for you to return."

Edward waved a hand and leaned against the warm stones next to the hearth, pulling the blanket more fully around his shoulders. "He won't ever want me back here," he said. "I am a danger to whoever rules England."

"That you are, old man," Tregloyne said. "I'm glad you finally recognize it." This time he didn't bother to lower his voice.

Edward either didn't hear him or pretended he didn't. "I am tired," he said. "I don't want to stay in England."

Wilmot said softly, "What do you want to do, majesty?"

The king's eyes were drooping. "I want quiet and safety. I want time: to confess, to repent, to make my peace with God. I have had enough of trying to rule an ungrateful people who so resent my friends that they rise up in rebellion against me." He opened one eye. "And I have had more than enough of Isabella. Tell my son I thank him for his timely rescue, and that I wish him well."

"But where do you want to go, majesty?" Wilmot said.

But the king was asleep.

"I know where he wants to go," Alaric said.

Jaufre understood immediately. "Can you get him there?"

Alaric looked almost beatific. "No one is looking for him. He's already dead."

"Oh," Wilmot said. "Alaric, of course. It would be the perfect place for him." He hesitated. "He cannot go alone, and I must return to the king."

"I will go with him," Alaric said, "and I will stay with him as long as he needs me." He paused, and said in a lower voice, "I have sins to repent me of, too."

Jaufre looked at Wilmot, and something in the other man's expression told Jaufre that that had been the plan all along.

✠

The next morning they put it to Edward as they watched for a sail. "A monastery," he said. "In Lombardy, you say?"

"Yes, sire. It is a good place, beautiful and peaceful. Wilmot says your son has provided sufficient coin so that we may travel in comfort. I will guide you there, and stay with you as long as you wish."

The king smiled. "It seems I have my freedom, and a place to go. Now all we need is a ship."

But the ship did not come that day. That evening, Tregloyne took Alaric aside and said, "Are you going to tell him? Are you going to tell either one of them?"

"Tell them what?" Alaric said.

"Jaufre told me that Edward recognized Robert's family name, but Edward couldn't remember why. You know why, don't you?"

Alaric's face was a perfect blank. "Do I?"

"The reason Edward knows the name of de Beauville is that he has heard the story of the lovely Ailene de Beauville," Tregloyne said, "who caught his father's eye and whom his father then caught with child. Unfortunately, she was married to one of his own knights, who couldn't bear the sight of his fourth child, so unlike his other three, and so packed him off to the Knights Templar as soon as he was old enough to hold a sword. The sword, I am betting, that was given to Robert de Beauville by Longshanks himself before he left Outremer. The sword Jaufre of Cambaluc carries to this day." He paused. "Edward of Caernarfon and Robert de Beauville were half-brothers. Jaufre is Edward's nephew."

"You have no proof of any of this," Alaric said.

"I don't need it. All I have to do is look at them. Edward is Jaufre in another thirty years, or would be if Edward's recent time had not worn on him so. Why not tell them?"

"What good would it do?" Alaric said.

Tregloyne, goaded, said, "Why, then, bring Jaufre to the king's attention in the first place?"

Alaric folded his arms and sighed. "I owed his father my life. It is a debt even yet unpaid. I had hoped—but Gilbert had already spent what we took from Ruad. There was none left to benefit Jaufre. So then I thought that if I brought Jaufre to Edward's attention, that perhaps Edward would show the boy some favor – a knighthood, some land perhaps. Royal bastards never starve."

Tregloyne snorted. "Jaufre's not the starving type."

Alaric's mouth twisted up in a half smile. "No. No, he isn't."

"Does Wilmot know?"

"Like you, Wilmot knew the moment he set eyes on Jaufre." He looked at Tregloyne, very stern. "We will leave it to him to tell the new king. If he does, then Jaufre will have to be told, I suppose, but that, too, I leave to Wilmot." He looked across the room at the man dozing in Tregloyne's chair. "As for Edward of Caernarfon, you heard him yourself. He only wants peace."

✚

The next day the *Faucon* came, and loaded a hold full of good English fleeces, one ex-Master of Glynnow, one ex-Knight Templar, and one ex-king, and set sail for Harfleur on the evening tide.

"Will we ever see Alaric again, do you think?" Johanna said.

They were standing at the top of the cliff, watching the ship sink below the horizon.

"I don't know," he said. He looked down at her and grinned. "We could always go visit him," he said.

She smiled. "We could," she said. "He's still a member of Wu Company, after all."

Hand in hand they walked home down the narrow cliff path.

20

London, December, 1327

Woman should gather roses ere
Time's ceaseless foot o'ertaketh her,
For if too long she make delay,
Her chance of love may pass away.

A FEW LADIES looked askance but Johanna proved she knew her audience well when the opening verse was greeted with a roar of male approval. Well, and wasn't it a man's world? Certainly it was best to let them think so. Smiling, she continued.

And well it is she seek it while
Health, strength, and youth around her smile.
To pluck the fruits of love in youth
Is each wise woman's rule forsooth,
For when age creepeth o'er us, hence
Go also the sweet joys of sense,
And ill doth she her days employ
Who lets life pass without love's joy.

Johanna's eyes met Jaufre's and she sang the last verse directly to him.

And if my counsel she despise,
Not knowing how 'tis just and wise,
Too late, alas! will she repent
When age is come, and beauty spent.

There was thunderous applause from the men, tepid applause from the women, and Johanna took the moment to wink surreptitiously at Edward's young queen, whose polite blankness eased into a brief but genuine smile. Nearby, Wilmot, dressed now in the livery of Edward III, gave Johanna a wry smile and a slight bow.

The full complement of Wu Company stood at her back, absent one. Alma, Hayat and Hari had returned for a long visit on Angelique's last trip to Glynnow for the year. Tiphaine had acquired a timbrel and had worked up a flourish of different accompaniments to their most requested songs. She stood very proud in her new blue robes, a red ribbon tying back her black curls. Hari hummed as well as ever, and Shasha, Firas and Jaufre gave body and soul to every chorus.

For an encore, Johanna sang of the village of Ferlec, where whatever you saw first upon waking was what you worshipped for the rest of the day, be it your wife, the rising sun, or your neighbor's pig. Always leave them laughing, she thought, and struck the final chord with a flourish as she laughed along with them.

Edward himself led the applause, and came forward to take her hands and raise her to her feet. "And what will you do to keep yourself occupied between songs, hmm?" he asked her, his brilliant blue eyes caressing the curves beneath the embroidery of her robe.

"Why, I believe I would like to raise horses, sire," Johanna said demurely.

"Then so you shall, my dear," Edward said, dropping a kiss on the back of the hand he still held. "So long as you pay me in song every Christmas. It is agreed?"

"It is, sire."

"Good." And then, because even at fifteen Edward Plantagenet was as much man as king, he turned Johanna's hand up and placed another kiss on the inside of her wrist. He raised his head and looked at her with a smile and a query in his eyes.

She met his smile with one of her own, and withdrew her hand gently from his to place it on Jaufre's wrist.

Edward gave up her hand with good grace, flicked Tiphaine's nose with a finger, and clapped his unacknowledged cousin on the back. "Congratulations, Jaufre, Master of Glynnow. You have won name, hearth and hand this day."

Edward had done his level best to make Jaufre accept a title. Jaufre had remained steadfast in his refusal, and when Wilmot reported that Jaufre and Wu Company were going to single-handedly double the tax revenue from that part of Cornwall, Edward desisted. All it cost him was an exclusive royal charter to buy and ship good English wool between Tregloyne and Harfleur.

Jaufre, whose eyes had darkened when Edward kissed Johanna's hand, responded to the death grip on his wrist and managed to reply to Edward's pleasantries with a reasonable amount of civility. Edward laughed out loud, interpreting the stilted phrases with no difficulty, and moved on.

Johanna sighed, and felt her body relax with the release of tension. "I was afraid you were going to hit him," she murmured.

Jaufre looked down at her, at the changeable gray eyes, at the pure texture of her skin, at the unbound chestnut hair tumbling from brow to breast, at the lithe curves beneath the Robe of a Thousand Larks. It was five years since they had left Cambaluc, to begin the long journey that would bring them adventure and sorrow, new friends as well as new enemies, and, at long last, a home.

He said, the warmth of a smile in his voice, "So was I. But how can I blame him? I want to take you to bed, too."

And they laughed, their voices blending together as they did in song, as their lives would down the long years at Glynnow. Wu Company laughed with them, and irresistibly so did the members of the court, even if they didn't know why.

And if they did not live happily ever after, well, that is only to be expected. There would be children, who bring their own heartaches with them into this world, and there would be prosperity, but only after great toil, and there would be safety, although it would be paid for with precious blood.

But let it here be said that Jaufre of Glynnow and Johanna his wife lived longer, laughed louder, and loved better than many of that time, and they would not have changed their place with kings.

Supplemental

Including the glossary, cast of characters, place names, historical notes, and the Silk and Song Bureau of Weights and Measures from all three books in *Silk and Song*.

Abraham of Acre – Wu Li's agent in Gaza.

Agalia – Jaufre's mother, Robert de Beauville's wife. Sold to Sheik Saghir bin Nazari as the Lycian Lotus.

Alaric de Claret – Ex-knight Templar.

Al-Idrisi – A Persian mapmaker of great renown.

Alma – An inmate of Sheik Mohammed's harem, a scholar.

Ambroise de L'Arête – Also known as The Blade. Lord of L'Arête by marriage.

Arabic and Persian – I have used names from both languages interchangeably, but mostly Arabic because they are most available.

Audouard – Second in command to Florian.

Angelique – Ship owner and captain, smuggler, sister to Alaric de Claret.

Anwar the Egyptian – Slave dealer in Kashgar.

Balasaga – An historical province of Persia, now Iran.

Bao – A personal seal. Chinese.

Basil the Frank – Wu Li's agent in Baghdad.

Bastak – A small town in central Persia, ten days' ride west of Kerman.

Bayan – Genghis Khan's favorite general. Friend to Marco Polo.

Beda – Bedouin.

Bernart – Page to Ambroise de L'Arête.

Bible – All verses quoted are from the Vulgate Bible, English translation via the website vulgate.org. The King James version was three hundred years down the road.

Biblioteca Nazionale Marciana – The National Library of St. Mark's, in Venice. I have advanced its existence by several centuries so Alma wouldn't drive everyone crazy that winter in Venice.

Blister – Foot-and-mouth disease, which produces blisters on cows and camels and anything with a split hoof. It is highly contagious and was indeed used as a bioweapon.

Bo He Dai – Fang's doorman.

Brescia – Then a city-state in Lombardy, Italy. Now just a city.

Caffa – Now Feodosia, Crimea.

Calicut – Now Kozhikode, India.

Cambaluc – Built by Kublai Khan. Became the basis for what is now the Forbidden City in Beijing, China.

Ceylon – Today, Sri Lanka.

Chang'an – Now Xi'an, China.

Cheche – Pronounced "shesh." A long scarf, usually indigo-dyed blue, worn by Tuaregs. It can be knotted many different ways to keep the sun out of the eyes and protect the neck and face from sunburn. The indigo leeched onto the face and hands of the wearer. Or, alternatively, depending on which story you believe, Tuaregs deliberately dyed their face and hands blue to protect themselves from the sun. I heard both in Morocco.

Chi Yuan – A powerful Mandarin at the court of the Great Khan, and Dai Fang's uncle.

Chiang – Edyk the Portuguese's manservant.

Cipangu – Now Japan.

Countries – France wasn't France as we know it in 1322, and thanks to Henry II of England's heritage and marriage they would be disputing boundaries with England for a

Hundred Years' War. Italy certainly wasn't Italy, being a haphazard collection of city-states like Venice that spent most of their time making bloody war on one another and who suffered greatly during the Hundred Years War at the hands of condottiere like John Hawkwood. Fortunately, my characters don't go to Germany so I don't have to try to explain the Holy Roman Empire or even mention Charlemagne, except here. I am relieved to report that England really was England. For convenience I refer to each by its modern name, and again I have moved up, pushed back and eliminated events to suit my plot. My book, my rules.

Currency – Tael: China. Bezants: Byzantium. Drachma: Arabic. England: Silver penny. France: Livre, and I cannot tell you how much it delights me that today this word in French means "book." Now that's currency. Florence: Florins. Venice: Accommodate all currencies but rely on gemstones. *In A Distant Mirror: The Calamitous 14th Century*, Barbara Tuchman writes, "…the non-specialist reader would be well advised not to worry about it, because the names of coins and currency mean nothing anyway except in terms of purchasing power." Surely a bargain in Baghdad that begins with a search for bezants to buy malachite beads which is concluded with a horse race sufficiently illuminates her statement.

Curzola – Now Korkula, an island in Croatia.

Dai Fang – Wu Li's second wife. Johanna's step-mother. Gokudo's lover.

Dayir – Aide to Bayan. Friend of Marco Polo. Ogodei's father.

Ambroise De L'Arête – Lord of Château L'Arête by marriage.

Deshi the Scout – Caravan master to Wu Li.

Edward I of England – King of England, 1272–1307. Known also as Longshanks. Yes, he was in Acre in 1271 at the same time as the Polos, and as fellow strangers in a strange land are surely drawn together in faraway places even today, Edward and the Polos could have met. Maffeo and Niccolo had already been to the court of the Khan and they could have dined out forever on tales of Cathay. Why not at table with kings? Marco Polo certainly did after he got home.

Edward II of England – King of England, 1307–1327. Oh my yes, lots of competing stories here. When you tour Nottingham Castle, the guide will tell you definitively that Edward II was killed in September 1327 by having a red-hot poker shoved up his rectum. Barbarity in the Middle Ages was not reserved for Mongols. But! In the 1800s a letter written to Edward III from a papal prelate was found, telling of Edward III's father killing his jailer and escaping into the night, eventually ending his days as a monk in Italy. It is even rumored that Edward III met with Edward II in Koblenz in 1338. Note: He was imprisoned by Isabella and Mortimer first in Kenilworth and then in Berkeley, but for the purposes of my plot I have imprisoned him only in Berkeley.

Edward III of England – King of England, 1327–1377. True, he was only fourteen in 1327, but fourteen then and fourteen now are two very different things. He was the heir to a throne and had his share of the Plantagenet good looks. Very little would have been denied him. He could have had Johanna on the nearest flat surface in five minutes and no one would have lifted a finger to stop him. But he was also a lover of all things Arthurian and the creator of the Order of the Garter in the Round Table's image, and I have chosen to imagine him as being amused by and respectful of Jaufre's prior claim.

Edyk the Portuguese – Trader residing in Cambaluc.

Ell – See *Bureau of Weights and Measures* above. The distance from a man's elbow to the tip of his middle finger, or about 18 inches. A standard unit of measurement for textiles in the Middle Ages, and never mind the differences between Scots, English, Flemish, Polish, German and French ells.

Eneas – Wu Li's agent in Alexandria.

Europe – A name I did not discover has been in use since

Anaximander until I was writing Book III. What a futile thing is research.

Fakhir – Wu Li's agent in Antioch.

Farhad bin Mohammed – Son of Sheik Mohammed of Talikan.

Fatima – Daughter of Malala and Ahmed, betrothed of Azar, friend to Johanna.

Félicien – Old lord of L'Arête.

Félicien – A Frank from Dijon. Goliard, or student traveling the world. Has studied liberal arts in Paris and medicine in Salerno.

Félicienne – Daughter to the lord of L'Arête.

Firas – A Nazari Ismaili from Alamut, the hereditary home of the Old Man of the Mountain, leader of the Assassins.

Florian – Lieutenant for Ambroise de L'Arête.

Shidibala Gegeen Khan – The Khan in Cambaluc when Johanna and company departed. I have waved my authorial wand and made his tenure in office even shorter than it actually was.

Gokudo – Samurai, now ronin, expert in naginata (spear). Family killed and exiled from Cipangu in 1192. Dai Fang's lover and hatchet man.

Giovanni Gradenigo – Ship's captain, and member of a powerful Venetian shipping family.

Grigori the Tatar – Wu Li's agent in Kabul.

Guilham – Page to Ambroise de L'Arête.

Gujarat – Now a province in northwest India.

Hari – Chughi monk, itinerant preacher, self-styled priest.

Hayat – An inmate of Sheik Mohammed's harem. A weaver.

Hasan – Wu Li's agent in Tabriz.

Hicca – A boy of Glynnow.

Hilde – Servant of L'Arête.

Ibn Battuta – Berber slave trader, 1304–1369, known for writing The Rihla (The Journey), an account of his extensive travels throughout the medieval, mostly Muslim world. I have advanced his first visit to Kabul purely for the convenience of my plot.

Ibn Tabib – Doctor in Kabul.

Philippe Imbert – Agent for the Gradenigo interests in Lyon.

Ishan – Stablemaster to Sheik Mohammed of Talikan.

Jaufre of Cambaluc – Son of Agalia and Robert de Beauville. Orphaned on the Silk Road, rescued by Wu Li, raised as Johanna's foster brother.

Jibran – Headman of the village of Aab.

Joan Burgh – English pilgrim on the Jerusalem Journey. Based on the real life Margery Kempe.

Johanna of Cambaluc – Daughter of Wu Li and Shu Ming, granddaughter of Marco Polo and Shu Lin. Known in Sheik Mohammed's harem as Nazirah.

John XXII – Pope in Avignon from 1316–1334.

Kabul – Now the capital of Afghanistan. Holdout against attack from every invading force from Alexander the Great on, including Genghis Khan, the USSR and the USA. In spite of being a mile high, highs average in the 60's (F) as soon as March.

Kadar – The chief eunuch in Sheik Mohammed's harem.

Kerra – A girl of Glynnow, Johanna's stablehand.

Khuree – The summer capital of the Mongols. Now Ulan Bator, Mongolia.

Kinsai – Now Hangzhou, or Hangchow, China.

Koran – Or Quran. All quotations from quran.com.

Lanchow – Now Lanzhou, China.

League – The distance one person could walk in an hour, also defined as about three miles. I have rounded up and down. The Khan's yambs were built every 25 miles, therefore in Silk and Song every eight leagues. The Khan's imperial mailmen rode 200 miles daily, hence sixty leagues. Close enough for government work and fiction.

The Levant – From Wikipedia: "A geographic and cultural region consisting of the eastern Mediterranean between Anatolia and Egypt... The Levant consists today of Lebanon, Syria, Jordan, Israel, Palestine, Cyprus and parts of southern

Turkey. Iraq and the Sinai Peninsula are also sometimes included."

Madhar – Wu Li's agent in Calicut.

Mangu – Cook in Wu Li's caravan.

Marco Polo – Venetian merchant, c.1254–1324. Traveled to China with his father and uncle where they spent twenty years working for Kublai Khan. He did say upon his deathbed, "I did not tell half of what I saw."

Did Marco leave a daughter behind when he finally went home? I'd be surprised if he didn't leave a dozen. In any edition of his memoir, no matter how bowdlerized, it is clear that he loved the ladies, and during the twenty years he was from home he must have gotten lucky at least a couple of times. If he didn't, yes, by Marco's own account Kublai Khan did in fact exact tributes of nubile young women from his various suzerainties, enjoy their company, and then award them as gifts to his vassals. This was deemed to be the highest honor. Marco was a personable and capable young man, high in the Khan's favor. It is reasonable to suppose he might have been so rewarded, so I have the taken the liberty to suppose it here.

The Travels of Marco Polo – Published as *Il Milione* in 1300, and Marco himself was nicknamed "Marco Milione" because of the exaggerated figures he used in description. His stories were at first disbelieved and derided, especially by comparison to Sir John Mandeville's book, which was of course the truth, the whole truth and nothing but the truth itself. Much later, when advanced scholarship discredited Mandeville as a fabulist and a plagiarist, Marco's far better-informed star (and story) rose by comparison. You can see Christopher Columbus' copy, with marginalia by Columbus himself, in the Biblioteca Columbina in Seville.

Donata Polo – Marco Polo's second wife. Mother of Fantina, Bellela, and Moreta.

Moreta Polo – Daughter of Marco and Donata Polo.

Middle Sea – The Mediterranean. Also called the Western Sea.

Mien – Now Myanmar, or Burma.

Mintan – A short-waisted, long-sleeved coat. Ottoman.

Mohammed – Sheik Mohammed bin Assad of Talikan. Father of Farhad.

Mongol battle tactics and strategy – Surrender or die. If you surrendered, you would continue to live, albeit under Mongol rule, which was, amazingly, pretty reasonable. If you fought, if you crossed them or betrayed them in any way, they would annihilate you with whatever means they had to hand. They mounted hundreds of thousands of soldiers with extensive training. Their engineers were superb. They didn't travel with siege engines, they built them from available materials when it came time to use them. They'd catapult anything into a city they thought would kill and spread terror: naphtha bombs, stoppered urns filled with poisonous snakes and spiders that burst upon impact, bodies dead from the plague (weapons that stretch back to antiquity, FYI, the Mongols didn't have to invent them). When the city fell, as it almost invariably did, the Mongols would send in execution squads to kill off any remaining survivors, including women and children. Sometimes they'd save the soldiers and the engineers and put them to work. Sometimes the conquered soldiers would be placed in front in the attack on the next target, keeping the Mongols' own soldiers in reserve until the besieged ran out of ammunition. You really, really didn't want to get on their bad side, and it astonishes me how many cities didn't just strike their colors at the first hint of a Mongol flag on the horizon.

Mongols and torture – Yes, they did those things. Those exact things. And more.

Mysore – Then as now, a city in northwest India.

Niu Gang – Wu Li's factotum.

Ogodei – Son of Dayir, friend to Wu Li. A captain of the ten thousand risen to one of the twelve barons of the Shiang. Named for Ghengis Khan's successor.

Paiza – The royal Mongol passport. The Mongols called it a gerrega. Also a yarlik.

Pascau – A boatman of Avignon.

Peter – Marco Polo's Mongol servant.

Philosophy – The words "science" and "scientists" would not be invented for another five hundred years. I have used "philosopher" here as a catch-all for anyone studying the hard sciences.

Rambahadur Raj – Havildar of the first caravan into Kabul in 1323.

Robert de Beauville – Knight Templar, Jaufre's father, Agalia's husband.

Messire Roland – A fencing master in Venice.

Roubin – Page to Ambroise de L'Arête.

Sarik – A headscarf. Ottoman.

Eremo di Sant' Alberto – The Hermitage of St. Albert in Pavia, Italy. A real place I shanghaied for my own fell purpose.

Shang-tu – The summer capital of the Mongols. Now Ulan Bator, Mongolia. Also called Khuree.

Shensi – Now Shaanxi, China.

Shidibala Gegeen Khan – The Khan in Cambulac when Johanna and company departed. I have waved my authorial wand and made his tenure in office even shorter than it actually was.

Shu Lin – Shu Ming's mother, Marco Polo's concubine, the Khan's gift to Marco Polo, Johanna's grandmother.

Shu Ming – Johanna's mother, Wu Li's wife, Shu Lin's daughter, Marco Polo's daughter. Shu Shao's adopted elder sister.

Shu Shao – Also called "Shasha." Johanna's foster sister. Nurse, friend, healer, wise woman.

Silk Road – The trade route(s) between Europe and China. "Silk Road" is a term that did not come into common use until the twentieth century. Here I use the more generic Road.

Giovanni Soranzo – Doge of Venice 1312–1328.

Talan – A boy of Glynnow, Johanna's stablehand.

Talikan – I have appropriated the name of today's tiny (pop. 43) village in northeast Iran for Sheik Mohammed's great walled city of 1323, which exists somewhere in Dana World south and west of the Terak Pass and south and east of the Caspian Sea.

Templars – Their order existed for nearly 200 years, from between the First and Second Crusades until their dissolution in 1307 (or 1312 or 1314, take your pick). They weren't all slaughtered, contrary to the fervent wishes of Philip the Fair of France, and after the dissolution many were allowed to join the Knights of the Hospital and other orders. As late as 1338, former Templars were still drawing pensions in England. Surely others, perhaps those who felt themselves more at risk, must have seen the writing on the wall and decamped early enough to escape the coming purge. It isn't much of a stretch to imagine them hiring their experienced swords as caravan guards after their Templar gig fell through. It is no stretch at all to imagine some of them absconding with whatever treasure was near to hand on their way out the door.

Time – See *Bureau of Weights and Measures* above. In Europe: divided into times for prayer. Matins: midnight. Lauds: 3am. Prime: Sunrise. Terce: Mid-morning. Sext: Noon. None: Mid-afternoon. Vespers: Sunset. Compline: Bedtime.

Tiphaine – Venetian street kid.

Tregloyne – Master of Glynnow in Cornwall, England.

Turgesh or *Turkic* – Turkey, or Turkish.

Umar al-Khayyam – Omar Khayyám, author of the *Rubáiyát of Omar Khayyám,* a verse of which Johanna translates so ably under Alma's direction.

Wilmot of Bavaria – Knight Templar.

Wu Cheng – Wu Li's brother. A eunuch who was gelded by his parents for advancement at court. Fell out of favor when the old Khan died and with the help of his brother went into business as a trader on the Road.

Wu Hai – Marco Polo's friend and Wu Li's father.

Wu Li – Johanna's father, Shu Ming's husband, and later Dai Fang's husband.

Zeilan – On what is now the Somali-Ethiopian border.

*

The *Silk and Song Bureau of Weights and Measures* – No two nations back in 1322 measured anything the same way, so here for the sake of narrative clarity and my sanity *time* is measured in minutes, hours, days, weeks, months and years, and no notice is taken of that error in Julius Caesar's 45 BC calendar that wouldn't be corrected until 1582 AD by Pope Gregory XIII.

Length is measured in fingers (about an inch), hands (about 4 inches), rods (16.5 feet) and leagues (3 miles).

Travel is measured in leagues, about three miles or the distance a man could walk in an hour.

Fabric is measured in ells from China to England. Smaller lengths are fingers (three-quarters of an inch) and hands (three to four inches).

Google "weights in the Middle Ages" and you get over 8 million hits. Here, I use drams (one ounce), gills (four ounces), cups (eight ounces), pints (16 ounces), quarts (32 ounces) and gallons (124 ounces) in ascending order of liquid measurement.

Dry weight pounds then ranged from 300 grams to 508 grams, so the hell with it, here it's 16 ounces or about 453 grams. Ten pounds is a tenweight, and yes, I just made that right up. A hundredweight is a hundred pounds.

Timeline

Fictional events are displayed in italics.

1215	Kublai Khan born
1254	Marco Polo born
1270	Edward I of England joins French King Louis IX on Crusade
1271	The Polos depart Venice for Chandu The beginning of the Ninth (and last) Crusade
1272	The end of the Ninth Crusade
1275	The Polos arrive in Chandu
1280	*Alaric the Templar born in Languedoc*
1281	*Robert de Beauville born in England*
1285	*Marco Polo given a concubine by Kublai Khan, the beautiful Shu Lin*
1289	*Marco Polo and Shu Lin have a daughter, Shu Ming*
1291	Acre falls to the Mameluks
1292	The Polos leave China *Kublai Khan holds Shu Lin and Shu Ming hostage against Marco Polo's return* *Marco commits them to the care of his merchant friend, Wu Hai* *Ogodei born to Daiyin*
1294	Kublai Khan dies

713

1294 *(cont'd)*	*Shu Lin dies*
	Wu Hai marries Shu Ming, age 5, to his son,
	Wu Li, age 9
1296	*Robert de Beauville joins the Knights Templar*
1302	The Templars lose Ruad
1306	*Agalia, a Greek merchant's daughter, marries*
	Robert de Beauville, ex-Templar, in Antioch
	Jaufre, their son, born
	Johanna born to Wu Li and Shu Ming
	Shu Shao, 12, becomes Johanna's foster sister
1307	*Wu Hai dies, Wu Li inherits all*
	Philip IV arrests all Knights Templar in France
	July – Edward I dies
1308	February 25 – Edward II crowned at
	Westminster
1309	March Pope Clement VI moves papacy to
	Avignon
	Papal bull dissolves the Knights Templar
	Giovanni Soranzo elected Doge of Venice
	November – Edward III born at Windsor
1312	*Wu Li, Shu Ming, and Johanna find Jaufre*
	east of Kashgar, the lone survivor of a caravan
	attacked by bandits
1314	March 18 – Knight Templar masters Jacques de
	Molay and Geoffroi de Charney burned at the
	stake in Paris by Philip IV
	Philip IV of France dies
	Battle of Bannockburn
1314–1317	Hard winters and wet summers
	Crops fail, Europeans starve and some resort to
	cannibalism
1316	August 7 – Pope John XXII crowned in Avignon
1320	*November – Shu Ming dies*
1321	*July – Wu Li marries Dai Fang*
1322	*Wu Li dies*

	April – Johanna, Jaufre and Shu Shao leave Cambaluc
	June – Arrive at Kashgar
	Firas, Hari and Félicien join the company
	August – The company crosses Terak Pass
1323	*Ogodei arrives at Talikan*
	Alaric joins the company
	October – Arrive at Gaza
	November – Arrive at Venice
1324	January 8 – Marco Polo dies
	January – Tiphaine joins the company
	May – The Wedding to the Sea
	Summer – Wu Company travels and trades through Lombardy
	September – Wu Company travels to Avignon
	October – Wu Company travels to Chartres
1325	*April – Wu Company travels to England*
1326	September – Isabella, Mortimer and Edward III cross the channel and land in Suffolk
	October – Edward III assumes his duties as heir
	November – Edward II captured by Isabella's forces
1327	January 24 – Edward II of England deposed in favor of Edward III with his mother as regent
	February 1 – Edward III crowned at Westminster
	April, July, September – Plots discovered to free Edward II
	September 21 – Edward II dies in Berkeley Castle

Acknowledgments

My profound gratitude to Michael Cattagio, reference librarian, retired (not so much). No one has ever been quicker on the draw when I ask for information I need right now.

Thanks also go to freelance editor and author Laura Anne Gilman, who coped womanfully with a manuscript delayed when I fell off a ladder in my garage and sprained my wrist so badly I couldn't type for three weeks. That will interfere with a story going forward; I can't believe I made my deadline. I wouldn't have but for Laura Anne's willingness to work nights and weekends. She also brags on Twitter (*@LAGilman*) when she gets to read a new Stabenow book before anyone else.

You know when an author realizes she has reached the *ne plus ultra* of her profession? When she discovers a cartographer among her fans. Dr. Cherie Northon (and I bet Thom had a hand in it, too), take a bow for the terrific map.

And a big shout-out to the readers who so recklessly spend their hard-earned after-tax dollars on my books. I couldn't do this without you, guys. Thanks.

Bibliography

My intent as a storyteller is always to entertain, but this book also required a great deal of research over many years, and was influenced by the work of many scholars, without whose heavy lifting this by-comparison light-hearted romp would not have been possible. Here's a list of just a few of the books that helped Johanna and Jaufre on their way.

Ackroyd, Peter. Foundation: The history of England from its earliest beginnings to the Tudors.
—— The Canterbury Tales: A Retelling.
Armstrong, Karen. Jerusalem: One City, Three Faiths.
Barber, Malcolm. The New Knighthood: A History of the Order of the Temple.
Bergreen, Laurence. Marco Polo: From Venice to Xanadu.
Bonavia, Judy. The Silk Road.
Boorstin, Daniel J. The Discoverers: A History of Man's Search to Know His World and Himself.
Brotton, Jerry. A History of the World in 12 Maps.
Brown, Lloyd A. The Story of Maps.
Brown, Michelle. The World of the Luttrell Psalter.
Burman, Edward. The Assassins.
—— The World before Columbus, 1100–1492.
Cahill, Thomas. Mysteries of the Middle Ages: The Rise of Feminism, Science and Art from the Cults of Catholic Europe.

Cantor, Norman. The Medieval Reader.

Caro, Ina. Paris to the Past: Traveling through French History by Train.

Cawthorne, Nigel. Sex Lives of the Popes.

Chareyron, Nicole. Pilgrims to Jerusalem in the Middle Ages.

Chute, Marchette. Geoffrey Chaucer of England.

Collis, Louise. Memoirs of a Medieval Woman: the Life and Times of Margery Kempe.

Cosman, Madeleine Pelner. Medieval Wordbook: More than 4,000 Terms and Expressions From Medieval Culture.

Costain, Thomas. The Three Edwards.

Coss, Peter. The Lady in Medieval England, 1000-1500.

Croutier, Alev Lytle. Harem: The World Behind the Veil.

Crowley, Roger. City of Fortune: How Venice Won and Lost a Naval Empire.

Dalrymple, William. In Xanadu: A Quest.

Dougherty, Martin. Weapons & Fighting Techniques of the Medieval Warrior, 1000–1500 AD.

Evangelisti, Silvia. Nuns: A History of Convent Life.

Foltz, Richard C. Religions of the Silk Road: Overland Trade and Cultural Exchange from Antiquity to the Fifteenth Century.

Fox, Sally, researched and edited by. The Medieval Woman: An Illuminated Book of Days.

Freeman, Margaret B. Herbs for the Medieval Household for Cooking, Healing and Divers Uses.

Garfield, Simon. On the Map: A Mind-Expanding Exploration of the Way the World Looks.

Gies, Frances and Joseph. Cathedral, Forge, and Waterwheel: Technology and Invention in the Middle Ages.

—— Life in a Medieval City.

—— Marriage and the Family in the Middle Ages.

Gillman, Ian, and Hans-Joachim Klimkeit. Christians in Asia before 1500.

Goldstone, Nancy. Four Queens: The Provençal Sisters Who Ruled Europe.

Grotenhuis, Elizabeth Ten, editor. Along the Silk Road.

Hansen, Valerie. The Silk Road: A New History.

Herrin, Judith. Byzantium: The Surprising Life of a Medieval Empire.

Hollister, Warren C, and Bennett, Judith M. Medieval Europe: A Short History.

Hopper, Vincent F. Chaucer's Canterbury Tales (Selected): An Interlinear Translation.

Hutton, Alfred. The Sword and the Centuries.

Johnson, Steven. The Ghost Map.

Jones, Dan. The Plantagenets: The Warrior Kings and Queens Who Made England.

Jones, Terry. Medieval Lives.

Lacey, Robert & Danny Danziger. The Year 1000: What Life Was Like at the Turn of the First Millennium.

Leon, Vicki. Uppity Women of Medieval Times.

Lewis, Raphaela. Everyday Life in Ottoman Turkey.

Leyser, Henrietta. Medieval Women: A Social History of Women in England 450-1500.

Man, John. Gutenberg: How One Man Remade the World with Words.

Manchester, William. A World Lit Only by Fire: The Medieval Mind and the Renaissance: Portrait of an Age.

Mayor, Adrienne. Greek Fire, Poison Arrows & Scorpion Bombs: Biological and Chemical Warfare in the Ancient World.

Miller, Malcolm. Chartres Cathedral.

Morier, James. The Adventures of Hajji Baba of Ispahan.

Mortimer, Ian. Medieval Intrigue: Decoding Royal Conspiracies.

—— The Time Traveler's Guide to Medieval England: A Handbook for Visitors to the Fourteenth Century.

Norwich, John Julius. A History of Venice.

Newman, Sharan. The Real History Behind the Templars.

Ohler, Norbert. The Medieval Traveller.

Polo, Marco. The Adventures of Marco Polo. Many editions.

Robinson, James. The Lewis Chessmen.

Rowling, Marjorie. Everyday Life of Medieval Travellers.

—— Life in Medieval Times.

Stark, Freya. The Valleys of the Assassins: and Other Persian Travels.

Starr, S. Frederick. Lost Enlightenment: Central Asia's Golden Age from the Arab Conquest to Tamerlane.

Trask, Willard R. Medieval Lyrics of Europe.

Tooley, Ronald Vere. Maps and Map-Makers.

Tuchman, Barbara. A Distant Mirror: The Calamitous 14th Century.

Turner, Jack. Spice: The History of a Temptation.

Weatherford, Jack. Genghis Khan and the Making of the Modern World.

Whitfield, Susan. Life Along the Silk Road.

Weis, René. The Yellow Cross: The Story of the Last Cathars' Rebellion Against the Inquisition, 1290-1320.

Wood, Frances. The Silk Road: Two Thousand Years in the Heart of Asia.

✧

The first historical novels I read were bestsellers in the fifties, and as such available in the sixties as tattered paperbacks in boat cubbies all over southcentral Alaska, which was how they swam into my ken. They include but are not limited to Anya Seton, Thomas B. Costain, Norah Lofts, Samuel Shellabarger, Georgette Heyer, Frank G. Slaughter, Grace Ingram, C. S. Forester, Rosemary Sutcliff and James Michener.

Nowadays I read Diana Gabaldon (*Outlander*), Sharon Kay Penman (the *Princes of Gwynedd* and the *Plantagenets* series), Sharan Newman (the *Catherine LeVendeur* series and one of two authors to be listed in both the fiction and non-fiction sections of this homage), Francine Matthews (aka Stephanie Barron and the author of the Jane Austen history mysteries but also of many other fine historical novels, including one that might inspire you to take a pry bar to a certain tomb in England), C.J.

Sansom (*Matthew Shardlake*), Imogen Robertson (*Westerman and Crowther*) and P. F. Chisholm (*Sir Robert Carey*), as well as the late Ariana Franklin (*Adelia Aguilar*), Ellis Peters (*Brother Cadfael*) and Elizabeth Peters (*Amelia Peabody*).

These are only a few among many. For a lifetime of enjoyment and for the inspiration to write my own, my heartfelt thanks to you all.

A letter from the publisher

We hope you enjoyed this book. We are an independent publisher dedicated to discovering brilliant books, new authors and great storytelling. If you want to hear more, why not join our community of book-lovers at:

www.headofzeus.com

We'll keep you up-to-date with our latest books, author blogs, tempting offers, chances to win signed editions, events across the UK and much more.

If you have any questions, feedback or just want to say hi, drop us a line on hello@headofzeus.com
or find us on social media:

t @HoZ_Books

f HeadofZeus